THE
GRANTA
Book of the
American
Long Story

THE
GRANTA
Book of the
American
Long Story

Edited by Richard Ford

Granta Books
London

Granta Publications, 2/3 Hanover Yard,
London N1 8BE

First published in Great Britain by
Granta Books 1998

Introduction ('Why Not a Novella?') and
selection copyright © 1998 by Richard Ford

For other copyrights see Acknowledgements

A CIP catalogue record for this book is available
from the British Library.

Typeset by M Rules
Printed and bound in Great Britain by
Mackays of Chatham plc

Contents

Acknowledgements

I appreciate the indispensable assistance of Ms Marisa Rubinow, who generously contributed her good sense and wisdom to this writing. I wish also to thank my friends Kenneth Holditch, Richard Howorth, Gary Fisketjon and Anthony Walton for their advice, and for suggesting long stories that were new to me. Finally, my thanks go to my friend Rea Hederman, and to Frances Coady who has aided this project immeasurably.

Richard Ford
13 March, 1998

Why Not a Novella?

RICHARD FORD

When I began to think of collecting these exceptional long stories written by Americans since the end of World War II, my thought was that for a long while I would be reading and thinking about novellas. Novella was the Latin-y sounding word long in use to refer to prose fictions of a certain, intermediate length; intermediate 'between' the modern prose forms that had achieved if not reliable definition, at least scholarly and readerly acceptance as entities—novels and short stories.

In past times, I had never thought about novellas in any but the most specific ways. Stories I liked by writers I admired had been called novellas by their authors or by somebody in authority. *The Great Gatsby* was famously *not* a novella. ('Clearly' it was a novel, even if a short one, and even if only because it was so wonderful and had made its author famous. Only a novel could do both). *Bartleby the Scrivener*, though, was one. So was *The Death of Ivan Ilytch* and *The Turn of the Screw*, *The Beast In the Jungle*, *Death in Venice*, *Noon wine*, and possibly even *The Dead*. They were all different from each other—different lengths, differing number of incidents, larger and smaller casts of characters. Each focussed a reader's attention and accounted for fictive time in dissimilar ways (*The Dead* took place during a single winter's evening; *Bartleby* depicted months). But all these novellas seemed substantial. All represented life's density and importance in ways that made the stories thematically weighty. They were simply not as long as novels.

Yet even though I'd believed that there *were* novellas, I had never thought there was actually something (other than length) anatomically characteristic about them—formal features, narrative strategies, subjects peculiarly appropriate to novellas—properties which might define a genre in the way, that say a dandelion's cell structure creates and explains only a dandelion.

I did think, from what I'd heard over years, that novellas were stories that somehow gained part of their excellence from being 'free' of the constraining length that typified regulation short stories. Novellas were free to cultivate more characters, invent more scenes, free to 'go more deeply' into more nitty issues, and to analyze action and motive more thoroughly so as to develop themes of greater importance; yet without getting caught up with the heavy lumber of a full-fledged novel. My limited understanding also seemed to imply that writing short stories and novels was each in its own way onerous, requiring in the first case great deftness, drastic economy, even sleight of hand, and in the second a sort of Great-Wall-of-China stamina that occasionally produced monuments but usually little that was commensurate with the effort. The novella, however, flourished free of these severities and was possibly for that very reason, a virtuous form, even fiction's most natural one.

This, I realized, hardly comprised a *theory* of the novella, since my assumptions originated always in indistinct, anecdotal sources: from long-ago teachers whose specialty had been something else; or from colleagues who'd written or were currently writing what they called a novella but who didn't want to go on out on a limb on the subject in case it turned out I knew more than they did, and who, in any event, didn't want to pronounce a definition that might queer their project half-way through.

Some of my colleagues of course had written very good novellas. Or at least they'd written longer-than-usual stories they or their publishers called novellas. Stanley Elkin had. Jim Harrison had written several. Tobias Wolff had. Jane Smiley. It occurred to me that before I finished with the present collection I'd want to ask them if they had some ideas about what a novella really was, something particular that had moved them to claim they'd written one.

It'd long been a commonplace that big American magazines wouldn't usually touch novellas. This was purportedly because of their long length. Short stories, on the other hand, had been kept alive by magazines since the last century. Book publishers *would* touch novellas but didn't really want to. (If Saul Bellow wrote one, or if Hemingway came back to life, then okay.) Other word was that the novella was a 'European form,' suited more to the 'European mind,' which I understood to mean a mind tolerant of things longer than Americans generally liked. (There was a lot of mention of Peter Handke in this context).

There was also the confusing matter of the *novelette*, which sounded to me like a diminutive novel wearing chorus girls' clothes. But it was a form of some form, and further muddied the water of definition (I didn't remember ever reading a novelette, although I sensed they were mostly stories of the frontier, and weren't very literary). And then there were 'short novels,' too, about which I knew nothing, except that *The Great Gatsby* seemed like it could be one.

These first thoughts about the novella occurred to me during a semester's teaching at a large college near Boston. And one afternoon I came round the English chairman's office to find out what he knew about novellas. He'd recently revealed over lunch at the faculty club that he was teaching a whole course the lengthy syllabus of which featured novellas. Surely, I thought, he would know the straight stuff. But when I sat down across from him and asked him what he knew, he grinned, turned sheepish, let his eyes roam around the papers on his desk, shook his head as if I'd brought up a sensitive subject (a friend we might've once known at the same time), then said rather perkily, 'Well, James *did* call it "our ideal, the beautiful and blest nouvelle," didn't he?' He blinked, then assumed a rather plaintive smile. (This was news to me about James.) 'He also called it "shapely," I believe. He said he wanted to "ride the *nouvelle* down-town and prance and curvet and caracole with it."' His eyes quickly found a jumbled stack of blue books on the desk top. 'I can't remember much more than that, though,' he said in conclusion. 'I really haven't thought about novellas as a form. I just like 'em. You know?'

'Oh right, me, too,' I said. 'You bet. I like 'em. I've always liked them.'

★

What I liked about novellas had, of course, always been occasioned by reading them. They were satisfyingly long but not too long; they were full; they seemed artful about staying out of definition's focus and were likely to be surprising about something important. But my appreciation took on greater complexity the moment I set out to write one of my own. In general, my degree of 'genre awareness' has always been rather unacute. My first short stories were written in contemplation of the rather traditional, realistic practices of Sherwood Anderson, Eudora Welty, Faulkner, Hemingway, Fitzgerald, Isaac Babel and Chekhov. Yet the first stories that truly shocked and delighted me were the decidedly 'anti-story' stories written by Donald Barthelme and Borges, Tomasso Landolphi and William Gass. In American literary annals these writers' ascent denoted a time of boisterous experimenting and questioning about what a short narrative might variously be and still be thought of as a 'story'—the 60s— although their sort of experimenting had gone on elsewhere in the world for decades. But because I liked these seemingly permissive anti-stories, I tried hard to write like Barthelme and Calvino. And of course I failed to produce anything even I could stomach, and eventually decided my 'talents' were suited best for the realistic tradition I'd started from, even if my feelings about genres remained permissive. To me, what made a story a story was the writer's calling it one. That was all. Short stories, if only because of their name, seemed to need to be short, although not for generic reasons but organic ones—because brevity suited certain writerly ambitions, generating and conducting intelligence in possibly more focussed ways than novels, about which I knew even less. Novels were just big swampy things that usually drew the writer out beyond the 50,000 word barrier and on to who knows where: *Magic Mountain* and Thomas Pynchon territory, although Walter Benjamin had written disparagingly that novels carried 'the incommensurable to extremes in the representation of human life.'

But setting out to write a novella, provisioned as I was with these unsensitized generic concerns, made the project seem eminently performable. And in fact the performing turned out to be rather easy, at least in formal terms. I simply wrote a longer story, one which would 'hold' more of the raw material I routinely collect to stock stories with, a story which became more important, more weighty than a short story much in the way a pocket battle ship is more important than a PT Boat. In writing such a long story I didn't have to restrain much of anything or streamline or think about holding back (not that this is so hard to do; the writing simply wasn't performed in those uniquely disciplined ways). Neither did I have to do the mental and clerical muscling up I always do prior to writing what I think of as a novel—preparation which *is* arduous, but which I perform primarily to assure myself I won't run out of material half-way through. But to me the important thing is that I didn't do anything very different, just let the story contain more and go on longer.

The story I wrote was about an American salesman who goes to Paris on business and meets a French woman whom he becomes infatuated but not intimate with. After a few days of this infatuation he goes back home to the north suburbs of Chicago, picks a boozy fight with his strong-willed but loving wife, and springs himself free to return to Paris, where he again sees the French woman though only to have everything in his life go to hell in a near-lethal handbasket. The story has four characters, two continents, two language groups, fifteen or so scenes, involves about a week's worth of fictive time and dramatizes its main character's descent into destructive solipsism about which it tries to be funny but also serious. The writing seemed for the most part 'novelistic;' pausing to drill down "under" various actions, letting scenes run on, not worrying about local economies, and letting the whole story go on to what felt to me like its natural end—which happened to be at page 103. It seemed large to me but not too large, free but not given up to abandon, and it also seemed to be precisely—a novella.

If a novella was anything more specific than that, then I (on record now as having written one), did not know what it could be. I suppose the procedure's a little like you and your wife deciding to have a baby, picking out a name that'll fit both sexes (Sydney, for instance) and knowing you'll love what you get no matter what it looks like.

★

An overview of the novella's history might put an interested observer in mind of the famous paintings of a humorous nature familiar from

American barbershops and fishing tackle stores of my youth, paintings showing an expensively panelled drawing room containing a number of chimpanzees dressed in 30s golfing attire—plus-fours, heavy knitted sweaters, floppy mob caps—all of them trying with the aid of various instruments of force (fireplace tongs, ballpeen hammers, big wooden mallets, nutcrackers, sand wedges) to crack a bunch of walnuts that had been left scattered on the floor. Only the walnuts have been mixed, by some mischievous soul, with several nice white golf balls which the chimps, unable to detect the difference, are also trying with grimaces of great strain and frustration to get to the middle of.

Novella. The word comes from Latin: *novus*, which means new (or young) and was originally applied to plants and animals, not stories. In the sixth century AD the word *novella* actually turns up meaning (and right away here's trouble) a newly planted tree, or else a series of supplementary laws instituted by the Emperor Justinian.

Giovanni Boccaccio is generally conceded either to have authored and collected the first cycle of novellas, in Italy in the fourteenth century. Or at least he's thought to have been the first to use a word *like* novella (novelle) to refer to the hundred stories that made up *The Decameron*, a famous book most of us have heard of but not read.

The Decameron is a collection of *written* stories dramatically 'recited' by a group of ten well-born, young Florentines who've fled the plague of 1348 and found an idyllic haven of pleasure and safety in the Tuscan highlands. The narrative frame ('cornice') within which these individual stories (the novellas themselves) are set has an overall narrator and an atmosphere of calamity, death and fearful escape, and the stories tend to be brief (2,500 words or twenty minutes recitation time), lightly diverting ones depicting the loves, fortunes, immoderations and greed of ordinary well-to-do life. The rich exiles pass their time sumptuously, drinking, listening to music and eating good food. And along the way they lace lyrics and ballads and mild bawdiness into their tales while the narrator supplies vivid descriptions of the plague and of nature, pronounces social commentary, and generally gives the entire cycle a unifying moral context, thus preventing it from seeming trivial or blasphemous to its Renaissance readership, accustomed by tradition to thinking of literature as mostly theological and philosophic.

The Decameron's novellas were written in prose and for that reason, and because they were often entertaining, were thought unusual and by some readers inartistically shabby. (*The Canterbury Tales*, one remembers, are about a pilgrimage to a holy martyr's grave and were written in more decorous iambic pentameter.) Boccaccio described his novellas as 'fables or parables or histories or whatever we want to call them,' and indeed they contained characters and events that link them and their form variously to French *lais* and *fabliaux* and even to Persian and Indian story cycles, though also specifically to the religious exemplum, an anecdotal narrative found in many cultures, wherein a character is made to represent some instructably good moral quality.

Boccaccio's stories were full of nonsense, jokes, foolishness even eroticism; they supposedly depicted actual events—news items, even—which had been fictionalized for discretion's sake, but they were also about events that were somehow un-heard of and new. In one story late in the cycle an abbess, Madonna Usimbalda, is roused from her bed by her sister nuns who are scheming to expose a young novice, Isabetta, who's taken a lover to her room. Usimbalda, as it happens, is herself in bed with a priest she's smuggled into the convent via a barrel. And in the hector of being suddenly exposed the abbess confusedly puts the priest's trousers over her head instead of her nun's veil. When the young Isabetta, upon being ashamedly caught herself, points out the abbess's folly (the pair of priestly suspenders dangling on either side of her head being the nice modern detail), she is then absolved, and the two women return to their lovers, while the Boccaccian narrator wryly notes that the other, scheming, lover-less nuns 'sought their solace secretly in the best way they know how.'

After Boccaccio and for several centuries, European writers continued to invent what they called novellas, even though the formal features and dramatic effects of these stories and cycles were hardly consistent. What were called novellas in Romance culture both substantiated Christian conduct as before yet, as Cervantes wrote about his own *Novelas Ejemplares* in 1613, they could also be diverting and harmless in the manner of 'billiard balls' (not so different from golf balls) and provide 'decent and pleasurable pastimes.'

Quite a number of thematic and formal characteristics of

Renaissance novellas have been debated by scholars over the years as a way of identifying a genre: the 'need' for a unifying framing structure (the pretext story within which other stories are narrated—think of the *Arabian Nights*, where a sadistic husband's intention to slay his wife encourages her to narrate nightly tales meant to postpone the evil moment); the need for internal unity among novellas organized routinely in groups of ten times ten; the need for brevity, stories which could be 'recited' in roughly twenty minutes; the need for stories to seem historically true. And more.

But as always literary laws are uncertain predictors of what writers will write, and some characteristics showed up in what was newly written, and many didn't. The rule of brevity, for example, gave way after the sixteenth century when printed books became more the norm and stories grew longer than the convenient twenty-minute recitation time. Much early scholarship in fact settled on a novella formula in which if only *some* of the formal elements appeared the genre could be satisfied. And in most ways the accuracies of definition have not improved much since then.

Novellas, variously spelled, went on being written in Europe after Cervantes' time and under Boccaccio's influence. In France from the fifteenth to the seventeenth centuries, novellas gradually became more focussed upon character and psychological inquiry, and used realistic dialog and word-play. But it was not until the late eighteenth century when Goethe published *Unterhaltungen Deutscher Ausgewanderten* (*Conversations of German Refugees*) that the novella commenced what might be called its salad days among readers and writers, and became important as a sort of national art form in Germany.

Goethe wrote *Unterhaltungen* at a time when the novella was a recognized but not especially popular prose form in Germany. But in 1795, on an invitation from his friend Friedrich Schiller, Goethe produced a suite of six stories grouped within the traditional Boccaccian narrative frame. In *Unterhaltungen*, an upper-class German family living near the Rhine flees the upheaval of the French revolution and, while taking refuge, consoles itself by sitting around listening to a priest recount fresh and purportedly factual stories of everyday life which contain twists of fate, unresolved mysteries, revelations about man's moral nature, and the occasional entertaining bit of Teutonic zaniness. Novellas—again—are the individual stories the priest tells.

Goethe never finished *Unterhaltungen* (Schiller's little magazine folded, in the way of little magazines). And nowhere in the cycle does the master actually use the word novella or *novelle* (although the exiled characters do actually discuss narrative proprieties, and years later Goethe would get around to pronouncing what became a famous definition). But critics—the Schlegels most prominently—soon wrote essays that ordained Goethe's story cycle as the official door-opener for a century of what would become novella fascination: writers writing them, readers reading them, critics feverishly trying to keep up with, define and improve them. It was the century in which Kleist wrote *The Marquis of O*, Tieck wrote *The Painting* and in which the unfair stereotype of Germans as a species of humans willing to go to great lengths to see their terms very, very well-defined, finally might not seem all that unfair.

German literary impulse in the nineteenth century has been scrupulously divided, mostly by nineteenth-century German writers and critics, into several succeeding 'periods,' each with its own school, manifesto and point of view about writing, art, home furnishings, etc. There's the early 'Romantic Period,' the homey 'Biedermeier Period,' the intense 'Period of Poetic Realism,' and the late period of literary 'Naturalism.' (Much of this chronology corresponds to similar if less well-organized literary movements in England and America following the French Revolution). And in Germany, the novella was the most popular literary form persisting through all these succeeding aesthetic tempers and styles. Seemingly legions of Germans wrote novellas in the nineteenth century. And plenty who wrote them also wrote torrents *about* them. In literary circles it became a kind of popular hobby to speculate about the true nature of the novella. The critic Theodore Mundt, in 1823, called the novella 'The German house pet.' And from the present moment, a hundred years after the novella's flourish was mostly over, one can see that it was German wrangling and repositioning, posturing and decrying about it which propelled at least the *word* into twentieth-century American usage, and also informed our albeit murky view of what *novella* might mean.

As in all previous moments in its history, there were points of critical agreement about the novella, even among the fractious nineteenth-century Germans. Goethe's eventual rather minimal definition from 1827, which said that a novella simply involves 'one authentic unheard-of event' suited the majority of readers. Most also agreed that novellas should generally be brief and concentrate on one dramatic, authentic-seeming situation, possibly a fated rather than a willed one, but which by its treatment reveals ordinary, modern, recognizable characters in spiritual and ethical conflict. Brevity (still important) might stress the symbolic importance of characters and events by minimizing milieu and motivation. Surprising twists of fate might occur. Intelligence versus passion, good sense versus unreason were subjects commonly put in play. Though quite often even these formal requirements were conspicuous by being ignored by German writers.

Even the great writer-critic Ludwig Tieck admitted that common features among his own novellas were difficult to find. There were rules; but was a novella, as Friedrich Schlegel wrote, just a streamlined novel? Was an Aristotelian turning point essential? Should characters actually *develop* or merely reveal themselves? Is fate the same as chance? Must a novella be realistic or could it be a fairy tale? Is the old framing story still necessary? How about a central symbol to organize things? These were the matters under vigorous assessment. Satires written in novella form satirizing the controversy over the novella soon became popular.

As one fertile period gave way to the next abundant one, heading toward the stew of uncertainty that would be our century, many German critics began to complain (familiarly to all us writers) that too many novella writers weren't observing the rules, and were writing too many loose, defective unserious stories that made the literary scene a maze (*ein Irrgarten*). Like men with badges, German literary critics inspected novella anthologies for the required symbols and leitmotifs. A critic named Paul Heyse in a letter to a colleague in 1875, actually expressed a wistful, though not-to-be-fulfilled longing for an old-fashioned *mittlepunkt* (turning point) among the many novellas he was then reading. A flourish had begun, and quick it was over.

In the 1880s, following the beginning of German Literary Naturalism, a movement in which social milieu rather than personal will became fashionable as a determinant of man's ambiguous character, many German scholars began to sense that a weakening in traditional ideas of human certainty (will, character, consequence) had made all well-regulated, realistic art forms less persuasive, even less writable. Meanwhile, most everything that remotely could be was being called a novella, though many of these looked like artless tales, studies, flimsy sketches, or worse, like something written by Maupassant—a short story. Eventually critics began to say what critics say when they can't make the world behave: that further speculation (about novellas) was a waste of time, that the great work had already been done, that the current scene looked drab, that ultimately the novella was over-rated, and it was time the truth was told.

Not that the fussing stopped, only that the novella's modern period of resurgence in Germany had ended. German writers went on writing novellas, but they wrote much less *about* them. Critical consensus became even harder to find. Some observers conjectured that a novella was a form nicely suited to stories of character disintegration, while others thought novellas were born of a time when life made sense. Some felt novellas were good at making rather succinct philosophical points, while others noticed that most novellas' philosophical themes stayed undeveloped. Eventually the form's brevity (again) became its feature most consistently agreed to, and in an intellectual climate gradually becoming merely scholarly Goethe's spare definition seemed safest: 'one authentic un-heard-of event'. And with the rise of the short story, the invention of literary psychology, the popularity of mass circulation news and the resulting enhancement of readers' appetite for the *actual*, the novella simply settled into a diminished place among other narrative inventions, while its critics went on arguing over and reinventing the past.

★

American writers are notoriously slippery when it comes to following literary rules. This tendency becomes exaggerated when the rules— such as those purportedly governing novellas—won't be still, keep disagreeing with other rules and give no promise to aid in the enjoyment much less the production of a good, old-fashioned novella for our time.

So far this century, nothing has occurred in America remotely proportionate to what happened to the novella in Germany during the last. Perhaps Americans are just not as literarily excitable as Germans. Still, World War I altered everyone's views about all artistic rules. American innovation in the arts became epidemic, while American notions about all things German changed drastically. Novels assumed enhanced grandeur as the supreme narrative achievement. The short story continued in popularity among readers, and what Americans called novellas became 'foredoomed,' Henry James wrote in his *Prefaces*, 'to editorial disfavor.'

And genre titles multiplied. Call it individualism, incipient pluralism or simple American uneasiness about what things are called, but Katherine Ann Porter titled both 'Noon Wine' and 'Pale Horse, Pale Rider,' *short novels*. The 'novelette' turned up again and again to represent more or less what a novella might also be. Henry James, Scott Fitzgerald, Nathaniel West, Edith Wharton all wrote what they or their reviewers called novellas, but in their stories these writers made no special effort to employ the traditional structuring and intellectual hardware (cyclical ordering, the framing device, turning point, the specific use of symbols). Plus, American writers didn't write much *about* novellas, didn't seem familiar with the last century's formalities, and didn't dispute them in learned journals. Europeans, of course, especially Germans and the French, have always considered imaginative writers to be intellectuals (something we Americans find puzzling, sometimes intimidating). The route to European literary greatness with some large exceptions still nominally requires erudition, a familiarity with history and the achievement of the ancients. Twentieth-century American prose writing, on the other hand, generally reflects in addition to an intense interest in self, a demotic, inductive impulse, a trust in practical experience as the path to truth, as well as a suspicion about the elitism of schoolishness—often, in fact, a suspicion about Europe. It isn't that Americans (particularly prose writers) have distrusted intelligence, but rather that they've seemed skeptical about institutions which might inhibit the all-important individual nature of creativity. 'In Paris,' Marcel Duchamp wrote in 1915, 'the young men of any generation act as the grandsons of some great men . . . [but you Americans], you don't give a damn about Shakespeare . . . you're not his grandson. So it is a perfect terrain for new developments.'

And so, a wide and lively debate over the novella didn't occur among important American writers before the 1940s, but mostly among critics and interpreters in universities, where one might say they were away from the action.

What twentieth-century American critics did with American novellas was chiefly interpret their American themes and view them formally as distinctive for their in-between condition and for their propensity for being great works of art. The poet Howard Nemerov, as late as 1963, observed that the novella (which he also liked to call the short novel) existed solidly in 'a tradition of masterpieces' composed by writers of still greater works (Melville, Mann, Virginia Woolf, Fitzgerald). Nemerov believed short novels resembled Greek dramas but also parables, and were adept at dramatizing the theme of identity among their rational middle-class protagonists. Yet when it came to pronouncing the form's intrinsic character which he thinks of as 'ideal,' Nemerov isn't very helpful. He hazily states that novellas somehow balance motive with circumstance, or have a tendency toward doublings within focussed dramatic situations, but then settles into a vague, summary dictum uttered by an apparently more eminent man of letters—in this case Nabokov—who wrote, in his autobiography, *Speak, Memory*—that 'there is, it would seem, in the dimensional scale of the world a kind of delicate meeting-place between imagination and knowledge, a point, arrived at by diminishing large things and enlarging small ones, that is intrinsically artistic.' It's hard to see how such a view wouldn't encompass everything that's ultimately beautiful.

Following World War II, during the period of literary re-surgence that followed Americans' exposure to Europe, and spurred by the great numbers attending American universities, scholars took fresh interest in the novella. It was an interest that started with the old German wranglings but sought to do for the American novella what the Europeans had failed to do with their own: spell out a definition for what a novella is.

Nothing much worked. American scholarship generally took the approach that there *was* a prose form that a few (though not that many) American writers still used and called a novella. In practice, the form usually contained as many as 50,000 words, but almost always fifteen thousand. Novellas were no longer usually published in framed cycles but singly, and didn't consistently exhibit the last century's structuring strategies or necessarily share its preoccupations with authenticity, fate, symbol, etc. New examples were, *Seize the Day*, *The Old Man and the Sea*, *The Ballad of the Sad Café*, *Good-bye, Columbus*. Some people thought *The Catcher in the Rye* was a novella, too, although a long one.

American critics *did*, however, argue that to qualify as a genre, novellas should produce unique effects and should handle their subjects in ways no other forms do. This view, basic to genre study, argues that unique principles of composition, often quite subtle, are common to each genre—novels, short stories—and that readers get more out of a story, perhaps even read it more correctly, if they can know what those principles are and respond to them as they read. It is not so different, if less vociferously argued, from what nineteenth-century Germans thought.

Elaborate critical attention has thus been turned on the question of whether, as one critic said, novellas are a class of narrations embodying a unique 'shaping purpose'; again, internal methods of making meaning and creating effects which are specific to whatever a novella is—something other than just a story of intermediate length. Novels, using this approach, are said to embody specific strategies of telling which the writer (knowingly or unknowingly) employs once he's chosen his genre. *Elaboration* is estimated to be the novel's principal narrative assignment. And by elaborating themes, characters, situations in a continuous untidy way, the novel comes to define its generic self. On the other hand, the short story's task is said to be *restriction* and *intensity*, and a true short story will radiate these and seek in the ways it develops subjects to make restriction and intense focus a virtue.

Novellas, again by being in-between novels and stories in length (although not necessarily in any other ways) are by theorists judged unique and generic because they create effects which are both intense (like stories) but have wide implications. *Bartleby, The Scrivener* again, might be a good example.

Predictably, the case for the novella's *shaping purpose* works when it works and doesn't when it doesn't. Any individual novella might expand its implications and restrict its formal terms in ways that seem to follow a theory. But all the unique effects one might nail down about novellas—intensification through repetition, simultaneous expansion of thematic implication—are often as noticeable in short stories, especially longer ones (*The Dead* would be an example here again). And when a story resists classification as does Faulkner's *The Bear*, where a diversity of structural features and effects—some quite intense and local, some broad, almost unchartable and sprawling—dramatize subjects as vast as history, identity, the extinguishment of nature by modern life, all in about a hundred pages, then the effects produced in fact favor both genres without inevitably ratifying a third.

'Specific difficulties, if they can be identified,' Nemerov wrote, 'are what define the form—without them it is not a form but only so many thousand words.' This is the old prosodist's claim to purity, and nicely theorizes how or why, for instance, a sestina makes its meaning. But most prose writers understand that writing stories (if not all of art) is a matter of compromise, and that purity has little to do with anything outside a writer's heart. Indeed, most writers I know would be more than happy to have their stories considered as 'only so many thousand words' if that meant someone would simply read them. And in the case of long prosy stories wherein the writer may be innocent of any specific genre definitions and goals, it's hard to believe that the selection of the word *novella* (occurring perhaps after the fact of creation) could determine the author's ability to manipulate his material and create characteristic effects. At best, such a formula would only explain how one specific set of difficulties became one specific book.

*

Following my months of reading, I decided to conduct the previously-mentioned informal poll among my colleagues and writer friends—people who might be expected to know a thing or two—about what they, be they practitioners or not, believe a novella might be. A poll seemed useful since no one I knew who'd written a novella had also written critically on the subject. In fact it seemed far-fetched that a group of American writers, from Ms Welty's generation to Ms Danticat's would ever discover themselves sitting around arguing about 'the novella,' calculating whether this story or that was certifiable based on some tweezing historical demands of framing structure, philosophical focus, turning points, shaping purpose, identity, doubling—all that. It seemed, well . . . un-American. Not that American writers are dim or more than usually wanting in curiosity or formal training, but rather (it's just my feeling) that no one would choose to wall-in his imagination that way merely to prove a point extrinsic, even irrelevant to the act of writing.

I also felt that American writers would resist any suggestion that value adhered to generic identification, or that novels, stories and whatever was in between could be aided simply as reading matter by the imputation of inherent generic signals and narrative goals distinct from those specific ones the writer had in mind. Most writers I know are champions of what Nemerov called 'the ecstasy of the unique,' and believe that each book they write contains its own peculiar reader-instruction-kit, and that the urge to make good books involves devising specific unmistakable instructions for each one.

My instinct also told me that while most of my colleagues probably felt at ease using the word 'novella,' and that while quite a few had certainly written stories intended to be novellas right from the start, others might've begun writing a story that eventually ran long, so that by the end the writer decided that *here* indeed was a novella, too—and indeed quite a noble form it was. 'Blest' even.

The results of my poll weren't very surprising. Everyone absolutely agreed that there was a contemporary prose form called a novella. All could name several, though there were some spiritless disagreements. Everyone seemed to believe there was a 'technical definition,' around somewhere, but no one knew if it could be found in a specific book. Several people said they would definitely know a novella if they saw one, and that between sixty and 120 printed pages would be about the right length. Four different people said they knew the Germans and

Henry James had played an important part in the novella's past, but they couldn't say how or when or if James and the Germans had done whatever it was together. One man who's written several good long stories said that recognizing a novella was like describing the way you'd hit a fast ball—always a difficult American trick. Another quite famous novelist and memoirist who'd never written a novella that he knew of, offered that a novella was something that didn't quite measure up to being a novel. And a very esteemed fiction editor who's published plenty of what he believes are novellas called upon the famous maxim by Randall Jarrell, who wrote that a novel is a prose narrative of a certain length that has something wrong with it. My editor friend said he believed that a novella must then have slightly less wrong with it. One friend said a novella fitted into a line of long prose forms, the longest of which was the novel, and the least long was the 'novellini.' (To be honest, most people didn't really want to talk about the subject very much.) Several people acted suspicious about why I wanted to know these things in the first place, as though I might be planning to expose their views and embarrass them. And one man advised that if he were me he wouldn't get involved in these kinds of 'academic matters' at all. He didn't say why.

Perhaps I'm at fault for thinking practitioners should have a word on the subject of the novella. Possibly, it's like expecting a man who owns a big ranch also to be an expert on geography. But that can happen. And I'm personally uncomfortable with readers finding significant strategies at work in my own stories and for me (and by extension my colleagues) to have nothing to say about it. Plus, it's interesting that in 1998, the word novella remains in at least timid use among American writers, and that intermediate length is its most agreed-upon defining quality. It's enough to make one wonder if there isn't something innately attractive about what modern novellas minimally are: their putative freedom and the vibrancy of their compromise condition; their history dotted with geniuses and masterpieces falling just short of being novels; and the form's insistence upon being considered best in isolation.

Many contemporary observers, American and European, have of course finally admitted definitional defeat. The words 'nebulous,' 'insoluble,' 'protean,' 'chameleon-like,' even 'nonsensical,' and 'enig-matique,' come along regularly in the critical literature. 'There are novellas,' Walter Pabst wrote in 1949, 'but there is no such genre as a novella.' Lenient readers, one remembers, have always said that if a story contained a few traits we associate with novellas, then why not call it one. Others argue novellas are the things you get when you lack the patience to write novels. And still more say that even though a def-inition is hopeless it's still fun to go on arguing. In a famous shrug, the German scholar Harry Steinhauer said that in his view, two centuries of novella study still 'have not brought forth a mouse.'

It is with this absent rodent in mind then I have decided , likewise with a shrug, and for purposes of the stories collected here, to set aside the term novella in favor of the less succinct, less memorable, but possibly less historically-infuriating and ultimately freeing expression, 'Long Story.' My wish for this anthology is, after all, that it address readers and writers who relish long stories, and that the collection free its audience to write and relish as suits its wishes, undistracted by off-stage wranglings over nomenclature.

As I've said, when I started this project, I intended to read novellas, but I also wanted to emerge with a good, spanking definition of the novella which I and others could use forever. And yet I could not through all my reading discern anything other than length to distin-guish these stories as a uniform genre, or to distinguish them consistently from their seemingly better-defined narrative cousins. Had I sculpted and restricted my choices, I'm sure I could've found stories that satisfied almost anyone's definition; although not every-one's. But then I'd have left stories out for reasons not intrinsic to them. And as a writer of stories myself, I don't find this defensible; in fact I find it contrary to the best impulse of art which is to be inclusive.

True, in this volume are long stories of varying longnessess and, yes, length is just another arbitrarily chosen attribute. But it's not a very troublesome attribute in contrast to the bad-fitting dog collars of schol-arship. Plus, the expression 'Long Story' isn't very pretentious, nor is it especially ambiguous. It isn't coercive, it isn't clearly wrong, it doesn't distract from the stories themselves, and it doesn't confer hazy inter-mediacy or inspire controversy. Almost everything the word 'novella' has meant over the centuries is not what it means in current writerly usage. And although letting a form be defined by whatever's left when you take away all that's *not* right about it certainly isn't very scientific, I can also assure you I have no conviction that even length is an inspired standard for what these stories have in common. Length certainly doesn't constitute a shaping purpose. (Something does, though, feel good about forcing a worn out literary term into retirement.)

Several of the eleven stories that follow have, on first publication, been called *novellas*. And out of courtesy I have not quizzed those authors who remain alive about what they meant by that. I actually have no brief against the word or objection to its survival. Maybe it's good for writers to use words they don't understand very well; maybe it keeps the language on its toes. I may even use it again myself when I don't have quite as much time as I've used up here. I'm not mad at the word. I just don't know what I might mean if I used it.

The esteemed fiction editor and *New Yorker* writer Roger Angell recently wrote that 'summing up fiction is a losing game.' And because I believe that, I've not done it here—not sought to micro-organize these stories or to phony up neat, self-congratulatory ways that they're secretly alike, or speculated about how they reflect their American-ness or their region or their ethnicity. Rather, I've just given them the stage more or less alone to be what they each uniquely are.

As with *The Granta Book of the American Short Story*, I've limited the period of my editorial notice to the years between World War II and almost today. This is convenient for me, since it's roughly the number of years I've been alive, and allows me a nominal 'interest' and familiarity. Included here is at least one long story from each decade since the 1940s, but as with the short-story volume, I make no claims for each story's aptness to its time, although its aptness could hardly be questionable.

Furthermore, I make no claims that the volume is exhaustive of its period or that I've read everything, only that I believe the stories I've chosen are excellent. People will disagree with me about my selections, particularly about writers I've left out, and I would only say that I'm pleased that these objecting readers care so passionately for literature as to have favorites.

Finally, keeping in mind the stories I didn't choose, I have observed that American writers since World War II have been less apt to write long stories, in contrast to short stories and novels, which they seem to write a lot. No doubt it is magazine space and publishing economies which are to blame. Yet even in the hands of truly exceptional writers, the long story often doesn't work out as well as the other prose forms. The character of those I read but didn't choose often seemed to be what I'm sure they were—short stories that grew long, their middles soft and not well-tended, their ends frequently unsuccessful at bringing to a close what their middles had come to contain. There may simply be some quality of the long story which makes it a difficult entity for any writer to hold in his mind at once—something perplexing about being both long and short at the same time—the very qualities a reader is likely to find pleasing in a long story when a good one comes along.

There isn't much more to say. I very much wished to include Norman Maclean's wonderful story, *A River Runs Through It*, but regrettably the University of Chicago Press declined to grant me permission. I've not included certain standards such as *The Old Man and The Sea*, and *Wise Blood* by Flannery O'Connor, because I felt they are likely to be available elsewhere and to be well-known already by British readers. Other famous long stories simply didn't hold up to fresh readings—particularly *The Ballad of the Sad Café*, Bellow's *Seize the Day*, Truman Capote's *Breakfast At Tiffany's*, all of which are much admired, but not by me.

At the end, it's just nice to have these stories here to read together— on a long train-ride, maybe. What critics feel as a strange unease about this rather formless form, new readers will, I hope, experience as interest, even pleasure. Reading is always a good way to define pleasure anew.

And so enough. More than enough, I'm sure. You have the book in hand now. It's finally got quiet. You can read.

THE
GRANTA
Book of the
American
Long Story

June Recital

EUDORA WELTY

Loch was in a tempest with his mother. She would keep him in bed and make him take Cocoa-Quinine all summer, if she had her way. He yelled and let her wait holding the brimming spoon, his eyes taking in the whole ironclad pattern, the checkerboard of her apron—until he gave out of breath, and took the swallow. His mother laid her hand on his pompadour cap, wobbled his scalp instead of kissing him, and went off to her nap.

'Louella!' he called faintly, hoping she would come upstairs and he could devil her into running to Loomis's and buying him an ice cream cone out of her pocket, but he heard her righteously bang a pot to him in the kitchen. At last he sighed, stretched his toes—so clean he despised the very sight of his feet—and brought himself up on his elbow to the window.

Next door was the vacant house.

His family would all be glad if it burned down; he wrapped it with the summer's love. Beyond the hackberry leaves of their own tree and the cedar row and the spready yard over there, it stretched its weathered side. He let his eyes rest or go flickering along it, as over something very well known indeed. Its left-alone contour, its careless stretching away into that deep backyard he knew by heart. The house's side was like a person's, if a person or giant would lie sleeping there, always sleeping.

A red and bottle-shaped chimney held up all. The roof spread falling to the front, the porch came around the side leaning on the curve, where it hung with bannisters gone, like a cliff in a serial at the Bijou. Instead of cowboys in danger, Miss Jefferson Moody's chickens wandered over there from across the way, flapped over the edge, and found the shade cooler, the dust fluffier to sit in, and the worms thicker under that blackening floor.

In the side of the house were six windows, two upstairs and four down, and back of the chimney a small stair window shaped like a keyhole—one made never to open; they had one like it. There were green shades rolled up to various levels, but not curtains. A table showed in the dining room, but no chairs. The parlor window was in the shadow of the porch and of thin, vibrant bamboo leaves, clear and dark as a pool he knew in the river. There was a piano in the parlor. In addition there were little fancy chairs, like Sunday School chairs or children's drug store chairs, turned this way and that, and the first strong person trying to sit down would break them one after the other. Instead of a door into the hall there was a curtain; it was made of beads. With no air the curtain hung still as a wall and yet you could see through it, if anybody should pass the door.

In that window across from his window, in the back upper room, a bed faced his. The foot was gone, and a mattress had partly slid down but was holding on. A shadow from a tree, a branch and its leaves, slowly traveled over the hills and hollows of the mattress.

In the front room there, the window was dazzling in afternoon; it was raised. Except for one tall post with a hat on it, that bed was out of sight. It was true, there was one person in the house—Loch would recall him sooner or later—but it was only Mr Holifield. He was the night watchman down at the gin, he always slept all day. A framed picture could be seen hanging on the wall, just askew enough so that it looked straightened every now and then. Sometimes the glass in the picture reflected the light outdoors and the flight of birds between branches of trees, and while it reflected, Mr Holifield was having a dream.

Loch could look across through cedars that missed one, in the line, and in a sweeping glance see it all—as if he possessed it—from its front porch to its shed-like back and its black-shadowed summerhouse—which was an entirely different love, odorous of black leaves that crumbled into soot; and its shade of four fig trees where he would steal the figs if July ever came. And above all the shade, which was dark as a boat, the blue sky flared—shooting out like a battle, and hot as fire. The hay riders his sister went with at night (went with against their father's will, slipped out by their mother's connivance) would ride off singing, 'Oh, It Ain't Gonna Rain No More.' Even under his shut eye-lids, that light and shade stayed divided from each other, but reversed.

Some whole days at a time, often in his dreams day and night, he would seem to be living next door, wild as a cowboy, absolutely by himself, without his mother or father coming in to feel his skin, or run a finger up under his cap—without one parent to turn on the fan and the other to turn it off, or them both together to pin a newspaper around the light at night to shade him out of their talk. And there was where Cassie could never bring him books to read, miserable girls' books and fairy tales.

It was the leaky gutter over there that woke Loch up, back in the spring when it rained. Splashy as a waterfall in a forest, it shook him with that agony of being *made* to wake up from a sound sleep to be taken away somewhere, made to go. It made his heart beat fast.

They could do what they wanted to to him but they could not take his pompadour cap off him or take his house away. He reached down under the bed and pulled up the telescope.

It was his father's telescope and he was allowed to look through it unmolested as long as he ran a temperature. It was what they gave him instead of his pea-shooter and cap pistol. Smelling of brass and the drawer of the library table where it came from, it was an object hith-erto brought out in the family group for eclipses of the moon; and the day the airplane flew over with a lady in it, and they all waited for it all day, wry and aching up at the sky; the telescope had been gripped in his father's hand like a big stick, some kind of protective weapon for what was to come.

Loch fixed the long brass tubes and shot the telescope out the window, propping the screen outward and letting more mosquitoes in, the way he was forbidden. He examined the size of the distant figs: like marbles yesterday, wine-balls today. Getting those would not be the same as stealing. On the other side of fury at confinement a sweet self-indulgence could visit him in his bed. He moved the glass lovingly toward the house and touched its roof, with the little birds on it cock-ing their heads.

With the telescope to his eye he even smelled the house strongly. Morgana was extra deep in smell this afternoon; the magnolias were open all over the tree at the last corner. They glittered like lights in the dense tree that loomed in the shape of a cave opening at the brought-up-close edge of the Carmichael roof. He looked at the thrush's nest, Woodrow Spight's old ball on the roof, the drift of faded election handbills on the porch—the vacant house again, the half of a china plate deep in the weeds; the chickens always went to that plate, and it was dry.

Loch trained the telescope to the back and caught the sailor and the girl in the moment they jumped the ditch. They always came the back way, swinging hands and running low under the leaves. The girl was the piano player at the picture show. Today she was carrying a paper sack from Mr Wiley Bowles' grocery.

Loch squinted; he was waiting for the day when the sailor took the figs. And see what the girl would hurry him into. Her name was Virgie Rainey. She had been in Cassie's room all the way through school, so that made her sixteen; she would ruin any nice idea. She looked like a tomboy but it was not the truth. She had let the sailor pick her up and carry her one day, with her fingers lifting to brush the leaves. It was she that had showed the sailor the house to begin with, she that started him coming. They were rusty old fig trees but the figs were the little sweet blue. When they cracked open, their pink and golden flesh would show, their inside flowers, and golden bubbles of juice would hang, to touch your tongue to first. Loch gave the sailor time, for it was he, Loch, who was in command of leniency here; he was giving him day after day.

He swayed on his knees and saw the sailor and Virgie Rainey in a clear blue-and-white small world run sparkling to the back door of the empty house.

And next would come the old man going by in the blue wagon, up as far as the Starks' and back to the Carmichaels' corner.

> *'Buttermilk?*
> *Buttermilk.*
> *Fresh dewberries and—*
> *Buttermilk.'*

That was Mr Fate Rainey and his song. He would take a long time to pass. Loch could study through the telescope the new flower in his horse's hat each day. He would go past the Starks' and circle the cemetery and niggertown, and come back again. His cry, with a song's tune, would come near, then far, and near again. Was it an echo—was an echo that? Or was it, for the last time, the call of somebody seeking about in a deep cave, 'Here—here! Oh, here am I!'

There was a sound that might have been a blue jay scolding, and that was the back door; they were just now going in off the back porch. When he saw the door prized open—the stretched screen billowing from being too freely leaned against—and let the people in, Loch felt the old indignation rise up. But at the same time he felt joy. For while the invaders did not see him, he saw them, both with the naked eye and through the telescope; and each day that he kept them to himself, they were his.

Louella appeared below on their steps and with a splash threw out the dirty dishwater in the direction of the empty house. But she would never speak, and he would never speak. He had not shared anybody in his life even with Louella.

After the door fell to at the sailor's heel, and the upstairs window had been forced up and propped, then silence closed over the house next door. It closed over just as silence did in their house at this time of day; but like the noisy waterfall it kept him awake—fighting sleep.

In the beginning, before he saw anyone, he would just as soon have lain there and thought of wild men holding his house in thrall, or of a giant crouched double behind the window that corresponded to his own. The big fig tree was many times a magic tree with golden fruit that shone in and among its branches like a cloud of lightning bugs— a tree twinkling all over, burning, on and off, off and on. The sweet golden juice to come—in his dream he put his tongue out, and then his mother would be putting that spoon in his mouth.

More than once he dreamed it was inside that house that the cave had moved, and the buttermilk man went in and out the rooms driving his horse with its red rose and berating its side with a whip that unfurled of itself; in the dream he was not singing. Or the horse itself, a white and beautiful one, was on its way over, approaching to ask some favor of him, a request called softly and intelligibly upward—which he was not decided yet whether to grant or deny. This call through the window had not yet happened—not quite. But someone had come.

He turned away. 'Cassie!' he cried.

Cassie came to his room. She said, 'Didn't I tell you what you could do? Trim up those Octagon Soap coupons and count them good if you want that jack-knife.' Then she went off again and slammed her door. He seemed to see her belatedly. She had been dressed up for whatever she was doing in her room like somebody in the circus, with colored spots on her, and hardly looked like his sister.

'You looked silly when you came in!' he called.

But over at the empty house was a stillness not of going off and leaving him but of coming nearer. Something was coming very close to him, there was something he had better keep track of. He had the feeling that something was being counted. Then he too must count. He could be wary enough that way, counting by ones, counting by fives, by tens. Sometimes he threw his arm across his eyes and counted without moving his lips, imagining that when he got to a certain amount he might give a yell, like 'Coming, ready or not!' and go down by the hackberry limb. He never had yelled, and his arm was a heavy weight across his face. Often that was the way he fell asleep. He woke up drenched with the afternoon fever breaking. Then his mother pulled him and pushed him as she put cool pillow cases on the pillows and pushed him back straight. She was doing it now.

'Now your powder.'

His mother, dressed up for a party, tilted the little pinked paper toward his stuck-out, protesting tongue, and guided the glass of water into his groping hand. Every time he got a powder swallowed, she said calmly, 'Dr Loomis only gives you these to satisfy me you're getting medication.' His father, when he came home from the office, would say, 'Well, if you've got malaria, son . . .' (kissing him) '. . . you've got malaria, that's all there is to it. Ha! Ha! Ha!'

'I've made you some junket, too,' she said with a straight face.

He made a noise calculated to sicken her, and she smiled at him.

'When I come back from Miss Nell Carlisle's I'll bring you all the news of Morgana.'

He could not help but smile at her—lips shut. She was almost his ally. She swung her little reticule at him and went off to the Rook party. By leaning far out he could see a lackadaisical, fluttery kind of parade, the ladies of Morgana under their parasols, all trying to keep cool while they walked down to Miss Nell's. His mother was absorbed into their floating, transparent colors. Miss Perdita Mayo was talking, and they were clicking their summery heels and drowning out— drowning out something. . . .

A little tune was playing on the air, and it was coming from the piano in the vacant house.

The tune came again, like a touch from a small hand that he had unwittingly pushed away. Loch lay back and let it persist. All at once tears rolled out of his eyes. He opened his mouth in astonishment. Then the little tune seemed the only thing in the whole day, the whole summer, the whole season of his fevers and chills, that was accountable: it was personal. But he could not tell why it was so.

It came like a signal, or a greeting—the kind of thing a horn would play out in the woods. He halfway closed his eyes. It came and trailed off and was lost in the neighborhood air. He heard it and then wondered how it went.

It took him back to when his sister was so sweet, to a long time ago. To when they loved each other in a different world, a boundless, trustful country all its own, where no mother or father came, either through sweetness or impatience—different altogether from his solitary world now, where he looked out all eyes like Argus, on guard everywhere.

A spoon went against a dish, three times. In her own room Cassie was carrying on some girls' business that, at least, smelled terrible to him, as bad as when she painted a hair-receiver with rosebuds and caught it on fire drying it. He heard Louella talking to herself in the lower hall. 'Louella!' he called, flat on his back, and she called up for him to favor her with some rest or she would give up the ghost right then. When he drew up to the window again, the first thing he saw was someone new, coming along the walk out front.

Here came an old lady. No, she was an old woman, round and unsteady-looking—unsteady the way he felt himself when he got out of bed—not on her way to a party. She must have walked in from out in the country. He saw her stop in front of the vacant house, turn herself, and go up the front walk.

Something besides countriness gave her her look. Maybe it came from her having nothing in her hands, no reticule or fan. She looked as if she could even be the one who lived in the house and had just stepped outside for a moment to see if it was going to rain and now, matter-of-factly, a little toilsomely with so much to do, was going back in.

But when she began to hasten, Loch got the idea she might be the sailor's mother come after her son. The sailor didn't belong in Morgana anyhow. Whoever she was, she climbed the steps and crossed the wobbly porch and put her hand to the front door, which she opened just as easily as Virgie Rainey had opened the back door. She went inside, and he saw her through the beady curtain, which made her outline quiver for a moment.

Suppose doors with locks and keys were ever locked—then nothing like this would have the chance to happen. The nearness of missing things, and the possibility of preventing them, made Loch narrow his eyes.

Three party ladies who were late and puffing, all hurrying together in a duck-like line, now passed. They just missed sight of the old woman—Miss Jefferson Moody, Miss Mamie Carmichael, and Miss Billy Texas Spights. They would have stopped everything. Then in the middle of the empty air behind everybody, butterflies suddenly crossed and circled each other, their wings digging and flashing like duelers' swords in the vacuum.

Though Loch was gratified with the outrage mounting—three people now were in the vacant house—and could consider whether the old woman might have come to rout out the other two and give them her tirade, he was puzzled when the chandelier lighted up in the parlor. He ran the telescope out the window again and put his frowning eye to it. He discovered the old woman moving from point to point all around the parlor, in and out of the little chairs, sidling along the piano. He could not see her feet; she behaved a little like a wind-up toy on wheels, rolling into the corners and edges of objects and being diverted and sent on, but never out of the parlor.

He moved his eye upstairs, up an inch on the telescope. There on a mattress delightfully bare—where he would love, himself, to lie, on a slant and naked, to let the little cottony tufts annoy him and to feel the mattress like billows bouncing beneath, and to eat pickles lying on his back—the sailor and the piano player lay and ate pickles out of an open sack between them. Because of the down-tilt of the mattress, the girl had to keep watch on the sack, and when it began to slide down out of reach that was when they laughed. Sometimes they held pickles stuck in their mouths like cigars, and turned to look at each other. Sometimes they lay just alike, their legs in an M and their hands joined between them, exactly like the paper dolls his sister used to cut out of folded newspaper and unfold to let him see. If Cassie would come in now, he would point out the window and she would remember.

And then, like the paper dolls sprung back together, they folded close—the real people. Like a big grasshopper lighting, all their legs and arms drew in to one small body, deadlike, with protective coloring.

He leaned back and bent his head against the cool side of the pillow and shut his eyes, and felt tired out. He clasped the cool telescope to his side, and with his fingernail closed its little eye.

'Poor old Telescope,' he said.

When he looked out again, everybody next door was busier.

Upstairs, the sailor and Virgie Rainey were running in circles around the room, each time jumping with outstretched arms over the broken bed. Who chased whom had nothing to do with it because they kept the same distance between them. They went around and around like the policeman and Charlie Chaplin, both intending to fall down.

Downstairs, the sailor's mother was doing something just as fanciful. She was putting up decorations. (Cassie would be happy to see that.) As if she were giving a party that day, she was dressing up the parlor with ribbons of white stuff. It was newspaper.

The old woman left the parlor time and time again and reappeared—in and out through the beads in the doorway—each time with an armful of old *Bugles* that had lain on the back porch in people's way for a long time. And from her gestures of eating crumbs or pulling bits of fluff from her bosom, Loch recognized that mother-habit: she had pins there. She pinned long strips of the newspaper together, first tearing them carefully and evenly as a school teacher. She made ribbons of newspaper and was hanging them all over the parlor, starting with the piano, where she weighted down the ends with a statue.

When Loch grew tired of watching one animated room he watched the other. How the two playing would whirl and jump over the old woman's head! That was the way the bed fell to begin with.

As Loch leaned his chin in his palm at the window and watched, it seemed strangely as if he had seen this whole thing before. The old woman was decorating the piano until it rayed out like a Christmas tree or a Maypole. Maypole ribbons of newspaper and tissue paper streamed and crossed each other from the piano to the chandelier and festooned again to the four corners of the room, looped to the backs of chairs here and there. When would things begin?

Soon everything seemed fanciful and beautiful enough to Loch; he thought she could stop. But the old woman kept on. This was only a part of something in her head. And in the splendor she fixed and pinned together she was all alone. She was not connected with anything else, with anybody. She was one old woman in a house not bent on dealing punishment. Though once when Woody Spights and his sister came by on skates, of course she came out and ran them away.

Once she left the house, to come right back. With her unsteady but purposeful walk, as if she were on a wheel that misguided her, she crossed the road to the Carmichael yard and came back with some green leaves and one bloom from the magnolia tree—carried in her skirt. She pulled the corners of her skirt up like a girl, and she was thin beneath in her old legs. But she zigzagged across the road—such a show-off, carefree way for a mother to behave, but mothers sometimes did. She lifted her elbows—as if she might skip! But nobody saw her: his forehead was damp. He heard a scream from the Rook party up at

Miss Nell's—it sounded like Miss Jefferson Moody shooting-the-moon. Nobody saw the old woman but Loch, and he told nothing.

She brought the bunch of green into the parlor and put it on the piano, where the Maypole crown would go. Then she took a step back and was as admiring as if somebody else had done it—nodding her head.

But after she had the room all decorated to suit her, she kept on, and began to stuff the cracks. She brought in more paper and put it in all the cracks at the windows. Now Loch realized that the windows in the parlor were both down, it was tight as a box, and she had been inside in the suffocating heat. A wave of hotness passed over his body. Furthermore, she made her way with a load of *Bugles* to the blind part of the wall where he knew the fireplace was. All the load went into the fireplace.

When she went out of the parlor again she came back slowly indeed. She was pushing a big square of matting along on its side; she wove and bent and struggled behind it, like a spider with something bigger than he can eat, pushing it into the parlor. Loch was suddenly short of breath and pressed forward, cramped inside, checkerboarding his forehead and nose against the screen. He both wanted the plot to work and wanted it to fail. In another moment he was shed of all the outrage and the possessiveness he had felt for the vacant house. This house was something the old woman intended to burn down. And Loch could think of a thousand ways she could do it better.

She could fetch a mattress—that would burn fine. Suppose she went upstairs now for the one they played on? Or pulled the other one, sheet and all, from under Mr Holifield (whose hat had imperceptibly turned on the bedpost; it changed like a weathercock)? If she went out of sight for a minute, he watched at the little stair window, but she did not go up.

She brought in an old quilt that the dogs there once slept on, that had hung over the line on the back porch until it was half light-colored and half dark. She climbed up on the piano stool, the way women climb, death-defying, and hung the quilt over the front window. It fell down. Twice more she climbed up with it and the third time it stayed. If only she did not block the window toward him! But if she meant to, she forgot. She kept putting her hand to her head.

Everything she did was wrong, after a certain point. She had got off the track. What she really wanted was a draft. Instead, she was keeping air away, and let her try to make fire burn in an airless room. That was the conceited thing girls and women would try.

But now she went to the blind corner of the parlor and when she came out she had a new and mysterious object in her hands.

At that moment Loch heard Louella climbing the back stairs, coming to peep in at him. He flung himself on his back, stretched out one arm, his hand on his heart and his mouth agape, as he did when he played dead in battle. He forgot to shut his eyes. Louella stood there a minute and then tiptoed off.

Loch then leapt to his knees, crawled out the window under the pushed-out screen, onto the hackberry branch, and let himself into the tree the old way.

He went out on a far-extending limb that took him nearest the vacant house. With him at their window the sailor and girl saw him and yet did not see him. He descended further. He found his place in the tree, a rustling, familiar old crotch where he used to sit and count up his bottle tops. He hung watching, sometimes by the hands and sometimes by the knees and feet.

The old woman was dirty. Standing still she shook a little—her hanging cheeks and her hands. He could see well now what she was holding there like a lamp. But he could not tell what it was—a small brown wooden box, shaped like the Obelisk. It had a door—she opened it. It made a mechanical sound. He heard it plainly through the boxed room which was like a sounding board; it was ticking.

She set the obelisk up on the piano, there in the crown of leaves; she pushed a statue out of the way. He listened to it ticking on and his hopes suddenly rose for her. Holding by the knees and diving head down, then swaying in the sweet open free air and dizzy as an apple on a tree, he thought: the box is where she has the dynamite.

He opened his arms and let them hang outward, and flickered his lashes in the June light, watching house, sky, leaves, a flying bird, all and nothing at all.

Little Sister Spights, aged two, that he had not seen cross the street since she was born, wandered under him dragging a skate.

'Hello, little bitty old sweet thing,' he murmured from the leaves. 'Better go back where you came from.'

And then the old woman stuck out a finger and played the tune.

He hung still as a folded bat.

II

Für Elise.

In her bedroom when she heard the gentle opening, the little phrase, Cassie looked up from what she was doing and said in response, 'Virgie Rainey, *danke schoen.*'

In surprise, but as slowly as in regret, she stopped stirring the emerald green. She got up from where she had been squatting in the middle of the floor and stepped over the dishes which were set about on the matting rug. She went quietly to her south window, where she lifted a curtain, spotting it with her wet fingers. There was not a soul in sight at the MacLain house but Old Man Holifield asleep with his gawky hightop shoes on and his stomach full as a robin's. His presence—he was the Holifield who was night watchman at the gin and slept here by day—never kept Cassie's mother from going right ahead and calling the MacLain house 'the vacant house.'

Whatever you called it, the house was something you saw without seeing it—it was part of the world again. That unpainted side changed passively with the day and the season, the way a natural place like the river bank changed. In cooler weather its windows would turn like sweetgum leaves, maroon when the late sun came up, and in winter it was bare and glinty, more exposed and more lonesome even than now. In summer it was an overgrown place. Leaves and their shadows pressed up to it, arc-light sharp and still as noon all day. It showed at all times that no woman kept it.

That rainless, windless June the bright air and the town of Morgana, life itself, sunlit and moonlit, were composed and still and china-like.

Cassie felt that now. Yet in the shade of the vacant house, though all looked still, there was agitation. Some life stirred through. It may have been *old* life.

Ever since the MacLains had moved away, that roof had stood (and leaked) over the heads of people who did not really stay, and a restless current seemed to flow dark and free around it (there would be some sound or motion to startle the birds), a life quicker than the Morrisons' life, more driven probably, thought Cassie uneasily.

Was it Virgie Rainey in there now? Where was she hiding, if she sneaked in and touched that piano? When did she come? Cassie felt teased. She doubted for a moment that she had heard *Für Elise*—she doubted herself, so easily, and she struck her chest with her fist, sighing, the way Parnell Moody always struck hers.

A line of poetry tumbled in her ears, or started to tumble.

> *'Though I am old with wandering . . .'*

She banged her hands on her hipbones, enough to hurt, flung around, and went back to her own business. On one bare foot with the other crossed over it, she stood gazing down at the pots and dishes in which she had enough colors stirred up to make a sunburst design. She was shut up in here to tie-and-dye a scarf. 'Everybody stay out!!!' said an envelope pinned to her door, signed with skull and crossbones.

You took a square of crepe de Chine, you made a point of the goods and tied a string around it in hard knots. You kept on gathering it in and tying it. Then you hung it in the different dyes. The strings were supposed to leave white lines in the colors, a design like a spiderweb. You couldn't possibly have any idea what you would get when you untied your scarf; but Missie Spights said there had never been one yet that didn't take the breath away.

Für Elise. This time there were two phrases, the *E* in the second phrase very flat.

Cassie edged back to the window, while her heart sank, praying that she would not catch sight of Virgie Rainey or, especially, that Virgie Rainey would not catch sight of her.

Virgie Rainey worked. Not at teaching. She played the piano for the picture show, both shows every night, and got six dollars a week, and was not popular any more. Even in her last year in consolidated high school—just ended—she worked. But when Cassie and she were little, they used to take music together in the MacLain house next door, from Miss Eckhart. Virgie Rainey played *Für Elise* all the time. And Miss Eckhart used to say, 'Virgie Rainey, *danke schoen.*' Where had Miss Eckhart ever gone? She had been Miss Snowdie MacLain's roomer.

'Cassie!' Loch was calling again.

'What!'

'Come here!'

'I can't!'

'Got something to show you!'

'I *ain't got time!*'

Her bedroom door had been closed all afternoon. But first her mother had opened it and come in, only to exclaim and not let herself be touched, and to go out leaving the smell of rose geranium behind for the fan to keep bringing at her. Then Louella had moved right in on her without asking and for ages was standing over her rolling up her hair on newspaper to make it bushy for the hayride that night. 'I cares if you don't.'

With her gaze at a judicious distance from the colors she dipped in, Cassie was now for a little time far away, perhaps up in September in college, where, however, tie-and-dye scarves would be out-of-uniform, though something to unfold and show.

But with *Für Elise* the third time, her uncritical self of the crucial present, this Wednesday afternoon, slowly came forward—as if called on. Cassie saw herself without even facing the mirror, for her small, solemn, unprotected figure was emerging staring-clear inside her mind. There she was now, standing scared at the window again in her petticoat, a little of each color of the rainbow dropped on her—bodice and flounce—in spite of reasonable care. Her pale hair was covered and burdened with twisty papers, like a hat too big for her. She balanced her head on her frail neck. She was holding a spoon up like a mean switch in her right hand, and her feet were bare. She had seemed to be favored and happy and she stood there pathetic—

homeless-looking—horrible. Like a wave, the gathering past came right up to her. Next time it would be too high. The poetry was all around her, pellucid and lifting from side to side,

> '*Though I am old with wandering*
> *Through hollow lands and hilly lands,*
> *I will find out where she has gone. . . .*'

Then the wave moved up, towered, and came drowning down over her stuck-up head.

Through the years Cassie had come just before Virgie Rainey for her music lesson, or, at intervals, just after her. To start with, Cassie was so poor in music and Virgie so good (the opposite of themselves in other things!) that Miss Eckhart with her methodical mind might have coupled them on purpose. They went on Mondays and Thursdays at 3:30 and 4:00 and, after school was out and up until the recital, at 9:30 and 10:00 in the morning. So punctual and so formidable was Miss Eckhart that all the little girls passed, one going and one coming, through the beaded curtains mincing like strangers. Only Virgie would let go the lights of mockery from her eyes.

Though she was tireless as a spider, Miss Eckhart waited so unbudgingly for her pupils that from the back she appeared asleep in her studio. How much later had it occurred to Cassie that 'the studio' itself, the only one ever heard of in Morgana, was nothing more than a room that was rented? Rented because poor Miss Snowdie MacLain needed the money?

Then it seemed a dedicated place. The black-painted floor was bare even of matting, so as not to deaden any sound of music. There was in the very center a dark squarish piano (ebony, they all thought) with legs twisted like elephant legs, bearing many pounds of sheet music on its back—just to look heavy there, Cassie thought, for whose music was it? The yellow keys, some split and others in the bass coffee-colored, always had a little film of sweat. There was a stool spun up high, with a seat worn away like a bowl. Beside it, Miss Eckhart's chair was the kind of old thing most people placed by their telephones.

There were gold chairs, their legs brittle and set the way pulled candy was, sliding across the floor at a touch, and forbidden—they were for the recital audience; their fragility was intentional. There were taboret tables with little pink statuettes and hydrangea-colored, horny shells. Beaded curtains in the doorway stirred and clicked now and then during a lesson, as if someone were coming, but it signified no more than the idle clicking redbirds made in the free outdoors, if it was not time for a pupil. (The MacLains lived largely upstairs, except for the kitchen, and came in at the side.) The beads were faintly sweet-smelling, and made you think of long strings of wine-balls and tiny candy bottles filled with violet liquid, and licorice sticks. The studio was in some ways like the witch's house in *Hansel and Gretel*, Cassie's mother said, 'including the witch.' On the right-hand corner of the piano stood a small, mint-white bust of Beethoven, all softened around the edges with the nose smoothed down, as if a cow had licked it.

Miss Eckhart, a heavy brunette woman whose age was not known, sat during the lessons on the nondescript chair, which her body hid altogether, in apparent disregard for body and chair alike. She was alternately very quiet and very alert, and sometimes that seemed to be because she hated flies. She held a swatter in her down-inclined lap, gracefully and tenderly as a fan, her hard, round, short fingers surprisingly forgetful-looking. All at once as you played your piece, making errors or going perfectly it did not matter, smack down would come the fly swatter on the back of your hand. No words would be passed, of triumph or apology on Miss Eckhart's part or of surprise or pain on yours. It did hurt. Virgie, her face hardening under the progress of her advancing piece, could manage the most oblivious look of all, though Miss Eckhart might strike harder and harder at the persistent flies. All her pupils let the flies in, when they trailed in and out for their lessons; not to speak of the MacLain boys, who left their door wide open to the universe when they went out to play.

Miss Eckhart might also go abruptly to her little built-on kitchen— she and her mother had no Negro and didn't use Miss Snowdie's; she did not say 'Excuse me,' or explain what was on the stove. And there were times, perhaps on rainy days, when she walked around and

around the studio, and you felt her pause behind you. Just as you
thought she had forgotten you, she would lean over your head, you
were under her bosom like a traveler under a cliff, her penciled finger
would go to your music, and above the bar you were playing she
would slowly write 'Slow.' Or sometimes, precipitant above you, she
would make a curly circle with a long tail, as if she might draw a cat,
but it would be her ' P' and the word would turn into 'Practice!!'

When you could once play a piece, she paid scant attention, and
made no remark; her manners were all very unfamiliar. It was only
time for a new piece. Whenever she opened the cabinet, the smell of
new sheet music came out swift as an imprisoned spirit, something
almost palpable, like a pet coon; Miss Eckhart kept the music locked
up and the key down her dress, inside the collar. She would seat herself and with a dipped pen add '$.25' to the bill on the spot. Cassie
could see the bills clearly, in elaborate handwriting, the 'z' in Mozart
with an equals-sign through it and all the 'y's' so heavily tailed they
went through the paper. It took a whole lesson for those tails to dry.

What was it she did when you played without a mistake? Oh, she
went over and told the canary something, tapping the bars of his cage
with her finger. 'Just listen,' she told him. 'Enough from *you* for today,'
she would call to you over her shoulder.

Virgie Rainey would come through the beads carrying a magnolia
bloom which she had stolen.

She would ride over on a boy's bicycle (her brother Victor's) from
the Raineys' with sheets of advanced music rolled naked (girls usually
had portfolios) and strapped to the boy's bar which she straddled, the
magnolia broken out of the Carmichaels' tree and laid bruising in the
wire basket on the handlebars. Or sometimes Virgie would come an
hour late, if she had to deliver the milk first, and sometimes she came
by the back door and walked in peeling a ripe fig with her teeth; and
sometimes she missed her lesson altogether. But whenever she came
on the bicycle she would ride it up into the yard and run the front
wheel bang into the lattice, while Cassie was playing the 'Scarf Dance.'
(In those days, the house looked nice, with latticework and plants
hiding the foundation, and a three-legged fern stand at the turn in the

porch to discourage skaters and defeat little boys.) Miss Eckhart would put her hand to her breast, as though she felt the careless wheel shake the very foundation of the studio.

Virgie carried in the magnolia bloom like a hot tureen, and offered it to Miss Eckhart, neither of them knowing any better: magnolias smelled too sweet and heavy for right after breakfast. And Virgie handled everything with her finger stuck out; she was conceited over a musician's cyst that appeared on her fourth finger.

Miss Eckhart took the flower but Virgie might be kept waiting while Cassie recited on her catechism page. Sometimes Miss Eckhart checked the questions missed, sometimes the questions answered; but every question she did check got a heavy 'V' that crossed the small page like the tail of a comet. She would draw her black brows together to see Cassie forgetting, unless it was to remember some nearly forgotten thing herself. At the exact moment of the hour (the alarm clock had a green and blue waterfall scene on its face) she would dismiss Cassie and incline her head toward Virgie, as though she was recognizing her only now, when she was ready for her; yet all this time she had held the strong magnolia flower in her hand, and its scent was filling the room.

Virgie would drift over to the piano, spread out her music, and make sure she was sitting just the way she wanted to be upon the stool. She flung her skirt behind her, with a double swimming motion. Then without a word from Miss Eckhart she would start to play. She played firmly, smoothly, her face at rest, the musician's cyst, of which she was in idleness so proud, perched like a ladybug, riding the song. She went now gently, now forcibly, never loudly.

And when she was finished, Miss Eckhart would say, 'Virgie Rainey, *danke schoen*.'

Cassie, so still her chest cramped, not daring to walk on the creaky floor down the hall, would wait till the end to run out of the house and home. She would whisper while she ran, with the sound of an engine, '*Danke schoen, danke schoen, danke schoen*.' It wasn't the meaning that propelled her; she didn't know then what it meant.

But then nobody knew for years (until the World War) what Miss Eckhart meant by '*Danke schoen*' and '*Mein lieber Kind*' and the rest, and who would dare ask? It was like belling the cat. Only Virgie had the nerve, only she could have found out for the others. Virgie said she did not know and did not care. So they just added that onto Virgie's name in the school yard. She was Virgie Rainey *Danke schoen* when she jumped hot pepper or fought the boys, when she had to sit down the very first one in the spelling match for saying 'E-a-r, ear, r-a-k-e, rake, ear-ache.' She was named for good. Sometimes even in the Bijou somebody cat-called that to her as she came in her high heels down the steep slant of the board aisle to switch on the light and open the piano. When she was grown she would tilt up her chin. Calm as a marble head, defamed with a spit-curl, Virgie's head would be proudly carried past the banner on the wall, past every word of 'It's Cool at the Bijou, Enjoy Typhoons of Alaskan Breezes,' which was tacked up under the fan. Rats ran under her feet, most likely, too; the Bijou was once Spights' Livery Stable.

'Virgie brings me good luck!' Miss Eckhart used to say, with a round smile on her face. Luck that might not be good was something else that was a new thought to them all.

Virgie Rainey, when she was ten or twelve, had naturally curly hair, silky and dark, and a great deal of it—uncombed. She was not sent to the barber shop often enough to suit the mothers of other children, who said it was probably dirty hair too—what could the children see of the back of her neck, poor Katie Rainey being so rushed for time? Her middy blouse was trimmed in a becoming red, her anchor was always loose, and her red silk lacers were actually ladies' shoestrings dipped in pokeberry juice. She was full of the airs of wildness, she swayed and gave way to joys and tempers, her own and other people's with equal freedom—except never Miss Eckhart's, of course.

School did not lessen Virgie's vitality; once on a rainy day when recess was held in the basement, she said she was going to butt her brains out against the wall, and the teacher, old Mrs McGillicuddy, had said, 'Beat them out, then,' and she had really tried. The rest of the fourth grade stood around expectant and admiring, the smell of open thermos bottles sweetly heavy in the close air. Virgie came with strange kinds of sandwiches—everybody wanted to swap her—stewed peach, or perhaps banana. In the other children's eyes she was as exciting as a gypsy would be.

Virgie's air of abandon that was so strangely endearing made even the Sunday School class think of her in terms of the future—she would go somewhere, somewhere away off, they said then, talking with their chins sunk in their hands—she'd be a missionary. (Parnell Moody used to be wild and now *she* was pious.) Miss Lizzie Stark's mother, old Mrs Sad-Talking Morgan, said Virgie would be the first lady governor of Mississippi, that was where she would go. It sounded worse than the infernal regions. To Cassie, Virgie was a secret love, as well as her secret hate. To Cassie she looked like an illustration by Reginald Birch for a serial in Etta Carmichael's *St Nicholas Magazine* called 'The Lucky Stone.' Her inky hair fell in the same loose locks— because it was dirty. She often took the very pose of that inventive and persecuted little heroine who coped with people she thought were witches and ogres (alas! they were not)—feet apart, head aslant, eyes glancing up sideways, ears cocked; but you could not tell whether Virgie would boldly interrupt her enemies or run off to her own devices with a forgetful smile on her lips.

And she smelled of flavoring. She drank vanilla out of the bottle, she told them, and it didn't burn her a bit. She did that because she knew they called her mother Miss Ice Cream Rainey, for selling cones at speakings.

Für Elise was always Virgie Rainey's piece. For years Cassie thought Virgie wrote it, and Virgie never did deny it. It was a kind of signal that Virgie had burst in; she would strike that little opening phrase off the keys as she passed anybody's piano—even the one in the café. She never abandoned *Für Elise*; long after she went on to the hard pieces, she still played that.

Virgie Rainey was gifted. Everybody said that could not be denied. To show her it was not denied, she was allowed to play all through school for the other children to march in and to play for Wand Drill. Sometimes they drilled to 'Dorothy, an Old English Dance,' and sometimes to *Für Elise*—everybody out of kilter.

'I guess they scraped up the money for music lessons somehow,' said Cassie's mother. Cassie, when she heard Virgie running her scales next door, would see a vision of the Rainey dining room—an interior which in life she had never seen, for she didn't go home from school with the Raineys—and sitting around the table Miss Katie Rainey and Old Man Fate Rainey and Berry and Bolivar Mayhew, some cousins, and Victor who was going to be killed in the war, and Virgie waiting; with Miss Katie scraping up nickels and pennies with an old bone-handled knife, patting them into shape like her butter, and each time—as the scale went up—just barely getting enough or—as it went down—not quite.

Cassie was Miss Eckhart's first pupil, the reason she 'took' being that she lived right next door, but she never had any glory from it. When Virgie began 'taking,' she was the one who made things evident about Miss Eckhart, her lessons, and all. Miss Eckhart, for all her being so strict and inexorable, in spite of her walk, with no give whatsoever, had a timid spot in her soul. There was a little weak place in her, vulnerable, and Virgie Rainey found it and showed it to people.

Miss Eckhart worshiped her metronome. She kept it, like the most precious secret in the teaching of music, in a wall safe. Jinny Love Stark, who was only seven or eight years old but had her tongue, did suggest that this was the only thing Miss Eckhart owned of the correct size to lock up there. Why there had ever been a real safe built into the parlor nobody seemed to know; Cassie remembered Miss Snowdie saying the Lord knew, in His infinite workings and wisdom, and some day, somebody would come riding in to Morgana and have need of that safe, after she was gone.

Its door looked like a tin plate there in the wall, the closed-up end of an old flue. Miss Eckhart would go toward it with measured step. Technically the safe was hidden, of course, and only she knew it was there, since Miss Snowdie rented it; even Miss Eckhart's mother, possibly, had no expectations of getting in. Yes, her mother lived with her.

Cassie, out of nice feeling, looked the other way when it was time for the morning opening of the safe. It seemed awful, and yet imminent, that because she was the first pupil she, Cassie Morrison, might be the one to call logical attention to the absurdity of a safe in which there were no jewels, in which there was the very opposite of a jewel. Then Virgie, one day when the metronome was set going in front of her—Cassie was just leaving—announced simply that she would not play another note with that thing in her face.

At Virgie's words, Miss Eckhart quickly—it almost seemed that was what she'd wanted to hear—stopped the hand and slammed the little door, bang. The metronome was never set before Virgie again.

Of course all the rest of them still got it. It came out of the safe every morning, as regularly as the canary was uncovered in his cage. Miss Eckhart had made an exception of Virgie Rainey; she had first respected Virgie Rainey, and now fell humble before her impudence.

A metronome was an infernal machine, Cassie's mother said when Cassie told on Virgie. 'Mercy, you have to keep moving, with that infernal machine. I want a song to *dip*.'

'What do you mean, dip? Could you have played the piano, Mama?'

'Child, I could have *sung*,' and she threw her hand from her, as though all music might as well now go jump off the bridge.

As time went on, Virgie Rainey showed her bad manners to Miss Eckhart still more, since she had won about the metronome. Once she had a little *Rondo* her way, and Miss Eckhart was so beset about it that the lesson was not like a real lesson at all. Once she unrolled the new *Étude* and when it kept rolling back up, as the *Étude* always did, she threw it on the floor and jumped on it, before Miss Eckhart had even seen it; that was heartless. After such showing off, Virgie would push her hair behind her ears and then softly lay her hands on the keys, as she would take up a doll.

Miss Eckhart would sit there blotting out her chair in the same way as ever, but inside her she was listening to every note. Such listening would have made Cassie forget. And half the time, the piece was only *Für Elise*, which Miss Eckhart could probably have played blindfolded and standing up with her back to the keys. Anybody could tell that Virgie was doing something to Miss Eckhart. She was turning her from a teacher into something lesser. And if she was not a teacher, what was Miss Eckhart?

At times she could not bring herself to swat a summer fly. And as little as Virgie, of them all, cared if her hand was rapped, Miss Eckhart would raise her swatter and try to bring it down and could not. You could see torment in her regard of the fly. The smooth clear music would move on like water, beautiful and undisturbed, under the hanging swatter and Miss Eckhart's red-rimmed thumb. But even boys hit Virgie, because she liked to fight.

There were times when Miss Eckhart's Yankeeness, if not her very origin, some last quality to fade, almost faded. Before some caprice of Virgie's, her spirit drooped its head. The child had it by the lead. Cassie saw Miss Eckhart's spirit as a terrifyingly gentle water-buffalo cow in the story of 'Peasie and Beansie' in the reader. And sooner or later, after taming her teacher, Virgie was going to mistreat her. Most of them expected some great scene.

There was in the house itself, soon, a daily occurrence to distress Miss Eckhart. There was now a second roomer at Miss Snowdie's. While Miss Eckhart listened to a pupil, Mr Voight would walk over their heads and come down to the turn of the stairs, open his bathrobe, and flap the skirts like an old turkey gobbler. They all knew Miss Snowdie never suspected she housed a man like that: he was a sewing machine salesman. When he flapped his maroon-colored bathrobe, he wore no clothes at all underneath.

It would be plain to Miss Eckhart or to anybody that he wanted, first, the music lesson to stop. They could not close the door, there was no door, there were beads. They could not tell Miss Snowdie even that he objected; she would have been agonized. All the little girls and the one little boy were afraid of Mr Voight's appearance at every lesson and felt nervous until it had happened and got over with. The one little boy was Scooter MacLain, the twin that took the free lessons; he kept mum.

Cassie saw that Miss Eckhart, who might once have been formidable in particular to any Mr Voights, was helpless toward him and his antics—as helpless as Miss Snowdie MacLain would have been, helpless as Miss Snowdie was, toward her own little twin sons—all since she had begun giving in to Virgie Rainey. Virgie kept the upper hand over Miss Eckhart even at the moment when Mr Voight came out to scare them. She only played on the stronger and clearer, and never pretended he had not come out and that she did not know it, or that she might not tell it, no matter how poor Miss Eckhart begged.

'Tell a soul what you have seen, I'll beat your hands until you scream,' Miss Eckhart had said. Her round eyes opened wide, her mouth went small. This was all she knew to say. To Cassie it was as idle as a magic warning in a story; she criticized the rhyme. She herself had told all about Mr Voight at breakfast, stood up at the table and waved her arms, only to have her father say he didn't believe it; that Mr Voight represented a large concern and covered seven states. He added his own threat to Miss Eckhart's: no picture show money.

Her mother's laugh, which followed, was as usual soft and playful but not illuminating. Her laugh, like the morning light that came in the window each summer breakfast time around her father's long head, slowly made it its solid silhouette where he sat against the day. He turned to his paper like Douglas Fairbanks opening big gates; it was indeed his; he published the *Morgana-MacLain Weekly Bugle* and Mr Voight had no place in it.

'Live and let live, Cassie,' her mother said, meaning it mischievously. She showed no repentance, such as Cassie felt, for her inconsistencies. She had sometimes said passionately, 'Oh, I hate that old MacLain house next door to me! I hate having it there all the time. I'm worn out with Miss Snowdie's cross!' Later on, when Miss Snowdie finally had to sell the house and move away, her mother said, 'Well, I see Snowdie gave up.' When she told bad news, she wore a perfectly blank face and her voice was helpless and automatic, as if she repeated a lesson.

Virgie told on Mr Voight too, but she had nobody to believe her, and so Miss Eckhart did not lose any pupils by that. Virgie did not know how to tell anything.

And for what Mr Voight did there were no ready words—what would you call it? 'Call it spontaneous combustion,' Cassie's mother said. Some performances of people stayed partly untold for lack of a name, Cassie believed, as well as for lack of believers. Mr Voight before so very long—it happened during a sojourn home of Mr MacLain, she remembered—was transferred to travel another seven states, ending the problem; and yet Mr Voight had done something that amounted to more than going naked under his robe and calling alarm like a turkey gobbler, it was more belligerent; and the least describable thing of all had been a look on his face; that was strange. Thinking of it now, and here in her room, Cassie found she had bared her teeth and set them, trying out the frantic look. She could not now, any more than then, really describe Mr Voight, but without thinking she could *be* Mr Voight, which was more frightening still.

Like a dreamer dreaming with reservations, Cassie moved over and changed the color for her scarf and moved back to the window. She reached behind her for a square of heavenly-hash in its platter and bit down on the marshmallow.

There was another man Miss Eckhart had been scared of, up until the last. (Not Mr King MacLain. They always passed without touching, like two stars, perhaps they had some kind of eclipse-effect on each other.) She had been sweet on Mr Hal Sissum, who clerked in the shoe department of Spights' store.

Cassie remembered him—who didn't know Mr Sissum and all the Sissums? His sandy hair, parted on the side, shook over his ear like a toboggan cap when he ambled forward, in his long lazy step, to wait on people. He teased people that came to buy shoes, as though that took the prize for the vainest, most outlandish idea that could ever come over human beings.

Miss Eckhart had pretty ankles for a heavy lady like herself. Mrs Stark said what a surprise it was for Miss Eckhart, of all people, to turn up with such pretty ankles, which made it the same as if she didn't have them. When she came in she took her seat and put her foot earnestly up on Mr Sissum's stool like any other lady in Morgana and he spoke to her very nicely. He generally invited the bigger ladies, like Miss Nell Loomis or Miss Gert Bowles, to sit in the children's chair, but he held back, with Miss Eckhart, and spoke very nicely to her about her feet and treated them as a real concern; he even brought out a choice of shoes. To most ladies he brought out one box and said, 'There's your shoe,' as though shoes were something predestined. He knew them all so well.

Miss Eckhart might have come over to his aisle more often, but she had an incomprehensible habit of buying shoes two or even four pairs at a time, to save going back, or to take precaution against never finding them again. She didn't know how to do about Mr Sissum at all.

But what could they either one have done? They couldn't go to church together; the Sissums were Presbyterians from the beginning of time and Miss Eckhart belonged to some distant church with a previously unheard-of name, the Lutheran. She could not go to the picture show with Mr Sissum because he was already at the picture show. He played the music there every evening after the store closed—he had to; this was before the Bijou afforded a piano, and he could play the cello. He could not have refused Mr Syd Sissum, who bought the stable and built the Bijou.

Miss Eckhart used to come to the political speakings in the Starks' yard when Mr Sissum played with the visiting band. Anybody could see him all evening then, high on the fresh plank platform behind his cello. Miss Eckhart, the true musician, sat on the damp night grass and listened. Nobody ever saw them really together any more than that. How did they know she was sweet on Mr Sissum? But they did.

Mr Sissum was drowned in the Big Black River one summer—fell out of his boat, all alone.

Cassie would rather remember the sweet soft speaking-nights in the Starks' yard. Before the speakings began, while the music was playing, Virgie and her older brother Victor ran wild all over everywhere, assaulting the crowd, where couples and threes and fives of people joined hands like paperdoll strings and wandered laughing and turning under the blossoming China trees and the heavy crape myrtles that were wound up in honeysuckle. How delicious it all smelled! Virgie let herself go completely, as anyone would like to do. Jinny Love Stark's swing was free to anybody and Virgie ran under the swingers, or jumped on behind, booting and pumping. She ran under sweethearts' twining arms, and nobody, even her brother, could catch her. She rolled the country people's watermelons away. She caught lightning bugs and tore out their lights for jewelry. She never rested as long as the music played except at last to throw herself hard and panting on the ground, her open mouth smiling against the trampled clover. Sometimes she made Victor climb up on the Starks' statue. Cassie remembered him, white face against dark leaves, a baseball cap turned backwards with the bill behind, and long black-stockinged legs wound over the snowy limbs of the goddess, and slowly, proudly sliding down.

But Virgie would not even watch him. She whirled in one direction till she fell down drunk, or turned about more slowly when they played *Vienna Woods*. She pushed Jinny Love Stark into her own lily bed. And all the time, she was eating. She ate all the ice cream she wanted. Now and then, in the soft parts of *Carmen* or before the storm in *William Tell*—even during dramatic pauses in the speaking— Mrs Ice Cream Rainey's voice could be heard quickly calling, 'Ice cream?' She had brought a freezer or two on Mr Rainey's wagon to the foot of the yard. This time of year it might be fig. Sometimes Virgie whirled around with a fig ice cream cone in each hand, held poised like daggers.

Virgie would run closer and closer circles around Miss Eckhart, who sat alone (her mother never came out that far) on a *Bugle*, all four pages unfolded on the grass, listening. Up above, Mr Sissum— who bent over his cello in the Bijou every night like an old sewing woman over the machine, like a shoe clerk over another foot to fit— shone in a Palm Beach coat and played straight-backed in the visiting band, and as fast as they did. The lock of hair was no longer hiding his eyes and nose; like the candidate for supervisor, he looked out.

Virgie put a loop of clover chain down over Miss Eckhart's head, her hat—her one hat—and all. She hung Miss Eckhart with flowers, while Mr Sissum plucked the strings up above her. Miss Eckhart sat on, perfectly still and submissive. She gave no sign. She let the clover chain come down and lie on her breast.

Virgie laughed delightedly and with her long chain in her hand ran around and around her, binding her up with clovers. Miss Eckhart let her head roll back, and then Cassie felt that the teacher was filled with terror, perhaps with pain. She found it so easy—ever since Virgie showed her—to feel terror and pain in an outsider; in someone you did not know at all well, pain made you wonderfully sorry. It was not so easy to be sorry about it in the people close to you—it came unwillingly; and how strange—in yourself, on nights like this, pain— even a moment's pain—seemed inconceivable.

Cassie's whole family would be at the speakings, of course, her father moving at large through the crowd or sometimes sitting on the platform with Mr Carmichael and Mr Comus Stark with the rolling head and Mr Spights. Cassie would try to stay in sight of her mother, but no matter how slightly she strayed, only to follow Virgie around the backyard and find croquet balls in the grass, or down the hill to get a free cone, when she got back to their place her mother would be gone. She always lost her mother. She would find Loch there, rolled in a ball asleep in his sailor suit, his cheek holding down the ribbon of her softly removed hat. When she was back again, 'I've just been through yonder to speak to my candidate,' she said. 'It's you that vanishes, Lady Bug, you that gets away.'

It appeared to Cassie that only the figure of Miss Eckhart, off there like a vast receptacle in its island of space, did not move or sway when the band played *Tales of Hoffmann*.

One time Mr Sissum gave Miss Eckhart something, a Billikin. The Billikin was a funny, ugly doll that Spights' store gave free to children with every pair of Billikin shoes. Never had Miss Eckhart laughed so hard, and with such an unfamiliar sound, as she laughed to see Mr Sissum's favor. Tears ran down her bright, distorted cheeks every time one of the children coming into the studio picked the Billikin up. When her laughter was exhausted she would sigh faintly and ask for the doll, and then soberly set it down on a little minaret table, as if it were a vase of fresh red roses. Her old mother took it one day and cracked it across her knee.

When Mr Sissum was drowned, Miss Eckhart came to his funeral like everybody else. The Loomises invited her to ride with them. She looked exactly the same as ever, round and solid, her back a ramrod in her dress that was the wrong season's length and her same hat, the home-made one with cambric flowers sticking up on it. But when the coffin was lowered into Mr Sissum's place in the Sissum lot under a giant magnolia tree, and Mr Sissum's preacher, Dr Carlyle, said burial service, Miss Eckhart broke out of the circle.

She pressed to the front, through Sissums from everywhere and all the Presbyterians, and went close to get a look; and if Dr Loomis had not caught her she would have gone headlong into the red clay hole. People said she might have thrown herself upon the coffin if they'd let her; just as, later, Miss Katie Rainey did on Victor's when he was brought back from France. But Cassie had the impression that Miss Eckhart simply wanted to see—to see what was being done with Mr Sissum.

As she struggled, her round face seemed stretched wider than it was long by a feeling that failed to match the feelings of everybody else. It was not the same as sorrow. Miss Eckhart, a stranger to their cemetery, where none of her people lay, pushed forward with her unstylish, winter purse swinging on her arm, and began to nod her head—sharply, to one side and then the other. She appeared almost little under the tree, but Mr Comus Stark and Dr Loomis looked more shrunken still by the side of her as they—sent by ladies—reached for her elbows. Her vigorous nods included them too, increasing in urgency. It was the way she nodded at pupils to bring up their rhythm, helping out the metronome.

Cassie remembered how Miss Snowdie MacLain's grip tightened on her hand and stayed tightened until Miss Eckhart got over it. But Cassie remembered her manners better than to seem to watch Miss Eckhart after one look; she stared down at her Billikin shoes. And her mother had slipped away.

It was strange that in Mr Sissum's life Miss Eckhart, as everybody said, had never known what to do; and now she did this. Her sharp nodding was like something to encourage them all—to say that she knew now, to do this, and that nobody need speak to her or touch her unless, if they thought best, they could give her this little touch at the elbows, the steer of politeness.

'*Pizzicato.*'

Once, Miss Eckhart gave out the word to define in the catechism lesson.

'*Pizzicato* is when Mr Sissum played the cello before he got drowned.'

That was herself: Cassie heard her own words. She had tried—she was as determined as if she'd been dared—to see how that sounded, spoken out like that to Miss Eckhart's face. She remembered how Miss Eckhart listened to her and did nothing but sit still as a statue, as she sat when the flowers came down over her head.

After the way she cried in the cemetery—for they decided it must have been crying she did—some ladies stopped their little girls from learning any more music; Miss Jefferson Moody stopped Parnell.

Cassie heard noises—a thump next door, the antiquated sound of thunder. There was nothing she could see—only Old Man Holifield's hat that idly made a half-turn on the bedpost, as if something, by a long grapevine, had jolted it.

One summer morning, a sudden storm had rolled up and three children were caught at the studio—Virgie Rainey, little Jinny Love Stark, and Cassie—though the two bigger girls might have run their short way home with newspapers over their hair.

Miss Eckhart, without saying what she was going to do, poked her finger solidly along the pile of music on top of the piano, pulled out a piece, and sat down on her own stool. It was the only time she ever performed in Cassie's presence except when she took the other half in duets.

Miss Eckhart played as if it were Beethoven; she struck the music open midway and it was in soft yellow tatters like old satin. The thunder rolled and Miss Eckhart frowned and bent forward or she leaned back to play; at moments her solid body swayed from side to side like a tree trunk.

The piece was so hard that she made mistakes and repeated to correct them, so long and stirring that it soon seemed longer than the day itself had been, and in playing it Miss Eckhart assumed an entirely different face. Her skin flattened and drew across her cheeks, her lips changed. The face could have belonged to someone else—not even to a woman, necessarily. It was the face a mountain could have, or what might be seen behind the veil of a waterfall. There in the rainy light it was a sightless face, one for music only—though the fingers kept slipping and making mistakes they had to correct. And if the sonata had an origin in a place on earth, it was the place where Virgie, even, had never been and was not likely ever to go.

The music came with greater volume—with fewer halts—and Jinny Love tiptoed forward and began turning the music. Miss Eckhart did not even see her—her arm struck the child, making a run. Coming from Miss Eckhart, the music made all the pupils uneasy, almost alarmed; something had burst out, unwanted, exciting, from the wrong person's life. This was some brilliant thing too splendid for Miss Eckhart, piercing and striking the air around her the way a Christmas firework might almost jump out of the hand that was, each year, inexperienced anew.

It was when Miss Eckhart was young that she had learned this piece, Cassie divined. Then she had almost forgotten it. But it took only a summer rain to start it again; she had been pricked and the music came like the red blood under the scab of a forgotten fall. The little girls, all stationed about the studio with the rushing rain outside, looked at one another, the three quite suddenly on some equal footing. They were all wondering—thinking—perhaps about escape. A mosquito circled Cassie's head, singing, and fastened on her arm, but she dared not move.

What Miss Eckhart might have told them a long time ago was that there was more than the ear could bear to hear or the eye to see, even in her. The music was too much for Cassie Morrison. It lay in the very heart of the stormy morning—there was something almost too violent about a storm in the morning. She stood back in the room with her whole body averted as if to ward off blows from Miss Eckhart's strong left hand, her eyes on the faintly winking circle of the safe in the wall. She began to think of an incident that had happened to Miss Eckhart instead of about the music she was playing; that was one way.

One time, at nine o'clock at night, a crazy Negro had jumped out of the school hedge and got Miss Eckhart, had pulled her down and threatened to kill her. That was long ago. She had been walking by herself after dark; nobody had told her any better. When Dr Loomis made her well, people were surprised that she and her mother did not move away. They wished she had moved away, everybody but poor Miss Snowdie; then they wouldn't always have to remember that a terrible thing once happened to her. But Miss Eckhart stayed, as though she considered one thing not so much more terrifying than another. (After all, nobody knew why she came!) It was because she was from so far away, at any rate, people said to excuse her, that she couldn't comprehend; Miss Perdita Mayo, who took in sewing and made everybody's trousseaux, said Miss Eckhart's *differences* were why shame alone had not killed her and killed her mother too; that differences were reasons.

Cassie thought as she listened, had to listen, to the music that perhaps more than anything it was the terrible fate that came on her that people could not forgive Miss Eckhart for. Yet things divined and endured, spectacular moments, hideous things like the black stranger jumping out of the hedge at nine o'clock, all seemed to Cassie to be by their own nature rising—and so alike—and crossing the sky and setting, the way the planets did. Or they were more like whole constellations, turning at their very centers maybe, like Perseus and Orion and Cassiopeia in her Chair and the Big Bear and Little Bear, maybe often upside down, but terribly recognizable. It was not just the sun and moon that traveled. In the deepening of the night, the rising sky lifted like a cover when Louella let it soar as she made the bed.

All kinds of things would rise and set in your own life, you could begin now to watch for them, roll back your head and feel their rays come down and reach your open eyes.

Performing, Miss Eckhart was unrelenting. Even when the worst of the piece was over, her fingers like foam on rocks pulled at the spent-out part with unstilled persistence, insolence, violence.

Then she dropped her hands.

'Play it again, Miss Eckhart!' they all cried in startled recoil, begging for the last thing they wanted, looking at her great lump of body.

'No.'

Jinny Love Stark gave them a grown-up look and closed the music. When she did, the other two saw it wasn't the right music at all, for it was some bound-together songs of Hugo Wolf.

'What were you playing, though?'

That was Miss Snowdie MacLain, standing in the door, holding streams of bead curtains in both hands.

'I couldn't say,' Miss Eckhart said, rising. 'I have forgotten.'

The pupils all ran out in the slackening rain without another word, scattering in three directions by the mimosa tree, its flowers like wet fur, which once grew in the yard of the now-vacant house.

★

Für Elise. It came again, but in a labored, foolish way. Was it a man, using one finger?

Virgie Rainey had gone straight from taking music to playing the piano in the picture show. With her customary swiftness and lightness she had managed to skip an interval, some world-in-between where Cassie and Missie and Parnell were, all dyeing scarves. Virgie had gone direct into the world of power and emotion, which was beginning to seem even bigger than they had all thought. She belonged now with the Gish and the Talmadge sisters. With her yellow pencil she hit the tin plate when the tent opened where Valentino lived.

Virgie sat nightly at the foot of the screen ready for all that happened at the Bijou, and keeping pace with it. Nothing proved too much for her or ever got too far ahead, as it certainly got ahead of Mr Sissum. When the dam broke everywhere at once, or when Nazimova cut off both feet with a saber rather than face life with Sinji, Virgie was instantly playing *Kamennoi-Ostrow.* Missie Spights said only one thing was wrong with having Virgie to play at the Bijou. She didn't work hard enough. Some evenings, she would lean back in her chair and let a whole forest fire burn in dead silence on the screen, and then when the sweethearts had found each other, she would switch on her light with a loud click and start up with creeping, minor runs—perhaps *Anitra's Dance.* But that had nothing to do with working hard.

The only times she played *Für Elise* now were for the advertisements; she played it moodily while the slide of the big white chicken on the watermelon-pink sky came on for Bowles' Gro., or the yellow horn on the streaky blue sky flashed on for the *Bugle,* with Cassie's father's picture as a young man inserted in the wavy beam of noise. *Für Elise* never got finished any more; it began, went a little way, and was interrupted by Virgie's own clamorous hand. She could do things with 'You've Got to See Mama Every Night,' and 'Avalon.'

By now, it was not likely she could play the opening movement of her Liszt concerto. That was the piece none of the rest of them could ever hope to play. Virgie would be heard from in the world, playing that, Miss Eckhart said, revealing to children with one ardent cry her lack of knowledge of the world. How could Virgie be heard from, in the world? And 'the world'! Where did Miss Eckhart think she was now? Virgie Rainey, she repeated over and over, had a gift, and she must go away from Morgana. From them all. From her studio. In the world, she must study and practice her music for the rest of her life. In repeating all this, Miss Eckhart suffered.

And all the time, it was on Miss Eckhart's piano that Virgie had to do her practicing. The Raineys' old borrowed piano was butted and half-eaten by the goats one summer day; something that could only happen at the Raineys'. But they had all known Virgie would never go, or study, or practice anywhere, never would even have her own piano, because it wouldn't be like her. They felt no less sure of that when they heard, every recital, every June, Virgie Rainey playing better and better something that was harder and harder, or watched this fill Miss Eckhart with stiff delight, curious anguish. The very place to prove Miss Eckhart crazy was on her own subject, piano playing: she didn't know what she was talking about.

When the Raineys, after their barn got blown away in a big wind, had no more money to throw away on piano lessons, Miss Eckhart said she would teach Virgie free, because she must not stop learning. But later she made her pick the figs off the trees in the backyard in summer and the pecans off the ground in the front yard in winter, for her lessons. Virgie said Miss Eckhart never gave her a one. Yet she always had nuts in her pocket.

Cassie heard a banging and a running next door, the obvious sound of falling. She shut her eyes.

'Virgie Rainey, *danke schoen*.' Once that was said in a dreadful voice, condemning. There were times in the studio when Miss Eckhart's mother would roll in; she had a wheelchair. The first years, she had kept to herself, rolling around no closer than the dining room, round and round with a whining wheel. She was old, and fair as a doll. Up close, her yellowish hair was powdery like goldenrod that had gone forgotten in a vase, turned white in its curls like Miss Snowdie's. She had wasting legs that showed knifelike down her long skirt, and clumsy-shaped, suffering feet that she placed just so out in front of her on the step of her chair, as if she wanted you to think they were pretty.

The mother rolled into the studio whenever she liked, as time went on; with her shepherdess curls she bobbed herself through the beads that opened to her easier than a door. She would roll a certain distance into the room, then stop the wheels and wait there. She was not so much listening to the lesson as watching it, and though she was not keeping time, it was all the more noticeable the way her hands would tip, tap against her chair; she had a brass thimble on one finger.

Ordinarily, Miss Eckhart never seemed disturbed by her mother's abrupt visits. She appeared gentler, more bemused than before, when old Mrs Eckhart made Parnell Moody cry, just by looking at Parnell too hard. Should daughters *forgive* mothers (with mothers under their heel)? Cassie would rather look at the two of them at night, separated by the dark and the distance between. For when from your own table you saw the Eckharts through their window in the light of a lamp, and Miss Eckhart with a soundless ebullience bouncing up to wait on her mother, sometimes you could imagine them back far away from Morgana, before they had troubles and before they had come to you— plump, bright, and sweet somewhere.

Once when Virgie was practicing on Miss Eckhart's piano, and before she was through, the old mother screamed, '*Danke schoen, danke schoen, danke schoen!*' Cassie heard and saw her.

She screamed with a shy look still on her face, as though through Virgie Rainey she would scream at the whole world, at least at all the music in the world and wasn't that all right? Then she sat there look-ing out the front window, half smiling, having mocked her daughter. Virgie, of course, kept on practicing—it was a Schumann 'forest piece.' She had a pomegranate flower (the marbelized kind, from the Moodys') stuck in her breast-pin, and it did not even move.

But when the song was smoothly finished, Miss Eckhart made her way among the little tables and chairs across the studio. Cassie thought she was going for a drink of water, or something for herself. When she reached her mother, Miss Eckhart slapped the side of her mouth. She stood there a moment more, leaning over the chair—while it seemed to Cassie that it must, after all, have been the mother that slapped the daughter—with the key from her bosom, slipped out, beginning to swing on its chain, back and forth, catching the light.

Then Miss Eckhart, with her back turned, asked Cassie and Virgie to stay for dinner.

Enveloping all that the pupils did—entering the house, parting the curtains, turning the music page, throwing up the wrist for a 'rest'—was the smell of cooking. But the smell was wrong, as the pitch of a note could be wrong. It was the smell of food nobody else had ever tasted.

Cabbage was cooked there by no Negro and by no way it was ever cooked in Morgana. With wine. The wine was brought on foot by Dago Joe, and to the front door. Some nice mornings the studio smelled like a spiced apple. But it was known from Mr Wiley Bowles, the grocer, that Miss Eckhart and her mother (whose mouth was still held crooked after the slap) ate pigs' brains. Poor Miss Snowdie!

Cassie yearned—she did want to taste the cabbage—that was really the insurmountable thing, and even the brains of a pig she would have put in her mouth that day. With that, Missie Spights might be flouted. But when Miss Eckhart said, 'Please—please, will you stay to dinner?' Virgie and Cassie twined arms and said 'No' together.

The war came and all through it and even after 1918 people said Miss Eckhart was a German and still wanted the Kaiser to win, and that Miss Snowdie could get along without her. But the old mother died, and Miss Snowdie said Miss Eckhart needed a friendly roof more than she did herself. Miss Eckhart raised the price of her lessons to six dollars a month. Miss Mamie Carmichael stopped her girls from taking, for this or for one thing or another, and then Miss Billy Texas Spights stopped Missie to be like her. Virgie stopped taking her free lessons when her brother Victor was killed in France, but that might have been coincidence, for Virgie had a birthday: she was fourteen. It might have been Virgie's stopping that took away Miss Eckhart's luck for good.

And when she stopped, Virgie's hand lost its touch—that was what they said. Perhaps nobody wanted Virgie Rainey to be anything in Morgana any more than they had wanted Miss Eckhart to be, and they were the two of them still linked together by people's saying that. How much might depend on people's being linked together? Even Miss

Snowdie had a little harder time than she had had already with Ran and Scooter, her bad boys, by being linked with roomers and music lessons and Germans.

The time came when Miss Eckhart had almost no pupils at all. Then she had only Cassie.

Her mother, Cassie had long known in her heart, could not help but despise Miss Eckhart. It was just for living so close to her, or maybe just for living, a poor unwanted teacher and unmarried. And Cassie's instinct told her her mother despised herself for despising. That was why she kept Cassie taking just a little longer after Miss Eckhart had been deserted by all the other mothers. It was more that than the money, which would go to Miss Snowdie on the rent bill. The child had to make up for her mother's abhorrence, to keep her mother as kind as she really was. While Miss Snowdie could stay kind through always being far away in her heart.

Cassie herself was well applauded when she played a piece. The recital audience always clapped more loudly for her than they did for Virgie; but then they clapped more loudly still for little Jinny Love Stark. It was Cassie who was awarded the Presbyterian Church's music scholarship that year to go to college—not Virgie. It made Cassie feel 'natural'; winning the scholarship over Virgie did not surprise her too much. The only reason for that which she put into words, to be self-effacing, was that the Raineys were Methodists; and yet she did not, basically, understand a slight. And now stretching ahead of her, as far as she could see, were those yellow Schirmer books: all the rest of her life.

But Miss Eckhart sent for Virgie and gave her a present that Cassie for many days could close her eyes and see. It was a little butterfly pin made of cut-out silver, like silver lace, to wear on her shoulder; the safety-catch wasn't any good.

But that didn't make Virgie say she loved Miss Eckhart or go on practicing as she told her. Miss Eckhart gave Virgie an armful of books that were written in German about the lives of the masters, and Virgie couldn't read a word; and Mr Fate Rainey tore out the Venusberg pictures and fed them to the pigs. Miss Eckhart tried all those things and was strict to the last in the way she gave all her love to Virgie Rainey and none to anybody else, the way she was strict in music; and for Miss Eckhart love was just as arbitrary and one-sided as music teaching.

Her love never did anybody any good.

Then one day, Miss Eckhart had to move out.

The trouble was that Miss Snowdie had had to sell the house. She moved with her two boys back to MacLain where she came from, seven miles away, and where her husband's people came from too. She sold the house to Mrs Vince Murphy. And soon Miss Eckhart was put out, with Mrs Vince Murphy retaining the piano and anything Miss Eckhart had or that Miss Snowdie had left for Miss Eckhart.

It was not long before Mrs Vince Murphy was struck by lightning and left the house to Miss Francine, who always kept meaning to fix up the house and take boarders, but had a beau then. She temporized by putting Mr Holifield in to see that nobody ran off with the bathtubs and what furniture there was. And the house 'ran down'—as they said alike of houses and clocks, thought Cassie, to put the seal on inferiority and carelessness and fainting hopes alike, and for ever.

Then stories began to be told of what Miss Eckhart had really done to her old mother. People said the old mother had been in pain for years, and nobody was told. What kind of pain they did not say. But they said that during the war, when Miss Eckhart lost pupils and they did not have very much to eat, she would give her mother paregoric to make sure she slept all night and not wake the street with noise or complaint, for fear still more pupils would be taken away. Some people said Miss Eckhart killed her mother with opium.

Miss Eckhart, in a room out at the old Holifields' on Morgan's Wood Road, got older and weaker, though not noticeably thinner, and would be seen from time to time walking into Morgana, up one side of the street and down the other and home. People said you could look at her and see she had broken. Yet she still had authority. She could still stop young, unknowing children like Loch on the street and ask them imperative questions, 'Where were you throwing that ball?' 'Are you trying to break that tree?' . . . Of course her only associates from first to last were children; not counting Miss Snowdie.

Where did Miss Eckhart come from, and where in the end did she go? In Morgana most destinies were known to everybody and seemed to go without saying. It was unlikely that anybody except Miss Perdita Mayo had asked Miss Eckhart where the Eckharts came from, where exactly in the world, and so received the answer. And Miss Perdita was so undependable: she couldn't tell you now, to save her life. And Miss Eckhart had gone down out of sight.

Once on a Sunday ride, Cassie's father said he bet a nickel that was old lady Eckhart hoeing peas out there on the County Farm, and he bet another nickel she could still do the work of ten nigger men.

Wherever she was, she had no people. Surely, by this time, she had nobody at all. The only one she had ever wanted to have for 'people' was Virgie Rainey *Danke schoen.*

Missie Spights said that if Miss Eckhart had allowed herself to be called by her first name, then she would have been like other ladies. Or if Miss Eckhart had belonged to a church that had ever been heard of, and the ladies would have had something to invite her to belong to . . . Or if she had been married to anybody at all, just the awfullest man—like Miss Snowdie MacLain, that everybody could feel sorry for.

Cassie knelt, and with hurrying hands untied all the knots in her scarf. She held it out in a square. Though she was not thinking of her scarf, it did surprise her; she didn't see indeed how she had ever made it. They had told her so. She hung it over the two posts of a chair to dry and as it fell softly over the ladder of the back she thought that somewhere, even up to the last, there could have been for Miss Eckhart a little opening wedge—a crack in the door. . . .

But if I had been the one to see it open, she thought slowly, I might have slammed it tight for ever. I might.

Her eyes lifted to the window where she saw a thin gray streak go down, like the trail of a match. The humming-bird! She knew him, one that came back every year. She stood and looked down at him. He was a little emerald bobbin, suspended as always before the opening four-o'clocks. Metallic and misty together, tangible and intangible, splendid and fairy-like, the haze of his invisible wings mysterious, like the ring around the moon—had anyone ever tried to catch him? Not she. Let him be suspended there for a moment each year for a hundred years—incredibly thirsty, greedy for every drop in every four-o'clock trumpet in the yard, as though he had them numbered—then dart.

'Like a military operation.'

Cassie's father always said the recital was planned that way, in all its tactics and dress. The preparations went on for many hot, secret weeks—all of May. 'You're not to tell anyone what the program is to be,' Miss Eckhart warned at every lesson and rehearsal, as if there were other music teachers, other classes, rivaling, and as if every year the program didn't begin with 'The Stubborn Rocking Horse' by the one boy and end with '*Marche Militaire*' for eight hands. What Virgie played in the recital one year, Cassie (gradually improving) would come to the next, and Missie Spights had it one more step in the future.

Miss Eckhart decided early in the spring what color each child should wear, with what color sash and hair ribbon, and sent written word to the mother. She explained to the children that it was important which color followed which. 'Think of God's rainbow and its order,' and she would shake her pencil in abrupt little beats in an arch overhead; but they had to think of Spights' store. The quartet, with four dresses in view at one time and in close conjunction, pushing one another, made Miss Eckhart especially apprehensive.

Account was kept in a composition book of each child's assigned color; Miss Eckhart made a little 'v' beside the name in token of the mother's agreement and regarded it as a promise. When the dress was reported finished, starched, and ironed, a line was drawn through that name.

In general, mothers were scared of Miss Eckhart then. Miss Lizzie Stark laughed about it, but she was as scared as anybody else. Miss Eckhart assumed that there would be a new dress for every pupil for the recital night, that Miss Perdita Mayo would make it, or if not Miss Perdita, who even with her sister could not make them all, then the pupil's own mother. The dress must be made with the fingers and the edges of bertha and flounce picoted, the sash as well; and—whatever happened—the costume must be saved for recital night. And this was the kind of thing that both Miss Perdita and most mothers understood immediately.

And it could seldom be worn again; certainly not to another recital—by then an 'old' dress. A recital dress was fuller and had more trimming than a Sunday dress. It was like a flower girl's dress in a wedding; once little Nina Carmichael's *was* a flower girl's dress, after Etta's wedding, but this was special dispensation. The dress should be organdie, with ruffles on skirt, bertha, and sleeves; it called for a satin or taffeta sash tied in a back bow with long tails, pointed like the tails of arrows, to hang over the stool and, if it could be afforded, to reach the floor.

All through May, Miss Eckhart would ask how far along the dresses had come. Cassie was uneasy, for her mother's way was to speak too late for Miss Perdita's list and plan to run the dress up herself at the last minute; but Cassie had to encourage Miss Eckhart. 'She's just evening my hem,' she would report, when the material would still be lying folded up with the newspaper-pattern borrowed from Miss Jefferson Moody, in the *armoire*.

As for the program, that was no problem; it existed readymade without discussion. Far back in the winter, Virgie Rainey would have been allotted a piece that was the most difficult Miss Eckhart could find in the music cabinet. Sometimes it was not as showy a thing as Teensie Loomis always had to have (before she got old and stopped taking), but always it was the hardest piece of all. It would be the test of what Virgie could do, to learn it; an ordeal was set for her each year and each year it was accomplished, with no yielding sign from Virgie that she had struggled. The rest of the program would lead up to this, and did not matter enough to be altered seriously from one year to the next. Just so everybody had a piece to play, and a new dress finished in time, and kept the secrets, there was nothing to do but endure May.

A week ahead of the night, the gold chairs were set in a solid row across the room, to look as if all were gold, and the extra chairs would appear one by one behind them until the room was filled. Miss Eckhart must have carried them in from the dining room first, and then, as she could get hold of them, from elsewhere. She carried them downstairs from Miss Snowdie's freely, of course, and then even from Mr Voight's, for no matter what Miss Eckhart thought of Mr Voight, she wouldn't hesitate to go in and take his chairs for the recital.

A second piano had to be rented from the Presbyterian Sunday School (through the Starks), hauled over in time for rehearsing the quartet all together, and of course tuned. There were programs to be printed (through the Morrisons), elaborate enough to include the opus numbers, the first, middle, and last name of each pupil, and flowing across the top in a script which resembled, as if for a purpose, Miss Eckhart's writing in the monthly bills, the full name of Miss Lotte Elisabeth Eckhart. Some little untalented Maloney would give the programs out at the door from a pink fruit plate.

On the day, gladiolas or carnations in princess-baskets were expected to arrive for each child, duly ordered from some Loomis florist-connections in Vicksburg and kept in buckets of water on the MacLains' shady back porch. They would be presented at the proper time—immediately after the bow—by Miss Eckhart. The pupil could hold the basket for the count of three—this had been rehearsed, using a black umbrella—then present it back to Miss Eckhart, who had in mind a crescent moon design on the floor which she would fill in basket by basket on the night. Jinny Love Stark always received a bouquet of Parma violets in a heart of leaves, and had to be allowed to keep it. She said, 'Ta-ta.' She never did give it up a single year, which hurt the effect.

For the recital was, after all, a ceremony. Better than school's being let out—for that presupposed examinations—or the opening political fireworks—the recital celebrated June. Both dread and delight were to come down on little girls that special night, when only certain sashes and certain flowers could possibly belong, and with only smart, pretty little girls to carry things out.

And Miss Eckhart pushed herself to quite another level of life for it. A blushing sensitivity sprang up in her every year at the proper time like a flower of the season, like the Surprise Lilies that came up with no leaves and overnight in Miss Nell's yard. Miss Eckhart stirred here and there, utterly carried away by matters that at other times interested her least—dresses and sashes, prominence and precedence, smiles and bows. It was strange, exciting. She called up the pictures on those little square party invitations, the brown bear in a frill and the black poodle standing on a chair to shave at a mirror. . . .

With recital night over, the sensitivity and the drive too would be over and gone. But then all trials would be ended. The limitless part of vacation would have come. Girls and boys could go barefooted alike in the mornings.

The night of the recital was always clear and hot; everyone came. The prospective audience turned out in full oppression.

Miss Eckhart and her pupils were not yet to be visible. It was up to Miss Snowdie MacLain to be at the door, and she was at the door, staunchly, as if she'd been in on things the whole time. She welcomed all female Morgana there in perfect innocence. By eight o'clock the studio was packed.

Miss Katie Rainey would always come early. She trembled with delight, like a performer herself, and she had milked with that hat on. She laughed with pleasure as she grew accustomed to it all, and through the recital she would stay much in evidence, the first to clap when a piece was over, and pleased equally with the music she listened to and the gold chair she sat on. And Old Man Fate Rainey, the buttermilk man, was the only father who came. He remained standing. Miss Perdita Mayo, who had made most of the recital dresses, was always on the front row to see that the bastings had all been pulled out after the dresses got home, and beside her was Miss Hattie Mayo, her quiet sister who helped her.

As the studio filled, Cassie, peeping around the sheet curtain (*they* were all herded in the dining room), bore the dread that her mother might not come at all. She was always late, perhaps because she lived so near. Miss Lizzie Stark, the most important mother there, who was just waiting for Jinny Love to get a little older to play better, would turn around in her chair down front to spot each of the other mothers. Knowing that too, and dressed beautifully in a becoming flowery dress just right for a mother on recital night, Cassie's mother could not walk across the two yards on time to save her life. And Cassie's *Rustle of Spring*, for instance, was very hard, harder than Missie Spights' piece; but it appeared that everything Miss Eckhart planned for, Cassie's mother could let go for nothing.

In the studio decorated like the inside of a candy box, with 'material' scalloping the mantel shelf and doilies placed under every movable object, now thus made immovable, with streamers of white ribbons and nosegays of pink and white Maman Cochet roses and the last MacLain sweetpeas dividing and re-dividing the room, it was as hot as fire. No matter that this was the first night of June; no electric fans were to whir around while music played. The metronome, ceremoniously closed, stood on the piano like a vase. There was no piece of music anywhere in sight.

When the first unreasoning hush—there was the usual series—fell over the audience, the room seemed to shake with the agitation of palmetto and feather fans alone, plus the occasional involuntary tick of the metronome within its doors. There was the mixture together of agitation and decoration which could make every little forthcoming child turn pale with a kind of ultimate dizziness. Whoever might look up at the ceiling for surcease would be floundered within a paper design stemming out of the chandelier, as complicated and as unavailing as a cut-out paper snowflake.

Now Miss Eckhart came into the room all changed, with her dark hair pulled low on her brow, and gestured for silence. She was wearing her recital dress, which made her look larger and closer-to than she looked at any other times. It was an old dress: Miss Eckhart disregarded her own rules. People would forget that dress between times and then she would come out in it again, the untidy folds not quite spotlessly clean, gathered about her bosom and falling heavy as a coat to the sides; it was a tawny crepe-back satin. There was a bodice of browning lace. It was as rich and hot and deep-looking as a furskin. The unexpected creamy flesh on her upper arms gave her a look of emerging from it.

Miss Eckhart, achieving silence, stood in the shadowy spot directly under the chandelier. Her feet, white-shod, shod by Mr Sissum for good, rested in the chalk circle previously marked on the floor and now, she believed, perfectly erased. One hand, with its countable little muscles so hard and ready, its stained, blue nails, went to the other hand and they folded quite still, holding nothing, until they lost their force by lying on her breast and made a funny little house with peaks and gables. Standing near the piano but not near enough to help, she presided but not with her whole heart on guard against disaster; while disaster was what remained on the minds of the little girls. Starting with the youngest, she called them out.

So they played, and except Virgie, all played their worst. They shocked themselves. Parnell Moody burst into tears on schedule. But Miss Eckhart never seemed to notice or to care. How forgetful she seemed at exactly the moments she should have been agonized! You expected the whip, almost, for forgetting to repeat before the second ending, or for failing to count ten before you came around the curtain at all; and instead you received a strange smile. It was as though Miss Eckhart, at the last, were grateful to you for *anything*.

When Hilda Ray Bowles' turn came and Miss Eckhart herself was to bend down and move the stool out twelve inches, she did it in a spirit of gentle, uninterrupted abstraction. She might be not moving a stool out for an overgrown girl at all, but performing some gentle ministration to someone else, someone who was not there; perhaps it was Beethoven, who wrote Hilda Ray's piece, and perhaps not.

Cassie played, and her mother—not betraying her, after all—was seated among the rest. At the end, she had creased her program into a little hat, for which Cassie could have fallen at her feet.

But recital night was Virgie's night, whatever else it was. The time Virgie Rainey was most wonderful in her life, to Cassie, was when she came out—her turn was just before the quartet—wearing a Christmas-red satin band in her hair with rosettes over the ears, held on by a new elastic across the back; she had a red sash drawn around under the arms of a starched white swiss dress. She was thirteen. She played the *Fantasia on Beethoven's Ruins of Athens*, and when she finished and got up and made her bow, the red of the sash was all over the front of her waist, she was wet and stained as if she had been stabbed in the heart, and a delirious and enviable sweat ran down from her forehead and cheeks and she licked it in with her tongue.

Cassie, who had slipped around to the front, was spellbound still when Miss Katie Rainey put a hand on her sash and to her pure terror said, 'Oh, but I wish Virgie had a sister!'

Then there was only the quartet, and with the last chord—sudden disintegration itself—laughter and teasing broke loose. All the children got a kiss or a token spank in congratulation and then ran free. Ladies waved and beckoned with their fans, conversation opened up. Flowers were lifted high, shown off, thrown, given, and pulled to giddy pieces by fingers freed for the summer. The MacLain twins, now crashing restraint, rushed downstairs in identical cowboy suits, pointing and even firing cap pistols. Two fans were set rumbling and walking on the floor, from which the dropped programs flew up like a flock of birds, while the decorations whipped and played all over. Neither piano was gone near except for punching out 'Sally in Her Shimmie Tail.' Little Jinny Stark, after all, fell, skinned her knee and bled profusely. It was like any other party.

'Punch and *Kuchen!*' Miss Eckhart came announcing.

The big MacLain dining room at the back, where Miss Snowdie only wintered her flowers for the most part, was thrown open tonight. Punch was being served from the MacLain punch bowl, one of Miss Snowdie's gifts from her husband—served impromptu by Miss Billy Texas Spights, who sprang for the ladle, and they drank it out of the twenty-four MacLain cups and the twelve Loomis. The little cakes that Miss Eckhart tirelessly brought out were sweet, light, and warm, their tops sprinkled with colored 'shot' that came (or so they'd thought) only out of glass pistols sold on trains. When the plate was empty you saw it was decorated with slipping flower garlands and rowdy babies, sprinkled with gold and now with golden crumbs.

Miss Eckhart's cheeks flooded with color as the guests accepted her sugar cookies and came back to lift their punch cups, with the drowned fruit in the bottom, again to her quick, brimming ladle. (*'I'll* give you more punch!' she cried, when Miss Billy Texas started counting.) Her hair was as low on her forehead as Circe's, on the fourth grade wall feeding her swine. She smiled, not on any particular one but on everyone, everywhere she looked and everywhere she went—for the party had spread out—from studio to dining room and back and out on the porch, where she called, 'What is this out here? You little girls come back inside and stay till you eat my *Kuchen* all up! The last crumb!' It made them laugh to hear her, when strictness was only a pretense.

Miss Lizzie Stark, although she had occasionally referred to Miss

Eckhart as 'Miss Do-daddle,' did not spare herself from wearing her most elaborate hat, one resembling a large wreath or a wedding cake, and it was constantly in the vision, turned this way and that like a floating balloon at a fair over the heads of the crowd. The canary sang; his cover was lifted off. Gradually the Maman Cochets bowed their little green stems over the vase's edge.

At the close of the evening, saying goodnight, people congratulated Miss Eckhart and her mother. Old Mrs Eckhart had sat near the door during the whole evening—had sat by Miss Snowdie at the door, when she welcomed them in. She wore a dark dress too, but it was sprigged. In the path of the talking and laughing mothers and the now wild children she sat blinking her eyes, but amenable, like a baby when he is wheeled out into the sunlight. While Miss Snowdie watched her kindly, she would hold her mouth in one evening-long smile; she was letting herself be looked at and herself, at the end, be thanked.

Miss Eckhart, breasting the pushing, departing children, moving among the swinging princess-baskets and the dropped fans of the suddenly weakened mothers, would be heard calling, 'Virgie Rainey? Virgie Rainey?' Then she would look down ceremoniously at the sleepiest and smallest child, who had only played 'Playful Kittens' that night. All her pupils on that evening partook of the grace of Virgie Rainey. Miss Eckhart would catch them running out the door, speaking German to them and holding them to her. In the still night air her dress felt damp and spotted, as though she had run a long way.

Cassie listened, but *Für Elise* was not repeated. She took up her ukulele from the foot of the bed. She screwed it into tune and played it, slurring the chords expertly and fanning with her fingers. She strolled around her scarf hanging up to dry, playing a chorus or two, and then wandered back to the window.

There she saw Loch go hanging on all fours like a monkey down the hackberry limb. Far on the other side of the tree he hung by his hands, perfectly still, diver-like—not going into any of his tricks. That was the way he stayed in bed taking quinine.

He was concerned not with tricks but with watching something inside the vacant house. Loch could see in. Cassie opened her mouth to cry out, but the cry wouldn't come.

Except for once, she had not answered Loch all day when he called her, and now the sight of his spread-eagled back in the white night drawers seemed as far from her as the morning star. It was gone from her, any way to shield his innocence, when his innocence was out there shining at her, cavorting—for Loch calmly reversed himself and hung by his knees; plunged upside down, he looked in at the old studio window, with his pompadour cap falling to earth and his hair spiking out all over his young boy's head.

Once Loch wandered over their house in a skirt, beating on a christening cup with a pencil. 'Mama, do you think I can ever play music too?' 'Why, of course, dear heart. You're *my* child. Just you bide your time.' (He was her favorite.) And he never could—bide or play. How Cassie had adored him! He didn't know one tune from another. 'Is this *Jesus Loves Me?*' he'd ask, interrupting his own noise. She looked out at him now as stricken as if she saw him hurt, from long ago, and silently performing tricks to tell her. She stood there at her window. Softly she was playing and singing, 'By the light, light, light, light, light of the silvery moon,' her favorite song.

She could never go for herself, never creep out on the shimmering bridge of the tree, or reach the dark magnet there that drew you inside, kept drawing you in. She could not see herself do an unknown thing. She was not Loch, she was not Virgie Rainey; she was not her mother. She was Cassie in her room, seeing the knowledge and torment beyond her reach, standing at her window singing—in a voice soft, rather full today, and halfway thinking it was pretty.

III

After a moment of blackness, upside down, Loch opened his eyes. Nothing had happened. The house he watched was all silence but for the progressing tick-tock that was different from a clock's. There were outer sounds. His sister was practicing on her ukulele again so she could sing to the boys. He heard from up the street the water-like sounds of the ladies' party, and off through the trees where the big boys were playing, sounds of the ball being knocked out—gay and removed as birdsong. But the tick-tock was sharper and clearer than all he could hear just now in the world, and at moments seemed to ring close, the way his own heartbeat rang against the bed he came out of.

His mother, had it been she in the vacant house, would have stopped those two Negroes straggling home with their unsold peas and made them come in off the street and do all that for her, and finish up in no time. But the sailor's mother was doing her work alone. She wanted things to suit herself, nobody else would have been able to please her; and she was taking her own sweet time. She was building a bonfire of her own in the piano and would set off the dynamite when she was ready and not before.

Loch knew from her actions that the contrivance down in the wires—the piano front had been taken away—was a kind of nest. She was building it like a thieving bird, weaving in every little scrap that she could find around her. He saw in two places the mustached face of Mr Drewsie Carmichael, his father's candidate for mayor—she found the circulars in the door. The litter on his bed, the Octagon Soap coupons, would have pleased her at that moment, and he would have turned them over to her.

Then Loch almost gave a yell; pride filled him, like a second yell, that he did not. Here down the street came Old Man Moody, the marshal, and Mr Fatty Bowles with him. They had taken the day off to go fishing in Moon Lake and came carrying their old fishing canes but no fish. Their pants and shoes were heavy with mud. They were cronies of old Mr Holifield and often came to wake him up, this time of day, and hound him off to the gin.

Loch skinned the cat over the limb and waited head down as they came tramping, sure enough, across the yard. In his special vision he saw that they could easily be lying on their backs in the blue sky and waving their legs pleasantly around, having nothing to do with law and order.

Old Man Moody and Mr Fatty Bowles divided at the pecan stump, telling a joke, joined, said 'Bread and butter,' and then clogged up the steps. The curtain at the front window flapped signaling in their faces.

They looked at each other anew. Their bodies and their faces grew smooth as fishes. They floated around the porch and flattened like fishes to nose at the window. There were round muddy spots on the seats of their pants; they squatted.

Well, there it is, thought Loch—the houseful. Two upstairs, one downstairs, and the two on the porch. And on the piano sat the ticking machine. . . . Directly below Loch a spotted thrush walked noisily in the weeds, pointing her beak ahead of her straight as a gun, just as busy in the world as people.

He held his own right hand ever so still as the old woman, unsteady as the Christmas angel in Mrs McGillicuddy's fourth-grade pageant, came forward with a lighted candle in her hand. It was a kitchen tallow candle; she must have taken it out of Mr Holifield's boxful against all the times the lights went out in Morgana. She came so slowly and held the candle so high that he could have popped it with a pea-shooter from where he was. Her hair, he saw, was cropped and white and lighted up all around. From the swaying, farthest length of a branch that would hold his weight, he could see how bright her big eyes were under their black circling brows, and how seldom they blinked. They were owl eyes.

She bent over, painfully, he felt, and laid the candle in the paper nest she had built in the piano. He too drew his breath in, protecting the flame, and as she pulled her aching hand back he pulled his. The newspaper caught, it was ablaze, and the old woman threw in the candle. Hands to thighs, she raised up, her work done.

Flames arrowed out so noiselessly. They ran down the streamers of paper, as double-quick as freshets from a loud gully-washer of rain. The room was criss-crossed with quick, dying yellow fire, there were pinwheels falling and fading from the ceiling. And up above, on the other side of the ceiling, they, the first two, were as still as mice.

The law still squatted. Mr Fatty's and Old Man Moody's necks stretched sideways, the fat and the thin. Loch could have dropped a caterpillar down onto either of their heads, which rubbed together like mother's and child's.

'So help me. She *done* it,' Mr Fatty Bowles said in a natural voice.

He lifted his arm, that had been hugging Old Man Moody's shoulders, and transferred to his own back pocket a slap that would have cracked Old Man Moody's bones. 'Bless her heart! She done it before our eyes. What would you have bet?'

'Not a thing,' said Old Man Moody. 'Watch. If it catches them old dried-out squares of matting, Booney Holifield's going to feel a little warm ere long.'

'Booney! Why, I done forgot him!'

Old Man Moody laughed explosively with shut lips.

'Wouldn't you say it's done caught now,' said Mr Fatty, pointing into the room with his old fishing knife.

'The house is on fire!' Loch cried at the top of his voice. He was riding his limb up and down and shaking the leaves.

Old Man Moody and Mr Fatty might have heard, for, a little as if they were insulted, they raised up, moved their fishing poles along, and deliberately chose the dining room window instead of the parlor window to get to work on.

They lifted the screen out, and Mr Fatty accidentally stepped through it. They inched the sash up with a sound that made them draw high their muck-coated heels. They could go in now: they opened their mouths and guffawed silently. They were so used to showing off, they almost called up Morgana then and there.

Mr Fatty Bowles started to squeeze himself over the sill into the room, but Old Man Moody was ready for that, pulled him back by the suspenders, and went first. He leap-frogged it. Inside, they both let go a holler.

'Look out! You're caught in the act!'

In the parlor, the old lady backed herself into the blind corner.

Old Man Moody and Mr Fatty made a preliminary run around the dining room table to warm up, and then charged the parlor. They trod down the barrier of sparky matting and stomped in. They boxed at the smoke, hit each other, and ran to put up the window. Then Loch heard their well-known coughs and the creep and crack of fire inside the room. The smoke mostly stayed inside, contained and still.

Loch skinned the cat again. Here came somebody else. It was a fine day! Presently he thought he knew the golden Panama hat, and the elastic spareness of the man under it. He used to live in that vacant house and had at that time promised to bring Loch a talking bird, one that could say 'Rabbits!' He had left and never returned. After all the years, Loch still wanted a bird like that. It was to his taste today.

'Nobody lives there now!' Loch called out of the leaves in an appropriate voice, for Mr Voight turned in just like home at the vacant house. 'If you go in, you'll blow up.'

There was no talking bird on his shoulder yet. It was a long time ago that Mr Voight had promised it. (And how often, Loch thought now with great surprise, he had remembered and cherished the promise!)

Mr Voight shook his head rapidly as though a far-away voice from the leaves bothered him only for a moment. He ran up the steps with a sound like a green stick along a fence. He, though, instead of running into the flapping barrier over the door, drifted around the porch to the side and leisurely took a look through the window. Everything made his shout alarming.

'Will you please tell me why you're trespassing here?'

'So help me!' said Mr Fatty Bowles, who was looking right at him, holding a burning hat.

Old Man Moody only said, '*Good* evening. Now I don't speak to you.'

'Answer me! Trespassing, are you?'

'Whoa. Your house is afire.'

'If my house is afire, then where's my folks gone?'

'Oh, *'tain't* your house no more, I forgot. It's Miss Francine Murphy's house. You're late, Captain.'

'What antics are these? Get out of my house. Put that fire out behind you. Tell me where they went. Never mind, I know where they went. All right, burn it down, who's to stop you?'

He slapped his hands on the boarding of the house, fanfare like, and must have glared at them between, at the window. He had inserted himself between Loch and what happened, and to tell the truth he made one too many.

Old Man Moody and Mr Fatty, exchanging murderous looks, ran hopping about the parlor, clapping their hats at the skittering flames, working in a team mad at itself, the way two people try to head off chickens in a yard. They jumped up and knocked at the same flame. They kicked and rubbed under their feet a spark they found by themselves, sometimes imaginary. Maybe because they'd let the fire almost go out, or because Mr Voight had come to criticize, they pretended this fire was bigger than it had ever been. They bit their underlips tightly as old people do in carrying out acts of rudeness. They didn't speak.

Mr Voight shook all over. He was laughing, Loch discovered. Now he watched the room like a show. 'That's it! That's it!' he said.

Old Man Moody and Mr Bowles together beat out the fire in the piano, fighting over it hard, banging and twanging the strings. Old Man Moody, no matter how his fun had been spoiled, enjoyed jumping up and down on the fierce-burning magnolia leaves. So they put the fire out, every spark, even the matting, which twinkled all over time and again before it went out for good. When a little tongue of flame started up for the last time, they quenched it together; and with a whistle and one more stamp each, they dared it, and it stayed out.

'That's it, boys,' said Mr Voight.

Then the old woman came out of the blind corner. 'Now who's this?' cried Mr Voight. In the center of the room she stopped. Without the law to stand over her, she might have clasped her empty hands and turned herself this way and that. But she did not; she was more desperate still. Loch hollered out again, riding the tree, his branch in both fists.

'Why don't you step on in, Captain?' called Mr Fatty Bowles, and he beckoned the old lady to him.

'Down to business here. Now I'd appreciate knowing why you done this, lady,' Old Man Moody said, rubbing his eyes and rimming them with black. 'Putting folks to all this trouble. Now what you got against us?'

'Cat's got her tongue,' said Mr Fatty.

'I'm an old man. But you're an old woman. *I* don't know why you done it. Unless of course it was for pure lack of good sense.'

'Where you come from?' asked Mr Fatty in his little tenor voice.

'You clowns.'

Mr Voight, who said that, now went lightly as a dragonfly around the porch and entered the house by the front door: it was not locked. He might have been waiting until all the beating about had been done by others—clowns—or perhaps he thought he was so valuable that he could burn up in too big a hurry.

Loch saw him step, with rather a flare, through the beads at the hall door and come into the parlor. He gazed serenely about the walls, pausing for a moment first, as though something had happened to them not that very hour but a long time ago. He was there and not there, for he alone was not at his wit's end. He went picking his feet carefully among the frills and flakes of burned paper, and wrinkled up his sharp nose; not from the smell, it seemed, but from wider, dissolving things. Now he stood at the window. His eyes rolled. Would he foam at the mouth? He did once. If he did not, Loch might not be sure about him; he remembered Mr Voight best as foaming.

'Do you place her, Captain?' asked Old Man Moody in a cautious voice. 'Who's this here firebug? You been places.'

Mr Voight was strolling about the room, and taking the poker he poked among the ashes. He picked up a seashell. The old lady advanced on him and he put it back, and as he came up he took off his hat. It looked more than polite. There close to the old lady's face he cocked his head, but she looked through him, a long way through Mr Voight. She could have been a lady on an opposite cliff, far away, out of eye range and earshot, but about to fall.

The tick-tock was very loud then. Just as Mr Fatty had forgotten Mr Booney Holifield, Loch had forgotten the dynamite. Now he could go back to expecting a blast. The fire had had a hard time, but fire could manage to connect itself with an everlasting little mechanism that could pound like that, right along, right in the room.

('Do you hear something, Mr Moody?' Loch could cry out right now. 'Mr Voight, listen.'—'All right, say—do you want your bird this minute?' might be the reply. 'We'll call everything off.')

'Man, what's that?' asked Mr Fatty Bowles, and 'Fatty boy, do you hear something ugly?' Old Man Moody asked at the same instant. At last they cocked their ears at the ticking that had been there in

the room with them all this time. They looked at each other and
then with hunched shoulders paraded around looking for the source
of it.

'It's a rattlesnake! No, it ain't! But it's close,' said Mr Fatty.

They looked high and low all over the room but they couldn't see
it right in front of their eyes and up just a little, on top of the piano.
That was honestly not a fair place, not where most people would put
a thing. They looked at each other harder and hurried faster, but all
they did was run on each other's heels and tip the chairs over. One of
the chair legs snapped like a chicken bone.

Mr Voight only got in their way, since he did not move an inch. He
was still standing before the eyes of the sailor's mother, looking at her
with lips puckered. It could be indeed that he knew her from his travels. He looked tired from these same travels now.

At last Old Man Moody, the smarter one of those two, spied what
they were looking for, the obelisk with its little moving part and its
door open. Once seen, that thing was so surely *it* that he merely
pointed it out to Mr Fatty. Mr Fatty tiptoed over and picked the
obelisk up and set it down again quickly. So .Old Man Moody
stumped over and picked it up and held it up on the diagonal, posing,
like a fisherman holding a funny-looking fish to have come out of
Moon Lake.

The old woman lifted her head and walked around Mr Voight to
Old Man Moody. She reached up and took the ticking thing right out
of his hand, and he turned it loose agreeably; Old Man Moody
seemed not taken by surprise by women.

The old woman held her possession to her, drawn to her big gray
breast. Her eyesight returned from far to close by. Then she stood
looking at the three people fixedly, as if she showed them her insides,
her live heart.

And then a little whir of her own voice: 'See . . . See, Mr MacLain.'

Nothing blew up, but Mr Voight (but she called him MacLain)
groaned.

'No, boys. I never saw her in my life,' he said.

He walked stiffly out of the room. He walked out of the house and
cater-cornered across the yard toward the MacLain Road. As he

reached the road itself, he put his hat on, and then he did not look as shabby, or as poor.

Loch clasped a leafy armful of the tree and sank his head in the green cool.

'Let *me* see your play-pretty,' Mr Fatty Bowles was saying with his baby-smile. He took the obelisk away from the old woman, and with a sudden change on his face threw it with all his might out the open window. It came straight toward Loch, and fell into the weeds below him. And still it ticked.

'You could have been a little too quick there, Fatty boy,' said Old Man Moody. 'Flinging evidence.'

'You ought to think about us. Listen and you'll hear it blow up. I'd rather have it blow up your wife's chickens.'

'Well, I wouldn't.'

And while they talked, the poor old woman tried it again. She was down on her knees cradling the lump of candle and the next moment had it lighted. She rose up, agitated now, and went running about the room, holding the candle above her, evading the men each time they tried to head her off.

This time, the fire caught her own hair. The little short white frill turned to flame.

Old Man Moody was so quick that he caught her. He came up with a big old rag from somewhere, and ran after the old woman with it. They both ran extraordinarily fast. He had to make a jump. He brought the cloth down over her head from behind, grimacing, as if all people on earth had to do acts of shame, some time. He hit her covered-up head about with the flat of his hand.

Old Man Moody and Mr Bowles brought the old woman between them out on the porch of the vacant house. She was quiet now, with the scorched black cloth covering her head; she herself held it on with both hands.

'Know what I'm going to have to do with you?' Old Man Moody was saying gently and conversationally, but she only stood there, all covered in wrinkled cloth with her little hands up, clawed, the way a locust shell would be found clinging to that empty door in August.

'It don't signify nothing what your name is now, or what you intended, old woman,' Mr Bowles told her as he got the fishing canes. 'We know where you belong at, and that's Jackson.'

'Come on ladylike. I'm sure you know how,' Old Man Moody said.

She came along but she did not answer either man anything.

'Maybe she aimed mischief at King MacLain after all,' said Mr. Fatty Bowles. 'She's a she, ain't she?'

'That'll be enough out of you for the rest of the day,' said Old Man Moody.

Among the leaves, Loch watched them come down the walk and head toward town. They went slowly, for the old woman took short, hesitant steps. Where would they take her now? Not later, to Jackson, but now? After they passed, he let go his hands and jumped out of the tree. It made a good noise when he hit ground. He turned a forward and a backward somersault and started walking on his hands around the tree trunk. He made noises like a goat, and a bobwhite, like the silly Moody chickens, and like a lion.

On his hands he circled the tree and the obelisk waited in the weeds, upright. He stood up and looked at it. Its ticker was outside it.

He felt charmed like a bird, for the ticking stick went like a tail, a tongue, a wand. He picked the box up in his hands.

'Now go on. Blow up.'

When he examined it, he saw the beating stick to be a pendulum that instead of hanging down stuck upwards. He touched it and stopped it with his finger. He felt its pressure, and the weight of the obelisk, which seemed about two pounds. He released the stick, and it went on beating.

Then he turned a little key in the side of the box, and that controlled it. The stick stopped and he poked it into place within the box, and shut the door of the thing.

It might not be dynamite: especially since Mr Fatty thought it was.

What was it?

He opened his shirt and buttoned it in. He thought he might take it up to his room. It was this; not a bird that knew how to talk.

★

The sand pile was before him now. He planed away the hot top layer and sat down. He held still for a while, while nothing was ticking. Nothing but the crickets. Nothing but the train going through, ticking its two cars over the Big Black bridge.

IV

Cassie moved to the front window, where she could see Old Man Moody and Mr Fatty Bowles carrying off the old woman. The old woman was half sick or dazed. She held on her head some nameless kitchen rag; she had no purse. In a gray housedress prophetic of an institution she was making her way along, about to be touched, prodded, any minute, but not worrying about it. She wore shoes without stockings—and she had such white, white ankles. When she saw the ankles, Cassie flung herself in full view at the window and gave a cry.

No heat lifted. Cassie rushed out of her room, down the stairs and out the front door.

To Loch's amazement his sister Cassie came running barefooted down the front walk in her petticoat and in full awareness turned toward town, crying, 'You can't take her! Miss Eckhart!'

She was too late for anybody to hear her, of course, but he creaked up out of the sand pile and ran out after her as if they had heard. He caught up with her and pulled at her petticoat. She turned, with her head still swimming high in the air, and cried softly, 'Oh, Mother!'

They looked at each other.

'Crazy.'

'Crazy yourself.'

'Back yonder,' said Loch presently, 'I can show you how ripe the figs are.' They withdrew as far as the tree. But it was only in time to see the sailor and Virgie Rainey run out, trying to escape by the back way. Virgie and the sailor saw them. Back into the house they ran, and then, in utter recklessness, out the front, the sailor first. The Morrisons had nowhere to go.

Old Man Moody's party was only now progressing again, for the old woman had fallen down and they had to hold her on her feet. Farther along, the ladies' Rook party was coming out of Miss Nell's with a pouring sound. The sailor faced both these ranks.

The marshal tagged him but he ran straight on into the wall of ladies, most of whom cried 'Why, Kewpie Moffitt!'—an ancient nickname he had outgrown. He whirled about-face and ran the other way, and since he was carrying his blouse and was naked from the waist up, his collar stood out behind him like the lowest-hung wings. At the Carmichael corner, he tried east and took west, and ran into the shadows of the short-cut to the river, where he would just about meet with Mr King MacLain, if he was not too late.

'Look at that!' Miss Billy Texas Spights called clearly. 'I see you, Virgie Rainey!'

'Mother!' Cassie called, just as clearly. She and Loch found themselves out in front again.

The front door of the empty house fell to with a frail sound behind Virgie Rainey. A haze of the old smoke lifted unhurryingly over her, brushed and hid her for a moment like a gauzy cloud. She was coming right out, though, in a home-made dress of apricot voile, carrying a mesh bag on a chain. She ran down the steps and walked clicking her heels out to the sidewalk—always Virgie clicked her heels as if nothing had happened in the past or behind her, as if she were free, whatever else she might be. The ladies hushed, holding on to their prizes and folded parasols. Virgie faced them as she turned toward town.

It was the hour, of course, for her to go to work. Once past the next corner, she could drink a Coca-Cola and eat a box of cakes at Loomis's drug store, as she did every evening for her supper; then she could vanish inside the Bijou.

She passed Cassie and Loch, cutting them, and kept going and caught up, as she had to, with the marshal, Patty Bowles, and the old woman.

'You're running the wrong way!' Miss Billy Texas Spights called loudly. 'Better run after that sailor boy!'

'Isn't he visiting the Flewellyns out in the country?' Miss Perdita Mayo was pleading to everybody. 'What ever became of his mother? I'd forgotten all about him!'

Pinning Loch tightly by the arms in front of her, Cassie could only think: we were spies too. And nobody else was surprised at anything—it was only we two. People saw things like this as they saw Mr MacLain come and go. They only hoped to place them, in their hour or their street or the name of their mothers' people. Then Morgana could hold them, and at last they were this and they were that. And when ruin was predicted all along, even if people had forgotten it was on the way, even if they mightn't have missed it if it hadn't appeared, still they were never surprised when it came.

'She'll stop for Miss Eckhart,' breathed Cassie.

Virgie went by. There was a meeting of glances between the teacher and her old pupil, that Cassie knew. She could not be sure that Miss Eckhart's eyes closed once in recall—they had looked so wide-open at everything alike. The meeting amounted only to Virgie Rainey's passing by, in plain fact. She clicked by Miss Eckhart and she clicked straight through the middle of the Rook party, without a word or the pause of a moment.

Old Man Moody and Fatty Bowles, dirty, their faces shining like the fish they didn't catch, took advantage of the path Virgie cut through the ladies and walked Miss Eckhart, unprotesting, on. Then the ladies brought their ranks safely to, and Miss Billy Texas, suddenly beside herself, cried once more, 'He went the *other* way, Virgie!'

'That's enough, Billy Texas,' said Miss Lizzie Stark. 'As if her mother didn't have enough on her, just burying her son.'

The noise of tin pans being beaten came from the distance, then little children's and Negro nurses' cries, 'Crazy! Crazy!'

Cassie turned on Loch, pulled him to her and shook him by the shoulders. He was wet as a dishrag. A row of those big salt-and-pepper-colored mosquitoes perched all along his forehead. 'What were you doing out of your bed, anyway?' she asked in a matter-of-fact, scolding voice. Loch gave her a long, gratified look. 'What have you got there inside your nighties, crazy?'

'None of your business.'

'Give it to me.'

'It's mine.'

'It is not. Let go.'

'You make me.'

'All right, I know what it is.'

'What is it? You do not.'

'You can't have that.'

'Get away from me.'

'I'll tell Mama and Papa.—You hit me! You hit a girl where she's tender.'

'Well, you know you can't have it.'

'All right then—did you see Mr MacLain? He's been gone since you were born.'

'Why, sure,' said Loch. 'I saw Mr MacLain.'

'Oh, Loch, why don't you beat off those mosquitoes!' She wept. 'Mother!' Even Loch flew from her, at once.

'Well, here I am,' said her mother.

'Oh!' After a moment she raised her head to say, 'And Mr King MacLain was here, and now he's gone.'

'Well. You've seen him before,' said her mother after a moment, breaking from her. 'That's no excuse for coming outdoors in your petticoat to cry.'

'You knew it would be this way, you were with them!'

There was no answer then either, and Cassie trudged through the yard. Loch stood near the sand pile. His lips clamped down, he held his bulging nightie and regarded it. She ran him back under the tree and into the house by the back door.

'What orphan-lookin' children is these here?' said Louella. 'Where yawl orphan come from? Yawl don't live here, yawl live at County Orphan. Gawn back.'

Cassie pushed Loch through the kitchen and then pulled him to a stop in the back hall. It was their father coming home.

'What's going on here! The house is on fire, the MacLain house! I see smoke!'

They could see him coming up the front walk, waving the rolled-up *Bugle* he brought home every night.

'Holifield! Holifield!'

Mr Holifield must have come to the window, for they heard, 'Did I hear my name called?' and they sighed with foreboding.

'It's gone out, Wilbur,' said their mother at the door.

'That house has been on fire *and* gone out, sir.' Their father was speaking loudly as he did from the platform at election time. 'You can read about it in tomorrow's *Bugle*.'

'Come in, Wilbur.'

They could see her finger tracing a little pattern on the screen door as she stood there in her party dress. 'Cassie says King MacLain was here and gone. That's as interesting as twenty fires.'

Cassie shivered.

'Maybe this will bestir Francine Murphy to take a step. *There's* a public guardian for you: Booney Holifield.'

Cassie was glad her father kept on. If there was anything that unsettled him it was for people not to be on the inside what their outward semblances led you to suppose. 'MacLain came to the wrong place this time. It might have caught *our* house: Booney Holifield!'

Their mother laughed. 'That old monkey,' she said. As far as she was concerned, the old man next door had just come alive, redeemed himself a little from being a Holifield.

The six-o'clock summer light shone just as usual on their father and mother meeting at the door.

'Come on.'

Cassie and Loch running up the back stairs heard the sigh of the door and the old, muffled laugh that came between their parents at this moment. No matter what had happened, or had started to happen, around them, they could come in the house and laugh about the old thing. Theirs was a laugh that hinted of some small but interesting object, a thing even their deliberate father could find—something that might be seizable and holdable as well as findable, as ridiculous and forbidden to children, as alive, as a stray kitten or a rabbit.

The children kept on going up the steep dark backstairs, so close on each other they prodded and nudged each other, both punishing and petting.

'Get back in bed like you were never out," Cassie advised. 'Pull the beggarlice off you.'

'But I think Mother saw me,' he said over his shoulder, going.

Cassie didn't answer.

She shivered and walked into her room. There was the scarf. It was

an old friend, part enemy. She brought it to her face, touched her lips
to it, breathed its smoky dye-smell, and passed it up her cheeks and
over her eyes. She pressed it against her forehead. She might have lost
it, might have run out with it . . . for she had visions of poor Miss
Eckhart wearing it away over her head; of Virgie waving it, brazenly,
in the air of the street; of too-knowing Jinny Love Stark asking,
'Couldn't you keep it?'

'Listen and I'll tell you what Miss Nell served at the party,' Loch's
mother said softly, with little waits in her voice. She was just a glimmer
at the foot of his bed.

'Ma'am.'

'An orange scooped out and filled with orange juice, with the top
put back on and decorated with icing leaves, a straw stuck in. A slice
of pineapple with a heap of candied sweet potatoes on it, and a little
handle of pastry. A cup made out of toast, filled with creamed chicken,
fairly warm. A sweet peach pickle with flower petals around it of dif-
ferent-colored cream cheese. A swan made of a cream puff. He had
whipped cream feathers, a pastry neck, green icing eyes. A pastry bis-
cuit the size of a marble with a little date filling.' She sighed abruptly.

'Were you hungry, Mama?' he said.

It was not really to him that his mother would be talking, but it was
he who tenderly let her, as they watched and listened to the swallows
just at dark. It was always at this hour that she spoke in this voice—not
to him or to Cassie or Louella or to his father, or to the evening, but
to the wall, more nearly. She bent seriously over him and kissed him
hard, and swayed out of the room.

There was singing in the street. He saw Cassie, a lesser but similar
gleam, go past his door. The hay wagon was coming up the street to
get her. He heard the girls and boys hail her, and her greeting the same
as theirs, as if nothing had happened up until now, heard them pull her
up. Ran MacLain from MacLain Courthouse, or was it his brother
Eugene, always called to Mrs Morrison, teasing, 'Come on! You come
with us!' Did they really want to take her? He heard the wagon creak
away. They were singing and playing on their ukuleles, some song of
which he couldn't be sure.

Presently Loch lifted up and gazed through the same old leaves, dark once more, and saw the vacant house looking the same as it ever did. A cloud lighted anew, low in the deep sky, a single long wing. The mystery he had felt like a golden and aimless bird had waited until now to fly over. Until now, when all else had been driven out. His body shook. Perhaps the fever would go now, and the chill come.

But Louella brought him his supper, and waited while he ate it, sitting quietly. She had made him chicken broth that sparkled like diamonds in the evening light, and then there would be the junket he hated, turning to water under his tongue.

'Louella, I don't want junket tonight. Louella, listen. Do you hear a thing ticking?'

'Hear it plain.'

She took his tray and sat down again, and he lay on his back, looking upward. High in the sky the quarter moon was bright. 'Reckon it's going to blow up in the night? You can see it. Look on the washstand.' All by itself, of its own accord, it might let fly its little door and start up. He thought he heard it now. Or was it his father's watch in the next room, already laid on the dresser for the night?

'I 'spec' it will, Loch, if you wants it to,' she said readily, and sat on in the dark. She added, 'Blow up? If it do, I'll wrang your neck. Next time you scoot down that tree and come back draggin' sompm. Listen that big bullfrog in the swamp, you want to listen to sompm might blow up.'

He listened, lying stretched and pointed in the four directions. His heart pumping the secret anticipation that parted his lips, he fell into space and floated. Even floating, he felt the pressure of his frown and heard his growling voice and the gnashing of his teeth. He dreamed close to the surface, and his dreams were filled with a color and a fury that the daytime that summer never held.

Later, in her moonlit bed, Cassie lay thinking. Her hair and the inner side of her arms still smelled of hay; she tasted the sweet summer dryness in her mouth. In the distances of her mind the wagon still rocked, rocking its young girls' burden, the teasing anxiety, the singing, the moon and stars and the moving roof of leaves, Moon Lake brimming and the boat on it, the smiling drowse of boys, and the way she herself had let nobody touch even her hand. And she thought back to the sailor beginning to run down the street, as strange a sight with his clothes partly missing as a mer-man from the lake, and around again to Miss Eckhart and Virgie coming together on the deadquiet sidewalk. What she was certain of was the distance those two had gone, as if all along they had been making a trip (which the sailor was only starting). It had changed them. They were deliberately terrible. They looked at each other and neither wished to speak. They did not even horrify each other. No one could touch them now, either.

Danke schoen . . . That much was out in the open. Gratitude—like rescue—was simply no more. It was not only past; it was outworn and cast away. Both Miss Eckhart and Virgie Rainey were human beings terribly at large, roaming on the face of the earth. And there were others of them—human beings, roaming, like lost beasts.

Into her head flowed the whole of the poem she had found in that book. It ran perfectly through her head, vanishing as it went, one line yielding to the next, like a torch race. All of it passed through her head, through her body. She slept, but sat up in bed once and said aloud, "*Because a fire was in my head.*" Then she fell back unresisting. She did not see except in dreams that a face looked in; that it was the grave, unappeased, and radiant face, once more and always, the face that was in the poem.

1947

The Long March

WILLIAM STYRON

1

One noon, in the blaze of a cloudless Carolina summer, what was left of eight dead boys lay strewn about the landscape, among the poison ivy and the pine needles and loblolly saplings. It was not so much as if they had departed this life but as if, sprayed from a hose, they were only shreds of bone, gut, and dangling tissue to which it would have been impossible ever to impute the quality of life, far less the capacity to relinquish it. Of course, though, these had really died quickly, no doubt before the faintest flicker of recognition, of wonder, apprehension, or terror had had time to register in their minds. But the shock, it occurred to Lieutenant Culver, who stood in the shady lee of an ambulance and watched the scene, must have been fantastic to those on the periphery of the explosion, those fifteen or so surviving marines who now lay on the ground beneath blankets, moaning with pain and fright, and who, not more than half an hour before, had been waiting patiently in line for their lunch before the two mortar shells misfired—how? why? the question already hung with a buzzing, palpable fury in the noontime heat—had plummeted down upon the chow-line and had deadened their ears and senses and had hurled them earthward where they lay now, alive but stricken in a welter of blood and brain, scattered messkits and mashed potatoes, and puddles of melting ice-cream. Moments ago in the confusion—just before he had stolen off from the Colonel's side to go behind a tree and get sick—Lieutenant Culver had had a glimpse of a young sweaty face grimed with dust, had heard the boy's voice, astonishing even in that moment of nausea because of its clear, unhysterical tone of explanation: 'Major, I tell you I was on the field phone and I tell you as soon

as they come out the tube I knew they were short rounds and so I
hollered . . .' Of course it had been an accident. But why? He heard
the Major shout something, then Culver had heard no more, retching
on the leaves with a sound that, for the moment, drowned out the
cries and whines of the wounded and the noise of trucks and ambu-
lances crashing up through the underbrush.

It was not that he had a weak stomach or that he was unacquainted
with carnage that allowed him to lose control. If anything, he prided
himself on his stomach, and as for blood he had seen a lot spilled on
Okinawa and had himself (although through no act of valour whatever) received a shrapnel wound—in the buttocks, a matter which
even in retrospect, as he had often been forced to remind his wife, possessed no elements of comedy at all. In this case it was simply that on
the one hand he himself had been shocked. The sight of death was the
sort of thing which in war-time is expected, which one protects oneself against, and which is finally excused or at least ignored, in the same
way that a beggar is ignored, or a head-cold, or a social problem. But
in training here in the States in peace-time (or what, this sweltering
summer in the early 1950s, passed as peace-time) one had felt no particular need for that type of self-defence, and the slick nude litter of
intestine and shattered blue bones, among which forks and spoons
peeked out like so many pathetic metal flowers, made a crazy, insult-
ing impact at Culver's belly, like the blow of a fist. And on the other
hand (and the pulsing ache at his brow now as he vomited helplessly
on to his shoes lent confirmation to what he'd been trying to deny
himself for months): he was too old, he was no longer an eager kid just
out of Quantico with a knife between his teeth. He was almost thirty,
he was old, and he was afraid.

Lieutenant Culver had been called back to the marines early that
spring. When, one Saturday morning, his wife had thrown the brown
envelope containing his orders on to the bed where he lay sleeping, he
experienced an odd distress which kept him wandering about, baffled
and mumbling to himself, for days. Like most of his fellow reserves he
had retained his commission after the last war. It was an insouciant gesture which he had assumed would in some way benefit him in case of
an all-out conflict, say, thirty years hence, but one which made no

provisions for such an eventuality as a police action in Korea. It had all come much too soon and Culver had felt weirdly as if he had fallen asleep in some barracks in 1945 and had awakened in a half-dozen years or so to find that the intervening freedom, growth, and serenity had been only a glorious if somewhat prolonged dream. A flood of protest had welled up in him, for he had put the idea of war out of his mind entirely, and the brief years since Okinawa had been the richest of his life. They had produced, among lesser things, a loving, tenderly passionate wife who had passed on to their little girl both some of her gentle nature and her wealth of butter-coloured hair; a law degree, the fruits of which he had just begun to realize, even though still some-what impecuniously, as one of the brightest juniors in a good New York law firm; a friendly beagle named Howard whom he took for hikes in Washington Square; a cat, whom he did not deign to call by name, and despised; and a record-player that played Haydn, Mozart and Bach.

Up until the day that his orders came—the day that he tried to forget and the one that Betsy, his wife, soon bitterly referred to as 'the day the roof fell in'—they had been living in a roomy walk-up in the Village and experiencing the prosaic contentment that comes from eating properly, indulging themselves with fair moderation in the pleasures of the city, and watching the growth of a child. This is not to say that they were either smug or dull. They had a bright circle of friends, mostly young lawyers and newspapermen and doctors and their wives. There were parties and occasional week-ends in the country, where everyone became frankly drunk. There were the usual household skirmishes, too, but these were infrequent and petered out quickly. Both of them were too sensible to allow some domestic mis-demeanour to develop into anything horrible; they were well adjusted and each of them found it easy to admit, long after the honeymoon, that they were deeply in love. Months later at camp, ensnared futilely in the coils of some administrative fly-paper, Culver would find him-self gazing up from his work and out across the smoky hot barrens of pine and sand, relieving his vast boredom in a day-dream of that van-ished simplicity and charm. His mind seemed to drift towards one recurrent vision. This was of the afternoons in winter when—bundled to the ears, the baby-carriage joggling bravely in the van and the melancholy beagle scampering at their heels—they took their Sunday stroll. On such days the city, its frantic heartbeat quieted and clothed in the sooty white tatters of a recent snow, seemed to have an Old World calm, and the people that passed them in the twilight appeared to be, like themselves, pink-cheeked and contented, no matter what crimson alarms flowered at the news-stands or what evil rumours sounded from distant radios. For Culver the waning Sunday light had not spelled out the promise of Monday morning's gloom but of Monday's challenge—and this was not because he was a go-getter but because he was happy. He was happy to walk through the chill and leafless dusk with his wife and his child and his dog. And he was happy to return home to warmth and peanut butter and liverwurst, to the familiar delight of the baby's good-night embrace, to the droll combat between beagle and cat, to music before sleep. Sometimes in these reveries Culver thought that it was the music, more than anything, which provided the key, and he recalled himself at a time which already seemed dark ages ago, surrounded by beer cans and attuned, in the nostalgic air of a winter evening, to some passage from some forgotten Haydn. It was one happy and ascending bar that he remembered, a dozen bright notes through which he passed in memory to an earlier, untroubled day at the end of childhood. There, like tumbling flowers against the sunny grass, their motions as nimble as the music itself, two lovely little girls played tennis, called to him voicelessly, as in a dream, and waved their arms.

The sordid little town outside the camp possessed the horror of recognition, for Culver had been there before. They left the baby with a sister and headed south where, on the outskirts of the town, they found a cramped room in a tourist cabin. They were there for two weeks. They searched vainly for a place to live, there was no more room at the camp. They turned away from bleak cell-like rooms offered at five times their value, were shown huts and chicken-coops by characters whose bland country faces could not hide the sparkle, in their calculating eyes, of venal lust. The ageing proprietress of the tourist camp was a scold and a cheat. And so they finally gave up. Betsy went home. He kissed her good-bye late one rainy afternoon in the bus station, surrounded by a horde of marines and by cheap suitcases and fallen candy wrappers and the sound of fretful children—all of the unlovely mementoes, so nightmarishly familiar, of leavetaking and of anxiety. Of war. He felt her tears against his cheek. It had been an evil day, and the rain that streamed against the windows, blurring a distant frieze of gaunt grey pines, had seemed to nag with both remembrance and foreboding—of tropic seas, storm-swept distances and strange coasts.

2

He had heard the explosion himself. They had been eating at their own chow-line in a command post set up in a grove of trees, when the noise came from off to the right, distant enough but still too close: a twin quick earth-shaking sound—*crump crump*. Then seconds later in the still of noon when even the birds had become quiet and only a few murmured voices disturbed the concentration of eating, a shudder had passed through the surrounding underbrush, like a faint hot wind. It was premonitory, perhaps, but still no one knew. The leaves rustled, ceased, and Culver had looked up from where he squatted against a tree to see fifty scattered faces peering towards the noise, their knives and forks suspended. Then from the galley among the trees a clatter broke the silence, a falling pan or kettle, and someone laughed, and the Colonel, sitting nearby, had said to the Major—what had he said? Culver couldn't remember, yet there had been something uneasy in his tone, even then, before anyone had known, and at least ten minutes before the radio corporal, a tobacco-chewing clown from Oklahoma named Hobbs, came trotting up brushing crumbs from his mouth, a message book clutched in one fat paw. He was popular in battalion headquarters, one of those favoured men who, through some simplicity or artlessness of nature, can manage a profane familiarity which in another would be insubordinate; the look of concern on his clown's face, usually so whimsical, communicated an added dread.

'I gotta flash red from Plumbob, Colonel, and it ain't no problem emergency. All hell's broke loose over in Third Battalion. They dropped in some short rounds on a chow-line and they want corpsmen and a doctor and the chaplain. Jesus, you should hear 'em down there.'

The Colonel had said nothing at first. The brief flicker of uneasiness in his eyes had fled, and when he put down his messkit and looked up at Hobbs it was only to wipe his hands on his handkerchief and squint casually into the sun, as if he were receiving the most routine of messages. It was absolutely typical of the man, Culver reflected. Too habitual to be an act yet still somehow too faintly self-conscious to be entirely natural, how many years and what strange interior struggle had gone into the perfection of such a gesture? It was good, Grade-A Templeton, perhaps not a distinctly top-notch performance but certainly, from where the critic Culver sat, deserving of applause: the frail, little-boned, almost pretty face peering upward with a look of attitudinized contemplation; the pensive bulge of tongue sliding inside the rim of one tanned cheek to gouge out some particle of food; small hands working calmly in the folds of the handkerchief—surely all this was more final, more commanding than the arrogant loud mastery of a Booth, more like the skill of Bernhardt, who could cow men by the mystery of her smallest twitch. Perhaps fifteen seconds passed before he spoke. Culver became irritated—at his own suspense, throbbing inside him like a heartbeat, and at the awesome silence which, as if upon order, had fallen over the group of five, detached from the bustle of the rest of the command post: the Colonel; Hobbs; Major Lawrence, the executive officer, now gazing at the Colonel with moist underlip and deferential anxiety; Captain Mannix; himself. Back off in the bushes a mockingbird commenced a shrill rippling chant and far away, amidst the depth of the silence, there seemed to be a single faint and terrible scream. Hobbs spat an auburn gob of tobacco-juice into the sand, and the Colonel spoke: 'Let me have that radio, Hobbs, and get me Plumbob One,' he said evenly, and then with no change of tone to the Major: 'Billy, send a runner over for Doc Patterson and you two get down there with the chaplain. Take my jeep. Tell the Doc to detach all his corpsmen. And you'd better chop-chop.'

The Major scrambled to his feet. He was youthful and handsome, a fine marine in his polished boots, his immaculate dungarees—donned freshly clean, Culver had observed, that morning. He was of the handsomeness preferred by other military men—regular features, clean-cut, rather athletic—but there was a trace of peace-time fleshiness in his cheeks which often lent to the corners of his mouth a sort of petulance, so that every now and again, his young uncomplicated face in deep concentration over some operations map or training schedule or order, he looked like a spoiled and arrogant baby of five. 'Aye-aye, sir,' he said and bent over the Colonel, bestowing upon him that third-person flattery which to Culver seemed perilously close to bootlicking and was thought to be considerably out of date, especially among the reserves. 'Does the Colonel want us to run our own problem as ordered, sir?' He was a regular.

Templeton took the headset from Hobbs, who lowered the radio down beside him in the sand. 'Yeah, Billy,' he said, without looking up, 'yeah, that'll be all right. We'll run her on time. Tell O'Leary to tell all companies to push off at thirteen-hundred.'

'Aye-aye, sir.' And the Major, boots sparkling, was off in a puff of pine needles and dust.

'Jesus,' Mannix said. He put down his messkit and nudged Culver in the ribs. Captain Mannix, the commanding officer of headquarters company, was Culver's friend and, for five months, his closest one. He was a dark heavy-set Jew from Brooklyn, Culver's age and a reserve, too, who had had to sell his radio store and leave his wife and two children at home. He had a disgruntled sense of humour which often seemed to bring a spark of relief not just to his own, but to Culver's feeling of futility and isolation. Mannix was a bitter man and, in his bitterness, sometimes recklessly vocal. He had long ago given up genteel accents, and spoke like a marine. It was easier, he maintained. 'Je-sus,' he whispered again, too loud, 'what'll Congress do about this? Look at Billy chop-chop.'

Culver said nothing. His tension eased off a bit, and he looked around him. The news had not seemed yet to have spread around the command post; the men began to get up and walk to the chow-line to clean their messgear, strolled back beneath the trees and flopped down, heads against their packs, for a moment's nap. The Colonel spoke in an easy, confidential voice with the other battalion commander: the casualties were confined, Culver gathered, to that outfit. It was a battalion made up mostly of young reserves and it was one in which, he suddenly thanked God, he knew no one. Then he heard the Colonel go on calmly—to promise more aid, to promise to come down himself, shortly. 'Does it look rough, Luke?' Culver heard him say, 'Hold on tight, Luke boy'—all in the cool and leisurely, almost bored, tones of a man to whom the greatest embarrassment would be a show of emotion, and to whom, because of this quality, had been given, in the midst of some strained and violent combat situation long ago, the name 'Old Rocky'. He was not yet forty-five, yet the adjective 'old' applied, for there was a grey sheen in his hair and a bemused, unshakeable look in his tranquil eyes that made him seem, like certain young ecclesiastics, prematurely aged and perhaps even wise. Culver saw him put the headset down and get up, walking off towards the operations tent with a springy, slim-hipped, boyish stride, calling out over his shoulder as he went: 'Mannix.' Simply that: Mannix. A voice neither harsh nor peremptory nor, on the other hand, particularly gentle. It was merely a voice which expected to be obeyed, and Culver felt Mannix's big weight against him as the Captain put a hand on his shoulder and prised himself up from the ground, muttering, 'Jesus, lemme digest a bit, Jack.'

Mannix despised the Colonel. Yet, Culver thought, as the Captain hulked stiff-kneed behind the Colonel and disappeared after him into the operations tent, Mannix despised everything about the Marine Corps. In this attitude he was like nearly all the reserves, it was true, but Mannix was more noisily frank in regard to his position. He detested Templeton not because of any slight or injustice, but because Templeton was a lieutenant colonel, because he was a regular, and because he possessed over Mannix—after six years of freedom—an absolute and unquestioned authority. Mannix would have hated any battalion commander, had he the benignity of Santa Claus, and Culver, listening to Mannix's frequently comical but often too audible complaints, as just now, was kept in a constant state of mild suspense—half amusement, half horror. Culver settled himself against the tree.

Apparently there was nothing, for the moment at least, that he could do. Above him an aeroplane droned through the stillness. A truck grumbled across the clearing, carrying a group of languid hospital corpsmen, was gone; around him the men lay against their packs in crumpled attitudes of sleep. A heavy drowsiness came over him, and he let his eyes slide closed. Suddenly he yearned, with all of the hunger of a schoolboy in a classroom on a May afternoon, to be able to collapse into slumber. For the three days they had been on the problem he had averaged only four hours of sleep a night—almost none last night— and gratefully he knew he'd be able to sleep this evening. He began to doze, dreaming fitfully of home, of white cottages, of a summer by the sea. *Long walk tonight*. And his eyes snapped open then—on what seemed to be the repeated echo, from afar, of that faint anguished shriek he had heard before—in the horrid remembrance that there would be no sleep tonight. For anyone at all. Only a few seconds had passed.

'Long walk tonight,' the voice repeated. Culver stared upward through a dazzling patchwork of leaves and light to see the broad pink face of Sergeant O'Leary, smiling down.

'Christ, O'Leary,' he said, 'don't remind me.'

The Sergeant, still grinning, gestured with his shoulder in the direction of the operations tent. 'The Colonel's really got a wild hair aint he?' He chuckled and reached down and clutched one of his feet, with an elaborate groan.

Culver abruptly felt cloaked in a gloom that was almost tangible, and he was in no mood to laugh. 'You'll be really holding that foot tomorrow morning,' he said, 'and that's no joke.'

The grin persisted. 'Ah, Mister Culver,' O'Leary said, 'don't take it so hard. It's just a little walk through the night. It'll be over before you know it.' He paused, prodding with his toe at the pine needles. 'Say,' he went on, 'what's this I heard about some short rounds down in Third Batt?'

'I don't know from nothing, O'Leary. I just read the papers.' Another truck came by, loaded with corpsmen, followed by a jeep in which sat the helmeted Major Lawrence, a look of sulky arrogance on his face, his arms folded at his chest like a legionnaire riding through a conquered city. 'But from what I understand,' Culver went on, turning back, 'quite a few guys got hurt.'

'That's tough,' O'Leary said. 'I'll bet you they were using that old stuff they've had stored on Guam ever since '45. Jesus, you'd think they'd have better sense. Why, I seen those shells stacked up high as a man out there just last year, getting rained on every day and getting the jungle rot and Jesus, they put tarps over 'em but five years is one hell of a long time to let 81-shells lay around. I remember once . . .' Culver let him talk, without hearing the words, and drowsed. O'Leary was an old-timer (though only a few years older than Culver), a regular who had just signed over for four more years, and it was impossible to dislike him. On Guadalcanal he had been only a youngster, but in the intervening years the Marine Corps had moulded him—perhaps by his own unconscious choice—in its image, and he had become as inextricably grafted to the system as any piece of flesh surgically laid on to arm or thigh. There was great heartiness and warmth in him but at the same time he performed all infantry jobs with a devoted, methodical competence. He could say sarcastically, 'The Colonel's really got a wild hair, ain't he?' but shrug his shoulders and grin, and by that ambivalent gesture sum up an attitude which only a professional soldier could logically retain: I doubt the Colonel's judgement a little, but I will willingly do what he says. He also shared with Hobbs, the radioman, some sort of immunity. And thus it had been last night, Culver recalled, that upon the Colonel's announcement about this evening's forced march—which was to take thirteen hours and extend the nearly thirty-six miles back to the main base— O'Leary had been able to give a long, audible, incredulous whistle, right in the Colonel's face, and elicit from the Colonel an indulgent smile; whereas in the same blackout tent and at virtually the same instant Mannix had murmured, 'Thirty-six miles, Jesus Christ,' in a tone, however, laden with no more disbelief or no more pain than O'Leary's whistle, and Culver had seen the Colonel's smile vanish, replaced on the fragile little face by a subtle, delicate shadow of irritation.

'You think that's too long?' the Colonel had said to Mannix then, turning slightly. There had been no hostility in his voice, or even reproof; it had, in fact, seemed merely a question candidly stated—although this might have been because two enlisted men had been in the tent, O'Leary, and some wizened, anonymous little private shivering over the radio. It was midsummer, but nights out in the swamps were fiercely, illogically cold, and from where they had set up the operations tent that evening—on a tiny patch of squashy marshland—the dampness seemed to ooze up and around them, clutching their bones in a chill which extra sweaters and field jackets and sweatshirts could not dislodge. A single kerosene pressure-lamp dangled from overhead—roaring like a pint-sized, encapsuled hurricane; it furnished the only light in the tent, and the negligible solace of a candle-like heat. It had the stark, desperate, manufactured quality of the light one imagines in an execution chamber; under it the Colonel's face, in absolute repose as he stared down for a brief, silent instant and awaited Mannix's reply, looked like that of a mannequin, chalky, exquisite, solitary beneath a store-window glare.

'No, sir,' Mannix said. He had recovered quickly. He peered up at the Colonel from his camp stool, expressionless. 'No, sir,' he repeated, 'I don't think it's too long, but it's certainly going to be some hike.'

The Colonel did something with his lips. It seemed to be a smile. He said nothing—bemused and mystifying—wearing the enigma of the moment like a cape. In the silence the tempestuous little lamp boiled and raged; far off in the swamp somewhere a mortar flare flew up with a short, sharp crack. O'Leary broke the quietness in the tent with a loud sneeze, followed, almost like a prolongation of the sneeze, by a chuckle, and said: 'Oh boy, Colonel, there're gonna be some sore feet Saturday morning.'

The Colonel didn't answer. He hooked his thumbs in his belt. He turned to the Major, who was brooding upward from the field desk, cheeks propped against his hands. 'I was sitting in my tent a while ago, Billy,' the Colonel said, 'and I got to thinking. I got to thinking about a lot of things. I got to thinking about the Battalion. I said to myself, "How's the Battalion doing?" I mean, "What kind of an outfit do I have here? Is it in good combat shape? If we were to meet an Aggressor enemy tomorrow would we come out all right?" Those were the queries I posed to myself. Then I tried to formulate an answer.' He paused, his eyes luminous and his lips twisted in a wry, contemplative smile as if he were indeed, again, struggling with the weight of the questions to which he had addressed himself. The Major was absorbed; he looked up at Templeton with an intent baby-blue gaze and parted mouth, upon which, against a pink cleft of the lower lip, there glittered a bead of saliva. 'Reluctantly,' the Colonel went on slowly, 'reluctantly, I came to this conclusion: the Battalion's been doping off.' He paused again. 'Doping off. Especially,' he said, turning briefly towards Mannix with a thin smile, 'a certain component unit known as Headquarters and Service Company.' He leaned back on the camp stool and slowly caressed the pewter-coloured surface of his hair. 'I decided a little walk might be in order for tomorrow night, after we secure the problem. Instead of going back to the base on the trucks. What do you think, Billy?'

'I think that's an excellent idea, sir. An excellent idea. In fact I've been meaning to suggest something like that to the Colonel for quite some time. As a means of inculcating a sort of group *esprit.*'

'It's what they need, Billy.'

'Full marching order, sir?' O'Leary put in seriously.

'No, that'd be a little rough.'

'Aaa-h,' O'Leary said, relieved.

Suddenly Culver heard Mannix's voice: 'Even so—'

'Even so, what?' the Colonel interrupted. Again, the voice was not hostile, only anticipatory, as if it already held the answer to whatever Mannix might ask or suggest.

'Well, even so, Colonel,' Mannix went on mildly, while Culver, suddenly taut and concerned, held his breath, 'even without packs thirty-six miles is a long way for anybody, much less for guys who've gone soft for the past five or six years. I'll admit my company isn't the hottest outfit in the world, but most of them are reserves—'

'Wait a minute, Captain, wait a minute,' the Colonel said. Once more the voice—as cool and as level as the marshy ground upon which they were sitting—carefully skirted any tone of reproach and was merely explicit: 'I don't want you to think I'm taking it out on the Battalion merely because of you, or rather H & S Company. But they aren't reserves. They're *marines. Comprehend?*' He arose from the chair. 'I think,' he went on flatly, almost gently, 'that there's one thing that we are all tending to overlook these days. We've been trying to differentiate too closely between two particular bodies of men that make up the Marine Corps. Technically it's true that a lot of these new men are reserves—that is, they have an "R" affixed at the end of the "USMC". But it's only a technical difference, you see. Because first and foremost they're *marines*. I don't want my marines doping off. They're going to *act* like marines. They're going to be *fit*. If they meet an Aggressor enemy next week they might have to march a long, long way. And that's what I want this hike to teach them. *Comprend?*' He made what could pass for the token of a smile and laid his hand easily and for a lingering second on Mannix's shoulder, in a sort of half-gesture of conciliation, understanding—something—it was hard to tell. It was an odd picture because from where he sat Culver was the only one in the tent who could see, at the same instant, both of their expressions. In the morbid, comfortless light they were like classical Greek masks, made of chrome or tin, reflecting an almost theatrical disharmony: the Colonel's fleeting grin sculpted cleanly and prettily in the unshadowed air above the Captain's darkened, downcast face where, for a flicker of a second, something outraged and agonized was swiftly graven and swiftly scratched out. The Colonel's smile was not complacent or unfriendly. It was not so much as if he had achieved a triumph but merely equilibrium, had returned once more to that devout, ordered state of communion which the Captain's words had ever so briefly disturbed. At that moment Culver almost liked the Colonel, in some negative way which had nothing to do with affection, but to which 'respect', though he hated the word, was the nearest approach. At least it was an honest smile, no matter how faint. It was the expression of a man who might be fatuous and a ham of sorts, but was not himself evil or unjust—a man who would like to overhear some sergeant say, 'He keeps a tight outfit, but he's straight.' In men like Templeton all emotions—all smiles, all anger— emanated from a priestlike, religious fervour, throbbing inwardly with the cadence of parades and booted footballs. By that passion rebels are ordered into quick damnation but simple doubters some- times find indulgence—depending upon the priest, who may be one inclined towards mercy, or who is one ever rapt in some litany of punishment and court martial. The Colonel was devout but inclined towards mercy. He was not a tyrant, and his smile was a sign that the Captain's doubts were forgiven, probably even forgotten. But only Culver had seen the Captain's face: a quick look of both fury and suffering, like the tragic Greek mask, or a shackled slave. Then Mannix flushed. 'Yes, sir,' he said.

The Colonel walked towards the door. He seemed already to have put the incident out of his mind. 'Culver,' he said, 'if you can ever make radio contact with Able Company tell them to push off at 0600. If you can't, send a runner down before dawn to see if they've got the word.' He gave the side of his thigh a rather self-conscious, gratuitous slap. 'Well, good night.'

There was a chorus of 'Good night, sirs', and then the Major went out, too, trailed by O'Leary. Culver looked at his watch: it was nearly three o'clock.

Mannix looked up. 'You going to try and get some sleep, Tom?'

'I've tried. It's too cold. Anyway, I've got to take over the radio watch from Junior here. What's your name, fellow?'

The boy at the radio looked up with a start, trembling with the cold. 'McDonald, sir.' He was very young, with pimples and a sweet earnest expression; he had obviously just come from boot camp, for he had practically no hair.

'Well, you can shove off and get some sleep, if you can find a nice warm pile of pine needles somewhere.' The boy sleepily put down his earphones and went out, fastening the blackout flap behind him.

'I've tried,' Culver repeated, 'but I just can't get used to sleeping on the ground any more. I'm getting old and rheumatic. Anyway, the Old Rock was in here for about two hours before you came, using up my sack time while he told the Major and O'Leary and me all about his Shanghai days.'

'He's a son of a bitch.' Mannix morosely cupped his chin in his hands, blinking into space, at the bare canvas wall. He was chewing on the butt of a cigar. The glare seemed to accentuate a flat Mongoloid cast in his face; he looked surly and tough and utterly exhausted. Shivering, he pulled his field jacket closer around his neck, and then, as Culver watched, his face broke out into the comical, exasperated smile which always heralded his bitterest moments of outrage—at the Marine Corps, at the system, at their helpless plight, the state of the world—tirades which, in their unqualified cynicism, would have been intolerable were they not always delivered with such gusto and humour and a kind of grisly delight. 'Thirty . . . six . . . *miles*,' he said slowly, his eyes alive and glistening, '*thirty . . . six . . . miles!* Christ on a crutch! Do you realize how far that is? Why that's as far as it is from Grand Central to Stamford, Connecticut! Why, man, I haven't walked a hundred consecutive yards since 1945. I couldn't go thirty-six miles if I were sliding downhill the whole way on a sled. And a *forced* march, mind you. You just don't stroll along, you know. That's like running. That's a regulation two-and-a-half miles per hour with only a ten-minute break each hour. So H & S Company is fouled up. So maybe it is. He can't take green troops like these and do that. After a couple of seven- or ten- or fifteen-mile conditioning hikes, maybe so. If they were young. And rested. Barracks-fresh. But this silly son of a bitch is going to have all these tired, flabby old men flapping around on the ground like a bunch of fish after the first two miles. Christ on a frigging crutch!'

'He's not a bad guy, Al,' Culver said, 'he's just a regular. Shot in the ass with the Corps. A bit off his nut, like all of them.'

But Mannix had made the march seem menacing, there was no doubt about that, and Culver—who for the moment had been regarding the hike as a sort of careless abstraction, a prolonged evening's stroll—felt a solid dread creep into his bones, along with the chill of the night. Involuntarily, he shuddered. He felt suddenly unreal and disoriented, as if through some curious second sight or seventh sense his surroundings had shifted, ever so imperceptibly, into another dimension of space and time. Perhaps he was just so tired. Freezing marsh and grass instead of wood beneath his feet, the preposterous cold in the midst of summer, Mannix's huge distorted shadow cast brutishly against the impermeable walls by a lantern so sinister that its raging noise had the sound of a typhoon at sea—all these, just for an instant, did indeed contrive to make him feel as if they were adrift at sea in a dazzling, windowless box, ignorant of direction or of any points of the

globe, and with no way of telling. What he had had for the last years—
wife and child and home—seemed to have existed in the infinite past
or, dreamlike again, never at all, and what he had done yesterday and
the day before, moving wearily with this tent from one strange thicket
to a stranger swamp and on to the green depths of some even stranger
ravine, had no sequence, like the dream of a man delirious with fever.
All time and space seemed for the moment to be enclosed within the
tent, itself unmoored and unhelmed upon a dark and compassless
ocean.

And although Mannix was close by, he felt profoundly alone.
Something that had happened that evening—something Mannix had
said, or suggested, perhaps not even that, but only a fleeting look in
the Captain's face, the old compressed look of torment mingled with
seething outrage—something that evening, without a doubt, had
added to the great load of his loneliness an almost intolerable burden.
And that burden was simply an anxiety, nameless for the moment and
therefore the more menacing. It was not merely the prospect of the
hike. Exhaustion had just made him vulnerable to a million shaky,
anonymous fears—fears which he might have resisted had he felt
strong and refreshed, or younger. His age was showing badly. All this
would have been easy at twenty-three. But he was thirty, and seventy-
two virtually sleepless hours had left him feeling bushed and defeated.
And there was another subtle difference he felt about his advanced
age—a new awakening, an awareness—and therein lay the reason for
his fears.

It was simply that after six years of an ordered and sympathetic
life—made the more placid by the fact that he had assumed he had put
war forever behind him—it was a shock almost mystically horrifying,
in its unreality, to find himself in this new world of frigid nights and
blazing noons, of disorder and movement and fanciful pursuit. He was
insecure and uprooted and the prey of many fears. Not for days but for
weeks, it seemed, the battalion had been on the trail of an invisible
enemy who always eluded them and kept them pressing on—across
swamps and blasted fields and past indolent, alien streams. This enemy
was labelled Aggressor, on maps brightly spattered with arrows and
symbolic tanks and guns, but although there was no sign of his

aggression he fled them nonetheless and they pushed the sinister chase, sending up shells and flares as they went. Five hours' pause, five hours in a tent somewhere, lent to the surrounding grove of trees a warm, homelike familiarity that was almost like permanence, and he left each command post feeling lonely and uprooted, as they pushed on after the spectral foe into the infinite strangeness of another swamp or grove. Fatigue pressed down on his shoulders like strong hands, and he awoke in the morning feeling weary, if he ever slept at all. Since their constant movement made the sunlight come from ever-shifting points of the compass, he was often never quite sure—in his steady exhaustion—whether it was morning or afternoon. The displacement and the confusion filled him with an anxiety which would not have been possible six years before, and increased his fatigue. The tent itself, in its tiny, momentary permanence, might have had all of the appeal of the home which he so desperately hungered for, had it not been so cold, and had it not seemed, as he sat there suddenly shivering with fear, so much more like a coffin instead.

Then it occurred to him that he was actually terrified of the march, of the thirty-six miles: not because of the length—which was beyond comprehension—but because he was sure he'd not be able to make it. The contagion of Mannix's fear had touched him. And he wondered then if Mannix's fear had been like his own: that no matter what his hatred of the system, of the Marine Corps, might be, some instilled, twisted pride would make him walk until he dropped, and his fear was not of the hike itself, but of dropping. He looked up at Mannix and said, 'Do you think you can make it, Al?'

Mannix heavily slapped his knee. He seemed not to have heard the question. The giddy sensation passed, and Culver got up to warm his hands at the lamp.

'I'll bet if Regiment or Division got wind of this they'd lower the boom on the bastard,' Mannix said.

'They have already. They said fine.'

'What do you mean? How do you know?'

'He said so, before you came in. He radioed to the base for permission, or so he said.'

'The bastard.'

'He wouldn't dare without it,' Culver said. 'What I can't figure out is why Regiment gave him the O.K. on it.'

'The swine. The little swine. It's not on account of H & S Company. You know that. It's because it's an exploit. He wants to be known as a tough guy, a boondocker.'

'There's one consolation, though,' said Culver, after a pause, 'if it'll help you any.'

'What, for God's sake?'

'Old Rocky, or whatever they call him, is going to hike along, too.'

'You think so?' Mannix said doubtfully.

'I know so. So do you. He wouldn't dare not push along with his men.'

Mannix was silent for a moment. Then he said viciously, as if obsessed with the idea that no act of Templeton's could remain untainted by a prime and calculated evil: 'But the son of a bitch! He's made for that sort of thing. He's been running around the boondocks for six years getting in shape while sane people like you and me were home living like humans and taking it easy. Billy Lawrence, too. They're both gung ho. These fat civilians can't take that sort of thing. My God! Hobbs! Look at that radioman, Hobbs. That guy's going to keel over two minutes out—' He rose suddenly to his feet and stretched, his voice stifled by the long, indrawn breath of a yawn. 'Aaa-h, f— it. I'm going to hit the sack.'

'Why don't you?'

'Fine bed. A poncho in a pile of poison ivy. My ass looks like a chessboard from chigger bites. Jesus, if Mimi could see me now.' He paused and pawed at his red-rimmed eyes. 'Yeah,' he said, blinking at his watch, 'I think I will.' He slapped Culver on the back, without much heartiness. 'I'll see you tomorrow, sport. Stay loose.' Then he lumbered from the tent, mumbling something: *be in for fifty years.*

Culver turned away from the lamp. He sat down at the field desk, strapping a black garland of wires and earphones around his skull. The wild, lost wail of the radio signal struck his ears, mingling with the roar, much closer now, of the lamp; alone as he was, the chill and cramped universe of the tent seemed made for no one more competent than a blind midget, and was on the verge of bursting with a

swollen obbligato of demented sounds. He felt almost sick with the
need for sleep and, with the earphones still around his head, he thrust
his face into his arms on the field desk. There was nothing on the
radio except the signal; far off in the swamp the companies were
sleeping wretchedly in scattered squads and platoons, tumbled about in
the cold and the dark, and dreaming fitful dreams. The radios were
dead everywhere, except for their signals: a crazy, tortured multitude
of wails on which his imagination played in exhaustion. They seemed
like the cries of souls in the anguish of hell, if he concentrated closely
enough, shrill cracklings, whines, barks and shrieks—a whole jungle
full of noise an inch from his eardrum and across which, like a thread
of insanity, was strung the single faint fluting of a dance-band clar-
inet—blown in from Florida or New York, some place beyond
reckoning. His universe now seemed even more contained: not merely
by the tiny space of the tent, but by the almost tangible fact of sound.
And it was impossible to sleep. Besides, something weighed heavily on
his mind; there was something he had forgotten, something he was
supposed to do . . .

Then suddenly he remembered the Colonel's instructions. He
cleared his throat and spoke drowsily into the mouthpiece, his head
still resting against his arms. 'This is Bundle Three calling Bundle
Able. This is Bundle Three calling Bundle Able. This is Bundle Three
calling Bundle Able. Do you hear me? Over . . .' He paused for a
moment, waiting. There was no answer. He repeated: 'This is Bundle
Three calling Bundle Able, this is Bundle Three calling Bundle Able,
this is . . .' And he snapped abruptly erect, thinking of Mannix, thinking: to hell with it: simply because the words made him feel juvenile
and absurd, as if he were reciting Mother Goose.

He *would* stay awake. And he thought of Mannix. Because Mannix
would laugh. Mannix appreciated the idiocy of those radio words, just
as in his own crazy way he managed to put his finger on anything
which might represent a symbol of their predicament. Like the radio
code. He had a violent contempt for the gibberish, the boy-scout
passwords which replaced ordinary conversation in the military world.
To Mannix they were all part of the secret language of a group of
morons, morons who had been made irresponsibly and dangerously

clever. He had despised the other side, also—the sweat, the exertion, and the final danger. It had been he, too, who had said, 'None of this Hemingway crap for me, Jack'; he was nobody's lousy hero, and he'd get out of this outfit some way. Yet, Culver speculated, who really was a hero anyway, any more? Mannix's disavowal of faith put him automatically out of the hero category, in the classical sense, yet if suffering was part of the hero's role, wasn't Mannix as heroic as any? On his shoulder there was a raw, deeply dented, livid scar, made the more conspicuous and, for that matter, more ugly, by the fact that its evil slick surface only emphasized the burly growth of hair around it. There were smaller scars all over his body. About them Mannix was neither proud nor modest, but just frank, and once while they were showering down after a day in the field, Mannix told him how he had gotten the scars, one day on Peleliu. 'I was a buck sergeant then. I got pinned down in a shell hole out in front of my platoon. Christ knows how I got there but I remember there was a telephone in the hole and—whammo!—the Nips began laying in mortar fire on the area and I got a piece right here.' He pointed to a shiny, triangular groove just above his knee. 'I remember grabbing that phone and hollering for them to for Christ's sake get the 81s up and knock out that position, but they were slow, Jesus they were slow! The Nips were firing for effect, I guess, because they were coming down like rain and every time one of the goddam things went off I seemed to catch it. All I can remember is hollering into that phone and the rounds going off and the zinging noise that shrapnel made. I hollered for 81s and I caught a piece in my hand. Then I hollered for at least a goddam rifle grenade and I caught a piece in the ass, right here. I hollered for 60s and guns and aeroplanes. Every time I hollered for something I seemed to catch some steel. Christ, I was scared. And hurting! Jesus Christ, I never hurt so much in my life. Then I caught this one right here'—he made a comical, contorted gesture, with a bar of soap, over his shoulder—'man, it was lights out then. I remembered thinking, "Al, you've had it," and just before I passed out I looked down at that telephone. You know, that frigging wire had been blasted right out of sight all that time.'

No, perhaps Mannix wasn't a hero, any more than the rest of them, caught up by wars in which, decade by half-decade, the combatant served peonage to the telephone and the radar and the thunderjet—a horde of cunningly designed, and therefore often treacherous, machines. But Mannix had suffered once, that 'once' being, in his own words, 'once too goddam many, Jack.' And his own particular suffering had made him angry, had given him an acute, if cynical, perception about their renewed bondage, and a keen nose for the winds that threatened to blow up out of the oppressive weather of their surroundings and sweep them all into violence. And he made Culver uneasy. His discontent was not merely peevish; it was rocklike and rebellious, and thus this discontent seemed to Culver to be at once brave and somehow full of peril.

He had first seen Mannix the revolutionary five months ago, soon after they had been called back to duty. He hadn't known him then. There were compulsory lectures arranged at first, to acquaint the junior officers with recent developments in what had been called 'the new amphibious doctrine'. The outlines of these lectures were appallingly familiar: the stuffy auditorium asprawl with bored lieutenants and captains, the brightly lit stage with its magnified charts and graphs, the lantern slides (at which point, when the lights went out, it was possible to sneak a moment's nap, just as in officers' school seven years ago), the parade of majors and colonels with their maps and pointers, and their cruelly tedious, doggedly memorized lectures: the whole scene, with its grave, professional air, seemed seedily portentous, especially since no one cared, save the majors and colonels, and no one listened. When Culver sat down, during the darkness of a lantern slide, next to the big relaxed mass which he dimly identified as a captain, he noticed that it was snoring. When the lights went up, Mannix still slept on, filling the air around him with a loud, tranquil blubber. Culver aroused him with a nudge. Mannix grumbled something, but then said, 'Thanks, Jack.' A young colonel had come on to the stage then. He had made many of the lectures that week. He had a curiously thick, throaty voice which would have made him sound like a yokel, except that his words were coolly, almost passionately put, and he bent forward over the lectern with a bleak and solemn attitude—a lean, natty figure with hair cut so close to his head that he appeared to be, from that distance, nearly bald. 'An SS man,' Mannix whispered, 'he's gonna come down here and cut your balls off. You Jewish?' He grinned and collapsed back, forehead against his hand, into quiet slumber. Culver couldn't recall what the colonel talked about: the movement of supplies, logistics, ship-to-shore movement, long-range planning, all abstract and vast, and an ardent glint came to his eyes when he spoke of the 'grandiose doctrine' which had been formulated since they, the reserves, had been away. 'You bet your life, Jack,' Mannix had whispered out of the shadows then. He seemed to have snapped fully awake and, following the lecture intently, he appeared to address his whispers not to Culver, or the colonel, but to the air. 'You bet your life they're grandiose,' he said, 'even if you don't know what grandiose means. I'll bet you'd sell your soul to be able to drop a bomb on somebody.' And then, aping the colonel's instructions to the corporal—one of the enlisted flunkies who, after each lecture, passed out the reams of printed and mimeographed tables and charts and résumés, which everyone promptly, when out of sight, threw away—he whispered in high, throaty, lilting mockery: 'Corporal, kindly pass out the atom bombs for inspection.' He smacked the arm of his seat, too hard; it could be heard across the auditorium, and heads turned then, but the colonel had not seemed to have noticed. 'Jesus,' Mannix rumbled furiously, 'Jesus Christ almighty,' while the colonel droned on, in his countrified voice: 'Our group destiny,' he said, 'amphibiously integrated, from any force thrown against us by Aggressor enemy.'

Later—towards the end of that week of lectures, after Mannix had spoken the calm, public manifesto which at least among the reserves had made him famous, and from then on the object of a certain awe, though with a few doubts about his balance, too—Culver had tried to calculate how he had gotten by with it. Perhaps it had to do with his size, his bearing. There was at times a great massive absoluteness in the way he spoke. He was huge, and the complete honesty and candour of his approach seemed to rumble forth, like notes from a sounding-board, in direct proportion to his size. He had suffered, too, and this suffering had left a persistent, unwhipped, scornful look in his eyes, almost like a stain, or rather a wound, which spells out its own warning and cautions the unwary to handle this tortured parcel of flesh with care. And he was an enormous man, his carriage was formidable. That skinny, bristle-haired colonel, Culver finally realized, had been taken aback past the point of punishment, or even reprimand, merely because of the towering, unavoidable, physical fact that he was facing not a student or a captain or a subordinate, but a stubborn and passionate man. So it was that, after a lecture on transport of supplies, when the colonel had called Mannix's name at random from a list to answer some generalized, hypothetical question, Mannix had stood up and said merely, 'I don't know, sir.' A murmur of surprise passed over the auditorium then, for the colonel, early in the hour, had made it plain that he had wanted at least an attempt at an answer—a guess—even though they might be unacquainted with the subject. But Mannix merely said, 'I don't know, sir,' while the colonel, as if he hadn't heard correctly, rephrased the question with a little tremor of annoyance. There was a moment's silence and men turned around in their seats to look at the author of this defiance. 'I don't know, sir,' he said again, in a loud but calm voice. 'I don't know what my first consideration would be in making a space table like that. I'm an infantry officer. I got an 0302.' The colonel's forehead went pinker under the glare of the lights. 'I stated earlier, Captain, that I wanted some sort of answer. None of you gentlemen is expected to know this subject pat, but you can essay *some kind of an answer.*' Mannix just stood there, solid and huge, blinking at the colonel. 'I just have to repeat sir,' he said finally, 'that I don't have the faintest idea what my first consideration would be. I never went to cargo-loading school. I'm an 0302. And I'd like to respectfully add, sir, if I might, that there's hardly anybody in this room who knows that answer, either. They've forgotten everything they ever learned seven years ago. Most of them don't even know how to take an M-1 apart. They're too old. They should be home with their family.' There was passion in his tone but it was controlled and straightforward—he had managed to keep out of his voice either anger or insolence—and then he fell silent. His words had the quality, the sternness, of an absolute and unequivocal fact, as if they had been some intercession for grace spoken across the heads of a courtroom by a lawyer so quietly convinced of his man's innocence that there was no need for gesticulations or frenzy. The colonel's eyes bulged incredulously at Mannix from across the rows of seats, but in the complete, astounded hush that had followed he was apparently at a loss for words. A bit unsteadily, he called out another name and Mannix sat down, staring stonily ahead.

It had been perhaps a court-martial offence, at least worthy of some reprimand, but that was all there was to it. Nothing happened, no repercussions, nothing. The thing had been forgotten; either that, or it had been stored away in the universal memory of colonels, where all such incidents are sorted out for retribution, or are forgotten. Whatever effect it had on the colonel, or whatever higher, even more important sources got wind of it, it had its effect on Mannix. And the result was odd. Far from giving the impression that he had been purged, that he had blown off excess pressure, he seemed instead more tense, more embittered, more in need to scourge something—his own boiling spirit, authority, anything.

Culver's vision of him at this time was always projected against Heaven's Gate, which was the name—no doubt ironically supplied at first by the enlisted men—of the pleasure-dome ingeniously erected amid a tangle of alluvial swampland, and for officers only. He and Mannix lived in rooms next to each other, in the bachelor quarters upstairs. The entire area was a playground which had all the casual opulence of a Riviera resort and found its focus in the sparkling waters of a swimming pool, set like an oblong sapphire amid flowered walks and a fanciful growth of beach umbrellas. There, at ten minutes past four each day, Mannix could be found, his uniform shed in an instant and a gin fizz in his hand—a sullen mountainous figure in a lurid sports shirt, across which a squadron of monstrous butterflies floated in luminous, unmilitary files. Both Mannix and Culver hated the place—its factitious luxury, its wanton atmosphere of alcohol and torpid ease and dances, the vacant professional talk of the regular officers and the constant teasing presence of their wives, who were beautiful and spoke in tender drawls and boldly flaunted at the wifeless reserves—in a proprietary, Atlanta-debutante fashion—their lecherous sort of chastity. The place seemed to offer up, like a cornucopia, the fruits of boredom, of footlessness and dissolution. It was, in Mannix's words, like a prison where you could have anything you wanted except happiness, and once, in a rare midnight moment when he allowed himself to get drunk, he got paper and wood together from his room and announced to Culver in an unsteady but determined voice that he was going to burn the place down. Culver held him off, but it was true: they were bound to the pleasures of the place by necessity—for there was no place to go for a hundred miles, even if they had wanted to go—and therefore out of futility. 'Goddam, it's degrading,' Mannix had said, making use of an adjective which indeed seemed to sum it all up. 'It's like sex now. Or the lack of it. Now maybe it's all right for a kid to go without sex, but it's degrading for someone like me almost thirty to go without making love for so long. It's simply degrading, that's all. I'd go for one of these regulars' pigs if it wasn't for Mimi . . . This whole mess is degrading. I know it's my own fault I stayed in the reserves, Jack, you don't have to tell me that. I was a nut. I didn't know I was going to get called out for every frigging international incident that came along. But, goddam, it's degrading'—and with a glum, subdued gesture he'd down the dregs of his drink—'it's degrading for a man my age to go sniffing around on my belly in the boondocks like a dog. And further more—' He looked scornfully about him, at the glitter and chrome, at the terrace by the pool where Japanese lanterns hung like a grove of pastel moons, and a girl's shrill and empty laugh uncoiled as bright as tinsel through the sluggish coastal dusk. It was a silent moment in a night sprinkled with a dusty multitude of Southern stars, and the distant bleating saxophone seemed indecisive and sad, like the nation and the suffocating summer, neither at peace nor at war. 'Furthermore, it's degrading to come out of the field each day and then be *forced* to go to a night club like this, when all you want to do is go home to your wife and family. Goddam, man, I've *gotta* get out!'

But underneath his rebellion, Culver finally knew, Mannix—like all of them—was really resigned. Born into a generation of conformists, even Mannix (so Culver sensed) was aware that his gestures were not symbolic, but individual, therefore hopeless, maybe even absurd, and that he was trapped like all of them in a predicament which one personal insurrection could, if anything, only make worse. 'You know,' he said once, 'I think I was really afraid just one time last war.' The phrase 'last war' had had, itself, a numb, resigned quality, in its lack of any particular inflection, like 'last week-end', or 'last movie I went to see'. They had been lying on the beach to which they fled each hot week-end. In that setting of coast and sea and lugubrious solitude they felt nearly peaceful, in touch with a tranquil force more important, and more lasting (or so it seemed on those sunlit afternoons), than war. Mannix had been, almost for the first time since Culver had known him, rested and subdued, and the sound of his voice had been a surprise after long, sun-laden hours of sleep and silence. 'That's the goddam truth,' he said thoughtfully, 'I was only afraid once. Really afraid, I mean. It was at a hotel in San Francisco. I think I really came closer to dying that night than I ever have in my life. We were drunk, you see, polluted, all of us. I think there were five of us, all of us boots just out of Dago. Kids. We were on the tenth floor of this hotel and in this room and I believe we were about as drunk as anyone could get. I remember going in to take a shower in the bathroom. It was late at night, past midnight, and after I took this shower, you see, I came out into the room buck naked. Two of those drunk guys were waiting for me. They grabbed me and pushed me towards the window. I was so loaded I couldn't battle. Then they pushed me out the window and held me by the heels while I dangled upside-down buck naked in space, ten floors above the street.' He paused and sucked at a beer can. 'Can you imagine that?' he went on slowly. 'How I felt? I got stone-sober in a second. Imagine being that high upside-down in space with two drunks holding on to your heels. I was heavy, man, just like now, you see. All I can remember is those teeny-weeny lights below and the tiny little people like ants down there and those two crazy drunk guys holding on to my wet slippery ankles, laughing like hell and trying to decide whether to let go or not. I just remember the cold wind blowing on my body and that dark, man, infinite darkness all around me, and my ankles beginning to slip out of their hands. I really saw Death then, and I think that all I could think of was that I was going to fall and smash myself on that hard, hard street below. That those crazy bastards were going to let me fall. I was praying, I guess. I remember the blood rushing to my brain and my ankles slipping, and that awful strange noise. And I was reaching out, man, clutching at thin air. Then I wondered what that noise was, that high loud noise, and then I realized it was me, screaming at the top of my voice, all over San Francisco.' He stopped talking then and scuffed at the sand with one calloused heel. 'They hauled me up somehow. It was those sober guys—I guess they were sober—the other two. They got me up. But every time I remember that moment a great big cold shudder runs up and down my spine.' He chuckled and chewed on his cigar but the laugh was half-hearted and listless, and he dug his elbows into the sand and resumed his quiet, placid gaze towards the horizon. Culver watched him: his bitterness dissolved in the hot salty air, slumped in the sand gazing wistfully out to sea, sun-glassed, hairy-chested, a cigar protruding from his face and a beer can warming in his hand, he seemed no longer the man who could sicken himself with resentment, but relaxed, pliable even, like a huge hairy baby soothed by the wash of elemental tides, ready to receive anything, all, into that great void in his soul which bitterness and rebellion had briefly left vacant—all—the finality of more suffering, or even death. War was in the offing. A promenade of waves, snow-crowned like lovely garlands in the dark hair of girls, swelled eastward towards Africa: past those smoky heights, more eastward still, the horizon seemed to give back repeated echoes of the sea, like far-off thunder, or guns. Culver remembered making a quick, contorted motion in the sand with his body, and being swept by a hot wave of anguish. It was loneliness and homesickness, but it was also fright. Across the rim of his memory two little girls playing on the sunny grass waved to him, were gone, pursued by a shower of uncapturable musical sounds. Mannix's resigned silence fed his loneliness. Suddenly he felt, like Mannix, upturned drunkenly above the abyss, blood rushing to his head, in terror clutching at the substanceless night. . . .

In the noonday light Sergeant O'Leary, his face brightly pink, was still talking. Culver snapped awake with a start. O'Leary grinned down at him—'Damn, Lieutenant, you're gonna crap out tonight if you're that tired now'—and Culver struggled for speech; time seemed to have unspooled past him in a great spiral, and for an instant— his mind still grappling with the memory of a hurried, chaotic nightmare—he was unable to tell where he was. He had the feeling that it should be the night before, and that he was still in the tent. 'Did I go to sleep, O'Leary?' he said, blinking upward.

'Yes, sir,' O'Leary said, and chuckled, 'you sure did.'

'How long?'

'Oh, just a second.'

'Christ, I *am* tired. I dreamt it was last night,' Culver said. He got to his feet. A truck moved through the clearing in a cloud of dust. There seemed to be new activity in the command post, and new confusion. Culver and O'Leary turned together then towards the operations tent; the Colonel had come out and was striding towards them, followed by Mannix.

'Culver, get your jeep and driver,' he said walking towards the road, not looking up. His voice was briskly matter-of-fact; he strode past them with short, choppy steps and the swagger stick in his hand made a quick tattoo, *slap-slap*-slapping against his dungaree pants. 'I want you and Captain Mannix to go with me down to Third Batt. See if we can help.' His voice faded.

Mannix trailed behind him, saying nothing, but his face seemed to Culver even more exhausted, and even more grimly taut, than it had been an hour before.

The road was a dusty cart-path that rambled footlessly across scrubby, fallow farmland. Shacks and cabins, long ago abandoned, lay along its way. They piled into the jeep, Mannix and Culver in the back, the Colonel in front next to the driver. They hadn't far to go— less than a mile—but the trip felt endless to Culver because the day, by now a fitful carousel of sleepy sounds, motions without meaning, seemed wildly, almost dangerously abstracted, as if viewed through drug-glazed eyes or eyes, like those of a mole, unacquainted with light. Dust billowed past them as they went. Above them a blue cloud-less sky in which the sun, pitched now at its summit, beat fearfully down, augured no rain for the day, or for the evening. Mannix said nothing; his silence prompted Culver to turn and look at him. He was gazing straight ahead with eyes that seemed to bore through the Colonel's neck. Tormented beast in the cul-de-sac, baffled fury, grief at the edge of defeat—his eyes made Culver suddenly aware of what they were about to see, and he turned dizzily away and watched the wreck of a Negro cabin float past through the swirling dust: shell-shattered doors and sagging walls, blasted façade—a target across which for one split second in the fantastic noon there seemed to crawl the ghosts of the bereaved and the departed, mourning wraiths come back to reclaim from the ruins some hot scent of honeysuckle, smell of cooking, murmurous noise of bees. Culver closed his eyes and drowsed, slack-jawed, limp, his stomach faintly heaving.

One boy's eyes lay gently closed, and his long dark lashes were washed in tears, as though he had cried himself to sleep. As they bent over him they saw that he was very young, and a breeze came up from the edges of the swamp, bearing with it a scorched odour of smoke and powder, and touched the edges of his hair. A lock fell across his brow with a sort of gawky, tousled grace, as if preserving even in that blank and mindless repose some gesture proper to his years, a callow charm. Around his curly head grasshoppers darted among the weeds. Below, beneath the slumbering eyes, his face had been blasted out of sight. Culver looked up and met Mannix's gaze. The Captain was sobbing helplessly. He cast an agonized look towards the Colonel, standing across the field, then down again at the boy, then at Culver. 'Won't they ever let us alone, the sons of bitches,' he murmured, weeping. 'Won't they ever let us alone?'

3

That evening at twilight, just before the beginning of the march, Mannix found a nail in his shoe. 'Look at it,' he said to Culver, 'what lousy luck.' They were sitting on an embankment bordering the road. The blue dusk was already scattered with stars, but evening had brought no relief to the heat of the day. It clung to them still, damp and stifling, enveloping them like an overcoat. The battalion, over a thousand men, was ready for the march. It stretched out in two files on either side of the road below them for more than a mile. Culver turned and looked down into Mannix's shoe: sure enough, a nail-end had penetrated the lining at the base of the heel, a sharp pinpoint of torture. Mannix inspected the bottom of his big dirty foot. He pulled off a flake of skin which the nail had already worn away. 'Of all the lousy luck,' he said, 'gimme a band-aid.'

'It'll wear right through, Al,' Culver said, 'you'd better get another pair of shoes. Try flattening it out with the end of your bayonet.'

Mannix hammered for a moment at the nail and then looked up in exasperation. 'It won't go all the way. Gimme that band-aid.' A rusty spatter of blood he had picked up at noon was still on the sleeve of his dungarees. He had become nervous and touchy. All that afternoon, after they had come back, he had seemed, like Culver, still shaken by the slaughter, still awed, and rather despondent. Finally, he had alternated moments of remote abstraction with quick outbursts of temper. The shock of the explosion seemed to have set something off in him. His mood had become vague and unpredictable, and he was able to shift from sour, uncommunicative gloom to violent anger in an instant. Culver had never seen him quite so cranky before, nor had he ever seen him so testily at odds with his men, to whom he usually had shown the breeziest good will. All afternoon he'd been after them, nagging, bellowing orders—only to fall suddenly into a profound and brooding silence. As he squatted in the weeds eating his evening meal two hours before, he had hardly said a word, except to murmur—irrelevantly, Culver thought—that his company 'had better goddam well shape up.' It puzzled Culver; the explosion seemed to have stripped off layers of skin from the Captain, leaving only raw nerves exposed.

Now he had become fretful again, touchily alert, and his voice was heavy with impatience. He mumbled as he plastered the band-aid on his foot. 'I wish they'd get this show on the road. That's the trouble with the Marine Corps, you always stand frigging around for half the night while they think up some grandiose doctrine. I wish to Christ I'd joined the Army. Man, if I'd have known what I was getting in for when I went down to that recruiting office in 1941, I'd have run off at the door.' He looked up from his foot and down towards the command group nearly at the head of the column. Three or four officers were clustered together on the road. The Colonel was among them, neat, almost jaunty, in new dungarees and boots. On his head there was a freshly clean utility cap with a spruce uptilted bill and a shiny little silver leaf. At his side he wore a pearl-handled .38 revolver, glistening with silver inlay. It was, as usual, loaded, though no one knew why, for he was never known to shoot it; the general feeling seemed to be that it was his emblematic prerogative, no more an affectation, certainly, than a visored hat encrusted with gilt, or grenades worn at the shoulder. The pistol—like the swagger stick; the nickname; the quizzical, almost tenderly contemplative air of authority—was part of the act, and to be sure, Culver reflected, the act was less offensive, less imperious than it might be. One simply learned soon to believe that the pistol 'belonged', just as the name 'Old Rocky' belonged; if such an act finally did no harm, if it only flattered his vanity, was the Colonel to be blamed, Culver asked himself, if he did nothing to mitigate the total impression?

Mannix watched him, too, watched the Colonel toe at the sand, thumbs hooked rakishly in his belt, a thin gentle smile on his face, adumbrated by the fading light: he looked youthful and fresh, nonchalant, displaying the studied casualness of an athlete before the stadium throng, confident of his own victory long before the race begins. Mannix gnawed at the end of a cigar, spat it out viciously. 'Look at the little jerk. He thinks he's gonna have us pooped out at the half-way mark—'

Culver put in, 'Look, Al, why don't you do something about that nail? If you told the Colonel he'd let you ride in—'

Mannix went fiercely on, in a husky whisper: 'Well he's not. He's a little sadist, but he's not gonna have Al Mannix crapped out. I'll walk anywhere that son of a bitch goes and a mile further. He thinks H & S Company's been doping off. Well, I'll show him. I wouldn't ask him to ride in if I'd been walking over broken glass. I'll—'

He paused. Culver turned and looked at him. They were both silent, staring at each other, embarrassed by the common understanding of their gaze. Each turned away; Mannix murmured something and began to tie his shoe. 'You're right, Al,' Culver heard himself saying. It seemed it was almost more than he could bear. Night was coming on. As in a stupor, he looked down the road at the battalion, the men lounging along the embankments with their rifles, smoking and talking in tired, subdued voices, smoke rising in giant blue clouds through the dusk, where swarms of gnats rose and fell in vivacious, panicky flight. In the swamp, frogs had begun a brainless chorale; their noise seemed perfectly suited to his sense of complete and final frustration. It was almost more than he could bear. So Mannix had felt it, too: not simply fear of suffering, nor exhaustion, nor the lingering horror, which gripped both of them, of that bloody wasteland in the noonday heat. But the other: the old atavism that clutched them, the voice that commanded, once again, *you will.* How stupid to think they had ever made their own philosophy; it was as puny as a house of straw, and at this moment—by the noise in their brains of those words, *you will*—it was being blasted to the winds like dust. They were as helpless as children. Another war, and years beyond reckoning, had violated their minds irrevocably. For six years they had slept a cataleptic sleep, dreaming blissfully of peace, awakened in horror to find that, after all, they were only marines, responding anew to the old commands. They were marines. Even if they were old. Bank clerks and salesmen and lawyers. Even if, right now, they were unutterably tired. They could no more *not* be determined to walk the thirty-six miles than they could, in the blink of an eye, turn themselves into beautiful nymphs. Culver was afraid he wasn't going to make it, and now he knew Mannix was afraid, and he didn't know what to feel—resentment or disgust—over the fact that his fear was mingled with a faint, fugitive pride.

Mannix looked up from his shoe and at the Colonel. 'You're goddam right, Jack, we're going to make it,' he said. 'My company's going to make it if I have to *drag in their bodies.*' There was a tone in his voice that Culver had never heard before.

Suddenly the Colonel's flat voice broke through the stillness: 'All right, Billy, let's saddle up.'

''Talion saddle up!' The Major's words were eager and shrill, became multiplied down the long mile. 'Smoking lamps out!' The blue cloud dissolved in the air, the gnats descended in a swarm and the voices passed on—*Saddle up, saddle up*—while the battalion rose to its feet, not all at once but in a steady gradual surge, like rows of corn snapping back erect after the passing of a wind. Mannix got to his feet, began to sideslip in a cloud of dust down the embankment towards his company directly below. It was at the head of the column, right behind the command group. Culver, moving himself now down the hill, heard Mannix's shout. It rang out in the dusk with deliberate authority, hoarse blunt command: 'All right, H & S Company, saddle up, saddle up! You people get off your asses and straighten up!' Culver passed by him on his way to the command group: he stood surrounded by a cloud of gnats, hulking enormously above the company, hands balanced lightly on his hips, poised forward badgering the men like some obsessed, rakehell Civil War general before a battle: 'All right, you people, we're gonna walk thirty-six miles tonight and I mean walk! First man I see drop out's gonna get police duty for two weeks, and that goes for everybody. You think I'm kidding you wait and see. There's gonna be trucks going in for those that can't make it but I don't want to see anyone from H & S Company climbing on! If an old man with as much flab as I've got can make it you people can too . . .' There was a note, almost, of desperation in his voice. Culver, passing along the line of bedraggled, mournful-looking men, so few of whom looked like fabled marines, heard the voice rise to a taut pitch close to frenzy; it was too loud, it worried Culver, and he wished to caution him: no longer just admonishing the men to a simple duty, it was the voice of a man wildly fanatic with one idea: to last. 'I want to hear no bitching out of you people! Take it easy on the water. You get shinsplints or blisters you see the corpsman, don't come crying to me. When we get in I want to see all of you people . . .' Not because the hike was good or even sensible, Culver thought, but out of hope of triumph, like a chain-gang convict who endures a flogging without the slightest whimper, only to spite the flogger. Culver joined the command group, heard the Colonel say to the Major: 'Looks like H & S Company's going to make it *en masse*, Billy.' It was just as Culver feared, for although his words were pleasant enough, his face, regarding Mannix for a brief moment, had a look of narrow scrutiny, as if he, too, had detected in the Captain's tone that note of proud and wilful submission, rebellion in reverse. But there was no emotion in his voice as he turned quickly, with a glance at his watch, and said, 'Let's move out, Billy.'

They started out without delay. A jeep, its headlamps lit, preceded them. The Colonel, in the lead, abreast of the Major and just ahead of Culver, plunged off into the deep dust of the road. He walked with a slinky-hipped, athletic stride, head down between his shoulders and slightly forward, arms bent and moving methodically; nothing broke the rhythm of his steps—ruts in the road or the deeply grooved tyre tracks—and Culver became quickly amazed, and rather appalled, at the pace he was setting. It was the pace of a trained hiker—determined, unhesitant, much closer to a trot now than a walk—and only a few minutes passed before Culver was gasping for breath. Sand lay thick in the road, hindering a natural step. They had not gone more than a couple of hundred yards; already he felt sweat trickling down his fore-head and beneath his arms. For a moment fear surged up in him unnaturally, and a crazy panic. He had been afraid of the march before, but his fear had been abstract and hazy; now so quickly fatigued, in what seemed a matter of seconds, he felt surely (as Mannix had pre-dicted) that he'd be unable to last the first hour. A panicky wash of blood came to his face and he struggled for breath, wanting to cry out—it passed. His mind groped for reason and the terror receded: once he adjusted to the shock of this pace, he realized, he'd be all right. Then the panic went away; as it did so, he found himself breath-ing easier, freed of that irrational fright. The Colonel pushed ahead in front of him with the absolute mechanical confidence of a wound-up, strutting tin soldier on a table top. Culver, panting a bit, heard his voice, as calm and unwinded as if he were sitting at a desk somewhere, addressed to the Major: 'We shoved off at nine on the dot, Billy. We should make the main road at ten and have a break.' 'Yes, sir,' he heard the Major say, 'we'll be ahead of the game.' Culver made a calculation then; by the operations map, which he knew so well, that was three and a half miles—a mile farther than the regulation distance for an hour's march. It was, indeed, like running. Pushing on through the sand, he felt a wave of hopelessness so giddy and so incomprehensible that it was almost like exhilaration—and he heard a noise—half-chuckle, half-groan—escape between his laboured breaths. Three and a half miles: the distance from Greenwich Village almost to Harlem. In his mind he measured that giddy parade of city blocks, an exhausting voyage even on wheels. It was like twisting a knife in his side but he went on with the mental yardstick—to imagine himself plodding that stretch up the sandless, comfortable receptive pavements of Fifth Avenue, past Fourteenth Street and the bleak vistas of the Twenties and the Thirties, hurrying onward north by the Library, twenty blocks more to the Plaza, and pressing still onward along the green acres of the Park . . . his thoughts recoiled. Three and a half miles. In an hour. With more than thirty-two still to go. A vision of Mannix came swimming back; Culver stumbled along after the dauntless Colonel, thinking, Christ on a crutch.

They hastened on. Night had fallen around them, tropic and sudden, lit now, as they descended across a thicket of swampy ground, only by the lights of the jeep. Culver had regained his wind but already his chest and back were awash in sweat, and he was thirsty. He took a vague comfort in the fact that others felt the same way, for behind him he heard canteens being unsnapped from their cases, rattling out of their cups, and the noise, in mid-march, of drinking—a choked, gurgling sound— then, faint to the rear, Mannix's angry voice: 'All right, goddammit, I told you people to hold on to your water! Put those goddam canteens back until the break!' Culver, craning his neck around, saw nothing—no Mannix, who had apparently dropped behind—nothing except a shadowy double line of men labouring through the sand, fading off far down the road into the general blackness. To the rear some marine made a joke, a remark; there was laughter and a snatch of song—*on top of old Smo-oky, all covered* . . . Then Mannix's voice again out of the dark: 'O.K. you people can grabass all you want but I'm telling you you'd better save your wind. If you want to talk all the way it's O.K. with me but you're gonna crap out if you do, and remember what I said . . .' His tone had become terse and vicious; it could have been the sound of a satrap of Pharaoh, a galley master. It had the forbidding quality of a strand of barbed wire or a lash made of thorns, and the voices, the song, abruptly ceased, as if they had been strangled. Still his words continued to sting and flay them—already, in this first hour, with the merciless accents of a born bully—and Culver, suddenly angered, had an impulse to drop back and try to make him let up.

'You people close it up now! Dammit, Shea, keep those men closed up there. They fall back they're gonna have to run to catch up! Goddammit, close it up now, you hear me! I mean *you*, Thompson, goddammit you aren't deaf! Close it up! *Close it up*, I said!' So it was that the voice, brutal and furious, continued the rest of the way.

And so it was that those first hours Culver recollected as being the most harrowing of all, even though the later hours brought more subtle refinements of pain. He reasoned that this was because during the first few miles or so he was at least in rough possession of his intellect, his mind lashing his spirit as pitilessly as his body. Later, he seemed to be involved in something routine, an act in which his brain, long past co-operation, played hardly any part at all. But during these early hours there was also the fact of Mannix. Superimposed upon Culver's own fantasies, his anger, his despair (and his own calm moments of rationalization, too) was his growing awareness of what was happening to the Captain. Later, Mannix's actions seemed to become mixed up and a part of the general scheme, the nightmare. But here at first Culver's mind was enough in focus for Mannix's transformation to emerge clearly, even if with the chill, unreal outlines of coming doom—like a man conversing, who might turn around briefly to a mirror and see behind him in the room no longer his familiar friend, but something else—a shape, a ghost, a horror—a wild and threatful face reflected from the glass.

They made the highway at ten o'clock, almost to the minute. When the Colonel looked at his watch and stopped and the Major raised his arm, shouting, 'Breather! Ten minutes!' Culver went over to the side of the road and sat down in the weeds. Blood was knocking angrily at his temples, behind his eyes, and he was thirsty enough to drink, with a greedy recklessness, nearly a third of his canteen. He lit a cigarette; it tasted foul and metallic and he flipped it away. His knees and thighs, unaccustomed to so much pounding, were stiff and fatigued; he stretched them out slowly into the dewy underbrush, looking upward at a placid cloud of stars. He turned. Up the road, threading its way through a barrier of outstretched legs and rifles, came a figure. It was Mannix. He was still muttering as he lumbered up and sank down beside him. 'Those goddam people, they won't keep it closed up. I have to dog them every minute. They're going to find themselves running the whole way if they don't keep closed up. Gimme a butt.' He was breathing heavily, and he passed the back of his hand over his brow to wipe the sweat away.

'Why don't you leave them alone?' Culver said. He gave the Captain a cigarette, which he lit, blowing the smoke out in a violent sort of choked puff.

'Dammit,' he replied, coughing, 'you *can't* leave them alone! They don't want to make this lousy hike. They'd just as soon crap out on the side and let the trucks haul them in. They'd just as soon take police duty. Man, they're reserves. They don't care who sees them crap out— me, anybody.' He fell back with a sigh into the weeds, arms over his eyes. 'F— it,' he said. Culver looked down at him. From the jeep's headlamps an oblong of yellow slanted across the lower part of his face. One corner of his mouth jerked nervously—a distasteful grimace, as if he had been chewing something sour. Exhausted, completely bushed, there was something in his manner—even in repose—which refused to admit his own exhaustion. He clenched his teeth convulsively together. It was as if his own fury, his own obsession now, held up, Atlas-like, the burden of his great weariness. 'Jesus,' he murmured, almost irrelevantly, 'I can't help thinking about those kids today, lying out there in the weeds.'

Culver rested easily for a moment, thinking too. He looked at his watch, with a sinking sensation: six of their ten minutes had already passed—so swiftly that they seemed not to have existed at all. Then he said, 'Well, for Christ's sake, Al, why don't you let them crap out? If you were getting screwed like these enlisted men are you'd crap out too, you wouldn't care. You don't have to chew them out like you've been doing. Let's face it, you don't really care if they make it. You. Me, maybe. But these guys . . . anybody else. What the hell.' He paused, fumbling for words, went on feebly, '*Do* you?'

Mannix rose up on his elbows then. 'You're damn right I do,' he said evenly. They turned towards the Colonel standing not far away; he and the Major, pointing a flashlight, were bent together over a map. Mannix hawked something up and spat. His voice became more controlled. 'You see that little jerk standing there?' he said. 'He thinks he's pulling something on us. Thirty-six miles. *Nobody* walks that far, stateside. *Nobody*. We never walked that far even with Edson, last war. See, that little jerk wants to make a name for himself—Old Rocky Templeton. Led the longest forced march in the history of the Corps—'

'But—' Culver started.

'He'd just love to see H & S Company crap out,' he went on tensely, 'he'd *love* it. It'd do something to his ego. Man, I can see him now'—and his voice lifted itself in a tone of sour mockery—'"Well, Cap'n Mannix, see where you had a little trouble last night getting your men in. Need a little bit more *esprit*, huh?"' His voice lowered, filled with venom. 'Well, screw *him* Jack. I'll get my company in if I have to carry them on my back—'

It was useless to reason with him. Culver let him go on until he had exhausted his bitter spurt of hatred, of poison, and until finally he lay back again with a groan in the weeds—only a moment before the cry came again: 'Saddle up! Saddle up!'

They pushed off once more. It was just a bit easier now, for they were to walk for two miles on the highway, there was no sand to hinder their steps, before turning back on to the side roads. Yet there was a comfortless feeling at the outset, too: legs cramped and aching from the moment's rest, he walked stooped and bent over, at the start, like an arthritic old man, and he was sweating again, dry with thirst, after only a hundred yards. How on earth, he wondered, gazing up for a second at the dim placid landscape of stars, would they last until the next morning, until nearly noon? A car passed them—a slick convertible bound for the North, New York perhaps—wherever, inevitably, for some civilian pleasure—and its fleet, almost soundless passage brought, along with the red pinpoint of its vanishing taillights, a new sensation of unreality to the night, the march: dozing, shrouded by the dark, its people seemed unaware of the shadowy walkers, had sped unceasingly on, like ocean voyagers oblivious of all those fishy struggles below them in the night, submarine and fathomless.

They plodded on, the Colonel pacing the march, but slower now, and Culver played desperately with the idea that the man would, somehow, tire, become exhausted himself. A wild fantasia of hopes and imaginings swept through his mind: that Templeton *would* become fatigued, having overestimated his own strength, *would* stop the march after an hour or so and load them on the trucks—like a stern father who begins a beating, only to become touched with if not remorse then leniency, and stays his hand. But Culver knew it was a hollow desire. They pushed relentlessly ahead, past shadowy pine groves, fields dense with the fragrance of alfalfa and wild strawberries, shuttered farmhouses, deserted rickety stores. Then this brief civilized vista they abandoned again, and for good, when without pause they plunged off again on to another road, into the sand. Culver had become bathed in sweat once more; they all had, even the Colonel, whose neat dunga-rees had a black triangular wet spot plastered at their back. Culver heard his own breath coming hoarsely again, and felt the old panic: he'd never be able to make it, he knew, he'd fall out on the side like the old man he was—but far back to the rear then he heard Mannix's huge voice, dominating the night: 'All right, goddammit, move out! We got sand here now. Move out and close it up! Close it up, I say, goddammit! Leadbetter, get that barn out of your ass and close it up! *Close it up*, I say!' They spurred Culver on, after a fashion, but fol-lowing upon those shouts, there was a faint, subdued chorus, almost inaudible, of moans and protests. They came only from Mannix's company, a muffled, sullen groan. To them Culver heard his own fitful breath add a groan—expressing something he could hardly put a name to: fury, despair, approaching doom—he scarcely knew. He stumbled on behind the Colonel, like a ewe who follows the slaugh-terhouse ram, dumb and undoubting, too panicked by the general chaos to hate its leader, or care.

At the end of the second hour, and three more miles, Culver was sobbing with exhaustion. He flopped down in the weeds, conscious now of a blister beginning at the bottom of his foot, as if it had been scraped by a razor.

Mannix was having trouble, too. This time when he came up, he was limping. He sat down silently and took off his shoe; Culver, gulp-ing avidly at his canteen, watched him. Both of them were too winded to smoke, or to speak. They were sprawled beside some waterway—

canal or stream; phosphorescent globes made a spooky glow among shaggy Spanish moss, and a rank and fetid odour bloomed in the darkness—not the swamp's decay, Culver realized, but Mannix's feet. 'Look,' the Captain muttered suddenly, 'that nail's caught me right in the heel.' Culver peered down by the glare of Mannix's flashlight to see on his heel a tiny hole, bleeding slightly, bruised about its perimeter and surrounded by a pasty white where the band-aid had been pulled away. 'How'm I going to do it with that?' Mannix said.

'Try beating that nail down again.'

'I tried, but the point keeps coming out. I'd have to take the whole frigging shoe apart.'

'Can't you put a piece of cloth over it or something?'

'I tried that, too, but it puts my foot off balance. It's worse than the nail.' He paused. 'Jesus Christ.'

'Look,' Culver said, 'try taking this strip of belt and putting it over it.' They debated, operated, talked hurriedly, and neither of them was aware of the Colonel, who had walked over through the shadows and was standing beside them. 'What's the matter, Captain?' he said.

They looked up, startled. Hands hooked as usual—Culver wanted to say 'characteristically'—in his belt, he stood serenely above them. In the yellow flashlight glow his face was red from exertion, still damp with sweat, but he appeared no more fatigued than a man who had sprinted a few yards to catch a bus. The faint smile hovered at the corners of his lips. Once more it was neither complacent nor superior but, if anything, almost benevolent, so that by the unnatural light, in which his delicate features became fiery red and again now, along the borders of his slim tapering fingers, nearly transparent, he looked still not so much the soldier but the priest in whom passion and faith had made an alloy, at last, of only the purest good intentions; above meanness or petty spite, he was leading a march to some humourless salvation, and his smile—his solicitous words, too—had at least a bleak sincerity.

'I got a nail in my shoe,' Mannix said.

The Colonel squatted down and inspected Mannix's foot, cupping it almost tenderly in his hand. Mannix appeared to squirm at the Colonel's touch. 'That looks bad,' he said after a moment, 'did you see the corpsman?'

'No, sir,' Mannix replied tensely, 'I don't think there's anything can be done. Unless I had a new pair of boondockers.'★

The Colonel ruminated, rubbing his chin, his other hand still holding the Captain's foot. His eyes searched the dark reaches of the surrounding swamp, where now the rising moon had laid a tranquil silver dust. Frogs piped shrilly in the night, among the cypress and the shallows and closer now, by the road and the stagnant canal, along which danced shifting pinpoints of fire—cigarettes that rose and fell in the hidden fingers of exhausted men. 'Well,' the Colonel finally said, 'well—' and paused. Again the act: indecision before decision, the waiting. 'Well,' he said, and paused again. The waiting. At that moment—in a wave that came up through his thirst, his throbbing lips, his numb sense of futility—Culver felt that he knew of no one on earth he had ever loathed so much before. And his fury was heightened by the knowledge that he did not hate the man—the Templeton with his shrewd friendly eyes and harmless swagger, that fatuous man whose attempt to convey some impression of a deep and subtle wisdom was almost endearing—not this man, but the Colonel, the marine: that was the one he despised. He didn't hate him for himself, nor even for his brutal march. Bad as it was, there were no doubt worse ordeals; it was at least a peaceful landscape they had to cross. But he did hate him for his perverse and brainless gesture: squatting in the sand, gently, almost indecently now, stroking Mannix's foot, he had too long been conditioned by the system to perform with grace a human act. Too ignorant to know that with this gesture—so nakedly human in the midst of a crazy, capricious punishment which he himself had imposed—he lacerated the Captain by his very touch. Then he spoke. Culver knew what he was going to say. Nothing could have been worse.

'Well,' he said, 'maybe you'd better ride in on one of the trucks.'

If there had been ever the faintest possibility that Mannix would ride in, those words shattered it. Mannix drew his foot away abruptly, as if the Colonel's hand were acid, or fire. 'No, sir!' he said fiercely—

★ A pair of heavy, thick shoes used in marching or field work, also in combat, by the U.S. Marine Corps.

too fiercely, the note of antagonism, now, was unmistakable—'No, sir! I'll make this frigging march.' Furiously, he began to put on his shoe. The Colonel rose to his feet, hooked his thumbs in his belt and gazed carelessly down.

'I think you're going to regret it,' he said, 'with that foot of yours.'

The Captain got up, limping off towards his company, over his retreating shoulder shot back a short, clipped burst of words at the Colonel—whose eyeballs rolled white with astonishment when he heard them—and thereby joined the battle.

'Who cares what you think,' he said.

4

Had the colonel entertained any immediate notions of retribution, he held them off, for at a quarter past four that morning—half-way through the march, when the first green light of dawn streaked the sky—Culver still heard Mannix's hoarse, ill-tempered voice, lashing his troops from the rear. For hours he had lost track of Mannix. As for the Colonel, the word had spread that he was no longer pacing the march but had gone somewhere to the rear and was walking there. In his misery, a wave of hope swelled up in Culver: if the Colonel had become fagged, and was walking no longer but sitting in his jeep somewhere, at least they'd all have the consolation of having suc-ceeded while their leader failed. But it was a hope, Culver knew, that was ill-founded. He'd be back there slogging away. The bastard could out-march twenty men, twenty raging Mannixes.

The hike had become disorganized, no slower but simply more spread out. Culver—held back by fatigue and thirst and the burning, enlarging pain in his feet— found himself straggling behind. From time to time he managed to catch up; at one point he discovered himself at the tail end of Mannix's company, but he no longer cared. The night had simply become a great solitude of pain and thirst, and an exhaustion so profound that it enveloped his whole spirit, and precluded thought.

A truck rumbled past, loaded with supine marines, so still they

appeared unconscious. Another passed, and another—they came all
night. But far to the front, long after each truck's passage, he could
hear Mannix's cry: 'Keep on, Jack! This company's walking in.' They
pushed on through the night, a shambling horde of zombies in
drenched dungarees, eyes transfixed on the earth in a sort of glazed,
avid concentration. After midnight it seemed to Culver that his mind
only registered impressions, and these impressions had no sequence but
were projected upon his brain in a scattered, disordered riot, like a
movie film pieced together by an idiot. His memory went back no
further than the day before; he no longer thought of anything so
unattainable as home. Even the end of the march seemed a fanciful
thing, beyond all possibility, and what small aspirations he now had
were only to endure this one hour, if just to attain the microscopic bliss
of ten minutes' rest and a mouthful of warm water. And bordering his
memory was ever the violent and haunting picture of the mangled
bodies he had seen—when? where? it seemed weeks, years ago,
beneath the light of an almost prehistoric sun; try as he could, to
dwell upon consoling scenes—home, music, sleep—his mind was
balked beyond that vision: the shattered youth with slumbering eyes,
the blood, the swarming noon.

Then at their next halt, their sixth—or seventh, eighth, Culver
had long ago lost count—he saw Mannix lying beside a jeep-towed
water-cart at the rear of his company. O'Leary was sprawled out next
to him, breath coming in long asthmatic groans. Culver eased himself
painfully down beside them and touched Mannix's arm. The light of
dawn, a feverish pale green, had begun to appear, outlining on
Mannix's face a twisted look of suffering. His eyes were closed.

'How you doing, Al?' Culver said, reaching up to refill his canteen.

'Hotsy-totsy,' he breathed, 'except for my frigging foot. How you
making it, boy?' His voice was listless. Culver looked down at
Mannix's shoe; he had taken it off, to expose heel and sock, where,
soaked up like the wick of a lantern, rose a dark streak of blood.

'Jesus,' Culver said, 'Al, for Christ sake now, you'd better ride in on
a truck.'

'Nail's out, sport. I finally stole me a pair of pliers, some radioman.
Had to run like hell to catch up.'

'Even so—' Culver began. But Mannix had fallen into an impervious silence. Up the road stretched a line of squatting men, Mannix's company. Most were sprawled in the weeds or the dust of the road in attitudes as stiff as death, yet some nearby sat slumped over their rifles, drinking water, smoking; there was a thin resentful muttering in the air. And the men close at hand—the faces he could see in the indecisive light—wore looks of agonized and silent protest. They seemed to be mutely seeking for the Captain, author of their misery, and they were like faces of men in bondage who had jettisoned all hope, and were close to defeat. In the weeds Mannix breathed heavily, mingling his with the tortured wheezes of O'Leary, who had fallen sound asleep. It was getting hot again. No one spoke. Then a fitful rumbling filled the dawn, grew louder, and along the line bodies stirred, heads turned, gazing eastward down the road at an oncoming, roaring cloud of dust. Out of the dust came a machine. It was a truck, and it passed them, and it rattled to a stop up in the midst of the company.

'Anyone crapped out here?' a voice called. 'I got room for ten more.'

There was a movement towards the truck; nearby, half a dozen men got to their feet, slung their rifles, and began to hobble up the road. Culver watched them tensely, hearing Mannix stir beside him, putting his shoe back on. O'Leary had awakened and sat up. Together the three of them watched the procession towards the truck: a straggle of limping men plodding as wretchedly as dog-pound animals towards that yawning vehicle in the smoky dawn, huge, green, and possessed of wheels—which would deliver them to freedom, to sleep, oblivion. Mannix watched them without expression, through inflamed eyes; he seemed so drugged, so dumb with exhaustion, that he was unaware of what was taking place. 'What happened to the Colonel?' he said absently.

'He went off in a jeep a couple of hours ago,' O'Leary said, 'said something about checking on the column of march.'

'What?' Mannix said. Again, he seemed unaware of the words, as if they—like the sight of this slow streaming exodus towards the truck—were making no sudden imprint on his mind, but were filtering into his consciousness through piles and layers of wool. A dozen more men arose and began a lame procession towards the truck. Mannix watched them, blinking. 'What?' he repeated.

'To check the column, sir,' O'Leary repeated. 'That's what he said.'

'He *did*?' Mannix turned with an angry, questioning look. 'Who's pacing the march, then?'

'Major Lawrence is.'

'He *is*?' Mannix rose to his feet, precariously, stiffly and in pain balancing himself not on the heel, but the toe only, of his wounded foot. He blinked in the dawn, gazing at the rear of the truck and the cluster of marines there, feebly lifting themselves into the interior. He said nothing and Culver, watching him from below, could only think of the baffled fury of some great bear cornered, bloody and torn by a foe whose tactics were no braver than his own, but simply more cunning. He bit his lips—out of pain perhaps, but as likely out of impotent rage and frustration, and he seemed close to tears when he said, in a tone almost like grief: '*He* crapped out! *He* crapped out!'

He came alive like a somnambulist abruptly shocked out of sleep, and he lunged forward on to the road with a wild and tormented bellow: 'Hey, you people, get off that goddamn truck!' He sprang into the dust with a skip and a jump, toiling down the road with hobbled leg and furious flailing arms. By his deep swinging gait, his terrible limp, he looked no more capable of locomotion than a wheel-chair invalid, and it would have been funny had it not seemed at the same time so full of threat and disaster. He pressed on. 'Off that truck, goddammit, I say! Off that truck. Saddle up. Saddle up now, I say! On your feet!' he yelled. 'Get off that goddam truck before I start kicking you people in the ass!' His words flayed and cowed them: a long concerted groan arose in the air, seemed to take possession of the very dawn; yet they debarked from the truck in terrified flight, scuttling down like mice from a sinking raft. 'Move the hell out of here!' he shouted at the truck driver, a skinny corporal, eyes bulging, who popped back into the cab in fright. 'Get that heap out of here!' The truck leaped off with a roar, enveloping the scene in blue smoke and a tornado of dust. Mannix, with windmilling arms, stood propped on his toe in the centre of the road, urged the men wildly on. 'Saddle up now! Let somebody else crap out O.K., but not you people, hear me!

Do you hear me! Goddammit, I mean it! Shea, get those people moving out up there! You people better face it, you got eighteen more miles to go . . .' Culver tried to stop him, but they had already begun to run.

Panic-stricken, limping with blisters and with exhaustion, and in mutinous despair, the men fled westward, whipped on by Mannix's cries. They pressed into the humid, sweltering light of the new day. Culver followed; O'Leary, without a murmur, puffed along beside him, while to the rear, with steady slogging footsteps, trailed the remnants of the battalion. Dust billowed up and preceded them, like Egypt's pillar of cloud, filling the air with its dry oppressive menace. It coated their lips and moist brows with white powdery grit, like a spray of plaster, and gave to the surrounding trees, the underbrush and vacant fields, a blighted pallor, as if touched by unseasonable frost. The sun rose higher, burning down at their backs so that each felt he bore on his shoulders not the burden of a pack but, almost worse, a portable oven growing hotter and hotter as the sun came up from behind the sheltering pines. They walked automatically, no longer with that light and tentative step in order to ease the pain in their feet, with the firm, dogged tread of robots; and if they were all like Culver they had long since parted with a sensation of motion below the hips, and felt there only a constant throbbing pain—of blisters and battered muscles and the protest of exhausted bones.

Then one time Culver saw the Colonel go by in a jeep, boiling along in a cloud of dust towards the head of the column. He caught a glimpse of him as he passed: he looked sweaty and tired, far from rested, and Culver wondered how justified Mannix's outrage had been, assigning to the Colonel that act of cowardice. So he hadn't been pacing the march, but God knows he must have been hiking along to the rear; and his doubts were bolstered by O'Leary's voice, coming painfully beside him: 'Old Captain Mannix's mighty pissed off at the Colonel.' He paused, wheezing steadily. 'Don't know if he's got a right to be that way. Old Colonel ain't gonna crap out without a reason. Colonel's kind of rough sometimes but he'll go with the troops.' Culver said nothing. They plodded ahead silently. Culver felt like cursing the Sergeant. How could he be so stupid? How could he, in the midst of this pain, yield up still only words of accord and respect and even admiration for the creator of such a wild and lunatic punishment? Only a man so firmly cemented to the system that all doubts were beyond countenance could say what O'Leary did—and yet—and yet God knows, Culver thought wearily, he could be right and himself and Mannix, and the rest of them, inescapably wrong. His mind was confused. A swarm of dust came up and filled his lungs. Mannix was screwing everything up horribly, and Culver wanted suddenly to sprint forward—in spite of the effort it took—reach the Captain, take him aside and tell him: *Al, Al, let up, you've already lost the battle.* Defiance, pride, endurance—none of these would help. He only mutilated himself by this perverse and violent rebellion; no matter what the Colonel was—coward and despot or staunch bold leader—he had him beaten, going and coming. Nothing could be worse than what Mannix was doing—adding to a disaster already ordained (Culver somehow sensed) the burden of his vicious fury. At least let up, the men had had enough. But his mind was confused. His kidneys were aching as if they had been pounded with a mallet, and he walked along now with his hands on his waist, like a professor lecturing in a classroom, coat-tails over his arms.

And for the first time he felt intolerably hot—with a heat that contributed to his mounting fury. At night they had sweated more from exertion; the coolness of the evening had been at least some solace, but the morning's sun began to flagellate him anew, adding curious sharp blades of pain to the furious frustration boiling inside him. Frustration at the fact that he was not independent enough, nor possessed of enough free will, was not *man* enough to say, to hell with it and crap out himself; that he was not man enough to disavow all his determination and endurance and suffering, cash in his chips, and by that act flaunt his contempt of the march, the Colonel, the whole bloody Marine Corps. But he was *not* man enough, he knew, far less simply a free man; he was just a marine—as was Mannix, and so many of the others—and they had been marines, it seemed, all their lives, would go on being marines forever; and the frustration implicit in this thought brought him suddenly close to tears. Mannix. A cold horror came over him. Far down, profoundly, Mannix was so much a marine that it could make him casually demented. The corruption begun years ago in his drill-field feet had climbed up, overtaken him, and had begun to rot his brain. Culver heard himself sobbing with frustration and outrage. The sun beat down against his back. His mind slipped off into fevered blankness, registering once more, on that crazy cinematic type, chaos, vagrant jigsaw images: Mannix's voice far ahead, hoarse and breaking now, then long spells of silence; halts beside stifling, windless fields, then a shady ditch into which he plunged, feverish and comatose, dreaming of a carnival tent where one bought, from a dozen barrels, all sorts of ice, chipped, crushed, and cubed, in various shapes and sizes. He was awakened by that terrible cry—*Saddle up, saddle up!*—and he set out again. The sun rose higher and higher. O'Leary, with a groan, dropped behind and vanished. Two trucks passed loaded with stiff, green-clad bodies motionless as corpses. The canteen fell off Culver's belt, somewhere, sometime; now he found though, to his surprise, that he was no longer thirsty and no longer sweating. This was dangerous, he recalled from some lecture, but at that moment the young marine vomiting at the roadside seemed more important, even more interesting. He stopped to help, thought better of it, passed on—through a strange crowd of pale and tiny butterflies, borne like bleached petals in shimmering slow-motion across the dusty road. At one point Hobbs, the radioman, cruised by in a jeep with a fishpole antenna; he was laughing, taunting the marchers with a song—*I got romance in my pants*—and he waved a jolly fat hand. A tanager rose, scarlet and beautiful, from a steaming thicket and pinwheeled upward, down again, and into the meadow beyond: there Culver thought, for a brief terrified moment, that he saw eight butchered corpses lying in a row, blood streaming out against the weeds. But it passed. Of course, he remembered, that was yesterday—or was it?—and then for minutes he tried to recall Hobbs's name, gave up the effort; it was along about this time, too, that he gazed at his watch, neither pleased nor saddened to find that it was not quite nine o'clock, began to wind it with careful absorption as he trudged along, and looked up to see Mannix looming enormously at the roadside.

'Get up,' the Captain was saying. He had hardly any voice left at all;

whatever he spoke with gave up only a rasp, a whisper. 'Get your ass off the deck,' he was saying, 'get up, I say.'

Culver stopped and watched. The marine lay back in the weeds. He was fat and he had a three-day growth of beard. He held up one bare foot, where there was a blister big as a silver dollar and a dead, livid white, the colour of toadstool; as the Captain spoke, the marine blandly peeled the skin away, revealing a huge patch of tender, pink, virgin flesh. He had a patient hillbilly voice and he was explaining softly, 'Ah just cain't go on, Captain, with a foot like this. Ah just cain't do it, and that's all there is to it.'

'You *can*, goddammit,' he rasped. 'I walked ten miles with a nail in my foot. If I can do it you can, too. Get up, I said. You're a marine . . .'

'Captain,' he went on patiently, 'Ah cain't help it about your nail. Ah may be a marine and all that but Ah ain't no goddamn fool . . .'

The Captain, poised on his crippled foot, made a swift, awkward gesture towards the man, as if to drag him to his feet; Culver grabbed him by the arm, shouting furiously: 'Stop it, Al! Stop it! Stop it! Stop it! Enough!' He paused, looking into Mannix's dull hot eyes. 'Enough!' he said, more quietly. 'Enough.' Then gently, 'That's enough, Al. They've just had enough.' The end was at hand, Culver knew, there was no doubt of that. The march had come to a halt again, the men lay sprawled out on the sweltering roadside. He looked at the Captain, who shook his head dumbly and suddenly ran trembling fingers over his eyes. 'O.K.,' he murmured, 'yeah . . . yes'—something incoherent and touched with grief—and Culver felt tears running down his cheeks. He was too tired to think—except: Old Al. Mannix. Goddam. 'They've had enough,' he repeated.

Mannix jerked his hand away from his face. 'O.K,' he croaked, 'Christ sake, I hear you. O.K. They've had enough, they've had enough. O.K. I heard you the first time. Let 'em crap out! I've did—done—' He paused, wheeled around. 'To hell with them all.'

He watched Mannix limp away. The Colonel was standing nearby up the road, thumbs hooked in his belt, regarding the Captain soberly. Culver's spirit sank like a rock. Old Al, he thought. You just couldn't win. Goddam. Old great soft scarred bear of a man.

★

If in defeat he appeared despondent, he retained one violent shred of life which sustained him to the end—his fury. It would get him through. He was like a man running a gauntlet of whips, who shouts outrage and defiance at his tormentors until he falls at the finish. Yet—as Culver could have long ago foretold—it was a fury that was uncontained; the old smoking bonfire had blazed up in his spirit. And if it had been out of control hours ago when he had first defied the Colonel, there was no doubt at all that now it could not fail to consume both of them. At least one of them. Culver, prone on his belly in the weeds, was hot with tension, and he felt blood pounding at his head when he heard the Colonel call, in a frosty voice: 'Captain Mannix, will you come here a minute?'

Culver was the closest at hand. There were six more miles to go. The break had extended this time to fifteen minutes—an added rest because, as Culver had heard the Colonel explain to the Major, they'd walk the last six miles without a halt. Another break, he'd said, with a wry weary grin, and they'd never be able to get the troops off the ground. Culver had groaned—another senseless piece of sadism—then reasoned wearily that it *was* a good idea. Probably. Maybe. Who knew? He was too tired to care. He watched Mannix walk with an awful hobbling motion up the road, face screwed up in pain and eyes asquint like a man trying to gaze at the sun. He moved at a good rate of speed but his gait was terrible to behold—jerks and spasms which warded off, reacted to, or vainly tried to control great zones and areas of pain. Behind him most of his men lay in stupefied rows at the edge of the road and waited for the trucks to come. They knew Mannix had finished, and they had crumpled completely. For the last ten minutes, in a listless fashion, he had assembled less than a third of the company who were willing to continue the march—diehards, athletes, and just those who, like Mannix himself, would make the last six miles out of pride and spite. Out of fury. It was a seedy, bedraggled column of people: of hollow, staring eyes and faces green with slack-jawed exhaustion; and behind them the remnants of the battalion made hardly more than two hundred men. Mannix struggled on up the road, approached the Colonel, and stood there propped on his toe, hands on his hips for balance.

The Colonel looked at him steadily for a moment, coldly. Mannix was no longer a simple doubter but the heretic, and was about to receive judgement. Yet there was still an almost paternal reluctance in Templeton's voice as he spoke, slowly and very softly, out of the troops' hearing: 'Captain Mannix, I want you to go in on the trucks.'

'No, sir,' Mannix said hoarsely, 'I'm going to make this march.'

The Colonel looked utterly whipped; grey bags of fatigue hung beneath his eyes. He seemed no longer to have enough strength to display his odd theatrical smile; his posture was taut and vaguely stooped, the unmistakable bent-kneed stance of a man with blisters, and Culver was forced to concede—with a sense of mountainous despair—that he *had* made the march after all, somewhere towards the rear and for legitimate reasons of his own, even if Mannix now was too blind, too outraged, to tell. *Goddam*, Culver heard himself moaning aloud, *if just he only hadn't made it*, but he heard the Colonel go on coolly: 'Not with that foot you aren't.' He glanced down. The Captain's ankle had swollen to a fat milky purple above the top of his shoe; he was unable to touch his heel to the ground even if he had wanted to. 'Not with that foot,' he repeated.

Mannix was silent, panting deeply—not as if taken aback at all, but only as if gathering wind for an outburst. He and the Colonel gazed at each other, twin profiles embattled against an escarpment of pines, the chaste blue sky of morning. 'Listen, Colonel,' he rasped, 'you ordered this goddam hike and I'm going to walk it even if I haven't got one goddam man left. You can crap out yourself for half the march—' Culver wanted desperately, somehow, by any means to stop him—not just because he was pulling catastrophe down on his head but because it was simply no longer worth the effort. Couldn't he see? That the Colonel didn't care and that was that? That with him the hike had had nothing to do with courage or sacrifice or suffering, but was only a task to be performed, that whatever he was he was no coward, he had marched the whole way—or most of it, any idiot could see that—and that he was as far removed from the vulgar battle, the competition, which Mannix had tried to promote as the frozen, remotest stars. He just didn't care. Culver strove, in a sick, heaving effort, to rise, to go and somehow separate them, but Mannix was charging on: 'You run your troops. Fine. O.K. But what's all this about crapping out—'

'Wait a minute, Captain, now—' the Colonel blurted ominously. 'For your information—'

'F— you and your information,' said Mannix in a hoarse, choked voice. He was almost sobbing. 'If you think—'

But he went no further, for the Colonel had made a curious, quick gesture—stage-gesture, fantastic and subtle, and it was like watching an old cowboy film to see the Colonel's hand go swiftly back to the handle of his pistol and rest there, his eyes cool and passionate and forbidding. It was a gesture of force which balked even the Captain. Mannix's face went pale—as if he had only just then realized the words which had erupted so heedlessly from his mouth—and he said nothing, only stood there sullen and beaten and blinking at the glossy white handle of the pistol as the Colonel went on: 'For your information, Captain, you aren't the only one who made this march. But I'm not *interested* in your observations. You quiet down now, hear? You march in, see? I order you confined to your quarters, and I'm going to see that you get a court martial. Do you understand? I'm going to have you tried for gross insubordination. I'll have you sent to Korea. *Keep your mouth shut.* Now get back to your company!' He was shaking with wrath; the hot morning light beat with piety and with vengeance from his grey, outraged eyes. 'Get back to your men,' he whispered, '*get back to your men!*'

Then he turned his back to the Captain and called down the road to the Major: 'All right, Billy, let's saddle up!'

So it was over, but not quite all. The last six miles took until past noon. Mannix's perpetual tread on his toe alone gave to his gait a ponderous, bobbing motion which resembled that of a man wretchedly spastic and paralysed. It lent to his face, too—whenever Culver became detached from his own misery long enough to glance at him—an aspect of deep, almost prayerfully passionate concentration— eyes thrown skyward and lips fluttering feverishly in pain—so that if one did not know he was in agony one might imagine that he was a communicant in rapture, offering up breaths of hot desire to the heavens. It was impossible to imagine such a distorted face; it was the painted, suffering face of a clown, and the heaving gait was a grotesque and indecent parody of a hopeless cripple, with shoulders gyrating like a seesaw and with flapping, stricken arms. The Colonel and the Major had long since outdistanced them, and Culver and Mannix walked alone. When the base came into sight, he was certain they were not going to make it. They trudged into the camp. Along the barren, treeless streets marines in neat khaki were going to lunch, and they turned to watch the mammoth gyrating Captain, so tattered and soiled—who addressed convulsive fluttering prayers to the sky, and had obviously parted with his senses. Then Mannix stopped suddenly and grasped Culver's arm. 'What the hell,' he whispered, 'we've made it.'

5

For a long while Culver was unable to sleep. He had lain naked on his bed for what seemed hours, but unconsciousness would not come; his closed eyes offered up only vistas of endless roads, steaming thickets, fields, tents—sunshine and darkness illogically commingled—and the picture, which returned to his mind with the unshakeable regularity of a scrap of music, of the boys who lay dead beneath the light of another noon. Try as he could, sleep would not come. So he dragged himself erect and edged towards the window, laboriously, because of his battered feet; it took him a full minute to do so, and his legs, like those of an amputee which possess the ghost of sensation, felt as if they were still in motion, pacing endless distances. He lowered himself into a chair and lighted a cigarette. Below, the swimming pool was grotto-blue, a miniature of the cloudless sky above, lit with shapes of dancing light as shiny as silver dimes. A squad of sunsuited maidens, officers' wives, splashed at its brink or ate ice-cream sundaes on the lawn, and filled the noontime with their decorous sunny laughter. It was hot and still. Far off above the pines, in the hot sunlight and over distant peace and civilization, brewed the smoky and threatful beginnings of a storm.

Culver let his head fall on his arm. Yes, they had had it—those eight boys—he thought, there was no doubt of that. In mindless slumber now, they were past caring, though diadems might drop or Doges surrender. They were ignorant of all. And that they had never grown old enough to know anything, even the tender miracle of pity, was perhaps a better ending—it was hard to tell. Faint warm winds came up from the river, bearing with them a fragrance of swamp and pine, and a last whisper of air passed through the trees, shuddered, died, became still; suddenly Culver felt a deep vast hunger for something he could not explain, nor ever could remember having known quite so achingly before. He only felt that all of his life he had yearned for something that was as fleeting and as incommunicable, in its beauty, as that one bar of music he remembered, or those lovely little girls with their ever joyful, ever sprightly dance on some far and fantastic lawn—serenity, a quality of repose—he could not call it by name, but only knew that, somehow, it had always escaped him. As he sat there, with the hunger growing and blossoming within him, he felt that he had hardly ever known a time in his life when he was not marching or sick with loneliness or afraid.

And so, he thought, they had all had it, in their various fashions. The Colonel had had his march and his victory, and Culver could not say still why he was unable to hate him. Perhaps it was only because he was a different kind of man, different enough that he was hardly a man at all, but just a quantity of attitudes so remote from Culver's world that to hate him would be like hating a cannibal, merely because he gobbled human flesh. At any rate, he had had it. And as for Mannix— well, *he'd* certainly had it, there was no doubt of *that*. Old Al, he thought tenderly. The man with the back unbreakable, the soul of pity—where was he now, great unshatterable vessel of longing, lost in the night, astray at mid-century in the neverendingness of war?

His hunger faded and died. He raised his head and gazed out the window. Over the pool a figure swan-dived against the sky, in crucified, graceless descent broke the water with a lumpy splash. A cloud passed over the day, darkening the lawn with a moment's sombre light. The conversation of the girls became subdued, civilized, general. Far off above the trees, on the remotest horizon, thunderheads bloomed, a squall. Later, towards sundown, they would roll landward over a shadowing reach of waves, borne nearer, ever more darkly across the coast, the green wild desolation of palmetto and cypress and pine—and here, where the girls pink and scanty in sunsuits would slant their tar-black eyes skyward in the gathering night, abandon pool and games and chatter with shrill cries of warning flee homeward like gawdy scraps of paper on the blast, voices young and lovely and lost in the darkness, the onrushing winds. One thing, Culver thought, was certain—they were in for a blow. Already there would be signals up and down the coast.

Abruptly he was conscious of a dry, parched thirst. He rose to his feet, put on a robe, and hobbled out into the hallway towards the water cooler. As he rounded the corner he saw Mannix, naked except for a towel around his waist, making his slow and agonized way down the hall. He was hairy and enormous and as he inched his way towards the shower room, clawing at the wall for support, his face with its clenched eyes and taut, drawn-down mouth was one of tortured and gigantic suffering. The swelling at his ankle was the size of a grapefruit, an ugly blue, and this leg he dragged behind him, a dead weight no longer capable of motion.

Culver started to limp towards him, said, 'Al—' in an effort to help him along, but just then one of the Negro maids employed in the place came swinging along with a mop, stopped, seeing Mannix, ceased the sing-song little tune she was humming, too, and said, 'Oh my, you poor man. What you been doin'? Do it hurt?' Culver halted.

'Do it hurt?' she repeated. 'Oh, I bet it does. Deed it does.' Mannix looked up at her across the short yards that separated them, silent, blinking. Culver would remember this: the two of them communicating across that chasm one unspoken moment of sympathy and understanding before the woman, spectacled, bandannaed, said again, 'Deed it does,' and before, almost at precisely the same instant, the towel slipped away slowly from Mannix's waist and fell with a soft flop to the floor; Mannix then, standing there, weaving dizzily and clutching for support at the wall, a mass of scars and naked as the day he emerged from his mother's womb, save for the soap which he held feebly in one hand. He seemed to have neither the strength nor the ability to lean down and retrieve the towel and so he merely stood there huge and naked in the slanting dusty light and blinked and sent towards the woman, finally, a sour, apologetic smile, his words uttered, it seemed to Culver, not with self-pity but only with the tone of a man who, having endured and lasted, was too weary to tell her anything but what was true.

'Deed it does,' he said.

1952

Goodbye, Columbus

PHILIP ROTH

The first time I saw Brenda she asked me to hold her glasses. Then she stepped out to the edge of the diving board and looked foggily into the pool; it could have been drained, myopic Brenda would never have known it. She dove beautifully, and a moment later she was swimming back to the side of the pool, her head of short-clipped auburn hair held up, straight ahead of her, as though it were a rose on a long stem. She glided to the edge and then was beside me. 'Thank you,' she said, her eyes watery though not from the water. She extended a hand for her glasses but did not put them on until she turned and headed away. I watched her move off. Her hands suddenly appeared behind her. She caught the bottom of her suit between thumb and index finger and flicked what flesh had been showing back where it belonged. My blood jumped.

That night, before dinner, I called her.

'Who are you calling?' my Aunt Gladys asked.

'Some girl I met today.'

'Doris introduced you?'

'Doris wouldn't introduce me to the guy who drains the pool, Aunt Gladys.'

'Don't criticize all the time. A cousin's a cousin. How did you meet her?'

'I didn't really meet her. I saw her.'

'Who is she?'

'Her last name is Patimkin.'

'Patimkin I don't know,' Aunt Gladys said, as if she knew anybody who belonged to the Green Lane Country Club. 'You're going to call her you don't know her?'

'Yes,' I explained. 'I'll introduce myself.'

'Casanova,' she said, and went back to preparing my uncle's dinner. None of use ate together: my Aunt Gladys ate at five o'clock, my cousin Susan at five-thirty, me at six, and my uncle at six-thirty. There is nothing to explain this beyond the fact that my aunt is crazy.

'Where's the suburban phone book?' I asked after pulling out all the books tucked under the telephone table.

'What?'

'The suburban phone book. I want to call Short Hills.'

'That skinny book? What, I gotta clutter my house with that, I never use it?'

'Where is it?'

'Under the dresser where the leg came off.'

'For God's sake,' I said.

'Call information better. You'll go yanking around there, you'll mess up my drawers. Don't bother me, you see your uncle'll be home soon. I haven't even fed *you* yet.'

'Aunt Gladys, suppose tonight we all eat together. It's hot, it'll be easier for you.'

'Sure, I should serve four different meals at once. You eat pot roast, Susan with the cottage cheese, Max has steak. Friday night is his steak night, I wouldn't deny him. And I'm having a little cold chicken. I should jump up and down twenty different times? What am I, a work-horse?'

'Why don't we all have steak, or cold chicken—'

'Twenty years I'm running a house. Go call your girl friend.'

But when I called, Brenda Patimkin wasn't home. She's having dinner at the club, a woman's voice told me. Will she be home after (my voice was two octaves higher than a choirboy's)? I don't know, the voice said, she may go driving golf balls. Who is this? I mumbled some words—nobody she wouldn't know I'll call back no message thank you sorry to bother . . . I hung up somewhere along in there. Then my aunt called me and I steeled myself for dinner.

She pushed the black whirring fan up to *High* and that way it managed to stir the cord that hung from the kitchen light.

'What kind of soda you want? I got ginger ale, plain seltzer, black raspberry, and a bottle cream soda I could open up.'

'None, thank you.'

'You want water?'

'I don't drink with my meals. Aunt Gladys, I've told you that every day for a year already—'

'Max could drink a whole case with his chopped liver only. He works hard all day. If you worked hard you'd drink more.'

At the stove she heaped up a plate with pot roast, gravy, boiled potatoes, and peas and carrots. She put it in front of me and I could feel the heat of the food in my face. Then she cut two pieces of rye bread and put that next to me, on the table.

I forked a potato in half and ate it, while Aunt Gladys, who had seated herself across from me, watched. 'You don't want bread,' she said, 'I wouldn't cut it it should go stale.'

'I *want* bread,' I said.

'You don't like the seeds, do you?'

I tore a piece of bread in half and ate it.

'How's the meat?' she said.

'Okay. Good.'

'You'll fill yourself with potatoes and bread, the meat you'll leave over I'll have to throw it out.'

Suddenly she leaped up from the chair. 'Salt!' When she returned to the table she plunked a salt shaker down in front of me—pepper wasn't served in her home: she'd heard on Galen Drake that it was not absorbed by the body, and it was disturbing to Aunt Gladys to think that anything she served might pass through a gullet, stomach, and bowel just for the pleasure of the trip.

'You're going to pick the peas out is all? You tell me that, I wouldn't buy with the carrots.'

'I love carrots,' I said, 'I love them.' And to prove it, I dumped half of them down my throat and the other half onto my trousers.

'Pig,' she said.

Though I am very fond of desserts, especially fruit, I chose not to have any. I wanted, this hot night, to avoid the conversation that revolved around my choosing fresh fruit over canned fruit, or canned fruit over fresh fruit; whichever I preferred, Aunt Gladys always had an abundance of the other jamming her refrigerator like stolen diamonds.

'He wants canned peaches, I have a refrigerator full of grapes I have to get rid of . . .' Life was a throwing off for poor Aunt Gladys, her greatest joys were taking out the garbage, emptying her pantry, and making threadbare bundles for what she still referred to as the Poor Jews in Palestine. I only hope she dies with an empty refrigerator, otherwise she'll ruin eternity for everyone else, what with her Velveeta turning green, and her navel oranges growing fuzzy jackets down below.

My Uncle Max came home and while I dialed Brenda's number once again, I could hear soda bottles being popped open in the kitchen. The voice that answered this time was high, cut, and tired. 'Hullo.'

I launched into my speech. 'Hello-Brenda-Brenda-you-don't-know-me-that-is-you-don't-know-my-name-but-I-held-your-glasses-for-you-this-afternoon-at-the-club . . . You-asked-me-to-I'm-not-a-member-my-cousin-Doris-is-Doris-Klugman-I-asked-who-you-were . . .' I breathed, gave her a chance to speak, and then went ahead and answered the silence on the other end. 'Doris? She's the one who's always reading *War and Peace*. That's how I know it's the summer, when Doris is reading *War and Peace*.' Brenda didn't laugh; right from the start she was a practical girl.

'What's your name?' she said.

'Neil Klugman. I held your glasses at the board, remember?'

She answered me with a question of her own, one, I'm sure, that is an embarrassment to both the homely and the fair. 'What do you look like?'

'I'm . . . dark.'

'Are you a Negro?'

'No,' I said.

'What *do* you look like?'

'May I come see you tonight and show you?'

'That's nice,' she laughed. 'I'm playing tennis tonight.'

'I thought you were driving golf balls.'

'I drove them already.'

'How about after tennis?'

'I'll be sweaty after,' Brenda said.

It was not to warn me to clothespin my nose and run in the

opposite direction; it was a fact, it apparently didn't bother Brenda, but she wanted it recorded.

'I don't mind,' I said, and hoped by my tone to earn a niche somewhere between the squeamish and the grubby. 'Can I pick you up?'

She did not answer a minute; I heard her muttering, 'Doris Klugman, Doris Klugman . . .' Then she said, 'Yes, Briarpath Hills, eight-fifteen.'

'I'll be driving a—' I hung back with the year, 'a tan Plymouth. So you'll know me. How will I know you?' I said with a sly, awful laugh.

'I'll be sweating,' she said and hung up.

Once I'd driven out of Newark, past Irvington and the packed-in tangle of railroad crossings, switchmen shacks, lumberyards, Dairy Queens, and used-car lots, the night grew cooler. It was, in fact, as though the hundred and eighty feet that the suburbs rose in altitude above Newark brought one closer to heaven, for the sun itself became bigger, lower, and rounder, and soon I was driving past long lawns which seemed to be twirling water on themselves, and past houses where no one sat on stoops, where lights were on but no windows open, for those inside, refusing to share the very texture of life with those of us outside, regulated with a dial the amounts of moisture that were allowed access to their skin. It was only eight o'clock, and I did not want to be early, so I drove up and down the streets whose names were those of eastern colleges, as though the township, years ago, when things were named, had planned the destinies of the sons of its citizens. I thought of my Aunt Gladys and Uncle Max sharing a Mounds bar in the cindery darkness of their alley, on beach chairs, each cool breeze sweet to them as the promise of afterlife, and after a while I rolled onto the gravel roads of the small park where Brenda was playing tennis. Inside my glove compartment it was as though the map of *The City Streets of Newark* had metamorphosed into crickets, for those mile-long tarry streets did not exist for me any longer, and the night noises sounded loud as the blood whacking at my temples.

I parked the car under the black-green canopy of three oaks, and walked towards the sound of the tennis balls. I heard an exasperated voice say, 'Deuce *again.*' It was Brenda and she sounded as though she was sweating considerably. I crackled slowly up the gravel and heard Brenda once more. 'My ad,' and then just as I rounded the path, catching a cuff full of burrs, I heard, 'Game!' Her racket went spinning up in the air and she caught it neatly as I came into sight.

'Hello,' I called.

'Hello, Neil. One more game,' she called. Brenda's words seemed to infuriate her opponent, a pretty brown-haired girl, not quite so tall as Brenda, who stopped searching for the ball that had been driven past her, and gave both Brenda and myself a dirty look. In a moment I learned the reason why: Brenda was ahead five games to four, and her cocksureness about there being just one game remaining aroused enough anger in her opponent for the two of us to share.

As it happened, Brenda finally won, though it took more games than she'd expected. The other girl, whose name sounded like Simp, seemed happy to end it at six all, but Brenda, shifting, running, up on her toes, would not stop, and finally all I could see moving in the darkness were her glasses, a glint of them, the clasp of her belt, her socks, her sneakers, and, on occasion, the ball. The darker it got the more savagely did Brenda rush the net, which seemed curious, for I had noticed that earlier, in the light, she had stayed back, and even when she had had to rush, after smashing back a lob, she didn't look entirely happy about being so close to her opponent's racket. Her passion for winning a point seemed outmatched by an even stronger passion for maintaining her beauty as it was. I suspected that the red print of a tennis ball on her cheek would pain her more than losing all the points in the world. Darkness pushed her in, however, and she stroked harder, and at last Simp seemed to be running on her ankles. When it was all over, Simp refused my offer of a ride home and indicated with a quality of speech borrowed from some old Katherine Hepburn movie that she could manage for herself; apparently her manor lay no further than the nearest briar patch. She did not like me and I her, though I worried it, I'm sure, more than she did.

'Who is *she?*'

'Laura Simpson Stolowitch.'

'Why don't you call her Stolo?' I asked.

'Simp is her Bennington name. The ass.'

'Is that where you go to school?' I asked.

She was pushing her shirt up against her skin to dry the perspiration. 'No. I go to school in Boston.'

I disliked her for the answer. Whenever anyone asks me where I went to school I come right out with it: Newark Colleges of Rutgers University. I may say it a bit too ringingly, too fast, too up-in-the-air, but I say it. For an instant Brenda reminded me of the pug-nosed little bastards from Montclair who come down to the library during vacations, and while I stamp out their books, they stand around tugging their elephantine scarves until they hang to their ankles, hinting all the while at 'Boston' and 'New Haven.'

'Boston University?' I asked, looking off at the trees.

'Radcliffe.'

We were still standing on the court, bounded on all sides by white lines. Around the bushes back of the court, fire-flies were cutting figure eights in the thorny-smelling air and then, as the night suddenly came all the way in, the leaves on the trees shone for an instant, as though they'd just been rained upon. Brenda walked off the court, with me a step behind her. Now I had grown accustomed to the dark, and as she ceased being merely a voice and turned into a sight again, some of my anger at her 'Boston' remark floated off and I let myself appreciate her. Her hands did not twitch at her bottom, but the form revealed itself, covered or not, under the closeness of her khaki Bermudas. There were two wet triangles on the back of her tiny-collared white polo shirt, right where her wings would have been if she'd had a pair. She wore, to complete the picture, a tartan belt, white socks, and white tennis sneakers.

As she walked she zipped the cover on her racket.

'Are you anxious to get home?' I said.

'No.'

'Let's sit here. It's pleasant.'

'Okay.'

We sat down on a bank of grass slanted enough for us to lean back without really leaning; from the angle it seemed as though we were preparing to watch some celestial event, the christening of a new star, the inflation to full size of a half-ballooned moon. Brenda zipped and unzipped the cover while she spoke; for the first time she seemed edgy. Her edginess coaxed mine back, and so we were ready now for what, magically, it seemed we might be able to get by without: a meeting.

'What does your cousin Doris look like?' she asked.

'She's dark—'

'Is she—'

'No,' I said. 'She has freckles and dark hair and she's very tall.'

'Where does she go to school?'

'Northampton.'

She did not answer and I don't know how much of what I meant she had understood.

'I guess I don't know her,' she said after a moment. 'Is she a new member?'

'I think so. They moved to Livingston only a couple of years ago.'

'Oh.'

No new star appeared, at least for the next five minutes.

'Did you remember me from holding your glasses?' I said.

'Now I do,' she said. 'Do you live in Livingston too?'

'No. Newark.'

'We lived in Newark when I was a baby,' she offered.

'Would you like to go home?' I was suddenly angry.

'No. Let's walk though.'

Brenda kicked a stone and walked a step ahead of me.

'Why is it you rush the net only after dark?' I said.

She turned to me and smiled. 'You noticed? Old Simp the Simpleton doesn't.'

'Why do you?'

'I don't like to be up too close, unless I'm sure she won't return it.'

'Why?'

'My nose.'

'What?'

'I'm afraid of my nose. I had it bobbed.'

'What?'

'I had my nose fixed.'

'What was the matter with it?'

'It was bumpy.'

'A lot?'

'No,' she said, 'I was pretty. Now I'm prettier. My brother's having his fixed in the fall.'

'Does he want to be prettier?'

She didn't answer and walked ahead of me again.

'I don't mean to sound facetious. I mean why's he doing it?'

'He *wants* to . . . unless he becomes a gym teacher . . . but he won't,' she said. 'We all look like my father.'

'Is he having his fixed?'

'Why are you so nasty?'

'I'm not. I'm sorry.' My next question was prompted by a desire to sound interested and thereby regain civility; it didn't quite come out as I'd expected—I said it too loud. 'How much does it cost?'

Brenda waited a moment but then she answered. 'A thousand dollars. Unless you go to a butcher.'

'Let me see if you got your money's worth.'

She turned again; she stood next to a bench and put the racket down on it. 'If I let you kiss me would you stop being nasty?'

We had to take about two too many steps to keep the approach from being awkward, but we pursued the impulse and kissed. I felt her hand on the back of my neck and so I tugged her towards me, too violently perhaps, and slid my own hands across the side of her body and around to her back. I felt the wet spots on her shoulder blades, and beneath them, I'm sure of it, a faint fluttering, as though something stirred so deep in her breasts, so far back it could make itself felt through her shirt. It was like the fluttering of wings, tiny wings no bigger than her breasts. The smallness of the wings did not bother me—it would not take an eagle to carry me up those lousy hundred and eighty feet that make summer nights so much cooler in Short Hills than they are in Newark.

2

The next day I held Brenda's glasses for her once again, this time not as momentary servant but as afternoon guest; or perhaps as both, which still was an improvement. She wore a black tank suit and went barefooted, and among the other women, with their Cuban heels and boned-up breasts, their knuckle-sized rings, their straw hats, which resembled immense wicker pizza plates and had been purchased, as I heard one deeply tanned woman rasp, 'from the cutest little *shvartze* when we docked at Barbados,' Brenda among them was elegantly simple, like a sailor's dream of a Polynesian maiden, albeit one with prescription sun glasses and the last name of Patimkin. She brought a little slurp of water with her when she crawled back towards the pool's edge, and at the edge she grabbed up with her hands and held my ankles, tightly and wet.

'Come in,' she said up to me, squinting. 'We'll play.'

'Your glasses,' I said.

'Oh break the goddam things. I hate them.'

'Why don't you have your eyes fixed?'

'There you go again.'

'I'm sorry,' I said. 'I'll give them to Doris.'

Doris, in the surprise of the summer, had gotten past Prince Andrey's departure from his wife, and now sat brooding, not, it turned out, over the lonely fate of poor Princess Liza, but at the skin which she had lately discovered to be peeling off her shoulders.

'Would you watch Brenda's glasses?' I said.

'Yes.' She fluffed little scales of translucent flesh into the air. 'Damn it.'

I handed her the glasses.

'Well, for God's sake,' she said, 'I'm not going to hold them. Put them down. *I'm* not her slave.'

'You're a pain in the ass, you know that, Doris?' Sitting there, she looked a little like Laura Simpson Stolowitch, who was, in fact, walking somewhere off at the far end of the pool, avoiding Brenda and me because (I liked to think) of the defeat Brenda had handed her the night before; or maybe (I didn't like to think) because of the strangeness of my presence. Regardless, Doris had to bear the weight of my indictment of both Simp and herself.

'Thank you,' she said. 'After I invite you up for the day.'

'That was yesterday.'

'What about last year?'

'That's right, your mother told you last year too—invite Esther's boy so when he writes his parents they won't complain we don't look after him. Every summer I get my day.'

'You should have gone with them. That's not our fault. You're not our charge,' and when she said it, I could just tell it was something she'd heard at home, or received in a letter one Monday mail, after she'd returned to Northampton from Stowe, or Dartmouth, or perhaps from that weekend when she'd taken a shower with her boyfriend in Lowell House.

'Tell your father not to worry. Uncle Aaron, the sport. I'll take care of myself,' and I ran on back to the pool, ran into a dive, in fact, and came up like a dolphin beside Brenda, whose legs I slid upon with my own.

'How's Doris?' she said.

'Peeling,' I said. 'She's going to have her skin fixed.'

'*Stop* it,' she said, and dove down beneath us till I felt her clamping her hands on the soles of my feet. I pulled back and then down too, and then, at the bottom, no more than six inches about the wiggling black lines that divided the pool into lanes for races, we bubbled a kiss into each other's lips. She was smiling there, at *me*, down at the bottom of the swimming pool of the Green Lane Country Club. Way above us, legs shimmied in the water and a pair of fins skimmed greenly by: my cousin Doris could peel away to nothing for all I cared, my Aunt Gladys have twenty feedings every night, my father and mother could roast away their asthma down in the furnace of Arizona, those penniless deserters— I didn't care for anything but Brenda. I went to pull her towards me just as she started fluttering up; my hand hooked onto the front of her suit and the cloth pulled away from her. Her breasts swam towards me like two pink-nosed fish and she let me hold them. Then, in a moment, it was the sun who kissed us both, and we were out of the water, too pleased with each other to smile. Brenda shook the wetness of her hair onto my face and with the drops that touched me I felt she had made a promise to me about the summer, and, I hoped, beyond.

'Do you want your sun glasses?'

'You're close enough to see,' she said. We were under a big blue umbrella, side-by-side on two chaise longues, whose plastic covers sizzled against our suits and flesh; I turned my head to look at Brenda and smelled that pleasant little burning odor in the skin of my shoulders. I turned back up to the sun, as did she, and, as we talked, and it grew hotter and brighter, the colors splintered under my closed eyelids.

'This is all very fast,' she said.

'Nothing's happened,' I said softly.

'No. I guess not. I sort of feel something has.'

'In eighteen hours?'

'Yes. I feel . . . pursued,' she said after a moment.

'You invited *me*, Brenda.'

'Why do you always sound a little nasty to me?'

'Did I sound nasty? I don't mean to. Truly.'

'You do! *You* invited *me*, Brenda. So what?' she said. 'That isn't what I mean anyway.'

'I'm sorry.'

'Stop apologizing. You're so automatic about it, you don't even mean it.'

'Now you're being nasty to me,' I said.

'No. Just stating the facts. Let's not argue. I like you.' She turned her head and looked as though she too paused a second to smell the summer on her own flesh. 'I like the way you look.' She saved it from embarrassing me with that factual tone of hers.

'Why?' I said.

'Where did you get those fine shoulders? Do you play something?'

'No,' I said. 'I just grew up and they came with me.'

'I like your body. It's fine.'

'I'm glad,' I said.

'You like mine, don't you?'

'No,' I said.

'Then it's denied you,' she said.

I brushed her hair flat against her ear with the back of my hand and then we were silent a while.

'Brenda,' I said, 'you haven't asked me anything about me.'

'How you feel? Do you want me to ask you how you feel?'

'Yes,' I said, accepting the back door she gave me, though probably not for the same reasons she had offered it.

'How *do* you feel?'

'I want to swim.'

'Okay,' she said.

We spent the rest of the afternoon in the water. There were eight of those long lines painted down the length of the pool and by the end of the day I think we had parked for a while in every lane, close enough to the dark stripes to reach out and touch them. We came back to the chairs now and then and sang hesitant, clever, nervous, gentle dithyrambs about how we were beginning to feel towards one another. Actually we did not have the feelings we said we had until we spoke them—at least I didn't; to phrase them was to invent them and own them. We whipped our strangeness and newness into a froth that resembled love, and we dared not play too long with it, talk too much of it, or it would flatten and fizzle away. So we moved back and forth from chairs to water, from talk to silence, and considering my unshakable edginess with Brenda, and the high walls of ego that rose, buttresses and all, between her and her knowledge of herself, we managed pretty well.

At about four o'clock, at the bottom of the pool, Brenda suddenly wrenched away from me and shot up to the surface. I shot up after her.

'What's the matter?' I said.

First she whipped the hair off her forehead. Then she pointed a hand down towards the base of the pool. 'My brother,' she said, coughing some water free inside her.

And suddenly, like a crew-cut Proteus rising from the sea, Ron Patimkin emerged from the lower depths we'd just inhabited and his immensity was before us.

'Hey, Bren,' he said, and pushed a palm flat into the water so that a small hurricane beat up against Brenda and me.

'What are you so happy about?' she said.

'The Yankees took two.'

'Are we going to have Mickey Mantle for dinner?' she said. 'When the Yankees win,' she said to me, treading so easily she seemed to have turned the chlorine to marble beneath her, 'we set an extra place for Mickey Mantle.'

'You want to race?' Ron asked.

'No, Ronald. Go race alone.'

Nobody had as yet said a word about me. I treaded unobtrusively as I could, as a third party, unintroduced, will step back and say nothing, awaiting the amenities. I was tired, however, from the afternoon's sport, and wished to hell brother and sister would not tease and chat much longer. Fortunately Brenda introduced me. 'Ronald, this is Neil Klugman. This is my brother, Ronald Patimkin.'

Of all things there in the fifteen feet water, Ron reached out his hand to shake. I returned the shake, not quite as monumentally as he apparently expected; my chin slipped an inch into the water and all at once I was exhausted.

'Want to race?' Ron asked me good-naturedly.

'Go ahead, Neil, race with him. I want to call home and tell them you're coming to dinner.'

'Am I? I'll have to call my aunt. You didn't say anything. My clothes—'

'We dine *au naturel*.'

'What?' Ronald said.

'Swim baby,' Brenda said to him and it ached me some when she kissed him on the face.

I begged out of the race, saying I had to make a phone call myself, and once upon the tiled blue border of the pool, looked back to see Ron taking the length in sleek, immense strokes. He gave one the feeling that after swimming the length of the pool a half dozen times he would have earned the right to drink its contents; I imagined he had, like my Uncle Max, a colossal thirst and a gigantic bladder.

Aunt Gladys did not seem relieved when I told her she'd have only three feedings to prepare that night. 'Fancy-shmancy' was all she said to me on the phone.

We did not eat in the kitchen; rather, the six of us—Brenda, myself,

Ron, Mr and Mrs Patimkin, and Brenda's little sister, Julie—sat around the dining room table, while the maid, Carlota, a Navaho-faced Negro who had little holes in her ears but no earrings, served us the meal. I was seated next to Brenda, who was dressed in what was *au naturel* for her: Bermudas, the close ones, white polo shirt, tennis sneakers and white socks. Across from me was Julie, ten, round-faced, bright, who before dinner, while the other little girls on the street had been play-ing with jacks and boys and each other, had been on the back lawn putting golf balls with her father. Mr Patimkin reminded me of my father, except that when he spoke he did not surround each syllable with a wheeze. He was tall, strong, ungrammatical, and a ferocious eater. When he attacked his salad—after drenching it in bottled French dressing—the veins swelled under the heavy skin of his forearm. He ate three helpings of salad, Ron had four, Brenda and Julie had two, and only Mrs Patimkin and I had one each. I did not like Mrs Patimkin, though she was certainly the handsomest of all of us at the table. She was disastrously polite to me, and with her purple eyes, her dark hair, and large, persuasive frame, she gave me the feeling of some captive beauty, some wild princess, who has been tamed and made the servant to the king's daughter—who was Brenda.

Outside, through the wide picture window, I could see the back lawn with its twin oak trees. I say oaks, though fancifully, one might call them sporting-goods trees. Beneath their branches, like fruit dropped from their limbs, were two irons, a golf ball, a tennis can, a baseball bat, basketball, a first-baseman's glove, and what was appar-ently a riding crop. Further back, near the scrubs that bounded the Patimkin property and in front of the small basketball court, a square red blanket, with a white O stitched in the center, looked to be on fire against the green grass. A breeze must have blown outside, for the net on the basket moved; inside we ate in the steady coolness of air by Westinghouse. It was a pleasure, except that eating among those Brobdingnags, I felt for quite a while as though four inches had been clipped from my shoulders, three inches from my height, and for good measure, someone had removed my ribs and my chest had set-tled meekly in towards my back.

There was not much dinner conversation; eating was heavy and

methodical and serious, and it would be just as well to record all that
was said in one swoop, rather than indicate the sentences lost in the
passing of food, the words gurgled into mouthfuls, the syntax chopped
and forgotten in heapings, spillings, and gorgings.

To RON: When's Harriet calling?

RON: Five o'clock.

JULIE: It *was* five o'clock.

RON: Their time.

JULIE: Why is it that it's earlier in Milwaukee? Suppose you took a
plane back and forth all day. You'd never get older.

BRENDA: That's right sweetheart.

MRS P.: What do you give the child misinformation for? Is that
why she goes to school?

BRENDA: I don't know why she goes to school.

MR P. (*lovingly*): College girl.

RON: Where's Carlota? Carlota!

MRS P.: Carlota, give Ronald more.

CARLOTA (*calling*): More what?

RON: Everything.

MR P.: Me too.

MRS P.: They'll have to *roll* you on the links.

MR P. (*pulling his shirt up and slapping his black, curved belly*): What are
you talking about? Look at that?

RON (*yanking his T-shirt up*): Look at *this*.

BRENDA (*to me*): Would you care to bare your middle?

ME (the choir boy again): No.

MRS P.: That's right, Neil.

ME: Yes. Thank you.

CARLOTA (*over my shoulder, like an unsummoned spirit*): Would *you* like
more?

ME: No.

MR P.: He eats like a bird.

JULIE: Certain birds eat a lot.

BRENDA: Which ones?

MRS P.: Let's not talk about animals at the dinner table. Brenda,
why do you encourage her?

RON: Where's Carlota, I gotta play tonight.

MR P.: Tape your wrist, don't forget.

MRS P.: Where do you live, Bill?

BRENDA: Neil.

MRS P.: Didn't I say Neil?

JULIE: You said 'Where do you live, *Bill?*'

MRS P.: I must have been thinking of something else.

RON: I hate tape. How the hell can I play in tape?

JULIE: Don't curse.

MRS P.: That's right.

MR P.: What is Mantle batting now?

JULIE: Three twenty-eight.

RON: Three twenty-five.

JULIE: Eight!

RON: Five, jerk! He got three for four in the second game.

JULIE: *Four* for four.

RON: That was an error, Minoso should have had it.

JULIE: *I* didn't think so.

BRENDA (*to me*): See?

MRS P.: See what?

BRENDA: I was talking to Bill.

JULIE: Neil.

MR P.: Shut up and eat.

MRS P.: A little less talking, young lady.

JULIE: *I* didn't say anything.

BRENDA: She was talking to me, sweetie.

MR P.: What's this *she* business. Is that how you call your mother? What's dessert?

The phone rings, and though we are awaiting desert, the meal seems at a formal end, for Ron breaks for his room, Julie shouts 'Harriet!' and Mr Patimkin is not wholly successful in stifling a belch, though the failure even more than the effort ingratiates him to me. Mrs Patimkin is directing Carlota not to mix the milk silverware and the meat silverware again, and Carlota is eating a peach while she listens; under the table I feel Brenda's fingers tease my calf. I am full.

★

We sat under the biggest of the oak trees while out on the basketball court Mr Patimkin played five and two with Julie. In the driveway Ron was racing the motor of the Volkswagen. 'Will somebody *please* move the Chrysler out from behind me?' he called angrily. 'I'm late as it is.'

'Excuse me,' Brenda said, getting up.

'I think I'm behind the Chrysler,' I said.

'Let's go,' she said.

We backed the cars out so that Ron could hasten on to his game. Then we reparked them and went back to watching Mr Patimkin and Julie.

'I like your sister,' I said.

'So do I,' she said. 'I wonder what she'll turn out to be.'

'Like you,' I said.

'I don't know,' she said. 'Better probably.' And then she added, 'or maybe worse. How can you tell? My father's nice to her, but I'll give her another three years with my mother . . . Bill,' she said, musingly.

'I didn't mind that,' I said. 'She's very beautiful, your mother.'

'I can't even think of her as my mother. She hates me. Other girls, when they pack in September, at least their mothers help them. Not mine. She'll be busy sharpening pencils for Julie's pencil box while I'm carrying my trunk around upstairs. And it's so obvious why. It's practically a case study.'

'Why?'

'She's jealous. It's so corny I'm ashamed to say it. Do you know my mother had the best back-hand in New Jersey? Really, she was the best tennis player in the state, man or woman. You ought to see the pictures of her when she was a girl. She was so healthy-looking. But not chubby or anything. She was soulful, truly. I love her in those pictures. Sometimes I say to her how beautiful the pictures are. I even asked to have one blown up so I could have it at school. "We have other things to do with our money, young lady, than spend it on old photographs." Money! My father's up to here with it, but whenever I buy a coat you should hear her. "You don't have to go to Bonwit's, young lady, Ohrbach's has the strongest fabrics of any of them." Who *wants* a strong fabric! Finally I get what I want, but not till she's had a chance to aggravate me. Money is a waste for her. She doesn't even know how to enjoy it. She still thinks we live in Newark.'

'But you get what you want,' I said.

'Yes. Him,' and she pointed out to Mr Patimkin who had just swished his third straight set shot through the basket to the disgruntlement, apparently, of Julie, who stamped so hard at the ground that she raised a little dust storm around her perfect young legs.

'He's not too smart but he's sweet at least. He doesn't treat my brother the way she treats me. Thank God, for that. Oh, I'm tired of talking about them. Since my freshman year I think every conversation I've ever had has always wound up about my parents and how awful it is. It's universal. The only trouble is they don't know it.'

From the way Julie and Mr Patimkin were laughing now, out on the court, no problem could ever have seemed less universal; but, of course, it was universal for Brenda, more than that, cosmic—it made every cashmere sweater a battle with her mother, and her life, which, I was certain, consisted to a large part of cornering the market on fabrics that felt soft to the skin, took on the quality of a Hundred Years' War . . .

I did not intend to allow myself such unfaithful thoughts, to line up with Mrs Patimkin while I sat beside Brenda, but I could not shake from my elephant's brain that she-still-thinks-we-live-in-Newark remark. I did not speak, however, fearful that my tone would shatter our post-dinner ease and intimacy. It had been so simple to be intimate with water pounding and securing all our pores, and later, with the sun heating them and drugging our senses, but now, in the shade and the open, cool and clothed on her own grounds, I did not want to voice a word that would lift the cover and reveal that hideous emotion I always felt for her, and is the underside of love. It will not always *stay* the underside—but I am skipping ahead.

Suddenly, little Julie was upon us. 'Want to play?' she said to me. 'Daddy's tired.'

'C'mon,' Mr Patimkin called. 'Finish for me.'

I hesitated—I hadn't held a basketball since high school—but Julie was dragging at my hand, and Brenda said, 'Go ahead.'

Mr Patimkin tossed the ball towards me while I wasn't looking and it bounced off my chest, leaving a round dust spot, like the shadow of a moon, on my shirt. I laughed, insanely.

'Can't you catch?' Julie said.

Like her sister, she seemed to have a knack for asking practical, infuriating questions.

'Yes.'

'Your turn,' she said. 'Daddy's behind forty-seven to thirty-nine. Two hundred wins.'

For an instant, as I placed my toes in the little groove that over the years had been nicked into a foul line, I had one of those instantaneous waking dreams that plague me from time to time, and send, my friends tell me, deadly cataracts over my eyes: the sun had sunk, crickets had come and gone, the leaves had blackened, and still Julie and I stood alone on the lawn, tossing the ball at the basket; 'Five hundred wins,' she called, and then when she beat me to five hundred she called, 'Now *you* have to reach it,' and I did, and the night lengthened, and she called, '*Eight* hundred wins,' and we played on and then it was eleven hundred that won and we played on and it never was morning.

'Shoot,' Mr Patimkin said. 'You're me.'

That puzzled me, but I took my set shot and, of course, missed. With the Lord's blessing and a soft breeze, I made the lay-up.

'You have forty-one. I go,' Julie said.

Mr Patimkin sat on the grass at the far end of the court. He took his shirt off, and in his undershirt, and his whole day's growth of beard, looked like a trucker. Brenda's old nose fitted him well. There was a bump in it, all right; up at the bridge it seemed as though a small eight-sided diamond had been squeezed in under the skin. I knew Mr Patimkin would never bother to have that stone cut from his face, and yet, with joy and pride, no doubt, had paid to have Brenda's diamond removed and dropped down some toilet in Fifth Avenue Hospital.

Julie missed her set shot, and I admit to a slight, gay, flutter of heart.

'Put a little spin on it,' Mr Patimkin told her.

'Can I take it again?' Julie asked me.

'Yes.' What with paternal directions from the sidelines and my own grudging graciousness on the court, there did not see much of a chance for me to catch up. And I wanted to, suddenly, I wanted to win, to run little Julie into the ground. Brenda was back on one elbow, under the tree, chewing on a leaf, watching. And up in the house, at the kitchen window, I could see that the curtain had swished back—the sun too low now to glare off electrical appliances—and Mrs Patimkin was looking steadily out at the game. And then Carlota appeared on the back steps, eating a peach and holding a pail of garbage in her free hand. She stopped to watch too.

It was my turn again. I missed the set shot and laughingly turned to Julie and said, 'Can I take it again?'

'No!'

So I learned how the game was played. Over the years Mr Patimkin had taught his daughters that free throws were theirs for the asking; he could afford to. However, with the strange eyes of Short Hills upon me, matrons, servants, and providers, I somehow felt I couldn't. But I had to and I did.

'Thanks a lot, Neil,' Julie said when the game was ended—at 100— and the crickets had come.

'You're welcome.'

Under the trees, Brenda smiled. 'Did you let her win?'

'I think so,' I said. 'I'm not sure.'

There was something in my voice that prompted Brenda to say, comfortingly, 'Even Ron lets her win.'

'It's all nice for Julie,' I said.

3

The next morning I found a parking space on Washington Street directly across from the library. Since I was twenty minutes early I decided to stroll in the park rather than cross over to work; I didn't particularly care to join my colleagues, who I knew would be sipping early morning coffee in the binding room, smelling still of all the orange crush they'd drunk that weekend at Asbury Park. I sat on a bench and looked out towards Broad Street and the morning traffic.

The Lackawanna commuter trains were rumbling in a few blocks to the north and I could hear them, I thought—the sunny green cars, old and clean, with windows that opened all the way. Some mornings, with time to kill before work, I would walk down to the tracks and watch the open windows roll in, on their sills the elbows of tropical suits and the edges of briefcases, the properties of businessmen arriving in town from Maplewood, the Oranges, and the suburbs beyond.

The park, bordered by Washington Street on the west and Broad on the east, was empty and shady and smelled of trees, night, and dog leavings; and there was a faint damp smell too, indicating that the huge rhino of a water cleaner had passed by already, soaking and whisking the downtown streets. Down Washington Street, behind me, was the Newark Museum—I could see it without even looking: two oriental vases in front like spittoons for a rajah, and next to it the little annex to which we had traveled on special buses as schoolchildren. The annex was a brick building, old and vine-covered, and always reminded me of New Jersey's link with the beginning of the country, with George Washington, who had trained his scrappy army—a little bronze tablet informed us children—in the very park where I now sat. At the far end of the park, beyond the Museum, was the bank building where I had gone to college. It had been converted some years before into an extension of Rutgers University; in fact, in what once had been the bank president's waiting room I had taken a course called Contemporary Moral Issues. Though it was summer now, and I was out of college three years, it was not hard for me to remember the other students, my friends, who had worked evenings in Bamberger's and Kresge's and had used the commissions they'd earned pushing ladies' out-of-season shoes to pay their laboratory fees. And then I looked out to Broad Street again. Jammed between a grimy-windowed bookstore and a cheesy luncheonette was the marquee of a tiny art theater—how many years had passed since I'd stood beneath that marquee, lying about the year of my birth so as to see Hedy Lamarr swim naked in *Ecstasy*; and then, having slipped the ticket taker an extra quarter, what disappointment I had felt at the frugality of her Slavic charm . . . Sitting there in the park, I felt a deep knowledge of Newark, an attachment so rooted that it could not help but branch out into affection.

Suddenly it was nine o'clock and everything was scurrying. Wobbly-heeled girls revolved through the doors of the telephone building across the way, traffic honked desperately, policeman barked, whistled, and waved motorists to and fro. Over at St Vincent's Church the huge dark portals swung back and those bleary-eyes that had risen early for Mass now blinked at the light. Then the worshipers had stepped off the church steps and were racing down the streets towards desks, filing cabinets, secretaries, bosses, and—if the Lord had seen fit to remove a mite of harshness from their lives—to the comfort of air-conditioners pumping at their windows. I got up and crossed over to the library, wondering if Brenda was awake yet.

The pale cement lions stood unconvincing guard on the library steps, suffering their usual combination of elephantiasis and arteriosclerosis, and I was prepared to pay them as little attention as I had for the past eight months were it not for a small colored boy who stood in front of one of them. The lion had lost all of its toes the summer before to a safari of juvenile delinquents, and now a new tormentor stood before him, sagging a little in his knees, and growling. He would growl, low and long, drop back, wait, then growl again. Then he would straighten up, and, shaking his head, he would say to the lion, 'Man, you's a coward . . .' Then, once again, he'd growl.

The day began the same as any other. From behind the desk on the main floor, I watched the hot high-breasted teen-age girls walk twitchingly up the wide flight of marble stairs that led to the main reading room. The stairs were an imitation of a staircase somewhere in Versailles, though in their toreador pants and sweaters these young daughters of Italian leatherworkers, Polish brewery hands, and Jewish furriers were hardly duchesses. They were not Brenda either, and any lust that sparked inside me through the dreary day was academic and time-passing. I looked at my watch occasionally, thought of Brenda, and waited for lunch and then for after lunch, when I would take over the Information Desk upstairs and John McKee, who was only twenty-one but wore elastic bands around his sleeves, would march starchily down the stairs to work assiduously at stamping books in and out. John McRubberbands was in his last year at Newark State Teachers College where he was studying at the Dewey Decimal System in prepa-

ration for his lifework. The library was not going to be my lifework, I
knew it. Yet, there had been some talk—from Mr Scapello, an old
eunuch who had learned somehow to disguise his voice as a man's—
that when I returned from my summer vacation I would be put in
charge of the Reference Room, a position that had been empty ever
since that morning when Martha Winney had fallen off a high stool in
the Encyclopedia Room and shattered all those frail bones that come
together to form what in a woman half her age we would call the hips.

I had strange fellows at the library and, in truth, there were many
hours when I never quite knew how I'd gotten there or why I stayed.
But I did stay and after a while waited patiently for that day when I
would go into the men's room on the main floor for a cigarette and,
studying myself as I expelled smoke into the mirror, would see that at
some moment during the morning I had gone pale, and that under my
skin, as under McKee's and Scapello's and Miss Winney's, there was a
thin cushion of air separating the blood from the flesh. Someone had
pumped it there while I was stamping out a book, and so life from
now on would be not a throwing off, as it was for Aunt Gladys, and
not a gathering in, as it was for Brenda, but a bouncing off, a numbness. I began to fear this, and yet, in my muscleless devotion to my
work, seemed edging towards it, silently, as Miss Winney used to edge
up to the *Britannica*. Her stool was empty now and awaited me.

Just before lunch the lion tamer came wide-eyed into the library.
He stood still for a moment, only his fingers moving, as though he
were counting the number of marble stairs before him. Then he
walked creepily about on the marble floor, snickering at the clink of
his taps and the way his little noise swelled up to the vaulted ceiling.
Otto, the guard at the door, told him to make less noise with his shoes,
but that did not seem to bother the little boy. He clacked on his tiptoes, high, secretively, delighted at the opportunity Otto had given
him to practice this posture. He tiptoed up to me.

'Hey,' he said, 'where's the heart section?'

'The what?' I said.

'The heart section. Ain't you got no heart section?'

He had the thickest sort of southern Negro dialect and the only
word that came clear to me was the one that sounded like heart.

'How do you spell it?' I said.

'*Heart*. Man, pictures. Drawing books. Where you got them?'

'You mean art books? Reproductions?'

He took my polysyllabic word for it. 'Yea, they's them.'

'In a couple places,' I told him. 'Which artist are you interested in?'

The boy's eyes narrowed so that his whole face seemed black. He started backing away, as he had from the lion. 'All of them . . .' he mumbled.

'That's okay,' I said. 'You go look at whichever ones you want. The next flight up. Follow the arrow to where it says Stack Three. You remember that? Stack Three. Ask somebody upstairs.'

He did not move; he seemed to be taking my curiosity about his taste as a kind of poll-tax investigation. 'Go ahead,' I said, slashing my face with a smile, 'right up there . . .'

And like a shot he was scuffling and tapping up towards the heart section.

After lunch I came back to the in-and-out desk and there was John McKee, waiting, in his pale blue slacks, his black shoes, his barber-cloth shirt with the elastic bands, and a great knit tie, green, wrapped into a Windsor knot, that was huge and jumped when he talked. His breath smelled of hair oil and his hair of breath and when he spoke, spittle cobwebbed the corners of his mouth. I did not like him and at times had the urge to yank back on his armbands and slingshoot him out past Otto and the lions into the street.

'Has a little Negro boy passed the desk? With a thick accent? He's been hiding in the art books all morning. You know what those boys *do* in there.'

'I saw him come in, John.'

'So did I. Has he gone *out* though.'

'I haven't noticed. I guess so.'

'Those are *very* expensive books.'

'Don't be so nervous, John. People are supposed to touch them.'

'There is touching,' John said sententiously, 'and there is touching. Someone should check on him. I was afraid to leave the desk here. You know the way they treat the housing projects we give them.'

'*You* give them?'

'The city. Have you seen what they do at Seth Boyden? They threw *beer* bottles, those big ones, on the *lawn*. They're taking over the city.'

'Just the Negro sections.'

'It's easy to laugh, you don't live near them. I'm going to call Mr Scapello's office to check the Art Section. Where did he ever find out about art?'

'You'll give Mr Scapello an ulcer, so soon after his egg-and-pepper sandwich. I'll check, I have to go upstairs anyway.'

'You know what they do in there,' John warned me.

'Don't worry, Johnny, *they're* the ones who'll get warts on their dirty little hands.'

'Ha ha. Those books happen to cost—'

So that Mr Scapello would not descend upon the boy with his chalky fingers, I walked up the three flights to Stack Three, past the receiving room where rheumy-eyed Jimmy Boylen, our fifty-one-year-old boy, unloaded books from a cart; past the reading room, where bums off Mulberry Street slept over *Popular Mechanics*; past the smoking corridor where damp-browed summer students from the law school relaxed, some smoking, others trying to rub the colored dye from their tort texts off their fingertips; and finally, past the periodical room, where a few ancient ladies who'd been motored down from Upper Montclair now huddled in their chairs, pince-nezing over yellowed, fraying society pages in old old copies of the Newark *News*. Up on Stack Three I found the boy. He was seated on the glass-brick floor holding an open book in his lap, a book, in fact, that was bigger than his lap and had to be propped up by his knees. By the light of the window behind him I could see the hundreds of spaces between the hundreds of tiny black corkscrews that were his hair. He was very black and shiny, and the flesh of his lips did not so much appear to be a different color as it looked to be unfinished and awaiting another coat. The lips were parted, the eyes wide, and even the ears seemed to have a heightened receptivity. He looked ecstatic—until he saw me, that is. For all he knew I was John McKee.

'That's okay,' I said before he could even move, 'I'm just passing through. You read.'

'Ain't nothing *to* read. They's pictures.'

'Fine.' I fished around the lowest shelves a moment, playing at work.

'Hey, mister,' the boy said after a minute, 'where is this?'

'Where is what?'

'Where is these pictures? These people, man, they sure does look cool. They ain't no yelling or shouting here, you could just see it.'

He lifted the book so I could see. It was an expensive large-sized edition of Gauguin reproductions. The page he had been looking at showed an 8½ × 11 print, in color, of three native women standing knee-high in a rose-colored stream. It *was* a silent picture, he was right.

'That's Tahiti. That's an island in the Pacific Ocean.'

'That ain't no place you could go, is it? Like a ree-*sort*?'

'You could go there, I suppose. It's very far. People live there . . .'

'Hey, *look*, look here at this one.' He flipped back to a page where a young brown-skinned maid was leaning forward on her knees, as though to dry her hair. 'Man,' the boy said, 'that's the fuckin life.' The euphoria of his diction would have earned him eternal banishment from the Newark Public Library and its branches had John or Mr Scapello—or, God forbid, the hospitalized Miss Winney—come to investigate.

'Who took these pictures?' he asked me.

'Gauguin. He didn't take them, he painted them. Paul Gauguin. He was a Frenchman.'

'Is he a white man or a colored man?'

'He's white.'

'Man,' the boy smiled, chuckled almost, 'I knew that. He don't *take* pictures like no colored men would. He's a good picture taker . . . *Look, look*, look here at this one. Ain't that the fuckin *life*?'

I agreed it was and left.

Later I sent Jimmy Boylen hopping down the stairs to tell McKee that everything was all right. The rest of the day was uneventful. I sat at the Information Desk thinking about Brenda and reminding myself that that evening I would have to get gas before I started up to Short Hills, which I could see now, in my mind's eye, at dusk, rose-colored, like a Gauguin stream.

★

When I pulled up to the Patimkin house that night, everybody but Julie was waiting for me on the front porch: Mr and Mrs, Ron, and Brenda, wearing a dress. I had not seen her in a dress before and for an instant she did not look like the same girl. But that was only half the surprise. So many of those Lincolnesque college girls turn out to be limbed for shorts alone. Not Brenda. She looked, in a dress, as though she'd gone through life so attired, as though she'd never worn shorts, or bathing suits, or pajamas, or anything but that pale linen dress. I walked rather bouncingly up the lawn, past the huge weeping willow, towards the waiting Patimkins, wishing all the while that I'd had my car washed. Before I'd even reached them, Ron stepped forward and shook my hand, vigorously, as though he hadn't seen me since the Diaspora. Mrs Patimkin smiled and Mr Patimkin grunted something and continued twitching his wrists before him, then raising an imaginary golf club and driving a ghost of a golf ball up and away towards the Orange Mountains, that are called Orange, I'm convinced, because in that various suburban light that's the *only* color they do not come dressed in.

'We'll be right back,' Brenda said to me. 'You have to sit with Julie. Carlota's off.'

'Okay,' I said.

'We're taking Ron to the airport.'

'Okay.'

'Julie doesn't want to go. She says Ron pushed her in the pool this afternoon. We've been waiting for you, so we don't miss Ron's plane. Okay?'

'*Okay.*'

Mr and Mrs Patimkin and Ron moved off, and I flashed Brenda just the hint of a glare. She reached out and took my hand for a moment.

'How do you like me?' she said.

'You're great to baby-sit for. Am I allowed all the milk and cake I want?'

'Don't be angry, baby. We'll be right back.' Then she waited a moment, and when I failed to deflate the pout from my mouth, she gave *me* a glare, no hints about it. 'I *meant* how do you like me in a dress!' Then she ran off towards the Chrysler, trotting in her high heels like a colt.

When I walked into the house, I slammed the screen door behind me.

'Close the other door too,' a little voice shouted. 'The air-conditioning.'

I closed the other door, obediently.

'Neil?' Julie called.

'Yes.'

'Hi. Want to play five and two?'

'No.'

'Why not?'

I did not answer.

'I'm in the television room,' she called.

'Good.'

'Are you supposed to stay with me?'

'Yes.'

She appeared unexpectedly through the dining room. 'Want to read a book report I wrote?'

'Not now.'

'What do you want to do?' she said.

'Nothing, honey. Why don't you watch TV?'

'All right,' she said disgustedly, and kicked her way back to the television room.

For a while I remained in the hall, bitten with the urge to slide quietly out of the house, into my car, and back to Newark, where I might even sit in the alley and break candy with my own. I felt like Carlota; no, not even as comfortable as that. At last I left the hall and began to stroll in and out of rooms on the first floor. Next to the living room was the study, a small knotty-pine room jammed with cater-cornered leather chairs and a complete set of *Information Please Almanacs*. On the wall hung three colored photo-paintings; they were the kind which, regardless of the subjects, be they vital or infirm, old or youthful, are characterized by bud-cheeks, wet lips, pearly teeth, and shiny, metallized hair. The subjects in this case were Ron, Brenda, and Julie at about ages fourteen, thirteen, and two. Brenda had long auburn hair, her diamond-studded nose, and no glasses; all combined to make her look a regal thirteen-year-old who'd just gotten smoke in her eyes.

Ron was rounder and his hairline was lower, but that love of spherical objects and lined courts twinkled in his boyish eyes. Poor little Julie was lost in the photo-painter's Platonic idea of childhood; her tiny humanity was smothered somewhere back of gobs of pink and white.

There were other pictures about, smaller ones, taken with a Brownie Reflex before photo-paintings had become fashionable. There was a tiny picture of Brenda on a horse another of Ron in bar mitzvah suit, *yamalkah*, and *tallas*; and two pictures framed together— one of a beautiful, faded woman, who must have been, from the eyes, Mrs Patimkin's mother, and the other of Mrs Patimkin herself, her hair in a halo, her eyes joyous and not those of a slowly aging mother with a quick and lovely daughter.

I walked through the archway into the dining room and stood a moment looking out at the sporting goods tree. From the television room that winged off the dining room, I could hear Julie listening to *This Is Your Life*. The kitchen, which winged off the other side, was empty, and apparently, with Carlota off, the Patimkins had had dinner at the club. Mr and Mrs Patimkin's bedroom was in the middle of the house, down the hall, next to Julie's, and for a moment I wanted to see what size bed those giants slept in—I imagined it wide and deep as a swimming pool—but I postponed my investigation while Julie was in the house, and instead opened the door in the kitchen that led down to the basement.

The basement had a different kind of coolness from the house, and it had a smell, which was something the upstairs was totally without. It felt cavernous down there, but in a comforting way, like the simulated caves children make for themselves on rainy days, in hall closets, under blankets, or in between the legs of dining room tables. I flipped on the light at the foot of the stairs and was not surprised at the pine paneling, the bamboo furniture, the ping-pong table, and the mirrored bar that was stocked with every kind and size of glass, ice bucket, decanter, mixer, swizzle stick, shot glass, pretzel bowl—all the bacchanalian paraphernalia, plentiful, orderly, and untouched, as it can be only in the bar of a wealthy man who never entertains drinking people, who himself does not drink, who, in fact, gets a fishy look from his wife when every several months he takes a shot of schnapps before dinner. I went behind the bar where there was an aluminum sink that had not seen a dirty glass, I'm sure, since Ron's bar mitzvah party, and would not see another, probably, until one of the Patimkin children was married or engaged. I would have poured myself a drink—just as a wicked wage for being forced into servantry—but I was uneasy about breaking the label on a bottle of whiskey. You had to break a label to get a drink. On the shelf back of the bar were two dozen bottles—twenty-three to be exact—of Jack Daniels, each with a little booklet tied to its collared neck informing patrons how patrician of them it was to drink the stuff. And over the Jack Daniels were more photos: there was a blown-up newspaper photo of Ron palming a basketball in one hand like a raisin; under the picture it said, '*Center, Ronald Patimkin, Millburn High School, 6'4", 217 pounds.*' And there was another picture of Brenda on a horse, and next to that, a velvet mounting board with ribbons and medals clipped to it: Essex County Horse Show 1949, Union County Horse Show 1950, Garden State Fair 1952, Morristown Horse Show 1953, and so on—all for Brenda, for jumping and running or galloping or whatever else young girls receive ribbons for. In the entire house I hadn't seen one picture of Mr Patimkin.

The rest of the basement, back of the wide pine-paneled room, was gray cement walls and linoleum floor and contained innumerable electrical appliances, including a freezer big enough to house a family of Eskimos. Beside the freezer, incongruously, was a tall old refrigerator; its ancient presence was a reminder to me of the Patimkin roots in Newark. This same refrigerator had once stood in the kitchen of an apartment in some four-family house, probably in the same neighborhood where I had lived all my life, first with my parents and then, when the two of them went wheezing off to Arizona, with my aunt and uncle. After Pearl Harbor the refrigerator had made the move up to Short Hills; Patimkin Kitchen and Bathroom Sinks had gone to war: no new barracks was complete until it had a squad of Patimkin sinks lined up in its latrine.

I opened the door of the old refrigerator; it was not empty. No longer did it hold butter, eggs, herring in cream sauce, ginger ale, tuna fish salad, an occasional corsage—rather it was heaped with fruit, shelves swelled with it, every color, every texture, and hidden within, every kind of pit. There were greengage plums, black plums, red plums, apricots, nectarines, peaches, long horns of grapes, black, yellow, red, and cherries, cherries flowing out of boxes and staining everything scarlet. And there were melons—cantaloupes and honeydews—and on the top shelf, half of a huge watermelon, a thin sheet of wax paper clinging to its bare red face like a wet lip. Oh Patimkin! Fruit grew in their refrigerator and sporting goods dropped from their trees!

I grabbed a handful of cherries and then a nectarine, and I bit right down to its pit.

'You better wash that or you'll get diarrhea.'

Julie was standing behind me in the pine-paneled room. She was wearing *her* Bermudas and *her* white polo shirt which was unlike Brenda's only in that it had a little dietary history of its own.

'What?' I said.

'They're not washed yet,' Julie said, and in such a way that it seemed to place the refrigerator itself out-of-bounds, if only for me.

'That's all right,' I said, and devoured the nectarine and put the pit in my pocket and stepped out of the refrigerator room, all in one second. I still didn't know what to do with the cherries. 'I was just looking around,' I said.

Julie didn't answer.

'Where's Ron going?' I asked, dropping the cherries into my pocket, among my keys and change.

'Milwaukee.'

'For long?'

'To see Harriet. They're in love.'

We looked at each other for longer than I could bear. 'Harriet?' I asked.

'Yes.'

Julie was looking at me as though she were trying to look behind me, and then I realized that I was standing with my hands out of sight. I brought them around to the front, and, I swear it, she did peek to see if they were empty.

We confronted one another again; she seemed to have a threat in her face.

Then she spoke. 'Want to play ping-pong?'

'God, yes,' I said, and made for the table with two long, bounding steps. 'You can serve.'

Julie smiled and we began to play.

I have no excuses to offer for what happened next. I began to win and I liked it.

'Can I take that one over?' Julie said. 'I hurt my finger yesterday and it just hurt when I served.'

'No.'

I continued to win.

'That wasn't fair, Neil. My shoelace came untied. Can I take it—'

'No.'

We played, I ferociously.

'Neil, you leaned over the table. That's illegal—'

'I didn't lean and it's not illegal.'

I felt the cherries hopping among my nickels and pennies.

'Neil, you gypped me out of a point. You have nineteen and I have eleven—'

'Twenty and *ten*,' I said. 'Serve!'

She did and I smashed my return past her—it zoomed off the table and skittered into the refrigerator room.

'You're a cheater!' she screamed at me. 'You cheat!' Her jaw was trembling as though she carried a weight on top of her pretty head. 'I *hate* you!' And she threw her racket across the room and it clanged off the bar, just as, outside, I heard the Chrysler crushing gravel in the driveway.

'The game isn't over,' I said to her.

'You cheat! And you were stealing fruit!' she said, and ran away before I had my chance to win.

Later that night, Brenda and I made love, our first time. We were sitting on the sofa in the television room and for some ten minutes had not spoken a word to each other. Julie had long since gone to a weepy bed, and though no one had said anything to me about her crying, I did not know if the child had mentioned my fistful of cherries, which, some time before, I had flushed down the toilet.

The television set was on and though the sound was off and the house quiet, the gray pictures still wiggled at the far end of the room. Brenda was quiet and her dress circled her legs, which were tucked back beneath her. We sat there for some while and did not speak. Then she went into the kitchen and when she came back she said that it sounded as though everyone was asleep. We sat a while longer, watching the soundless bodies on the screen eating a silent dinner in someone's silent restaurant. When I began to unbutton her dress she resisted me, and I like to think it was because she knew how lovely she looked in it. But she looked lovely, my Brenda, anyway, and we folded it carefully and held each other close and soon there we were, Brenda falling, slowly but with a smile, and me rising.

How can I describe loving Brenda? It was so sweet, as though I'd finally scored that twenty-first point.

When I got home I dialed Brenda's number, but not before my aunt heard and rose from her bed.

'Who are you calling at this hour? The doctor?'

'No.'

'What kind phone calls, one o'clock at night?'

'Shhh!' I said.

'He tells *me* shhh. Phone calls one o'clock at night, we haven't got a big enough bill,' and then she dragged herself back into the bed, where with a martyr's heart and bleary eyes she had resisted the downward tug of sleep until she'd heard my key in the door.

Brenda answered the phone.

'Neil?' she said.

'Yes,' I whispered. 'You didn't get out of bed, did you?'

'No,' she said. 'the phone is next to the bed.'

'Good. How is it in bed?'

'Good. Are you in bed?'

'Yes,' I lied, and tried to right myself by dragging the phone by its cord as close as I could to my bedroom.

'I'm in bed with you,' she said.

'That's right,' I said, 'and I'm with you.'

'I have the shades down, so it's dark and I don't see you.'

'I don't see you either.'

'That was so nice, Neil.'

'Yes. Go to sleep, sweet, I'm here,' and we hung up without good-
byes. In the morning, as planned, I called again, but I could hardly
hear Brenda or myself for that matter, for Aunt Gladys and Uncle Max
were going on a Workmen's Circle picnic in the afternoon, and there
was some trouble about grape juice that had dripped all night from a
jug in the refrigerator and by morning had leaked out onto the floor.
Brenda was still in bed and so could play our game with some success,
but I had to pull down all the shades of my senses to imagine myself
beside her. I could only pray our nights and mornings would come,
and soon enough they did.

4

Over the next week and a half there seemed to be only two people in
my life: Brenda and the little colored kid who liked Gauguin. Every
morning before the library opened, the boy was waiting; sometimes
he seated himself on the lion's back, sometimes under his belly, sometimes he just stood around throwing pebbles at his mane. Then he
would come inside, tap around the main floor until Otto stared him
up on tiptoes, and finally headed up the long marble stairs that led to
Tahiti. He did not always stay to lunch time, but one very hot day he
was there when I arrived in the morning and went through the door
behind me when I left at night. The next morning, it was, that he did
not show up, and as though in his place, a very old man appeared,
white, smelling of Life Savers, his nose and jowls showing erupted
veins beneath them. 'Could you tell me where I'd find the art
section?'

'Stack Three,' I said.

In a few minutes, he returned with a big brown-covered book in
his hand. He placed it on my desk, withdrew his card from a long
moneyless billfold and waited for me to stamp out the book.

'Do you want to take this book *out*?' I said.

He smiled.

I took his card and jammed the metal edge into the machine; but I did not stamp down. 'Just a minute,' I said. I took a clipboard from under the desk and flipped through a few pages, upon which were games of battleship and tick-tack-toe that I'd been playing through the week with myself. 'I'm afraid there's a hold on this book.'

'A what?'

'A hold. Someone's called up and asked that we hold it for them. Can I take your name and address and drop a card when it's free . . .'

And so I was able, not without flushing once or twice, to get the book back in the stacks. When the colored kid showed up later in the day, it was just where he'd left it the afternoon before.

As for Brenda, I saw her every evening and when there was not a night game that kept Mr Patimkin awake and in the TV room, or a Hadassah card party that sent Mrs Patimkin out of the house and brought her in at unpredictable hours, we made love before the silent screen. One muggy, low-skied night Brenda took me swimming at the club. We were the only ones in the pool, and all the chairs, the cabañas, the lights, the diving boards, the very water seemed to exist only for our pleasure. She wore a blue suit that looked purple in the lights and down beneath the water it flashed sometimes green, sometimes black. Late in the evening a breeze came up off the golf course and we wrapped ourselves in one huge towel, pulled two chaise longues together, and despite the bartender, who was doing considerable pacing back and forth by the bar window, which overlooked the pool, we rested side by side on the chairs. Finally the bar light itself flipped off, and then, in a snap, the lights around the pool went down and out. My heart must have beat faster, or something, for Brenda seemed to guess my sudden doubt—*we should go*, I thought.

She said: 'That's okay.'

It was very dark, the sky was low and starless, and it took a while for me to see, once again, the diving board a shade lighter than the night, and to distinguish the water from the chairs that surrounded the far side of the pool.

I pushed the straps of her bathing suit down but she said no and

rolled an inch away from me, and for the first time in the two weeks
I'd known her she asked me a question about me.

'Where are your parents?' she said.

'Tucson,' I said. 'Why?'

'My mother asked me.'

I could see the life guard's chair now, white almost.

'Why are you still here? Why aren't you with them?' she asked.

'I'm not a child any more, Brenda,' I said, more sharply than I'd
intended. 'I just can't go wherever my parents are.'

'But then why do you stay with your aunt and uncle?'

'They're not my parents.'

'They're better?'

'No. Worse. I don't *know* why I stay with them.'

'Why?' she said.

'Why don't I know?'

'Why do you stay? You do know, don't you?'

'My job, I suppose. It's convenient from there, and it's cheap, and it
pleases my parents. My aunt's all right really . . . Do I really have to
explain to your mother why I live where I do?'

'It's not for my mother. I want to know. I wondered why you
weren't with your parents, that's all.'

'Are you cold?' I asked.

'No.'

'Do you want to go home?'

'No, not unless you do. Don't you feel well, Neil?'

'I feel all right,' and to let her know that I was still me, I held her to
me, though that moment I was without desire.

'Neil?'

'What?'

'What about the library?'

'Who wants to know that?'

'My father,' she laughed.

'And you?'

She did not answer a moment. 'And me,' she said finally.

'Well, what about it? Do I like it? It's okay. I sold shoes once and
like the library better. After the Army they tried me for a couple

months at Uncle Aaron's real estate company—Doris' father—and I like the library better than that . . .'

'How did you get a job *there*?'

'I worked there for a little while when I was in college, then when I quit Uncle Aaron's, oh, I don't know . . .'

'What did you take in college?'

'At Newark Colleges of Rutgers University I majored in philosophy. I am twenty-three years old. I—'

'Why do you sound nasty again?'

'Do I?'

'Yes.'

I didn't say I was sorry.

'Are you planning on making a career of the library?'

'Bren, I'm not planning anything. I haven't planned a thing in three years. At least for the year I've been out of the Army. In the Army I used to plan to go away weekends. I'm—I'm not a planner.' After all the truth I'd suddenly given her, I shouldn't have ruined it for myself with that final lie. I added, 'I'm a liver.'

'I'm a pancreas,' she said.

'I'm a—'

And she kissed the absurd game away; she wanted to be serious.

'Do you love me, Neil?'

I did not answer.

'I'll sleep with you whether you do or not, so tell me the truth.'

'That was pretty crude.'

'Don't be prissy,' she said.

'No, I mean a crude thing to say about me.'

'I don't understand,' she said, and she didn't, and that she didn't pained me; I allowed myself the minor subterfuge, however, of forgiving Brenda her obtuseness. 'Do you?' she said.

'No.'

'I want you to.'

'What about the library?'

'What about it?' she said.

Was it obtuseness again? I thought not—and it wasn't, for Brenda said, 'When you love me, there'll be nothing to worry about.'

'Then of course I'll love you.' I smiled.

'I know you will,' she said. 'Why don't you go in the water, and I'll wait for you and close my eyes, and when you come back you'll surprise me with the wet. Go ahead.'

'You like games, don't you?'

'Go ahead. I'll close my eyes.'

I walked down to the edge of the pool and dove in. The water felt colder than it had earlier, and when I broke through and was headed blindly down I felt a touch of panic. At the top again, I started to swim the length of the pool and then turned at the end and started back, but suddenly I was sure that when I left the water Brenda would be gone. I'd be alone in this damn place. I started for the side and pulled myself up and ran to the chairs and Brenda was there and I kissed her.

'God,' she shivered, 'You didn't stay long.'

'I know.'

'My turn,' she said, and then she was up and a second later I heard a little crack of water and then nothing. Nothing for quite a while.

'Bren,' I called softly, 'are you all right?' but no one answered.

I found her glasses on the chair beside me and held them in my hands. 'Brenda?'

Nothing.

'Brenda?'

'No fair calling,' she said and gave me her drenched self. 'Your turn,' she said.

This time I stayed below the water for a long while and when I surfaced again my lungs were ready to pop. I threw my head back for air and above me saw the sky, low like a hand pushing down, and I began to swim as though to move out from under its pressure. I wanted to get back to Brenda, for I worried once again—and there was no evidence, was there?—that if I stayed away too long she would not be there when I returned. I wished that I had carried her glasses away with me, so she would have to wait for me to lead her back home. I was having crazy thoughts, I knew, and yet they did not seem uncalled for in the darkness and strangeness of that place. Oh how I wanted to call out to her from the pool, but I knew she would not answer and I forced myself to swim the length a third time, and then a fourth, but midway through the fifth I felt a weird fright again, had momentary thoughts of my own extinction, and that time when I came back I held her tighter than either of us expected.

'Let go, let go,' she laughed, 'my turn—'

'But Brenda—'

But Brenda was gone and this time it seemed as though she'd never come back. I settled back and waited for the sun to dawn over the ninth hole, prayed it would if only for the comfort of its light, and when Brenda finally returned to me I would not let her go, and her cold wetness crept into me somehow and made me shiver. 'That's it, Brenda. Please, no more games,' I said, and then when I spoke again I held her so tightly I almost dug my body into hers, 'I love you,' I said, 'I do.'

So the summer went on. I saw Brenda every evening: we went swimming, we went for walks, we went for rides, up through the mountains so far and so long that by the time we started back the fog had begun to emerge from the trees and push out into the road, and I would tighten my hands on the wheel and Brenda would put on her glasses and watch the white line for me. And we would eat—a few nights after my discovery of the fruit refrigerator Brenda led me to it herself. We would fill huge soup bowls with cherries, and in serving dishes for roast beef we would heap slices of watermelon. Then we would go up and out the back doorway of the basement and onto the back lawn and sit under the sporting goods tree, the light from the TV room the only brightness we had out there. All we would hear for a while were just the two of us spitting pits. 'I wish they would take root overnight and in the morning there'd just be watermelons and cherries.'

'If they took root in this yard, sweetie, they'd grow refrigerators and Westinghouse Preferred. I'm not being nasty,' I'd add quickly, and Brenda would laugh, and say she felt like a greengage plum, and I would disappear down into the basement and the cherry bowl would now be a greengage plum bowl, and then a nectarine bowl, and then a peach bowl, until, I have to admit it, I cracked my frail bowel, and would have to spend the following night, sadly, on the wagon. And then too we went out for corned beef sandwiches, pizza, beer and

shrimp, ice cream sodas, and hamburgers. We went to the Lions Club
Fair one night and Brenda won a Lions Club ashtray by shooting
three baskets in a row. And when Ron came home from Milwaukee
we went from time to time to see him play basketball in the semi-pro
summer league, and it was those evenings that I felt a stranger with
Brenda, for she knew all the player's names, and though for the most
part they were gawky-limbed and dull, there was one named Luther
Ferrari who was neither, and whom Brenda had dated for a whole
year in high school. He was Ron's closest friend and I remembered his
name from the Newark *News*: he was one of the great Ferrari brothers, All State all of them in at least two sports. It was Ferrari who called
Brenda Buck, a nickname which apparently went back to her ribbon-
winning days. Like Ron, Ferrari was exceedingly polite, as though it
were some affliction of those over six feet three; he was gentlemanly
towards me and gentle towards Brenda, and after a while I balked
when the suggestion was made that we go to see Ron play. And then
one night we discovered that at eleven o'clock the cashier of the
Hilltop Theatre went home and the manager disappeared into his
office, and so that summer we saw the last quarter of at least fifteen
movies, and then when we were driving home—driving Brenda
home, that is—we would try to reconstruct the beginnings of the
films. Our favorite last quarter of a movie was *Ma and Pa Kettle in the
City*, our favorite fruit, greengage plums, and our favorite, our only,
people, each other. Of course we ran into others from time to time,
some of Brenda's friends, and occasionally, one or two of mine. One
night in August we even went to a bar out on Route 6 with Laura
Simpson Stolowitch and her fiancé, but it was a dreary evening. Brenda
and I seemed untrained in talking to others, and so we danced a great
deal, which we realized was one thing we'd never done before. Laura's
boyfriend drank stingers pompously and Simp—Brenda wanted me to
call her Stolo but I didn't—Simp drank a tepid combination of something like ginger ale and soda. Whenever we returned to the table,
Simp would be talking about 'the dance' and her fiancé about 'the film,'
until finally Brenda asked him 'Which film?' and then we danced till
closing time. And when we went back to Brenda's we filled a bowl
with cherries which we carried into the TV room and ate sloppily for

a while; and later, on the sofa, we loved each other and when I moved from the darkened room to the bathroom I could always feel cherry pits against my bare soles. At home, undressing for the second time that night, I would find red marks on the undersides of my feet.

And how did her parents take all of this? Mrs Patimkin continued to smile at me and Mr Patimkin continued to think I ate like a bird. When invited to dinner I would, for his benefit, eat twice what I wanted, but the truth seemed to be that after he'd characterized my appetite that first time, he never really bothered to look again. I might have eaten ten times my normal amount, have finally killed myself with food, he would still have considered me not a man but a sparrow. No one seemed distressed by my presence, though Julie had cooled considerably; consequently, when Brenda suggested to her father that at the end of August I spend a week of my vacation at the Patimkin house, he pondered a moment, decided on the five iron, made his approach shot, and said yes. And when she passed onto her mother the decision of Patimkin Sink, there wasn't much Mrs Patimkin could do. So, through Brenda's craftiness, I was invited.

On that Friday morning that was to be my last day of work, my Aunt Gladys saw me packing my bag and she asked where I was going. I told her. She did not answer and I thought I saw awe in those red-rimmed hysterical eyes—I had come a long way since that day she'd said to me on the phone, 'Fancy-shmancy.'

'How long you going, I should know how to shop I wouldn't buy too much. You'll leave me with a refrigerator full of milk it'll go bad it'll stink up the refrigerator—'

'A week,' I said.

'A *week?*' she said. 'They got room for a week?'

'Aunt Gladys, they don't live over the store.'

'I lived over a store I wasn't ashamed. Thank God we always had a roof. We never went begging in the streets,' she told me as I packed the Bermudas I'd just bought, 'and your cousin Susan we'll put through college, Uncle Max should live and be well. We didn't send her away to camp for August, she doesn't have shoes when she wants them, sweaters she doesn't have a drawerful—'

'I didn't say anything, Aunt Gladys.'

'You don't get enough to eat here? You leave over sometimes I show your Uncle Max your plate it's a shame. A child in Europe could make a four-course meal from what you leave over.'

'Aunt Gladys.' I went over to her. 'I get everything I want here. I'm just taking a vacation. Don't I deserve a vacation?'

She held herself to me and I could feel her trembling. 'I told your mother I would take care of her Neil she shouldn't worry. And now you go running—'

I put my arms around her and kissed her on the top of her head. 'C'mon,' I said, 'you're being silly. I'm not running away. I'm just going away for a week, on a vacation.'

'You'll leave their telephone number God forbid you should get sick.'

'Okay.'

'Millburn they live?'

'Short Hills. I'll leave the number.'

'Since when do Jewish people live in Short Hills? They couldn't be real Jews believe me.'

'They're real Jews,' I said.

'I'll see it I'll believe it.' She wiped her eyes with the corner of her apron, just as I was zipping up the sides of the suitcase. 'Don't close the bag yet. I'll make a little package with some fruit in it, you'll take with you.'

'Okay, Aunt Gladys,' and on the way to work that morning I ate the orange and the two peaches that she'd put in a bag for me.

A few hours later Mr Scapello informed me that when I returned from my vacation after Labor Day, I would be hoisted up onto Martha Winney's stool. He himself, he said, had made the same move some twelve years ago, and so it appeared that if I could manage to maintain my balance I might someday be Mr Scapello. I would also get an eight-dollar increase in salary which was five dollars more than the increase Mr Scapello had received years before. He shook my hand and then started back up the long flight of marble stairs, his behind barging against his suit jacket like a hoop. No sooner had he left my side than I smelled spearmint and looked up to see the old man with veiny nose and jowls.

'Hello, young man,' he said pleasantly. 'Is the book back?'

'What book?'

'The Gauguin. I was shopping and I thought I'd stop by to ask. I haven't gotten the card yet. It's two weeks already.'

'No,' I said, and as I spoke I saw that Mr Scapello had stopped midway up the stairs and turned as though he'd forgotten to tell me something. 'Look,' I said to the old man, 'it should be back any day.' I said it with a finality that bordered on rudeness, and I alarmed myself, for suddenly I saw what would happen: the old man making a fuss, Mr Scapello gliding down the stairs, Mr Scapello scampering up to the stacks, Scapello scandalized, Scapello profuse, Scapello presiding at the ascension of John McKee to Miss Winney's stool. I turned to the old man, 'Why don't you leave your phone number and I'll try to get a hold of it this afternoon—' but my attempt at concern and courtesy came too late, and the man growled some words about public servants, a letter to the Mayor, snotty kids, and left the library, thank God, only a second before Mr Scapello returned to my desk to remind me that everyone was chipping in for a present for Miss Winney and that if I liked I should leave a half dollar on his desk during the day.

After lunch the colored kid came in. When he headed past the desk for the stairs, I called over to him. 'Come here,' I said. 'Where are you going?'

'The heart section.'

'What book are you reading?'

'That Mr Go-again's book. Look, man, I ain't doing nothing wrong. I didn't do *no* writing in *anything*. You could search me—'

'I know you didn't. Listen, if you like that book so much why don't you please take it home? Do you have a library card?'

'No, sir, I didn't take *nothing*.'

'No, a library card is what we give to you so you can take books home. Then you won't have to come down here every day. Do you go to school?'

'Yes, sir. Miller Street School. But this here's summertime. It's okay I'm not in school. I ain't *supposed* to be in school.'

'I know. As long as you go to school you can *have* a library card.

You could take the book home.'

'What you keep telling me take that book home for? At home somebody dee-*stroy* it.'

'You could hide it someplace, in a desk—'

'Man,' he said, squinting at me, 'why don't you want me to come round here?'

'I didn't say you shouldn't.'

'I *likes* to come here. I likes them stairs.'

'I like them too,' I said. 'But the trouble is that someday somebody's going to take that book out.'

He smiled. 'Don't you worry,' he said to me. 'Ain't nobody done that yet,' and he tapped off to the stairs and Stack Three.

Did I perspire that day! It was the coolest of the summer, but when I left work in the evening my shirt was sticking to my back. In the car I opened my bag, and while the rush-hour traffic flowed down Washington Street, I huddled in the back and changed into a clean shirt so that when I reached Short Hills I'd look as though I was deserving of an interlude in the suburbs. But driving up Central Avenue I could not keep my mind on my vacation, or for that matter on my driving: to the distress of pedestrians and motorists, I ground gears, overshot crosswalks, hesitated at green and red lights alike. I kept thinking that while I was on vacation that jowly bastard would return to the library, that the colored kid's book would disappear, that my new job would be taken away from me, that, in fact my old job—but then why should I worry about all that: the library wasn't going to be *my* life.

5

'Ron's getting married!' Julie screamed at me when I came through the door. 'Ron's getting married!'

'Now?' I said.

'Labor Day! He's marrying Harriet, he's marrying Harriet.' She began to sing it like a jump-rope song, nasal and rhythmic. 'I'm going to be a sister-in-law!'

'Hi,' Brenda said, 'I'm going to be a sister-in-law.'

'So I hear. When did it happen?'

'This afternoon he told us. They spoke long distance for forty minutes last night. She's flying here next week, and there's going to be a *huge* wedding. My parents are flittering all over the place. They've got to arrange everything in about a day or two. And my father's taking Ron in the business—but he's going to have to start at two hundred a week and then work himself up. That'll take till October.'

'I thought he was going to be a gym teacher.'

'He was. But now he has responsibilities . . .'

And at dinner Ron expanded on the subject of responsibilities and the future.

'We're going to have a boy,' he said, to his mother's delight, 'and when he's about six months old I'm going to sit him down with a basketball in front of him, and a football, and a baseball, and then whichever one he reaches for, that's the one we're going to concentrate on.'

'Suppose he doesn't reach for any of them,' Brenda said.

'Don't be funny, young lady,' Mrs Patimkin said.

'I'm going to be an aunt,' Julie sang, and she stuck her tongue out at Brenda.

'When is Harriet coming?' Mr Patimkin breathed through a mouthful of potatoes.

'A week from yesterday.'

'Can she sleep in my room?' Julie cried. '*Can* she?'

'No, the guest room—' Mrs Patimkin began, but then she remembered me—with a crushing side glance from those purple eyes, and she said, 'Of course.'

Well, I did eat like a bird. After dinner my bag was carried—by me—up to the guest room which was across from Ron's room and right down the hall from Brenda. Brenda came along to show me the way.

'Let me see your bed, Bren.'

'Later,' she said.

'Can we? Up here?'

'I think so,' she said. 'Ron sleeps like a log.'

'Can I stay the night?'

'I don't know.'

'I could get up early and come back in here. We'll set the alarm.'

'It'll wake everybody up.'

'I'll remember to get up. I can do it.'

'I better not stay up here with you too long,' she said. 'My mother'll have a fit. I think she's nervous about your being here.'

'So am I. I hardly know them. Do you think I should really stay a whole week?'

'A whole week? Once Harriet gets here it'll be so chaotic you can probably stay two months.'

'You think so?'

'Yes.'

'Do you want me to?'

'Yes,' she said, and went down the stairs so as to ease her mother's conscience.

I unpacked my bag and dropped my clothes into a drawer that was empty except for a packet of dress shields and a high school yearbook. In the middle of my unpacking, Ron came clunking up the stairs.

'Hi,' he called into my room.

'Congratulations,' I called back. I should have realized that any word of ceremony would provoke a handshake from Ron; he interrupted whatever it was he was about to do in his room, and came into mine.

'Thanks.' He pumped me. 'Thanks.'

Then he sat down on my bed and watched me as I finished unpacking. I have one shirt with a Brooks Brothers label and I let it linger on the bed a while; the Arrows I heaped in the drawer. Ron sat there rubbing his forearm and grinning. After a while I was thoroughly unsettled by the silence.

'Well,' I said, 'that's something.'

He agreed, to *what* I don't know.

'How does it feel?' I asked, after another longer silence.

'Better. Ferrari smacked it under the boards.'

'Oh. Good,' I said. 'How does getting married feel?'

'Ah, okay, I guess.'

I leaned against the bureau and counted stitches in the carpet.

Ron finally risked a journey into language. 'Do you know anything about music?' he asked.

'Something, yes.'

'You can listen to my phonograph if you want.'

'Thanks, Ron. I didn't know you were interested in music.'

'Sure. I got all the Andre Kostelanetz records ever made. You like Mantovani? I got all of him too. I like semi-classical a lot. You can hear my Columbus record if you want . . .' he dwindled off. Finally he shook my hand and left.

Downstairs I could hear Julie singing. 'I'm going to be an a-a-aunt,' and Mrs Patimkin saying to her, 'No, honey, you're going to be a sister-in-law. Sing that, sweetheart,' but Julie continued to sing, 'I'm going to be an a-a-aunt,' and then I heard Brenda's voice joining hers, singing, 'We're going to be an a-a-aunt,' and then Julie joined that, and finally Mrs Patimkin called to Mr Patimkin, 'Will you make her stop encouraging her . . .' and soon the duet ended.

And then I heard Mrs Patimkin again. I couldn't make out the words but Brenda answered her. Their voices grew louder; finally I could hear perfectly. 'I need a houseful of company at a time like this?' It was Mrs Patimkin. 'I asked you, Mother.' 'You asked your father. I'm the one you should have asked first. He doesn't know how much extra work this is for me . . .' 'My God, Mother, you'd think we didn't have Carlota and Jenny.' 'Carlota and Jenny can't do everything. This is not the Salvation Army!' 'What the hell does that mean?' 'Watch your tongue, young lady. That may be very well for your college friends.' 'Oh, *stop* it, Mother!' 'Don't raise your voice to me. When's the last time you lifted a finger to help around here?' 'I'm not a slave . . . I'm a daughter.' 'You ought to learn what a day's work means.' 'Why?' Brenda said. '*Why?*' 'Because you're lazy,' Mrs Patimkin answered, 'and you think the world owes you a living.' 'Whoever said *that?*' 'You ought to earn some money and buy your own clothes.' 'Why? Good God, Mother, Daddy could live off the stocks alone, for God's sake. What are you complaining about?' 'When's the last time you washed the dishes!' 'Jesus Christ!' Brenda flared, 'Carlota washes the dishes!' 'Don't Jesus Christ me!' 'Oh, Mother!' and Brenda was crying. 'Why the hell are you like this!'

'That's it,' Mrs Patimkin said 'cry in front of your company . . .' 'My *company* . . .' Brenda wept, 'why don't you go yell at him too . . . why is everyone so nasty to me . . .'

From across the hall I heard Andre Kostelanetz let several thousand singing violins loose on 'Night and Day.' Ron's door was open and I saw he was stretched out, colossal, on his bed; he was singing along with the record. The words belonged to 'Night and Day,' but I didn't recognize Ron's tune. In a minute he picked up the phone and asked the operator for a Milwaukee number. While she connected him, he rolled over and turned up the volume on the record player, so that it would carry the nine hundred miles west.

I heard Julie downstairs. 'Ha ha, Brenda's crying, ha ha, Brenda's crying.'

And then Brenda was running up the stairs. 'Your day'll come, you little bastard!' she called.

'*Brenda!*' Mrs Patimkin called.

'*Mommy!*' Julie cried. 'Brenda cursed at me!'

'What's going *on* here!' Mr Patimkin shouted.

'You call *me*, Mrs P?' Carlota shouted.

And Ron, in the other room, said, 'Hello, Har, I told them . . .'

I sat down on my Brooks Brothers shirt and pronounced my own name out loud.

'Goddam her!' Brenda said to me as she paced up and down my room.

'Bren, do you think I should go—'

'Shhh . . .' She went to the door of my room and listened. 'They're going visiting, thank God.'

'Brenda—'

'Shhh . . . They've gone.'

'Julie too?'

'Yes,' she said. 'Is Ron in his room? His door is closed.'

'He went out.'

'You can't hear anybody move around here. They all creep around in *sneakers*. Oh Neil.'

'Bren, I asked you, maybe I should just stay through tomorrow and then go.'

'Oh, it isn't you she's angry about.'

'I'm not helping any.'

'It's Ron, really. That he's getting married just has her flipped. And me. Now with that goody-good Harriet around she'll just forget I ever exist.'

'Isn't that okay with you?'

She walked off to the window and looked outside. It was dark and cool; the trees rustled and flapped as though they were sheets that had been hung out to dry. Everything outside hinted at September, and for the first time I realized how close we were to Brenda's departure for school.

'Is it, Bren?' but she was not listening to me.

She walked across the room to a door at the far end of the room. She opened it.

'I thought that was a closet,' I said.

'Come here.'

She held the door back and we leaned into the darkness and could hear the strange wind hissing in the eaves of the house.

'What's in here?' I said.

'Money.'

Brenda went into the room. When the puny sixty-watt bulb was twisted on, I saw that the place was full of old furniture—two wing chairs with hair-oil lines at the back, a sofa with a paunch in its middle, a bridge table, two bridge chairs with their stuffing showing, a mirror whose backing had peeled off, shadeless lamps, lampless shades, a coffee table with a cracked glass top, and a pile of rolled up shades.

'What is this?' I said.

'A storeroom. Our old furniture.'

'How old?'

'From Newark,' she said. 'Come here.' She was on her hands and knees in front of the sofa and was holding up its paunch to peek beneath.

'Brenda, what the hell are we doing here? You're getting filthy.'

'It's not here.'

'*What?*'

'The money. I told you.'

I sat down on a wing chair, raising some dust. It had begun to rain outside, and we could smell the fall dampness coming through the vent that was outlined at the far end of the storeroom. Brenda got up from the floor and sat down on the sofa. Her knees and Bermudas were dirty and when she pushed her hair back she dirtied her forehead. There among the disarrangement and dirt I had the strange experience of seeing us, *both* of us, placed among disarrangement and dirt: we looked like a young couple who had just moved into a new apartment; we had suddenly taken stock of our furniture, finances, and future, and all we could feel any pleasure about was the clean smell of outside, which reminded us we were alive, but which, in a pinch, would not feed us.

'What money?' I said again.

'The hundred-dollar bills. From when I was a little girl . . .' and she breathed deeply. 'When I was little and we'd just moved from Newark, my father took me up here one day. He took me into this room and told me that if anything should ever happen to him, he wanted me to know where there was some money that I should have. He said it wasn't for anybody else but me, and that I should never tell anyone about it, not even Ron. Or my mother.'

'How much was it?'

'Three hundred-dollar bills. I'd never seen them before. I was nine, around Julie's age. I don't think we'd been living here a month. I remember I used to come up here about once a week, when no one was home but Carlota, and crawl under the sofa and make sure it was still here. And it always was. He never mentioned it once again. Never.'

'Where is it? Maybe someone stole it.'

'I don't know, Neil. I suppose he took it back.'

'When it was gone,' I said, 'my God, didn't you tell him? Maybe Carlota—'

'I never knew it was gone, until just now. I guess I stopped looking at one time or another . . . And then I forgot about it. Or just didn't think about it. I mean I always had enough, I didn't need this. I guess one day *he* figured I wouldn't need it.'

Brenda paced up to the narrow, dust-covered window and drew her initials on it.

'Why did you want it now?' I said.

'I don't know . . .' she said and went over and twisted the bulb off.

I didn't move from the chair and Brenda, in her tight shorts and shirt, seemed naked standing there a few feet away. Then I saw her shoulders shaking. 'I wanted to find it and tear it up in little pieces and put the goddam pieces in her purse! If it was there, I swear it, I would have done it.'

'I wouldn't have let you, Bren.'

'Wouldn't you have?'

'No.'

'Make love to me, Neil. Right now.'

'Where?'

'Do it! *Here*. On this cruddy cruddy cruddy sofa.'

And I obeyed her.

The next morning Brenda made breakfast for the two of us. Ron had gone off to his first day of work—I'd heard him singing in the shower only an hour after I'd returned to my own room; in fact, I had still been awake when the Chrysler had pulled out of the garage, carrying boss and son down to the Patimkin works in Newark. Mrs Patimkin wasn't home either; she had taken her car and had gone off to the Temple to talk to Rabbi Kranitz about the wedding. Julie was on the back lawn playing at helping Carlota hang the clothes.

'You know what I want to do this morning?' Brenda said. We were eating a grapefruit, sharing it rather sloppily, for Brenda couldn't find a paring knife, and so we'd decided to peel it down like an orange and eat the segments separately.

'What?' I said.

'Run,' she said. 'Do you ever run?'

'You mean on a track? God, yes. In high school we had to run a mile every month. So we wouldn't be Momma's boys. I think the bigger your lungs get the more you're supposed to hate your mother.'

'I want to run,' she said, 'and I want you to run. Okay?'

'Oh, Brenda . . .'

But an hour later, after a breakfast that consisted of another grapefruit, which apparently is all a runner is supposed to eat in the morning, we had driven the Volkswagen over to the high school, behind which was a quarter-mile track. Some kids were playing with a dog out in the grassy center of the track, and at the far end, near the woods, a figure in white shorts with slits in the side, and no shirt, was twirling, twirling, and then flinging a shot put as far as he could. After it left his hand he did a little eagle-eyed tap dance while he watched it arch and bend and land in the distance.

'You know,' Brenda said, 'you look like me. Except bigger.'

We were dressed similarly, sneakers, sweat socks, khaki Bermudas, and sweat shirts, but I had the feeling that Brenda was not talking about the accidents of our dress—if they were accidents. She meant, I was sure, that I was somehow beginning to look the way she wanted me to. Like herself.

'Let's see who's faster,' she said, and then we started along the track. Within the first eighth of a mile the three little boys and their dog were following us. As we passed the corner where the shot putter was, he waved at us; Brenda called 'Hi!' and I smiled, which, as you may or may not know, makes one engaged in serious running feel inordinately silly. At the quarter mile the kids dropped off and retired to the grass, the dog turned and started the other way, and I had a tiny knife in my side. Still I was abreast of Brenda, who as we started on the second lap, called 'Hi!' once again to the lucky shot putter, who was reclining on the grass now, watching us, and rubbing his shot like a crystal ball. Ah, I thought, there's the sport.

'How about us throwing the shot put?' I panted.

'After,' she said, and I saw beads of sweat clinging to the last strands of hair that shagged off her ear. When we approached the half mile Brenda suddenly swerved off the track onto the grass and tumbled down; her departure surprised me and I was still running.

'Hey, Bob Mathias,' she called, 'let's lie in the sun . . .'

But I acted as though I didn't hear her and though my heart pounded in my throat and my mouth was dry as a drought, I made my legs move, and swore I would not stop until I'd finished one more lap. As I passed the shot putter for the third time, I called 'Hi!'

She was excited when I finally pulled up alongside of her. 'You're good,' she said. My hands were on my hips and I was looking at the ground and sucking air—rather, air was sucking me, I didn't have much to say about it.

'Uh-huh,' I breathed.

'Let's do this every morning,' she said. 'We'll get up and have two grapefruit, and then you'll come out here and run. I'll time you. In two weeks you'll break four minutes, won't you, sweetie? I'll get Ron's stop watch.' She was so excited—she'd slid over on the grass and was pushing my socks up against my wet ankles and calves. She bit my kneecap.

'Okay,' I said.

'Then we'll go back and have a real breakfast.'

'Okay.'

'You drive back,' she said, and suddenly she was up and running ahead of me, and then we were headed back in the car.

And the next morning, my mouth still edgy from the grapefruit segments, we were at the track. We had Ron's stop watch and a towel for me, for when I was finished.

'My legs are a little sore,' I said.

'Do some exercises,' Brenda said. 'I'll do them with you.' She heaped the towel on the grass and together we did deep knee bends, and sit-ups, and push-ups, and some high-knee raising in place. I felt overwhelmingly happy.

'I'm just going to run a half today, Bren. We'll see what I do . . .' and I heard Brenda click the watch, and then when I was on the far side of the track, the clouds trailing above me like my own white, fleecy tail, I saw that Brenda was on the ground, hugging her knees, and alternately checking the watch and looking out at me. We were the only ones there, and it all reminded me of one of those scenes in race-horse movies, where an old trainer like Walter Brennan and a young handsome man clock the beautiful girl's horse in the early Kentucky morning, to see if it really is the fastest two-year-old alive. There were differences all right—one being simply that at the quarter mile Brenda shouted out to me, 'A minute and fourteen seconds,' but it was pleasant and exciting and clean and when I finished Brenda was standing up and waiting for me. Instead of a tape to break I had Brenda's sweet flesh to meet, and I did, and it was the first time she said that she loved me.

We ran—I ran—every morning, and by the end of the week I was running a 7:02 mile, and always at the end there was the little click of the watch and Brenda's arms.

At night, I would read in my pajamas, while Brenda, in her room, read, and we would wait for Ron to go to sleep. Some nights we had to wait longer than others, and I would hear the leaves swishing outside, for it had grown cooler at the end of August, and the air-conditioning was turned off at night and we were all allowed to open our windows. Finally Ron would be ready for bed. He would stomp around his room and then he would come to the door in his shorts and T-shirt and go into the bathroom where he would urinate loudly and brush his teeth. After he brushed his teeth I would go in to brush mine. We would pass in the hall and I would give him a hearty and sincere 'Good-night.' Once in the bathroom, I would spend a moment admiring my tan in the mirror; behind me I could see Ron's jock straps hanging out to dry on the Hot and Cold knobs of the shower. Nobody ever questioned their tastefulness as adornment, and after a few nights I didn't even notice them.

While Ron brushed his teeth and I waited in my bed for my turn, I could hear the record player going in his room. Generally, after coming in from basketball, he would call Harriet—who was now only a few days away from us—and then would lock himself up with *Sports Illustrated* and Mantovani; however, when he emerged from his room for his evening toilet, it was not a Mantovani record I would hear playing, but something else, apparently what he'd once referred to as his Columbus record. I *imagined* that was what I heard, for I could not tell much from the last moments of sound. All I heard were bells moaning evenly and soft patriotic music behind them, and riding over it all, a deep kind of Edward R. Murrow gloomy voice: '*And so goodbye, Columbus,*' the voice intoned, '*. . . goodbye, Columbus . . . goodbye . . .*' Then there would be silence and Ron would be back in his room; the light would switch off and in only a few minutes I would hear him rumbling down into that exhilarating, restorative, vitamin-packed sleep that I imagined athletes to enjoy.

One morning near sneaking-away time I had a dream and when I awakened from it, there was just enough dawn coming into the room

for me to see the color of Brenda's hair. I touched her in her sleep, for
the dream had unsettled me; it had taken place on a ship, an old sailing
ship like those you see in pirate movies. With me on the ship was the
little colored kid from the library—I was the captain and he my mate,
and we were the only crew members. For a while it was a pleasant
dream; we were anchored in the harbor of an island in the Pacific and
it was very sunny. Up on the beach there were beautiful bare-skinned
Negresses, and none of them moved; but suddenly *we* were moving,
our ship, out of the harbor, and the Negresses moved slowly down to
the shore and began to throw leis at us and say 'Goodbye, Columbus . . .
goodbye, Columbus . . . goodbye . . .' and though we did not want to
go, the little boy and I, the boat was moving and there was nothing we
could do about it, and he shouted at me that it was my fault and I
shouted it was his for not having a library card, but we were wasting
our breath, for we were further and further from the island, and soon
the natives were nothing at all. Space was all out of proportion in the
dream, and things were sized and squared in no way I'd ever seen
before, and I think it was that more than anything else that steered me
into consciousness. I did not want to leave Brenda's side that morning,
and for a while I played with the little point at the nape of her neck,
where she'd had her hair cut. I stayed longer than I should have, and
when finally I returned to my room I almost ran into Ron who was
preparing for his day at Patimkin Kitchen and Bathroom Sinks.

6

That morning was supposed to have been my last at the Patimkin
house; however, when I began to throw my things into my bag late in
the day, Brenda told me I could unpack—somehow she'd managed to
inveigle another week out of her parents, and I would be able to stay
right through till Labor Day, when Ron would be married; then, the
following morning Brenda would be off to school and I would go
back to work. So we would be with each other until the summer's last
moment.

This should have made me overjoyed, but as Brenda trotted back down the stairs to accompany her family to the airport—where they were to pick up Harriet—I was not joyful but disturbed, as I had been more and more with the thought that when Brenda went back to Radcliffe, that would be the end for me. I was convinced that even Miss Winney's stool was not high enough for me to see clear up to Boston. Nevertheless, I tossed my clothing back into the drawer and was able, finally, to tell myself that there'd been no hints of ending our affair from Brenda, and any suspicions I had, any uneasiness, was spawned in my own uncertain heart. Then I went into Ron's room to call my aunt.

'Hello?' she said.

'Aunt Gladys,' I said, 'how are you?'

'You're sick.'

'No, I'm having a fine time. I wanted to call you, I'm going to stay another week.'

'Why?'

'I told you. I'm having a good time. Mrs Patimkin asked me to stay until Labor Day.'

'You've got clean underwear?'

'I'm washing it at night. I'm okay, Aunt Gladys.'

'By hand you can't get it clean.'

'It's clean enough. Look, Aunt Gladys, I'm having a wonderful time.'

'*Shmutz* he lives in and I shouldn't worry.'

'How's Uncle Max?' I asked.

'What should he be? Uncle Max is Uncle Max. You, I don't like the way your voice sounds.'

'Why? Do I sound like I've got on dirty underwear?'

'Smart guy. Someday you'll learn.'

'What?'

'What do you mean *what*? You'll find out. You'll stay there too long you'll be too good for us.'

'Never, sweetheart,' I said.

'I'll see it I'll believe it.'

'Is it cool in Newark, Aunt Gladys?'

'It's snowing,' she said.

'Hasn't it been cool all week?'

'You sit around all day it's cool. For me it's not February, believe me.'

'Okay, Aunt Gladys. Say hello to everybody.'

'You got a letter from your mother.'

'Good. I'll read it when I get home.'

'You couldn't take a ride down you'll read it?'

'It'll wait. I'll drop them a note. Be a good girl,' I said.

'What about your socks?'

'I go barefoot. Goodbye, honey.' And I hung up.

Down in the kitchen Carlota was getting dinner ready. I was always amazed at how Carlota's work never seemed to get in the way of her life. She made household chores seem like illustrative gestures of whatever it was she was singing, even, if as now, it was 'I Get a Kick out of You.' She moved from the oven to the automatic dishwasher—she pushed buttons, turned dials, peeked in the glass-doored oven, and from time to time picked a big black grape out of a bunch that lay on the sink. She chewed and chewed, humming all the time, and then, with a deliberated casualness, shot the skin and the pit directly into the garbage disposal unit. I said hello to her as I went out the back door, and though she did not return the greeting, I felt a kinship with one who, like me, had been partially wooed and won on Patimkin fruit.

Out on the lawn I shot baskets for a while; then I picked up an iron and drove a cotton golf ball limply up into the sunlight; then I kicked a soccer ball towards the oak tree; then I tried shooting foul shots again. Nothing diverted me—I felt open-stomached, as though I hadn't eaten for months, and though I went back inside and came out with my own handful of grapes, the feeling continued, and I knew it had nothing to do with my caloric intake; it was only a rumor of the hollowness that would come when Brenda was away. The fact of her departure had, of course, been on my mind for a while, but overnight it had taken on a darker hue. Curiously, the darkness seemed to have something to do with Harriet, Ron's intended, and I thought for a time that it was simply the reality of Harriet's arrival that had dramatized the passing of time: we had been talking about it and now suddenly it was here—just as Brenda's departure would be here before we knew it.

But it was more than that: the union of Harriet and Ron reminded me that separation need not be a permanent state. People could marry each other, even if they were young! And yet Brenda and I had never mentioned marriage, except perhaps for that night at the pool when she'd said, 'When you love me, everything will be all right.' Well, I loved her, and she me, and things didn't seem all right at all. Or was I inventing troubles again? I supposed I should really have thought my lot improved considerably; yet, there on the lawn, the August sky seemed too beautiful and temporary to bear, and I wanted Brenda to marry me. Marriage, though, was not what I proposed to her when she drove the car up the driveway, alone, some fifteen minutes later. That proposal would have taken a kind of courage that I did not think I had. I did not feel myself prepared for any answer but 'Hallelujah!' Any other kind of yes wouldn't have satisfied me, and any kind of no, even one masked behind the words, 'Let's wait, sweetheart,' would have been my end. So I imagine that's why I proposed the surrogate, which turned out finally to be far more daring than I knew it to be at the time.

'Harriet's plane is late, so I drove home,' Brenda called.

'Where's everyone else?'

'They're going to wait for her and have dinner at the airport. I have to tell Carlota,' and she went inside.

In a few minutes she appeared on the porch. She wore a yellow dress that cut a wide-bottomed U across her shoulders and neck, and showed where the tanned flesh began above her breasts. On the lawn she stepped out of her heels and walked barefoot over to where I was sitting under the oak tree.

'Women who wear high heels all the time get tipped ovaries,' she said.

'Who told you that?'

'I don't remember. I like to think everything's ship-shape in there.'

'Brenda, I want to ask you something . . .'

She yanked the blanket with the big O on it over to us and sat down.

'What?' she said.

'I know this is out of the blue, though really it's not . . . I want you to buy a diaphragm. To go to a doctor and get one.'

She smiled. 'Don't worry, sweetie, we're careful. Everything is okay.'

'But that's the safest.'

'We're safe. It'd be a waste.'

'Why take chances?'

'But we *aren't*. How many things do you need.'

'Honey, it isn't bulk I'm interested in. It's not even safety,' I added.

'You just want me to own one, is that it? Like a walking stick, or a pith helmet—'

'Brenda, I want you to own one for . . . for the sake of pleasure.'

'Pleasure? Whose? The doctor's?'

'Mine,' I said.

She did not answer me, but rubbed her fingers along the ridge of her collarbone to wipe away the tiny globes of perspiration that had suddenly formed there.

'No, Neil, it's silly.'

'Why?'

'Why? It just is.'

'You know why it's silly, Brenda—because *I* asked you to do it?'

'That's sillier.'

'If you asked *me* to buy a diaphragm we'd have to go straight to the Yellow Pages and find a gynecologist open on a Saturday afternoon.'

'I would never ask you to do that, baby.'

'It's the truth,' I said, though I was smiling. 'It's the truth.'

'It's not,' she said, and got up and walked over to the basketball court, where she walked on the white lines that Mr Patimkin had laid the day before.

'Come back here,' I said.

'Neil, it's silly and I don't want to talk about it.'

'Why are you being so selfish?'

'Selfish? You're the one who's being selfish. It's your pleasure . . .'

'That's right. My pleasure. Why not!'

'Don't raise your voice. Carlota.'

'Then get the hell over here,' I said.

She walked over to me, leaving white footprints on the grass. 'I didn't think you were such a creature of the flesh,' she said.

'Didn't you?' I said. 'I'll tell you something that you ought to know. It's not even the pleasures of the flesh I'm talking about.'

'Then frankly, I don't know *what* you're talking about. Why you're even bothering. Isn't what we use sufficient?'

'I'm bothering just because I want you to go to a doctor and get a diaphragm. That's all. No explanation. Just do it. Do it because I asked you to.'

'You're not being reasonable—'

'Goddamit, Brenda!'

'Goddamit yourself!' she said and went up into the house.

I closed my eyes and leaned back and in fifteen minutes, or maybe less, I heard somebody stroking at the cotton golf ball. She had changed into shorts and a blouse and was still barefoot.

We didn't speak with each other, but I watched her bring the club back of her ear, and then swing through, her chin tilted up with the line of flight a regular golf ball would have taken.

'That's five hundred yards,' I said.

She didn't answer but walked after the cotton ball and then readied for another swing.

'Brenda. Please come here.'

She walked over, dragging the club over the grass.

'What?'

'I don't want to argue with you.'

'Nor I with you,' she said. 'It was the first time.'

'Was it such an awful thing for me to ask?'

She nodded.

'Bren, I know it was probably a surprise. It was for me. But we're not children.'

'Neil, I just don't want to. It's not because you asked me to, either. I don't know where you get that from. That's not it.'

'Then why is it?'

'Oh everything. I just don't feel *old* enough for all that equipment.'

'What does age have to do with it?'

'I don't mean age. I just mean—well, *me*. I mean it's so conscious a thing to do.'

'Of course it's conscious. That's exactly it. Don't you see? It would change us.'

'It would change me.'

'Us. Together.'

'Neil, how do you think I'd feel lying to some doctor.'

'You can go to Margaret Sanger, in New York. They don't ask any questions.'

'You've done this before?'

'No,' I said. 'I just know. I read Mary McCarthy.'

'That's exactly right. That's just what I'd feel like, somebody out of *her*.'

'Don't be dramatic,' I said.

'You're the one who's being dramatic. You think there would be something affairish about it, then. Last summer I went with this whore who I sent out to buy—'

'Oh, Brenda, you're a selfish egotistical bitch! You're the one who's thinking about "last summer," about an end for us. In fact, that's the whole thing, isn't it—'

'That's right, I'm a bitch. I want this to end. That's why I ask you to stay another week, that's why I let you sleep with me in my own house. What's the *matter* with you! Why don't you and my mother take turns—one day she can plague me, the next you—'

'Stop it!'

'Go to hell, all of you!' Brenda said, and now she was crying and I knew when she ran off I would not see her, as I didn't, for the rest of the afternoon.

Harriet Ehrlich impressed me as a young lady singularly unconscious of a motive in others or herself. All was surfaces, and she seemed a perfect match for Ron, and too for the Patimkins. Mrs Patimkin, in fact, did just as Brenda prophesied: Harriet appeared, and Brenda's mother lifted one wing and pulled the girl in towards the warm underpart of her body, where Brenda herself would have liked to nestle. Harriet was built like Brenda, although a little chestier, and she nodded her head insistently whenever anyone spoke. Sometimes she would even say the last few words of your sentence with you, though that was infrequent; for the most part she nodded and kept her hands folded. All evening, as the Patimkins planned where the newlyweds should live, what furniture they should buy, how soon they should have a baby—all through this I kept thinking that Harriet was wearing white gloves, but she wasn't.

Brenda and I did not exchange a word or a glance; we sat, listening, Brenda somewhat more impatient than me. Near the end Harriet began calling Mrs Patimkin 'Mother,' and once, 'Mother Patimkin,' and that was when Brenda went to sleep. I stayed behind, mesmerized almost by the dissection, analysis, reconsideration, and finally, the embracing of the trivial. At last Mr and Mrs Patimkin tumbled off to bed, and Julie, who had fallen asleep on her chair, was carried into her room by Ron. That left us two non-Patimkins together.

'Ron tells me you have a very interesting job.'

'I work in the library.'

'I've always liked reading.'

'That'll be nice, married to Ron.'

'Ron likes music.'

'Yes,' I said. What had I *said*?

'You must get first crack at the best-sellers,' she said.

'Sometimes.' I said.

'Well,' she said, flapping her hands on her knees, 'I'm sure we'll all have a good time together. Ron and I hope you and Brenda will double with us soon.'

'Not tonight.' I smiled. 'Soon. Will you excuse me?'

'Good night. I like Brenda very much.'

'Thank you,' I said as I started up the stairs.

I knocked gently on Brenda's door.

'I'm sleeping.'

'Can I come in?' I asked.

Her door opened an inch and she said, 'Ron will be up soon.'

'We'll leave the door open. I only want to talk.'

She let me in and I sat in the chair that faced the bed.

'How do you like your sister-in-law?'

'I've met her before.'

'Brenda, you don't have to sound so damn terse.'

She didn't answer and I just sat there yanking the string on the shade up and down.

'Are you still angry?' I asked at last.

'Yes.'

'Don't be,' I said. 'You can forget about my suggestion. It's not worth it if this is what's going to happen.'

'What did you expect to happen?'

'Nothing. I didn't think it would be so horrendous.'

'That's because you can't understand my side.'

'Perhaps.'

'No perhaps about it.'

'*Okay*,' I said. 'I just wish you'd realize what it is you're getting angry about. It's not my suggestion, Brenda.'

'No? What is it?'

'It's me.'

'Oh don't start that again, will you? I can't win, no matter what I say.'

'Yes, you can,' I said. 'You have.'

I walked out of her room, closing the door behind me for the night.

When I got downstairs the following morning there was a great deal of activity. In the living room I heard Mrs Patimkin reading a list to Harriet while Julie ran in and out of rooms in search of a skate key. Carlota was vacuuming the carpet; every appliance in the kitchen was bubbling, twisting, and shaking. Brenda greeted me with a perfectly pleasant smile and in the dining room, where I walked to look out at the back lawn and the weather, she kissed me on the shoulder.

'Hello,' she said.

'Hello.'

'I have to go with Harriet this morning,' Brenda told me. 'So we can't run. Unless you want to go alone.'

'No. I'll read or something. Where are you going?'

'We're going to New York. Shopping. She's going to buy a wedding dress. For after the wedding. To go away in.'

'What are *you* going to buy?'

'A dress to be maid of honor in. If I go with Harriet then I can go to Bergdorf's without all that Ohrbach's business with my mother.'

'Get me something, will you?' I said.

'Oh, Neil, are you going to bring that up again!'

'I was only *fooling*. I wasn't even thinking about that.'

'Then why did you say it?'

'Oh Jesus!' I said, and went outside and drove my car down into Millburn Center where I had some eggs and coffee.

When I came back, Brenda was gone, and there were only Carlota, Mrs Patimkin, and myself in the house. I tried to stay out of whichever rooms they were in, but finally Mrs Patimkin and I wound up sitting opposite each other in the TV room. She was checking off names on a long sheet of paper she held; next to her, on the table, were two thin phone books which she consulted from time to time.

'No rest for the weary,' she said to me.

I smiled hugely, embracing the proverb as though Mrs Patimkin had just then coined it. 'Yes. Of course,' I said. 'Would you like some help? Maybe I could help you check something.'

'Oh, no,' she said with a little head-shaking dismissal, 'it's for Hadassah.'

'Oh,' I said.

I sat and watched her until she asked, 'Is your mother in Hadassah?'

'I don't know if she is now. She was in Newark.'

'Was she an active member?'

'I guess so, she was always planting trees in Israel for someone.'

'Really?' Mrs Patimkin said. 'What's her name?'

'Esther Klugman. She's in Arizona now. Do they have Hadassah there?'

'Wherever there are Jewish women.'

'Then I guess she is. She's with my father. They went there for their asthma. I'm staying with my aunt in Newark. She's not in Hadassah. My Aunt Sylvia is, though. Do you know her, Aaron Klugman and Sylvia? They belong to your club. They have a daughter, my cousin Doris—' I couldn't stop myself '—They live in Livingston. Maybe it isn't Hadassah my Aunt Sylvia belongs to. I think it's some TB organization. Or cancer. Muscular dystrophy, maybe. I know she's interested in *some* disease.'

'That's very nice,' Mrs Patimkin said.

'Oh yes.'

'They do very good work.'

'I know.'

Mrs Patimkin, I thought, had begun to warm to me; she let the purple eyes stop peering and just look out at the world for a while without judging. 'Are you interested in B'nai Brith?' she asked me. 'Ron is joining, you know, as soon as he gets married.'

'I think I'll wait till then,' I said.

Petulantly, Mrs Patimkin went back to her lists, and I realized it had been foolish of me to risk lightheartedness with her about Jewish affairs. 'You're active in the Temple, aren't you?' I asked with all the interest I could muster.

'Yes,' she said.

'What Temple do *you* belong to?' she asked in a moment.

'We used to belong to Hudson Street Synagogue. Since my parents left, I haven't had much contact.'

I didn't know whether Mrs Patimkin caught a false tone in my voice. Personally I thought I had managed my rueful confession pretty well, especially when I recalled the decade of paganism prior to my parent's departure. Regardless, Mrs Patimkin asked immediately—and strategically it seemed—'We're all going to Temple Friday night. Why don't you come with us? I mean, are you orthodox or conservative?'

I considered. 'Well, I haven't gone in a long time . . . I sort of switch . . .' I smiled. 'I'm just Jewish,' I said well-meaningly, but that too sent Mrs Patimkin back to her Hadassah work. Desperately I tried to think of something that would convince her I wasn't an infidel. Finally I asked: 'Do you know Martin Buber's work?'

'Buber . . . Buber,' she said, looking at her Hadassah list. 'Is he orthodox or conservative?' she asked.

'. . . He's a philosopher.'

'Is he *reformed*?' she asked, piqued either at my evasiveness or at the possibility that Buber attended Friday night services without a hat, and Mrs Buber had only one set of dishes in her kitchen.

'Orthodox,' I said faintly.

'That's very nice,' she said.

'Yes.'

'Isn't Hudson Street Synagogue orthodox?' she asked.

'I don't know.'

'I thought you belonged there.'

'I was bar-mitzvahed.'

'And you don't know that it's orthodox?'

'Yes. I do. It is.'

'Then *you* must be.'

'Oh, yes, I am,' I said. 'What are you?' I popped, ushing.

'Orthodox. My husband is conservative,' which meant, I took it, that he didn't care. 'Brenda is nothing, as you probably know.'

'Oh?' I said. 'No, I didn't know that.'

'She was the best Hebrew student I've ever seen,' Mrs Patimkin said, 'but then, of course, she got too big for her britches.'

Mrs Patimkin looked at me, and I wondered whether courtesy demanded that I agree. 'Oh, I don't know,' I said at last, 'I'd say Brenda is conservative. Maybe a little reformed . . . '

The phone rang, rescuing me, and I spoke a silent orthodox prayer to the Lord.

'Hello,' Mrs Patimkin said. '. . . no . . . I can *not*, I have all the Hadassah calls to make . . .'

I acted as though I were listening to the birds outside, though the closed windows let no natural noises in.

'Have Ronald drive them up . . . But we can't wait, not if we want it on time . . .'

Mrs Patimkin glanced up at me; then she put one hand over the mouthpiece. 'Would you ride down to Newark for me?'

I stood. 'Yes. Surely.'

'Dear?' she said back into the phone, 'Neil will come for it . . . No, *Neil*, Brenda's friend . . . Yes . . . Goodbye.

'Mr Patimkin has some silver patterns I have to see. Would you drive down to his place and pick them up?'

'Of course.'

'Do you know where the shop is?'

'Yes.'

'Here,' she said, handing a key ring to me, 'take the Volkswagen.'

'My car is right outside.'

'Take these,' she said.

Patimkin Kitchen and Bathroom Sinks was in the heart of the Negro section of Newark. Years ago, at the time of the great immigration, it had been the Jewish section, and still one could see the little fish stores, the kosher delicatessens, the Turkish baths, where my grandparents had shopped and bathed at the beginning of the century. Even the smells had lingered: whitefish, corned beef, sour tomatoes—but now, on top of these, was the grander greasier smell of auto wrecking shops, the sour stink of a brewery, the burning odor from a leather factory; and on the streets, instead of Yiddish, one heard the shouts of Negro children playing at Willie Mays with a broom handle and half a rubber ball. The neighborhood had changed: the old Jews like my grandparents had struggled and died, and their offspring had struggled and prospered, and moved further and further west, towards the edge of Newark, then out of it, and up the slope of the Orange Mountains, until they had reached the crest and started down the other side, pouring into Gentile territory as the Scotch-Irish had poured through the Cumberland Gap. Now, in fact, the Negroes were making the same migration, following the steps of the Jews, and those who remained in the Third Ward lived the most squalid of lives and dreamed in their fetid mattresses of the piny smell of Georgia nights.

I wondered, for an instant only, if I would see the colored kid from the library on the streets here. I didn't, of course, though I was sure he lived in one of the scabby, peeling buildings out of which dogs, children, and aproned women moved continually. On the top floors, windows were open, and the very old, who could no longer creak down the long stairs to the street, sat where they had been put, in the screenless windows, their elbows resting on fluffless pillows, and their heads tipping forward on their necks, watching the push of the young and the pregnant and the unemployed. Who would come after the Negroes? Who was left? No one, I thought, and someday these streets, where my grandmother drank hot tea from an old *jahrzeit* glass, would be empty and we would all of us have moved to the crest of the Orange Mountains, and wouldn't the dead stop kicking at the slats in their coffins then?

I pulled the Volkswagen up in front of a huge garage door that said across the front of it:

PATIMKIN KITCHEN AND BATHROOM SINKS
'Any Size—Any Shape'

Inside I could see a glass-enclosed office; it was in the center of an immense warehouse. Two trucks were being loaded in the rear, and Mr Patimkin, when I saw him, had a cigar in his mouth and was shouting at someone. It was Ron, who was wearing a white T-shirt that said Ohio State Athletic Association across the front. Though he was taller than Mr Patimkin, and almost as stout, his hands hung weakly at his sides like a small boy's; Mr Patimkin's cigar locomoted in his mouth. Six Negroes were loading one of the trucks feverishly, toss-ing—my stomach dropped—sink bowls at one another.

Ron left Mr Patimkin's side and went back to directing the men. He thrashed his arms about a good deal, and though on the whole he seemed rather confused, he didn't appear to be at all concerned about anybody dropping a sink. Suddenly I could see myself directing the Negroes—I would have an ulcer in an hour. I could almost hear the enamel surfaces shattering on the floor. And I could hear myself: 'Watch it, you guys. Be careful, will you? *Whoops!* Oh, please be— *watch* it! Watch! Oh!' Suppose Mr Patimkin should come up to me and say, 'Okay, boy, you want to marry my daughter, let's see what you can do.' Well, he would see: in a moment that floor would be a shattered mosaic, a crunchy path of enamel. 'Klugman, what kind of worker are you? You work like you eat!' 'That's right, that's right, I'm a sparrow, let me go.' 'Don't you even know how to load and unload?' 'Mr Patimkin, even breathing gives me trouble, sleep tires me out, let me go, let me go . . .'

Mr Patimkin was headed back to the fish bowl to answer a ringing phone, and I wrenched myself free of my reverie and headed towards the office too. When I entered, Mr Patimkin looked up from the

phone with his eyes; the sticky cigar was in his free hand—he moved
it at me, a greeting. From outside I heard Ron call in a high voice,
'You can't all go to lunch at the same time. We haven't got all day!'

'Sit down,' Mr Patimkin shot at me, though when he went back to
his conversation I saw there was only one chair in the office, his.
People did not sit at Patimkin Sink—here you earned your money the
hard way, standing up. I busied myself looking at the several calendars
that hung from filing cabinets; they showed illustrations of women so
dreamy, so fantastically thighed and uddered, that one could not think
of them as pornographic. The artist who had drawn the calendar girls
for 'Lewis Construction Company,' and 'Earl's Truck and Auto
Repair,' and 'Grossman and Son, Paper Box' had been painting some
third sex I had never seen.

'Sure, sure, sure,' Mr Patimkin said into the phone. 'Tomorrow,
don't tell me tomorrow. Tomorrow the world could blow up.'

At the other end someone spoke. Who was it? Lewis from the
construction company? Earl from truck repair?

'I'm running a business, Grossman, not a charity.'

So it was Grossman being browbeaten at the other end.

'Shit on that,' Mr Patimkin said. 'You're not the only one in town,
my good friend,' and he winked at me.

Ah-ha, a conspiracy against Grossman. Me and Mr Patimkin. I
smiled as collusively as I knew how.

'All right then, we're here till five . . . No later.'

He wrote something on a piece of paper. It was only a big X.

'My kid'll be here,' he said. 'Yea, he's in the business.'

Whatever Grossman said on the other end, it made Mr Patimkin
laugh. Mr Patimkin hung up without a goodbye.

He looked out the back to see how Ron was doing.

'Four years in college he can't unload a truck.'

I didn't know what to say but finally chose the truth. 'I guess I
couldn't either.'

'You could learn. What am I, a genius? I learned. Hard work never
killed anybody.'

To that I agreed.

Mr Patimkin looked at his cigar. 'A man works hard he's got

something. You don't get anywhere sitting on your behind, you know . . . The biggest men in the country worked hard, believe me. Even Rockefeller. Success don't come easy . . .' He did not say this so much as he mused it out while he surveyed his dominion. He was not a man enamored of words, and I had the feeling that what had tempted him into this barrage of universals was probably the combination of Ron's performance and my presence—me, the outsider who might one day be an insider. But did Mr Patimkin even consider that possibility? I did not know; I only knew that these few words he did speak could hardly transmit all the satisfaction and surprise he felt about the life he had managed to build for himself and his family.

He looked out at Ron again. 'Look at him, if he played basketball like that they'd throw him the hell off the court.' But he was smiling when he said it.

He walked over to the door. 'Ronald, let them go to lunch.'

Ron shouted back, 'I thought I'd let some go now, and some later.'

'Why?'

'Then somebody'll always be—'

'No fancy deals here,' Mr Patimkin shouted. 'We all go to lunch at once.'

Ron turned back. 'All right, boys, lunch!'

His father smiled at me. 'Smart boy? Huh?' He tapped his head. 'That took brains, huh? He ain't got the stomach for business. He's an idealist,' and then I think Mr Patimkin suddenly realized who *I* was, and eagerly corrected himself so as not to offend. 'That's all right, you know, if you're a schoolteacher, or like you, you know, a student or something like that. Here you need a little of the *gonif* in you. You know what that means? *Gonif?*'

'Thief,' I said.

'You know more than my own kids. They're *goyim*, my kids, that's how much they understand.' He watched the Negro loading gang walk past the office and shouted out to them, 'You guys know how long an hour is? All right, you'll be back in an hour!'

Ron came into the office and of course shook my hand.

'Do you have that stuff for Mrs Patimkin?' I asked.

'Ronald, get him the silver patterns.' Ron turned away and Mr

Patimkin said, 'When I got married we had forks and knives from the five and ten. This kid needs gold to eat off,' but there was no anger; far from it.

I drove to the mountains in my own car that afternoon, and stood for a while at the wire fence watching the deer lightly prance, coyly feed, under the protection of signs that read, DO NOT FEED THE DEER, *By Order of South Mountain Reservation.* Alongside me at the fence were dozens of kids; they giggled and screamed when the deer licked the popcorn from their hands, and then were sad when their own excitement sent the young loping away towards the far end of the field where their tawny-skinned mothers stood regally watching the traffic curl up the mountain road. Young white-skinned mothers, hardly older than I, and in many instances younger, chatted in their convertibles behind me, and looked down from time to time to see what their children were about. I had seen them before, when Brenda and I had gone out for a bite in the afternoon, or had driven up here for lunch: in clotches of three and four they sat in the rustic hamburger joints that dotted the Reservation area while their children gobbled hamburgers and malteds and were given dimes to feed the jukebox. Though none of the little ones were old enough to read the song titles, almost all of them could holler out the words, and they did, while the mothers, a few of whom I recognized as high school mates of mine, compared suntans, supermarkets, and vacations. They looked immortal sitting there. Their hair would always stay the color they desired, their clothes the right texture and shade; in their homes they would have simple Swedish modern when that was fashionable, and if huge, ugly baroque ever came back, out would go the long, midget-legged marble coffee table and in would come Louis Quatorze. These were the goddesses, and if I were Paris I could not have been able to choose among them, so microscopic were the differences. Their fates had collapsed them into one. Only Brenda shone. Money and comfort would not erase her singleness—they hadn't yet, or had they? What was I loving, I wondered, and since I am not one to stick scalpels into myself, I wiggled my hand in the fence and allowed a tiny-nosed buck to lick my thoughts away.

When I returned to the Patimkin house, Brenda was in the living room looking more beautiful that I had ever seen her. She was modeling her new dress for Harriet and her mother. Even Mrs Patimkin seemed softened by the sight of her; it looked as though some sedative had been injected into her, and so relaxed the Brenda-hating muscles around her eyes and mouth.

Brenda, without glasses, modeled in place; when she looked at me it was a kind of groggy, half-waking look I got, and though others might have interpreted it as sleepiness it sounded in my veins as lust. Mrs Patimkin told her finally that she'd bought a very nice dress and I told her she looked lovely and Harriet told her she was very beautiful and that *she* ought to be the bride, and then there was an uncomfortable silence while all of us wondered who ought to be the groom.

Then when Mrs Patimkin had let Harriet out to the kitchen, Brenda came up to me and said, 'I *ought* to be the bride.'

'You ought, sweetheart.' I kissed her, and suddenly she was crying.

'What is it, honey?' I said.

'Let's go outside.'

On the lawn, Brenda was no longer crying but her voice sounded very tired.

'Neil, I called Margaret Sanger Clinic,' she said. 'When I was in New York.'

I didn't answer.

'Neil, they *did* ask if I was married. God, the woman sounded like my mother . . .'

'What did you say?'

'I said *no*.'

'What did she say?'

'I don't know. I hung up.' She walked away and around the oak tree. When she appeared again she'd stepped out of her shoes and held one hand on the tree, as though it were a Maypole she were circling.

'You can call them back,' I said.

She shook her head. 'No, I can't. I don't even know why I called in the first place. We were shopping and I just walked away, looked up the number, and called.'

'Then you can go to a doctor.'

She shook again.

'Look, Bren,' I said, rushing to her, 'we'll go together, to a doctor. In New York—'

'I don't want to go to some dirty little office—'

'We won't. We'll go to the most posh gynecologist in New York. One who gets *Harper's Bazaar* for the reception room. How does that sound?'

She bit her lower lip.

'You'll come with me?' she asked.

'I'll come with you.'

'To the office?'

'Sweetie, your husband wouldn't come to the office.'

'No?'

'He'd be working.'

'But you're not,' she said.

'I'm on vacation,' I said, but I had answered the wrong question. 'Bren, I'll wait and when you're all done we'll buy a drink. We'll go out to dinner.'

'Neil, I shouldn't have called Margaret Sanger—it's not right.'

'It is, Brenda. It's the most right thing we can do.' She walked away and I was exhausted from pleading. Somehow I felt I could have convinced her had I been a bit more crafty; and yet I did not want it to be craftiness that changed her mind. I was silent when she came back, and perhaps it was just that, my *not* saying anything, that prompted her finally to say, 'I'll ask Mother Patimkin if she wants us to take Harriet too . . .'

7

I shall never forget the heat and mugginess of that afternoon we drove into New York. It was four days after the day she'd called Margaret Sanger—she put it off and put it off, but finally on Friday, three days before Ron's wedding and four before her departure, we were heading through the Lincoln Tunnel, which seemed longer and fumier than ever, like Hell with tiled walls. Finally we were in New York and smothered again by the thick day. I pulled around the policeman who directed traffic in his shirt sleeves and up onto the Port Authority roof to park the car.

'Do you have cab fare?' I said.

'Aren't you going to come with me?'

'I thought I'd wait in the bar. Here, downstairs.'

'You can wait in Central Park. His office is right across the street.'

'Bren, what's the diff—' But when I saw the look that invaded her eyes I gave up the air-conditioned bar to accompany her across the city. There was a sudden shower while our cab went crosstown, and when the rain stopped the streets were sticky and shiny, and below the pavement was the rumble of the subways, and in all it was like entering the ear of a lion.

The doctor's office was in the Squibb Building, which is across from Bergdorf Goodman's and so was a perfect place for Brenda to add to her wardrobe. For some reason we had never once considered her going to a doctor in Newark, perhaps because it was too close to home and might allow for possibilities of discovery. When Brenda got to the revolving door she looked back at me; her eyes were very watery, even with her glasses, and I did not say a word, afraid what a word, any word, might do. I kissed her hair and motioned that I would be across the street by the Plaza fountain, and then I watched her revolve through the doors. Out on the street the traffic moved slowly as though the humidity were a wall holding everything back. Even the fountain seemed to be bubbling boiling water on the people who sat at its edge, and in an instant I decided against crossing the street, and turned south on Fifth and began to walk the steaming pavement towards St Patrick's. On the north steps a crowd was gathered; everyone was watching a model being photographed. She was wearing a lemon-colored dress and had her feet pointed like a ballerina, and as I passed into the church I heard some lady say, 'If I ate cottage cheese *ten* times a day, I couldn't be that skinny.'

It wasn't much cooler inside the church, though the stillness and the flicker of the candles made me think it was. I took a seat at the rear and while I couldn't bring myself to kneel, I did lean forward onto the back of the bench before me, and held my hands together and closed

my eyes. I wondered if I looked like a Catholic, and in my wonderment I began to make a little speech to myself. Can I call the
self-conscious words I spoke prayer? At any rate, I called my audience
God. God, I said, I am twenty-three years old. I want to make the best
of things. Now the doctor is about to wed Brenda to me, and I am not
entirely certain this is all for the best. What is it I love, Lord? Why have
I chosen? Who is Brenda? The race is to the swift. Should I have
stopped to think?

I was getting no answers, but I went on. If we meet You at all, God,
it's that we're carnal, and acquisitive, and thereby partake of You. I am
carnal, and I know You approve, I just know it. But how carnal can I
get? I am acquisitive. Where do I turn now in my acquisitiveness?
Where do we meet? Which prize is You?

It was an ingenious meditation, and suddenly I felt ashamed. I got
up and walked outside, and the noise of Fifth Avenue met me with an
answer:

Which prize do you think, *schmuck*? Gold dinnerware, sporting-
goods trees, nectarines, garbage disposals, bumpless noses, Patimkin
Sink, Bonwit Teller—

But damn it, God, that *is* You.

And God only laughed, that clown.

On the steps around the fountain I sat in a small arc of a rainbow
that the sun had shot through the spray of the water. And then I saw
Brenda coming out of the Squibb Building. She carried nothing with
her, like a woman who's only been window shopping, and for a
moment I was glad that in the end she had disobeyed my desire.

As she crossed the street, though, that little levity passed, and then
I was myself again.

She walked up before me and looked down at where I sat; when
she inhaled she filled her entire body, and then let her breath out with
a 'Whew!'

'Where is it?' I said.

My answer, at first, was merely that victorious look of hers, the one
she'd given Simp the night she'd beaten her, the one I'd gotten the
morning I finished the third lap alone. At last she said, 'I'm wearing it.'

'Oh, Bren.'

'He said shall I wrap it or will you take it with you?'

'Oh Brenda, I love you.'

We slept together that night, and so nervous were we about our new toy that we performed like kindergartners, or (in the language of that country) like a lousy double-play combination. And then the next day we hardly saw one another at all, for with the last-minute wedding preparations came scurrying, telegramming, shouting, crying, rushing—in short, lunacy. Even the meals lost their Patimkin fullness, and were tortured out of Kraft cheese, stale onion rolls, dry salami, a little chopped liver, and fruit cocktail. It was hectic all weekend, and I tried as best I could to keep clear of the storm, at whose eye, Ron, clumsy and smiling, and Harriet, flittering and courteous, were being pulled closer and closer together. By Sunday night fatigue had arrested hysteria and all of the Patimkins, Brenda included, had gone off to an early sleep. When Ron went into the bathroom to brush his teeth I decided to go in and brush mine. While I stood over the sink he checked his supports for dampness; then he hung them on the shower knobs and asked me if I would like to listen to his records for a while. It was not out of boredom and loneliness that I accepted; rather a brief spark of lockerroom comradery had been struck there among the soap and the water and the tile, and I thought that perhaps Ron's invitation was prompted by a desire to spend his last moments as a Single Man with another Single Man. If I was right, then it was the first real attestation he'd given to my masculinity. How could I refuse?

I sat on the unused twin bed.

'You want to hear Mantovani?'

'Sure,' I said.

'Who do you like better, him or Kostelanetz?'

'It's a toss-up.'

Ron went to his cabinet. 'Hey, how about the Columbus record? Brenda ever play it for you?'

'No. I don't think so.'

He extracted a record from its case, and like a giant with a sea shell, placed it gingerly on the phonograph. Then he smiled at me and leaned back onto his bed. His arms were behind his head and his eyes fixed on the ceiling. 'They give this to all the seniors. With the year-book—' but he hushed as soon as the sound began. I watched Ron and listened to the record.

At first there was just a roll of drums, then silence, then another drum roll—and then softly, a marching song, the melody of which was very familiar. When the song ended, I heard the bells, soft, loud, then soft again. And finally there came a Voice, bowel-deep and historic, the kind one associates with documentaries about the rise of Fascism.

'The year, 1956. The season, fall. The place, Ohio State University . . .'

Blitzkrieg! Judgment Day! The Lord had lowered his baton, and the Ohio State Glee Club were lining out the Alma Mater as if their souls depended on it. After one desperate chorus, they fell, still screaming, into bottomless oblivion, and the Voice resumed:

'The leaves had begun to turn and redden on the trees. Smoky fires line Fraternity Row, as pledges rake the leaves and turn them to a misty haze. Old faces greet new ones, new faces meet old, and another year has begun . . .'

Music. Glee Club in great comeback. Then the Voice: 'The place, the banks of the Olentangy. The event, Homecoming Game, 1956. The opponent, the ever dangerous Illini . . .'

Roar of crowd. New voice—Bill Stern: 'Illini over the ball. The snap. Linday fading to pass, he finds a receiver, he passes long *long* down field—and IT'S INTERCEPTED BY NUMBER 43, HERB CLARK OF OHIO STATE! Clark evades one tackler, he evades another as he comes up to midfield. Now he's picking up blockers, he's down to the 45, the 40, the 35—'

And as Bill Stern egged on Clark, and Clark, Bill Stern, Ron, on his bed, with just a little body-english, eased Herb Clark over the goal.

'And it's the Buckeyes ahead now, 21 to 19. *What a game!*'

The Voice of History baritoned in again: 'But the season was up and down, and by the time the first snow had covered the turf, it was the sound of dribbling and the cry *Up and In!* that echoed through the fieldhouse . . .'

Ron closed his eyes.

'The Minnesota game,' a new, high voice announced, 'and for some of our seniors, their last game for the red and white . . . The players are ready to come out on the floor and into the spotlight. There'll be a big hand of appreciation from this capacity crowd for some of the boys who won't be back next year. Here comes Larry Gardner, big Number 7, out onto the floor; Big Larry from Akron, Ohio . . .'

'Larry—' announced the P.A. system; 'Larry,' the crowed roared back.

'And here comes Ron Patimkin dribbling out. Ron, Number 11, from Short Hills, New Jersey. Big Ron's last game, and it'll be some time before Buckeye fans forget him . . .'

Big Ron tightened on his bed as the loudspeaker called his name; his ovation must have set the nets to trembling. Then the rest of the players were announced, and then basketball season was over, and it was Religious Emphasis Week, the Senior Prom (Billy May blaring at the gymnasium roof), Fraternity Skit Night, E.E. Cummings reading to students (verse, silence, applause); and then, finally, commencement:

'The campus is hushed this day of days. For several thousand young men and women it is a joyous yet a solemn occasion. And for their parents a day of laughter and a day of tears. It is a bright green day, it is June the seventh of the year one thousand nine hundred and fifty-seven and for these young Americans the most stirring day of their lives. For many this will be their last glimpse of the campus, of Columbus, for many many years. Life calls us, and anxiously if not nervously we walk out into the world and away from the pleasures of these ivied walls. But not from its memories. They will be the concomitant, if not the fundament, of our lives. We shall choose husbands and wives, we shall choose jobs and homes, we shall sire children and grandchildren, but we will not forget you, Ohio State. In the years ahead we will carry with us always memories of thee, Ohio State . . .'

Slowly, softly, the OSU band begins the Alma Mater, and then the bells chime that last hour. Soft, very soft, for it is spring.

There was goose flesh on Ron's veiny arms as the Voice continued. 'We offer ourselves to you then, world, and come at you in search of Life. And to you, Ohio State, to you Columbus, we say thank you, thank you and goodbye. We will miss you, in the fall, in the winter, in the spring, but some day we shall return. Till then, goodbye, Ohio State, goodbye, red and white, goodbye Columbus . . . goodbye, Columbus . . . goodbye . . .'

Ron's eyes were closed. The band was upending its last truckload of nostalgia, and I tiptoed from the room, in step with the 2163 members of the Class of '57.

I closed my door, but then opened it and looked back at Ron: he was still humming on his bed. Thee! I thought, my brother-in-law!

The wedding.

Let me begin with the relatives.

There was Mrs Patimkin's side of the family: her sister Molly, a tiny buxom hen whose ankles swelled and ringed her shoes, and who would remember Ron's wedding if for no other reason than she'd martyred her feet in three-inch heels, and Molly's husband, the butter and egg man, Harry Grossbart, who had earned his fortune with barley and corn in the days of Prohibition. Now he was active in the Temple and whenever he saw Brenda he swatted her on the can; it was a kind of physical bootlegging that passed, I guess, for familial affection. Then there was Mrs Patimkin's brother, Marty Kreiger, the Kosher Hot-Dog King, an immense man, as many stomachs as he had chins, and already, at fifty-five, with as many heart attacks as chins and stomachs combined. He had just come back from a health cure in the Catskills, where he said he'd eaten nothing but All-Bran and had won $1500 at gin rummy. When the photographer came by to take pictures, Marty put his hand on his wife's pancake breasts and said, 'Hey, how about a picture of this!' His wife, Sylvia, was a frail, spindly woman with bones like a bird's. She had cried throughout the ceremony, and sobbed openly, in fact, when the rabbi had pronounced Ron and Harriet 'man and wife in the eyes of God and the State of New Jersey.' Later, at dinner, she had hardened enough to slap her husband's hand as it reached out for a cigar. However, when he reached across to hold her breast she just looked aghast and said nothing.

Also there were Mrs Patimkin's twin sisters, Rose and Pearl, who both had white hair, the color of Lincoln convertibles, and nasal voices, and husbands who followed after them but talked only to each other, as though, in fact, sister had married sister, and husband had married husband. The husbands, named Earl Klein and Manny Kartzman, sat next to each other during the ceremony, then at dinner, and once, in fact, while the band was playing between courses, they rose, Klein and Kartzman, as though to dance, but instead walked to the far end of the hall where together they paced off the width of the floor. Earl, I learned later, was in the carpet business, and apparently he was trying to figure how much money he would make if the Hotel Pierre favored him with a sale.

On Mr Patimkin's side there was only Leo, his half-brother. Leo was married to a woman named Bea whom nobody seemed to talk to. Bea kept hopping up and down during the meal and running over to the kiddie table to see if her little girl, Sharon, was being taken care of. 'I told her not to take the kid. Get a baby-sitter, I said.' Leo told me this while Brenda danced with Ron's best man, Ferrari. 'She says what are we, millionaires? No, for Christ sake, but my brother's kids gets married, I can have a little celebration. No, we gotta *shlep* the kid with us. Aah, it gives her something to do! . . .' He looked around the hall. Up on the stage Harry Winters (né Weinberg) was leading his band in a medley from *My Fair Lady*; on the floor, all ages, all sizes, all shapes were dancing. Mr Patimkin was dancing with Julie, whose dress had slipped down from her shoulders to reveal her soft small back, and long neck, like Brenda's. He danced in little squares and was making considerable effort not to step on Julie's toes. Harriet, who was, as everyone said, a beautiful bride, was dancing with her father. Ron danced with Harriet's mother, Brenda with Ferrari, and I had sat down for a while in the empty chair beside Leo so as not to get maneuvered into dancing with Mrs Patimkin, which seemed to be the direction towards which things were moving.

'You're Brenda's boy friend? Huh?' Leo said.

I nodded—earlier in the evening I'd stopped giving blushing explanations. 'You gotta deal there, boy,' Leo said, 'you don't louse it up.'

'She's very beautiful,' I said.

Leo poured himself a glass of champagne, and then waited as though he expected a head to form on it; when one didn't, he filled the glass to the brim.

'Beautiful, not beautiful, what's the difference. I'm a practical man. I'm on the bottom, so I gotta be. You're Aly Khan you worry about marrying movie stars. I wasn't born yesterday . . . You know how old I was when I got married? Thirty-five years old. I don't know what the hell kind of hurry I was in.' He drained his glass and refilled it. 'I'll tell you something, one good thing happened to me in my whole life. Two maybe. Before I came back from overseas I got a letter from my wife—she wasn't my wife then. My mother-in-law found an apartment for us in Queens. Sixty-two fifty a month it cost. That's the last good thing that happened.'

'What was the first?'

'What first?'

'You said *two* things,' I said.

'I don't remember. I say two because my wife tells me I'm sarcastic and a cynic. That way maybe she won't think I'm such a wise guy.'

I saw Brenda and Ferrari separate, and so excused myself and started for Brenda, but just then Mr Patimkin separated from Julie and it looked as though the two men were going to switch partners. Instead the four of them stood on the dance floor and when I reached them they were laughing and Julie was saying, 'What's so funny!' Ferrari said 'Hi' to me and whisked Julie away, which sent her into peals of laughter.

Mr Patimkin had one hand on Brenda's back and suddenly the other one was on mine. 'You kids having a good time?' he said.

We were sort of swaying, the three of us, to 'Get Me to the Church on Time.'

Brenda kissed her father. 'Yes,' she said. 'I'm so drunk my head doesn't even need my neck.'

'It's a fine wedding, Mr Patimkin.'

'You want anything just ask me . . .' he said, a little drunken himself. 'You're two good kids . . . How do you like that brother of yours getting married? . . . Huh? . . . Is that a girl or is that a girl?'

Brenda smiled, and though she apparently thought her father had spoken of her, I was sure he'd been referring to Harriet.

'You like weddings, Daddy?' Brenda said.

'I like my kids' weddings . . .' He slapped me on the back. 'You two kids, you want anything? Go have a good time. Remember,' he said to

Brenda, 'you're my honey . . .' Then he looked at me. 'Whatever my Buck wants is good enough for me. There's no business too big it can't use another head.'

I smiled, though not directly at him, and beyond I could see Leo sopping up champagne and watching the three of us; when he caught my eye he made a sign with his hand, a circle with his thumb and fore-finger, indicating, 'That a boy, that a boy!'

After Mr Patimkin departed, Brenda and I danced closely, and we only sat down when the waiters began to circulate with the main course. The head table was noisy, particularly at our end where the men were almost all team-mates of Ron's, in one sport or another; they ate a fantastic number of rolls. Tank Feldman, Ron's roommate, who had flown in from Toledo, kept sending the waiter back for rolls, for celery, for olives, and always to the squealing delight of Gloria Feldman, his wife, a nervous, undernourished girl who continually looked down the front of her gown as though there was some sort of construction project going on under her clothes. Gloria and Tank, in fact, seemed to be self-appointed precinct captains at our end. They proposed toasts, burst into wild song, and continually referred to Brenda and me as 'love birds.' Brenda smiled at this with her eyeteeth and I brought up a cheery look from some fraudulent auricle of my heart.

And the night continued: we ate, we drank, we danced—Rose and Pearl did the Charleston with one another (while their husbands examined woodwork and chandeliers), and then I did the Charleston with none other than Gloria Feldman, who made coy, hideous faces at me all the time we danced. Near the end of the evening, Brenda, who'd been drinking champagne like her Uncle Leo, did a Rita Hayworth tango with herself, and Julie fell asleep on some ferns she'd whisked off the head table and made into a mattress at the far end of the hall. I felt a numbness creep into my hard palate, and by three o'clock people were dancing in their coats, shoeless ladies were wrap-ping hunks of wedding cake in napkins for their children's lunch, and finally Gloria Feldman made her way over to our end of the table and said, freshly, 'Well, our little Radcliffe smarty, what have *you* been doing all summer?'

'Growing a penis.'

Gloria smiled and left as quickly as she'd come, and Brenda without another word headed shakily away for the ladies' room and the rewards of overindulgence. No sooner had she left than Leo was beside me, a glass in one hand, a new bottle of champagne in the other.

'No sign of the bride and groom?' he said, leering. He'd lost most of his consonants by this time and was doing the best he could with long, wet vowels. 'Well, you're next, kid, I see it in the cards . . . You're nobody's sucker . . .' And he stabbed me in the side with the top of the bottle, spilling champagne onto the side of my rented tux. He straightened up, poured more onto his hand and glass, but then suddenly he stopped. He was looking into the lights which were hidden beneath a long bank of flowers that adorned the front of the table. He shook the bottle in his hand as though to make it fizz. 'The son of a bitch who invented the fluorescent bulb should drop dead!' He set the bottle down and drank.

Up on the stage Harry Winters brought his musicians to a halt. The drummer stood up, stretched, and they all began to open up cases and put their instruments away. On the floor, relatives, friends, associates, were holding each other around the waists and the shoulders, and small children huddled around their parents' legs. A couple of kids ran in and out of the crowd, screaming at tag, until one was grabbed by an adult and slapped soundly on the behind. He began to cry, and couple by couple the floor emptied. Our table was a tangle of squashed everything: napkins, fruits, flowers; there were empty whiskey bottles, droopy ferns, and dishes puddled with unfinished cherry jubilee, gone sticky with the hours. At the end of the table Mr Patimkin was sitting next to his wife, holding her hand. Opposite them, on two bridge chairs that had been pulled up, sat Mr and Mrs Ehrlich. They spoke quietly and evenly, as though they had known each other for years and years. Everything had slowed down now, and from time to time people would come up to the Patimkins and Ehrlichs, wish them *mazel tov*, and then drag themselves and their families out into the September night, which was cool and windy, someone said, and reminded me that soon would come winter and snow.

'They never wear out, those things, you know that.' Leo was

pointing to the fluorescent lights that shone through the flowers. 'They last for years. They could make a car like that if they wanted, that could never wear out. It would run on water in the summer and snow in the winter. But they wouldn't do it, the big boys . . . Look at me,' Leo said, splashing his suit front with champagne. 'I sell a good bulb. You can't get the kind of bulb I sell in the drugstores. It's a quality bulb. But I'm the little guy. I don't even own a car. His brother, and I don't even own an automobile. I take a train wherever I go. I'm the only guy I know who wears out three pairs of rubbers every winter. Most guys get new ones when they lose the old ones. I wear them out, like shoes. Look,' he said, leaning into me, 'I could sell a crappy bulb, it wouldn't break my heart. But it's not good business.'

The Ehrlichs and Patimkins scraped back their chairs and headed away, all except Mr Patimkin who came down the table towards Leo and me.

He slapped Leo on the back. 'Well, how you doing, *shtarke*?'

'All right, Ben. All right . . .'

'You have a good time?'

'You had a nice affair, Ben, it must've cost a pretty penny, believe me . . .'

Mr Patimkin laughed. 'When I make out my income tax I go to see Leo. He knows just how much money I spent . . . You need a ride home?' he asked me.

'No, thanks. I'm waiting for Brenda. We have my car.'

'Good night,' Mr Patimkin said.

I watched him step down off the platform that held the head table, and then start towards the exit. Now the only people in the hall—the shambles of a hall—were myself, Leo, and his wife and child who slept, both of them, with their heads pillowed on a crumpled tablecloth at a table down on the floor before us. Brenda still wasn't around.

'When you got it,' Leo said, rubbing his fingers together, 'you can afford to talk like a big shot. Who needs a guy like me any more. Salesmen, you spit on them. you can go to the supermarket and buy anything. Where my wife shops you can buy sheets and pillowcases. Imagine, a grocery store! Me, I sell to gas stations, factories, small businesses, all up and down the east coast. Sure, you can sell a guy in a gas

station a crappy bulb that'll burn out in a week. For inside the pumps
I'm talking, it takes a certain kind of bulb. A utility bulb. All right, so
you sell him a crappy bulb, and then a week later he puts in a new one,
and while he's screwing it in he still remembers your name. Not me.
I sell a quality bulb. It lasts a month, five weeks, before it even flick-
ers, then it gives you another couple of days, dim maybe, but so you
shouldn't go blind. It hangs on, it's a quality bulb. Before it even burns
out you notice it's getting darker, so you put a new one in. What
people don't like is when one minute it's sunlight and the next dark.
Let it glimmer a few days and they don't feel so bad. Nobody ever
throws out my bulb—they figure they'll save them, can always use
them in a pinch. Sometimes I say to a guy, you ever throw out a bulb
you bought from Leo Patimkin? You gotta use psychology. That's
why I'm sending my kid to college. You don't know a little psychology these days, you're licked . . .'

He lifted an arm and pointed out to his wife; then he slumped
down in his seat. 'Aaach!' he said, and drank off half a glass of champagne. 'I'll tell you, I go as far as New London, Connecticut. That's as
far as I'll go, and when I come home at night I stop first for a couple
of drinks. Martinis. Two I have, sometimes three. That seems fair,
don't it? But to her a little sip or a bathtubful, it smells the same. She
says it's bad for the kid if I come home smelling. The kid's a baby, for
God's sake, she thinks that's the way I'm *supposed* to smell. A forty-
eight-year-old man with a three-year-old kid! She'll give me a
thrombosis that kid. My wife, she wants me to come home early and
play with the kid before she goes to bed. Come home, she says, and *I'll*
make you a drink. Hah! I spend all day sniffing gas, leaning under
hoods with grimy *poilishehs* in New London, trying to force a lousy
bulb into a socket—I'll screw it in myself, I tell them—and she thinks
I want to come home and drink a martini from a jelly glass! How long
are you going to stay in bars, she says. Till a Jewish girl is Miss
Rheingold!

'Look,' he went on after another drink, 'I love my kid like Ben loves
his Brenda. It's not that I don't want to play with her. But if I play with
the kid and then at night get into bed with my wife, then she can't
expect fancy things from me. It's one or the other. I'm no movie star.'

Leo looked at his empty glass and put it on the table; he tilted the bottle up and drank the champagne like soda water. 'How much do you think I make a week?' he said.

'I don't know.'

'Take a guess.'

'A hundred dollars.'

'Sure, and tomorrow they're gonna let the lions out of the cage in Central Park. What do you think I make?'

'I can't tell.'

'A cabdriver makes more than me. That's a fact. My wife's brother is a cabdriver, *he* lives in Kew Gardens. And he don't take no crap, no sir, not those cabbies. Last week it was raining one night and I said the hell with it, I'm taking a cab. I'd been all day in Newton, Mass. I don't usually go so far, but on the train in the morning I said to myself, stay on, go further, it'll be a change. And I know all the time I'm kidding myself. I wouldn't even make up the extra fare it cost me. But I stay on. And at night I still had a couple boxes with me, so when the guy pulls up at Grand Central there's like a genie inside me says get in. I even threw the bulbs in, not even caring if they broke. And this cabbie says, Whatya want to do, buddy, rip the leather? Those are brand new seats I got. No, I said. Jesus Christ, he says, some goddam people. I get in and give him a Queens address which ought to shut him up, but no, all the way up the Drive he was Jesus Christing me. It's hot in the cab, so I open a window and *then* he turns around and says, Whatya want to do, give me a cold in the neck? I just got over a goddam cold . . .' Leo looked at me, bleary-eyed. 'This city is crazy! If I had a little money I'd get out of here in a minute. I'd go to California. They don't need bulbs out there it's so light. I went to New Guinea during the war from San Francisco. *There*,' he burst, 'there is the other good thing that happened to me, that night in San Francisco with this Hannah Schreiber. That's the both of them, you asked me I'm telling you—the apartment my mother-in-law got us, and this Hannah ·Schreiber. One night was all. I went to a B'nai Brith dance for servicemen in the basement of some big temple, and I met her. I wasn't married then, so don't make faces.'

'I'm not.'

'She had a nice little room by herself. She was going to school to be a teacher. Already I knew something was up because she let me feel inside her slip in the cab. Listen to me, I sound like I'm always in cabs. Maybe two other times in my life. To tell the truth I don't even enjoy it. All the time I'm riding I'm watching the meter. Even the pleasures I can't enjoy!'

'What about Hannah Schreiber?'

He smiled, flashing some gold in his mouth. 'How do you like that name? She was only a girl, but she had an old lady's name. In the room she says to me she believes in oral love. I can still hear her: Leo Patimkin, I believe in oral love. I don't know what the hell she means. I figure she was one of those Christian Scientists or some cult or something. So I said, But what about for soldiers, guys going overseas who may get killed, God forbid.' He shrugged his shoulders. 'The smartest guy in the world I wasn't. But that's twenty years almost, I was still wet behind the ears. I'll tell you, every once in a while my wife—you know, she does for me what Hannah Schreiber did. I don't like to force her, she works hard. That to her is like a cab to me. I wouldn't force her. I can remember every time, I'll bet. Once after a Seder, my mother was still living, she should rest in peace. My wife was up to here with Mogen David. In fact, *twice* after Seders. Aachhh! Everything good in my life I can count on my fingers! God forbid someone should leave me a million dollars, I wouldn't even have to take off my shoes. I got a whole other hand yet.'

He pointed to the fluorescent bulbs with the nearly empty champagne bottle. 'You call that a light? That's a light to *read* by? It's purple, for God's sake! Half the blind men in the world ruined themselves by those damn things. You know who's behind them? The optometrists! I'll tell you, if I could get a couple hundred for all my stock and the territory, I'd sell tomorrow. That's right, Leo A. Patimkin, one semester accounting, City College nights, will sell equipment, territory, good name. I'll buy two inches in the *Times*. The territory is from here to everywhere. I go where I want, my own boss, no one tells me what to do. You know the Bible? "Let there be a light—and there's Leo Patimkin!" That's my trademark, I'll sell that too. I tell them that slogan, the *poilishehs*, they think I'm making it up. What good is it to be smart unless you're in on the ground floor! I got more brains in my pinky than Ben got in his whole *head*. Why is it he's on top and I'm on the bottom! *Why!* Believe me, if you're born lucky, you're lucky!' And then he exploded into silence.

I had the feeling that he was going to cry, so I leaned over and whispered to him, 'You better go home.' He agreed, but I had to raise him out of his seat and steer him by one arm down to his wife and child. The little girl could not be awakened, and Leo and Bea asked me to watch her while they went out into the lobby to get their coats. When they returned, Leo seemed to have dragged himself back to the level of human communication. He shook my hand with real feeling. I was very touched.

'You'll go far,' he said to me. 'You're a smart boy, you'll play it safe. Don't louse things up.'

'I won't.'

'Next time we see you it'll be *your* wedding,' and he winked at me. Bea stood alongside, muttering goodbye all the while he spoke. He shook my hand again and then picked the child out of her seat, and they turned towards the door. From the back, round-shouldered, burdened, child-carrying, they looked like people fleeing a captured city.

Brenda, I discovered, was asleep on a couch in the lobby. It was almost four o'clock and the two of us and the desk clerk were the only ones in the hotel lobby. At first I did not waken Brenda, for she was pale and wilted and I knew she had been sick. I sat beside her, smoothing her hair back off her ears. How would I ever come to know her, I wondered, for as she slept I felt I knew no more of her than what I could see in a photograph. I stirred her gently and in a half-sleep she walked beside me out to the car.

It was almost dawn when we came out of the Jersey side of the Lincoln Tunnel. I switched down to my parking lights, and drove on to the Turnpike, and there out before me I could see the swampy meadows that spread for miles and miles, watery, blotchy, smelly, like an oversight of God. I thought of that other oversight, Leo Patimkin, half-brother to Ben. In a few hours he would be on a train heading north, and as he passed Scarsdale and White Plains, he would belch and taste champagne and let the flavor linger in his mouth. Alongside him on the seat, like another passenger, would be cartons of bulbs. He would get off at New London, or maybe, inspired by the sight of his half-brother, he would stay on again, hoping for some new luck further north. For the world was Leo's territory, every city, every swamp, every road and highway. He could go on to Newfoundland if he wanted, Hudson Bay, and on up to Thule, and then slide down the other side of the globe and rap on frosted windows on the Russian steppes, if he wanted. But he wouldn't. Leo was forty-eight years old and he had learned. He pursued discomfort and sorrow, all right, but if you had a heartful by the time you reached New London, what new awfulness could you look forward to in Vladivostok?

The next day the wind was blowing the fall in and the branches of the weeping willow were fingering at the Patimkin front lawn. I drove Brenda to the train at noon, and she left me.

8

Autumn came quickly. It was cold and in Jersey the leaves turned and fell overnight. The following Saturday I took a ride up to see the deer, and did not even get out of the car, for it was too brisk to be standing at the wire fence, and so I watched the animals walk and run in the dimness of the late afternoon, and after a while everything, even the objects of nature, the trees, the clouds, the grass, the weeds, reminded me of Brenda, and I drove back down to Newark. Already we had sent our first letters and I had called her late one night, but in the mail and on the phone we had some difficulty discovering one another; we had not the style yet. That night I tried her again, and someone on her floor said she was out and would not be in till late.

Upon my return to the library I was questioned by Mr Scapello about the Gauguin book. The jowly gentleman *had* sent a nasty letter about my discourtesy, and I was only able to extricate myself by offering a confused story in an indignant tone. In fact, I even managed to turn it around so that Mr Scapello was apologizing to me as he led me up to my new post, there among the encyclopedias, the bibliographies, the indexes and guides. My bullying surprised me, and I wondered if some of it had not been learned from Mr Patimkin that morning I'd heard him giving Grossman an earful on the phone. Perhaps I was more of a businessman than I thought. Maybe I could learn to become a Patimkin with ease . . .

Days passed slowly; I never did see the colored kid again, and when, one noon, I looked in the stacks, Gauguin was gone, apparently charged out finally by the jowly man. I wondered what it had been like that day the colored kid had discovered the book was gone. Had he cried? For some reason I imagined that he had blamed it on me, but then I realized that I was confusing the dream I'd had with reality. Chances were he had discovered someone else, Van Gogh, Vermeer . . . But no, they were not his kind of artists. What had probably happened was that he'd given up on the library and gone back to playing Willie Mays in the streets. He was better off, I thought. No sense in carrying dreams of Tahiti in your head, if you can't afford the fare.

Let's see, what else did I do? I ate, I slept, I went to the movies, I sent broken-spined books to the bindery—I did everything I'd ever done before, but now each activity was surrounded by a fence, existed alone, and my life consisted of jumping from one fence to the next. There was no flow, for that had been Brenda.

And then Brenda wrote saying that she could be coming in for the Jewish holidays which were only a week away. I was so overjoyed I wanted to call Mr and Mrs Patimkin, just to tell them of my pleasure. However, when I got to the phone and had actually dialed the first two letters, I knew that at the other end there would be silence; if there was anything said, it would only be Mrs Patimkin asking, 'What is it you want?' Mr Patimkin had probably forgotten my name.

That night, after dinner, I gave Aunt Gladys a kiss and told her she shouldn't work so hard.

'In less than a week it's Rosh Hashana and he thinks I should take a vacation. Ten people I'm having. What do you think, a chicken cleans itself? Thank God, the holidays come once a year, I'd be an old woman before my time.'

But then it was only nine people Aunt Gladys was having, for only two days after her letter Brenda called.

'Oy, Gut!' Aunt Gladys called. 'Long *distance!*'

'Hello?' I said.

'Hello, sweetie?'

'Yes,' I said.

'What *is* it?' Aunt Gladys tugged at my shirt. 'What is it?'

'It's for me.'

'Who?' Aunt Gladys said, pointing into the receiver.

'Brenda,' I said.

'Yes?' Brenda said.

'Brenda?' Aunt Gladys said. 'What does she call long distance, I almost had a heart attack.'

'Because she's in Boston,' I said. 'Please, Aunt Gladys . . .'

And Aunt Gladys walked off, mumbling, 'These kids . . .'

'Hello,' I said again into the phone.

'Neil, how are you?'

'I love you.'

'Neil, I have bad news. I can't come in this week.'

'But, honey, it's the Jewish holidays.'

'Sweet*heart*,' she laughed.

'Can't you say that, for an excuse?'

'I have a test Saturday, and a paper, and you know if I went home I wouldn't get anything done . . .'

'You would.'

'Neil, I just *can't*. My mother'd make me go to Temple, and I wouldn't even have enough time to see *you*.'

'Oh God, Brenda.'

'Sweetie?'

'Yes?'

'Can't you come up here?' she asked.

'I'm working.'

'The Jewish holidays,' she said.

'Honey, I can't. Last year I didn't take them off, I can't all—'

'You can say you had a conversion.'

'Besides, my aunt's having all the family for dinner, and you know what with my parents—'

'Come up, Neil.'

'I can't just take two days off, Bren. I just got promoted and a raise—'

'The hell with the raise.'

'Baby, it's my job.'

'Forever?' she said.

'No.'

'Then come. I've got a hotel room.'

'For me?'

'For us.'

'Can you do that?'

'No and yes. People do it.'

'Brenda, you tempt me.'

'Be tempted.'

'I could take a train Wednesday right from work.'

'You could stay till Sunday night.'

'Bren, I can't. I still have to be back to work on Saturday.'

'Don't you ever get a day *off*?' she said.

'Tuesdays,' I said glumly.

'God.'

'And Sunday,' I added.

Brenda said something but I did not hear her, for Aunt Gladys called, 'You talk all day long distance?'

'Quiet!' I shouted back to her.

'Neil, will you?'

'Damn it, yes,' I said.

'Are you angry?'

'I don't think so. I'm going to come up.'

'Till Sunday.'

'We'll see.'

'Don't feel upset, Neil. You sound upset. It is the Jewish holidays. I mean you *should* be off.'

'That's right,' I said. 'I'm an orthodox Jew, for God's sake. I ought to take advantage of it.'

'That's right,' she said.

'Is there a train around six?'

'Every hour, I think.'

'Then I'll be on the one that leaves at six.'

'I'll be on the station,' she said. 'How will I know you?'

'I'll be disguised as an orthodox Jew.'

'Me too,' she said.

'Good night, love,' I said.

Aunt Gladys cried when I told her I was going away for Rosh Hashana.

'And I was preparing a big meal,' she said.

'You can still prepare it.'

'What will I tell your mother?'

'I'll tell her, Aunt Gladys. Please. You have no right to get upset . . .'

'Someday you'll have a family you'll know what it's like.'

'I have a family now.'

'What's a matter,' she said, blowing her nose, 'That girl couldn't come home to see her family it's the holidays?'

'She's in school, she just can't—'

'If she loved her family she'd find time. We don't live six hundred years.'

'She does love her family.'

'Then one day a year you could break your heart and pay a visit.'

'Aunt Gladys, you don't understand.'

'Sure,' she said, 'when I'm twenty-three years old I'll understand everything.'

I went to kiss her and she said, 'Go away from me, go run to Boston . . .'

The next morning I discovered that Mr Scapello didn't want me to leave on Rosh Hashana either, but I unnerved him, I think, by hinting that his coldness about my taking the two days off might just be so much veiled anti-Semitism, so on the whole he was easier to manage. At lunch time I took a walk down to Penn Station and picked up a train schedule to Boston. That was my bedtime reading for the next three nights.

She did not look like Brenda, at least for the first minute. And probably to her I did not look like me. But we kissed and held each other, and it was strange to feel the thickness of our coats between us.

'I'm letting my hair grow,' she said in the cab, and that in fact was all she said. Not until I helped her out of the cab did I notice the thin gold band shining on her left hand.

She hung back, strolling casually about the lobby while I signed the register 'Mr and Mrs Neil Klugman,' and then in the room we kissed again.

'Your heart's pounding,' I said to her.

'I know,' she said.

'Are you nervous?'

'No.'

'Have you done this before?' I said.

'I read Mary McCarthy.'

She took off her coat and instead of putting it in the closet, she tossed it across the chair. I sat down on the bed; she didn't.

'What's the matter?'

Brenda took a deep breath and walked over to the window, and I thought that perhaps it would be best for me to ask nothing—for us to get used to each other's presence in quiet. I hung her coat and mine in the empty closet, and left the suitcases—mine and hers—standing by the bed.

Brenda was kneeling backwards in the chair, looking out the window as though out the window was where she'd rather be. I came up behind her and put my hands around her body and held her breasts, and when I felt the cool draft that swept under the sill, I realized how long it had been since that first warm night when I had put my arms around her and felt the tiny wings beating in her back. And then I realized why I'd really come to Boston—it had been long enough. It was time to stop kidding about marriage.

'Is something the matter?' I said.

'Yes.'

It wasn't the answer I'd expected; I wanted no answer really, only to soothe her nervousness with my concern.

But I asked, 'What is it? Why didn't you mention it on the phone?'

'It only happened today.'

'School?'

'Home. They found out about us.'

I turned her face up to mine. 'That's okay. I told my aunt I was coming here too. What's the difference.'

'About the summer. About our sleeping together.'

'Oh?'

'Yes.'

'. . . Ron?'

'No.'

'That night, you mean, did Julie—'

'No,' she said, 'it wasn't *anybody*.'

'I don't get it.'

Brenda got up and walked over to the bed where she sat down on the edge. I sat in the chair.

'My mother found the thing.'

'The diaphragm?'

She nodded.

'When?' I asked.

'The other day, I guess.' She walked to the bureau and opened her purse. 'Here, you can read them in the order I got them.' She tossed an envelope at me; it was dirty-edged and crumpled, as though it had been in and out of her pockets a good many times. 'I got this one this morning,' she said. 'Special delivery.'

I took out the letter and read:

PATIMKIN KITCHEN AND BATHROOM SINKS
'Any Size—Any Shape'

Dear Brenda—

Don't pay any Attention to your Mother's Letter when you get it. I love you honey if you want a coat I'll buy You a coat. You could always have anything you wanted. We have every faith in you so you won't be too upset by what your mother says in her Letter. Of course she is a little hystericall because of the shock and she has been Working so hard for Hadassah. She is a Woman and it is hard for her to understand some of the Shocks in life. Of course I can't say We weren't all surprised because from the beginning I was nice to him and Thought he would appreciate the nice vacation we supplied for him. Some People never turn out the way you hope and pray but I am willing to forgive and call Buy Gones, Buy Gones, You have always up till now been a good Buck and got good scholastic Grades and Ron has always been what we wanted a Good Boy, most important, and a Nice boy. This late in my life believe me I am not going to start hating my own flesh and blood. As for your mistake it takes Two to make a mistake and now that you will be away at school and from him and what you got involved in you will probably do all right I have every faith you will. You have to have faith in your children like in a Business or any serious undertaking and there is nothing that is so bad that we can't forgive especially when Our own flesh and blood is involved. We have a nice close nitt family and why not???? Have a nice Holiday and in Temple I will say a Prayer for you as I do every year. On Monday I want you to go into Boston and buy a coat. Whatever you need because I know how Cold it gets up where you are . . . Give my regards to Linda and remember to bring her home with you on Thanksgiving like last year. You two had such a nice time. I have always never said bad things about any of your friends or Rons and that this should happen is only the exception that proves the rule. Have a Happy Holiday.

YOUR FATHER

And then it was signed BEN PATIMKIN, but that was crossed out and written beneath 'Your Father' were again, like an echo, the words, 'Your Father.'

'Who's Linda?' I asked.

'My roommate, last year.' She tossed another envelope to me. 'Here. I got this one in the afternoon. Air Mail.'

The letter was from Brenda's mother. I started to read it and then put it down a moment. 'You got this *after*?'

'Yes,' she said. 'When I got his I didn't know what was happening. Read hers.'

I began again.

Dear Brenda:

I don't even know how to begin. I have been crying all morning and have had to skip my board meeting this afternoon because my eyes are so red. I never thought this would happen to a daughter of mine. I wonder if you know what I mean, if it is at least on your conscience, so I won't have to degrade either of us with a description. All I can say is that this morning when I was cleaning out the drawers and putting away your summer clothing I came upon something in your bottom drawer, *under* some sweaters which you probably remember leaving there. I cried the minute I saw it and I haven't stopped crying yet. Your father called a while ago and now he is driving home because he heard how upset I was on the phone.

I don't know what we ever did that you should reward us this way. We gave you a nice home and all the love and respect a child needs. I always was proud when you were a little girl that you could take care of yourself so well. You took care of Julie so beautifully it was a treat to see, when you were only fourteen years old. But you drifted away from your family, even though we sent you to the best schools and gave you the best money could buy. Why you should reward us this way is a question I'll carry with me to the grave.

About your friend I have no words. He is his parents' responsibility and I cannot imagine what kind of home life he had that he could act that way. Certainly that was a fine way to repay us for the hospitality we were nice enough to show to him, a perfect stranger. That the two of you should be carrying on like that in our very house I will never in my life be able to understand. Times certainly have changed since I was a girl that this kind of thing could go on. I keep asking myself if at least you didn't think of us while you were doing that. If not for me, how could you do this to your father? God forbid Julie should ever learn of this.

God only knows what you have been doing all these years we put our trust in you.

You have broken your parents' hearts and you should know that. This is some thank you for all we gave you.

MOTHER

She only signed 'Mother' once, and that was in an extraordinarily miniscule hand, like a whisper.

'Brenda,' I said.

'What?'

'Are you starting to cry?'

'No. I cried already.'

'Don't start again.'

'I'm trying not to, for God's sake.'

'Okay . . . Brenda, can I ask you one question?'

'What?'

'Why did you leave it home?'

'Because I didn't plan on using it here, that's why.'

'Suppose I'd come up. I mean I have come up, what about that?'

'I thought I'd come down first.'

'So then couldn't you have carried it down then? Like a tooth-brush?'

'Are you trying to be funny?'

'No. I'm just asking you why you left it home.'

'I told you,' Brenda said. 'I thought I'd come home.'

'But, Brenda, that doesn't make any sense. Suppose you did come home, and then you came back again. Wouldn't you have taken it with you then?'

'I don't *know*.'

'Don't get angry,' I said.

'You're the one who's angry.'

'I'm upset, I'm not angry.'

'I'm upset then too.'

I did not answer but walked to the window and looked out. The stars and moon were out, silver and hard, and from the window I could see over to the Harvard campus where lights burned and then seemed to flicker when the trees blew across them.

'Brenda . . .'

'What?'

'Knowing how your mother feels about you, wasn't it silly to leave it home? Risky?'

'What does how she feels about me have to do with it?'

'You can't trust her.'

'Why can't I?'

'Don't you see. You *can't.*'

'Neil, she was only cleaning out the drawers.'

'Didn't you know she would?'

'She never did before. Or maybe she did. Neil, I couldn't think of everything. We slept together night after night and nobody heard or noticed—'

'Brenda, why the hell are you willfully confusing things?'

'I'm not!'

'Okay,' I said softly. 'All right.'

'It's you who's confusing things,' Brenda said. 'You act as though I wanted her to find it.'

I didn't answer.

'Do you believe *that?*' she said, after neither of us had spoken for a full minute.

'I don't know.'

'Oh, Neil, you're *crazy.*'

'What was crazier than leaving that damn thing around?'

'It was an oversight.'

'Now it's an oversight, before it was deliberate.'

'It was an oversight about the drawer. It wasn't an oversight about leaving it,' she said.

'Brenda, sweetheart, wouldn't the safest, smartest, easiest, simplest thing been to have taken it with you? Wouldn't it?'

'It didn't make any difference either way.'

'Brenda, this is the most frustrating argument of my life!'

'You keep making it seem as though I *wanted* her to find it. Do you think I need this? Do you? I can't even go home any more.'

'Is that so?'

'Yes!'

'No,' I said. 'You can go home—your father will be waiting with two coats and a half-dozen dresses.'

'What about my mother?'

'It'll be the same with her.'

'Don't be absurd. How can I face them!'

'Why can't you face them? Did you do anything wrong?'

'Neil, look at the reality of the thing, will you?'

'*Did* you do anything wrong?'

'Neil, *they* think it's wrong. They're my parents.'

'But do you think it's wrong—'

'That doesn't *matter.*'

'It does to me, Brenda . . .'

'Neil, why are *you* confusing things? You keep accusing me of things.'

'Damn it, Brenda, you're guilty of some things.'

'*What?*'

'Of leaving that damn diaphragm there. How can you call it an oversight!'

'Oh, Neil, don't start any of that psychoanalytic crap!'

'Then why else did you do it? You wanted her to find it!'

'Why?'

'I don't know, Brenda, *why?*'

'Oh!' she said, and she picked up the pillow and threw it back on to the bed.

'What happens now, Bren?' I said.

'What does that mean?'

'Just that. What happens now?'

She rolled over on to the bed and buried her head in it.

'Don't start crying,' I said.

'I'm *not.*'

I was still holding the letters and took Mr Patimkin's from its envelope.

'Why does your father capitalize all these letters?'

She didn't answer.

'"As for your mistake,"' I read aloud to Brenda, '"it takes Two to make a mistake and now that you will be away at school and from him and what you got involved in you will probably do all right I have every faith you will. Your father. Your father."'

She turned and looked at me; but silently.

'"I have always never said bad things about any of your friends or Rons and that this should happen is only the exception that proves the rule. Have a Happy Holiday."' I stopped; in Brenda's face there was positively no threat of tears; she looked, suddenly, solid and decisive. 'Well, what are you going to do?' I asked.

'Nothing.'

'Who are you going to bring home Thanksgiving—Linda?' I said, 'or me?'

'Who *can* I bring home, Neil?'

'I don't know, who can you?'

'Can I bring you home?'

'I don't know,' I said, 'can you?'

'Stop repeating the question!'

'I sure as hell can't give you the answer.'

'Neil, be realistic. After this, can I bring you home? Can you see us all sitting around the table?'

'I can't if you can't, and I can if you can.'

'Are you going to speak Zen, for God's sake!'

'Brenda, the choices aren't mine. You can bring Linda or me. You can go home or not go home. That's another choice. Then you don't even have to worry about choosing between me and Linda.'

'Neil, you don't understand. They're still my parents. They did send me to the best schools, didn't they? They have given me everything I've wanted, haven't they?'

'Yes.'

'Then how can I not go home? I *have* to go home.'

'Why?'

'You don't understand. Your parents don't bother you any more. You're lucky.'

'Oh, sure. I live with my crazy aunt, that's a real bargain.'

'Families are different. You don't understand.'

'Goddamit, I understand more than you think. I understand why the hell you left that thing lying around. Don't you? Can't you put two and two together?'

'Neil, what are you talking about! You're the one who doesn't understand. You're the one who from the very beginning was accusing me of things? Remember? Isn't it so? Why don't you have your eyes fixed? Why don't you have this fixed, that fixed? As if it were my fault that I *could* have them fixed. You kept acting as if I was going to run away from you every minute. And now you're doing it again, telling me I planted that thing on purpose.'

'I loved you, Brenda, so I cared.'

'I loved *you*. That's why I got that damn thing in the first place.'

And then we heard the tense in which we'd spoken and we settled back into ourselves and silence.

A few minutes later I picked up my bag and put on my coat. I think Brenda was crying too when I went out the door.

Instead of grabbing a cab immediately, I walked down the street and out towards the Harvard Yard which I had never seen before. I entered one of the gates and then headed out along a path, under the tired autumn foliage and the dark sky. I wanted to be alone, in the dark; not because I wanted to think about anything, but rather because, for just a while, I wanted to think about nothing. I walked clear across the Yard and up a little hill and then I was standing in front of the Lamont Library, which, Brenda had once told me, had Patimkin Sinks in its rest rooms. From the light of the lamp on the path behind me I could see my reflection in the glass front of the building. Inside, it was dark and there were no students to be seen, no librarians. Suddenly, I wanted to set down my suitcase and pick up a rock and heave it right through the glass, but of course I didn't. I simply looked at myself in the mirror the light made of the window. I was only that substance, I thought, those limbs, that face that I saw in front of me. I looked, but the outside of me gave up little information about the inside of me. I wished I could scoot around to the other side of the window, faster than light or sound or Herb Clark on Homecoming Day, to get behind that image and catch whatever it was that looked through those eyes. What was it inside me that had turned pursuit and clutch-ing into love, and then turned it inside out again? What was it that had turned winning into losing, and losing—who knows—into winning? I was sure I had loved Brenda, though standing there, I knew I could-n't any longer. And I knew it would be a long while before I made love to anyone the way I had made love to her. With anyone else, could I summon up such a passion? Whatever spawned my love for her, had that spawned such lust too? If she had only been slightly *not* Brenda . . . but then would I have loved her? I looked hard at the image of me, at that darkening of the glass, and then my gaze pushed through it, over the cool floor, to a broken wall of books, imperfectly shelved.

I did not look very much longer, but took a train that got me into Newark just as the sun was rising on the first day of the Jewish New Year. I was back in plenty of time for work.

1959

A Long Day in November

ERNEST J. GAINES

1

Somebody is shaking me but I don't want get up now, because I'm tired and I'm sleepy and I don't want get up now. It's warm under the cover here, but it's cold up there and I don't want get up now.

'Sonny?' I hear.

But I don't want get up, because it's cold up there. The cover is over my head and I'm under the sheet and the blanket and the quilt. It's warm under here and it's dark, because my eyes's shut. I keep my eyes shut because I don't want get up.

'Sonny?' I hear.

I don't know who's calling me, but it must be Mama because I'm home. I don't know who it is because I'm still asleep, but it must be Mama. She's shaking me by the foot. She's holding my ankle through the cover.

'Wake up, honey,' she says.

But I don't want get up because it's cold up there and I don't want get cold. I try to go back to sleep, but she shakes my foot again.

'Hummm?' I say.

'Wake up, honey,' I hear.

'Hummm?' I say.

'I want you get up and wee-wee,' she says.

'I don't want wee-wee, Mama,' I say.

'Come on,' she says, shaking me. 'Come on. Get up for Mama.'

'It's cold up there,' I say.

'Come on,' she says. 'Mama won't let her baby get cold.'

I pull the sheet and blanket from under my head and push them back over my shoulder. I feel the cold and I try to cover up again, but

Mama grabs the cover before I get it over me. Mama is standing 'side the bed and she's looking down at me, smiling. The room is dark. The lamp's on the mantelpiece, but it's kind of low. I see Mama's shadow on the wall over by Gran'mon's picture.

'I'm cold, Mama,' I say.

'Mama go'n wrap his little coat round her baby,' she says.

She goes over and get it off the chair where all my clothes's at, and I sit up in the bed. Mama brings the coat and put it on me, and she fastens some of the buttons.

'Now,' she says. 'See? You warm.'

I gap' and look at Mama. She hugs me real hard and rubs her face against my face. My mama's face is warm and soft, and it feels good.

'I want my socks on,' I say. 'My feet go'n get cold on the floor.'

Mama leans over and get my shoes from under the bed. She takes out my socks and slip them on my feet. I gap' and look at Mama pulling my socks up.

'Now,' she says.

I get up but I can still feel that cold floor. I get on my knees and look under the bed for my pot.

'See it?' Mama says.

'Hanh?'

'See it under there?'

'Hanh?'

'I bet you didn't bring it in,' she says. 'Any time you sound like that you done forgot it.'

'I left it on the chicken coop,' I say.

'Well, go to the back door,' Mama says. 'Hurry up before you get cold.'

I get off my knees and go back there, but it's too dark and I can't see. I come back where Mama's sitting on my bed.

'It's dark back there, Mama,' I say. 'I might trip over something.'

Mama takes a deep breath and gets the lamp off the mantelpiece, and me and her go back in the kitchen. She unlatches the door, and I crack it open and the cold air comes in.

'Hurry,' Mama says.

'All right.'

I can see the fence back of the house and I can see the little pecan tree over by the toilet. I can see the big pecan tree over by the other fence by Miss Viola Brown's house. Miss Viola Brown must be sleeping because it's late at night. I bet you nobody else in the quarter's up now. I bet you I'm the only little boy up. They got plenty stars in the air, but I can't see the moon. There must be ain't no moon tonight. That grass is shining—and it must be done rained. That pecan tree's shadow's all over the back yard.

I get my tee-tee and I wee-wee. I wee-wee hard, because I don't want get cold. Mama latches the door when I get through wee-wee-ing.

'I want some water, Mama,' I say.

'Let it out and put it right back in, huh?' Mama says.

She dips up some water and pours it in my cup, and I drink. I don't drink too much at once, because the water makes my teeth cold. I let my teeth warm up, and I drink some more.

'I got enough,' I say.

Mama drinks the rest and then me and her go back in the front room.

'Sonny?' she says.

'Hanh?'

'Tomorrow morning when you get up me and you leaving here, hear?'

'Where we going?' I ask.

'We going to Gran'mon,' Mama says.

'We leaving us house?' I ask.

'Yes,' she says.

'Daddy leaving too?'

'No,' she says. 'Just me and you.'

'Daddy don't want leave?'

'I don't know what your daddy wants,' Mama says. 'But for sure he don't want me. We leaving, hear?'

'Uh-huh,' I say.

'I'm tired of it,' Mama says.

'Hanh?'

'You won't understand, honey,' Mama says. 'You too young still.'

'I'm getting cold, Mama,' I say.

'All right,' she says. She goes and put the lamp up, and comes back and sit on the bed 'side me. 'Let me take your socks off,' she says.

'I can take them off,' I say.

Mama takes my coat off and I take my socks off. I get back in bed and Mama pulls the cover up over me. She leans over and kiss me on the jaw, and then she goes back to her bed. Mama's bed is over by the window. My bed is by the fireplace. I hear Mama get in the bed. I hear the spring, then I don't hear nothing because Mama's quiet. Then I hear Mama crying.

'Mama?' I call.

She don't answer me.

'Mama?' I call her.

'Go to sleep, baby,' she says.

'You crying?' I ask.

'Go to sleep,' Mama says.

'I don't want you to cry,' I say.

'Mama's not crying,' she says.

Then I don't hear nothing and I lay quiet, but I don't turn over because my spring'll make noise and I don't want make no noise because I want hear if my mama go'n cry again. I don't hear Mama no more and I feel warm in the bed and I pull the cover over my head and I feel good. I don't hear nothing no more and I feel myself going back to sleep.

Billy Joe Martin's got the tire and he's rolling it in the road, and I run to the gate to look at him. I want go out in the road, but Mama don't want me to play out there like Billy Joe Martin and the other children . . . Lucy's playing 'side the house. She's jumping rope with— I don't know who that is. I go 'side the house and play with Lucy. Lucy beats me jumping rope. The rope keeps on hitting me on the leg. But it don't hit Lucy on the leg. Lucy jumps too high for it . . . Me and Billy Joe Martin shoots marbles and I beat him shooting . . . Mama's sweeping the gallery and knocking the dust out of the broom on the side of the house. Mama keeps on knocking the broom against the wall. Must be got plenty dust in the broom.

Somebody's beating on the door. Mama, somebody's beating on the door. Somebody's beating on the door, Mama.

'Amy, please let me in,' I hear.

Somebody's beating on the door, Mama. Mama, somebody's beating on the door.

'Amy, honey; honey, please let me in.'

I push the cover back and I listen. I hear Daddy beating on the door.

'Mama?' I say. 'Mama, Daddy's knocking on the door. He want come in.'

'Go back to sleep, Sonny,' Mama says.

'Daddy's out there,' I say. 'He want come in.'

'Go back to sleep, I told you,' Mama says.

I lay back on my pillow and listen.

'Amy,' Daddy says, 'I know you woke. Open the door.'

Mama don't answer him.

'Amy, honey,' Daddy says. 'My sweet dumpling, let me in. It's freezing out here.'

Mama still won't answer Daddy.

'Mama?' I say.

'Go back to sleep, Sonny,' she says.

'Mama, Daddy want come in,' I say.

'Let him crawl through the key hole,' Mama says.

It gets quiet after this, and it stays quiet a little while, and then Daddy says:

'Sonny?'

'Hanh?'

'Come open the door for your daddy.'

'Mama go'n whip me if I get up,' I say.

'I won't let her whip you,' Daddy says. 'Come and open the door like a good boy.'

I push the cover back and I sit up in the bed and look over at Mama's bed. Mama's under the cover and she's quiet like she's asleep. I get on the floor and get my socks out of my shoes. I get back in the bed and slip them on, and then I go and unlatch the door for Daddy. Daddy comes in and rubs my head with his hand. His hand is hard and cold.

'Look what I brought you and your mama,' he says.

'What?' I ask.

Daddy takes a paper bag out of his jumper pocket.

'Candy?' I say.

'Uh-huh.'

Daddy opens the bag and I stick my hand in there and take a whole handful. Daddy wraps the bag up again and sticks it in his pocket.

'Get back in that bed, Sonny,' Mama says.

'I'm eating candy,' I say.

'Get back in that bed like I told you,' Mama says.

'Daddy's up with me,' I say.

'You heard me, boy?'

'You can take your candy with you,' Daddy says. 'Get back in the bed.'

He follows me to the bed and tucks the cover under me. I lay in the bed and eat my candy. The candy is hard, and I sound just like Paul eating corn. I bet you little old Paul is some cold out there in that back yard. I hope he ain't laying in that water like he always do. I bet you he'll freeze in that water in all this cold. I'm sure glad I ain't a pig. They ain't got no mama and no daddy and no house.

I hear the spring when Daddy gets in the bed.

'Honey?' Daddy says.

Mama don't answer him.

'Honey?' he says.

Mama must be gone back to sleep, because she don't answer him.

'Honey?' Daddy says.

'Get your hands off me,' Mama says.

'Honey, you know I can't keep my hands off you,' Daddy says.

'Well, just do,' Mama says.

'Honey, you don't mean that,' Daddy says. 'You know 'fore God you don't mean that. Come on, say you don't mean it. I can't shut these eyes till you say you don't mean it.'

'Don't touch me,' Mama says.

'Honey,' Daddy says. Then he starts crying. 'Honey, please.'

Daddy cries a good little while, and then he stops. I don't chew on my candy while Daddy's crying, but when he stops I chew on another piece.

'Go to sleep, Sonny,' he says.

'I want eat my candy,' I say.

'Hurry then. You got to go to school tomorrow.'

I put another piece in my mouth and chew on it.

'Honey?' I hear Daddy saying. 'Honey, you go'n wake me up to go
to work?'

'I do hope you stop bothering me,' Mama says.

'Wake me up round four thirty, hear, honey?' Daddy says. 'I can cut
'bout six tons tomorrow. Maybe seven.'

Mama don't say nothing to Daddy, and I feel sleepy again. I finish
chewing my last piece of candy and I turn on my side. I feel good
because the bed is warm. But I still got my socks on.

'Daddy?' I call.

'Go to sleep,' Daddy says.

'My socks still on,' I say.

'Let them stay on tonight,' Daddy says. 'Go to sleep.'

'My feet don't feel good in socks,' I say.

'Please go to sleep, Sonny,' Daddy says. 'I got to get up at four thirty,
and it's hitting close to two now.'

I don't say nothing, but I don't like to sleep with my socks on. But
I stay quiet. Daddy and Mama don't say nothing, either, and little bit
later I hear Daddy snoring. I feel drowsy myself.

I run around the house in the mud because it done rained and I feel
the mud between my toes. The mud is soft and I like to play in it. I try
to get out the mud, but I can't get out. I'm not stuck in the mud, but
I can't get out. Lucy can't come over and play in the mud because her
mama don't want her to catch cold . . . Billy Joe Martin shows me his
dime and puts it back in his pocket. Mama bought me a pretty little
red coat and I show it to Lucy. But I don't let Billy Joe Martin put his
hand on it. Lucy can touch it all she wants, but I don't let Billy Joe
Martin put his hand on it . . . Me and Lucy get on the horse and ride
up and down the road. The horse runs fast, and me and Lucy bounce
on the horse and laugh . . . Mama and Daddy and Uncle Al and
Gran'mon's sitting by the fire talking. I'm outside shooting marbles,
but I hear them. I don't know what they talking about, but I hear
them. I hear them. I hear them. I hear them.

I don't want wake up, but I'm waking up. Mama and Daddy's talking. I want go back to sleep, but they talking too loud. I feel my foot in the sock. I don't like socks on when I'm in the bed. I want go back to sleep, but I can't. Mama and Daddy talking too much.

'Honey, you let me oversleep,' Daddy says. 'Look here, it's going on seven o'clock.'

'You ought to been thought about that last night,' Mama says.

'Honey, please,' Daddy says. 'Don't start a fuss right off this morning.'

'Then don't open your mouth,' Mama says.

'Honey, the car broke down,' Daddy says. 'What I was suppose to do, it broke down on me. I just couldn't walk away and not try to fix it.'

Mama's quiet.

'Honey,' Daddy says, 'don't be mad with me. Come on, now.'

'Don't touch me,' Mama says.

'Honey, I got to go to work. Come on.'

'I mean it,' she says.

'Honey, how can I work without touching you? You know I can't do a day's work without touching you some.'

'I told you not to put your hands on me,' Mama says. I hear her slap Daddy on the hand. 'I mean it,' she says.

'Honey,' Daddy says, 'this is Eddie, your husband.'

'Go back to your car,' Mama says. 'Go rub against it. You ought to be able to find a hole in it somewhere.'

'Honey, you oughtn't talk like that in the house,' Daddy says. 'What if Sonny hear you?'

I stay quiet and I don't move because I don't want them to know I'm woke.

'Honey, listen to me,' Daddy says. 'From the bottom of my heart I'm sorry. Now, come on.'

'I told you once,' Mama says, 'you not getting on me. Go get on your car.'

'Honey, respect the child,' Daddy says.

'How come you don't respect him?' Mama says. 'How come you don't come home sometime and respect him? How come you don't leave that car alone and come home and respect him? How come you don't respect him? You the one need to respect him.'

'I told you it broke down,' Daddy says. 'I was coming home when it broke down on me. I even had to leave it out on the road. I made it here quick as I could.'

'You can go back quick as you can, for all I care,' Mama says.

'Honey, you don't mean that,' Daddy says. 'I know you don't mean that. You just saying that because you mad.'

'Just don't touch me,' Mama says.

'Honey, I got to get out and make some bread for us,' Daddy says.

'Get out if you want,' Mama says. 'They got a jailhouse for them who don't support their family.'

'Honey, please don't talk about a jail,' Daddy says. 'It's too cold. You don't know how cold it is in a jailhouse this time of the year.'

Mama's quiet.

'Honey?' Daddy says.

'I hope you let me go back to sleep,' Mama says. 'Please.'

'Honey, don't go back to sleep on me,' Daddy says. 'Honey—'

'I'm getting up,' Mama says. 'Damn all this.'

I hear the springs mash down on the bed boards. My head's under the cover, but I can just see Mama pushing the cover down the bed. Then I hear her walking across the floor and going back in the kitchen.

'Oh, Lord,' Daddy says. 'Oh, Lord. The suffering a man got to go through in this world. Sonny?' he says.

'Don't wake that baby up,' Mama says, from the door.

'I got to have somebody to talk to,' Daddy says. 'Sonny?'

'I told you not to wake him up,' Mama says.

'You don't want talk to me,' Daddy says. 'I need somebody to talk to. Sonny?' he says.

'Hanh?'

'See what you did?' Mama says. 'You woke him up, and he ain't going back to sleep.'

Daddy comes across the floor and sits down on the side of the bed. He looks down at me and passes his hand over my face.

'You love your daddy, Sonny?' he says.

'Uh-huh.'

'Please love me,' Daddy says.

I look up at Daddy and he looks at me, and then he just falls down on me and starts crying.

'A man needs somebody to love him,' he says.

'Get love from what you give love,' Mama says, back in the kitchen. 'You love your car. Go let it love you back.'

Daddy shakes his face in the cover.

'The suffering a man got to go through in this world,' he says. 'Sonny, I hope you never have to go through all this.'

Daddy lays there 'side me a long time. I can hear Mama back in the kitchen. I hear her putting some wood in the stove, and then I hear her lighting the fire. I hear her pouring water in the tea kettle, and I hear when she sets the kettle on the stove.

Daddy raises up and wipes his eyes. He looks at me and shakes his head, then he goes and puts his overalls on.

'It's a hard life,' he says. 'Hard, hard. One day, Sonny—you too young right now—but one day you'll know what I mean.'

'Can I get up, Daddy?'

'Better ask your mama,' Daddy says.

'Can I get up, Mama?' I call.

Mama don't answer me.

'Mama?' I call.

'Your paw standing in there,' Mama says. 'He the one woke you up.'

'Can I get up, Daddy?'

'Sonny, I got enough troubles right now,' Daddy say.

'I want get up and wee-wee,' I say.

'Get up,' Mama says. 'You go'n worry me till I let you get up anyhow.'

I crawl from under the cover and look at my feet. I got just one sock on and I look for the other one under the cover. I find it and slip it on and then I get on the floor. But that floor is still cold. I hurry up and put on my clothes, and I get my shoes and go and sit on the bed to put them on.

Daddy waits till I finish tying up my shoes, and me and him go back in the kitchen. I get in the corner 'side the stove and Daddy comes over and stands 'side me. The fire is warm and it feels good.

Mama is frying salt meat in the skillet. The skillet's over one hole and the tea kettle's over the other one. The water's boiling and the tea kettle is whistling. I look at the steam shooting up to the loft.

Mama goes outside and gets my pot. She holds my pot for me and I wee-wee in it. Then Mama carries my pot in the front room and puts it under my bed.

Daddy pours some water in the wash basin and washes his face, and then he washes my face. He dumps the water out the back door, and me and him sit at the table. Mama brings the food to the table. She stands over me till I get through saying my blessing, and then she goes back to the stove. Me and Daddy eat.

'You love your daddy?' he says.

'Uh-huh,' I say.

'That's a good boy,' he says. 'Always love your daddy.'

'I love Mama, too. I love her more than I love you.'

'You got a good mama,' Daddy says. 'I love her, too. She the only thing keep me going—'cluding you, too.'

I look at Mama standing 'side the stove, warming.

'Why don't you come to the table and eat with us,' Daddy says.

'I'm not hungry,' Mama says.

'I'm sorry, baby,' Daddy says. 'I mean it.'

Mama just looks down at the stove and don't answer Daddy.

'You got a right to be mad,' Daddy says. 'I ain't nothing but a' old rotten dog.'

Daddy eats his food and looks at me across the table. I pick up a piece of meat and chew on it. I like the skin because the skin is hard. I keep the skin a long time.

'Well, I better get going,' Daddy says. 'Maybe if I work hard I'll get me a couple tons.'

Daddy gets up from the table and goes in the front room. He comes back with his jumper and his hat on. Daddy's hat is gray and it got a hole on the side.

'I'm leaving, honey,' he tells Mama.

Mama don't answer Daddy.

'Honey, tell me "'Bye, old dog," or something,' Daddy says. 'Just don't stand there.'

Mama still don't answer him, and Daddy jerks his cane knife out the wall and goes on out. I chew on my meat skin. I like it because it's hard.

'Hurry up, honey,' Mama says. 'We going to Mama.'

Mama goes in the front room and I stay at the table and eat. I finish eating and I go in the front room where Mama is. Mama's pulling a big bundle of clothes from under the bed.

'What's that, Mama?' I ask.

'Us clothes,' she says.

'We go'n take us clothes down to Gran'mon?'

'I'm go'n try,' Mama says. 'Find your cap and put it on.

I see my cap hanging on the chair and I put it on and fasten the strap under my chin. Mama fixes my shirt in my pants, and then she goes and puts on her overcoat. Her overcoat is black and her hat is black. She puts on her hat and looks in the looking glass. I can see her face in the glass. Look like she want cry. She comes from the dresser and looks at the big bundle of clothes on the floor.

'Where's your pot?' she says. 'Find it.'

I get my pot from under the bed.

'Still got some wee-wee in it,' I say.

'Go to the back door and dump it out,' Mama says.

I go back in the kitchen and open the door. It's cold out there, and I can see the frost all over the grass. The grass is white with frost. I dump the wee-wee out and come back in the front.

'Come on,' Mama says.

She drags the big bundle of clothes out on the gallery and I shut the door. Mama squats down and puts the bundle on her head, and then she stands up and me and her go down the steps. Soon's I get out in the road I can feel the wind. It's strong and it's blowing in my face. My face is cold and one of my hands is cold.

It's red over there back of the trees. Mr Guerin's house is over there. I see Mr Guerin's big old dog. He must be don't see me and Mama because he ain't barking at us.

'Don't linger back too far,' Mama says.

I run and catch up with Mama. Me and Mama's the only two people walking in the road now.

I look up and I see the tree in Gran'mon's yard. We go little farther and I see the house. I run up ahead of Mama and hold the gate open for her. After she goes in I let the gate slam.

Spot starts barking soon's he sees me. He runs down the steps at me and I let him smell my pot. Spot follows me and Mama back to the house.

'Gran'mon?' I call.

'Who that out there?' Gran'mon asks.

'Me,' I say.

'What you doing out there in all that cold for, boy?' Gran'mon says. I hear Gran'mon coming to the door fussing. She opens the door and looks at me and Mama.

'What you doing here with all that?' she asks.

'I'm leaving him, Mama,' Mama says.

'Eddie?' Gran'mon says. 'What he done you now?'

'I'm just tired of it,' Mama says.

'Come in here out that cold,' Gran'mon says. 'Walking out there in all that weather . . .'

We go inside and Mama drops the big bundle of clothes on the floor. I go to the fire and warm my hands. Mama and Gran'mon come to the fire and Mama stands at the other end of the fireplace and warms her hands.

'Now what that no good nigger done done?' Gran'mon asks.

'Mama, I'm just tired of Eddie running up and down the road in that car,' Mama says.

'He beat you?' Gran'mon asks.

'No, he didn't beat me,' Mama says. 'Mama, Eddie didn't get home till after two this morning. Messing around with that old car somewhere out on the road all night.'

'I told you,' Gran'mon says. 'I told you when that nigger got that car that was go'n happen. I told you. No—you wouldn't listen. I told you. Put a fool in a car and he becomes a bigger fool. Where that yellow thing at now?'

'God telling,' Mama says. 'He left with his cane knife.'

'I warned you 'bout that nigger,' Gran'mon says. 'Even 'fore you married him. I sung at you and sung at you. I said, "Amy, that nigger ain't no good. A yellow nigger with a gap like that 'tween his front teeth ain't no good." But you wouldn't listen.'

'Can me and Sonny stay here?' Mama asks.

'Where else can y'all go?' Gran'mon says. 'I'm your mon, ain't I? You think I can put you out in the cold like he did?'

'He didn't put me out, Mama, I left,' Mama says.

'You finally getting some sense in your head,' Gran'mon says. 'You ought to been left that nigger years ago.'

Uncle Al comes in the front room and looks at the bundle of clothes on the floor. Uncle Al's got on his overalls and got just one strap hooked. The other strap's hanging down his back.

'Fix that thing on you,' Gran'mon says. 'You not in a stable.'

Uncle Al fixes his clothes and looks at me and Mama at the fire.

'Y'all had a round?' he asks Mama.

'Eddie and that car again,' Mama says.

'That's all they want these days,' Gran'mon says. 'Cars. Why don't they marry them cars? No. When they got their troubles, they come running to the womenfolks. When they ain't got no troubles and when their pockets full of money they run jump in the car. I told you that when you was working to help him get that car.'

Uncle Al stands 'side me at the fireplace, and I lean against him and look at the steam coming out a piece of wood. Lord knows I get tired of Gran'mon fussing all the time.

'Y'all moving in with us?' Uncle Al asks.

'For a few days,' Mama says. 'Then I'll try to find another place somewhere in the quarter.'

'We got plenty room here,' Uncle Al says. 'This old man here can sleep with me.'

Uncle Al gets a little stick out of the corner and hands it to me so I can light it for him. I hold it to the fire till it's lit, and I hand it back to Uncle Al. Uncle Al turns the pipe upside down in his mouth and holds the fire to it. When the pipe's good and lit, Uncle Al gives me the little stick and I throw it back in the fire.

'Y'all ate anything?' Gran'mon asks.

'Sonny ate,' Mama says. 'I'm not hungry.'

'I reckon you go'n start looking for work now?' Gran'mon says.

'There's plenty cane to cut,' Mama says. 'I'll get me a cane knife and go out tomorrow morning.'

'Out in all that cold?' Gran'mon says.

'They got plenty women cutting cane,' Mama says. 'I don't mind. I done it before.'

'You used to be such a pretty little thing, Amy,' Gran'mon says. 'Long silky curls. Prettiest little face on this whole plantation. You could've married somebody worth something. But, no, you had to go throw yourself away to that yellow nigger who don't care for nobody, 'cluding himself.'

'I loved Eddie,' Mama says.

'Poot,' Gran'mon says.

'He wasn't like this when we married,' Mama says.

'Every nigger from Bayonne like this now, then, and forever,' Gran'mon says.

'Not then,' Mama says. 'He was the sweetest person . . .'

'And you fell for him?' Gran'mon says.

'. . . He changed after he got that car,' Mama says. 'He changed overnight.'

'Well, you learned your lesson,' Gran'mon says. 'We all get teached something no matter how old we get. "Live and learn," what they say.'

'Eddie's all right,' Uncle Al says. 'He—'

'You keep out of this, Albert,' Gran'mon says. 'It don't concern you.'

Uncle Al don't say no more, and I can feel his hand on my shoulder. I like Uncle Al because he's good, and he never talk bad about Daddy. But Gran'mon's always talking bad about Daddy.

'Freddie's still there,' Gran'mon says.

'Mama, please,' Mama says.

'Why not?' Gran'mon says. 'He always loved you.'

'Not in front of him,' Mama says.

Mama leaves the fireplace and goes to the bundle of clothes. I can hear her untying the bundle.

'Ain't it 'bout time you was leaving for school?' Uncle Al asks.

'I don't want go,' I say. 'It's too cold.'

'It's never too cold for school,' Mama says. 'Warm up good and let Uncle Al button your coat for you.'

I get closer to the fire and I feel the fire hot on my pants. I turn around and warm my back. I turn again, and Uncle Al leans over and buttons up my coat. Uncle Al's pipe almost gets in my face, and it don't smell good.

'Now,' Uncle Al says. 'You all ready to go. You want take a potato with you?'

'Uh-huh.'

Uncle Al leans over and gets me a potato out of the ashes. He knocks all the ashes off and puts the potato in my pocket.

'Wait,' Mama says. 'Mama, don't you have a little paper bag?'

Gran'mon looks on the mantelpiece and gets a paper bag. There's something in the bag, and she takes it out and hands the bag to Mama. Mama puts the potato in the bag and puts it in my pocket. Then she goes and gets my book and tucks it under my arm.

'Now you ready,' she says. 'And remember, when you get out for dinner come back here. Don't you forget and go up home now. You hear, Sonny?'

'Uh-huh.'

'Come on,' Uncle Al says. 'I'll open the gate for you.'

''Bye, Mama,' I say.

'Be a good boy,' Mama says. 'Eat your potato at recess. Don't eat it in class now.'

Me and Uncle Al go out on the gallery. The sun is shining but it's still cold out there. Spot follows me and Uncle Al down the walk. Uncle Al opens the gate for me and I go out in the road. I hate to leave Uncle Al and Spot. And I hate to leave Mama—and I hate to leave the fire. But I got to, because they want me to learn.

'See you at twelve,' Uncle Al says.

I go up the quarter and Uncle Al and Spot go back to the house. I see all the children going to school. But I don't see Lucy. When I get to her house I'm go'n stop at the gate and call her. She must be don't want go to school, cold as it is.

It still got some ice in the water. I better not walk in the water. I'll get my feet wet and Mama'll whip me.

When I get closer I look and I see Lucy and her mama on the gallery. Lucy's mama ties her bonnet for her, and Lucy comes down the steps. She runs down the walk toward the gate. Lucy's bonnet is red and her coat is red.

'Hi,' I say.

'Hi,' she says.

'It's some cold,' I say.

'Unnn-hunnnn,' Lucy says.

Me and Lucy walk side by side up the quarter. Lucy's got her book in her book sack.

'We moved,' I say. 'We staying with Gran'mon now.'

'Y'all moved?' Lucy asks.

'Uh-huh.'

'Y'all didn't move,' Lucy says. 'When y'all moved?'

'This morning.'

'Who moved y'all?' Lucy asks.

'Me and Mama,' I say. 'I'm go'n sleep with Uncle Al.'

'My legs getting cold,' Lucy says.

'I got a potato,' I say. 'In my pocket.'

'You go'n eat it and give me piece?' Lucy says.

'Uh-huh,' I say. 'At recess.'

Me and Lucy walk up the quarter, and Lucy stops and touches the ice with her shoe.

'You go'n get your foot wet,' I say.

'No, I'm not,' Lucy says.

Lucy breaks the ice with her shoe and laughs. I laugh and I break a piece of ice with my shoe. Me and Lucy laugh and I see the smoke coming out of Lucy's mouth. I open my mouth and go, 'Haaaa,' and plenty smoke comes out of my mouth. Lucy laughs and points at the smoke.

Me and Lucy go on up the quarter to the schoolhouse. Billy Joe Martin and Ju-Ju and them's playing marbles right by the gate. Over 'side the schoolhouse Shirley and Dottie and Katie's jumping rope. On the other side of the schoolhouse some more children playing 'Patty-cake, patty-cake, baker-man' to keep warm. Lucy goes where Shirley and them's jumping rope and asks them to play. I stop where Billy Joe Martin and them's at and watch them shoot marbles.

2

It's warm inside the schoolhouse. Bill made a big fire in the heater, and I can hear it roaring up the pipes. I look out the window and I can see the smoke flying across the yard. Bill sure knows how to make a good fire. Bill's the biggest boy in school, and he always makes the fire for us.

Everybody's studying their lesson, but I don't know mine. I wish I knowed it, but I don't. Mama didn't teach me my lesson last night, and she didn't teach it to me this morning, and I don't know it.

'Bob and Rex in the yard. Rex is barking at the cow.' I don't know what all this other reading is. I see 'Rex' again, and I see 'cow' again—but I don't know what all the rest of it is.

Bill comes up to the heater and I look up and see him putting another piece of wood in the fire. He goes back to his seat and sits down 'side Juanita. Miss Hebert looks at Bill when he goes back to his seat. I look in my book at Bob and Rex. Bob's got on a white shirt and blue pants. Rex is a German police dog. He's white and brown. Mr Bouie's got a dog just like Rex. He don't bite though. He's a good dog. But Mr Guerin's old dog'll bite you for sure. I seen him this morning when me and Mama was going down to Gran'mon's house.

I ain't go'n eat dinner at us house because me and Mama don't stay there no more. I'm go'n eat at Gran'mon's house. I don't know where Daddy go'n eat dinner. He must be go'n cook his own dinner.

I can hear Bill and Juanita back of me. They whispering to each other, but I can hear them. Juanita's some pretty. I hope I was big so I could love her. But I better look at my lesson and don't think about other things.

'First grade,' Miss Hebert says.

We go up to the front and sit down on the bench. Miss Hebert looks at us and make a mark in her roll book. She puts the roll book down and comes over to the bench where we at.

'Does everyone know his lesson today?' she asks.

'Yes, Ma'am,' Lucy says, louder than anybody else in the whole schoolhouse.

'Good,' Miss Hebert says. 'And I'll start with you today, Lucy. Hold your book in one hand and begin.'

'"Bob and Rex are in the yard,"' Lucy reads. '"Rex is barking at the cow. The cow is watching Rex."'

'Good,' Miss Hebert says. 'Point to barking.'

Lucy points.

'Good. Now point to watching.'

Lucy points again.

'Good,' Miss Hebert says. 'Shirley Ann, let's see how well you can read.'

I look in the book at Bob and Rex. 'Rex is barking at the cow. The cow is looking at Rex.'

'William Joseph,' Miss Hebert says.

I'm next, I'm scared. I don't know my lesson and Miss Hebert go'n whip me. Miss Hebert don't like you when you don't know your lesson. I can see her strap over there on the table. I can see the clock and the little bell, too. Bill split the end of the strap, and them little ends sting some. Soon 's Billy Joe Martin finishes, then it's me. I don't know . . . Mama ought to been . . . 'Bob and Rex' . . .

'Eddie,' Miss Hebert says.

I don't know my lesson. I don't know my lesson. I don't know my lesson. I feel warm. I'm wet. I hear the wee-wee dripping on the floor. I'm crying. I'm crying because I wee-wee on myself. My clothes's wet. Lucy and them go'n laugh at me. Billy Joe Martin and them go'n tease me. I don't know my lesson. I don't know my lesson. I don't know my lesson.

'Oh, Eddie, look what you've done,' I think I hear Miss Hebert saying. I don't know if she's saying this, but I think I hear her say it. My eyes's shut and I'm crying. I don't want look at none of them, because I know they laughing at me.

'It's running under that bench there now,' Billy Joe Martin says. 'Look out for your feet back there, it's moving fast.'

'William Joseph,' Miss Hebert says. 'Go over there and stand in that corner. Turn your face to the wall and stay there until I tell you to move.'

I hear Billy Joe Martin leaving the bench, and then it's quiet. But I don't open my eyes.

'Eddie,' Miss Hebert says, 'go stand by the heater.'

I don't move, because I'll see them, and I don't want see them.

'Eddie?' Miss Hebert says.

But I don't answer her, and I don't move.

'Bill?' Miss Hebert says.

I hear Bill coming up to the front and then I feel him taking me by the hand and leading me away. I walk with my eyes shut. Me and Bill stop at the heater, because I can feel the fire. Then Bill takes my book and leaves me standing there.

'Juanita,' Miss Hebert says, 'get a mop, will you, please.'

I hear Juanita going to the back, and then I hear her coming back to the front. The fire pops in the heater, but I don't open my eyes. Nobody's saying anything, but I know they all watching me.

When Juanita gets through mopping up the wee-wee she carries the mop back to the closet, and I hear Miss Hebert going on with the lesson. When she gets through with the first graders, she calls the second graders up there.

Bill comes up to the heater and puts another piece of wood in the fire.

'Want turn around?' he asks me.

I don't answer him, but I got my eyes open now and I'm looking down at the floor. Bill turns me round so I can dry the back of my pants. He pats me on the shoulder and goes back to his seat.

After Miss Hebert gets through with the second graders, she tells the children they can go out for recess. I can hear them getting their coats and hats. When they all leave I raise my head. I still see Bill and Juanita and Veta sitting there. Bill smiles at me, but I don't smile back. My clothes's dry now, and I feel better. I know the rest of the children go'n tease me, though.

'Bill, why don't you and the rest of the seventh graders put your arithmetic problems on the board,' Miss Hebert says. 'We'll look at them after recess.'

Bill and them stand up, and I watch them go to the blackboard in the back.

'Eddie?' Miss Hebert says.

I turn and I see her sitting behind her desk. And I see Billy Joe Martin standing in the corner with his face to the wall.

'Come up to the front,' Miss Hebert says.

I go up there looking down at the floor, because I know she go'n whip me now.

'William Joseph, you may leave,' Miss Hebert says.

Billy Joe Martin runs over and gets his coat, and then he runs outside to shoot marbles. I stand in front of Miss Hebert's desk with my head down.

'Look up,' she says.

I raise my head and look at Miss Hebert. She's smiling, and she don't look mad.

'Now,' she says. 'Did you study your lesson last night?'

'Yes, ma'am,' I say.

'I want the truth, now,' she says. 'Did you?'

It's a sin to story in the churchhouse, but I'm scared Miss Hebert go'n whip me.

'Yes, ma'am,' I say.

'Did you study it this morning?' she asks.

'Yes, ma'am,' I say.

'Then why didn't you know it?' she asks.

I feel a big knot coming up in my throat and I feel like I'm go'n cry again. I'm scared Miss Hebert go'n whip me, that's why I story to her.

'You didn't study your lesson, did you?' she says.

I shake my head. 'No, ma'am.'

'You didn't study it last night either, did you?'

'No, ma'am,' I say. 'Mama didn't have time to help me. Daddy wasn't home. Mama didn't have time to help me.'

'Where is your father?' Miss Hebert asks.

'Cutting cane.'

'Here on this place?'

'Yes, ma'am,' I say.

Miss Hebert looks at me, and then she gets out a pencil and starts writing on a piece of paper. I look at her writing and I look at the clock and the strap. I can hear the clock. I can hear Billy Joe Martin and them shooting marbles outside. I can hear Lucy and them jumping rope, and some more children playing 'Patty-cake'.

'I want you to give this to your mother or your father when you get

home,' Miss Hebert says. 'This is only a little note saying I would like
to see them sometime when they aren't too busy.'

'We don't live home no more,' I say.

'Oh?' Miss Hebert says. 'Did you move?'

'Me and Mama,' I say. 'But Daddy didn't.'

Miss Hebert looks at me, and then she writes some more on the
note. She puts her pencil down and folds the note up.

'Be sure to give this to your mother,' she says. 'Put it in your pocket
and don't lose it.'

I take the note from Miss Hebert, but I don't leave the desk.

'Do you want to go outside?' she asks.

'Yes, ma'am.'

'You may leave,' she says.

I go over and get my coat and cap, and then I go out in the yard. I
see Billy Joe Martin and Charles and them shooting marbles over by
the gate. I don't go over there because they'll tease me. I go 'side the
schoolhouse and look at Lucy and them jumping rope. Lucy ain't
jumping right now.

'Hi, Lucy,' I say.

Lucy looks over at Shirley and they laugh. They look at my pants
and laugh.

'You want a piece of potato?' I ask Lucy.

'No,' Lucy says. 'And you not my boyfriend no more, either.'

I look at Lucy and I go stand 'side the wall in the sun. I peel my
potato and eat it. And look like soon 's I get through, Miss Hebert
comes to the front and says recess is over.

We go back inside, and I go to the back and take off my coat and
cap. Bill comes back there and hang the things up for us. I go over to
Miss Hebert's desk and Miss Hebert gives me my book. I go back to
my seat and sit down 'side Lucy.

'Hi, Lucy,' I say.

Lucy looks at Shirley and Shirley puts her hand over her mouth and
laughs. I feel like getting up from there and socking Shirley in the
mouth, but I know Miss Hebert'll whip me. Because I got no business
socking people after I done wee-wee on myself. I open my book and
look at my lesson so I don't have to look at none of them.

3

It's almost dinner time, and when I get home I ain't coming back here either, now. I'm go'n stay there. I'm go'n stay right there and sit by the fire. Lucy and them don't want play with me, and I ain't coming back up here. Miss Hebert go'n touch that little bell in a little while. She getting ready to touch it right now.

Soon 's Miss Hebert touches the bell all the children run go get their hats and coats. I unhook my coat and drop it on the bench till I put my cap on. Then I put my coat on, and I get my book and leave.

I see Bill and Juanita going out the schoolyard, and I run and catch up with them. Time I get there I hear Billy Joe Martin and them coming up behind us.

'Look at that baby,' Billy Joe Martin says.

'Piss on himself,' Ju-Ju says.

'Y'all leave him alone,' Bill says.

'Baby, baby, piss on himself,' Billy Joe Martin sings.

'What did I say now?' Bill says.

'Piss on himself,' Billy Joe Martin says.

'Wait,' Bill says. 'Let me take off my belt.'

'Good-bye, piss pot,' Billy Joe Martin says. Him and Ju-Ju run down the road. They spank their hind parts with their hands and run like horses.

'They just bad,' Juanita says.

'Don't pay them no mind,' Bill says. 'They'll leave you alone.'

We go on down the quarter and Bill and Juanita hold hands. I go to Gran'mon's gate and open it. I look at Bill and Juanita going down the quarter. They walking close together, and Juanita done put her head on Bill's shoulder. I like to see Bill and Juanita like that. It makes me feel good. But I go in the yard and I don't feel good any more. I know old Gran'mon go'n start her fussing. Lord in Heaven knows I get tired of all this fussing, day and night. Spot runs down the walk to meet me. I put my hand on his head and me and him go back to the gallery. I make him stay on the gallery, because Gran'mon don't want him inside. I pull the door open and I see Gran'mon and Uncle Al sitting by the fire. I look for my mama, but I don't see her.

'Where Mama?' I ask Uncle Al.

'In the kitchen,' Gran'mon says. 'But she talking to somebody.'

I go back to the kitchen.

'Come back here,' Gran'mon says.

'I want see my mama,' I say.

'You'll see her when she come out,' Gran'mon says.

'I want see my mama now,' I say.

'Don't you hear me talking to you, boy?' Gran'mon hollers.

'What's the matter?' Mama asks. Mama comes out of the kitchen and Mr Freddie Jackson comes out of there, too. I hate Mr Freddie Jackson. I never did like him. He always want to be round my mama.

'That boy don't listen to nobody,' Gran'mon says.

'Hi, Sonny,' Mr Freddie Jackson says.

I look at him standing there, but I don't speak to him. I take the note out of my pocket and hand it to my mama.

'What's this?' Mama says.

'Miss Hebert sent it.'

Mama unfolds the note and take it to the fireplace to read it. I can see her mouth working. When she gets through reading, she folds the note up again.

'She want see me or Eddie sometime when we free,' Mama says. 'Sonny been doing pretty bad in his class.'

'I can just see that nigger husband of yours in a schoolhouse,' Gran'mon says. 'I doubt if he ever went to one.'

'Mama, please,' Mama says.

Mama helps me off with my coat and I go to the fireplace and stand 'side Uncle Al. Uncle Al pulls me between his legs and he holds my hand out to the fire.

'Well?' I hear Gran'mon saying.

'You know how I feel 'bout her,' Mr Freddie Jackson says. 'My house opened to her and Sonny any time she want come there.'

'Well?' Gran'mon says.

'Mama, I'm still married to Eddie,' Mama says.

'You mean you still love that yellow thing,' Gran'ma says. 'That's what you mean, ain't it?'

'I didn't say that,' Mama says. 'What would people say, out one house and in another one the same day?'

'Who care what people say?' Gran'mon says. 'Let people say what they big enough to say. You looking out for yourself, not what people say.'

'You understand, don't you, Freddie?' Mama says.

'I think I do,' he says. 'But like I say, Amy, any time—you know that.'

'And there ain't no time like right now,' Gran'mon says. 'You can take that bundle of clothes down there for her.'

'Let her make up her own mind, Rachel,' Uncle Al says. 'She can make up her own mind.'

'If you know what's good for you you better keep out of this,' Gran'mon says. 'She my daughter and if she ain't got sense enough to look out for herself, I have. What you want to do, go out in that field cutting cane in the morning?'

'I don't mind it,' Mama says.

'You done forgot how hard cutting cane is?' Gran'mon says. 'You must be done forgot.'

'I ain't forgot,' Mama says. 'But if the other women can do it, I suppose I can do it, too.'

'Now you talking back,' Gran'mon says.

'I'm not talking back, Mama,' Mama says. 'I just feel it ain't right to leave one house and go to another house the same day. That ain't right in nobody's book.'

'Maybe she's right, Mrs Rachel,' Mr Freddie Jackson says.

'Her trouble is she's still in love with that mariny,' Gran'mon says. 'That's what your trouble is. You ain't satisfied 'less he got you doing all the work while he rip and run up and down the road with his other nigger friends. No, you ain't satisfied.'

Gran'mon goes back in the kitchen fussing. After she leaves the fire, everything gets quiet. Everything stays quiet a minute, and then Gran'mon starts singing back in the kitchen.

'Why did you bring your book home?' Mama says.

'Miss Hebert say I can stay home if I want,' I say. 'We had us lesson already.'

'You sure she said that?' Mama says.

'Uh-huh.'

'I'm go'n ask her, you know.'

'She said it,' I say.

Mama don't say no more, but I know she still looking at me, but I don't look at her. Then Spot starts barking outside and everybody look that way. But nobody don't move. Spot keeps on barking, and I go to the door to see what he's barking at. I see Daddy coming up the walk. I pull the door and go back to the fireplace.

'Daddy coming, Mama,' I say.

'Wait,' Gran'mon says, coming out the kitchen. 'Let me talk to that nigger. I'll give him a piece of my mind.'

Gran'mon goes to the door and pushes it open. She stands in the door and I hear Daddy talking to Spot. Then Daddy comes up to the gallery.

'Amy in there, Mama?' Daddy says.

'She is,' Gran'mon says.

I hear Daddy coming up the steps.

'And where you think you going?' Gran'mon asks.

'I want speak to her,' Daddy says.

'Well, she don't want speak to you,' Gran'mon says. 'So you might 's well go right on back down them steps and march right straight out of my yard.'

'I want speak to my wife,' Daddy says.

'She ain't your wife no more,' Gran'mon says. 'She left you.'

'What you mean she left me?' Daddy says.

'She ain't up at your house no more, is she?' Gran'mon says. 'That look like a good enough sign to me that she done left.'

'Amy?' Daddy calls.

Mama don't answer him. She's looking down in the fire. I don't feel good when Mama's looking like that.

'Amy?' Daddy calls.

Mama still don't answer him.

'You satisfied?' Gran'mon says.

'You the one trying to make Amy leave me,' Daddy says. 'You ain't never liked me—from the starting.'

'That's right, I never did,' Gran'mon says. 'You yellow, you got a gap 'tween your teeth, and you ain't no good. You want me to say more?'

'You always wanted her to marry somebody else,' Daddy says.

'You right again,' Gran'mon says.

'Amy?' Daddy calls. 'Can you hear me, honey?'

'She can hear you,' Gran'mon says. 'She's standing right there by that fireplace. She can hear you good 's I can hear you, and nigger, I can hear you too good for comfort.'

'I'm going in there,' Daddy says. 'She got somebody in there and I'm going in there and see.'

'You just take one more step toward my door,' Gran'mon says, 'and it'll take a' undertaker to get you out of here. So help me, God, I'll get that butcher knife out of that kitchen and chop on your tail till I can't see tail to chop on. You the kind of nigger like to rip and run up and down the road in your car long 's you got a dime, but when you get broke and your belly get empty you run to your wife and cry on her shoulder. You just take one more step toward this door, and I bet you somebody'll be crying at your funeral. If you know anybody who care that much for you, you old yellow dog.'

Daddy is quiet a while, and then I hear him crying. I don't feel good, because I don't like to hear Daddy and Mama crying. I look at Mama, but she's looking down in the fire.

'You never liked me,' Daddy says.

'You said that before,' Gran'mon says. 'And I repeat, no, I never liked you, don't like you, and never will like you. Now, get out my yard 'fore I put the dog on you.'

'I want see my boy,' Daddy says, 'I got a right to see my boy.'

'In the first place, you ain't got no right in my yard,' Gran'mon says.

'I want see my boy,' Daddy says. 'You might be able to keep me from seeing my wife, but you and nobody else can keep me from seeing my son. Half of him is me and I want see my—I want see him.'

'You ain't leaving?' Gran'mon asks Daddy.

'I want see my boy,' Daddy says. 'And I'm go'n see my boy.'

'Wait,' Gran'mon says. 'Your head hard. Wait till I come back. You go'n see all kind of boys.'

Gran'mon comes back inside and goes to Uncle Al's room. I look toward the wall and I can hear Daddy moving on the gallery. I hear Mama crying and I look at her. I don't want see my mama crying, and I lay my head on Uncle Al's knee and I want cry, too.

'Amy, honey,' Daddy calls, 'ain't you coming up home and cook me something to eat? It's lonely up there without you, honey. You don't know how lonely it is without you. I can't stay up there without you, honey. Please come home . . .'

I hear Gran'mon coming out of Uncle Al's room and I look at her. Gran'mon's got Uncle Al's shotgun and she's putting a shell in it.

'Mama?' Mama screams.

'Don't worry,' Gran'mon says. 'I'm just go'n shoot over his head. I ain't go'n have them sending me to the pen for a good-for-nothing nigger like that.'

'Mama, don't,' Mama says. 'He might hurt himself.'

'Good,' Gran'mon says. 'Save me the trouble of doing it for him.'

Mama runs to the wall. 'Eddie, run,' she screams. 'Mama got the shotgun.'

I hear Daddy going down the steps. I hear Spot running after him barking. Gran'mon knocks the door open with the gun barrel and shoot. I hear Daddy hollering.

'Mama, you didn't?' Mama says.

'I shot two miles over that nigger's head,' Gran'mon says. 'Long-legged coward.'

We all run out on the gallery, and I see Daddy out in the road crying. I can see the people coming out on the galleries. They looking at us and they looking at Daddy. Daddy's standing out in the road crying.

'Boy, I would've like to seen old Eddie getting out of this yard,' Uncle Al says.

Daddy's walking up and down the road in front of the house, and he's crying.

'Let's go back inside,' Gran'mon says. 'We won't be bothered with him for a while.'

It's cold, and me and Uncle Al and Gran'mon go back inside. Mr Freddie Jackson and Mama don't come back in right now, but after a little while they come in, too.

'Oh, Lord,' Mama says.

Mama starts crying and Mr Freddie Jackson takes her in his old arms. Mama lays her head on his old shoulder, but she just stays there a little while and then she moves.

'Can I go lay 'cross your bed, Uncle Al?' Mama asks.

'Sure,' Uncle Al says.

I watch Mama going to Uncle Al's room.

'Well, I better be going,' Mr Freddie Jackson says.

'Freddie?' Gran'mon calls him, from the kitchen.

'Yes, ma'am?' he says.

'Come here a minute,' Gran'mon says.

Mr Freddie Jackson goes back in the kitchen where Gran'mon is. I get between Uncle Al's legs and look at the fire. Uncle Al rubs my head with his hand. Mr Freddie Jackson comes out of the kitchen and goes in Uncle Al's room where Mama is. He must be sitting down on the bed because I can hear the springs.

'Gran'mon shot Daddy?' I ask.

Uncle Al rubs my head with his hand.

'She just scared him,' he says. 'You like your daddy?'

'Uh-huh.'

'Your daddy's a good man,' Uncle Al says. 'A little foolish, but he's okay.'

'I don't like Mr Freddie Jackson,' I say.

'How come?' Uncle Al says.

'I just don't like him,' I say. 'I just don't like him. I don't like him to hold my mama, neither. My daddy suppose to hold my mama. He ain't suppose to hold my mama.'

'You want go back home?' Uncle Al asks.

'Uh-huh,' I say. 'But me and Mama go'n stay here now. I'm go'n sleep with you.'

'But you rather go home and sleep in your own bed, huh?'

'Yes,' I say. 'I pull the cover 'way over my head. I like to sleep under the cover.'

'You sleep like that all the time?' Uncle Al asks.

'Uh-huh.'

'Even in the summertime, too?' Uncle Al says.

'Uh-huh,' I say.

'Don't you ever get too warm?' Uncle Al says.

'Uh-uh,' I say. 'I feel good 'way under there.'

Uncle Al rubs my head and I look down in the fire.

'Y'all come on in the kitchen and eat,' Gran'mon calls.

Me and Uncle Al go back in the kitchen and sit down at the table. Gran'mon already got us food dished up. Uncle Al bows his head and I bow my head.

'Thank Thee, Father, for this food Thou has given us,' Uncle Al says.

I raise my head and start eating. We having spaghetti for dinner. I pick up a string of spaghetti and suck it up in my mouth. I make it go *loo-loo-loo-loo-loo-loo-loop.* Uncle Al looks at me and laugh. I do it again, and Uncle Al laughs again.

'Don't play with my food,' Gran'mon says. 'Eat it right.'

Gran'mon is standing 'side the stove looking at me. I don't like old Gran'mon. Shooting at my daddy—I don't like her.

'Taste good?' Uncle Al asks.

'Uh-huh,' I say.

Uncle Al winks at me and wraps his spaghetti on his fork and sticks it in his mouth. I try to wrap mine on my fork, but it keeps falling off. I can just pick up one at a time.

Gran'mon starts singing her song again. She fools round the stove a little while, and then she goes in the front room. I get a string of spaghetti and suck it up in my mouth. When I hear her coming back I stop and eat right.

'Still out there,' she says. 'Sitting on that ditch bank crying like a baby. Let him cry. But he better not come back in this yard.'

Gran'mon goes over to the stove and sticks a piece of wood in the fire. She starts singing again:

> *Oh, I'll be there,*
> *I'll be there,*
> *When the roll is called in Heaven, I'll be there.*

Uncle Al finishes his dinner and waits for me. When I finish eating, me and him go in the front room and sit at the fire.

'I want go to the toilet, Uncle Al,' I say.

I get my coat and cap and bring them to the fireplace, and Uncle Al helps me get in them. Uncle Al buttons up my coat for me, and I go out on the gallery. I look out in the road and I see Daddy sitting out on the ditch bank. I go round the house and go back to the toilet. The grass is dry like hay. There ain't no leaves on the trees. I see some birds in the tree. The wind's moving the birds's feathers. I bet you them little birds's some cold. I'm glad I'm not a bird. No daddy, no mama—I'm glad I'm not a bird.

I open the door and go in the toilet. I get up on the seat and pull down my pants. I squat over the hole—but I better not slip and fall in there. I'll get all that poo-poo on my feet, and Gran'mon'll kill me if I tramp all that poo-poo in her house.

I try hard and my poo-poo come. It's long. I like to poo-poo. Sometimes I poo-poo on my pot at night. Mama don't like for me to go back to the toilet when it's late. Scared a snake might bite me.

I finish poo-poo-ing and I jump down from the seat and pull up my pants. I look in the hole and I see my poo-poo. I look in the top of the toilet, but I don't see any spiders. We got spiders in us toilet. Gran'mon must be done killed all her spiders with some Flit.

I push the door open and I go back to the front of the house. I go round the gallery and I see Daddy standing at the gate looking in the yard. He sees me.

'Sonny?' he calls.

'Hanh?'

'Come here, baby,' he says.

I look toward the door, but I don't see nobody and I go to the gate where Daddy is. Daddy pushes the gate open and grabs me and hugs me to him.

'You still love your daddy, Sonny?' he asks.

'Uh-huh,' I say.

Daddy hugs me and kisses me on the face.

'I love my baby,' he says. 'I love my baby. Where your mama?'

'Laying 'cross Uncle Al's bed in his room,' I say. 'And Mr Freddie Jackson in there, too.'

Daddy pushes me away real quickly and looks in my face.

'Who else in there?' he asks. 'Who?'

'Just them,' I say. 'Uncle Al's in Gran'mon's room by the fire, and Gran'mon's in the kitchen.'

Daddy looks toward the house.

'This the last straw,' he says. 'I'm turning your Gran'mon in this minute. And you go'n be my witness. Come on.'

'Where we going?' I ask.

'To that preacher's house,' Daddy says. 'And if he can't help me, I'm going back in the field to Madame Toussaint.'

Daddy grabs my hand and me and him go up the quarter. I can see all the children going back to school.

'. . . Lock her own daughter in a room with another man and got her little grandson there looking all the time,' Daddy says. 'She ain't so much Christian as she put out to be. Singing round that house every time you bat your eyes and doing something like that in broad daylight. Step it up, Sonny.'

'I'm coming fast as I can,' I say.

'I'll see about that,' Daddy says. 'I'll see about that.'

When me and Daddy get to Reverend Simmons's house, we go up on the gallery and Daddy knocks on the door. Mrs Carey comes to the door to see what we want.

'Mrs Carey, is the Reverend in?' Daddy asks.

'Yes,' Mrs Carey says. 'Come on in.'

Me and Daddy go inside and I see Reverend Simmons sitting at the fireplace. Reverend Simmons got on his eyeglasses and he's reading the Bible. He turns and looks at us when we come in. He takes off his glasses like he can't see us too good with them on, and he looks at us again. Mrs Carey goes back in the kitchen and me and Daddy go over to the fireplace.

'Good evening, Reverend,' Daddy says.

'Good evening,' Reverend Simmons says. 'Hi, Sonny.'

'Hi,' I say.

'Reverend, I hate busting in on you like this, but I need your help,'

Daddy says. 'Reverend, Amy done left me and her mama got her down at her house with another man and—'

'Now, calm down a second,' Reverend Simmons says. He looks toward the kitchen. 'Carey, bring Mr Howard and Sonny a chair.'

Mrs Carey brings the chairs and goes right on back in the kitchen again. Daddy turns his chair so he can be facing Reverend Simmons.

'I come in pretty late last night 'cause my car broke down on me and I had to walk all the way—from the other side of Morgan up there,' Daddy says. 'When I get home me and Amy get in a little squabble. This morning we squabble again, but I don't think too much of it. You know a man and a woman go'n have their little squabbles every once in a while. I go to work in the field. Work like a dog. Cutting cane right and left—trying to make up lost time I spent at the house this morning. When I come home for dinner—hungry 's a dog—my wife, neither my boy is there. No dinner—and I'm hungry 's a dog. I go in the front room and all their clothes gone. Lord, I almost go crazy. I don't know what to do. I run out the house because I think she still mad at me and done gone down to her mama. I go down there and ask for her, and first thing I know here come Mama Rachel shooting at me with Uncle Al's shotgun.'

'I can't believe that,' Reverend Simmons says.

'If I'm telling a lie I hope to never rise from this chair,' Daddy says. 'And I reckon she would've got me if I wasn't moving fast.'

'That don't sound like Sister Rachel,' Reverend Simmons says.

'Sound like her or don't sound like her, she did it,' Daddy says. 'Sonny right over there. He seen every bit of it. Ask him.'

Reverend Simmons looks at me but he don't ask me nothing. He just clicks his tongue and shakes his head.

'That don't sound like Sister Rachel,' he says. 'But if you say that's what she did, I'll go down there and talk to her.'

'And that ain't all,' Daddy says.

Reverend Simmons waits for Daddy to go on.

'She got Freddie Jackson locked up in a room with Amy,' Daddy says.

Reverend Simmons looks at me and Daddy, then he goes over and gets his coat and hat from against the wall. Reverend Simmons's coat is long and black. His hat is big like a cowboy's hat.

'I'll be down the quarter, Carey,' he tells Mrs. Simmons. 'Be back quick as I can.'

We go out of the house and Daddy holds my hand. Me and him and Reverend Simmons go out in the road and head on back down the quarter.

'Reverend Simmons, I want my wife back,' Daddy says. 'A man can't live by himself in this world. It too cold and cruel.'

Reverend Simmons don't say nothing to Daddy. He starts humming a little song to himself. Reverend Simmons is big and he can walk fast. He takes big old long steps and me and Daddy got to walk fast to keep up with him. I got to run because Daddy's got my hand.

We get to Gran'mon's house and Reverend Simmons pushes the gate open and goes in the yard.

'Me and Sonny'll stay out here,' Daddy says.

'I'm cold, Daddy,' I say.

'I'll build a fire,' Daddy says. 'You want me build me and you a little fire?'

'Uh-huh.'

'Help me get some sticks, then,' Daddy says.

Me and Daddy get some grass and weeds and Daddy finds a big chunk of dry wood. We pile it all up and Daddy gets a match out his pocket and lights the fire.

'Feel better?' he says.

'Uh-huh.'

'How come you not in school this evening?' Daddy asks.

'I wee-weed on myself,' I say.

I tell Daddy because I know Daddy ain't go'n whip me.

'You peed on yourself at school?' Daddy asks. 'Sonny, I thought you was a big boy. That's something little babies do.'

'Miss Hebert want see you and Mama,' I say.

'I don't have time to see nobody now,' Daddy says. 'I got my own troubles. I just hope that preacher in there can do something.'

I look up at Daddy, but he's looking down in the fire.

'Sonny?' I hear Mama calling me.

I turn and I see Mama and all of them standing out there on the gallery.

'Hanh?' I answer.

'Come in here before you catch a death of cold,' Mama says.

Daddy goes to the fence and looks across the pickets at Mama.

'Amy,' he says, 'please come home. I swear I ain't go'n do it no more.'

'Sonny, you hear me talking to you?' Mama calls.

'I ain't go'n catch cold,' I say. 'We got a fire. I'm warm.'

'Amy, please come home,' Daddy says. 'Please, honey. I forgive you. I forgive Mama. I forgive everybody. Just come home.'

I look at Mama and Reverend Simmons talking on the gallery. The others ain't talking; they just standing there looking out in the road at me and Daddy. Reverend Simmons comes out the yard and over to the fire. Daddy comes to the fire where me and Reverend Simmons is. He looks at Reverend Simmons but Reverend Simmons won't look back at him.

'Well, Reverend?' Daddy says.

'She say she tired of you and that car,' Reverend Simmons says.

Daddy falls down on the ground and cries.

'A man just can't live by himself in this cold, cruel world,' he says. 'He got to have a woman to stand by him. He just can't make it by himself. God, help me.'

'Be strong, man,' Reverend Simmons says.

'I can't be strong with my wife in there and me out here,' Daddy says. 'I need my wife.'

'Well, you go'n have to straighten that out the best way you can,' Reverend Simmons says. 'And I talked to Sister Rachel. She said she didn't shoot to hurt you. She just shot to kind of scare you away.'

'She didn't shoot to hurt me?' Daddy says. 'And I reckon them things was jelly beans I heard zooming just three inches over my head?'

'She said she didn't shoot to hurt you,' Reverend Simmons says. He holds his hands over the fire. 'This fire's good, but I got to get on back up the quarter. Got to get my wood for tonight. I'll see you people later. And I hope everything comes out all right.'

'Reverend, you sure you can't do nothing?' Daddy asks.

'I tried, son,' Reverend Simmons says. 'Now we'll leave it in God's hand.'

'But I want my wife back now,' Daddy says. 'God take so long to—'

'Mr Howard, that's blasphemous,' Reverend Simmons says.

'I don't want blaspheme Him,' Daddy says. 'But I'm in a mess. I'm in a big mess. I want my wife.'

'I'd suggest you kneel down sometime,' Reverend Simmons says. 'That always helps in a family.'

Reverend Simmons looks at me like he's feeling sorry for me, then he goes on back up the quarter. I can see his coattail hitting him round the knees.

'You coming in this yard, Sonny?' Mama calls.

'I'm with Daddy,' I say.

Mama goes back in the house and Gran'mon and them follow her.

'When you want one of them preachers to do something for you, they can't do a doggone thing,' Daddy says. 'Nothing but stand up in that churchhouse and preach 'bout Heaven. I hate to go to that old hoo-doo woman, but I reckon there ain't nothing else I can do. You want go back there with me, Sonny?'

'Uh-huh.'

'Come on,' Daddy says.

Daddy takes my hand and me and him leave the fire. When I get 'way down the quarter I look back and see the fire still burning. We cross the railroad tracks and I can see the people cutting cane. They got plenty cane all on the ground.

'Get me piece of cane, Daddy,' I say.

'Sonny, please,' Daddy says. 'I'm thinking.'

'I want piece of two-ninety,' I say.

Daddy turns my hand loose and jumps over the ditch. He finds a piece of two-ninety and jumps back over. Daddy takes out a little pocketknife and peels the cane. He gives me a round and he cut him off a round and chew it. I like two-ninety cane because it's soft and sweet and got plenty juice in it.

'I want another piece,' I say.

Daddy cuts me off another round and hands it to me.

'I'll be glad when you big enough to peel your own cane,' he says.

'I can peel my own cane now,' I say.

Daddy breaks me off three joints and hands it to me. I peel the cane with my teeth. Two-ninety cane is soft and it's easy to peel.

Me and Daddy go round the bend, and then I can see Madame Toussaint's house. Madame Toussaint's got a' old house, and look like it want to fall down any minute. I'm scared of Madame Toussaint. Billy Joe Martin say Madame Toussaint's a witch, and he say one time he seen Madame Toussaint riding a broom.

Daddy pulls Madame Toussaint's little old broken-down gate open and we go in the yard. Me and Daddy go far as the steps, but we don't go up on the gallery. Madame Toussaint's got plenty trees round her house, little trees and big trees. And she got plenty moss hanging on every tree. I see a pecan over there on the ground but I'm scared to go and pick it up. Madame Toussaint'll put bad mark on me and I'll turn to a frog or something. I let Madame Toussaint's little old pecan stay right where it is. And I go up to Daddy and let him hold my hand.

'Madame Toussaint?' Daddy calls.

Madame Toussaint don't answer. Like she ain't there.

'Madame Toussaint?' Daddy calls again.

'Who that?' Madame Toussaint answers.

'Me,' Daddy says. 'Eddie Howard and his little boy Sonny.'

'What you want, Eddie Howard?' Madame Toussaint calls from in her house.

'I want talk to you,' Daddy says. 'I need little advice on something.'

I hear a dog bark three times in the house. He must be a big old dog because he's sure got a heavy voice. Madame Toussaint comes to the door and cracks it open.

'Can I come in?' Daddy says.

'Come in, Eddie Howard,' Madame Toussaint says.

Me and Daddy go up the steps and Madame Toussaint opens the door for us. Madame Toussaint's a little bitty little old woman and her face is brown like cowhide. I look at Madame Toussaint and I walk close 'side Daddy. Me and Daddy go in the house and Madame Toussaint shuts the door and comes back to her fireplace. She sits down in her big old rocking chair and looks at me and Daddy. I look round Daddy's leg at Madame Toussaint, but I let Daddy hold my hand. Madame Toussaint's house don't smell good. It's too dark in here. It don't smell good at all. Madame Toussaint ought to have a window or something open in her house.

'I need some advice, Madame Toussaint,' Daddy says.

'Your wife left you,' Madame Toussaint says.

'How you know?' Daddy asks.

'That's all you men come back here for,' Madame Toussaint says. 'That's how I know.'

Daddy nods his head. 'Yes,' he says. 'She done left me and staying with another man.'

'She left,' Madame Toussaint says. 'But she's not staying with another man.'

'Yes, she is,' Daddy says.

'She's not,' Madame Toussaint says. 'You trying to tell me my business?'

'No, ma'am,' Daddy says.

'I should hope not,' Madame Toussaint says.

Madame Toussaint ain't got but three old rotten teeth in her mouth. I bet you she can't peel no cane with them old rotten teeth. I bet you they'd break off in a hard piece of cane.

'I need advice, Madame Toussaint,' Daddy says.

'You got money?' Madame Toussaint asks.

'I got some,' Daddy says.

'How much?' she asks Daddy. She's looking up at Daddy like she don't believe him.

Daddy turns my hand loose and sticks his hand down in his pocket. He gets all his money out his pocket and leans over the fire to see how much he's got. I see some matches and piece of string and some nails in Daddy's hand. I reach for the piece of string and Daddy taps me on the hand with his other hand.

'I got about seventy-five cents,' Daddy says. 'Counting them pennies.'

'My price is three dollars,' Madame Toussaint says.

'I can cut you a load of wood,' Daddy says. 'Or make grocery for you. I'll do anything in the world if you can help me, Madame Toussaint.'

'Three dollars,' Madame Toussaint says. 'I got all the wood I'll need this winter. Enough grocery to last me till summer.'

'But this all I got,' Daddy says.

'When you get more, come back,' Madame Toussaint says.

'But I want my wife back now,' Daddy says. 'I can't wait till I get more money.'

'Three dollars is my price,' Madame Toussaint says. 'No more, no less.'

'But can't you give me just a little advice for seventy-five cents?' Daddy says. 'Seventy-five cents worth? Maybe I can start from there and figure something out.'

Madame Toussaint looks at me and looks at Daddy again.

'You say that's your boy?' she says.

'Yes, ma'am,' Daddy says.

'Nice-looking boy,' Madame Toussaint says.

'His name's Sonny,' Daddy says.

'Hi, Sonny,' Madame Toussaint says.

'Say "Hi" to Madame Toussaint,' Daddy says. 'Go on.'

'Hi,' I say, sticking close to Daddy.

'Well, Madame Toussaint?' Daddy says.

'Give me the money,' Madame Toussaint says. 'Don't complain to me if you not satisfied.'

'Don't worry,' Daddy says. 'I won't complain. Anything to get her back home.'

Daddy leans over the fire again and picks the money out of his hand. Then he reaches it to Madame Toussaint.

'Give me that little piece of string,' Madame Toussaint says. 'It might come in handy sometime in the future. Wait,' she says. 'Run it 'cross the left side of the boy's face three times, then pass it to me behind your back.'

'What's that for?' Daddy asks.

'Just do like I say,' Madame Toussaint says.

'Yes, ma'am,' Daddy says. Daddy turns to me. 'Hold still, Sonny,' he says. He rubs the little old dirty piece of cord over my face, and then he sticks his hand behind his back.

Madame Toussaint reaches in her pocket and takes out her

pocketbook. She opens it and puts the money in. She opens another little compartment and stuffs the string down in it. Then she snaps the pocketbook and puts it back in her pocket. She picks up three little green sticks she got tied together and starts poking in the fire with them.

'What's the advice?' Daddy asks.

Madame Toussaint don't say nothing.

'Madame Toussaint?' Daddy says.

Madame Toussaint still don't answer him, she just looks down in the fire. Her face is red from the fire. I get scared of Madame Toussaint. She can ride all over the plantation on her broom. Billy Joe Martin say he seen her one night riding 'cross the houses. She was whipping her broom with three switches.

Madame Toussaint raises her head and looks at Daddy. Her eyes's big and white, and I get scared of her. I hide my face 'side Daddy's leg.

'Give it up,' I hear her say.

'Give what up?' Daddy says.

'Give it up,' she says.

'What?' Daddy says.

'Give it up,' she says.

'I don't even know what you talking 'bout,' Daddy says. 'How can I give up something and I don't even know what it is?'

'I said it three times,' Madame Toussaint says. 'No more, no less. Up to you now to follow it through from there.'

'Follow what from where?' Daddy says. 'You said three little old words: "Give it up." I don't know no more now than I knowed 'fore I got here.'

'I told you you wasn't go'n be satisfied,' Madame Toussaint says.

'Satisfied?' Daddy says. 'Satisfied for what? You gived me just three little old words and you want me to be satisfied?'

'You can leave,' Madame Toussaint says.

'Leave?' Daddy says. 'You mean I give you seventy-five cents for three words? A quarter a word? And I'm leaving? No, Lord.'

'Rollo?' Madame Toussaint says.

I see Madame Toussaint's big old black dog get up out of the corner and come where she is. Madame Toussaint pats the dog on the head with her hand.

'Two dollars and twenty-five cents more and you get all the advice you need,' Madame Toussaint says.

'Can't I get you a load of wood and fix your house for you or something?' Daddy says.

'I don't want my house fixed and I don't need no more wood,' Madame Toussaint says. 'I got three loads of wood just three days ago from a man who didn't have money. Before I know it I'll have wood piled up all over my yard.'

'Can't I do anything?' Daddy says.

'You can leave,' Madame Toussaint says. 'I ought to have somebody else dropping round pretty soon. Lately I've been having men dropping in three times a day. All of them just like you. What they can do to make their wives love them more. What they can do to keep their wives from running round with some other man. What they can do to make their wives give in. What they can do to make their wives scratch their backs. What they can do to make their wives look at them when they talking to her. Get out my house before I put the dog on you. You been here too long for seventy-five cents.'

Madame Toussaint's big old jet-black dog gives three loud barks that makes my head hurt. Madame Toussaint pats him on the back to calm him down.

'Come on, Sonny,' Daddy says.

I let Daddy take my hand and we go over to the door.

'I still don't feel like you helped me very much, though,' Daddy says.

Madame Toussaint pats her big old jet-black dog on the head and she don't answer Daddy. Daddy pushes the door open and we go outside. It's some cold outside. Me and Daddy go down Madame Toussaint's old broken-down steps.

'What was them words?' Daddy asks me.

'Hanh?'

'What she said when she looked up out of that fire?' Daddy asks.

'I was scared,' I say. 'Her face was red and her eyes got big and white. I was scared. I had to hide my face.'

'Didn't you hear what she told me?' Daddy asks.

'She told you three dollars,' I say.

'I mean when she looked up,' Daddy says.

'She say, "Give it up,"' I say.

'Yes,' Daddy says. '"Give it up." Give what up? I don't even know what she's talking 'bout. I hope she don't mean give you and Amy up. She ain't that crazy. I don't know nothing else she can be talking 'bout. You don't know, do you?'

'Uh-uh,' I say.

'"Give it up,"' Daddy says. 'I don't even know what she's talking 'bout. I wonder who them other men was she was speaking of. Johnny and his wife had a fight the other week. It might be him. Frank Armstrong and his wife had a round couple weeks back. Could be him. I wish I knowed what she told them.'

'I want another piece of cane,' I say.

'No,' Daddy says. 'You'll be pee-ing in bed all night tonight.'

'I'm go'n sleep with Uncle Al,' I say. 'Me and him go'n sleep in his bed.'

'Please, be quiet, Sonny,' Daddy says. 'I got enough troubles on my mind. Don't add more to it.'

Me and Daddy walk in the middle of the road. Daddy holds my hand. I can hear a tractor—I see it across the field. The people loading cane on the trailer back of the tractor.

'Come on,' Daddy says. 'We going over to Frank Armstrong.'

Daddy totes me 'cross the ditch on his back. I ride on Daddy's back and I look at the stubbles where the people done cut the cane. Them rows some long. Plenty cane's laying on the ground. I can see cane all over the field. Me and Daddy go over where the people cutting cane.

'How come you ain't working this evening?' a man asks Daddy. The man's shucking a big armful of cane with his cane knife.

'Frank Armstrong round anywhere?' Daddy asks the man.

'Farther over,' the man says. 'Hi, youngster.'

'Hi,' I say.

Me and Daddy go 'cross the field. I look at the people cutting cane. That cane is some tall. I want another piece, but I might wee-wee in Uncle Al's bed.

Me and Daddy go over where Mr Frank Armstrong and Mrs Julie's cutting cane. Mrs Julie got overalls on just like Mr Frank got. She's even wearing one of Mr Frank's old hats.

'How y'all?' Daddy says.

'So–so, and yourself?' Mrs Julie says.

'I'm trying to make it,' Daddy says. 'Can I borrow your husband there a minute?'

'Sure,' Mrs Julie says. 'But don't keep him too long. We trying to reach the end 'fore dark.'

'It won't take long,' Daddy says.

Mr Frank and them got a little fire burning in one of the middles. Me and him and Daddy go over there. Daddy squats down and let me slide off his back.

'What's the trouble?' Mr Frank asks Daddy.

'Amy left me, Frank,' Daddy says.

Mr Frank holds his hands over the fire.

'She left you?' he says.

'Yes,' Daddy says. 'And I want her back, Frank.'

'What can I do?' Mr Frank says. 'She's no kin to me. I can't go and make her come back.'

'I thought maybe you could tell me what you and Madame Toussaint talked about,' Daddy says. 'That's if you don't mind, Frank.'

'What?' Mr Frank says. 'Who told you I talked with Madame Toussaint?'

'Nobody,' Daddy says. 'But I heard you and Julie had a fight, and I thought maybe you went back to her for advice.'

'For what?' Mr Frank says.

'So you and Julie could make up,' Daddy says.

'Well, I'll be damned,' Mr Frank says. 'I done heard everything. Excuse me, Sonny. But your daddy's enough to make anybody cuss.'

I look up at Daddy, and I look back in the fire again.

'Please, Frank,' Daddy says. 'I'm desperate. I'm ready to try any-thing. I'll do anything to get her back in my house.'

'Why don't you just go and get her?' Mr Frank says. 'That makes sense.'

'I can't,' Daddy says. 'Mama won't let me come in the yard. She even took a shot at me once today.'

'What?' Mr Frank says. He looks at Daddy, and then he just bust out laughing. Daddy laughs little bit, too.

'What y'all talked about, Frank?' Daddy asks. 'Maybe if I try the same thing, maybe I'll be able to get her back, too.'

Mr Frank laughs at Daddy, then he stops and just looks at Daddy.

'No,' he says. 'I'm afraid my advice won't help your case. You got to first get close to your wife. And your mother-in-law won't let you do that. No, mine won't help you.'

'It might,' Daddy says.

'No, it won't,' Mr Frank says.

'It might,' Daddy says. 'What was it?'

'All right,' Mr Frank says. 'She told me I wasn't petting Julie enough.'

'Petting her?' Daddy says.

'You think he knows what we talking 'bout?' Mr Frank asks Daddy.

'I'll get him piece of cane,' Daddy says.

They got a big pile of cane right behind Daddy's back, and he crosses the row and gets me a stalk of two-ninety. He breaks off three joints and hands it to me. He throws the rest of the stalk back.

'So I start petting her,' Mr Frank says.

'What you mean "petting her"?' Daddy says. 'I don't even know what you mean now.'

'Eddie, I swear,' Mr Frank says. 'Stroking her. You know. Like you stroke a colt. A little horse.'

'Oh,' Daddy says. 'Did it work?'

'What you think?' Mr Frank says, grinning. 'Every night, a little bit. Turn your head, Sonny.'

'Hanh?'

'Look the other way,' Daddy says.

I look down the row toward the other end. I don't see nothing but cane all over the ground.

'Stroke her a little back here,' Mr Frank says. I hear him hitting on his pants. 'Works every time. Get along now like two peas in one pod. Every night when we get in the bed—' I hear him hitting again. '—couple little strokes. Now everything's all right.'

'You was right,' Daddy says. 'That won't help me none.'

'My face getting cold,' I say.

'You can turn round and warm,' Daddy says.

I turn and look at Mr Frank. I bite off piece of cane and chew it.

'I told you it wouldn't,' Mr Frank says. 'Well, I got to get back to work. What you go'n do now?'

'I don't know,' Daddy says. 'If I had three dollars she'd give me some advice. But I don't have a red copper. You wouldn't have three dollars you could spare till payday, huh?'

'I don't have a dime,' Mr Frank says. 'Since we made up, Julie keeps most of the money.'

'You think she'd lend me three dollars till Saturday?' Daddy asks.

'I don't know if she got that much on her,' Mr Frank says. 'I'll go over and ask her.'

I watch Mr Frank going 'cross the rows where Mrs Julie's cutting cane. They start talking, and then I hear them laughing.

'You warm?' Daddy asks.

'Uh-huh.'

I see Mr Frank coming back to the fire.

'She don't have it on her but she got it at the house,' Mr Frank says. 'If you can wait till we knock off.'

'No,' Daddy says. 'I can't wait till night. I got to try to borrow it from somebody now.'

'Why don't you go 'cross the field and try Johnny Green,' Mr Frank says. 'He's always got some money. Maybe he'll lend it to you.'

'I'll ask him,' Daddy says. 'Get on, Sonny.'

Me and Daddy go back 'cross the field. I can hear Mr Johnny Green singing, and Daddy turns that way and we go down where Mr Johnny is. Mr Johnny stops his singing when he sees me and Daddy. He chops the top off a' armful of cane and throws it 'cross the row. Mr Johnny's cutting cane all by himself.

'Hi, Brother Howard,' Mr Johnny says.

'Hi,' Daddy says. Daddy squats down and let me slide off.

'Hi there, little Brother Sonny,' Mr Johnny says.

'Hi,' I say.

'How you?' Mr Johnny asks.

'I'm all right,' I say.

'That's good,' Mr Johnny says. 'And how you this beautiful, God-sent day, Brother Howard?'

'I'm fine,' Daddy says. 'Johnny, I want know if you can spare me 'bout three dollars till Saturday?'

'Sure, Brother Howard,' Mr Johnny says. 'You mind telling me just why you need it? I don't mind lending a good brother anything, long 's I know he ain't wasting it on women or drink.'

'I want pay Madame Toussaint for some advice,' Daddy says.

'Little trouble, Brother?' Mr Johnny asks.

'Amy done left me, Johnny,' Daddy says. 'I need some advice. I just got to get her back.'

'I know what you mean, Brother,' Mr Johnny says. 'I had to visit Madame—you won't carry this no farther, huh?'

'No,' Daddy says.

'Couple months ago I had to take a little trip back there to see her,' Mr Johnny says.

'What was wrong?' Daddy asks.

'Little misunderstanding between me and Sister Laura,' Mr Johnny says.

'She helped?' Daddy asks.

'Told me to stop spending so much time in church and little more time at home,' Mr Johnny says. 'I couldn't see that. You know, far back as I can go in my family my people been good church members.'

'I know that,' Daddy says.

'My pappy was a deacon and my mammy didn't miss a Sunday long as I can remember,' Mr Johnny says. 'And that's how I was raised. To fear God. I just couldn't see it when she first told me that. But I thought it over. I went for a long walk back in the field. I got down on my knees and looked up at the sky. I asked God to show me the way—to tell me what to do. And He did, He surely did. He told me to do just like Madame Toussaint said. Slack up going to church. Go twice a week, but spend the rest of the time with her. Just like that He told me. And I'm doing exactly what He said. Twice a week. And, Brother Howard, don't spread this round, but the way Sister Laura been acting here lately, there might be a little Johnny next summer sometime.'

'No?' Daddy says.

'Uhnnnn-hunh,' Mr Johnny says.

'I'll be doggone,' Daddy says. 'I'm glad to hear that.'

'I'll be the happiest man on this whole plantation,' Mr Johnny says.

'I know how you feel,' Daddy says. 'Yes, I know how you feel. But that three, can you lend it to me?'

'Sure, Brother,' Mr Johnny says. 'Anything to bring a family back together. Nothing more important in this world than family love. Yes, indeed.'

Mr Johnny unbuttons his top overalls pocket and takes out a dollar.

'Only thing I got is five, Brother Howard,' he says. 'You wouldn't happen to have some change, would you?'

'I don't have a red copper,' Daddy says. 'But I'll be more than happy if you can let me have that five. I need some grocery in the house, too.'

'Sure, Brother,' Mr Johnny says. He hands Daddy the dollar. 'Nothing looks more beautiful than a family at a table eating something the little woman just cooked. But you did say Saturday didn't you, Brother?'

'Yes,' Daddy says. 'I'll pay you back soon 's I get paid. You can't ever guess how much this means to me, Johnny.'

'Glad I can help, Brother,' Mr Johnny says. 'Hope she can do likewise.'

'I hope so too,' Daddy says. 'Anyhow, this a start.'

'See you Saturday, Brother,' Mr Johnny says.

'Soon 's I get paid,' Daddy says. 'Hop on, Sonny, and hold tight. We going back.'

4

Daddy walks up on Madame Toussaint's gallery and knocks on the door.

'Who that?' Madame Toussaint asks.

'Me. Eddie Howard,' Daddy says. He squats down so I can slide off his back. I slide down and let Daddy hold my hand.

'What you want, Eddie Howard?' Madame Toussaint asks.

'I got three dollars,' Daddy says. 'I still want that advice.'

Madame Toussaint's big old jet-black dog barks three times, and then I hear Madame Toussaint coming to the door. She peeps through the keyhole at me and Daddy. She opens the door and let me and Daddy come in. We go to the fireplace and warm. Madame Toussaint comes to the fireplace and sits down in her big old rocking chair. She looks up at Daddy. I look for big old Rollo, but I don't see him. He must be under the bed or hiding somewhere in the corner.

'You got three dollars?' Madame Toussaint asks Daddy.

'Yes,' Daddy says. He takes out the dollar and shows it to Madame Toussaint.

Madame Toussaint holds her hand up for it.

'This is five,' Daddy says. 'I want two back.'

'You go'n get your two,' Madame Toussaint says.

'Come to think of it,' Daddy says, 'I ought to just owe you two and a quarter, since I done already gived you seventy-five cents.'

'You want advice?' Madame Toussaint asks Daddy. Madame Toussaint looks like she's getting mad with Daddy now.

'Sure,' Daddy says. 'But since—'

'Then shut up and hand me your money,' Madame Toussaint says.

'But I done already—' Daddy says.

'Get out my house, nigger,' Madame Toussaint says. 'And don't come back till you learn how to act.'

'All right,' Daddy says, 'I'll give you three more dollars.'

He hands Madame Toussaint the dollar.

Madame Toussaint gets her pocketbook out her pocket. Then she leans close to the fire so she can look down in it. She sticks her hand in the pocketbook and gets two dollars. She looks at the two dollars a long time. She stands up and gets her eyeglasses off the mantelpiece and puts them on her eyes. She looks at the two dollars a long time, then she hands them to Daddy. She sticks the dollar bill Daddy gived her in the pocketbook, then she takes her eyeglasses off and puts them back on the mantelpiece. Madame Toussaint sits in her big old rocking chair and starts poking in the fire with the three sticks again. Her face gets red from the fire, her eyes get big and white. I turn my head and hide behind Daddy's leg.

'Go set fire to your car,' Madame Toussaint says.

'What?' Daddy says.

'Go set fire to your car,' Madame Toussaint says.

'You talking to me?' Daddy says.

'Go set fire to your car,' Madame Toussaint says.

'Now, just a minute,' Daddy says. 'I didn't give you my hard-earned three dollars for that kind of foolishness. I dismiss that seventy-five cents you took from me, but not my three dollars that easy.'

'You want your wife back?' Madame Toussaint asks Daddy.

'That's what I'm paying you for,' Daddy says.

'Then go set fire to your car,' Madame Toussaint says. 'You can't have both.'

'You must be fooling,' Daddy says.

'I don't fool,' Madame Toussaint says. 'You paid for advice and I'm giving you advice.'

'You mean that?' Daddy says. 'You mean I got to go burn up my car for Amy to come back home?'

'If you want her back there,' Madame Toussaint says. 'Do you?'

'I wouldn't be standing here if I didn't,' Daddy says.

'Then go and burn it up,' Madame Toussaint says. 'A gallon of coal oil and a penny box of match ought to do the trick. You got any gas in it?'

'A little bit—if nobody ain't drained it,' Daddy says.

'Then you can use that,' Madame Toussaint says. 'But if you want her back there you got to burn it up. That's my advice to you. And if I was you I'd do it right away. You can never tell.'

'Tell about what?' Daddy asks.

'She might be sleeping in another man's bed a week from now,' Madame Toussaint says. 'This man loves her and he's kind. And that's what a woman wants. That's what they need. You men don't know this, but you better learn it before it's too late.'

'What's that other man's name?' Daddy asks. 'Can it be Freddie Jackson?'

'It can,' Madame Toussaint says. 'But it don't have to be. Any man that'd give her love and kindness.'

'I love her,' Daddy says. 'I give her kindness. I'm always giving her love and kindness.'

'When you home, you mean,' Madame Toussaint says. 'How about when you running up and down the road in your car? How do you think she feels then?'

Daddy don't say nothing.

'You men better learn,' Madame Toussaint says. 'Now, if you want her, go and burn it. If you don't want her, go and get drunk off them two dollars and sleep in a cold bed tonight.'

'You mean she'll come back tonight?' Daddy asks.

'She's ready to come back right now,' Madame Toussaint says. 'Poor little thing.'

I look round Daddy's leg at Madame Toussaint. Madame Toussaint's looking in the fire. Her face ain't red no more; her eyes ain't big and white, either.

'She's not happy where she is,' Madame Toussaint says.

'She's with her mama,' Daddy says.

'You don't have to tell me my business,' Madame Toussaint says. 'I know where she is. And I still say she's not happy. She much rather be back in her own house. Women like to be in their own house. That's their world. You men done messed up the outside world so bad that they feel lost and out of place in it. Her house is her world. Only there she can do what she want. She can't do that in anybody else house— mama or nobody else. But you men don't know any of this. Y'all never know how a woman feels, because you never ask how she feels. Long 's she there when you get there you satisfied. Long 's you give her two or three dollars every weekend you think she ought to be satisfied. But keep on. One day all of you'll find out.'

'Couldn't I sell the car or something?' Daddy asks.

'You got to burn it,' Madame Toussaint says. 'How come your head so hard?'

'But I paid good money for that car,' Daddy says. 'It wouldn't look right if I just jumped up and put fire to it.'

'You, get out my house,' Madame Toussaint says, pointing her finger at Daddy. 'Go do what you want with your car. It's yours. But just don't come back here bothering me for no more advice.'

'I don't know,' Daddy says.

'I'm through talking,' Madame Toussaint says. 'Rollo? Come here, baby.'

Big old jet-black Rollo comes up and puts his head in Madame Toussaint's lap. Madame Toussaint pats him on the head.

'That's what I got to do, hanh?' Daddy says.

Madame Toussaint don't answer Daddy. She starts singing a song to Rollo:

> *Mama's little baby,*
> *Mama's little baby.*

'He bad?' Daddy asks.

> *Mama's little baby,*
> *Mama's little baby.*

'Do he bite?' Daddy asks.

Madame Toussaint keeps on singing:

> *Mama's little baby,*
> *Mama's little baby.*

'Come on,' Daddy says. 'I reckon we better be going.'

Daddy squats down and I climb up on his back. I look down at Madame Toussaint patting big old jet-black Rollo on his head.

Daddy pushes the door open and we go outside. It's cold outside. Daddy goes down Madame Toussaint's three old broken-down steps and we go out in the road.

'I don't know,' Daddy says.

'Hanh?'

'I'm talking to myself,' Daddy says. 'I don't know about burning up my car.'

'You go'n burn up your car?' I ask.

'That's what Madame Toussaint say to do,' Daddy says.

'You ain't go'n have no more car?'

'I reckon not,' Daddy says. 'You want me and Mama to stay together?'

'Uh-huh.'

'Then I reckon I got to burn it up,' Daddy says. 'But I sure hope there was another way out. I put better than three hundred dollars in that car.'

Daddy walks fast and I bounce on his back.

'God, I wish there was another way out,' Daddy says. 'Don't look like that's right for a man to just jump up and set fire to something like that. What you think I ought to do?'

'Hanh?'

'Go back to sleep,' Daddy says. 'I don't know what I'm educating you for.'

'I ain't sleeping,' I say.

'I don't know,' Daddy says. 'That don't look right. All Frank Armstrong had to do was pop Julie on the butt little bit every night 'fore she went to sleep. All Johnny had to do was stop going to church so much. Neither one of them had to burn down anything. Johnny didn't have to burn down the church; Frank didn't have to burn down the bed—nothing. But me, I got to burn up my car. She charged all us the same thing—no, she even charged me seventy-five cents more, and I got to burn up a car I can still get some use out. Now, that don't sound right, do it?'

'Hanh?'

'I can't figure it,' Daddy says. 'Look like I ought to be able to sell it for little something. Get some of my money back. Burning it, I don't get a red copper. That just don't sound right to me. I wonder if she was fooling. No. She say she wasn't. But maybe that wasn't my advice she seen in that fireplace. Maybe that was somebody else advice. Maybe she gived me the wrong one. Maybe it belongs to the man coming back there after me. They go there three times a day, she can get them mixed up.'

'I'm scared of Madame Toussaint, Daddy,' I say.

'Must've been somebody else,' Daddy says. 'I bet it was. I bet you anything it was.'

I bounce on Daddy's back and I close my eyes. I open them and I see me and Daddy going 'cross the railroad tracks. We go up the quarter to Gran'mon's house. Daddy squats down and I slide off his back.

'Run in the house to the fire,' Daddy says. 'Tell your mama come to the door.'

Soon 's I come in the yard, Spot runs down the walk and starts barking. Mama and all of them come out on the gallery.

'My baby,' Mama says. Mama comes down the steps and hugs me to her. 'My baby,' she says.

'Look at that old yellow thing standing out in that road,' Gran'mon says. 'What you ought to been done was got the sheriff on him for kidnap.'

Me and Mama go back on the gallery.

'I been to Madame Toussaint's house,' I say.

Mama looks at me and looks at Daddy out in the road. Daddy comes to the gate and looks at us on the gallery.

'Amy?' Daddy calls. 'Can I speak to you a minute? Just one minute?'

'You don't get away from my gate, I'm go'n make that shotgun speak to you,' Gran'mon says. 'I didn't get you at twelve o'clock, but I won't miss you now.'

'Amy, honey,' Daddy calls. 'Please.'

'Come on, Sonny,' Mama says.

'Where you going?' Gran'mon asks.

'Far as the gate,' Mama says. 'I'll talk to him. I reckon I owe him that much.'

'You leave this house with that nigger, don't ever come back here again,' Gran'mon says.

'You oughtn't talk like that, Rachel,' Uncle Al says.

'I talk like I want,' Gran'mon says. 'She's my daughter; not yours, neither his.'

Me and Mama go out to the gate where Daddy is. Daddy stands outside the gate and me and Mama stand inside.

'Lord, you look good, Amy,' Daddy says. 'Honey, didn't you miss me? Go on and say it. Go on and say how bad you missed me.'

'That's all you want say to me?' Mama says.

'Honey, please,' Daddy says. 'Say you missed me. I been grieving all day like a dog.'

'Come on, Sonny,' Mama says. 'Let's go back inside.'

'Honey,' Daddy says. 'Please don't turn your back on me and go back to Freddie Jackson. Honey, I love you. I swear 'fore God I love you. Honey, you listening?'

'Come on, Sonny,' Mama says.

'Honey,' Daddy says, 'if I burn the car like Madame Toussaint say, you'll come back home?'

'What?' Mama says.

'She say for Daddy—'

'Be still, Sonny,' Mama says.

'She told me to set fire to it and you'll come back home,' Daddy says. 'You'll come back, honey?'

'She told you to burn up your car?' Mama says.

'If I want you to come back,' Daddy says. 'If I do it, you'll come back?'

'If you burn it up,' Mama says. 'If you burn it up, yes, I'll come back.'

'Tonight?' Daddy says.

'Yes; tonight,' Mama says.

'If I sold it?' Daddy says.

'Burn it,' Mama says.

'I can get about fifty for it,' Daddy says. 'You could get couple dresses out of that.'

'Burn it,' Mama says. 'You know what burn is?'

Daddy looks across the gate at Mama, and Mama looks right back at him. Daddy nods his head.

'I can't argue with you, honey,' he says. 'I'll go and burn it right now. You can come see if you want.'

'No,' Mama says, 'I'll be here when you come back.'

'Couldn't you go up home and start cooking some supper?' Daddy asks. 'I'm just 's hungry as a dog.'

'I'll cook when that car is burnt,' Mama says. 'Come on, Sonny.'

'Can I go see Daddy burn his car, Mama?' I ask.

'No,' Mama says. 'You been in that cold long enough.'

'I want see Daddy burn his car,' I say. I start crying and stomping so Mama'll let me go.

'Let him go, honey,' Daddy says. 'I'll keep him warm.'

'You can go,' Mama says. 'But don't come to me if you start that coughing tonight, you hear?'

'Uh-huh,' I say.

Mama makes sure all my clothes's buttoned good, then she let me go. I run out in the road where Daddy is.

'I'll be back soon 's I can, honey,' Daddy says. 'And we'll straighten out everything, hear?'

'Just make sure you burn it,' Mama says. 'I'll find out.'

'Honey, I'm go'n burn every bit of it,' Daddy says.

'I'll be here when you come back,' Mama says. 'How you figuring on getting up there?'

'I'll go over and see if George Williams can't take me,' Daddy says.

'I don't want Sonny in that cold too long,' Mama says. 'And you keep your hands in your pockets, Sonny.'

'I ain't go'n take them out,' I say.

Mama goes back up the walk toward the house. Daddy stands there just watching her.

'Lord, that's a sweet little woman,' he says, shaking his head. 'That's a sweet little woman you see going back to that house.'

'Come on, Daddy,' I say. 'Let's go burn up the car.'

Me and Daddy walk away from the fence.

'Let me get on your back and ride,' I say.

'Can't you walk sometime,' Daddy says. 'What you think I'm educating you for—to treat me like a horse?'

5

Mr George Williams drives his car to the side of the road, then we get out.

'Look like we got company,' Mr George Williams says.

Me and Daddy and Mr George Williams go over where the people is. The people got a little fire burning, and some of them's sitting on the car fender. But most of them's standing round the little fire.

'Welcome,' somebody says.

'Thanks,' Daddy says. 'Since this is my car you sitting on.'

'Oh,' the man says. He jumps up and the other two men jump up, too. They go over to the little fire and stand round it.

'We didn't mean no harm,' one of them say.

Daddy goes over and peeps in the car. Then he opens the door and gets in. I go over to the car where he is.

'Go stand 'side the fire,' Daddy says.

'I want get in with you,' I say.

'Do what I tell you,' Daddy says.

I go back to the fire, and I turn and look at Daddy in the car. Daddy passes his hand all over the car; then he just sit there quiet-like. All the people round the fire look at Daddy in the car. I can hear them talking real low.

After a little while, Daddy opens the door and gets out. He comes over to the fire.

'Well,' he says, 'I guess that's it. You got a rope?'

'In the trunk,' Mr George Williams says. 'What you go'n do, drag it off the highway?'

'We can't burn it out here,' Daddy says.

'He say he go'n burn it,' somebody at the fire says.

'I'm go'n burn it,' Daddy says. 'It's mine, ain't it?'

'Easy, Eddie,' Mr George Williams says.

Daddy is mad but he don't say any more. Mr George Williams looks at Daddy, then he goes over to his car and gets the rope.

'Ought to be strong enough,' Mr George Williams says.

He hands Daddy the rope, then he goes and turns his car around. Everybody at the fire looks at Mr George Williams backing up his car.

'Good,' Daddy says.

Daddy gets between the cars and ties them together. Some of the people come over and watch him.

'Y'all got a side road anywhere round here?' he asks.

'Right over there,' the man says. 'Leads off back in the field. You ain't go'n burn up that good car for real, is you?'

'Who field this is?' Daddy asks.

'Mr Roger Medlow,' the man says.

'Any colored people got fields round here anywhere?' Daddy asks.

'Old man Ned Johnson 'bout two miles farther down the road,' another man says.

'Why don't we just take it on back to the plantation?' Mr George Williams says. 'I doubt if Mr Claude'll mind if we burnt it there.'

'All right,' Daddy says. 'Might as well.'

Me and Daddy get in his car. Some of the people from the fire run up to Mr George Williams's car. Mr George Williams tells them something, and I see three of them jumping in. Mr George Williams taps on the horn, then we get going. I sit 'way back in the seat and look at Daddy. Daddy's quiet. He's sorry because he got to burn up his car.

We go 'way down the road, then we turn and go down the quarter. Soon 's we get down there, I hear two of the men in Mr George Williams's car calling to the people. I sit up in the seat and look out at them. They standing on the fenders, calling to the people.

'Come on,' they saying. 'Come on to the car-burning party. Free. Everybody welcome. Free.'

We go farther down the quarter, and the two men keep on calling.

'Come on, everybody,' one of them says.

'We having a car-burning party tonight,' the other one says. 'No charges.'

The people start coming out on the galleries to see what all the racket is. I look back and I see some out in the yard, and some already out in the road. Mr George Williams stops in front of Gran'mon's house.

'You go'n tell Amy?' he calls to Daddy. 'Maybe she like to go, since you doing it all for her.'

'Go tell your mama come on,' Daddy says.

I jump out the car and run in the yard.

'Come on, everybody,' one of the men says.

'We having a car-burning party tonight,' the other one says. 'Everybody invited. No charges.'

I pull Gran'mon's door open and go in. Mama and Uncle Al and Gran'mon's sitting at the fireplace.

'Mama, Daddy say come on if you want see the burning,' I say.

'See what burning?' Gran'mon asks. 'Now don't tell me that crazy nigger going through with that.'

'Come on, Mama,' I say.

Mama and Uncle Al get up from the fireplace and go to the door.

'He sure got it out there,' Uncle Al says.

'Come on, Mama,' I say. 'Come on, Uncle Al.'

'Wait till I get my coat,' Mama says. 'Mama, you going?'

'I ain't missing this for the world,' Gran'mon says. 'I still think he's bluffing.'

Gran'mon gets her coat and Uncle Al gets his coat; then we go on outside. Plenty people standing round Daddy's car now. I can see more people opening doors and coming out on the galleries.

'Get in,' Daddy says. 'Sorry I can't take but two. Mama, you want ride?'

'No, thanks,' Gran'mon says. 'You might just get it in your head to run off in that canal with me in there. Let your wife and child ride. I'll walk with the rest of the people.'

'Get in, honey,' Daddy says. 'It's getting cold out there.'

Mama takes my arm and helps me in; then she gets in and shuts the door.

'How far down you going?' Uncle Al asks.

'Near the sugar house,' Daddy says. He taps on the horn and Mr George Williams drives away.

'Come on, everybody,' one of the men says.

'We having a car-burning party tonight,' the other one says. 'Everybody invited.'

Mr George Williams drives his car over the railroad tracks. I look back and I see plenty people following Daddy's car. I can't see Uncle Al and Gran'mon, but I know they back there, too.

We keep going. We get almost to the sugar house, then we turn down another road. The other road is bumpy and I have to bounce on the seat.

'Well, I reckon this's it,' Daddy says.

Mama don't say nothing to Daddy.

'You know it ain't too late to change your mind,' Daddy says. 'All I got to do is stop George and untie the car.'

'You brought matches?' Mama asks.

'All right,' Daddy says. 'All right. Don't start fussing.'

We go a little farther and Daddy taps on the horn. Mr George Williams stops his car. Daddy gets out his car and go and talk with Mr George Williams. Little bit later I see Daddy coming back.

'Y'all better get out here,' he says. 'We go'n take it down the field a piece.'

Me and Mama get out. I look down the headland and I see Uncle Al and Gran'mon and all the other people coming. Some of them even got flashlights because it's getting dark now. They come where me and Mama's standing. I look down the field and I see the cars going down the row. It's dark, but Mr George Williams got bright lights on his car. The cars stop and Daddy get out his car and go and untie the rope. Mr George Williams goes and turns around and come back to the headland where all the people standing. Then he turns his lights on Daddy's car so everybody can see the burning. I see Daddy getting some gas out the tank.

'Give me a hand down here,' Daddy calls. But that don't even sound like Daddy's voice.

Plenty people run down the field to help Daddy. They get round the car and start shaking it. I see the car leaning; then it tips over.

'Well,' Gran'mon says. 'I never would've thought it.'

I see Daddy going all round the car with the can, then I see him splashing some inside the car. All the other people back back to give him room. I see Daddy scratching a match and throwing it in the car. He scratches another one and throw that one in the car, too. I see little bit fire, then I see plenty.

'I just do declare,' Gran'mon says. 'I must be dreaming. He's a man after all.'

Gran'mon the only person talking; everybody else is quiet. We stay there a long time and look at the fire. The fire burns down and Daddy and them go and look at the car again. Daddy picks up the can and pours some more gas on the fire. The fire gets big. We look at the fire some more.

'Never thought that was in Eddie,' somebody says real low.

'You not the only one,' somebody else says.

'He loved that car more than he loved anything.'

'No, he must love her more,' another person says.

The fire burns down again. Daddy and them go and look at the car. They stay there a good while, then they come out to the headland where we standing.

'What's that, George?' Mama asks.

'The pump,' Mr George Williams says. 'Eddie gived it to me for driving him to get his car.'

'Hand it here,' Mama says.

Mr George Williams looks at Daddy, but he hands the pump to Mama. Mama goes on down the field with the pump and throws it in the fire. I watch Mama coming back.

'When Eddie gets paid Saturday he'll pay you,' Mama says. 'You ready to go home, Eddie?'

Daddy nods his head.

'Sonny,' Mama says.

I go where Mama is and Mama takes my hand. Daddy raises his head and looks at the people standing round looking at us.

'Thank y'all,' he says.

Me and Mama go in Gran'mon's house and pull the big bundle out on the gallery. Daddy picks the bundle up and puts it on his head, then we go up the quarter to us house. Mama opens the gate and me and Daddy go in. We go inside and Mama lights the lamp.

'You hungry?' Mama asks Daddy.

'How can you ask that?' Daddy says. 'I'm starving.'

'You want eat now or after you whip me?' Mama says.

'Whip you?' Daddy asks. 'What I'm go'n be whipping you for?'

Mama goes back in the kitchen. She don't find what she's looking for, and I hear her going outside.

'Where Mama going, Daddy?'

'Don't ask me,' Daddy says. 'I don't know no more than you.'

Daddy gets some kindling out of the corner and puts it in the fire-place. Then he pours some coal oil on the kindling and lights a match to it. Me and Daddy squat down on the fireplace and watch the fire burning.

I hear the back door shut, then I see Mama coming in the front room. Mama's got a great big old switch.

'Here,' she says.

'What's that for?' Daddy says.

'Here. Take it,' Mama says.

'I ain't got nothing to beat you for, Amy,' Daddy says.

'You whip me,' Mama says, 'or I turn right round and walk on out that door.'

Daddy stands up and looks at Mama.

'You must be crazy,' Daddy says. 'Stop all that foolishness, Amy, and go cook me some food.'

'Get your pot, Sonny,' Mama says.

'Shucks,' I say. 'Now where we going? I'm getting tired walking in all that cold. 'Fore you know it I'm go'n have whooping cough.'

'Get your pot and stop answering me back, boy,' Mama says.

I go to my bed and pick up the pot again.

'Shucks,' I say.

'You ain't leaving here,' Daddy says.

'You better stop me,' Mama says, going to the bundle.

'All right,' Daddy says. 'I'll beat you if that's what you want.'

Daddy gets the switch off the floor and I start crying.

'Lord, have mercy,' Daddy says. 'Now what?'

'Whip me,' Mama says.

'Amy, whip you for what?' Daddy says. 'Amy, please, just go back there and cook me something to eat.'

'Come on, Sonny,' Mama says. 'Let's get out of this house.'

'All right,' Daddy says. Daddy hits Mama two times on the legs. 'That's enough,' he says.

'Beat me,' Mama says.

I cry some more. 'Don't beat my mama,' I say. 'I don't want you to beat my mama.'

'Sonny, please,' Daddy says. 'What y'all trying to do to me—run me crazy? I burnt up the car—ain't that enough?'

'I'm just go'n tell you one more time,' Mama says.

'All right,' Daddy says. 'I'm go'n beat you if that's what you want.'

Daddy starts beating Mama, and I cry some more; but Daddy don't stop beating her.

'Beat me harder,' Mama says. 'I mean it. I mean it.'

'Honey, please,' Daddy says.

'You better do it,' Mama says. 'I mean it.'

Daddy keeps on beating Mama, and Mama cries and goes down on her knees.

'Leave my mama alone, you old yellow dog,' I say. 'You leave my mama alone.' I throw the pot at him but I miss him, and the pot go bouncing 'cross the floor.

Daddy throws the switch away and runs to Mama and picks her up. He takes Mama to the bed and begs her to stop crying. I get on my own bed and cry in the cover.

I feel somebody shaking me, and I must've been sleeping. 'Wake up,' I hear Daddy saying.

I'm tired and I don't feel like getting up. I feel like sleeping some more.

'You want some supper?' Daddy asks.

'Uh-huh.'

'Get up then,' Daddy says.

I get up. I got all my clothes on and my shoes on.

'It's morning?' I ask.

'No,' Daddy says. 'Still night. Come on back in the kitchen and eat supper.'

I follow Daddy in the kitchen and me and him sit down at the table. Mama brings the food to the table and she sits down, too.

'Bless this food, Father, which we're about to receive, the nurse of our bodies, for Christ sake, amen,' Mama says.

I raise my head and look at Mama. I can see where she's been crying. Her face is all swole. I look at Daddy and he's eating. Mama and Daddy don't talk, and I don't say nothing, either. I eat my food. We eating sweet potatoes and bread. I'm having a glass of clabber, too.

'What a day,' Daddy says.

Mama don't say nothing. She's just picking over her food.

'Mad?' Daddy says.

'No,' Mama says.

'Honey?' Daddy says.

Mama looks at him.

'I didn't beat you because you did us thing with Freddie Jackson, did I?' Daddy says.

'No,' Mama says.

'Well, why then?' Daddy says.

'Because I don't want you to be the laughingstock of the plantation,' Mama says.

'Who go'n laugh at me?' Daddy says.

'Everybody,' Mama says. 'Mama and all. Now they don't have nothing to laugh about.'

'Honey, I don't mind if they laugh at me,' Daddy says.

'I do mind,' Mama says.

'Did I hurt you?'

'I'm all right,' she says.

'You ain't mad no more?' Daddy says.

'No,' Mama says. 'I'm not mad.'

Mama picks up a little bit of food and puts it in her mouth.

'Finish eating your supper, Sonny,' she says.

'I got enough,' I say.

'Drink your clabber,' Mama says.

I drink all my clabber and show Mama the glass.

'Go get your book,' Mama says. 'It's on the dresser.'

I go in the front room to get my book.

'One of us got to go to school with him tomorrow,' I hear Mama saying. I see her handing Daddy the note. Daddy waves it back. 'Here,' she says.

'Honey, you know I don't know how to act in no place like that,' Daddy says.

'Time to learn,' Mama says. She gives Daddy the note. 'What page your lesson on, Sonny?'

I turn to the page, and I lean on Mama's leg and let her carry me over my lesson. Mama holds the book in her hand. She carries me over my lesson two times, then she makes me point to some words and spell some words.

'He knows it,' Daddy says.

'I'll take you over it again tomorrow morning,' Mama says. 'Don't let me forget it now.'

'Uh-uh.'

'Your daddy'll carry you over it tomorrow night,' Mama says. 'One night me, one night you.'

'With no car,' Daddy says, 'I reckon I'll be round plenty now. You think we'll ever get another one, honey?'

Daddy's picking in his teeth with a broom straw.

'When you learn how to act with one,' Mama says. 'I ain't got nothing against cars.'

'I guess you right, honey,' Daddy says. 'I was going little too far.'

'It's time for bed, Sonny,' Mama says. 'Go in the front room and say your prayers to your daddy.'

Me and Daddy leave Mama back there in the kitchen. I put my book on the dresser and I go to the fireplace where Daddy is. Daddy puts another piece of wood on the fire and plenty sparks shoot up in the chimley. Daddy helps me to take off my clothes. I kneel down and lean against his leg.

'Start off,' Daddy says. 'I'll catch you if you miss something.'

'Lay me down to sleep,' I say. 'I pray the Lord my soul to keep. If I should die before I wake, I pray the Lord my soul to take. God bless Mama and Daddy. God bless Gran'mon and Uncle Al. God bless the church. God bless Miss Hebert. God bless Bill and Juanita.' I hear Daddy gaping. 'God bless everybody else. Amen.'

I jump up off my knees. Them bricks on the fireplace make my knees hurt.

'Did you tell God to bless Johnny Green and Madame Toussaint?' Daddy says.

'No,' I say.

'Get down there and tell Him to bless them, too,' Daddy says.

'Old Rollo, too?'

'That's up to you and Him for that,' Daddy says. 'Get back down there.'

I get back on my knees. I don't get on the bricks because they make my knees hurt. I get on the floor and lean against the chair.

'And God bless Mr Johnny Green and Madame Toussaint,' I say.

'All right,' Daddy says. 'Warm up good.'

Daddy goes over to my bed and pulls the cover back.

'Come on,' he says. 'Jump in.'

I run and jump in the bed. Daddy pulls the cover up to my neck.

'Good night, Daddy.'

'Good night,' Daddy says.

'Good night, Mama.'

'Good night, Sonny,' Mama says.

I turn on my side and look at Daddy at the fireplace. Mama comes out of the kitchen and goes to the fireplace. Mama warms up good and goes to the bundle.

'Leave it alone,' Daddy says. 'We'll get up early tomorrow and get it.'

'I'm going to bed,' Mama says. 'You coming now?'

'Uh-hunnnnn,' Daddy says.

Mama comes to my bed and tucks the cover under me good. She leans over and kisses me and tucks the cover some more. She goes over to the bundle and gets her nightgown, then she goes in the kitchen and puts it on. She comes back and puts her clothes she took off on a chair 'side the wall. Mama kneels down and says her prayers, then she gets in the bed and covers up. Daddy stands up and takes off his clothes. I see Daddy in his big old long white BVD's. Daddy blows out the lamp, and I hear the spring when Daddy gets in the bed. Daddy never says his prayers.

'Sleepy?' Daddy says.

'Uh-uhnnn,' Mama says.

I hear the spring. I hear Mama and Daddy talking low, but I don't know what they saying. I go to sleep some, but I open my eyes again. It's some dark in the room. I hear Mama and Daddy talking low. I like Mama and Daddy. I like Uncle Al, but I don't like old Gran'mon too much. Gran'mon's always talking bad about Daddy. I don't like old Mr Freddie Jackson, either. Mama say she didn't do her and Daddy's thing with Mr Freddie Jackson. I like Mr George Williams. We went riding 'way up the road with Mr George Williams. We got Daddy's car and brought it all the way back here. Daddy and them turned the car over and Daddy poured some gas on it and set it on fire. Daddy ain't got no more car now . . . I know my lesson. I ain't go'n wee-wee on myself no more. Daddy's going to school with me tomorrow. I'm go'n show him I can beat Billy Joe Martin shooting marbles. I can shoot all over Billy Joe Martin. And I can beat him running, too. He thinks he can run fast. I'm go'n show Daddy I can beat him running . . . I don't know why I had to say, 'God bless Madame Toussaint'. I don't like her. And I don't like old Rollo, either. Rollo can bark some loud. He made my head hurt with all that loud barking. Madame Toussaint's old house don't smell good. Us house smell good. I hear the spring on Mama and Daddy's bed. I get 'way under the cover. I go to sleep little bit, but I wake up. I go to sleep some more. I hear the spring on Mama and Daddy's bed. I hear it plenty now. It's some dark under here. It's warm. I feel good 'way under here.

1963

The Making of Ashenden

STANLEY ELKIN

I've been spared a lot, one of the blessed of the earth, at least one of its lucky, that privileged handful of the dramatically prospering, the sort whose secrets are asked, like the hundred-year-old man. There is no secret, of course; most of what happens to us is simple accident. Highish birth and a smooth network of appropriate connection like a tea service written into the will. But surely something in the blood too, locked into good fortune's dominant genes like a blast ripening in a time bomb. Set to go off, my good looks and intelligence, yet exceptional still, take *away* my mouthful of silver spoon and lapful of luxury. Something my own, not passed on or handed down, something seized, wrested—my good character, hopefully, my taste perhaps. What's mine, what's mine? Say taste—the soul's harmless appetite.

I've money, I'm rich. The heir to four fortunes. Grandfather on Mother's side was a Newpert. The family held some good real estate in Rhode Island until they sold it for many times what they gave for it. Grandmother on Father's side was a Salts, whose bottled mineral water, once available only through prescription and believed indispensable in the cure of all fevers, was the first product ever to be reviewed by the Food and Drug Administration, a famous and controversial case. The government found it to contain nothing that was actually *detrimental* to human beings, and it went public, so to speak. Available now over the counter, the Salts made more money from it than ever.

Mother was an Oh. *Her* mother was the chemical engineer who first discovered a feasible way to store oxygen in tanks. And Father was Noel Ashenden, who though he did not actually invent the matchbook, went into the field when it was still a not very flourishing novelty, and whose slogan, almost a poem, 'Close Cover Before

Striking' (a simple stroke, as Father liked to say), obvious only after
someone else has already thought of it (the Patent Office refused to
issue a patent on what it claimed was merely an instruction, but
Father's company had the message on its matchbooks before his com-
petitors even knew what was happening), removed the hazard from
book matches and turned the industry and Father's firm particularly
into a flaming success overnight—Father's joke, not mine. Later, when
the inroads of Ronson and Zippo threatened the business, Father
went into seclusion for six months and when he returned to us he had
produced another slogan: 'For Our Matchless Friends.' It saved the
industry a second time and was the second and last piece of work in
Father's life.

There are people who gather in the spas and watering places of this
world who pooh-pooh our fortune. Après ski, cozy in their wools,
handsome before their open hearths, they scandalize amongst themselves in whispers. 'Imagine,' they say, 'saved from ruin because of
some cornball sentiment available in every bar and grill and truck
stop in the country. It's not, not . . .'

Not what? Snobs! Phooey on the First Families. On railroad, steel
mill, automotive, public utility, banking and shipping fortunes, on all
hermetic legacy, morganatic and blockbuster blood-lines that change
the maps and landscapes and alter the mobility patterns, your jungle
wheeling and downtown dealing a stone's throw from warfare. I come
of good stock—real estate, mineral water, oxygen, matchbooks: earth,
water, air and fire, the old elementals of the material universe, a belly-
button economics, a linchpin one.

It is as I see it a perfect genealogy, and if I can be bought and sold
a hundred times over by a thousand men in this country—people in
your own town could do it, providents and trailers of hunch, I bless
them, who got into this or went into that when it was eight cents a
share—I am satisfied with my thirteen or fourteen million. Wealth is
not after all the point. The genealogy is. That bridge-trick nexus that
brought Newpert to Oh, Salts to Ashenden and Ashenden to Oh,
love's lucky longshots which, paying off, permitted me as they permit
every human life! (I have this simple, harmless paranoia of the good-
natured man, this cheerful awe.) Forgive my enthusiasm, that I go on

like some secular patriot wrapped in the simple flag of self, a professional descendant, every day the closed-for-the-holiday banks and post offices of the heart. And why not? Aren't my circumstances superb? Whose are better? No boast, no boast. I've had it easy, served up on all life's silver platters like a satrap. And if my money is managed for me and I do no work—less work even than Father, who at least came up with those two slogans, the latter in a six-month solitude that must have been hell for that gregarious man ('For Our Matchless Friends': no slogan finally but a broken code, an extension of his own hospitable being, simply the Promethean gift of fire to a guest)—at least I am not 'spoiled' and have in me still alive the nerve endings of gratitude. If it's miserly to count one's blessings, Brewster Ashenden's a miser.

This will give you some idea of what I'm like:

On Having an Account in a Swiss Bank: I never had one, and suggest you stay away from them too. Oh, the mystery and romance is all very well, but never forget that your Swiss bank offers no premiums, whereas for opening a savings account for $5,000 or more at First National City Bank of New York or other fine institutions you get wonderful premiums—picnic hampers, Scotch coolers, Polaroid cameras, Hudson's Bay blankets from L. L. Bean, electric shavers, even lawn furniture. My managers always leave me a million or so to play with, and this is how I do it. I suppose I've received hundreds of such bonuses. Usually I give them to friends or as gifts at Christmas to doormen and other loosely connected personnel of the household, but often I keep them and use them myself. I'm not stingy. Of course I can afford to buy any of these things—and I do, I enjoy making purchases—but somehow nothing brings the joy of existence home to me more than these premiums. Something from nothing—the two-suiter from Chase Manhattan and my own existence, luggage a bonus and life a bonus too. Like having a film star next to you on your flight from the Coast. There are treats of high order, adventure like cash in the street.

Let's enjoy ourselves, I say; let's have fun. Lord, let us live in the sand by the surf of the sea and play till cows come home. We'll have a house on the Vineyard and a brownstone in the Seventies and a *pied-à-terre* in a world capital when something big is about to break. (Put the Cardinal in the back bedroom where the sun gilds the bay at afternoon tea and give us the courage to stand up to secret police at the door, to top all threats with threats of our own, the nicknames of mayors and ministers, the fast comeback at the front stairs, authority on us like the funny squiggle the counterfeiters miss.) Re-Columbus us. Engage us with the overlooked, a knowledge of optics, say, or a gift for the tides. (My pal, the heir to most of the vegetables in inland Nebraska, has become a superb amateur oceanographer. The marine studies people invite him to Wood's Hole each year. He has a wave named for him.) Make us good at things, the countertenor and the German language, and teach us to be as easy in our amateur standing as the best man at a roommate's wedding. Give us hard tummies behind the cummerbund and long swimmer's muscles under the hound's tooth so that we may enjoy our long life. And may all our stocks rise to the occasion of our best possibilities, and our humanness be bullish too.

Speaking personally I am glad to be a heroic man.

I am pleased that I am attractive to women but grateful I'm no bounder. Though I'm touched when married women fall in love with me, as frequently they do, I am rarely to blame. I never encourage these fits and do my best to get them over their derangements so as not to lose the friendships of their husbands when they are known to me, or the neutral friendship of the ladies themselves. This happens less than you might think, however, for whenever I am a houseguest of a married friend I usually make it a point to bring along a girl. These girls are from all walks of life—models, show girls, starlets, actresses, tennis professionals, singers, heiresses and the daughters of the diplomats of most of the nations of the free world. *All* walks. They tend, however, to conform to a single physical type, and are almost always tall, tan, slender and blond, the girl from Ipanema as a wag friend of mine has it. They are always sensitive and intelligent and good at sailing and the Australian crawl. They are never blemished in any way, for even something like a tiny beauty mark on the inside of a thigh or above the shoulder blade is enough to put me off, and their breaths must be as sweet at three in the morning as they are at noon. (I never see a woman who is dieting for diet sours the breath.) Arm hair, of course, is repellent to me though a soft blond down is now and then acceptable. I know I sound a prig. I'm not. I am—well, classical, drawn by perfection as to some magnetic, Platonic pole, idealism and beauty's true North.

But if I'm demanding about the type I fall in love with—I *do* fall in love, I'm not Don Juan—I try to be charming to all women, the flawed as well as the unflawed. I know that times have changed and that less is expected of gentlemen these days, that there's more 'open-ness' between the sexes and that in the main, this is a healthy development. Still, in certain respects I am old-fashioned—I'm the first to admit it—and not only find myself incapable of strong language in the presence of a lady (I rarely use it myself at any time, even a 'damn' even a 'hell') but become enraged when someone else uses it and immediately want to call him out. I'm the same if there's a child about or a man over the age of fifty-seven if he is not vigorous. The leopard cannot change his spots. I'm a gentleman, an opener of doors and doffer of hats and after you firster, meek in the elevator and kind to the help. I maintain a fund which I use for the abortions of girls other men have gotten into trouble; if the young lady prefers, I have a heart-to-heart with the young man. And although I've no sisters, I have a brother's temperament, all good counsel and real concern. Even without a sister of my own—or a brother either for that matter; I'm an only child—I lend an ear and do for other fellows' sisses the moral forks.

Still, there's fun in me, and danger too. I'm this orphan now but that's recent (Father and Mother died early this year, Mother first and Father a few days later—Father, too, was courteous to women), and I'm afraid that when they were alive I gave my parents some grisly moments with my exploits, put their hearts in their mouths and gray in their hair. I have been a fighter pilot for the RAF (I saw some action at Suez) and a mercenary on the *Biafran* side, as well as a sort of free-lance spy against some of your South American and Greek juntas. (I'm not polit-ical, but the average generalissimo cheats at cards. It's curious, I've noticed that though they steal the picture cards they rarely play them; I suppose it's a class thing—your military man would rather beat you with a nine than a king.) I am Johnny-on-the-spot at disasters—I was in Managua for the earthquake—lending a hand, pulling my oar, the sort of man who knocks your teeth out if he catches you abusing the water ration in the lifeboat and then turns around and offers his own meager mouthful to a woman or a man over fifty-seven. Chavez is my friend and the Chicago Seven, though I had to stop seeing them because of the foul language. (I love Jerry Rubin too much to tear his head off, and I could see that's what it would come to.) And here and there I've had Mafiosi for friends—wonderful family men, the Cosa Nostra, I respect that. And the astronauts, of course; I spent a weightless weekend with them in an anti-gravity chamber in Houston one time, coming down only to take a long-distance phone call from a girl in trouble. And, let's see, sixty hours in the bathysphere with Cousteau, fathoms below where the ordinary fish run. So I have been weightless and I have been gravid, falling in free-fall like a spider down its filament and paid out in rappel. And in the Prix de this and Prix de t'other, all the classic combats of moving parts (my own moving parts loose as a toy yet to be assembled), uninsurable at last, taking a stunt man's risks, a darer gone first, blinded in the world's uncharted caves and deafened beneath its waterfalls, the earth itself a sort of Jungle Gym finally, my playground, swimming at your own risk.

Last winter I fought a duel. I saw a man whipping his dog and called him out. Pistols at fourteen paces. The fellow—a prince, a wastrel—could get no one to act as his second so I did it myself, giving him pointers, calling the adjustments for windage, and at last standing still for him as one of those FBI paper silhouettes, my vitals (we were on a beach, I wore no shirt, just my bathing suit, the sun, rising over his shoulder, spotlighting me) clear as marked meat on a butcher's diagram, my Valentine heart vaulting toward the barrel of his pistol. He fired and missed and I threw my pistol into the sea. He wept, and I took him back to the house and gave him a good price for his dog. And running with the bulls at Pamplona—not in front of them, *with* them—and strolling at two a.m. through the Casbah like a fellow down Main Street, and standing on top of a patrol car in Harlem talking through the bull horn to the sniper. And dumb things too.

Father called me home from Tel Aviv a few weeks before he died.

He was sitting on a new bed in his room wearing only his pajama tops. He hadn't shaved, the gray stubble latticing his lower face in an old man's way, like some snood of mortality. There was a glass in his hand, his one-hundred-dollar bill rolled tight around the condensation. (He always fingered one, a tic.)

'Say hello to your mother.'

I hadn't seen her. Like many people who have learned the secret of living together, Father and Mother slept in separate suites, but now twin beds, Father in one, Mother in the other, had replaced Father's fourposter. A nightstand stood between them—I remembered it from Grandmother Newpert's summer house in Edgarton—on which, arranged like two entrenched armies, were two sets of medicines, Father's bright ceremonial pills and May Day capsules, and Mother's liquids in their antique apothecary bottles (she supplied the druggist with these bottles herself, insisting out of her willful aesthetic sense that all her prescriptions be placed in them), with their water glasses and a shiny artillery of teaspoons. Mother herself seemed to be sleeping. Perhaps that's why I hadn't noticed her, or perhaps it was the angle, Father's bed being the closer as I walked into the room. Or perhaps it was her condition itself, sickness an effacement. I hesitated.

'It's all right,' Father said. 'She's awake. You're not disturbing her.'

'Her eyes are closed,' I said softly to Father.

'I have been seeing double in the morning, Brewster darling,' Mother said. 'It gives me megrim to open them.'

'Mother, you naughty slugabed,' I teased. Sometimes being a gentleman can be a pain in the you-know-where, to oneself as well as to others. Well, it's often fatuous, and in emergency it always is, as anything is in emergency short of an uncivilized scream, but what can you do, a code is a code. One dresses for dinner in the jungle and surrenders one's sword to the enemy and says thank you very much and refuses the blindfold. 'Shame on you, sweetheart, the sun up these several hours and you still tucked in.'

'It's cancer, Son,' Father said in a low tone not meant for Mother.

'Lazybones,' I scolded, swallowing hard.

'Oh, I *do* want to see you, Brewster,' Mother said. 'Perhaps if I opened just *one* little eye—'

'Not at all, you sweet dear. If you must lie in bed all day I think it best that you do some honest sleeping. I'll still be here when you finally decide to get up.'

'There, that's better,' Mother said, opening her right eye and scowling at me.

'Please, honeybunch, you'll see double and get megrim.'

'Brewster, it's lovely. It makes you twice as handsome, twice as tall.'

'Please, Mother—'

'Let her, Brew. This is a deathbed.'

'Father!'

'Why are you so shocked, Brewster? It had to happen someday.'

'I think I'll close it now.'

'Really, Father, a *death*bed . . .'

'Since it upsets him so.'

'Well, death*beds* then.'

'But I reserve the right to open it again whenever I choose. If a cat can look at a king . . .'

'Father, aren't you being—that's right, darling, shut it, shut it tight—the slightest bit melodramatic?'

'Oh, for Lord's sake, Brew, don't be prissy. Mother and I are going, she of cancer, I of everything. Rather than waste the little time we have left together, we might try to get certain things straight.'

'When Father called you back from overseas he arranged with Mrs Lucas to have these twin deathbeds set up in here.'

Mrs Lucas is the housekeeper. She used to give me my baths when I was a child. I always try to remember to bring her a picnic hamper or some other especially nice premium from the bank when I come home for a visit. Over the years Mrs Lucas has had *chaises longues*, card tables, hammocks and many powerful flashlights from me—a small fortune in merchandise.

'What were you doing in the Middle East in the first place? Those people aren't your sort, Brew.'

'He did it for you, darling. He thought that by putting both deathbeds in the same room you wouldn't have to shuffle back and forth between one chamber and the next. It's a time-space thing, Noel said. Isn't that right, Noel?'

'Something like that. Yes, Nora.'

'Father, the Jewish are darned impressive. They run their military like a small family business. The Arabs can't touch them.'

'Arabs, Jews. In my time a country club was a country club. I don't understand anything anymore.'

'Don't quarrel, Noel, Brew. Brew, you're the reason we decided to have deathbeds in the first place. Well, my family has always had them, of course. None of this hole-and-corner hospital stuff for them. I don't speak against hospitals, mind you, they're all very well if you're going to get better, but, goodness, if you're really dying it's so much more pleasant for the immediate family if they can be saved from those drafty, smelly hospital corridors. Grandmother Oh herself, though she invented the oxygen tank, refused the tent when her time came if it meant going to a hospital.'

'Brr.'

'Are you addressing me, Father?'

'What? No, no, I have a chill.'

'Let me help you.' I lifted his legs into the bed gently, took the glass out of his hand and set it down, unpeeling the $100 bill as if it were a beer label. I placed his head back on the pillow and, smoothing the sheets, started to cover him when he grinned.

'Close cover before striking,' he said hoarsely. That broke the ice and we all laughed.

'Nothing important ever gets said in a hospital,' Father said after a while. 'There's too much distraction. The room, the gadgets, the flowers and who sent what, the nurses coming in for one thing or another. Nothing important gets said.'

I nodded.

'Mother's right, Brewster. The deathbed has been a tradition in our family. This twin bed business is a little vulgar, perhaps, but it can't be helped. We'll have a deathbed vigil. It's a leisure thing. It's elegant.'

'Please, Father, let's not have any more of this morbid stuff about dying,' I said, getting the upper hand on myself. 'It's my notion you're both goldbricking, that you'll be out on the links again in no time, your handicap lower than ever.'

'It's heart, Brew,' Father said gloomily. 'It's Ménière's disease. It's TB and a touch of MS that hangs on like a summer cold. It's a spot of Black Lung.'

'Black Lung?'

'Do you know how many matches I've struck in my time?'

'I wouldn't be surprised, Father, if there were another slogan in you yet. "I Would Rather Light an Ashenden Match Than Curse the Darkness." How's that?'

'Too literary. What the smoker wants is something short and sweet. No, there'll be no more slogans. Let others carry on my work. I'm tired.'

'There's this Israeli ace,' I said as a stopgap, 'Izzy Heskovitz, who's . . .'

'What's this about a duel, Brewster?' Father asked.

'Oh, did you hear about that? I should have thought the Prince would have wanted it hushed up, after what happened.'

'After what happened? He thinks you're mad. And so do I. Exposing yourself like that, offering a target like a statesman in an open car, then tossing your pistol into the sea. It was irresponsible. Were you trying to kill yourself?'

'It was a question of honor.'

'With you, Brewster, everything is a question of honor.'

'Everything is.'

'Stuff and nonsense.'

'I'm looking for myself.'

'Brewster, you are probably the last young man in America still looking for himself,' Father said. 'As a man who has a certain experience with slogans, I have some sense of when they have lost their currency.'

'Father, you are probably the last *old* man in America to take to a deathbed.'

'Touché, Brew. He's got you there, Noel,' Mother said.

'Thank you, Mother, but all I intended was to point out that obsolescence runs in our family. I am the earth, water, fire and air heir. Let the neon, tin and tungsten scions prepare themselves for the newfangled. I have pride and I have honor. My word is my bond and I'll marry a virgin. And I agree with you, Father, about the sanctity of the deathbed, though I shall continue, out of chivalry and delicacy, to maintain the imposture that this . . . these'—I took in the twin beds—'is . . . are . . . not that . . . those.'

'You're marvelous, Brewster. I . . .'

'Is something wrong, Father?'

'I . . . we . . . your mother and I . . .'

'Father?'

'I love you, Son.'

'I love *you*, sir,' I told him. I turned to Mother. She had opened one eye again. It was wet and darting from one side to the other like an eye in REM sleep. I understood that she was trying to choose my real image from the two that stood before her. In a moment her eye had decided. It stared off, focused about four yards to my right. I smiled to reassure her that she had chosen correctly and edged slowly to my right, an Indian in reverse, unhiding, trying to appear in her line of sight like a magician's volunteer in an illusion. 'And all I have to say to *you*, you great silly, is that if you're not out of bed soon I'll not answer for your zinnias and foxgloves. I noticed when the taxi brought me up the drive that Franklin, as usual, has managed to make a botch of the front beds.'

'Franklin is old, Son,' Mother said. 'He isn't well.'

'Franklin's a rogue, Mother. I don't know why you encourage him. I'm certain he's going to try to trade Mrs Lucas the three hundred feet of lovely rubber garden hose I brought him for her Scotch cooler so that he can have a place to hide his liquor.'

Mother closed her eye; Father grinned. I wrung out Father's hundred-dollar bill and handed it back to him. Excusing myself, I promised to return when they had rested. 'Brr,' Father said.

'Were you speaking to me, Father? '

'It's the chill again,' he said.

I went to my room, called up their doctors and had long, discouraging talks with them. Then I phoned some specialist friends of mine at Mass General and a good man at Barnes in St Louis and got some additional opinions. I asked about Franklin, too.

I kept the vigil. It was awful, but satisfying, too, in a way. It lasted five weeks and in that time we had truth and we had banter, and right up to the end each of us was able to tell the difference. Only once, a few days after Mother's death (her vision returned at the end: 'I can see, Brewster,' she said, 'I can see far and I can see straight.' These were not her last words; I'll not tell you her last words, for they were meant only for Father and myself, though I have written them down else-where to preserve for my children should I ever have them) did Father's spirits flag. He had gotten up from his bed to attend the funeral—through a signal courtesy to an out-of-stater, the Governor of Massachusetts permitted Mother to be buried on Copp's Hill Burying Ground near the Old North Church in Boston—and we had just returned to the house. Mrs Lucas and Franklin were weeping, and I helped Father upstairs and back into his deathbed. He was too weak to put his pajamas on. 'You know, Brew,' he said, 'I sure wish you hadn't thrown that d—d pistol into the ocean.'

'Oh Father,' I said, 'never mind. Tomorrow when you're stronger we'll go to town and buy a fresh brace and stroll the woods and shoot the birds from their trees just as we used to.'

He was dead in his own tree a few days later. I sensed it coming and had moved into the room with him, where I lay next to him all night in the twin bed, only Grandmother Newpert's nightstand between us, Mother's effects—the lovely old apothecary bottles and her drinking glass and medicine spoons—having been cleared away. I was awake the entire night, hanging on his broken breath and old man's groans like a detective in films on the croaks of a victim. I listened for a message from the coma and tried to parse delirium as if it were only a sort of French. Shall a man of honor and pride still searching for himself in his late thirties deny the sibyl in a goner's gasps? (I even asked one or two questions, pressing him in his terminal pain, pursuing him through the mazes of his dissolution, his deathbed my Ouija board.)

Then, once, just before dawn, a bird twittered in the garden and Father came out of it. For fifteen minutes he talked sense, speaking rapidly and with an astonishing cogency that was more mysterious somehow than all his moans and nightmares. He spoke of ways to expedite the probating of the two wills, of flaws in the nature of his estate, instructing me where to consolidate and where to trim. He told me the names of what lawyers to trust, which brokers to fire. In five minutes he laid down principles which would guarantee our fortune for a hundred years. Then, at the end, there was something personal, but after what had gone before, I thought it a touch lame, like a P.S. inquiring about your family's health at the end of a business letter. He wished me well and hoped I would find some nice girl, settle down, and raise fine children. I was to give them his love.

I thought this was the end, but in a few moments he came round again.

'Franklin *is* a rogue,' he said. 'For many years now he and Mrs Lucas have been carrying on an affair below stairs. That time during the war when Mrs Lucas was supposed to have gone to stay with her sister in Delaware she really went away to have Franklin's child. The scoundrel refused to marry her and would have had money from us to abort the poor thing. It was Mrs Lucas who wouldn't hear of it, but the baby died anyway. Mrs Lucas loves him. It's for her sake we never let him go when he screwed up in the garden.'

Those were Father's last words. Then he beckoned me to rise from my bed and approach him. He put out his right hand. I shook it and he died. The hundred-dollar bill he always held came off in my palm when the final paroxysm splayed his fingers.

The grief of the rich is clubby, expensive. (I don't mean *my* grief. My grief was a long gloom, persistent as grudge.) We are born week-enders anyway, but in death we are particularly good to each other, traveling thousands of miles to funerals, flying up from Rio or jamming the oceanic cables with our expensive consolation. (Those wires from the President to the important bereaved—that's our style, too.) We say it with flowers, wreaths, memorial libraries, offering the wing of a hospital as casually as someone else a chicken leg at a picnic. And why not? There aren't that many of us—never mind that there are a thousand who can buy and sell me. Scarcer we are than the Eskimaux, vanishing Americans who got rich slow.

So I did not wonder at the crowds who turned up at Mother's funeral and then went away the long distances only to return a few days later for Father's. Or at the clothes. Couturiers of Paris and London and New York—those three splendid cities, listed always together and making a sound on the page like a label on scent—taxed to the breaking point to come up with dresses in death's delicious high fashion, the rich taking big casualties that season, two new mourning originals in less than two weeks and the fitter in fits. The men splendid in their decent dark. Suits cunningly not black, *off* black, proper, the longitudes of their decency in their wiry pinstripes, a gent's torso bound up in vest and crisscrossed by watch chains and Phi Beta Kappa keys in the innocent para-militarism of the civilian respectable, men somehow more vital at the graveside in the burdensome clothes than in Bermudas on beaches or dinner jackets in hotel suites with cocktails in their hands, the band playing on the beach below and the telephone ringing.

And all the women were beautiful, gorgeous, grieving's colors good for them, aloof mantles which made them seem (though I knew better) unattainable, virgins again, yet sexy still as secret drinkers. God, how I lusted when I was with them! I could barely put two words together for them or accept their condolences without feeling my importunate, inopportune blood thicken, my senses as ticklish as if Persian whores had gotten to them. Which added to my gloom, of course, because I was dishonoring my parents in their death as I never had while they lived.

Only the necessity to cope saved me from some sacrilege. (Oh, the confidence of lust! Surely that's the basis of its evil. The assumptions it permits one, glossing reality like a boy in the dark, touching himself and thinking of his mother's bridge guests.) Somehow, however, I managed to see my tailor, somehow got the arrangements made, somehow wrote the necessary checks and visited the near-at-hand safe-deposit boxes before they were red-flagged, somehow got through the inventories, spoke to the obituary people at the *Times*, prepared the eulogies somehow, and fielded all the questions of the well-meaning that are asked at times like these.

'Will there be a foundation, do you suppose, Ashenden?' asked an old friend of the family who had himself been an heir for as long as we had known him. (And oh, the effect of that 'Ashenden'! It was the first time one had been thus addressed, at least officially, since one's roommates at boarding school and college, thinking of their own inheritances, had used it.)

'I don't know, sir. It's too early to tell. I shall have to wait until the estate is properly probated before I can be certain what there is.'

'Of course, of course,' he said, 'but it's never too soon to start *thinking* about a foundation, fixing your goals.'

'Yes, sir.'

'Let me give you a little advice on that score. The arts. There are those who swear by diseases and the various social ills, but I'm not one of them. And of the arts I think the *performing* arts give you your best return. You get invited backstage.'

'I'll have to look into it.'

'Look into it.'

And one of Mother's friends wondered if marriage was in the offing. 'Now you really *are* eligible, Brewster,' she said. 'Oh, you were before, of course, but now you must certainly feel a bit of pressure to put your affairs in order and begin to think about the next generation.'

It was a rude thing to say (though something like these had been almost Father's last words to me), but the truth was I did feel it. Perhaps that was what my shameful lust had been about, nature's way of pointing me to my duty. My search for myself seemed trivial child's play now. Honor did subsist in doing right by the generations. I know what you're thinking: Who's this impostor, this namby with no will of his own? If he's so rich, why ain't he smart? Meaning glacial, indifferent, unconscious of the swath of world he cuts as the blade of what it leaves bleeding—the cosmos as rich man's butter pat. Listen, disdain's easy, a mug's game, but look close at anything and you'll break your heart.

I was inconsolable, grave at the graveside, beside myself like a fulfillment of Mother's prophetic double vision.

'People lose parents,' a Securities and Exchange Commission cousin told me. (Yes, yes, it's nothing, only nature bottoming out.) 'Sons lose mothers,' he said, his gray hair trimmed that morning, wet looking. 'Fathers die.'

'Don't look,' I said wildly, 'shut an eye. I am beside myself.'

I keened like a widow, a refugee from hardest times, a daughter with the Cossacks, a son chopped in the thresher. I would go about in black, I thought, and be superstitious. My features will thicken and no one will know how old I am.

'There, there,' he told me, 'there, there.'

'There, there. There, there,' said this one and that.

My pals did not know what to make of me.

'My God, Ashenden,' one said, a roommate from boarding school, 'have you seen the will? Is it awful?'

'I've been left everything,' I told him coolly.

He nudged me in the ribs. I would have called him out had I not been in mourning.

Only the sight of Mrs Lucas saved me. The thought of that brave woman's travail enabled me to control myself at last. I no longer wept openly and settled into a silent, stand-offish grimness, despair like an ingrown toenail on a man of fashion.

The weekends began.

All my adult life I have been a guest in other people's houses, following the sun and seasons like a migratory bird, an instinct in me, the rich man's cunning feel for ripeness, some oyster-in-an-r-month notion working there which knows without reference to anything outside itself when to pack the tennis racket, when to bring along the German field glasses to look at a friend's birds, the telescope to stare at his stars, the wet suit to swim in beneath his waters when the exotic fish are running. It's not in the *Times* when the black dinner jacket comes off and the white one goes on; it's something surer, subtler, the delicate guidance system of the privileged, my playboy astronomy.

The weekends began, and the midweeks and week- and two-week stretches in the country. I was very grateful to my friends' sense of what I needed then. Where I was welcome before, I was now actively pursued. My friends were marvelous, and not a mean motive between them. If I can't say as much for myself.

In the luggage now with the bandboxes of equipment, the riding boots and golf clubs and hiker's gear, was a lover's wardrobe: shirts like the breasts of birds, custom ties that camouflaged themselves against their backgrounds or stood out like dye in the sea, ascots like bunting for the throat's centennial, the handmade jackets and perfect trousers and tack room leathers. I dressed to kill, slay should I meet her, the mother of my children. (These were my mourning togs, mind.) And if I brought the best that could be had, it was not out of vanity but only respect for that phantom girl who would be so exquisite herself, so refined and blessed with taste that it would have been as dangerous for her to look at the undistinguished as for another to stare directly into the eclipse. So it was actually humility that made me dress as I did, simple self-effacement, the old knight's old modesty, shyness so capitulative that prostration was only a kind of militant attention, a death-defying leap to the earth. And since I had never met her, nor knew her name, nor had a clue to where she might be, I traveled alone, for the first time taking along no guest of the guest. Which my friends put down to decency, the thirty- or sixty- or ninety-day celibacy of the orphaned. But it wasn't that.

It was a strange period of my life. My friends, innocent of my intentions and honoring what they supposed to be my bereavement, omitted to invite any girls for me at all, and I found myself on this odd bachelor circuit, several times meeting the same male guest I had met at someone else's house a few weeks before. We crossed each other's paths like traveling salesmen with identical territories. And I rode and hunted and fished and stayed up all hours playing whist or backgammon or chess with my hosts or the other male guest, settled before fires with sherry and cognac, oddly domestic, as if what I owed the generations was a debt already paid, a trip in the time machine, keeping late hours in libraries until the odor of leather actually became offensive to me. On the few occasions I retired early it was at my host's instructions. (I am an obedient guest.) The next morning there was to be an excursion in the four-wheel drive to investigate property he had acquired in backwoods forty miles off—a lodge, an abandoned watchtower, twice an old lighthouse. And always, nodding my approval if the purchase had been made or giving my judicious advice if it hadn't, I had this sense that I'd had the night before in the library; that the property in question was *my* property, that I was already what I was dressed to become.

I was not bored; I was distraught.

A strange thing happened. It occurred to me that perhaps my old fastidiousness regarding the inviolability of a friend's wife was wrong, morally wrong. Had not these women made overtures, dropped hints, left doors ajar so that returning to my room with a book I could see them in nightgowns beside bedlamps; hadn't they smiled sweetly and raised arms? Perhaps I had been a prig, had placed too high a value on myself by insisting on the virginity of my intended. Perhaps it was my fate to figure in a divorce. I decided that henceforth I must not be so stand-offish with my friends' wives.

So I stroked their knees beneath the whist table and put down their alarm to surprise. I begged off going on the excursions and stayed home with them when my friend and the other guest climbed into the jeep. I followed the wife all about the house and cornered her in stairwells and gardens.

'I'm no prig,' I told Nan Bridge, and clasped her breast and bit her ear.

'What the hell do you think you're doing, buster?' she shouted.

'Four months ago I would have called you out for that,' I told her lamely and left her house that afternoon and went to the next three days early, determined to be more careful.

I was staying with Courtney and Buffy Surface in Connecticut. Claiming a tennis elbow, I excused myself from the doubles early in the first set. Courtney and I were partners against Buffy and Oscar Bobrinage, the other houseguest. My plan was for Buffy to drop out and join me. I sat under a wide umbrella in the garden, and in a few minutes someone came up behind me. 'Where does it hurt? I'll rub it for you.'

'No thank you, Oscar.'

'No trouble, Brewster.'

'I've a heating pad from Chase Manhattan in my suitcase, Osc,' I told him dejectedly.

That night I was more obvious. I left the library and mentioned as casually as I could that I was going out for a bit of air. It has been my observation that the predisposition for encounter precedes encounter, that one must set oneself as one would a table. I never stroll the strand in moonlight except when I'm about the heart's business, or cross bridges toward dawn unless I mean to save the suicides. There are natural laws, magnetism. A wish pulls fate.

I passed the gazebo and wondered about the colors of the flowers in the dark, the queer consolidation of noon's bright pigment, yellow sunk in on yellow a thousand times as if struck by gravity. I thought of popular songs, their tunes and words. I meant for once to do away with polite conversation should Buffy appear, to stun her with my need and force. (Of all my friends Buffy was the most royally aloof. She had maddening ways of turning aside any question or statement that was the least bit threatening.)

I heard the soft crunch of gravel. 'Oscar?'

'No, it's Buffy. Were you looking for Oscar?'

'I thought he might be looking for me.'

'*Voilà du joli*,' Buffy said. She knew the idioms of eleven modern languages.

I gazed into her eyes. 'How are you and Courtney, Buffy?'

'*Mon dieu! ¿Qué pasa? Il est onze heures et demi*,' she said.

'Buffy, how are you and *Courtney*?'

'Courtney's been off erythromycin five days now and General Parker says there's no sign of redness. God bless wonder drugs. *Darauf kannst du Gift nehmen*.'

'Do you ever think of Madrid, Buffy?' Once, in a night club in Madrid on New Year's Eve she had kissed me. It was before she and Courtney met, but my memory of such things is long lasting and profound. I never forget the blandest intimacy. '*Do* you?'

'Oh, Brewster, I have every hope that when Juan Carlos is restored the people will accept him.'

'Buffy, we kissed each other on New Year's Eve in Madrid in 1966 before you ever heard of Courtney Surface.'

'*Autres temps, autres moeurs*.'

'I can't accept that, Buff. Forgive me, dear, but when I left the game this morning you stayed behind to finish out the set *against* Courtney. Yes, and before that you were Oscar's partner. Doesn't this indicate to you a certain aberrant competitiveness between you and your husband?'

'Oh, but darling, we play for *money*. *Pisica blândă pgarie rău*. Didn't you know that? We earn each other's birthday presents. We've an agreement: we don't buy a gift unless we win the money for it from the other fellow. I'll tell you something, *entre nous*. I get ripped off because I throw games. I do. I take dives. I go into the tank. *Damit kannst du keinen Blumentopf verlieren*. Isn't that *awful*? Aren't I *terrible*? But that's how Courtney got the money together to buy me Nancy's Treehouse. Have you seen her? She's the *most* marvelous beast. I was just going out to the stables to check on her when I ran into you. If you'd like to accompany me come along *lo más pronto posible*.'

'No.'

'*De gustibus*.'

'That's *not a* modern language, Buffy.'

'People *grow*, darling.'

'Buffy, as your houseguest I *demand* that you listen to me. I am almost forty years old and I am one of the three or four dozen truly civilized men in the world and I have been left a fortune. A fortune! And though I have always had the use of the money, I have never till now had the control of it. Up to now I have been an adventurer. The adventures, God save me, were meant to teach me life. Danger builds strong bodies twelve ways, I thought. Action and respite have been the pattern of my existence, Buffy. Through shot and shell on hands and knees one day, and breakfast in bed at the Claridge the next. I have lived my life a fighter pilot, beefed up like a gladiator, like a stuffed goose, like a Thanksgiving turkey. I am this civilized . . . *thing*. Trained and skilled and good. I mean *good*, Buffy, a strict observer till night before last of every commandment there is. Plus an eleventh—honor thy world, I mean. I've done that. I'm versed in it, up to my ears in it as you are in idioms. I was an environmentalist a decade before it was an issue. When I first noticed the deer were scrawnier than they'd been when I was a boy and the water in the rivers where I swam no longer tasted like peaches.

'I've been a scholar of the world—oh, an amateur, I grant you, but a scholar just the same. I understand things. I know literature and math and science and art. I know *everything*. How paper is made, glass blown, marble carved, things about furniture, stuff about cheese. This isn't a boast. With forty years to do it in and nothing to distract you like earning a living or raising a family, you can learn almost all there is *to* learn if you leave out the mystery and the ambiguity. If you omit the riddles and finesse the existential.

'No, *wait*! I'm perfectly aware that I'm barking up the wrong tree—

do you have that idiom, my dear?—but looky, looky, I'm speaking my heart. I'm in mourning, Buff. Here's how I do it. By changing my life. By taking this precious, solipsistic civilization of mine—Buffy, listen to me, dear; *it's not enough that there are only three or four dozen truly civilized men in the world*—this precious civilization of mine and passing it on to sons, daughters, all I can get.'

'*Was ist los?*' she said miserably.

'Time and tide.'

'*Pauvre garçon.*'

'Buffy, *pauvre garçon* me no *pauvres garçons.*'

She looked at me for a moment with as much feeling as I had looked at her. 'Jane Löes Lipton.'

'What? '

'Jane Löes Lipton. A friend of my sister Milly.'

'What about her? '

'Ah.'

'Ah?'

'She'll be Comte de Survillieur's houseguest this month. Do you know the Comte?'

'We did a hitch together in the Foreign Legion.'

'Go. Pack. I'll phone Paris. Perhaps Milly can get you an invitation. *In bocca al lupo.*'

I missed her at the Comte de Survillieur's, and again at Liège, and once more at Cap Thérèse and the Oktoberfest at München. All Europe was talking about her—the fabulous Jane Löes Lipton. One had only to mention her name to elicit one of those round Henry James 'Ah's.' Nor did it surprise me that until the evening in Buffy Surface's garden I had never heard of her: I had been out of society for three or four months. These things happen quickly, these brush fires of personality, some girl suddenly taken up and turned into a household word (if you can call a seventy-room castle a household or 'Ah' a word). Once or twice I had seen an old woman or even a child given this treatment. Normally I avoided such persons. When their fame was justified at all it was usually predicated on some quirkishness, nothing more substantial than some lisp of the character—a commitment to astrology, perhaps, or a knack for mimicry, or skill at bridge. I despise society, but who else will deal with me? I can't run loose in the street with the sailors or drink with the whores. I would put off everyone but a peer.

Still . . . Jane Löes Lipton. Ah. I hadn't met her, but from what I could gather from my peers' collective inarticulateness when it came to Miss (that much was established) Lipton, she was an 'authentic,' an 'original,' a 'beauty,' a 'prize.' And it was intriguing, too, how I happened to keep missing her, for once invited to the Comte's—where I behaved; where, recovering my senses, I no longer coveted my neighbor's wife and rededicated myself to carrying on the good work of my genes and environment in honorable ways—I had joined a regular touring company of the rich and favored. We were like the Ice Capades, like an old-time circus, occasionally taking on personnel, once in a while dropping someone off—a car pool of the heavily leisured. How I happened, as I say, to keep on missing her though we were on the same circuit now, going around—no metaphor but a literal description—in the same circles—and it is *too* a small world, at our heights, way up there where true North consolidates and collects like fog, it is—was uncanny, purest contretemps, a melodrama of bad timing. We were on the same guest lists, often the same floors or wings (dowagers showed me house plans, duchesses did; I saw the seating arrangements and croquet combinations), co-sponsors of the same charity balls and dinners. Twice it was I who fell out of lockstep and had to stay longer than I expected or leave a few days early, but every other time it was Jane who canceled out at the last minute. Was this her claim on them, I wondered? A Monroeish temperament, some pathological inability to keep appointments, honor commitments (though always her check for charity arrived, folded in her letter of regret), the old high school strategy of playing hard to get? No. And try to imagine how *this* struck me, knowing what you do about me, when I heard it. 'Miss Löes Lipton called to say she will not be able to join your Lordship this weekend due to an emergency outbreak of cholera among the children at the Sisters of Cecilia Mission in Lobos de Afuera.' That was the message the Duke's secretary brought him at Liège.

'She's Catholic?' I asked.

'What? Jane? Good Lord, I shouldn't think so.'

Then, at Cap Thérèse, I learned that she had again begged off. I expressed disappointment and inquired of Mrs Steppington whether Miss Lipton were ill.

'Ah, Jane. Ill? Jane's strong as a horse. No, dear boy, there was a plane crash at Dar es Salaam and Jane went there to help the survivors. She's visiting in hospital with them now. For those of them who have children—mostly wogs, I expect—she's volunteered to act as a sort of governess. I can almost see her, going about with a lot of nig-nog kids in tow, teaching them French, telling them the Greek myths, carrying them to whatever museums they have in such places, giving them lectures in art history, then fetching them watercolors—and oils too, I shouldn't doubt—so they can have a go at it. Oh, it *will* be a bore not having her with us. She's a frightfully good sailor and I had hoped to get her to wear my silks in the regatta.'

Though it was two in the morning in Paris, I went to my room and called the Comte de Survillieur.

'Comte. Why couldn't Jane Löes Lipton make it month before last?'

'What's that?' The connection was bad.

'Why did Miss Löes Lipton fail to show up when she was expected at Deux Oiseaux?'

'Who?'

'Jane Löes Lipton.'

'Ah.'

'Why wasn't she there?'

'Who's this?'

'Brewster Ashenden. I apologize for ringing up so late, but I have to know.'

'Indians.'

'Indians?'

'Yes. American Indians I think it was. Had to do some special pleading for them in Washington when a bill came up before your Congress.'

'HR eleven seventy-four.'

'*Qu'est-ce que c'est?*'

'The bill. Law now. So Jane was into HR eleven seventy-four.'

'Ah, what isn't Jane into? You know, I think she's become something of a snob? She has no time for her old friends since undertaking these crusades of hers. She told the Comtesse as much—something about finding herself.'

'She said *that*?'

'Well, she was more poetic, possibly, but that's how it came down to me. I know what *you're* after,' the Comte said roguishly. 'You're in love with her.'

'I've never even met her.'

'You're in love with her. Half Europe is. But unless you're a black or redskin, or have arranged in some other way to cripple yourself, you haven't a chance. Arse over tip in love, *mon cher* old comrade.'

We rang off.

In the following weeks I heard that Jane Löes Lipton had turned up in Hanoi to see if there weren't some way of getting negotiations off dead center; that she had published a book that broke the code in Oriental rugs; that she had directed an underground movie in Sweden which despite its frank language and graphic detail was so sensitive it was to be distributed with a G rating; and that she was back in America visiting outdoor fairs and buying up paintings depicting clowns and rowboats turned over on beaches for a show she was putting together for the Metropolitan entitled 'Shopping Center Primitive: Collectors' Items for the Twenty-Third Century.' One man said she could be seen in Dacca on Bangladesh Television in a series called 'Cooking Nutritious Meals on the Pavement for Large Families from Garbage and Without Fire,' and another that she had become a sort of spiritual adviser to the statesmen of overdeveloped nations. Newspapers reported her on the scene wherever the earth quaked or the ships foundered or the forests burned.

Certainly she could not have had so many avatars. Certainly most was rumor, speculation knit from Jane's motives and sympathies. Yet I heard people never known to lie, Rock-of-Gibraltarish types who didn't get the point of jokes, swear to their testimony Where there's smoke there's fire. If most was exaggerated, much was true.

Ah, Jane, Candy Striper to the Cosmos, Gray Lady of the Ineffable, when would I meet you, swap traveler's tales of what was to be found in those hot jungles of self-seeking, those voyages to the center of the soul and other uncharted places, the steeps and deeps and lost coves and far shelves of being? Ah, Jane, oh Löes Lipton, half Europe loves you.

I went to London and stayed in the Bottom, the tall new hotel there. Lonely as Frank Sinatra on an album cover I went up to their revolving cocktail lounge on the fiftieth floor, the Top of the Bottom, and ran into Freddy Plympton.

'She's here.'

'Jane Löes Lipton? I've heard *that* one before.' (We hadn't been talking of her. How did I know that's who he meant? I don't know, I knew.)

'No, no, she is, at my country place. She's there now. She's exhausted, poor dear, and tells me her doctor has commanded her to resign temporarily from all volunteer fire departments. So she's here. I've got her. She's with Lady Plympton right this moment. I had to come to town on business or I'd be with her. I'm going back in the morning. Ever meet her? Want to come down?'

'She's there? She's really there?'

'Want to come down?'

There's been too much pedigree in this account, I think. (Be kind. Put it down to metaphysics, not vanity. In asking Who? I'm wondering What? Even the trees have names, the rocks and clouds and grasses do. The world's a picture post card sent from a far hotel. 'Here's my room, this is what the stamps in this country look like, that's the strange color of the sand here, the people all wear these curious hats.') Bear with me.

Freddy Plympton is noble. The family is old—whose isn't, eh? we were none of us born yesterday; look it up in *Burke's Peerage* where it gets three pages, in *Debrett* where it gets four—and his great estate, Duluth, is one of the finest in England. Though he could build a grander if he chose. Freddy's real wealth comes from the gambling casinos he owns. He is an entrepreneur of chance, a fortune teller. The biggest gaming palaces and highest stakes in Europe, to say nothing of hotels in Aruba and boats beyond the twelve-mile limit and a piece of the action in church bingo basements and punchboards all over the world, the newsprint for which is supplied from his own forests in Norway and is printed on his own presses. Starting from scratch, from choosing odds-or-evens for cash with his roommate at Harrow, a sheikh's son with a finger missing from his left hand—he was left-handed—which made him constitutionally unable to play the game ('He thought "even," you see,' Freddy explains), taking the boy, neither of them more than fourteen, to the cleaners in the third form. It, the young sheikh's deformity, was Freddy's initial lesson in what it means to have the house odds in your favor and taught him never to enter any contest in which he did not have the edge.

Freddy has one passion, and it is not gambling. 'Gambling's my work, old bean,' he says. (He uses these corny aristocratic epithets. They make him seem fatuous but are as functional to his profession as a drawl to a hired gun.) 'I'm no gambler at all, actually. I'm this sort of mathematician. Please don't gamble with me, please don't accept my bets. We're friends and I'm ruthless. Not vicious—ruthless. I will never surrender an advantage. Since I know the odds and respect them, to ignore them would be a sort of cheating, and since I'm honorable I couldn't think of that. Don't play with me. We're friends. I was never the sheikh's friend, never the friend of any of those feet-off-the-ground *Fleugenmensch* sons of rich men I lived with at Harrow and Cambridge and who gave me my stake. Where I was meditative they were speculative. I like you, as I like anyone who doesn't confuse his need with his evidence. Let's never gamble. Promise. *Promise?'*

So he has a passion, but it isn't gambling. It's animals—beasts, rather. Duluth contains perhaps the most superb private zoo in the world, a huge game park, larger than Whipsnade and much more dangerous. Where Whipsnade hedges with moats and illusions, at Duluth the animals are given absolute freedom. An enormous, camouflaged electrified fence, the largest in the world, runs about the entire estate. ('We control the current. The jolt merely braces the larger animals and only stuns the smaller, puts them unconscious. I've installed an auxiliary electrical plant for when there are power failures'.) Although from time to time a few of the animals have fought and occasionally killed each other, an attempt has been made to introduce as near perfect an

ecological balance as possible, vegetarians and carnivores who find
the flesh of the beasts with whom they must live inimical, some almost
religious constraint in the jaws and digestion, some once-burned,
twice-sorry instinct passed on from generation to generation that protects and preserves his herds.

It was an ancestor of Plympton's who began the park, and as a result
of the care he and his successors put into selecting and arranging the
animals, some of the most incredible and lovely juxtapositions in the
world are to be found there. (Freddy told me that Henri Rousseau
painted his 'Sleeping Gypsy' while he was a guest on the estate.) From
the beginning a single rule has determined the constituency of the
zoo: all the beasts collected there must have appeared on the Plympton
heraldry. Lions, bears, elephants, unicorns ('a pure white rhinoceros
actually'), leopards, jackals ('One old boy helped to do in Becket, old
boy'), pandas, camels, sheep and apes. The family is an old one, the list
long.

Though Plympton and I had known each other for years—we're
the same age—this was the first time I had been invited to Duluth. I
drove down with him the next morning, and of course it was not of
the fabulous game park that I was thinking—I was not sure I even
approved of it—but of Jane. I gave myself away with my questions.

'She's ill, you say?'

'Did I? I thought I said tired. What she told me, anyway. Looks
ruddy healthy, in fact. Tanner than I've ever seen her.'

'Is she alone?'

'What, is there a *man* with her, you mean? No, no, Ashenden.
She's quite singular.'

'How did she happen to drop in on you?'

'I'm not in it at all, dear chap. I'm a businessman and gamekeeper.
My life's quite full. I suppose that may actually have had something to
do with it, in fact. She called from Heathrow day before yesterday. Said
she was in England and wanted someplace to rest, Lord, I hope she's
not put off by my bringing you down. Never thought of that aspect of
it before.'

'I won't bother her.'

'No, of course you won't,' he said smiling. 'Sorry I suggested that.

Just thinking out loud. A man concerned with animals must always be conscious of who goes into the cage with whom. It's a social science, zoology is, very helpful in making up parties. I suppose mine, when I trouble to give them, are among the most *gemütlich* in Europe. Indeed, now I think of it, I must have realized as soon as I saw you last night that you'd be acceptable to Jane, or I'd never have asked you. Have you known her long? '

'We've never met.'

'What, never met and so keen?' I smiled lamely and Freddy patted my knee. 'I understand. I do. I feel you hoping. And I quite approve. Just don't confuse your hope with your evidence.' He studied me for a moment. 'But then you wouldn't, would you, or I'd not be so fond of you.'

'You do understand quite a lot, Freddy.'

'Who, me? I'm objective, is all. Yearning, I can smell yearning a mile off.'

'I shall have to shower.'

'Not at all, not at all. It stinks only when untempered by reason. In your case I smell reason a mile off, too. Eminently suitable, eminently,' he pronounced. 'I wouldn't bet against it,' he added seriously, and I felt so good about this last that I had to change the subject. I questioned him about Duluth, which till then I hadn't even thought of. Now, almost superstitiously, I refused to think about Jane. Every time he gave me an opening I closed it, choosing, as one does who has so much at stake and success seems within his grasp, to steer clear of the single thing that is of any interest to him. We spoke trivially the whole time, and my excitement and happiness were incandescent.

'How many miles do you get to the gallon in this Bentley of yours, Plympton? ' I asked, and even before he could answer I turned to look out the window and exclaim, 'Look, look at the grass, so green it is. That's your English climate for you. If rain's the price a nation must pay to achieve a grass that green, then one must just as well pay up and be still about it. Who's your tailor? I'm thinking of having some things made.'

When we left the M-4 and came to the turnoff that would bring us at last to Duluth I put my hand on Plympton's sleeve. 'Freddy, listen, I know I must sound like a fool, but could you just introduce us and give me some time alone with her? We've so many friends in common—and perhaps other things as well—that I know there won't be any awkwardness. My God, I've been pursuing her for months. Who knows when I'll have such an opportunity again? I know my hope's showing, and I hope—look, there I go again—you won't despise me for it, but I have to talk to her. I have to.'

'Then you shall,' he said, and we turned onto the road that took us across the perimeter of the estate and drove for five miles and came to a gate where a gatekeeper greeted Lord Plympton and a chauffeur who seemed to materialize out of the woods got in and took the wheel while Freddy and I moved to the back seat, and we drove together through the lovely grounds for another fifteen or twenty minutes and passed through another gate, though I did not see it until we were almost on it—the queer, camouflaged electric fence—and through the windows I could hear the coughing of apes and the roar of lions and the bleating of lambs and the wheezes and grunts and trebles and basses of a hundred beasts—though I saw none—and at last, passing through a final gate, came to the long, curving, beautiful driveway of the beautiful house and servants came to take our bags and others to open doors and an older woman in a long gown—Plympton kissed her and introduced her as his wife, the Lady Plympton I'd never met ('She came with guanacos on her crest, dear fellow, with the funny panda and the gravid slug. I married her—ha ha—to fill out the set'), and he bolted upstairs beckoning me to follow. 'Come on, come on,' he said, 'can't wait to get here, then hangs back like a boy at his first ball,' and I bounded up the stairs behind him, and overtook him. 'Wherever are you going? You don't know the way. Go on, go on, left, left,' he called. 'When you come to the end of the hall turn right into the Richard Five wing. It's the first apartment past the Ballroom of Time. You'll see the clocks,' and I left him behind, only to come to the door, *her* door, and stop outside it.

Plympton came up behind me. 'I knew you wouldn't,' he said, and knocked on the door gently, 'Jane,' he called softly. 'Jane? Are you decent, darling?'

'Yes,' she said. Her voice was beautiful.

'Shall I push open the door?'

'Yes,' she said, 'would you just?'

He shoved me gently inside, but did not cross the threshold himself. 'Here's Brewster Ashenden for you,' he said, and turned and left.

I could not see her clearly. No lights were on and the curtains were still drawn. I stood in the center of the room and waited for a command. I was physically excited, a fact which I trusted the darkness to shield from Jane. Neither of us said anything.

Then I spoke boldly. 'He's right. I trust he's right. I pray he is.'

'He?'

'Plympton. "Here's Brewster Ashenden for you," he said.'

'Did he? That was presumptuous of him, then.'

'I am Brewster Ashenden of the earth, air, fire and water Ashendens and this moment is very important to me. I'm first among eligible men, Miss Löes Lipton. Though that sounds a boast, it is not. I have heard of your beauty and your character. Perhaps you have heard something of mine.'

'I never listen to gossip. And anyway hearsay is inadmissible in court . . . ship.'

I knew she was going to say that. *It was exactly what I would have replied had she made the speech I had just made!* Do you know what it means to have so profound a confirmation—to have, that is, all one's notions, beliefs, hunches and hypotheses suddenly and entirely endorsed? My God, I was like Columbus standing in the New round World, like the Wrights right and aloft over Kitty Hawk! For someone like myself it was like having my name cleared! I'm talking about redemption. *To be right!* That's everything in life, you know. To be right, absolutely right, one hundred percent correct in all the essentials, that's all we want. And whoever is? Brewster Ashenden—once. I had so much to tell her.

I began to talk, a mile a minute, filling her in, breathlessly bringing her up to date, a Greek stranger's after-dinner talk in a king's gold palace on an inaccessible island in a red and distant sea. A necessary entertainment. Until then I had not known my life had been a story.

Then, though I could not see it in the dark room, she held up her hand for me to stop. It was exactly where I would have held up *my* hand had Jane been speaking.

'Yes,' she said of my life, 'it was the same with me.'

Neither of us could speak for a time. Then, gaily, 'Oh, Brewster, think of all the—'

'—coastlines?' I said.

'Yes,' she said, 'yes. All the coastlines, bays, sounds, capes and peninsulas, the world's beaches scribbled round all the countries and continents and islands. All the Cannes and Hamptons yet to be. Shores in Norway like a golden lovely dust. Spain's wild hairline, Portugal's long face like an impression on coins. The nubbed antlers of Scandinavia and the great South American porterhouse. The French teapot and Italian boot and Australia like a Scottie in profile.'

'Asia running like a watercolor, dripping Japan and all the rest,' we said together.

'Yes, yes,' she said. 'God, I love the world.'

'There's no place like it.'

'Let me wash up on seashores and eat the local specialties, one fish giving way to another every two or three hundred miles along the great continuous coasts like an exquisite, delicious evolution. Thank God for money and jet airplanes. Let me out at the outpost. Do you feel that way?'

'What, are you kidding? An earth, fire, air and water guy like me? I do, I do.'

'Family's important,' she said.

'You bet it is.'

She giggled. 'My grandfather, a New Yorker, was told to go west for his health. Grandfather hated newspapers, he didn't trust them and said all news—even of wars, heavy weather and the closing markets—was just cheap gossip. He thought all they were good for, since he held that calendars were vulgar, was the date printed at the top of the page. In Arizona he had the New York *Times* sent to him daily, though of course it always arrived a day or two late. So for him the eleventh was the ninth or the tenth, and he went through the last four years of his life a day or two behind actual time. Grandfather's Christmas and New Year's were celebrated after everyone else's. He went to church on Easter Tuesday.'

'Easter Tuesday, that's very funny.'

'I love the idiosyncratic; it is all that constitutes integrity. Difference, nuance, hues and shade. Spectra, Brewster. That's why we travel, perhaps, why we're found on all this planet's exotic strands, cherishing peculiarities, finding lost causes, chipping in to save the primitive wherever it occurs—'

'Listen to her talk. Is that a sweetheart?'

'—refusing to let it die, though the old ways are the worst ways and unhealthy, bad for the teeth and the balanced diet and the comfort and the longevity. Is that selfish?'

'I think so.'

'Yes,' she said pensively. 'Of course it is. All taste's a cruelty at last. We impede history with our Sierra Clubs and our closed societies. We'll have to answer for that, I suppose. Oh, well . . . Brewster, do you have uncles? Tell me about your uncles.'

'I had an Uncle Clifford who believed that disease could be communicated only by a draft when one was traveling at high speeds. He wore a paper bag over his head even in a closed car. He cut out holes for the eyes, for despite his odd notion he dearly loved to travel and watch the scenery go by. Even going up in elevators he wore his paper bag, though he strolled at ease through the contagion wards of hospitals dispensing charity to the poor.'

'Marvelous.'

'Yes.'

'Brewster, this is important. Do you know things? People should know facts.'

'I know them.'

'I knew you knew them.'

'I love you, Miss Löes Lipton.'

'Jane,' she said.

'Jane.'

She was weeping. I didn't try to comfort her, but stood silently in place until she was through. I knew she was going to tell me to open the curtains, for this part of the interview was finished.

'Open the curtains, Brewster.'

I went to the bay and pulled the drawstring and light came into the room and flooded it and I turned to the chair in which Jane was sitting and saw her face for the first time. She looked exactly as I knew she would look, though I had never seen a photograph of her or yet been to any of the houses in which her portraits were hung. All that was different was that there was a darkish region under her eyes and her skin had an odd tan.

'Oh,' I said, 'you've a spot of *lupus erythematosus* there, don't you?'

'You *do* know things, Brewster.'

'I recognized the wolflike shadow across the eyes.'

'It's always fatal.'

'I know.'

'The body develops antibodies against itself.'

'I know.'

'It's as if I were allergic to my own chemistry.'

'I know, I know.' I went toward her blinded by my tears. I kissed her, her lips and the intelligent, wolfish mask across her beautiful face. 'How much time is there?' I asked.

Jane shrugged.

'It isn't fair. It isn't.'

'Yes. Well,' she said.

'Marry me, Jane.'

She shook her head.

'You've got to.'

'No,' she said.

'Because of this fatal disease? That doesn't matter to me. I beg your pardon, Jane, if that sounds callous. I don't mean that your mortality doesn't matter to me. I mean that now that I've found you I can't let you go, no matter how little time you might have left.'

'Do you think that's why I refused you? Because I'm going to die? Everyone dies. I refuse you because of what you are and because of what I am.'

'But we're the same. We know each other inside out.'

'No. There's a vast gulf between us.'

'No, Jane. I know what you're going to say before you say it, what you're going to do before you do it.'

'No.'

'Yes. I swear. Yes.' She smiled, and the wolf mask signal of her disease made her uncanny. 'You mean because I don't know why you refuse me? Is that what you mean?' She nodded. 'Then you see I *do* know. I knew that it was because I didn't know why you refused me. Oh, I'm so confused. I'm—wait. Oh. Is it what I think it is?' She nodded. 'Oh, my God. Jane, *please*. I wasn't thinking. You let me go on. I was too hasty in telling you my life. It's because you're pure and I'm not. That's it, isn't it? Isn't that it?' She nodded. 'Jane, I'm a *man*,' I pleaded. 'It's different with a man. Listen,' I said, 'I *can* be pure. I can be again. I *will* be.'

'There isn't time.'

'There *is*, there *is*.'

'If I thought there were . . . Oh, Brewster, if I really thought there *were*—' she said, and broke off.

'There *is*. I make a vow. I make a holy vow.' I crossed my heart.

She studied me. 'I believe you,' she said finally. 'That is, I believe you seriously *wish* to undo what you have done to yourself. I believe in your penitent spirit, I mean. No. Don't kiss me. You must be continent henceforth. Then . . .'

'We'll see?'

'We'll see.'

'The next time, Jane, the next time you see me, I swear I will have met your conditions.'

I bowed and left and was told where I was to sleep by a grinning Plympton. He asked if, now that I had seen Jane, I would like to go with him on a tour of the estate.

'Not just yet, Freddy, I think.'

'Jane gave you something to think about, did she?'

'Something like that.'

Was ever any man set such a task by a woman? To undo defilement and regain innocence, to take an historical corruption and will it annulled, whisking it out of time as if it were a damaged egg going by on a conveyor belt. And not given years—Jane's disease was progressive, the mask a manifestation of one of its last stages—nor deserts to do it in. Not telling beads or contemplating from some Himalayan hillside God's extensive Oneness. No, nor chanting a long, cunning train of boxcar mantras as it moves across the mind's trestle and over

the soul's deep, dangerous drop. No, no, and no question either of
simply distributing the wealth or embracing the leper or going about
in rags (I still wore my mourning togs, that lover's wardrobe, those
Savile Row whippery flags of self) or doing those bows and scrapes
that were only courtesy's moral minuet, and no time, no time at all for
the long Yoga life, the self's spring cleaning that could drag on years.
What had to be done had to be done now, in these comfortable
Victorian quarters on a velvet love seat or in the high fourposter,
naked cherubs climbing the bedposts, the burnished dimples of their
wooden behinds glistening in the light from the fresh laid fire. By a
gilded chamber pot, beneath a silken awning, next to a window with
one of the loveliest views in England.

That, at least, I could change. I drew the thick drapes across the
bayed glass and, influenced perhaps by the firelight and the Baker
Street ambience, got out my carpet slippers and red smoking jacket. I
really had to laugh. This won't do, I thought. How do you expect to
bring about these important structural changes and get that dear dying
girl to marry you if the first thing you do is to impersonate Sherlock
Holmes? Next you'll be smoking opium and scratching on a fiddle.
Get down to it, Ashenden, get down to it.

But it was pointless to scold when no alternative presented itself to
me. How *did* one get down to it? How does one undefile the defiled?
What acts of *kosher* and exorcism? Religion (though I am not *irreli-
gious*) struck me as beside the point. It was Jane I had offended, not
God. What good would it have done to pray for His forgiveness?
And what sacrilege to have prayed for hers! Anyway, I understood that
I already had her forgiveness. Jane wanted a virgin. In the few hours
that remained I had to become one.

I thought pure thoughts for three hours. Images of my mother: one
summer day when I was a child and we collected berries together for
beach plum jelly; a time in winter when I held a simple cat's cradle of
wool which my mother was carding. I thought of my tall father in a
Paris park when I was ten, and of the pictures we posed each other for,
waiting for the sun to come out before we tripped the shutter. And
recollected mornings in chapel in school in New England—I was
seven, I was eight—the chaplain describing the lovely landscapes of

Heaven and I, believing, wanting to die. I recalled the voices of guides
in museums I toured with my classmates, and thought about World's
Fairs I had attended. The '36 Olympics, sitting on the bench beside
the New Zealand pole vaulter. I remembered perfect picnics, Saturday
matinees in Broadway theaters, looking out the window lying awake
in comfortable compartment berths on trains, horseback riding on a
fall morning in mountains, sailing with Father. All the idylls. I remembered, that is, my virginity, sorting out for the first time in years the
decent pleasures of comfort and wonder and respect. But—and I was
enjoying myself, I could feel the smile on my face—what did it
amount to? I was no better than a gangster pleading his innocence
because he had once *been* innocent.

I thought *impure* thoughts, reading off my long-time bachelor's
hundred conquests, parsing past, puberty and old fantasy, reliving all
the engrams of lust in gazebo, band shell, yacht and penthouse, night
beaches at low tide, rooms, suites, shower stalls, bedrooms on crack
trains, at the carpeted turnings of stairs, and once in a taxi and once on
a butcher's block at dawn in Les Halles—all the bachelor's emergency
landing fields, all his makeshift landscapes, propinquitous to grandeur
and history, in Flanders Fields, rooms with views, by this ocean or by
that, this tall building or that public monument, my backstage lovemaking tangential as a town at the edge of a map. Oh love's landmarks,
oh its milestones, sex altering place like sunset. Oh the beds and oh the
walls, the floors and bridges—and me a gentleman!—the surfaces softened by Eros, contour stones and foam rubber floors of forests,
everywhere but the sky itself a zone for dalliance, my waterfalls of
sperm, our Laguardias of hum and droned groan. Recalling the settings first, the circumstances, peopling them only afterwards and even
then only piecemeal, a jigsaw, Jack-the-Ripper memory of hatcheck
girl thigh and night club singer throat and heiress breast, the salty
hairs of channel swimmers and buttocks of horseback riders and
knuckles of pianists and strapless tans of models—sex like flesh's cross-
word, this limb and that private like the fragments in a multiple choice.
And only after that gradually joining arm to shoulder, shoulder to
neck, neck to face, Ezekielizing my partners, dem bones, dem bones
gon' walk aroun'.

Yes? No. The smile was *still* on my face. And there in that Victorian counting house, I, lust's miser, its Midas, touching gold and having it gold still, an ancient Pelagian, could not overcome my old unholy gratitude for flesh, and so lost innocence again, even as I resisted, the blood rushing where it would, filling the locks of my body. 'Make me clean,' I prayed, 'help me to make one perfect act of contrition, break my nasty history's hold on me, pull a fast one at this eleventh hour.'

A strange thing happened. The impure thoughts left me and my blood retreated and I began to remember those original idylls, my calendar youth, the picnic and berry hunts, and all those placid times before fires, dozing on a couch, my head in Mother's lap and her hands in my hair like rain on the roof and, My God, my little weewee was stiff, and it was stiff now too!

It was what I'd prayed for: shame like a thermal inversion, the self-loathing that *is* purity. The sailing lessons and horseback rides and lectures and daytrips came back tainted. I saw how pleased I'd been, how smug. Why, I'm free, I thought, and was. 'I've licked it, Jane,' I said. 'I'm pure, holy as a wafer, my heart pink as rare meat. I was crap. Look at me now.'

If she won't have me, I thought, it's not my fault. I rushed out to show myself to her and tell her what I'd discovered. I ran over it again to see if I had it straight. 'Jane,' I'd say, 'I'm bad, unsavory from the word go, hold your nose. To be good subsists in such understanding. So innocence is knowledge, not its lack. See, morality's easy, clear, what's the mystery?' But when I stepped outside my suite the house was dark. Time had left me behind. The long night of the soul goes by in a minute. It must have been three or four in the morning. I couldn't wake Jane; she was dying of *lupus erythematosus* and needed her rest. I didn't know where Plympton slept or I would have roused him. Too exhilarated by my virtue to sleep, I went outside.

But it was not 'outside' as you and I know it. Say rather it was a condition, like the out-of-doors in a photograph, the colors fixed and temperature unfelt, simply not factors, the wind stilled and the air light, and so wide somehow that he could walk without touching it. It was as if he moved in an enormous diorama of nature, a crèche of the elements. Brewster Ashenden was rich. He had lain on his back on Ontario turf farms and played the greens of St Andrews and Burning Tree, but he had never felt anything like Duluth's perfect grass, soft and springy as theater seats, and even in moonlight green as billiard cloth. The moon, perfectly round and bright as a tennis shoe—he could make out its craters, like the eternally curving seams of a Spalding— enabled him to see perfectly, the night no more than the vaguest atmosphere, distant objects gyroscopically stilled like things glimpsed through the whirling blades of a fan.

What he saw was like the landscapes behind madonnas in classical paintings—one missed only the carefully drawn pillars and far, tiny palaces—blue-hilled horizons, knolls at the end of space, complex shores that trailed eccentrically about flat, blackish planes of water with boulders rising from them. He thought he perceived distant fields, a mild husbandry, the hay in, the crops a sloping green and blue debris in the open fields, here and there ledges keyholed with caves, trees in the middle distance as straight as the land they grew from. It was a geography of eclectic styles and landscapes, even the sky a hybrid—here clear and black and starred, there roiling with a brusque signature of cloud or piled in strata like folded linen or the interior of rock.

He walked away from the castle, pulled toward the odd, distant galleries. His mood was a fusion of virtue and wonder. He felt solitary but not lonely, and if he remembered that he walked unprotected through the largest game preserve this side of the Kenyan savannah, there was nothing in his bold step to indicate this. He strode powerfully toward those vistas he had seen stretching away in every direction from the manor. Never had he seemed to himself so fulfilled, and never, unless in dreams, had such seeming distances been so easily negotiated, the scenery changing every hundred yards or so, the hills that had appeared so remote easily climbed and giving way at their crests to tiny valleys and plains or thick, sudden clots of jungle. This trick of perspective was astonishing, reminding him of cunning golf courses, sudden doglegs, sand traps, unexpected waterholes. Everything was as distinctively charactered as foreign countries, natural borders. He remembered miniature golf courses to which he had been taken as a child, each hole dominated by some monolithic feature, a windmill, perhaps, a gingerbread house, a bridge, complicated networks of banked plains that turned on themselves, culs-de-sac. He thought that Duluth might be deceptively large or deceptively small, and he several miles or only a few thousand feet from the main house—which had already disappeared behind him.

As he came, effortlessly as in any paradise, to each seamed, successive landscape, the ease of his arrivals added to his sense of strength, and each increment of strength to his sense of purity, so that his exercise fed his feelings about his heart and happiness. Though he had that day made the long drive from London, had his interview with Jane (as exhausting as it was stimulating) and done the hardest thinking of his life, though he had not slept (even in London he had tossed and turned all night, kept awake by the prospect of finally meeting Jane) in perhaps forty hours, he wasn't tired. He wondered if he would ever be tired again. Or less gay than now. For what he felt, he was certain, was not mood but something deeper, a stability, as the out-of-doors was, as space was. He could make plans. If Jane would have him (she would; they had spoken code this afternoon, signaled each other a high language of commitment, no small talk but the cryptic, sacred speech of government flashing its secret observations over mountains and under seas, the serious ventriloquism of outpost), they could plan not to plan, simply to live, to be. In his joy he had forgotten her death, her rare, personal disease in which self fled self in ultimate allergy. *Lupus erythematosus.* It was not catching, but he would catch it. He would catch *her.* There was no need to survive her. Together they would grow the wolf mask across their eyes, death's big spreading butterfly. It didn't matter. They'd have their morality together, the blessed link-up between appropriate humans, anything permissible between consenting man and consenting woman—anything, any bold or timid configuration, whatever the one craved and the other yielded, whatever whatsoever, love's sanctified arrangements, not excluding the deathbed itself. What need had he to survive her—though he'd probably not die until she did—now that he had at last a vehicle for his taste, his marriage?

He was in a sort of clearing. Though he knew he had not retraced his steps nor circled around, it seemed familiar. He stood on uneven ground and could see a line of low frigid mountains in the distance. High above him and to his right the great tear of the moon, like the drain of day, sucked light. At his feet there appeared the remains of—what? A feast? A picnic? He bent down to investigate and found a few clay shards of an old jug, a bit of yellow wood like the facing on some stringed instrument and a swatch of faded, faintly Biblical cloth, broadly striped as the robe of a prophet. As he fingered this debris he smelled what was unmistakably bowel.

'Have I stepped in something?' He stood and raised his shoe, but his glance slid off it to the ground where he saw two undisturbed lumps, round as hamburger, of congealing lion waste. It came to him at once. 'I *knew* it was familiar! "The Sleeping Gypsy." This is where it was painted!' He looked suspiciously at the mangled mandolin facing, the smashed jug and the tough cloth, which he now perceived had been forcibly torn. My God, he thought, the lion must have eaten the poor fellow. The picture had been painted almost seventy-five years earlier, but he understood from his reading that lions often returned to the scenes of their most splendid kills, somehow passing on to succeeding generations this odd, historical instinct of theirs. Nervously he edged away, and though the odor of lion dung still stung his nostrils, it was gradually replaced by more neutral smells. Clearly, however, he was near the beasts.

He turned but still could not see the castle. He was not yet frightened. From what he had already seen of Duluth he understood that it was a series of cunningly stitched enclaves, of formal, transistorized prospects that swallowed each other transitionlessly. It seemed to be the antithesis of a maze, a surface of turned corners that opened up on fresh surprises. He thought of himself as walking along an enormous Möbius strip, and sooner or later he would automatically be brought back to his starting point. If he was a little uneasy it was only because of the proximity of the animals, whose presence he felt and smelled rather than saw or heard.

Meanwhile, quickening his pace, he came with increasing frequency to experience a series of déjà vus, puzzling at first but then suddenly and disappointingly explicable. He had hoped, as scenes

became familiar to him, that he was already retracing his steps, but a
few seconds' perusal of each place indicated otherwise. These were not
places he had ever been, only places he had seen. Certainly, he
thought, the paintings! Here's Cranach the Elder's 'Stag Hunt.'
Unmistakably. And a few moments later—I'll be darned, Jean Honore
Fragonard's 'A Game of Hot Cockles.' And then Watteau's 'Embarking
for Cythera,' will you look at that? There was E. Melvin Bolstad's
'Sunday in the Country' and then El Greco's 'View of Toledo' without Toledo. Astonishing, Ashenden thought, really worthwhile. Uh
oh, I don't think I care for that Constable, he thought; why'd they use
that? Perhaps because it was here. Gosh, isn't that a Thomas Hart
Benton? However did they manage that odd rolling effect? That's
really lovely. I'll have to ask Plympton the name of his landscaper. Jane
and I will certainly be able to use him once we're settled. Now he was
more determined than ever to get rid of Franklin.

And so it went. He strolled through wide-windowed Wyeths and
gay, open-doored Dufys and through Hoppers—I'll have to come
back and see that one with the sun on it—scratchy Segonzacs and dap-
pled Renoirs and faintly heaving Cézannes, and across twilled Van
Gogh grasses and faint Utrillo fields and precise Audubon fens, and
one perfect, wild Bosch dell. It was thrilling. I am in art, thought
Brewster Ashenden, pleased to have been prepared for it by his education and taste.

He continued on until he came to a small jewel of a pond mounted
in a setting of scalloped shoreline with low thin trees that came up
almost to the water. It was the Botticelli 'Birth of Venus,' which, like
El Greco's 'View of Toledo' without Toledo, was without either Venus
Zephyr, Ohloris, or the Hour of Spring. Nevertheless it was delight-
ful, and he took a seat on a mound of earth and rested, thinking of
Jane and listening to the sea in a large shell he had found on the
beach.

'I'm glad,' he said, speaking from the impulse of his mood now that
his wanderings were done and the prospect of his—their—death had
become a part of his taste and filled his eyes with tears, 'I'm glad to
have lived in the age of jet travel, and to have had the money for tick-
ets.' He grew contemplative. 'There has never been a time in my life,'

he said, 'when I have not had my own passport, and never a period of
more than four months when I was not immune to all the indigenous
diseases of place for which there are shots. I am grateful—not that I'd
ever lord it over my forebears—that I did not live in the time of sailing ships. Noble as those barks were, they were slow, slow. And
Dramamine not invented. This, for all its problems, is the best age to
be rich in. I've seen a lot in my time.'

Then, though he couldn't have told you the connection, Ashenden
said a strange thing for someone at that moment and in that setting. '*I
am not a jerk*,' he said, 'I am not so easily written off. Profound guys
like me often seem naïve. Perhaps I'm a fool of the gods. That remains
to be seen. But answers are mostly simple, wisdom is.' He was melancholy now and rose, as if by changing position he hoped to shake off
this new turn in his mood. He looked once more at the odd pool and
spoke a sort of valedictory. 'This is a nice place. Jane would enjoy it. I
wish I still had those two folding chairs the Bank of America gave me
for opening an account of five thousand dollars. We could come here
tomorrow on a picnic.'

He did not know whether to go around the pond or cut through
the thin trees, but finally determined not to go deeper into the forest.
Though he suspected the animals must be all around him, it was very
quiet and he wondered again about them. They would be asleep, of
course, but didn't his presence mean anything to them? Had their
queer captivity and the unusual circumstances in which they lived so
accustomed them to man that one could walk among them without
disturbing them at all? But I am in art, he thought, and thus in nature
too, and perhaps I've already caught Jane's illness and the wolf mask is
working someplace under my skin, making me no more significant
here than the presence of the trees or the angles of the hills.

Walking around the other side of the pond, he noticed that the trees
had changed. They were sparser, more ordinary. Ahead he spied a bluff
and moved toward it. Soon he was again in a sort of clearing and here
he smelled the smells.

The odor of beasts is itself a kind of meat—a dream avatar of alien
sirloin, strange chops and necks, oblique joints and hidden livers and
secret roasts. There are nude juices in it, and licy furs, and all the flesh's

vegetation. It is friction which rubs the fleshly chemistry, releasing it, sending skyhigh the queer subversive gasses of oblique life forms. It is noxious. Separated as we are from animals in zoos by glass cages and fenced-off moats, and by the counter odors of human crowds, melting ice cream, peanut shells crushed underfoot, snow cones, mustard, butts of bun—all the detritus of a Sunday outing—we rarely smell it. What gets through is dissipated, for a beast in civilization does not even smell like a beast in the wild. Already evolution has begun its gentling work, as though the animals might actually feel compunction, some subtle, aggravating modesty. But in Plympton's jungle the smells were uninhibited, biological, profane. Their acidity brought tears to Ashenden's eyes and he had to rub them.

When he took his hands away he saw where he was. He had entered, he knew, the last of the pictures. Although he could not at first identify it, much was familiar. The vegetation, for example, was unmistakably Rousseau, with here and there a Gauguin calabash or stringy palm. There were other palms, hybrid as the setting itself, queer gigantic leaves flying from conventional European trunks. The odor was fierce but he couldn't leave. At his feet were thick Rousseauvian candelabras of grass, and before him vertical pagoda clusters of enormous flowers, branches dangerously bent under the weight of heavy leaves like the notched ears of elephants. Everywhere were fernlike trees, articulated as spine or rib cage, a wide net of the greenly skeletal and the crossed swords of tall grasses. There were rusts and tawns and huge wigwam shapes and shadows like the entrances to caves, black as yawns. The odor was even more overpowering than before, and had he not seen the vegetation he would have thought himself at the fermented source of the winish world. Yet the leaves and grasses and bushes and flowers were ripe. He reached out and touched a leaf in a low branch and licked his hand: it was sweet. Still, the place stank. The smell was acrid, actually hot. Here the forest was made impenetrable by its very odor and he started to back off. Unable either to turn away from it completely or to look at it directly, he was forced to squint, and immediately he had a striking perception.

Seen through his almost closed eyes, the trees and vegetation lost their weird precision and articulation and became conventional, transformed into an ordinary arbor. Only then, half blinded, he saw at last where he was. It was Edward Hicks's 'The Peaceable Kingdom,' and unquestionably the painter had himself been squinting when he painted it. It was one of Ashenden's favorite paintings, and he was thrilled to be where lion and fox and leopard and lamb and musk ox and goat and tiger and steer had all lain together. The animals were gone now but must have been here shortly before. He guessed that the odor was the collective conflagration of their bowels, their guts' bonfire. I'll have to be careful where I step, he thought, and an enormous bear came out of the woods toward him.

It was a Kamchatkan Brown from the northeastern peninsula of the U.S.S.R. between the Bering and Okhotsk seas, and though it was not yet full grown it weighed perhaps seven hundred pounds and was already taller than Ashenden. It was female, and what he had been smelling was its estrus, not shit but lust, not bowel but love's gassy chemistry, the atoms and hormones and molecules of passion, vapors of impulse and the endocrinous spray of desire. What he had been smelling was secret, underground rivers flowing from hidden sources of intimate gland, and what the bear smelled on Brewster was the same.

Ashenden did not know this; indeed, he did not even know that it was female, or what sort of bear it was. Nor did he know that where he stood was not the setting for Hicks's painting (that was actually in a part of the estate where he had not yet been), but had he discovered his mistake he would still have told you that he was in art, that his error had been one of grace, ego's flashy optimism, its heroic awe. He would have been proud of having given the benefit of the doubt to the world, his precious blank check to possibility.

All this changed with the sudden appearance of the bear. Not *all*. He still believed—this in split seconds, more a reaction than a belief, a first impression chemical as the she-bear's musk—that the confrontation was noble, a challenge (there's going to be a hell of a contest, he thought), a coming to grips of disparate principles. In these first split seconds operating on that edge of instinct which is still the will, he believed not that the bear was emblematic, or even that he was, but that the two of them there in the clearing—remember, he thought he stood in 'The Peaceable Kingdom'—somehow made for symbolism, or at least for meaning. As the bear came closer, however, he was disabused of even this thin hope, and in that sense the contest was already over and the bear had won.

He was terrified, but it must be said that there was in his terror (an emotion entirely new to him, nothing like his grief for his parents nor his early anxieties about the value of his usefulness or life's, no even his fears that he would never find Jane Löes Lipton, and so inexpert at terror, so boyish with it that he was actually like someone experiencing a new drive) a determination to survive that was rooted in principle, as though he dedicated his survival to Jane, reserving his life as a holdup victim withholds the photographs of loved ones. Even as the bear came closer this did not leave him. So there was something noble and generous even in his decision to bolt. He turned and fled. The bear would have closed the gap between them and been on him in seconds had he not stopped. Fortunately, however, he realized almost as soon as he began his sprint that he could never outrun it. (This was the first time, incidentally, that he thought of the bear as *bear*, the first time he used his man's knowledge of his adversary.) He remembered that bears could cruise at thirty miles an hour, that they could climb trees. (And even if they couldn't would any of those frail branches already bowed under their enormous leaves have supported his weight?) The brief data he recalled drove him to have more. (This also reflex, subliminal, as he jockeyed for room and position in the clearing, a rough bowl shape perhaps fifty feet across, as his eye sought possible exits, narrow places in the trees that the bear might have difficulty negotiating, as he considered the water—but of course they swam, too—a hundred yards off through a slender neck of path like a firebreak in the jungle.) He turned and faced the bear and it stopped short. They were no more than fifteen feet from each other.

It suddenly occurred to him that perhaps the bear was tame.

'Easy, Ivan,' he crooned, 'easy boy, easy Ivan,' and the bear hearing his voice, a gentle, low, masculine voice, whined. Misconstruing the response, recalling another fact, that bears have weak eyesight, at the same time that he failed to recall its corollary, that they have keen hearing and a sharp sense of smell like perfect pitch, Ashenden took it to be the bear's normal conversational tone with Plympton. 'No, no, Ivan,' he said, 'it isn't Freddy, it's not your master. Freddy's sleeping. I'm Brewster, I'm your master's friend, old Bruin. I'm Brewster Ashenden. I won't hurt you, fellow.' The bear, excited by Ashenden's playful tone, whined once more, and Brewster, who had admitted he wasn't Plympton out of that same stockpile of gentlemanly forth-rightness that forbade deception of any creature, even this bear, moved cautiously closer so that the animal might see him better and correct any false impression it might still have of him.

It was Ashenden's false impression that was corrected. He halted before he reached the bear (he was ten feet away and had just remem-bered its keen hearing and honed smell) and knew, not from anything it did, not from any bearish lurch or bearish bearing, that it was not tame. This is what he saw:

A black patent-leather snout like an electric socket.

A long and even elegant run of purplish tongue, mottled, seasoned as rare delicatessen meat, that lolled idiotic inches out of the side of its mouth.

A commitment of claw (they were nonretractile, he remembered) the color of the heads of hammers.

A low black piping of lip.

A shallow mouth, a logjam of teeth.

Its solemn oval of face, direct and expressionless as a goblin's.

Ears, high on its head and discrete as antlers.

Its stolid, plantigrade stance, a flash as it took a step toward him of the underside of its smooth, hairless paws, vaguely like the bottoms of carpet slippers.

A battering ram of head and neck, pendent from a hump of muscle on its back, high as a bull's or buffalo's.

The coarse shag upholstery of its blunt body, greasy as furniture.

He knew it was not tame even when it settled dog fashion on the ground and its short, thick limbs seemed to disappear, its body hiding in its body. And he whirled suddenly and ran again and the bear was after him. Over his shoulder he could see, despite its speed, the slow, ponderous meshing of muscle and fat behind its fur like children rustling a curtain, and while he was still looking at this the bear felled him. He was not sure whether it had raised its paw or butted him or collided with him, but he was sent sprawling—a grand, amusing, almost painless fall.

He found himself on the ground, his limbs spraddled, like someone old and sitting on a beach, and it was terrible to Ashenden that for all his sudden speed and the advantage of surprise and the fact that the bear had been settled dog fashion and even the distance he had been sent flying, he was no more than a few feet from the place where he had begun his run.

Actually, it took him several seconds before he realized that he no longer saw the bear.

'Thank God,' he said, 'I'm saved,' and with a lightning stroke the bear reached down from behind Ashenden's back and tore away his fly, including the underwear. Then, just as quickly, it was in front of him. 'Hey,' Ashenden cried, bringing his legs together and covering himself with his hands. The tear in his trousers was exactly like the inside seam along the thigh and crotch of riding pants.

'əəng,' said the bear in the International Phonetic Alphabet.

Brewster scrambled to his knees while the bear watched him.

'oohwm.'

'All right,' Ashenden said, 'back off!' His voice was as sharp and commanding as he could make it. 'Back *off*, I said!'

'KHAēr KHOŏnn.

'Go,' he commanded. 'Go on. Shoo. Shoo, you.' And still barking orders at it—he had adopted the masterful, no-nonsense style of the animal trainer—he rose to his feet and actually shoved the bear as hard as he could. Surprisingly it yielded and Brewster, encouraged, punched it with all his considerable strength on the side of its head. It shook itself briefly and, as if it meant to do no more than simply alter its position, dropped to the ground, rolled over—the movement like the practiced effort of a cripple, clumsy yet incredibly powerful—and sat up. It was sitting in much the same position as Ashenden's a moment before, and it was only then that he saw its sex billowing the heavy curtain of hair that hung above its groin: a swollen, grotesque ring of vulva the color and texture of an ear and crosshatched with long loose hairs; a distended pucker of vagina, a black tunnel of oviduct, an inner tube of cunt. Suddenly the she-bear strummed itself with a brusque downbeat of claw and moaned. Ashenden moved back and the bear made another gesture, oddly whorish and insistent. It was as if it beckoned Ashenden across a barrier not of animal and man but of language—Chinese, say, and Rumanian. Again it made its strange movement, and this time barked its moan, a command, a grammar of high complication, of difficult, irregular case and gender and tense, a classic of aberrant syntax. Which was exactly as Ashenden took it, like a student of language who for the first time finds himself hearing in real and ordinary life a unique textbook usage. O God, he thought, I understand Bear!

He did not know what to do, and felt in his pockets for weapons and scanned the ground for rocks. The bear, watching him, emitted a queer growl and Ashenden understood *that*, too. She had mistaken his rapid, reflexive frisking for courtship, and perhaps his hurried glances at the ground for some stagy, bumpkin shyness.

'Look here,' Ashenden said, 'I'm a man and you're a bear,' and it was precisely as he had addressed those wives of his hosts and fellow guests who had made overtures to him, exactly as he might put off all those girls whose station in life, inferior to his own, made them ineligible. There was reproof in his declaration, yet also an acknowledgment that he was flattered, and even, to soften his rejection, a touch of gailant regret. He turned as he might have turned in a drawing room or at the landing of a staircase, but the bear roared and Ashenden, terrorized, turned back to face it. If before he had made blunders of grace, now, inspired by his opportunities—close calls arbitrarily exalted or debased men—he corrected them and made a remarkable speech.

'You're in rut. There are evidently no male bears here. Listen, you look familiar. I've seen your kind in circuses. You must be Kamchatkan. You stand on your hind legs in the center ring and wear an apron and a dowdy hat with flowers on it that stand up stiff as pipes. You wheel a cub in a carriage and do jointed, clumsy curtseys, and the muzzle's just for show, reassurance, state law and municipal ordinance and an increment of the awful to suggest your beastliness as the apron and hat your matronliness. Your decals are on the walls of playrooms and nurseries and in the anterooms of pediatricians' offices. So there must be something domestic in you to begin with, and it is to that which I now appeal, madam.'

The bear, seated and whimpering throughout Ashenden's speech, was in a frenzy now, still of noise, not yet of motion, though it strummed its genitalia like a guitar, and Brewster, the concomitant insights of danger on him like prophecy, shuddered, understanding that though he now appreciated his situation he had still made one mistake. No, he thought, *not* madam. If there were no male bears—and wouldn't there be if she were in estrus?—it was because the bear was not yet full-grown and had not till now needed mates. It was this which alarmed him more than anything he had yet realized. It meant that these feelings were new to her, horrid sensations of mad need, ecstasy *in extremis*. She would kill him.

The bear shook itself and came toward him, and Brewster realized that he would have to wrestle it. Oh Jesus, he thought, is this how I'm to be purified? Is *this* the test? Oh, Lord, first I was in art and now I am in allegory. Jane, I swear, I shall this day be with you in Paradise! When the bear was inches away it threw itself up on its hind legs and the two embraced each other, the tall man and the slightly taller bear, and Brewster, surprised at how light the bear's paws seemed on his shoulders, forgot his fear and began to ruminate. See how strong I am, how easily I support this beast. But then I am beast too, he thought. There's wolf in me now, and that gives me strength. What this means, he thought, is that my life has been too crammed with civilization.

Meanwhile they went round and round like partners in a slow dance. I have been too proud of my humanism, perhaps, and all along not paid enough attention to the base. This is probably a good lesson for me. I'm very privileged. I think I won't be too gentle with poor dying Jane. That would be wrong. On her deathbed we'll roll in the hay. Yes, he thought, there must be positions not too uncomfortable for dying persons. I'll find out what these are and send her out in style. We must not be too fastidious about ourselves, or stuck-up because we aren't dogs.

All the time he was thinking this he and the bear continued to circle, though Ashenden had almost forgotten where he was, and with whom. But then the bear leaned on him with all her weight and he began to buckle, his dreamy confidence and the thought of his strength deserting him. The bear whipped its paw behind Ashenden's back to keep him from falling, and it was like being dipped, supported in a dance, the she-bear leading and Brewster balanced against the huge beamy strength of her paw. With her free paw she snagged one sleeve of Ashenden's Harris tweed jacket and started to drag his hand toward her cunt.

He kneed her stomach and kicked at her crotch.

'ärng.'

'Let go,' he cried, 'let go of me,' but the bear, provoked by the pleasure of Ashenden's harmless, off-balance blows and homing in on itself, continued to pull at his arm caught in the sling of his sleeve, and in seconds had plunged Brewster's hand into her wet nest.

There was a quality of steamy mound, a transitional texture between skin and meat, as if the bear's twat were something butchered perhaps, a mysterious cut tumid with blood and the color of a strawberry ice-cream soda, a sexual steak. Those were its lips. He had grazed them with his knuckles going in, and the bear jerked forward, a shudder of flesh, a spasm, a bump, a grind. Frenzied, it drew his hand on. He made a fist but the bear groaned and tugged more fiercely at Ashenden's sleeve. He was inside. It was like being up to his wrist in dung, in a hot jello of baking brick fretted with awful straw. The bear's vaginal muscles contracted; the pressure was terrific, and the bones in his hand massively cramped. He tried to pull his fist out but it was welded to the bear's cunt. Then the bear's muscles relaxed and he forced his fist open inside her, his hand opening in a thick medium of mucoid strings, wet gutty filaments, moist pipes like the fingers for terrible gloves. Appalled, he pulled back with all his might and his wrist and hand, greased by bear, slid out, trailing a horrible suction, a concupiscent comet. He waved the hand in front of his face and the stink came off his fingertips like flames from a shaken candelabra, an odor of metal fruit, of something boiled years, of the center of the earth, filthy laundry, powerful as the stench of jewels and rare metals, of atoms and the waves of light.

'Oh Jesus,' he said, gagging, 'oh Jesus, oh God.'

'û(r)m,' the bear said, 'wrənff.'

Brewster sank to his knees in a position of prayer and the bear abruptly sat, its stubby legs spread, her swollen cunt in her lap like a bouquet of flowers.

It was as if he had looked up the dress of someone old. He couldn't look away and the bear, making powerful internal adjustments, obscenely posed, flexing her muscular rut, shivering, her genitalia suddenly and invisibly engined, a performance coy and proud. Finally he managed to turn his head, and with an almost lazy power and swiftness the bear reached out with one paw and plucked his cock out of his torn trousers. Ashenden winced—not in pain, the paw's blow had been gentle and as accurate as a surgical thrust, his penis hooked, almost comfortable, a heel in a shoe, snug in the bear's curved claws smooth and cool as piano keys—and looked down.

'OERəKH.'

His penis was erect. 'That's Jane's, not yours!' he shouted. 'My left hand doesn't know what my right hand is doing!'

The bear snorted and swiped with the broad edge of her forepaw against each side of Ashenden's peter. Her fur, lanolized by estrus, was incredibly soft, the two swift strokes gestures of forbidden brunette possibility.

And of all the things he'd said and thought and felt that night, this was the most reasonable, the most elegantly strategic: that he would have to satisfy the bear, make love to the bear, fuck the bear. And this was the challenge which had at last defined itself, the test he'd longed for and was now to have. Here was the problem: Not whether it was possible for a mere man of something less than one hundred and eighty pounds to make love to an enormous monster of almost half a ton; not whether a normal man like himself could negotiate the barbarous terrains of the beast or bring the bear off before it killed him; but merely how he, Brewster Ashenden of the air, water, fire and earth Ashendens, one of the most fastidious men alive, could bring himself to do it—how, in short, he could get it up for a bear!

But he had forgotten, and now remembered: it was *already* up. And if he had told the bear it was for Jane and not for it, he had spoken in frenzy, in terror and error and shock. It occurred to him that he had not been thinking of Jane at all, that she was as distant from his mind at this moment as the warranties he possessed for all the electric blankets, clock radios and space heaters he'd picked up for opening accounts in banks, as distant as the owner's manuals stuffed into drawers for all that stuff, as forgotten as all the tennis matches he'd played on the grass courts of his friends, as the faults in those matches, as all the strolls to fences and nets to retrieve opponents' balls, the miles he'd walked doing such things. Then why was he hard? And he thought of hanged men, of bowels slipped *in extremis*, of the erectile pressures of the doomed, of men in electric chairs or sinking in ships or singed in burning buildings, of men struck by lightning in open fields, and of all the random, irrelevant erections he'd had as an adolescent (once as he leaned forward to pick up a bowling ball in the basement alley of a friend from boarding school), hardness there when you woke up in the morning, pressures on the kidney that triggered the organ next to it, that signaled the one next to *it*, that gave the blood its go-ahead, the invisible nexus of conditions. 'That's Jane's' he'd said, 'not yours. My left hand doesn't know what my right hand is doing.' Oh, God. It *didn't*. He'd lied to a bear! He'd brought Jane's name into it like a lout in a parlor car. There was sin around like weather, like knots in shoes.

'*What the hell am I talking about?*' he yelled, and charged the bear.

And it leaned back from its sitting position and went down on its back slowly, slowly, its body sighing backward, ajar as a door stirred by wind, and Ashenden belly-flopped on top of it—with its paws in the air he was a foot taller than the bear at either end, and this contributed to his sin, as if it were some child he tumbled—pressed on its swollen pussy as over a barrel. He felt nothing.

His erection had withered. The bear growled contemptuously. '*Foreplay, foreplay,*' Brewster hissed, and plunged his hand inside the bear. I'm doing this to save my life, he thought. I'm doing this to pass tests. This is what I call a challenge and a half.

The bear permitted the introduction of his hand and hugged him firmly, yet with a kind of reserve as though conscious of Ashenden's eggshell mortality. His free hand was around her neck while the other moved around inside the bear insinuatingly. He felt a clit like a baseball. One hand high and one low, his head, mouth closed, buried in the mound of fur just to the side of the bear's neck, he was like a man doing the Australian crawl.

The bear shifted. Still locked together, the two of them rolled over and over through the peaceable kingdom. For Ashenden it was like being run over, but she permitted him to come out on top. His hand had taken a terrific wrenching however, and he knew he had to get it out before it swelled and he was unable to move it. Jesus, I've stubbed my hand, he thought, and began to withdraw it gently, gingerly, through a booby-trapped channel of obstacle grown agonizing by his injury, a minefield of pain. The bear lay stock still as he reeled in his hand, climbing out of her cunt as up a rope. (Perhaps this feels good to her, he thought tenderly.) At last, love's Little Jack Horner, it was out and Ashenden, his hand bent at almost a right angle to his wrist, felt disarmed. What he had counted on—without realizing he counted on it—was no longer available to him. He would not be able to manipulate the bear, would not be able to get away with merely jerking it off. It was another illusion stripped away. He would have to screw the animal conventionally.

Come on, he urged his cock, wax, grow, *grow*. He pleaded with his penis, taking it in his good hand and rubbing it desperately, polishing it like an heirloom, Aladdinizing it uselessly. Meanwhile, tears in his own, he looked deep into the bear's eyes and stalled by blowing crazy kisses to it off his broken hand, saying foolish things, making it incredible promises, keeping up a lame chatter like the pepper talk around an infield.

'Just a minute. Hold on a sec. I'm almost ready. It's going to be something. It's really . . . I've just got to . . . Look, there's really nothing to worry about. Everything's going to work out fine. I'm going to be a man for you, darling. Just give me a chance, will you? Listen,' he said, 'I love you. I don't think I can live without you. I want you to marry me.' He didn't know what he was saying, unconsciously selecting, with a sort of sexual guile he hadn't known he possessed, phrases from love, the compromising sales talk of romantic stall. He had been maidenized, a game, scared bride at the bedside. Then he began to hear himself, to listen to what he was saying. He'd never spoken this way to a woman in his life. Where did he get this stuff? Where did it come from? It was the shallow language of two-timers, of drummers with farm girls, of whores holding out and gigolos holding in, the conversation of cuckoldry, of all amorous greed. It was base and cheap and tremendously exciting and suddenly Ashenden felt a stirring, the beginning of a faint lust. He moved to the spark like an arsonist and gazed steadily at the enormous hulk of impatient bear, at its black eyes cute as checkers on a snowman. Yes, he thought, afraid he'd lose it, *yes. I am the wuver of the teddy bear, big bwown bear's wittle white man.*

He unbuckled his pants and let them drop and stepped out of his underwear feeling moonlight on his ass. He moved out of his jacket and tore off his shirt, his undershirt. He ran up against the bear. He slapped at it with his dick. He turned his back to it and moved the spread cheeks of his behind up and down the pelt. He climbed it, impaling himself on the strange softness of the enormous toy. He kissed it.

Pet, pet, he thought. '*Pet,*' he moaned, his eyes closed now. 'My pet, my pet.' Yes, he thought, yes. And remembered, suddenly, *saw,* all the animals he had ever petted, all the furry underbellies, writhing, inviting his nails, all the babies whose rubbery behinds he'd squeezed, the little girls he'd drawn toward him and held between his knees to comfort or tell a secret to, their hair tickling his face, all small boys whose heads he'd rubbed and cheeks pinched between his fingers. We are all sodomites, he thought. There is disparity at the source of love. We are all sodomites, all pederasts, all dikes and queens and mother fuckers.

'Hey bear,' he whispered, 'd'ja ever notice how all the short, bald, fat men get all the tall, good-looking blondes?' He was stiffening fast. 'Hey bear, ma'am,' he said, leaning naked against her fur, bare-assed and upright on a bear rug, 'there's something darling in a difference. Why me—take *me.* There's somethin' darlin' in a difference, how else would water come to fire or earth to air?' He cupped his hand over one of its cute little ears and rubbed his palm gently over the bristling fur as over the breast buds of a twelve-year-old-girl. 'My life, if you want to know, has been a sodomy. What fingers in what pies, what toes in what seas! I have the tourist's imagination, the day-tripper's vision. Fleeing the ordinary, crossing state lines, greedy at Customs and impatient for the red stamps on my passports like lipstick kisses on an envelope from a kid in the summer camp. Yes, and there's wolf in me too now. God, how I honor a difference and crave the unusual, life like a link of mixed boxcars.' He put a finger in the lining of the bear's silken ear. He kissed its mouth and vaulted his tongue over her teeth, probing with it for the roof of her mouth. Then the bear's tongue was in his throat, not horrible, only strange, the cunning length and marvelous flexibility an avatar of flesh, as if life were in it like an essence sealed in a tube, and even the breath, the taste of living, rutting bear, delicious to him as the taste of poisons vouchsafed not to kill him, as the taste of a pal's bowel or a parent's fats and privates.

He mooned with the giant bear, insinuating it backwards, guiding it as he would a horse with subtle pressures, squeezes, words and hugs. The bear responded, but you do not screw a bear as you would a woman and, seeing what he was about to do, she suddenly resisted. Now he was the horse—this too—and the bear the guide, and she crouched, a sort of semi-squat, and somehow shifted her cunt, sending it down her body and up behind her as a tap dancer sends a top hat down the length of her arm. With her head stretching out, pushing up and outward like the thrust of a shriek, cantilevering impossibly and looking over her shoulder, she signaled Ashenden behind her.

He entered her from the rear, and oddly he had never felt so male, so much the man, as when he was inside her. Their position reinforced this, the bear before him, stooped, gymnastically leaning forward as in the beginning of a handstand, and he behind as if he drove sled dogs. He might have been upright in a chariot, some Greek combination of man and bear exiled in stars for a broken rule. So good was it all that he did not even pause to wonder how he fit. He fit, that's all. Whether swollen beyond ordinary length himself or adjusted to by some stretch-sock principle of bear cunt (like a ring in a dime store that snugs any finger), he fit. 'He fit, he fit and that was it,' he crooned happily, and moved this way and that in the warm syrups of the beast, united with her, ecstatic, transcendent, not knowing where his cock left off and the bear began. Not deadened, however, not like a novocained presence of tongue in the mouth or the alien feel of a scar, in fact never so filled with sensation, every nerve in his body alive with delight, even his broken hand, even that, the nerves rearing, it seemed, hind-legged almost, revolting under their impossible burden of pleasure, vertiginous at the prospect of such orgasm, counseling Ashenden to back off, go slow, back off or the nerves would burst, a new lovely energy like love's atoms split. And even before he came, he felt addicted, hooked; where would his next high come from, he wondered almost in despair, and how you gonna keep 'em down on the farm, and what awfulness must follow such rising expectations?

And they went at it for ten minutes more and he and the bear came together.

'əōōōŏŭ(r)reñg hwhu ä ä c̱h ouhw ouhw nnng,' said the bear.

'əōōōŏŭ(r)reñg hwhu ä ä c̱hc̱h *ouhw* ouhw *nnñg*!' groaned Ashenden, and fell out of the bear and lay on his back and looked at the stars.

And he lay like that for half an hour, catching his breath, feeling his nerves coalesce, consolidating once more as a man, his hard-on declining, his flesh turning back into flesh, the pleasure lifting slow as fever. And thinking. So. I'm a sodomite. But not just any ordinary sodomite with a taste for sheep or a thing for cows, some carnivore's harmless extension of appetite that drives him to sleep with what he eats. No. I'm kinky for bears.

And then, when he was ready, when at last he could once more feel his injured hand, he pushed himself up on his elbows and looked around. The bear was gone, though he thought he saw its shape reclined beside a tree. He stood up and looked down and examined himself. When he put his clothes back on, they hung on him like flayed skin and he was conscious of vague withdrawal symptoms in his nuts. He moved into the moonlight. His penis looked as if it had been dipped in blood. Had it still been erect the blood might perhaps have gone unnoticed, a faint flush; no longer distended, it seemed horrid, wet, thick as paint. He cupped his hand beneath himself and caught one drop in his palm. He shook his head. 'My God,' he said, 'I haven't just screwed a bear, I've fucked a virgin!'

Now his old honor came back to chide him. He thought of Jane dying in the castle, of the wolf mask binding her eyes like a dark handkerchief on the vision of a condemned prisoner, of it binding his own and of the tan beard across his face like a robber's bandanna.

Ashenden shuddered. But perhaps it was not contagious unless from love and honor's self-inflicted homeopathy. Surely he would not *have* to die with her. All he had to do was tell her that he had failed the test, that he had not met her conditions. Then he knew that he would never tell her this, that he would tell her nothing, that he would not even see her, that tomorrow—today, in an hour or so when the sun was up—he would have Plympton's man take him to the station, that he would board a train, go to London, rest there for a day or two, take in a show, perhaps go to the zoo, book passage to someplace far, someplace wild, further and wilder than he had ever been, look it over, get its feel, with an idea of maybe settling down one day. He'd better get started. He had to change.

He remembered that he was still exposed and thought to cover himself lest someone see him, but first he'd better wipe the blood off his penis. There was a fresh handkerchief in his pocket, and he took it out, unfolded it and strolled over to the pond. He dipped the handkerchief in the water and rubbed himself briskly, his organ suddenly tingling with a new surge of pleasure, but a pleasure mitigated by twinges of pain. There was soreness, a bruise. He placed the handkerchief back in his pocket and handled himself lightly, as one goes over a tire to find a puncture. There was a small cut on the underside of his penis that he must have acquired from the bear. Then the blood could have been mine, he thought. Maybe *I* was the virgin. Maybe *I* was. It was good news. Though he was a little sad. *Post-coitum tristesse*, he thought. It'll pass.

He started back through art to the house, but first he looked over his shoulder for a last glimpse of the sleeping bear. And he thought again of how grand it had been, and wondered if it was possible that something might come of it. And seeing ahead, speculating about the generations that would follow his own, he thought, Air. Water, he thought. Fire, Earth, he thought . . . And *honey*.

1973

The Old Forest

PETER TAYLOR

I was already formally engaged, as we used to say, to the girl I was going to marry. But still I sometimes went out on the town with girls of a different sort. And during the very week before the date set for the wedding, in December, I was in an automobile accident at a time when one of those girls was with me. It was a calamitous thing to have happen—not the accident itself, which caused no serious injury to anyone, but the accident plus the presence of that girl.

As a matter of fact, it was not unusual in those days—forty years ago and a little more—for a well-brought-up young man like me to keep up his acquaintance, until the very eve of his wedding, with some member of what we facetiously and somewhat arrogantly referred to as the Memphis demimonde. (That was merely to say with a girl who was not in the Memphis debutante set.) I am not even sure how many of us knew what the word 'demimonde' meant or implied. But once it had been applied to such girls, it was hard for us to give it up. We even learned to speak of them individually as demimondaines—and later corrupted that to demimondames. The girls were of course a considerably less sophisticated lot than any of this sounds, though they were bright girls certainly and some of them even highly intelligent. They read books, they looked at pictures, and they were apt to attend any concert or play that came to Memphis. When the old San Carlo Opera Company turned up in town, you could count on certain girls of the demimonde being present in their block of seats, and often with a score of the opera in hand. From that you will understand that they certainly weren't the innocent, untutored types that we generally took to dances at the Memphis Country Club and whom we eventually looked forward to marrying.

These girls I refer to would, in fact, very frequently and very frankly say to us that the MCC (that's how we always spoke of the Club) was the last place they wanted to be taken. There was one girl in particular, not so smart as some of the others perhaps and certainly less restrained in the humor she sometimes poked at the world we boys lived in, an outspoken girl, who was the most vociferous of all in her disdain for the Country Club. I remember one night, in one of those beer gardens that became popular in Memphis in the late thirties, when this girl suddenly announced to a group of us, '*I* haven't lost anything at the MCC. That's something you boys can bet your daddy's bottom dollar on.' We were gathered—four or five couples—about one of the big wooden beer-garden tables with an umbrella in its center, and when she said that, all the other girls in the party went into a fit of laughter. It was a kind of giggling that was unusual for them. The boys in the party laughed, too, of course, but we were surprised by the way the girls continued to giggle among themselves for such a long time. We were out of college by then and thought we knew the world pretty well; most of us had been working for two or three years in our fathers' business firms. But we didn't see why this joke was so very funny. I suppose it was too broad for us in its reference. There is no way of knowing, after all these years, if it was too broad for our sheltered minds or if the rest of the girls were laughing at the vulgar tone of the girl who had spoken. She was, you see, a little bit coarser than the rest, and I suspect they were laughing at the way she had phrased what she said. For us boys, anyhow, it was pleasant that the demimondaines took the lighthearted view they did about not going to the MCC, because it was the last place most of us would have wished to take them. Our *other* girls would have known too readily who they were and would not willingly or gracefully have endured their presence. To have brought one of those girls to the Club would have required, at any rate, a boy who was a much bolder and freer spirit than I was at twenty-three.

To the liberated young people of today all this may seem a corrupting factor in our old way of life—not our snobbery so much as our continuing to see those demimonde girls right up until the time of marriage. And yet I suspect that in the Memphis of today customs concerning serious courtship and customs concerning unacknowledged love affairs have not been entirely altered. Automobile accidents occur there still, for instance, the reports of which in the newspaper do not mention the name of the driver's 'female companion,' just as the report of my accident did not. If the driver is a 'scion of a prominent local family' with his engagement to be married already announced at an MCC party, as well as in the Sunday newspaper, then the account of his automobile collision is likely to refer to the girl in the car with him only as his 'female companion.' Some newspaper readers might, I know, assume this to be a reference to the young man's fiancée. That is what is intended, I suppose—*for* the general reader. But it would almost certainly not have been the case—not in the Memphis, Tennessee, of 1937.

The girl with me in my accident was a girl whose origins nobody knew anything about. But she was a perfectly decent sort of girl, living independently in a respectable rooming house and working at a respectable job. That was the sort of girl about whom the Memphis newspapers felt obliged to exercise the greatest care when making any reference to her in their columns. It was as though she were their special ward. Such a girl must be protected from any blaze of publicity. Such a girl must not suffer from the misconduct of any Memphis man or group of men—even newspaper publishers. That was fine for the girl, of course, and who could possibly resent it? It was splendid for her, but I, the driver of the car, had to suffer considerable anguish just because of such a girl's presence in the car and suffer still more because of her behavior afterward. Moreover, the response of certain older men in town to her subsequent behavior would cause me still further anguish and prolong my suffering by several days. Those men were the editors of the city's two newspapers, along with the lawyers called in by my father to represent me if I should be taken to court. There was also my father himself, and the father of my fiancée, *his* lawyer (for some reason or other), and, finally, no less a person than the mayor of Memphis, all of whom one would ordinarily have supposed to be indifferent to the caprices of such a girl. They were the civic leaders and merchant princes of the city. They had great matters on their minds. They were, to say the least, an imposing group in the eyes of a young man who had just the previous year entered his father's cotton-brokerage firm, a young man who was still learning how to operate under the pecking order of Memphis's male establishment.

The girl in question was named Lee Ann Deehart. She was a quite beautiful, fair-haired, hazel-eyed girl with a lively manner, and surely she was far from stupid. The thing she did which drew attention from the city fathers came very near, also, to changing the course of my entire life. I had known Lee Ann for perhaps two years at the time, and knew her to be more level-headed and more reserved and self-possessed than most of her friends among the demimondaines. It would have been impossible for me to predict the behavior she was guilty of that winter afternoon. Immediately after the collision, she threw open the door on her side of the car, stepped out onto the road-side, and fled into the woods of Overton Park, which is where the accident took place. And from that time, and during the next four days, she was unheard from by people who wished to question her and protect her. During that endless-seeming period of four days no one could be certain of Lee Ann Deehart's whereabouts.

The circumstances of the accident were rather complicated. The colli-sion occurred just after three o'clock on a very cold Saturday afternoon—the fourth of December. Although at that time in my life I was already a member of my father's cotton firm, I was nevertheless—and strange as it may seem—enrolled in a Latin class out at Southwestern College, which is on the north side of Overton park. (We were reading Horace's *Odes!*) The class was not held on Saturday afternoon, but I was on my way out to the college to study for a test that had been scheduled for Monday. My interest in Latin was regarded by my father and mother as one of my 'anomalies'—a remnant of many 'anomalies' I had annoyed them with when I was in my teens and was showing some signs of 'not turning out well.' It seemed now of course that I had 'turned out well' after all, except that nobody in the family and nobody among my friends could understand why I went on showing this interest in Latin. I was not able to explain to them why. Any more than I was able to explain why to myself. It clearly had nothing to do with anything else in my life at that period. Furthermore, in the classroom and under the strict eye of our classics professor, a rotund, mustachioed little man hardly four feet in height (he had to sit on a large Latin dictionary in order to be comfortable at his desk), I didn't excel. I was often embarrassed by having to own up to Professor Bartlett's accusation that I had not so much as glanced at the assigned odes before coming to class. Sometimes other members of the class would be caught helping me with the translation, out in the hallway, when Professor Bartlett opened his classroom door to us. My real excuse for neglecting the assignments made by that earnest and admirable little scholar was that too many hours of my life were consumed by my job, by my courtship of the society girl I was going to marry, and by my old, bad habits of knocking about town with my boyhood cronies and keeping company with girls like Lee Ann Deehart.

Yet I had persisted with my Horace class throughout that fall (against the advice of nearly everyone, including Professor Bartlett). On that frigid December afternoon I had resolved to mend my ways as a student. I decided I would take my Horace and go out to Professor Bartlett's classroom at the college and make use of his big dictionary in preparing for Monday's test. It was something we had all been urged to do, with the promise that we would always find the door unlocked. As it turned out, of course, I was destined not to take the test on Monday and never to enter Professor Bartlett's classroom again.

It happened that just before I was setting out from home that afternoon I was filled suddenly with a dread of the silence and the peculiar isolation of a college classroom building on a weekend afternoon. I telephoned my fiancée and asked her to go along with me. At the other end of the telephone line, Caroline Braxley broke into laughter. She said that I clearly had no conception of all the things she had to do within the next seven days before we were to be married. I said I supposed I ought to be helping in some way, though until now she had not asked me so much as to help address invitations to the wedding. 'No indeed,' said my bride-to-be, 'I want to do everything myself. I wouldn't have it any other way.'

Caroline Braxley, this capable and handsome bride-to-be of mine, was a very remarkable girl, just as today, as my wife, she seems to me a very remarkable woman of sixty. She and I have been married for forty-one years now, and her good judgment in all matters relating to our marriage has never failed her—or us. She had already said to me before that Saturday afternoon that a successful marriage depended in part on the two persons' developing and maintaining a certain number of separate interests in life. She was all for my keeping up my golf, my hunting, my fishing. And, unlike my own family, she saw no reason that I shouldn't keep up my peculiar interest in Latin, though she had to confess that she thought it almost the funniest thing she had ever heard of a man of my sort going in for.

Caroline liked any sort of individualism in men. But I already knew her ways sufficiently well to understand that there was no use trying to persuade her to come along with me to the college. I wished she would come with me, or maybe I wished even more she would try to persuade me to come over to her house and help her with something in preparation for the wedding. After I had put down the telephone, it even occurred to me that I might simply drive over to her house and present myself at her front door. But I knew what the expression on her face would be, and I could even imagine the sort of thing she would say: 'No man is going to set foot in my house this afternoon, Nat Ramsey! *I'm* getting married next Saturday, in case the fact has slipped your mind. Besides, you're coming here for dinner tonight, aren't you? And there are parties every night next week!'

This Caroline Braxley of mine was a very tall girl. (Actually taller than she is nowadays. We have recently measured ourselves and found that each of us is an inch shorter than we used to be.) One often had the feeling that one was looking up at her, though of course she wasn't really so tall as that. Caroline's height and the splendid way she carried herself were one of her first attractions for me. It seems to me now that I was ever attracted to tall girls—that is, when there was the possibility of falling in love. And I think this was due in part to the fact that even as a boy I was half in love with my father's two spinster sisters, who were nearly six feet in height and were always more attentive to me than to the other children in the family.

Anyhow, only moments after I had put down the telephone that Saturday, when I still sat with my hand on the instrument and was thinking vaguely of rushing over to Caroline's house, the telephone underneath my hand began ringing. Perhaps, I thought, it was Caroline calling back to say that she had changed her mind. Instead, it was Lee Ann Deehart. As soon as she heard my voice, she began telling me that she was bored to death. Couldn't I think of something fun she and I could do on this dreary winter afternoon? I laughed aloud at her. 'What a shameless wench you are, Lee Ann!' I said.

'Shameless? How so?' she said with pretended innocence.

'As if you weren't fully aware,' I lectured her, 'that I'm getting married a week from today!'

'What's that got to do with the price of eggs in Arkansas?' She laughed. 'Do you think, old Nat, *I* want to marry you?'

'Well,' I explained, 'I happen to be going out to the college to cram for a Latin test on Monday.'

I could hear her laughter at the other end. 'Is your daddy going to let you off work long enough to take your Latin test?' she asked with heavy irony in her voice. It was the usual way those girls had of making fun of our dependence on our fathers.

'Ah, yes,' I said tolerantly.

'And is he going to let you off next Saturday, too,' she went on, 'long enough to get married?'

'Listen,' I said, 'I've just had an idea. Why don't you ride out to the college with me, and fool around some while I do my Latin?' I suppose I didn't really imagine she would go, but suddenly I had thought again of the lonely isolation of Dr Bartlett's classroom on a Saturday afternoon. I honestly wanted to go ahead out there. It was something I somehow felt I had to do. My preoccupation with the study of Latin poetry, ineffectual student though I was, may have represented a perverse wish to experience the isolation I was at the same time dreading or may have represented a taste for morbidity left over from my adolescence. I can allow myself to speculate on all that now, though it would not have occurred to me to do so at the time.

'Well,' said Lee Ann Deehart presently, to my surprise and delight, 'it couldn't be more boring out there than sitting here in my room is.'

'I'll pick you up in fifteen minutes,' I said quickly. And I hung up the telephone before she could possibly change her mind. Thirty minutes later, we were driving through Overton park on our way to the college. We had passed the Art Gallery and were headed down the hill toward the low ground where the Park Pond is. Ahead of us, on the left, were the gates to the Zoo. And on beyond was the point where the road crossed the streetcar tracks and entered a densely wooded area which is actually the last surviving bit of the primeval forest that once grew right up to the bluffs above the Mississippi River. Here are giant oak and yellow poplar trees older than the memory of the earliest white settler. Some of them surely may have been mature trees when Hernando de Soto passed this way, and were very old trees indeed when General Jackson, General Winchester, and Judge John Overton purchased this land and laid out the city of Memphis. Between the Art Gallery and the pond there used to be, in my day, a little spinney of woods which ran nearly all the way back to what was left of the old forest. It was just when I reached this spinney, with Lee Ann beside me, that I saw a truck approaching us on the wrong side of the icy road. There was a moderately deep snow on the ground, and the park roads had, to say the least, been imperfectly cleared. On the ice and the packed snow, the driver of the truck had clearly lost control of his vehicle. When he was within about seventy-five feet of us, Lee Ann said, 'Pull off the road, Nat!'

Lee Ann Deehart's beauty was of the most feminine sort. She was a tiny, delicate-looking girl, and I had noticed, when I went to fetch her that day, in her fur-collared coat and knitted cap and gutta-percha boots she somehow seemed smaller than usual. And I was now struck by the tone of authority coming from this small person whose diminutive size and whose role in my life were such that it wouldn't have occurred to me to heed her advice about driving a car—or about anything else, I suppose. I remember feeling something like: This is an ordeal that I must, and that I want, to face in my own way. It was as though Professor Bartlett himself were in the approaching truck. It seemed my duty not to admit any weakness in my own position. At least I *thought* that was what I felt.

'Pull off the road, Nat!' Lee Ann urged again. And my incredible reply to her was 'He's on *my* side of the road! Besides trucks are not allowed in the park!' And in reply to this Lee Ann gave only a loud snicker.

I believe I did, in the last seconds, try to swing the car off onto the shoulder of the road. But the next thing I really remember is the fierce impact of the two vehicles' meeting.

It was a relatively minor sort of collision, or seemed so at the moment. Since the driver of the truck, which was actually a converted Oldsmobile sedan—and a rather ancient one at that—had the good sense not to put on his brakes and to turn off her motor, the crash was less severe than it might have been. Moreover, since I *had* pulled a little to the right it was not a head-on meeting. It is worth mentioning, though, that it was sufficiently bad to put permanently out of commission the car I was driving, which was not my own car (my car was in the shop, being refurbished for the honeymoon trip) but an aging Packard limousine of my mother's, which I knew she would actually be happy to see retired. I don't remember getting out of the car at all and I don't remember Lee Ann's getting out. The police were told by the driver of the truck, however, that within a second after the impact Lee Ann had thrown open her door, leaped out onto the snow-covered shoulder, jumped the ditch beyond, and run up the incline and into the spinney. The truck driver's account was corroborated by two ice skaters on the pond, who also saw her run through the leafless trees of the spinney and on across a narrow stretch of the public golf course which divides the spinney from the old forest. They agreed that, considering there was a deep snow on the ground and that she was wearing those gutta-percha boots, she traveled at a remarkable speed.

I didn't even know she was out of the car until I got around on the other side and saw the door there standing open and saw her tracks in the snow, going down the bank. I suppose I was too dazed even to follow the tracks with my eyes down the bank and up the other side of the ditch. I must have stood there for several seconds, looking down blankly at the tracks she had left just outside the car door. Presently I looked up at the truck driver, who was standing before me. I know now his eyes must have been following Lee Ann's progress. Finally he turned his eyes to me, and I could tell from his expression that I wasn't a pleasant sight. 'Is your head hurt bad?' he asked. I put my hand up to my forehead and when I brought it down it was covered with blood. That was when I passed out. When I came to, they wouldn't let me get up. Besides the truck driver, there were two policemen and the two ice skaters standing over me. They told me that an ambulance was on the way.

At the hospital, the doctor took four stitches in my forehead; and that was it. I went home and lay down for a couple of hours, as I had been told to do. My parents and my two brothers and my little sister and even the servants were very much concerned about me. They hovered around in a way I had never before seen them do—not even when somebody was desperately sick. I suppose it was because a piece of violence like this accident was a very extraordinary thing in our quiet Memphis life in those years. They were disturbed, too, I soon realized, by my silence as I lay there on the daybed in the upstairs sitting room and particularly by my being reticent to talk about the collision. I had other things on my mind. Every so often I would remember Lee Ann's boot tracks in the snow. And I would begin to wonder where she was now. Since I had not found an opportunity to telephone her, I could only surmise that she had somehow managed to get back to the rooming house where she lived. I had not told anyone about her presence in the car with me. And as I lay there on the daybed, with the family and servants coming and going and making inquiries about how I felt, I would find myself wondering sometimes how and whether or not I could tell Caroline Braxley about Lee Ann's being with me that afternoon. It turned out the next day—or, rather, on Monday morning—that the truck driver had told the two policemen and then, later, repeated to someone who called from one of the newspapers that there had been a girl with me in the car. As a matter of fact, I learned that this was the case on the night of the accident, but as I lay there in the upstairs sitting room during the afternoon I didn't yet know it.

Shortly before five o'clock Caroline Braxley arrived at our house, making a proper sick call but also with the intention of taking me back to dinner with her parents and her two younger sisters. Immediately after she entered the upstairs sitting room, and almost before she and I had greeted each other, my mother's houseboy and sometime chauffeur came in, bringing my volume of Horace. Because Mother had thought it might raise my spirits, she had sent him down to the service garage where the wrecked car had been taken to fetch it for me. Smiling sympathetically, he placed it on a table near the daybed and left the room. Looking at the book, Caroline said to me with a smile that expressed a mixture of sympathy and reproach, 'I hope you see now what folly your pursuit of Latin poetry is.' And suddenly, then, the book on the table appeared to me as an alien object. In retrospect it seems to me that I really knew then that I would never open it again.

I went to dinner that night at Caroline's house, my head still in bandages. The Braxley family treated me with a tenderness equal to that I had received at home. At table, the servingman offered to help my plate for me, as though I were a sick child. I could have enjoyed all this immensely, I think, since I have always been one to relish loving, domestic care, if only I had not been worrying and speculating all the while about Lee Ann. As I talked genially with Caroline's family during the meal and immediately afterward before the briskly burning fire at the end of the Braxleys' long living room, I kept seeing Lee Ann's boot tracks in the snow. And then I would see my own bloody hand as I took it down from my face before I fainted. I remember still having the distinct feeling, as I sat there in the bosom of the Braxley family, that it had not been merely my bloody hand that had made me faint but my bloody hand plus the tracks in the deep snow. In a way, it is strange that I remember all these impressions so vividly after forty years, because it is not as though I have lived an uneventful life during the years since. My Second World War experiences are what I perhaps ought to remember best—those, along with the deaths of my two younger brothers in the Korean War. Even worse, really, were the deaths of my two parents in a terrible fire that destroyed our house on Central Avenue when they had got to be quite old, my mother leaping from a second-story window, my father asphyxiated inside the house. And I can hardly mention without being overcome with emotion the accidental deaths that took two of my and Caroline's children when they were in their early teens. It would seem that with all these disasters to remember, along with the various business and professional crises I have had, I might hardly be able to recall that earlier episode. But I think that, besides its coming at that impressionable period of my life and the fact that one just does remember things better from one's youth, there is the undeniable fact that life *was* different in those times. What I mean to say is that all these later, terrible events took place in a world where acts of terror are, so to speak, all around us—everyday occurrences—and are brought home to us audibly and pictorially on radio and television almost every hour. I am not saying that some of these ugly acts of terror did not need to take place or were not brought on by what our world was like in those days. But I am saying that the context was different. Our tranquil, upper-middle-class world of 1937 did not have the rest of the world crowding in on it so much. And thus when something only a little ugly did crowd in or when we, often unconsciously, reached out for it, the contrasts seemed sharper. It was not just in the Braxleys' household or in my own family's that everything seemed quiet and well ordered and unchanging. The households were in a context like themselves. Suffice it to say that though the Braxleys' house in Memphis was situated on East Parkway and our house on Central Avenue, at least two miles across town from each other, I could in those days feel perfectly safe, and *was* relatively safe, in walking home many a night from Caroline's house to our house at two in the morning. It was when we young men in Memphis ventured out with the more adventurous girls of the demimonde that we touched on the unsafe zones of Memphis. And there were girls still more adventurous, of course, with whom some of my contemporaries found their way into the very most dangerous zones. But we did think of it that way, you see, thought of it in terms of the girls being the adventurous ones, whom we followed or didn't follow.

Anyhow, while we were sitting there before the fire, with the portrait of Caroline's paternal grandfather peering down at us from above the mantel and with her father in his broad-lapelled, double-breasted suit standing on the marble hearth, occasionally poking at the logs with the brass poker or sometimes kicking a log with the toe of his wing-tipped shoes, suddenly I was called to the telephone by the Negro servingman who had wanted to help my plate for me. As he preceded me the length of the living room and then gently guided me across the hall to the telephone in the library, I believe he would have put his hand under my elbow to help me—as if a real invalid—if I had allowed him to. As we passed through the hall, I glanced through one of the broad, etched sidelights beside the front door and caught a glimpse of the snow on the ground outside. The weather had turned even colder. There had been no additional snowfall, but even at a glance you could tell how crisply frozen the old snow was on its surface. The servingman at my elbow was saying, 'It's your daddy on the phone. I'd suppose he just wants to know how you'd be feeling by now.'

But I knew in my heart it wasn't that. It was as if that glimpse of the crisp snow through the front-door sidelight had told me what it was. When I took up the telephone and heard my father's voice pronouncing my name, I knew almost exactly what he was going to say. He said that his friend the editor of the morning paper had called him and reported that there had been a girl in the car with me, and though they didn't of course plan to use her name, probably wouldn't even run the story until Monday, they would have to *know* her name. And would have to assure themselves she wasn't hurt in the crash. And that she was unharmed after leaving the scene. Without hesitation I gave my father Lee Ann Deehart's name, as well as her address and telephone number. But I made no further explanation to Father, and he asked me for none. The only other thing I said was that I'd be home in a little while. Father was silent a moment after that. Then he said, 'Are you all right?'

I said, 'I'm fine.'

And he said, 'Good. I'll be waiting up for you.'

I hung up the telephone, and my first thought was that before I left Caroline tonight I'd have to tell her that Lee Ann had been in the car with me. Then, without thinking almost, I dialed Lee Ann's rooming-house number. It felt very strange to be doing this in the Braxleys' library. The woman who ran the rooming house said that Lee Ann had not been in since she left with me in the afternoon.

As I passed back across the wide hallway and caught another glimpse of the snow outside, the question arose in my mind for the first time: *Had* Lee Ann come to some harm in those woods? More than the density of the underbrush, more than its proximity to the Zoo, where certain unsavory characters often hung out, it was the great size and antiquity of the forest trees somehow and the old rumors that white settlers had once been ambushed there by Chickasaw Indians that made me feel that if anything had happened to the girl, it had happened there. And on the heels of such thoughts I found myself wondering for the first time if all this might actually lead to my beautiful, willowy Caroline Braxley's breaking off our engagement. I returned to the living room, and at the sight of Caroline's tall figure at the far end of the room, placed between that of her mother and that of her father, the conviction became firm in me that I would have to tell her about Lee Ann before she and I parted that night. And as I drew nearer to her, still wondering if something ghastly had happened to Lee Ann there in the old forest, I saw the perplexed and even suspicious expression on Caroline's face and presently observed similar expressions on the faces of her two parents. And from that moment began the gnawing wonder which would be with me for several days ahead: What precisely would Caroline consider sufficient provocation for breaking off our engagement to be married? I had no idea, really. Would it be sufficient that I had had one of those unnamed 'female companions' in the car with me at the time of the accident? I knew of engagements like ours which had been broken with apparently less provocation. Or would it be the suspicious-seeming circumstances of Lee Ann's leaping out of the car and running off through the snow? Or might it be the final, worst possibility—that of delicate little Lee Ann Deehart's having actually met with foul play in that infrequently entered area of underbrush and towering forest trees?

Broken engagements were a subject of common and considerable interest to girls like Caroline Braxley. Whereas a generation earlier a broken engagement had been somewhat of a scandal—an engagement that had been formally announced at a party and in the newspaper, that is—it did not necessarily represent that in our day. Even in our day, you see, it meant something quite different from what it had once meant. There was, after all, no written contract and it was in no sense so unalterably binding as it had been in our parents' day. For us it was not considered absolutely dishonorable for either party to break off the plans merely because he or she had had a change of heart. Since the boy was no longer expected literally to ask the father for the girl's hand (though he would probably be expected to go through the form, as I had done with Mr Braxley), it was no longer a breach of contract between families. There was certainly nothing like a dowry any longer—not in Memphis—and there was only rarely any kind of property settlement involved, except in cases where both families were extraordinarily rich. The thought pleased me—that is, the ease with which an engagement might be ended. I suppose in part I was simply preparing myself for such an eventuality. And there in the Braxleys' long living room in the very presence of Caroline and Mr and Mrs Braxley themselves, I found myself indulging in a perverse fantasy, a fantasy in which Caroline had broken off our engagement and I was standing up pretty well, was even seeking consolation in the arms, so to speak, of a safely returned Lee Ann Deehart.

But all at once I felt so guilty for my private indiscretion that actually for the first time in the presence of my prospective in-laws I put my arm about Caroline Braxley's waist. And I told her that I felt so fatigued by events of the afternoon that probably I ought now to go ahead home. She and her parents agreed at once. And they agreed among themselves that they each had just now been reflecting privately that I looked exhausted. Mrs Braxley suggested that under the circumstances she ought to ask Robert to drive me home. I accepted. No other suggestion could have seemed so welcome. Robert was the same servingman who had offered to help my plate at dinner and who had so gently guided me to the telephone when my father called. Almost at once, after I got into the front seat of the car beside him— in his dark chauffeur's uniform and cap—I fell asleep. He had to wake me when we pulled up to the side door of my father's house. I remember how warmly I thanked him for bringing me home, even shaking his hand, which was a rather unusual thing to do in those days. I felt greatly refreshed and restored and personally grateful to Robert for it. There was not, in those days in Memphis, any time or occasion when one felt more secure and relaxed than when one had given oneself over completely to the care and protection of the black servants who surrounded us and who created and sustained for the most part the luxury which distinguished the lives we lived then from the lives we live now. They did so for us, whatever their motives and however degrading our demands and our acceptance of their attentions may have been to them.

At any rate, after my slumber in the front seat beside Robert I felt sufficiently restored to face my father (and his awareness of Lee Ann's having been in the car) with some degree of equanimity. And before leaving the Braxleys' house I had found a moment in the hallway to break the news to Caroline that I had not been alone in the car that afternoon. To my considerable surprise she revealed, after a moment's hesitation, that she already knew that had been the case. Her father, like my father, had learned it from one of the newspaper editors—only he had learned it several hours earlier than my father had. I was obliged to realize as we were saying good night to each other that she, along with her two parents, had known all evening that Lee Ann had been with me and had fled into the woods of Overton Park—that she, Caroline, had as a matter of fact known the full story when she came to my house to fetch me back to her house to dinner. 'Where is Lee Ann now?' she asked me presently, holding my two hands in her own and looking at me directly in the eye. 'I don't know,' I said. Knowing how much she knew, I decided I must tell her the rest of it, holding nothing back. I felt that I was seeing a new side to my fiancée and that unless I told her the whole truth there might be something of this other side of her that wouldn't be revealed to me. 'I tried to telephone her after I answered my father's call tonight. But she was not in her room and had not been in since I picked her up at two o'clock.' And I told Caroline about Lee Ann's telephoning me (after Caroline and I had talked in the early afternoon) and about my inviting her to go out to the college with me. Then I gave her my uncensored version of the accident, including the sight of Lee Ann's footprints in the snow.

'How did she sound on the telephone?' she asked.

'What do you mean by that?' I said impatiently. 'I just told you she wasn't home when I called.'

'I mean earlier—when she called you.'

'But why do you want to know that? It doesn't matter, does it?'

'I mean, did she sound depressed? But it doesn't matter for the moment.' She still held my hands in hers. 'You do know, don't you,' she went on after a moment, 'that you are going to have to *find* Lee Ann? And you probably are going to need help.'

Suddenly I had the feeling that Caroline Braxley was someone twenty years older than I; but, rather than sounding like my parents or her parents, she sounded like one or another of the college teachers I had had—even like Dr Bartlett, who once had told me that I was going to need outside help if I was going to keep up with the class. To reassure myself, I suppose, I put my arm about Caroline's waist again and drew her to me. But in our good-night kiss there was a reticence on her part, or a quality that I could only define as conditional or possibly probational. Still, I knew now that she knew everything, and I suppose that was why I was able to catch such a good nap in the car on the way home.

Girls who had been brought up the way Caroline had, in the Memphis of forty years ago, knew not only what was going to be expected of them in making a marriage and bringing up a family there in Memphis—a marriage and a family of the kind their parents had had—they knew also from a fairly early time that they would have to contend with girls and women of certain sorts before and frequently after they were married: with girls, that is, who had no conception of what it was to have a certain type of performance expected of them, or girls of another kind (and more like themselves) who came visiting in Memphis from Mississippi or Arkansas—pretty little plantation girls, my mother called them—or from Nashville or from the olds towns of West Tennessee. Oftentimes these other girls were their cousins, but that made them no less dangerous. Not being on their home ground—in their own country, so to speak—these Nashville or Mississippi or West Tennessee or Arkansas girls did not bother to abide by the usual rules of civilized warfare. They were marauders. But girls like Lee Ann Deehart were something else again. They were the Trojan horse, more or less, established in the very citadel. They were the fifth column, and were perhaps the most dangerous of all. At the end of a brilliant debutante season, sometimes the most eligible bachelor of all those on the list would still remain uncommitted, or even secretly committed to someone who had never seen the inside of the Memphis Country Club. This kind of thing, girls like Caroline Braxley understood, was not to be tolerated—not if the power of moral woman included the power to divine the nature of any man's commitment and the power to test the strength and nature of another kind of woman's power. Young people today may say that

that old-fashioned behavior on the part of girls doesn't matter today, that girls don't have those problems anymore. But I suspect that in Memphis, if not everywhere, there must be something equivalent even nowadays in the struggle of women for power among themselves.

Perhaps, though, to the present generation these distinctions I am making won't seem significant, after all, or worth my bothering so much about—especially the present generation outside of Memphis and the Deep South. Even in Memphis the great majority of people might say, Why is this little band of spoiled rich girls who lived here. forty years ago so important as to deserve our attention? In fact, during the very period I am writing about it is likely that the majority of people in Memphis felt that way. I think the significant point is that those girls took themselves seriously—girls like Caroline—and took seriously the forms of the life they lived. They imagined they knew quite well who they were and they imagined that that was important. They were what, at any rate, those girls like Lee Ann were not. Or they claimed to be what those girls like Lee Ann didn't claim to be and what very few people nowadays claim to be. They considered themselves the heirs to something, though most likely they could not have said what: something their forebears had brought to Memphis with them from somewhere else—from the country around Memphis and from other places, from the country towns of West Tennessee, from Middle Tennessee and East Tennessee, from the Valley of Virginia, from the Piedmont, even from the Tidewater. Girls like Caroline thought they were the heirs to something, and that's what the other girls didn't think about themselves, though probably they were, and probably the present generation, in and out of Memphis—even the sad generation of the sixties and seventies—is heir to more than it thinks it is, in the matter of manners, I mean to say, and of general behavior. And it is of course because these girls like Caroline are regarded as mere old-fashioned society girls that the present generation tends to dismiss them, whereas if it were their fathers we were writing about, the story would, shocking though it is to say, be taken more seriously by everyone. Everyone would recognize now that the fathers and grandfathers of these girls were the sons of the old plantation South come to town and converted or half-converted into modern Memphis businessmen, only with a certain something held over from the old order that made them both better and worse than businessmen elsewhere. They are the authors of much good and much bad in modern Memphis—and modern Nashville and modern Birmingham and modern Atlanta, too. The good they mostly brought with them from life in cities elsewhere in the nation, the thing they were imitating when they constructed the new life in Memphis. And why not judge their daughters and wives in much the same way? Isn't there a need to know what they were like, too? One thing those girls did know they were heirs to was the old, country manners and the insistence upon old, country connections. The first evidence of this that comes to mind is the fact that they often spoke of girls like Lee Ann as 'city girls,' by which they meant that such girls didn't usually have the old family connections back in the country on the cotton farms in West Tennessee, in Mississippi, in Arkansas, or back in Nashville or in Jonesboro or in Virginia.

When Robert had let me out at our side door that night and I came into the house, my father and mother both were downstairs. It was still early of course, but I had the sense of their having waited up for me to come in. They greeted me as though I were returning from some dangerous mission. Each of them asked me how the Braxleys 'seemed.' Finally Mother insisted upon examining the stitches underneath the bandage on my forehead. After that, I said that I thought I would hit the hay. They responded to that with the same enthusiasm that Mr and Mrs Braxley had evidenced when I told them I thought I should go ahead home. Nothing would do me more good than a good night's sleep, my parents agreed. It was a day everybody was glad to have come to an end.

After I got upstairs and in my room, it occurred to me that my parents both suddenly looked very old. That seems laughable to me now almost, because my parents were then ten or fifteen years younger than I am today. I look back on them now as a youngish couple in their early middle age, whose first son was about to be married and about whose possible infidelity they were concerned. But indeed what an old-fashioned pair they seem to me in the present day, waiting up for their children to come in. Because actually they stayed downstairs a

long while after I went up to bed, waiting there for my younger
brothers and my little sister to come in, all of whom were out on their
separate dates. In my mind's eye I can see them there, waiting as parents had waited for hundreds of years for their grown-up children to
come home at night. They would seem now to be violating the rights
of young individuals and even interfering with the maturing process.
But in those times it seemed only natural for parents to be watchful
and concerned about their children's first flight away from the nest. I
am referring mainly to my parents' waiting up for my brothers and my
sister, who were in their middle teens, but also as I lay in my bed I felt,
myself, more relaxed knowing that they were downstairs in the front
room speculating upon what Lee Ann's disappearance meant and alert
to whatever new development there might be. After a while, my
father came up and opened the door to my room. I don't know how
much later it was. I don't think I had been to sleep, but I could not tell
for sure even at the time—my waking and sleeping thoughts were so
much alike that night. At any rate, Father stepped inside the room and
came over to my bed.

'I have just called down to the police station,' he said, 'and they say
they have checked and that Lee Ann has still not come back to her
rooming house. She seems to have gone into some sort of hiding.' He
said this with wonderment and with just the slightest trace of irritation
in his voice. 'Have you any notion, Nat, why she *might* want to go into
hiding?'

The next day was Sunday, December 5. During the night it had turned
bitterly cold, the snow had frozen into a crisp sheet that covered most
of the ground. At about nine o'clock in the morning another snow
began falling. I had breakfast with the family, still wearing the bandage
on my forehead. I sat around in my bathrobe all morning, pretending
to read the newspaper. I didn't see any report of the accident, and my
father said it wouldn't appear till Monday. At ten o'clock, I dialed Lee
Ann's telephone number. One of the other girls who roomed in the
house answered. She said she thought Lee Ann hadn't come in last
night and she giggled. I asked her if she would make sure about it. She
left the phone and came back presently to say in a whisper that there

was no doubt about it: Lee Ann had not slept in her bed. I knew she was whispering so that the landlady wouldn't hear.

. . . And then I had a call from Caroline, who wanted to know how my head was this morning and whether or not there had been any word about Lee Ann. After I told her what I had just learned, we were both silent for a time. Finally she said she had intended to come over and see how I was feeling but her father had decreed that nobody should go out in such bad weather. It would just be inviting another automobile wreck, he said. She reported that her parents were not going to church, and I said that mine weren't either. We agreed to talk later and to see each other after lunch if the weather improved. Then I could hear her father's voice in the background, and she said that he wanted to use the telephone.

At noon the snow was still falling. My father stood at a front window in the living room, wearing his dark smoking jacket. He predicted that it might be the deepest snowfall we had ever had in Memphis. He said that people in other parts of the country didn't realize how much cold weather came all the way down the Mississippi Valley from Minneapolis to Memphis. I had never heard him pay so much attention to the weather and talk so much about it. I wondered if, like me, he was really thinking about the old forest out in Overton Park and wishing he were free to go out there and make sure there was no sign of Lee Ann Deehart's having come to grief in those ancient woods. I wonder now if there weren't others besides us who were thinking of the old forest all day that day. I knew that my father, too, had been on the telephone that morning—and he was on it again during a good part of the afternoon. In retrospect, I am certain that all day that day he was in touch with a whole circle of friends and colleagues who were concerned about Lee Ann's safety. It was not only the heavy snow that checked his freedom—and mine, too, of course—to go out and search those woods and put his mind at rest on the possibility at least. It was more than just this snow, which the radio reported as snarling up and halting all traffic. What prevented him was his own unwillingness to admit fully to himself and to others that this particular danger was really there; what prevented him and perhaps all the rest of us was the fear that the answer to the gnawing question of

Lee Ann's whereabouts might really be out there within that immemorial grove of snow-laden oaks and yellow poplars and hickory trees. It is a grove, I believe, that men in Memphis have feared and wanted to destroy for a long time and whose destruction they are still working at even in this latter day. It has only recently been saved by a very narrow margin from a great highway that men wished to put through there—saved by groups of women determined to save this last bit of the old forest from the axes of modern men. Perhaps in old pioneer days, before the plantation and the neoclassic towns were made, the great forests seemed woman's last refuge from the brute she lived alone with in the wilderness. Perhaps all men in Memphis who had any sense of their past felt this, though they felt more keenly (or perhaps it amounts to the same feeling) that the forest was woman's greatest danger. Men remembered mad pioneer women, driven mad by their loneliness and isolation, who ran off into the forest, never to be seen again, or incautious women who allowed themselves to be captured by Indians and returned at last so mutilated that they were unrecognizable to their husbands or who at their own wish lived out their lives among their savage captors. I think that if I had said to my father (or to myself), 'What is it that's so scary about the old forest?', he (or I) would have answered, 'There's nothing at all scary about it. But we can't do anything today because of the snow. It's the worst snow in history!' I think that all day long my father—like me—was busily not letting himself believe that anything awful had happened to Lee Ann Deehart, or that if it had it certainly hadn't happened in those woods. Not just my father and me, though. Caroline's father, too, and all their friends—their peers. And the newspapermen and the police. If they waited long enough, it would come out all right and there would be no need to search the woods even. And it turned out, in the most literal sense, that they—we—were right. Yet what guilty feelings must not everyone have lived with—lived with in silence—all that snowbound day.

At two o'clock, Caroline called again to say that because of the snow, her aunt was canceling the dinner party she had planned that night in honor of the bride and groom. I remember as well as anything else that terrible day how my mother and father looked at each other when they received this news. Surely they were wondering, as I had to also, if this was but the first gesture of withdrawal. There was no knowing what their behavior or the behavior of any of us that day meant. The day simply dragged on until the hour when we could decently go to bed. It was December, and we were near the shortest day of the year, but that day had seemed the longest day of my life.

On Monday morning, two uniformed policemen were at our house before I had finished my breakfast. When I learned they were waiting in the living room to see me, I got up from the table at once. I wouldn't let my father go in with me to see them. Mother tried to make me finish my eggs before going in, but I only laughed at her and kissed her on the top of the head as I left the breakfast room. The two policemen were sitting in the very chairs my parents had sat in the night before. This somehow made the interview easier from the outset. I felt initially that they were there to help me, not to harass me in any way. They had already, at the break of dawn, been out to Overton Park. (The whole case—if case it was—had of course been allowed to rest on Sunday.) And along with four other policemen they had conducted a full-scale search of the old forest. There was no trace of Lee Ann Deehart there. They had also been to her rooming house on Tutwiler Avenue and questioned Mrs Troxler, whose house it was, about all of Lee Ann's friends and acquaintances and about the habits of her daily life. They said that they were sure the girl would turn up but that the newspapers were putting pressure on them to explain her disappearance and—more particularly—to explain her precipitate flight from the scene of the accident.

I spent that day with the police, leaving them only for an hour at lunchtime, when they dropped me off at my father's office on Front Street, where I worked. There I made a small pretense of attending to some business for the firm while I consumed a club sandwich and milk shake that my father or one of my uncles in the firm had had sent up for me. At the end of the hour, I jogged down the two flights of steep wooden stairs and found the police car waiting for me at the curb, just outside the entrance. At some time during the morning, one of the policemen had suggested that they might have a bulldozer or some other piece of machinery brought in to crack the ice on the Overton Park Pond and then drag the pond for Lee Ann's body. But I had pointed out that the two skaters had returned to the pond after the accident and skated there until dark. There was no hole in the ice anywhere. Moreover, the skaters had reported that when the girl left the scene she did not go by way of the pond but went up the rise and into the wooded area. There was every indication that she had gone that way, and so the suggestion that the pond be dragged was dismissed. And we continued during the rest of the morning to make the rounds of the rooming houses and apartments of Lee Ann's friends and acquaintances, as well as the houses of the parents with whom some of them lived. In the afternoon we planned to go to the shops and offices in which some of the girls worked and to interview them there concerning Lee Ann's whereabouts and where it was they last had seen her. It seemed a futile procedure to me. But while I was eating my club sandwich alone in our third-floor walkup office I received a shocking telephone call.

Our offices, like most of the other cotton factors' offices, were in one of the plain-faced, three- and four-story buildings put up on Front Street during the middle years of the last century, just before the Civil War. Cotton men were very fond of those offices, and the offices did possess a certain rough beauty that anyone could see. Apparently there had been few, if any, improvements or alterations since the time they were built. All the electrical wiring and all the plumbing, such as they were, were 'exposed.' The wooden stairsteps and the floors were rough and splintery and extremely worn down. The walls were whitewashed and the ceilings were twelve or fourteen feet in height. But the chief charm of the rooms was the tall windows across the front of the buildings—wide sash windows with small windowlights, windows looking down onto Front Street and from which you could catch glimpses of the brown Mississippi River at the foot of the bluff, and even of the Arkansas shoreline on the other side. I was sitting on a cotton trough beside one of those windows, eating my club sandwich, when I heard the telephone ring back in the inner office. I remember that when it rang my eyes were on a little stretch of the Arkansas shoreline roughly delineated by its scrubby trees and my thoughts

were on the Arkansas roadhouses where we often went with the demimonde girls on a Saturday night. At first I thought I wouldn't answer
the phone. I let it ring for a minute or two. It went on ringing—
persistently. Suddenly I realized that a normal business call would have
stopped ringing before now. I jumped down from my perch by the
window and ran back between the cotton troughs to the office. When
I picked up the receiver, a girl's voice called my name before I spoke.

'Yes,' I said. The voice had sounded familiar, but I knew it wasn't
Caroline's. Aand it wasn't Lee Ann's. I couldn't identify it exactly,
though I did say to myself right away that it was one of the city girls.

'Nat,' the voice said, 'Lee Ann wants you to stop trying to trail her.'

'Who is this?' I said. 'Where is Lee Ann?'

'Never mind,' the girl on the other end of the line said. 'We're not
going to let you find her, and you're making her very uncomfortable
with your going around with the police after her and all that.'

'The police aren't "after her",' I said. 'They just want to be sure
she's all right.'

'She'll be all right,' the voice said, 'if you'll lay off and stop chasing
her. Don't you have any decency at all? Don't you have a brain in your
head? Don't you know what this is like for Lee Ann? We all thought
you were her friend.'

'I am,' I said. 'Just let me speak to Lee Ann.'

But there was a click in the telephone, and no one was there any
longer.

I turned back into the room where the cotton troughs were. When
I saw my milk-shake carton and the sandwich paper up by the
window, and remembered how the girl had called my name as soon as
I picked up the telephone, I felt sure that someone had been watching
me from down in the street or from a window across the way. Without
going back to my lunch, I turned quickly and started down the stairs
toward the street. But when I looked at my watch, I realized it was
time for the policemen to pick me up again. And there they were, of
course, waiting at the entrance to our building. When I got into the
police car, I didn't tell them about my call. And we began our rounds
again, going to the addresses where some of Lee Ann's friends worked.

Lee Ann Deehart and other girls like her that we went about with, as I have indicated, were not literally ladies of any Memphis demi-monde. Possibly they got called that first by the only member of our generation in Memphis who had read Marcel Proust, a literary boy who later became a college professor and who wanted to make his own life in Memphis—and ours—seem more interesting than it was. Actually, they were girls who had gone to the public high schools, and more often than not to some school other than Central High, which during those Depression years had a degree of acceptance in Memphis society. As anyone could have observed on that morning when I rode about town with the policemen, those girls came from a variety of backgrounds. We went to the houses of some of their parents, some of whom were day laborers who spoke in accents of the old Memphis Irish, descendants of the Irish who were imported to build the rail-roads to Texas. Today some of the girls would inevitably have been black. But they were the daughters also of bank clerks and salesmen and of professional men, too, because they made no distinction among themselves. The parents of some of them had moved to Memphis from cities in other sections of the country or even from Southern small towns. The girls were not interested in such distinctions of origin, were not conscious of them, had not been made aware of them by their parents. They would have been highly approved of by the present generation of young people. Like the present generation in general, these girls—Lee Ann included—tended to be bookish and artistic in a middlebrow sort of way, and some of them had real intellectual aspi-rations. They did not care who each other's families were or where they had gone to school. They met and got to know each other in roadhouses, on double dates, and in the offices and stores where they worked. As I have said, they tended to be bookish and artistic. If they had found themselves in Proust's Paris, instead of in our Memphis of the 1930s, possibly they would have played some role in the intellec-tual life of the place. But of course this is only my ignorant speculation. It is always impossible to know what changes might have been wrought in people under circumstances of the greatest or slight-est degree of difference from the actual.

The girls we saw that afternoon at their places of work were gen-erally more responsive to the policemen's questions than to my own.

And I became aware that the two policemen—youngish men in their late thirties, for whom this special assignment was somehow distasteful—were more interested in protecting these girls from any embarrassment than in obtaining information about Lee Ann. With all but one of the half-dozen girls we sought out, the policemen sent me in to see the girl first, to ask her if she would rather be questioned by them in her place of business or in the police car. In each case the girl treated my question concerning this as an affront, but always she finally sent word back to the policemen to come inside. And in each case I found myself admiring the girl not only for her boldness in dealing with the situation (they seemed fearless in their talk with the police and refused absolutely to acknowledge close friendship with Lee Ann, insisting—all of them—that they saw her only occasionally at night spots, sometimes with me, sometimes with other young men, that they had no idea who her parents were or where she came to Memphis from) but also for a personal, feminine beauty that I had never before been fully aware of. Perhaps I saw or sensed it now for the first time because I had not before seen them threatened or in danger. It is true, I know, that the effect of all this questioning seemed somehow to put them in jeopardy. Perhaps I saw now how much more vulnerable they were than were the girls in the set my parents more or less intended me to travel in. There was a delicacy about them, a frailty even, that didn't seem to exist in other girls I knew and that contrasted strangely—and disturbingly—with the rough surroundings of the roadhouses they frequented at night and the harsh, businesslike atmosphere of the places where they worked. Within each of them, moreover, there seemed a contrast between the delicate beauty of their bodies, their prettily formed arms and legs, their breasts and hips, their small feet and hands, their soft natural hair—hair worn so becomingly, groomed, in each case, on their pretty little heads to direct one's eyes first of all to the fair or olive complexion and the nicely proportioned features of the face—a contrast, that is to say, between this physical beauty and a bookishness and a certain toughness of mind and a boldness of spirit which were unmistakable in all of them.

The last girl we paid a call on that afternoon was one Nancy Minnifee, who happened to be the girl who was always frankest and crudest in making jokes about families like my own and who had made the crack that the other girls had laughed at so irrepressibly in the beer garden: 'I haven't lost anything at the MCC.' Or it may not have been that she just happened to be the last we called on. Perhaps out of dread of her jokes I guided the police last of all to the farm-implement warehouse where Nancy was a secretary. Or perhaps it wasn't so much because of her personality as because I knew she was Lee Ann's closest friend and I somehow dreaded facing her for that reason. Anyway, at the warehouse she was out on the loading platform with a clipboard and pencil in her hands when we drove up.

'That's Nancy Minnifee up there,' I said to the two policemen in the front seat. I was sitting in the backseat alone. I saw them shake their heads. I knew that it was with a certain sadness and a personal admiration that they did so. Nancy was a very pretty girl, and they hated the thought of bothering this lovely creature with the kind of questions they were going to ask. They hated it without even knowing she was Lee Ann's closest friend. Suddenly I began seeing all those girls through the policemen's eyes, just as next day, when I would make a similar expedition in the company of my father and the newspaper editor, I'd see the girls through their eyes. The worst of it, somehow, for the policemen, was that the investigation wasn't really an official investigation but was something the newspapers had forced upon the police in case something had happened which they hadn't reported. The girl hadn't been missing long enough for anyone to declare her 'officially' missing. Yet the police, along with the mayor's office and the newspaper editor, didn't want to risk something's having happened to a girl like Lee Ann. They—all of them—thought of such girls, in a sense, as their special wards. It would be hard to say why they did. At any rate, before the police car had fully stopped I saw Nancy Minnifee up there on the platform. She was wearing a fur-collared overcoat but no hat or gloves. Immediately she began moving along the loading platform toward us, holding the clipboard up to shield her eyes from the late-afternoon winter sun. She came down the steps to the graveled area where we were stopped, and when the policeman at the wheel of the car ran down his window she bent forward and put her arm on his door. The casual way she did it seemed almost familiar—indeed, almost provocative. I found myself resenting her manner, because I was afraid she would give the wrong impression. The way she leaned on the door reminded me of the prostitutes down on Pontotoc Street when we, as teenage boys, used to stop in front of their houses and leave the motor running because we were afraid of them.

'I've been expecting you two gentlemen,' Nancy said, smiling amiably at the two policemen and pointedly ignoring my presence in the backseat. The policemen broke into laughter.

'I suppose your friends have been calling ahead,' the driver said. Then Nancy laughed as though he had said something very funny.

'I could draw you a map of the route you've taken this afternoon,' she said. She was awfully polite in her tone, and the two policemen were awfully polite, too. But before they could really begin asking her their questions she began giving them her answers. She hadn't seen Lee Ann since several days before the accident. She didn't know anything about where she might be. She didn't know anything about her family. She had always understood that Lee Ann came from Texas.

'That's a big state,' the policeman who wasn't driving said.

'Well, I've never been there,' she said, 'but I'm told it's a mighty big state.'

The three of them burst into laughter again. Then the driver said quite seriously, 'But we understand you're her best friend.'

'I don't know her any better than most of the other girls do,' she said. 'I can't imagine who told you that.' Now for the first time she looked at me in the backseat. 'Hello, Nat,' she said. I nodded to her. I couldn't imagine why she was lying to them. But I didn't tell her, as I hadn't told the other girls or the police, about the call I had had in the cotton office. I knew that she must know all about it, but I said nothing.

When we had pulled away, the policeman who was driving the car said, 'This Lee Ann must be all right or these girls wouldn't be closing ranks so. They've got too much sense for that. They're smart girls.'

Presently the other policeman turned his head halfway around, though not looking directly at me, and asked, 'She wouldn't be pregnant by any chance, would she?'

'Uh-uh,' I said. It was all the answer it seemed to me he deserved. But then I couldn't resist echoing what he had said. 'They've got too much sense for that. They're smart girls.' He looked all the way around at me now and gave me what I am sure he thought was a straight look.

'Damn right they are,' said the driver, glancing at his colleague with a frown on his forehead and speaking with a curled lip. 'Get your mind out of the gutter, Fred. After all, they're just kids, all of them.'

We rode on in silence after that. For the first time in several hours, I thought of Caroline Braxley, and I wondered again whether or not she would break our engagement.

When the policemen let me off at my office at five o'clock, I went to my car and drove straight to the apartment house at Crosstown where Nancy Minnifee lived. I was waiting for Nancy in the parking lot when she got home. She invited me inside, but without a smile.

'I want to know where Lee Ann is,' I said as soon as she had closed the door.

'Do you imagine I'd tell you if I knew?' she said.

I sat myself down in an upholstered chair as if I were going to stay there till she told me. 'I want to know what the hell's going on,' I said with what I thought was considerable force, 'and why you told such lies to those policemen.'

'If you don't know that now, Nat,' she said, sitting down opposite me, 'you probably won't ever know.'

'She wouldn't be pregnant by any chance, would she?' I said, without really having known I was going to say it.

Nancy's mouth dropped open. Then she laughed aloud. Presently she said, 'Well, one thing's certain, Nat. It wouldn't be any concern of yours if she were.'

I pulled myself up out of the big chair and left without another word's passing between us.

Lee Ann Deehart and Nancy Minnifee and that whole band of girls that we liked to refer to as the girls of the Memphis demimonde were of course no more like the ladies of the demimonde as they appear in French literature than *they* were like some band of angels. And I hardly need say—though it does somehow occur to me to say—their manners and morals bore no resemblance whatsoever to those of the mercenary, filthy-mouthed whores on Pontotoc Street. I might even say that their manners were practically indistinguishable from those of the girls we knew who had attended Miss Hutchinson's School and St Mary's and Lausanne and were now members of the debutante set. The fact is that some of them—only a few perhaps—were from families that were related by blood, and rather closely related, to the families of the debutante set, but families that, for one reason or another, now found themselves economically in another class from their relatives. At any rate, they were all freed from old restraints put upon them by family and community, liberated in each case, so it seems to me, by sheer strength of character, liberated in many respects, but above all else—and I cannot say how it came about—liberated sexually. The most precise thing I can say about them is that they, in their little band, were like hordes of young girls today. It seems to me that in their attitude toward sex they were at least forty years ahead of their time. But I cannot say how it came about. Perhaps it was an individual thing with each of them—or partly so. Perhaps it was because they were the second or third generation of women in Memphis who were working in offices. They were not promiscuous—not most of them—but they slept with the men they were in love with and they did not conceal the fact. The men they were in love with were usually older than we were. Generally speaking, the girls merely amused themselves with us, just as we amused ourselves with them. There was a wonderful freedom in our relations which I have never known anything else quite like. And though I may not have had the most realistic sense of what their lives were, I came to know what I did know through my friendship with Lee Ann Deehart.

She and I first met, I think, at one of those dives where we all hung out. Or it may have been at some girl's apartment. I suspect we both would have been hard put to it to say where it was or exactly when. She was simply one of the good-looking girls we ran around with. I remember dancing with her on several occasions before I had any idea what her name was. We drifted into our special kind of friendship because, as a matter of fact, she was the good friend of Nancy Minnifee, whom my own close friend Bob Childress got very serious about for a time. Bob and Nancy may even have been living together for a while in Nancy's apartment. I think Bob, who was one of six or eight boys of approximately my background who used to go about with these girls, would have married Nancy if she'd consented to have him. Possibly it was at Nancy's apartment that I met Lee Ann. Anyway, we did a lot of double dating, the four of us, and had some wonderful times going to the sort of rough night spots that we all liked and found sufficiently exciting to return to again and again. We would be dancing and drinking at one of those places until about two in the morning, when most of them closed. At that hour most of us would take our girls home, because we nearly all of us had jobs—the girls and the boys, too—which we had to report to by eight or nine in the morning.

Between Lee Ann and me, as between most of the boys and their girls, I think, there was never a serious affair. That is, we never actually—as the young people today say—'had sex.' But in the car on the way home or in the car parked outside her rooming house or even outside the night spot, as soon as we came out, we would regularly indulge in what used to be known as 'heavy necking.' Our stopping at that I must attribute first of all to Lee Ann's resistance, though also, in part, to a hesitation I felt about insisting with such a girl. You see, she was in all respects like the girls we called 'nice girls,' by which I suppose we really meant society girls. And most of us accepted the restriction that we were not to 'go to bed' with society girls. They were the girls we were going to marry. These girls were not what those society girls would have termed shopgirls. They had much better taste in their clothes and in their general demeanor. And, as I have said, in the particular group I speak of there was at least an intellectual strain. Some of them had been to college for as much as a year or two, whereas others seemed hardly to have finished high school. Nearly all of them read magazines and books that most of us had never heard of. And they found my odd addiction to Latin poetry the most interesting thing about me. Most of them belonged to a national book club, from which they received a new book each month, and they nearly all bought records and listened to classical music. You would see them sometimes in groups at the Art Gallery. Or whenever there was an opera or a good play at the city auditorium they were all likely to be there in a group—almost never with dates. If you hadn't known who they were, you might easily have mistaken them for some committee from the Junior League or for an exceptionally pretty group of school-teachers—from some fashionable girls' school probably.

But mostly, of course, one saw them with their dates at one of the roadhouses, over in Arkansas or down in Mississippi or out east on the Bristol Highway, or yet again at one of the places we called the 'town joints.' They preferred going to those roadhouses and town joints to going to the Peabody Hotel Roof or the Claridge—as I suppose nearly everyone else did, really, including society girls like Caroline. You would, as a matter of fact, frequently see girls like Caroline at such places. At her request, I had more than once taken Caroline to a town joint down on Adams Street called The Cellar and once to a road-house called The Jungle, over in Arkansas. She had met some of the city girls there and said she found them 'dead attractive.' And she once recognized them at a play I took her to see and afterward expressed interest in them and asked me to tell her what they were like.

The fact may be that neither the roadhouses nor the town joints were quite as tough as they seemed. Or they weren't as tough as for the demimonde girls, anyway. Because the proprietors clearly had protec-tive feelings about them. At The Jungle, for instance, the middle-aged couple who operated the place, an extremely obese couple who were forever grinning in our direction and who were usually barefoot (we called them Ma and Pa), would often come and stand by our table—one or the other of them—and sing the words to whatever was playing on the jukebox. Often as not, one of them would be standing there during the entire evening. Sometimes Ma would talk to us about her two little daughters, whom she kept in a private school in Memphis, and Pa, who was a practicing taxidermist, would talk to us about the dogs whose mounted heads adorned the walls on every side of the dimly lit room. All this afforded us great privacy and safety. No drunk or roughneck would come near our table while either Ma or Pa was close by. We had similar protection at other places. At The Cellar, for instance, old Mrs Power was the sole proprietor. She had a huge goiter on her neck and was never known to smile. Not even in our direction. But it was easy to see that she watched our table like a hawk, and if any other patron lingered near us even momentarily she would begin moving slowly toward us. And whoever it was would catch one glimpse of her and move on. We went to these places quite regularly, though some of the girls had their favorites and dislikes among them. Lee Ann would never be taken to The Cellar. She would say only that the place depressed her. And Caroline, when I took her there, felt an instant dislike for The Jungle. She would shake her head afterward and say she would never go back and have those dogs' eyes staring down through the darkness at her.

On the day after I made the rounds with the policemen, I found myself following almost the same routine in the company of my father and the editor of the morning paper, and, as a matter of fact, the mayor of Memphis himself. The investigation or search was, you see, still entirely unofficial. And men like my father and the mayor and the editor wanted to keep it so. That's why after that routine and off-the-record series of questionings by the police they preferred to do a bit of investigation themselves rather than entrust the matter to someone else. As I have said, that generation of men in Memphis evidenced feelings of responsibility for such girls—for 'working girls of a superior kind,' as they phrased it—which I find somewhat difficult to explain. For it wasn't just the men I drove about town with that day. Or the dozen or so men who gathered for conference in our driveway before we set out—that is, Caroline's father, his lawyer, the driver of the other vehicle, his lawyer, my father's lawyer, ministers from three church denominations, the editor of the afternoon newspaper, and still others. That day, when I rode about town with my father and the two other men in our car, I came as near as I ever had or ever would to receiving a satisfactory explanation of the phenomenon. They were a generation of American men who were perhaps the last to grow up in a world where women were absolutely subjected and under the absolute protection of men. While my father wheeled his big Cadillac through the side streets on which some of the girls lived and then along the wide boulevards of Memphis, they spoke of the changes they had seen. In referring to the character of the life girls like Lee Ann led—of which they showed a far greater awareness than I would have supposed they possessed—they agreed that this was the second or third generation there of women who had lived as independently, as freely as these girls did. I felt that what they said was in no sense as derogatory or critical as it would have been in the presence of their wives or daughters. They spoke almost affectionately and with a certain sadness of such girls. They spoke as if these were daughters of dead brothers of their own or of dead companions-in-arms during the First World War. And it seemed to me that they thought of these girls as the daughters of men who had abdicated their authority and responsibility as fathers, men who were not strangers or foreign to them, though they were perhaps of a different economic class. The family names of the girls were familiar to them. The fathers of these girls were Americans of the great hinterland like themselves, even Southerners like themselves. I felt that they were actually cousins of ours who had failed as fathers somehow, had been destined to fail, even required to do so in a changing world. And so these men of position and power had to act as surrogate fathers during a transitional period. It was a sort of communal fatherhood they were acting out. Eventually, they seemed to say, fathers might not be required. I actually heard my father saying, 'That's what the whole world is going to be like someday.' He meant like the life such girls as Lee Ann were making for themselves. I often think nowadays of Father's saying that whenever I see his prediction being fulfilled by the students in the university where I have been teaching for twenty years now, and I wonder if Father did really believe his prediction would come true.

Yet while he and the other two men talked their rather sanguine talk that day, I was thinking of a call I had had the night before after I came back from seeing Nancy Minnifee. One of the servants answered the telephone downstairs in the back part of the house, and she must have guessed it was something special. Because instead of buzzing the buzzer three times, which was the signal when a call was for me, the maid came up the backstairs and tapped gently on my door. 'It's for you, Nat,' she said softly. 'Do you want to take it downstairs?'

There was nothing peculiar about her doing this, really. Since I didn't have an extension phone in my room, I had a tacit understanding with the servants that I preferred to take what I considered my private calls down in that quarter of the house. And so I followed the maid down the back stairway and shut myself in the little, servants' dining room that was behind the great white-tiled kitchen. I answered the call on the wall phone there.

A girl's voice, which wasn't the same voice I had heard on the office telephone at noon, said, 'Lee Ann doesn't want another day like this one, Nat.'

'Who is this?' I said, lowering my voice to be sure even the servants didn't hear me. 'What the hell is going on?' I asked. 'Where is Lee Ann?'

'She's been keeping just one apartment or one rooming house ahead of you all day.'

'But why? Why is she hiding this way?'

'All I want to say is she's had about enough. You let up on pursuing her so.'

'It's not me,' I protested. 'There's nothing I can do to stop them.'

Over the phone there came a contemptuous laugh. 'No. And you can't get married till they find her, can you?' Momentarily I thought I heard Lee Ann's voice in the background. 'Anyhow,' the same voice continued, 'Lee Ann's had about as much as she can take of all this. She was depressed as it was when she called you in the first place. Why else do you think she would call you, Nat? She was desperate for some comic relief.'

'Relief from what?'

'Relief from her depression, you idiot.'

'But what's she depressed about?' I was listening carefully to the voice, thinking it was that of first one girl and then another.

'Nat, we don't always have to have something to be depressed about. But Lee Ann will be all right, if you'll let her alone.'

'But what is she depressed about?' I persisted. I had begun to think maybe it was Lee Ann herself on the phone, disguising her voice.

'About life in general, you bastard! Isn't that enough?' Then I knew it wasn't Lee Ann, after all.

'Listen,' I said, 'let me speak to Lee Ann. I want to speak to Lee Ann.'

And then I heard whoever it was I was talking with break off the connection. I quietly replaced the receiver and went upstairs again.

In those days, I didn't know what it was to be depressed—not, anyway, about 'life in general.' Later on, you see, I did know. Later on, after years of being married, and having three children and going to grown-up Memphis dinner parties three or four times a week, and working in the cotton office six days a week, I got so depressed about life in general that I sold my interest in the cotton firm to a cousin of mine (my father and uncles were dead by then) and managed to make Caroline understand that what I needed was to go back to school for a while so that we could start our life all over. I took degrees at three universities, which made it possible for me to become a college professor. That may be an awful revelation about myself—I mean to say, awful that what decided me to become a teacher was that I was so depressed about life in general. But I reasoned that being an English professor—even if I was relegated to teaching composition and simpleminded survey courses—would be something useful and would throw us in with a different kind of people. (Caroline tried to persuade me to go into the sciences, but I told her she was just lucky that I didn't take up classics again.) Anyway, teaching has made me see a lot of young people over the years, in addition to my own children, and I think it is why, in retrospect, those Memphis girls I'm writing about still seem interesting to me after all these many years.

But the fact is I was still so uneasy about the significance of both those calls from Lee Ann's friends that I was unwilling to mention them to Caroline that night. At first I thought I would tell her, but as soon as I saw her tall and graceful figure in her white, pleated evening dress and wearing the white corsage I had sent, I began worrying again about whether or not she might still break off the engagement. Besides, we had plenty of other matters to discuss, including the rounds I had made with the two policemen that day and her various activities in preparation for the wedding. We went to a dinner that one of my aunts gave for us at the Memphis Country Club that night. We came home early and spent twenty minutes or so in her living room, telling

each other how much we loved each other and how we would let
nothing on earth interfere with our getting married. I felt reassured, or
I tried to feel so. It seemed to me, though, that Caroline still had not
really made up her mind. It worried me that she didn't have more to
say about Lee Ann. After I got home, I kept waking all night and wondering what if that had not been Lee Ann's voice I had heard in the
background and what if she never surfaced again. The circumstances
of her disappearance would have to be made public, and that would
certainly be too embarrassing for Caroline and her parents to ignore.

Next day, I didn't tell my father and his two friends, the editor and
the mayor, about either of the two telephone calls. I don't know why
I didn't, unless it was because I feared they might begin monitoring all
my calls. I could not tolerate the thought of having them hear the
things that girl said to me.

In preference to interviewing the girls whose addresses I could give
them, those three middle-aged men seemed much more interested in
talking to the girls' rooming-house landladies, or their apartment landlords, or their mothers. They did talk to some of the girls themselves,
though, and I observed that the girls were so impressed by having these
older men want to talk to them that they could hardly look at them
directly. What I think is that the girls were *afraid* they would tell them
the truth. They would reply to their questions respectfully, if evasively,
but they were apt to keep their eyes on me. This was not the case,
however, with the mothers and the landlords and the landladies. There
was an immediate rapport between these persons and the three men.
There hardly needed to be any explanation required of the unofficial
nature of the investigation or of the concern of these particular men
about such a girl as Lee Ann. One woman who told them that Lee
Ann had roomed with her for a time described her as being always a
moody sort of girl. 'But lots of these girls living on their own are
moody,' she said.

'Where did Miss Deehart come from?' my father asked. 'Who were
her people?'

'She always claimed she came from Texas,' the woman said. 'But she
could never make it clear to me where it was in Texas.'

Later the mayor asked Lee Ann's current landlady, Mrs Troxler, where she supposed Lee Ann might have gone. 'Well,' Mrs Troxler said, 'a girl, a decent girl, even among these modern girls, generally goes to her mother when there's trouble. Women turn to women,' she said, 'when there's real trouble.'

The three men found no trace of Lee Ann, got no real clue to where she might have gone. When finally we were leaving the editor at his newspaper office on Union Avenue, he hesitated a moment before opening the car door. 'Well,' he began, but he sat for a moment beating his leg thoughtfully with a newspaper he had rolled up in his hand. 'I don't know,' he said. 'It's going to be a matter for the police, after all, if we can't do any better than this.' I still didn't say anything about my telephone calls. But the calls were worrying me a good deal, and that night I told Caroline.

And when I had told her about the calls and told her how the police and my father and his friends had failed to get any information from the girls, Caroline, who was then sitting beside me on the couch in her living room, suddenly took my hand in hers and, putting her face close to mine and looking me directly in the eye, said, 'Nat, I don't want you to go to work at all tomorrow. Don't make any explanation to your father or to anybody. Just get up early and come over here and get me. I want you to take me to meet some of those girls.' Then she asked me which of the girls she might possibly have met on the rare occasions when I had taken her dancing at The Jungle or at The Cellar. And before I left that night she got me to tell her all I knew about 'that whole tribe of city girls.' I told her everything, including an account of my innocent friendship with Lee Ann Deehart, as well as an account of my earlier relations, which were not innocent, with a girl named Fern Morris. When, next morning, I came to fetch Caroline for our expedition, there were only three girls that she wanted to be taken to see. One of the three was of course Fern Morris.

There was something that had happened to me the day before, when I was going about Memphis with my father and his two friends, that I could not tell Caroline about. You see, I had been imagining, each place we went, how as we came in the front door Lee Ann was hurriedly, quietly going out the back. This mental picture of her in flight I found not merely appealing but strangely exciting. And it seemed to me I was discovering what my true feelings toward Lee Ann had been during the past two years. I had never dared insist upon the occasional advances I had naturally made to her, because she had always seemed too delicate, too vulnerable, for me to think of suggesting a casual sexual relationship with her. She had seemed too clever and too intelligent for me to deceive her about my intentions or my worth as a person. And I imagined I relished the kind of restraint there was between us because it was so altogether personal and not one placed upon us by any element or segment of society, or by any outside circumstances whatever. It kept coming to my mind as we stood waiting for an answer to the pressure on each doorbell that she was the girl I ought and wanted to be marrying. I realized the absolute folly of such thoughts and the utter impossibility of any such conclusion to present events. But still such feelings and thoughts had kept swimming in and out of my head all that day. I kept seeing Lee Ann in my mind's eye and hearing her soft, somewhat husky voice. I kept imagining how her figure would appear in the doorway before us. I saw her slender ankles, her small breasts, her head of ash-blond hair, which had a way of seeming to fall about her face when she talked but which with one shake of her head she could throw back into perfect place. But of course when the door opened there was the inevitable landlady or mother or friend. And when the next day came and I saw Caroline rolling up her sleeves, so to speak, to pitch in and settle this matter once and for all, then my thoughts and fantasies of the day before seemed literally like something out of a dream that I might have had.

The first two girls Caroline had wanted to see were the two that she very definitely remembered having met when I had taken her—'on a lark'—to my favorite night spots. She caught them both before they went to work that morning, and I was asked to wait in the car. I felt like an idiot waiting out there in the car, because I knew I'd been seen from some window as I gingerly hopped out and opened the door for Caroline when she got out—and opened it again when she returned. But there was no way around it. I waited out there, playing the car radio even at the risk of running down the battery.

When she came back from seeing the first girl, whose name was Lucy Phelan, Caroline was very angry. She reported that Lucy Phelan had pretended not to remember ever having met her. Moreover, Lucy had pretended that she knew Lee Ann Deehart only slightly and had no idea where she could be or what her disappearance meant. As Caroline fumed and I started up the car, I was picturing Lee Ann quietly tiptoeing out the backdoor of Lucy's rooming house just as Lucy was telling Caroline she scarcely knew the girl or while she was insisting that she didn't remember Caroline. As Caroline came back down the walk from the big Victorian house to the car, Lucy, who had stepped out onto the narrow porch that ran across the front of the house and around one corner of it, squatted down on her haunches at the top of the wooden porch steps and waved to me from behind Caroline's back. Though I knew it was no good, I pretended not to see her there. As I put the car into second gear and we sped away down the block, I took a quick glance back at the house. Lucy was still standing on the porch and waving to me the way one waves to a little child. She knew I had seen her stooping and waving moments before. And knew I would be stealing a glance now.

For a short time Caroline seemed undecided about calling on the second girl. But she decided finally to press on. Lucy Phelan she remembered meeting at The Cellar. The next girl, Betsy Morehouse, she had met at The Jungle and at a considerably more recent time. Caroline was a dog fancier in those days and she recalled a conversation with Betsy about the mounted dogs' heads that adorned the walls of The Jungle. They both had been outraged. When she mentioned this to me there in the car, I realized for the first time that by trying to make these girls acknowledge an acquaintance with her she had hoped to make them feel she was almost one of them and that they would thus be more likely to confide in her. But she failed with Betsy Morehouse, too. Betsy lived in an apartment house—an old residence, that is, converted into apartments—and when Caroline got inside the entrance-hall door she met Betsy, who was just then coming down the stairs. Betsy carried a purse and was wearing a fur coat and overshoes. When Caroline got back to the car and told me about it, I could not help feeling that Betsy had had a call from Lucy Phelan and even perhaps that Lee Ann herself was hiding in her apartment, having just arrived there from Lucy's. Because Betsy didn't offer to take Caroline back upstairs to her apartment for a talk. Instead, they sat down on two straight-backed chairs in the entrance hall and exchanged their few words there. Betsy at once denied the possibility of Caroline's ever having met her before. She denied that she had, herself, ever been to The Jungle. I knew this to be a lie, of course, but I didn't insist upon it to Caroline. I said that perhaps both she and I were mistaken about Betsy's being there on the night I had taken Caroline. As soon as Caroline saw she would learn nothing from Betsy, she got up and began to make motions of leaving. Betsy followed her to the door. But upon seeing my car out at the curb—so Caroline believed—she turned back, saying that she had remembered a telephone call she had to make. Caroline suspected that the girl didn't want to have to face me with her lie. That possibly was true. But my thought was that Betsy just might, also, have a telephone call she wanted to make.

There was now no question about Caroline's wanting to proceed to the third girl's house. This was the girl I had told her about having had a real affair with—the one I had gone with before Lee Ann and I had become friends. Caroline knew that she and Fern Morris had never met, but she counted on a different psychology with Fern. Most probably she had hoped it wouldn't be necessary for her to go to see Fern. She had been sure that one of those two other girls would give her the lead she needed. But as a last resort she was fully prepared to call on Fern Morris and to take me into the house with her.

Fern was a girl who still lived at home with her mother. She was in no sense a mama's girl or even a home-loving girl, since she was unhappy unless she went out on a date every night of her life. Perhaps she was not so clever and not so intellectual as most of her friends—if reading books, that is, on psychology and on China and every new volume of Andre Maurois indicated intellectuality. And though she was not home-loving, I suppose you would have to say she was more domestic than the other girls were. She had never 'held down' a job. Rather, she stayed at home in the daytime and kept house for her mother, who was said to 'hold down' a high-powered job under Boss Crump down at City Hall. Mrs Morris was a very sensible woman, who put no restrictions on her grown-up daughter and was glad to have her as a housekeeper. She used to tell me what a good cook and housekeeper Fern was and how well fixed she would leave her when she died. I really believe Mrs Morris hoped our romance might end in matrimony, and, as a matter of fact, it was when I began to suspect that Fern, too, was entertaining such notions that I stopped seeing her and turned my attentions to Lee Ann Deehart.

Mrs Morris still seemed glad to see me when I arrived at their bungalow that morning with Caroline and when I proceeded to introduce Caroline to her as my fiancée. Fern herself greeted me warmly. In fact, when I told her that Caroline and I were going to be married (though she must certainly have already read about it in the newspaper) she threw her arms about my neck and kissed me, 'Oh, Natty,' she said, 'I'm so happy for you. Really I am. But poor Lee Ann.' And in later life, especially in recent years, whenever Caroline has thought I was being silly about some other woman, usually a woman she considers her mental and social inferior, she has delighted in addressing me as 'Natty.' On more than one such occasion I have even had her say to me, 'I am so happy for you, Natty. Really I am.'

The fact is, Mrs Morris was just leaving the house for work when we arrived. And so there was no delay in Caroline's interview with Fern. 'I assume you know about Lee Ann's disappearance?' Caroline began as soon as we had seated ourselves in the little front parlor, with which I was very familiar.

'Of course I do,' said Fern, looking at me and laughing gleefully.

'You think it's a laughing matter, then?' Caroline asked.

'I do indeed. It's all a big joke,' Fern said at once. It was as though she had her answers all prepared. 'And a very successful joke it is.'

'Successful?' both Caroline and I asked. We looked at each other in dismay.

'It's only my opinion, of course. But I think she only wants to make you two suffer.'

'Suffer?' I said. This time Caroline was silent.

Fern was now addressing me directly. 'Everybody knows Caroline is not going to marry you until Lee Ann turns up safe.'

'Everybody?' Both of us again.

'Everybody in the world practically,' said Fern.

Caroline's face showed no expression. Neither, I believe, did mine.

'Fern, do you know where Lee Ann is?' Caroline asked gently.

Fern Morris, her eyes on me, shook her head, smiling.

'Do you know where her people are?' Caroline asked. 'And whether she's with them or hiding with her friends?'

Fern shook her head again, but now she gazed directly at Caroline. 'I'm not going to tell you anything!' she asserted. But after a moment she took a deep breath and said, still looking at Caroline, 'You're a smart girl. I think you'll likely be going to Lee Ann's room in that place where she lives. If you do go there, and if you are a smart girl, you'll look in the left-hand drawer of Lee Ann's dressing table.' Fern had an uneasy smile on her face after she had spoken, as if Caroline had got her to say something she hadn't really meant to say, as if she felt guilty for what she had just done.

Caroline had us out of there in only a minute or so and on our way to Lee Ann's rooming house.

It was a red-brick bungalow up in north Memphis. It looked very much like the one that Fern lived in but was used as a rooming house. When Mrs Troxler opened the front door to us, Caroline said, 'We're friends of Lee Ann's, and she wants us to pack a suitcase and bring it to her.'

'You know where she is, then?' Mrs Troxler asked. 'Hello, Nat.' she said, looking at me over Caroline's shoulder.

'Hello, Mrs Troxler,' I said. I was so stunned by what I had just heard Caroline say that I spoke in a whisper.

'She's with her mother—or with her family, at least,' Caroline said. By now she had slipped into the hallway, and I had followed without Mrs Troxler's really inviting us in.

'Where are her family?' Mrs Troxler asked, giving way to Caroline's forward thrust. 'She never volunteered to tell me anything about them. And I never think it's my business to ask.'

Caroline nodded her head at me, indicating that I should lead the way to Lee Ann's room. I knew that her room was toward the back of the house and I headed in that direction.

'I'll have to unlock the room for you,' said Mrs Troxler. 'There have been a number of people coming here and wanting to look about her room. And so I keep it locked.'

'A number of people?' asked Caroline casually.

'Yes. Nat knows. There were the police. And then there were some other gentlemen. Nat knows about it, though he didn't come in. And there were two other girls. The girls just seemed idly curious, and so I've taken to locking the door. Where do her people live?'

'I don't know,' said Caroline. 'She's going to meet us down town at the bus station and take a bus.'

When Mrs Troxler had unlocked the door she asked, 'Is Lee Ann all right? Do you think she will be coming back here?'

'She's fine,' Caroline said, 'and I'm sure she'll be coming back. She just wants a few things.'

'Yes, I've wondered how she's been getting along without a change of clothes. I'll fetch her suitcase. I keep my roomers' luggage in my storage closet down the hall.' We waited till she came back with a piece of plaid luggage, and then we went into the room and closed the door. Caroline went to the oak dresser and began pulling things out and stuffing them in the bag. I stood by, watching, hardly able to believe what I saw Caroline doing. When she had closed the bag, she looked up at me as if to say, 'What are you waiting for?' She had not gone near the little mahogany dressing table, and I had not realized that was going to be my part. I went over and opened the left-hand drawer. The only thing in the drawer was a small snapshot. I took it up and examined it carefully. I said nothing to Caroline, just handed her the picture. Finally I said, 'Do you know who that is? And where the picture was taken?' She recognized the woman with the goiter who ran The Cellar. The picture had been taken with Mrs Power standing in one of the flower beds against the side of the house. The big cut stones of the house were unmistakable. After bringing the snapshot up close to her face and peering into it for ten seconds or so, Caroline looked at me and said, 'That's her family.'

By the time we had stopped the car in front of The Cellar, I had told Caroline all that I knew about Lee Ann's schooling and about how it was that, though she had a 'family' in Memphis, no one had known her when she was growing up. She had been to one boarding school in Shreveport, Louisiana, to one in East Texas, and to still another in St Charles, Missouri. I had heard her make references to all

of those schools. 'They kept her away from home,' Caroline speculated. 'And so when she had finished school she wasn't prepared for the
kind of "family" she had. That's why she moved out on them and
lived in a rooming house.'

She reached that conclusion while I was parking the car at the
curb, near the front entrance to the house. Meanwhile, I was preparing myself mentally to accompany Caroline to the door of the old
woman's living quarters, which were on the main floor and above The
Cellar. But Caroline rested her hand on the steering wheel beside
mine and said, 'This is something I have to do without you.'

'But I'd like to see Lee Ann if she's here,' I said.

'I know you would,' said Caroline. 'Of course you would.'

'But, Caroline,' I said, 'I've made it clear that ours was an innocent—'

'I know,' she said. 'That's why I don't want you to see her again.'
Then she took Lee Ann's bag and went up to the front entrance of the
house.

The main entrance to The Cellar was to the side of and underneath
the high front stoop of the old house. Caroline had to climb a flight of
ten or twelve stone steps to reach the door to the residence. From the
car I saw a vague figure appear at one of the first-floor windows. I was
relatively certain that it was Lee Ann I saw. I could barely restrain
myself from jumping from the car and running up that flight of steps
and forcing myself past Caroline and into the house. During the hundred hours or so since she had fled into the woods of Overton Park,
Lee Ann Deehart had come to represent feelings of mine that I didn't
try to comprehend. The notion I had had yesterday that I was in love
with her and wanted to marry her didn't really adequately express the
emotions that her disappearance had stirred in me. I felt that I had
never looked at her really or had any conception of what sort of
person she was or what her experience in life was like. Now it seemed
I would never know. I suddenly realized—at that early age—that there
was experience to be had in life that I might never know anything
about except through hearsay and through books. I felt that this was
my last moment to reach out and understand something of the world
that was other than my own narrow circumstances and my own

narrow nature. When, nearly fifteen years later, I came into a comfortable amount of money—after my father's death—I made my extraordinary decision to go back to the university and prepare myself to become a teacher. But I knew then, at thirty-seven, that I was only going to try to comprehend intellectually the world about me and beyond me and that I had failed somehow at some time to reach out and grasp direct experience of a larger life which no amount of intellectualizing could compensate for. It may be that the moment of my great failure was when I continued to sit there in the car and did not force my way into the house where the old woman with the goiter lived and where it now seemed Lee Ann had been hiding for four days.

I was scarcely aware of the moment when the big front door opened and Caroline was admitted to the house. She was in there for nearly an hour. During that time I don't know what thoughts I had. It was as though I ceased to exist for the time that Lee Ann Deehart and Caroline Braxley were closeted together. When Caroline reappeared on the high stone stoop of the house, I was surprised to see she was still carrying Lee Ann's suitcase. But she would soon make it all clear. It *was* Lee Ann who received her at the door. No doubt she had seen that Caroline was carrying her own piece of luggage. And no doubt Caroline had counted on just that mystification and its efficacy, because Caroline is an extremely clever psychologist when she sets her mind to it. At any rate, in that relatively brief interview between them Caroline learned that all she had surmised about Lee Ann was true. Moreover, she learned that Lee Ann had fled the scene of the accident because she feared that the publicity would reveal to everyone who her grandmother was.

Lee Ann had crossed the little strip of snow-covered golf course and had entered the part of the woods where the old-forest trees were. And something had made her want to remain there for a while. She didn't know what it was. She had leaned against one of the trees, feeling quite content. It had seemed to her that she was not alone in the woods. And whatever the other presences were, instead of interfering with her reflections they seemed to wish to help her clear her thoughts. She stood there for a long time—perhaps for an hour or more. At any rate, she remained there until all at once she realized how cold she had grown and realized that she had no choice but to go back to the real world. Yet she wasn't going back to her room or to her pretty possessions there. That wasn't the kind of freedom she wanted any longer. She was going back to her grandmother. But still she hoped to avoid the publicity that the accident might bring. She decided to go, first of all, and stay with some of her friends, so that her grandmother would not suppose she was only turning to her because she was in trouble. And while making this important change in her life she felt she must be protected by her friends. She wanted to have an interval of time to herself and she wanted, above all, not to be bothered during that time by the silly society boy in whose car she had been riding.

During the first days she had gone from one girl's house to another. Finally she went to her grandmother. In the beginning she had, it was true, been mightily depressed. That was why she had telephoned me to start with, and had wanted someone to cheer her up. But during these four days she had much time for thinking and had overcome all her depression and had no other thought but to follow through with the decision to go and live openly with her old grandmother in her quarters above The Cellar.

Caroline also, in that single interview, learned other things about Lee Ann which had been unknown to me. She learned that Lee Ann's own mother had abandoned her in infancy to her grandmother but had always through the years sent money back for her education. She had had—the mother—an extremely successful career as a buyer for a woman's clothing store in Lincoln, Nebraska. But she had never tried to see her daughter and had never expressed a wish to see her. The only word she ever sent was that the children were not her dish, but that she didn't want it on her conscience that, because of her, some little girl in Memphis, Tennessee, had got no education and was therefore the domestic slave of some man. When Caroline told me all of this about the mother's not caring to see the daughter, it brought from her her first emotional outburst with regard to the whole business. But that was at a later time. The first thing she had told me when she returned to the car was that once Lee Ann realized that her place of hiding could no longer be concealed, she was quickly and easily persuaded to speak to the newspaper editor on the telephone and to tell him that she was safe and well. But she did this only after Caroline had first spoken to the editor herself, and obtained a promise from him that there would be no embarrassing publicity for Lee Ann's grand-mother.

The reason Caroline had returned with Lee Ann's suitcase was that Lee Ann had emptied it there in her grandmother's front parlor and had asked that we return to her rooming house and bring all of her possessions to her at her grandmother's. We obliged her in this, making appropriate, truthless explanations to her landlady, whom Lee Ann had meanwhile telephoned and given whatever little authority Mrs Troxler required in order to let us remove her things. It seemed to me that the poor woman scarcely listened to the explanations we gave. Another girl was already moving into the room before we had well got Lee Ann's things out. When we returned to the grandmother's house with these possessions in the car, Caroline insisted upon making an endless number of trips into the house, carrying everything herself. She was firm in her stipulation that Lee Ann and I not see each other again.

The incident was closed then. I could be certain that there would be no broken engagement—not on Caroline's initiative. But from that point—from that afternoon—my real effort and my real concern would be to try to understand why Caroline had not been so terribly enraged or so sorely wounded upon first discovering that there had been another girl with me in the car at the time of the accident, and by the realization that I had not immediately disclosed her presence, that she had not at least once threatened to end the engagement. What her mental processes had been during the past four days, know-ing now as I did that she was the person with whom I was going to spend the rest of my life, became of paramount interest to me.

But at that age I was so unquestioning of human behavior in general and so accepting of events as they came, and so without perception or reflection regarding the binding and molding effect upon people of the circumstances in which they are born, that I actually might not have found Caroline's thoughts of such profound interest and so vitally important to be understood had not Caroline, as soon as we were riding down Adams Street and were out of sight of The Cellar and of Mrs Power's great stone house above it, suddenly requested that I drive her out to the Bristol Highway, and once we were on the Bristol Highway asked me to drive as fast and as far out of town as I could or would, to drive and drive until she should beg me to turn around and take her home; and had she not, as soon as we were out of town and beyond city speed limits, where I could press down on the accelerator and send us flying along the three-lane strip of concrete which cut through the endless expanse of cotton fields and swamps on either side, had she not then at last, after talking quietly about Lee Ann's mother's sending back the money for her education, burst into weeping that began with a kind of wailing and grinding of teeth that one ordinarily associates more with a very old person in very great physical pain, a wailing that became mixed almost immediately with a sort of hollow laughter in which there was no mirth. I commenced slowing the car at once. I was searching for a place where I could pull off to the side of the road. But through her tears and her harsh, dry laughter she hissed at me, 'Don't stop! Don't stop! Go on. Go on. Go as far and as fast as you can, so that I can forget this day and put it forever behind me!' I obeyed her and sped on, reaching out my right hand to hold her two hands that were resting in her lap and were making no effort to wipe away her tears. I was not looking at her—only thinking thoughts of a kind I had never before had. It was the first time I had ever witnessed a victim of genuine hysteria. Indeed, I wasn't to hear such noises again until six or seven years later, during the Second World War. I heard them from men during days after a battle, men who had stood with great bravery against the enemy—particularly, as I remember now, men who had been brought back from the first onslaught of the Normandy invasion, physically whole but shaken in their souls. I think that during the stress of the four previous days Caroline Braxley had shed not a tear of self-pity or of shame and had not allowed herself a moment of genuine grief for my possible faithlessness to her. She had been far too busy with thinking—with thinking her thoughts of how to cope with Lee Ann's unexplained disappearance, with, that is, its possible effect upon her own life. But now the time had come when her checked emotions could be checked no longer.

The Bristol Highway, along which we were speeding as she wept hysterically, was a very straight and a very wide roadway for those days. It went northeast from Memphis. As its name implied, it was the old road that shot more or less diagonally across the long hinterland that is the state of Tennessee. It was the road along which many of our ancestors had first made their way from Virginia and the Carolinas to Memphis, to settle in the forest wilderness along the bluffs above the Mississippi River. And it occurred to me now that when Caroline said go as fast and as far as you can she really meant to take us all the way back into our past and begin the journey all over again, not merely from a point of four days ago or from the days of our childhood but from a point in our identity that would require a much deeper delving and a more radical return.

When we had got scarcely beyond the outskirts of Memphis, the most obvious signs of her hysteria had abated. Instead, however, she began to speak with a rapidity and in tones I was not accustomed to in her speech. This began after I had seen her give one long look over her shoulder and out the rear window of the car. Sensing some significance in that look and sensing some connection between it and the monologue she had now launched upon, I myself gave one glance into the rearview mirror. What met my eye was the skyline of modern Memphis beyond the snow-covered suburban rooftops—the modern Memphis of 1937, with its two or three high-rise office buildings. It was not clear to me immediately what there was in that skyline to inspire all that followed. She was speaking to me openly about Lee Ann and about her own feelings of jealousy and resentment of the girl—of *that* girl and of all those other girls, too, whose names and personalities and way of life had occupied our thoughts and had seemed to threaten our future during the four-day crisis that had followed my accident in the park.

'It isn't only Lee Ann that disturbs me,' she said. 'It began with her, of course. It began not with what she might be to you but with her freedom to jump out of your car, her freedom *from* you, her freedom to run off into the woods—with her capacity, which her special way of living provided her, simply to vanish, to remove herself from the eyes of the world, literally to disappear from the glaring light of day while the whole world, so to speak, looked on.'

'*You* would like to be able to do that?' I interrupted. It seemed so unlike her role as I understood it.

'*Any*body would, wouldn't they?' she said, not looking at me but at the endless stretch of concrete that lay straight ahead. '*Men* have always been able to do it,' she said. 'In my own family, for as many generations back as our family stories go, there have been men who seemed to disappear from the face of the earth just because they wanted to. They used to write "Gone to Texas" on the front door and leave the house and the farm to be sold for taxes. They walked out on dependent old parents and on sweethearts or even on wives and little children. And though they were considered black sheep for doing so, they were something of heroes, too. It seemed romantic to the rest of us that they had gone Out West somewhere and got a new start or had begun life over. But there was never a woman in our family who did that! There was no way it could happen. Or perhaps in some rare instance it did happen and the story hasn't come down to us. Her name simply isn't recorded in our family annals or reported in stories told around the fire. The assumption of course is that she is a streetwalker in Chicago or she resides in a red-plush whorehouse in Cheyenne. But with girls like Lee Ann and Lucy and Betsy it's all different. They have made their break with the past. Each of them had had the strength and intelligence to make the break for herself. But now they have formed a sort of league for their own protection. How I do admire and envy them! And how little you understand them, Nat. How little you understand Lee Ann's loneliness and depression and bravery. She and all the others are wonderful—even Fern. They occupy the real city of Memphis as none of the rest of us do. They treat men just as they please. And not the way men are treated in *our* circles. And men like them better for it. Those girls have learned to enjoy life together and to be mutually protective, but they enjoy a protection also, I hope you have observed, a kind of communal protection, from men who admire their very independence, from a league of men, mind you, not from individual men, from the police and from men like my father and your father, from men who would never say openly how much they admire them. Naturally we fear them. Those of us who are not like them in temperament—or in intelligence, because there is no use in denying it—we must fear them and find a means to give delaying action. And of course the only way we know is the age-old way!'

She became silent for a time now. But I knew I was going to hear what I had been waiting to hear. If I had been the least bit impatient with her explanation of Lee Ann and her friends, it was due in part to my impatience to see if she would explain *herself* to me. We were now speeding along the Bristol Highway at the very top speed the car would go. Except when we were passing through some crossroad or village I consciously kept the speed above ninety. In those days there was no speed limit in Tennessee. There were merely signs placed every so often along the roadside saying 'Speed Limit: Please Drive Carefully.' I felt somehow that, considering Caroline's emotional state and my own tension, it would be altogether unreasonable, it would constitute careless and unsafe driving, for me to reduce our speed to anything below the maximum capability of the car. And when we did of necessity slow down for some village or small town it was precisely at though we had arrived at some at once familiar and strange point in the past. And on each occasion I think we both experienced a sense of danger and disappointment. It was as though we expected to experience a satisfaction in having gone so far. But the satisfaction was not to be had. When we had passed that point, I felt only the need to press on at an even greater speed. And so we drove on and on, at first north and east through the wintry cotton land and cornland, past the old Orgill Plantation, the mansion house in plain view, its round brick columns on which the plaster was mostly gone, and now and then another white man's antebellum house, and always at the roadside or on the horizon, atop some distant ridge, a variety of black men's shacks and cabins, each with a little streamer of smoke rising from an improvised tin stovepipe or from an ill-made brick chimney bent away from the cabin at a precarious angle.

We went through the old villages of Arlington and Mason and the town of Brownsville—down streets of houses with columned porticoes and double galleries—and then we turned south to Bolivar, whose very name told you when it was built, and headed back to Memphis through Grand Junction and La Grange. (Mississippi towns

really, though north of the Tennessee line.) I had slowed our speed
after Bolivar, because that was where Caroline began her second
monologue. The tone and pace of her speech were very different
now. Her speech was slow and deliberate, her emotions more under
control than usual, as she described what she had felt and thought in
the time since the accident and explained how she came to reach the
decision to take the action she had—that is, action toward searching
out and finding Lee Ann Deehart. Though I had said nothing on the
subject of what she had done about Lee Ann and not done about our
engagement, expressed no request or demand for any explanation
unless it was by my silence, when she spoke now it was almost as
though Caroline were making a courtroom defense of accusations
hurled at her by me. 'I finally saw there was only one thing for me to
do and saw why I had to do it. I saw that the only power in the world
I had for saving myself lay in my saving you. And I saw that I could
only save you by "saving" Lee Ann Deehart. At first, of course, I
though I would have to break our engagement, or at least postpone
the wedding for a year. That's what *every*body thought, of course—
everybody in the family.'

'Even your father and mother?' I could not help interjecting. It had
seemed to me that Caroline's parents had—of all people—been most
sympathetic to me.

'Yes, even my mother and father,' she went on, rather serenely now.
'They could not have been more sympathetic to you personally.
Mother said that, after all, you were a mere man. Father said that, after
all, you were only human. But circumstances were circumstances, and
if some disaster had befallen Lee Ann, if she was murdered or if she
was pregnant or if she was a suicide or whatever other horror you can
conjure up, and it all came out, say, on our wedding day or came out
afterward, for that matter—well, what then? *They* and *I* had to think
of that. On the other hand, as I kept thinking, what if the wedding was
called off? What then for me? The only power I had to save myself was
to save you, and to save you by rescuing Lee Ann Deehart. It always
came to that, and comes to that still. Don't you see, it was a question
of how very much I had to lose and how little power I had to save
myself. Because *I* had not set *my*self free the way those other girls have.

One makes that choice at a much earlier age than this, I'm afraid. And so I knew already, Nat, and I know now what the only kind of power I can ever have must be.'

She hesitated then. She was capable of phrasing what she said much more precisely. But it would have been indelicate, somehow, for her to have done so. And so I said it for her in my crude way: 'You mean the power of a woman in a man's world.'

She nodded and continued. 'I had to protect *that*. Even if it had been *I* that broke our engagement, Nat, or even if you and I had been married before some second scandal broke, still I would have been a jilted, a rejected girl. And some part of my power to protect myself would be gone forever. Power, or strength, is what everybody must have some of if he—if she—is to survive in any kind of world. I have to protect and use whatever strength I have.'

Caroline went on in that voice until we were back in Memphis and at her father's house on East Parkway. She kissed me before we got out of the car there, kissed me for my silence, I believe. I had said almost nothing during the whole of the long ride. And I think she has ever since been grateful to me for the silence I kept. Perhaps she mistook it for more understanding than I was capable of at the time. At any rate, I cannot help believing that it has much to do with the support and understanding—rather silent though it was—which she gave me when I made the great break in my life in my late thirties. Though it clearly meant that we must live on a somewhat more modest scale and live among people of a sort she was not used to, and even meant leaving Memphis forever behind us, the firmness with which she supported my decision, and the look in her eyes whenever I spoke of feeling I must make the change, seemed to say to me that she would dedicate her pride of power to the power of freedom I sought.

1979

Rosa

CYNTHIA OZICK

Rosa Lublin, a madwoman and a scavenger, gave up her store—she smashed it up herself—and moved to Miami. It was a mad thing to do. In Florida she became a dependent. Her niece in New York sent her money and she lived among the elderly, in a dark hole, a single room in a 'hotel.' There was an ancient dresser-top refrigerator and a one-burner stove. Over in a corner a round oak table brooded on its heavy pedestal, but it was only for drinking tea. Her meals she had elsewhere, in bed or standing at the sink—sometimes toast with a bit of sour cream and half a sardine, or a small can of peas heated in a Pyrex mug. Instead of maid service there was a dumbwaiter on a shrieking pulley. On Tuesdays and Fridays it swallowed her meager bags of garbage. Squads of dying flies blackened the rope. The sheets on her bed were just as black—it was a five-block walk to the laundromat. The streets were a furnace, the sun an executioner. Every day without fail it blazed and blazed, so she stayed in her room and ate two bites of a hard-boiled egg in bed, with a writing board on her knees; she had lately taken to composing letters.

She wrote sometimes in Polish and sometimes in English, but her niece had forgotten Polish; most of the time Rosa wrote to Stella in English. Her English was crude. To her daughter Magda she wrote in the most excellent literary Polish. She wrote on the brittle sheets of abandoned stationery that inexplicably turned up in the cubbyholes of a blistered old desk in the lobby. Or she would ask the Cuban girl in the receptionist's cage for a piece of blank billing paper. Now and then she would find a clean envelope in the lobby bin; she would meticulously rip its seams and lay it out flat: it made a fine white square, the fresh face of a new letter.

The room was littered with these letters. It was hard to get them mailed—the post office was a block farther off than the laundromat, and the hotel lobby's stamp machine had been marked 'Out of Order' for years. There was an oval tin of sardines left open on the sink counter since yesterday. Already it smelled vomitous. She felt she was in hell. 'Golden and beautiful Stella,' she wrote to her niece. 'Where I put myself is in hell. Once I thought the worst was the worst, after that nothing could be the worst. But now I see, even after the worst there's still more.' Or she wrote: 'Stella, my angel, my dear one, a devil climbs into you and ties up your soul and you don't even know it.'

To Magda she wrote: 'You have grown into a lioness. You are tawny and you stretch apart your furry toes in all their power. Whoever steals you steals her own death.'

Stella had eyes like a small girl's, like a doll's. Round, not big but pretty, bright skin underneath, fine pure skin above, tender eyebrows like rainbows and lashes as rich as embroidery. She had the face of a little bride. You could not believe from all this beauty, these doll's eyes, these buttercup lips, these baby's cheeks, you could not believe in what harmless containers the bloodsucker comes.

Sometimes Rosa had cannibal dreams about Stella: she was boiling her tongue, her ears, her right hand, such a fat hand with plump fingers, each nail tended and rosy, and so many rings, not modern rings but old-fashioned junkshop rings. Stella liked everything from Rosa's junkshop, everything used, old, lacy with other people's history. To pacify Stella, Rosa called her Dear One, Lovely, Beautiful; she called her Angel; she called her all these things for the sake of peace, but in reality Stella was cold. She had no heart. Stella, already nearly fifty years old, the Angel of Death.

The bed was black, as black as Stella's will. After a while Rosa had no choice, she took a bundle of laundry in a shopping cart and walked to the laundromat. Though it was only ten in the morning, the sun was killing. Florida, why Florida? Because here they were shells like herself, already fried from the sun. All the same she had nothing in common with them. Old ghosts, old socialists: idealists. The Human Race was all they cared for. Retired workers, they went to lectures, they frequented the damp and shadowy little branch library. She saw them walking with Tolstoy under their arms, with Dostoyevsky. They knew good material. Whatever you wore they would feel between their fingers and give a name to: faille, corduroy, herringbone, shantung, jersey, worsted, velour, crepe. She heard them speak of bias, grosgrain, the 'season,' the 'length.' Yellow they called mustard. What was pink to everyone else, to them was sunset; orange was tangerine; red, hot tomato. They were from the Bronx, from Brooklyn, lost neighborhoods, burned out. A few were from West End Avenue. Once she met an ex-vegetable-store owner from Columbus Avenue; his store was on Columbus Avenue, his residence not far, on West Seventieth Street, off Central Park. Even in the perpetual garden of Florida, he reminisced about his flowery green heads of romaine lettuce, his glowing strawberries, his sleek avocados.

It seemed to Rosa Lublin that the whole peninsula of Florida was weighted down with regret. Everyone had left behind a real life. Here they had nothing. They were all scarecrows, blown about under the murdering sunball with empty rib cages.

In the laundromat she sat on a cracked wooden bench and watched the round porthole of the washing machine. Inside, the surf of detergent bubbles frothed and slapped her underwear against the pane.

An old man sat cross-legged beside her, fingering a newspaper. She looked over and saw that the headlines were all in Yiddish. In Florida the men were of higher quality than the women. They knew a little more of the world, they read newspapers, they lived for international affairs. Everything that happened in the Israeli Knesset they followed. But the women only recited meals they used to cook in their old lives—kugel, pirogen, latkes, blintzes, herring salad. Mainly the women thought about their hair. They went to hairdressers and came out into the brilliant day with plantlike crowns the color of zinnias. Sea-green paint on the eyelids. One could pity them: they were in love with rumors of their grandchildren, Katie at Bryn Mawr, Jeff at Princeton. To the grandchildren Florida was a slum, to Rosa it was a zoo.

She had no one but her cold niece in Queens, New York.

'Imagine this,' the old man next to her said. 'Just look, first he has Hitler, then he has Siberia, he's in a camp in Siberia! Next thing he gets away to Sweden, then he comes to New York and he peddles. He's a peddler, by now he's got a wife, he's got kids, so he opens a little store—just a little store, his wife is a sick woman, it's what you call a bargain store—'

'What?' Rosa said.

'A bargain store on Main Street, a place in Westchester, not even the Bronx. And they come in early in the morning, he didn't even hang out his shopping bags yet, robbers, muggers, and they choke him, they finish him off. From Siberia he lives for this day!'

Rosa said nothing.

'An innocent man alone in his store. Be glad you're not up there anymore. On the other hand, here it's no paradise neither. Believe me, when it comes to muggers and stranglers, there's no utopia nowhere.'

'My machine's finished,' Rosa said. 'I have to put in the dryer.' She knew about newspapers and their evil reports: a newspaper item herself. WOMAN AXES OWN BIZ. Rosa Lublin, 59, owner of a secondhand furniture store on Utica Avenue, Brooklyn, yesterday afternoon deliberately demolished . . . The *News* and the *Post*. A big photograph, Stella standing near with her mouth stretched and her arms wild. In the *Times*, six lines.

'Excuse me, I notice you speak with an accent.'

Rosa flushed. 'I was born somewhere else, not here.'

'I also was born somewhere else. You're a refugee? Berlin?'

'Warsaw.'

'I'm also from Warsaw! 1920 I left. 1906 I was born.'

'Happy birthday,' Rosa said. She began to pull her things out of the washing machine. They were twisted into each other like mixed-up snakes.

'Allow me,' said the old man. He put down his paper and helped her untangle. 'Imagine this,' he said. 'Two people from Warsaw meet in Miami, Florida. In 1910 I didn't dream of Miami, Florida.'

'My Warsaw isn't your Warsaw,' Rosa said.

'As long as your Miami, Florida, is my Miami, Florida.' Two whole long rows of glinting dentures smiled at her; he was proud to be a flirt.

Together they shoved the snarled load into the dryer. Rosa put in two quarters, and the thundering hum began. They heard the big snaps on the belt of her dress with the blue stripes, the one that was torn in the armpit, under the left sleeve, clanging against the caldron's metal sides.

'You read Yiddish?' the old man said.

'No.'

'You can speak a few words maybe?'

'No.' My Warsaw isn't your Warsaw. But she remembered her grandmother's cradle-croonings: her grandmother was from Minsk. *Unter Reyzls vigele shteyt a klorvays tsigele.* How Rosa's mother despised those sounds! When the drying cycle ended, Rosa noticed that the old man handled the clothes like an expert. She was ashamed for him to touch her underpants. *Under Rosa's cradle there's a clear-white little goat . . .* But he knew how to find a sleeve, wherever it might be hiding.

'What is it,' he asked, 'you're bashful?'

'No.'

'In Miami, Florida, people are more friendly. What,' he said, 'you're still afraid? Nazis we ain't got, even Ku Kluxers we ain't got. What kind of person are you, you're still afraid?'

'The kind of person,' Rosa said, 'is what you see. Thirty-nine years ago I was somebody else.'

'Thirty-nine years ago I wasn't so bad myself. I lost my teeth without a single cavity,' he bragged. 'Everything perfect. Periodontal disease.'

'*I* was a chemist almost. A physicist,' Rosa said. 'You think I wouldn't have been a scientist?' The thieves who took her life! All at once the landscape behind her eyes fell out of control: a bright field flashed; then a certain shadowy corridor leading to the laboratory supplies closet. The closet opened in her dreams also. Always she was hurtling down a veiled passage toward the closet. Retorts and microscopes were ranged on the shelves. Once, walking there, she was conscious of the coursing of her own ecstasy—her new brown shoes, laced and sober, her white coat, her hair cut short in bangs: a serious person of seventeen, ambitious, responsible, a future Marie Curie! One of her teachers in the high school praised her for what he said was a 'literary style'—oh, lost and kidnapped Polish!—and now she wrote and spoke English as helplessly as this old immigrant. From Warsaw! Born 1906! She imagined what bitter ancient alley, dense with stalls, cheap clothes strung on outdoor racks, signs in jargoned Yiddish. Anyhow they called her refugee. The Americans couldn't tell her apart from this fellow with his false teeth and his dewlaps and his rakehell reddish toupee bought God knows when or where—Delancey Street, the Lower East Side. A dandy. Warsaw! What did he know? In school she had read Tuwim: such delicacy, such loftiness, such *Polishness.* The Warsaw of her girlhood: a great light: she switched it on, she wanted to live inside her eyes. The curve of the legs of her mother's bureau. The strict leather smell of her father's desk. The white tile tract of the kitchen floor, the big pots breathing, a narrow tower stair next to the attic . . . the house of her girlhood laden with a thousand books. Polish, German, French; her father's Latin books; the shelf of shy literary periodicals her mother's poetry now and then wandered through, in short lines like heated telegrams. Cultivation, old civilization, beauty, history! Surprising turnings of streets, shapes of venerable cottages, lovely aged eaves, unexpected and gossamer turrets, steeples, the gloss, the antiquity! Gardens. Whoever speaks of Paris has never seen Warsaw. Her father, like her mother, mocked at Yiddish; there was not a particle of ghetto left in him, not a grain of rot. Whoever yearns for an aristocratic sensibility, let him switch on the great light of Warsaw.

'Your name?' her companion said.

'Lublin, Rosa.'

'A pleasure,' he said. 'Only why backwards? I'm an application form? Very good. You apply, I accept.' He took command of her shopping cart. 'Wherever is your home is my direction that I'm going anyhow.'

'You forgot to take your laundry,' Rosa said.

'Mine I did day before yesterday.'

'So why did you come here?'

'I'm devoted to Nature. I like the sound of a waterfall. Wherever it's cool it's a pleasure to sit and read my paper.'

'What a story!' Rosa snorted.

'All right, so I go to have a visit with the ladies. Tell me, you like concerts?'

'I like my own room, that's all.'

'A lady what wants to be a hermit!'

'I got my own troubles,' Rosa said.

'Unload on me.'

In the street she plodded beside him dumbly; a led animal. Her shoes were not nice, she should have put on the other ones. The sunlight was smothering—cooked honey dumped on their heads: one lick was good, too much could drown you. She was glad to have someone to pull the cart.

'You got internal warnings about talking to a stranger? If I say my name, no more a stranger. Simon Persky. A third cousin to Shimon Peres, the Israeli politician. I have different famous relatives, plenty of family pride. You ever heard of Betty Bacall, who Humphrey Bogart the movie star was married to, a Jewish girl? Also a distant cousin. I could tell you the whole story of my life experience, beginning with Warsaw. Actually it wasn't Warsaw, it was a little place a few miles out of town. In Warsaw I had uncles.'

Rosa said again, 'Your Warsaw isn't my Warsaw.'

He stopped the cart. 'What is this? A song with one stanza? You think I don't know the difference between generations? I'm seventy-one, and you, you're only a girl.'

'Fifty-eight.' Though in the papers, when they told how she smashed up her store, it came out fifty-nine. Stella's fault, Stella's black will, the Angel of Death's arithmetic.

'You see? I told you! A girl!'

'I'm from an educated family.'

'Your English ain't better than what any other refugee talks.'

'Why should I learn English? I didn't ask for it, I got nothing to do with it.'

'You can't live in the past,' he advised. Again the wheels of the cart were squealing. Like a calf, Rosa followed. They were approaching a self-service cafeteria. The smells of eggplant, fried potatoes, mush-rooms, blew out as if pumped. Rosa read the sign:

KOLLINS KOSHER KAMEO:

EVERYTHING ON YOUR PLATE AS PRETTY AS A PICTURE:

REMEMBRANCES OF NEW YORK AND THE

PARADISE OF YOUR MATERNAL KITCHEN:

DELICIOUS DISHES OF AMBROSIA AND NOSTALGIA:

AIR CONDITIONED THRU-OUT

'I know the owner,' Persky said. 'He's a big reader. You want tea?'
'Tea?'

'Not iced. The hotter the better. This is physiology. Come in,
you'll cool off. You got some red face, believe me.'

Rosa looked in the window. Her bun was loose, strings dangling on
either side of her neck. The reflection of a ragged old bird with worn
feathers. Skinny, a stork. Her dress was missing a button, but maybe
the belt buckle covered this shame. What did she care? She thought of
her room, her bed, her radio. She hated conversation.

'I got to get back,' she said.

'An appointment?'

'No.'

'Then have an appointment with Persky. So come, first tea. If you
take with an ice cube, you're involved in a mistake.'

They went in and chose a tiny table in a corner—a sticky disk on
a wobbly plastic pedestal. 'You'll stay, I'll get,' Persky said.

She sat and panted. Silverware tapped and clicked all around. No
one here but old people. It was like the dining room of a convalescent
home. Everyone had canes, dowager's humps, acrylic teeth, shoes cut
out for bunions. Everyone wore an open collar showing mottled skin,
ferocious clavicles, the wrinkled foundations of wasted breasts. The
air-conditioning was on too high; she felt the cooling sweat licking
from around her neck down, down her spine into the crevice of her
bottom. She was afraid to shift; the chair had a wicker back and a black
plastic seat. If she moved even a little, an odor would fly up: urine, salt,
old woman's fatigue. She left off panting and shivered. What do I care?
I'm used to everything. Florida, New York, it doesn't matter. All the
same, she took out two hairpins and caught up the hanging strands;
she shoved them into the core of her gray knot and pierced them

through. She had no mirror, no comb, no pocketbook; not even a handkerchief. All she had was a Kleenex pushed into her sleeve and some coins in the pocket of her dress.

'I came out only for the laundry,' she told Persky—with a groan he set down a loaded tray: two cups of tea, a saucer of lemon slices, a dish of eggplant salad, bread on what looked like a wooden platter but was really plastic, another plastic platter of Danish. 'Maybe I didn't bring enough to pay.'

'Never mind, you got the company of a rich retired taxpayer. I'm a well-off man. When I get my Social Security, I spit on it.'

'What line of business?'

'The same what I see you got one lost. At the waist. Buttons. A shame. That kind's hard to match, as far as I'm concerned we stopped making them around a dozen years ago. Braided buttons is out of style.'

'Buttons?' Rosa said.

'Buttons, belts, notions, knickknacks, costume jewelry. A factory. I thought my son would take it over but he wanted something different. He's a philosopher, so he became a loiterer. Too much education makes fools. I hate to say it, but on account of him I had to sell out. And the girls, whatever the big one wanted, the little one also. The big one found a lawyer, that's what the little one looked for. I got one son-in-law in business for himself, taxes, the other's a youngster, still on Wall Street.'

'A nice family,' Rosa bit off.

'A loiterer's not so nice. Drink while it's hot. Otherwise it won't reach to your metabolism. You like eggplant salad on top of bread and butter? You got room for it, rest assured. Tell me, you live alone?'

'By myself,' Rosa said, and slid her tongue into the tea. Tears came from the heat.

'My son is over thirty, I still support him.'

'My niece, forty-nine, not married, she supports me. '

'Too old. Otherwise I'd say let's make a match with my son, let her support him too. The best thing is independence. If you're able-bodied, it's a blessing to work.' Persky caressed his chest. 'I got a bum heart.'

Rosa murmured, 'I had a business, but I broke it up.'

'Bankruptcy?'

'Part with a big hammer,' she said meditatively, 'part with a piece of construction metal I picked up from the gutter.'

'You don't look that strong. Skin and bones.'

'You don't believe me? In the papers they said an ax, but where would I get an ax? '

'That's reasonable. Where would you get an ax?' Persky's finger removed an obstruction from under his lower plate. He examined it: an eggplant seed. On the floor near the cart there was something white, a white cloth. Handkerchief. He picked it up and stuffed it in his pants pocket. Then he said, 'What kind of business?'

'Antiques. Old furniture. Junk. I had a specialty in antique mirrors. Whatever I had there, I smashed it. See,' she said, '*now* you're sorry you started with me!'

'I ain't sorry for nothing,' Persky said. 'If there's one thing I know to understand, it's mental episodes. I got it my whole life with my wife.'

'You're not a widower?'

'In a manner of speaking.'

'Where is she?'

'Great Neck, Long Island. A private hospital, it don't cost me peanuts.' He said, 'She's in a mental condition.'

'Serious?'

'It used to be once in a while, now it's a regular thing. She's mixed up that she's somebody else. Television stars. Movie actresses. Different people. Lately my cousin, Betty Bacall. It went to her head.'

'Tragic,' Rosa said.

'You see? I unloaded on you, now you got to unload on me.'

'Whatever I would say, you would be deaf.'

'How come you smashed up your business?'

'It was a store. I didn't like who came in it.'

'Spanish? Colored?'

'What do I care who came? Whoever came, they were like deaf people. Whatever you explained to them, they didn't understand.' Rosa stood up to claim her cart. 'It's very fine of you to treat me to the Danish, Mr. Persky. I enjoyed it. Now I got to go.'

'I'll walk you.'

'No, no, sometimes a person feels to be alone.'

'If you're alone too much,' Persky said, 'you think too much.'

'Without a life,' Rosa answered, 'a person lives where they can. If all they got is thoughts, that's where they live.'

'You ain't got a life?'

'Thieves took it.'

She toiled away from him. The handle of the cart was a burning rod. A hat, I ought to have worn a hat! The pins in her bun scalded her scalp. She panted like a dog in the sun. Even the trees looked exhausted: every leaf face downward under a powder of dust. Summer without end, a mistake!

In the lobby she waited before the elevator. The 'guests'—some had been residents for a dozen years—were already milling around, groomed for lunch, the old women in sundresses showing their thick collarbones and the bluish wells above them. Instead of napes they had rolls of wide fat. They wore no stockings. Brazen blue-marbled sinews strangled their squarish calves; in their reveries they were again young women with immortal pillar legs, the white legs of strong goddesses; it was only that they had forgotten about impermanence. In their faces, too, you could see everything they were not noticing about themselves—the red gloss on their drawstring mouths was never meant to restore youth. It was meant only to continue it. Flirts of seventy. Everything had stayed the same for them: intentions, actions, even expectations—they had not advanced. They believed in the seamless continuity of the body. The men were more inward, running their lives in front of their eyes like secret movies.

A syrup of cologne clogged the air. Rosa heard the tearing of envelopes, the wing-shudders of paper sheets. Letters from children: the guests laughed and wept, but without seriousness, without belief. Report-card marks, separations, divorces, a new coffee table to match the gilt mirror over the piano, Stuie at sixteen learning to drive, Millie's mother-in-law's second stroke, rumors of the cataracts of half-remembered acquaintances, a cousin's kidney, the rabbi's ulcer, a daughter's indigestion, burglary, perplexing news of East Hampton parties, psychoanalysis . . . the children were rich, how was this possible from such poor parents? It was real and it was not real. Shadows on a wall; the shadows stirred, but you could not penetrate the wall. The guests were detached; they had detached themselves. Little by little they were forgetting their grandchildren, their aging children. More and more they were growing significant to themselves. Every wall of the lobby a mirror. Every mirror hanging thirty years. Every table surface a mirror. In these mirrors the guests appeared to themselves as they used to be, powerful women of thirty, striving fathers of thirty-five, mothers and fathers of dim children who had migrated long ago, to other continents, inaccessible landscapes, incomprehensible vocabularies. Rosa made herself brave; the elevator gate opened, but she let the empty car ascend without her and pushed the cart through to where the black Cuban receptionist sat, maneuvering clayey sweat balls up from the naked place between her breasts with two fingers.

'Mail for Lublin, Rosa,' Rosa said.

'Lublin, you lucky today. Two letters.'

'Take a look where you keep packages also.'

'You a lucky dog, Lublin,' the Cuban girl said, and tossed an object into the pile of wash.

Rosa knew what was in that package. She had asked Stella to send it; Stella did not easily do what Rosa asked. She saw immediately that the package was not registered. This angered her: Stella the Angel of Death! Instantly she plucked the package out of the cart and tore the wrapping off and crumpled it into a standing ashtray. Magda's shawl! Suppose, God forbid, it got lost in the mail, what then? She squashed the box into her breasts. It felt hard, heavy; Stella had encased it in some terrible untender rind; Stella had turned it to stone. She wanted to kiss it, but the maelstrom was all around her, pressing toward the dining room. The food was monotonous and sparse and often stale; still, to eat there increased the rent. Stella was all the time writing that she was not a millionaire; Rosa never ate in the dining room. She kept the package tight against her bosom and picked through the crowd, a sluggish bird on ragged toes, dragging the cart.

In her room she breathed noisily, almost a gasp, almost a squeal, left the laundry askew in the tiny parody of a vestibule, and carried the box and the two letters to the bed. It was still unmade, fish-smelling, the covers knotted together like an umbilical cord. A shipwreck. She let herself down into it and knocked off her shoes—oh, they were scarred; that Persky must have seen her shame, first the missing button, afterward the used-up shoes. She turned the box round and round—a rectangular box. Magda's shawl! Magda's swaddling cloth. Magda's shroud. The memory of Magda's smell, the holy fragrance of the lost babe. Murdered. Thrown against the fence, barbed, thorned, electrified; grid and griddle; a furnace, the child on fire! Rosa put the shawl to her nose, to her lips. Stella did not want her to have Magda's shawl all the time; she had such funny names for having it—trauma, fetish, God knows what: Stella took psychology courses at the New School at night, looking for marriage among the flatulent bachelors in her classes.

One letter was from Stella and the other was one of those university letters, still another one, another sample of the disease. But in the box, Magda's shawl! The box would be last, Stella's fat letter first (fat meant trouble), the university letter did not matter. A disease. Better to put away the laundry than to open the university letter.

Dear Rosa [Stella wrote]:

All right, I've done it. Been to the post office and mailed it. Your idol is on its way, separate cover. Go on your knees to it if you want. You make yourself crazy, everyone thinks you're a crazy woman. Whoever goes by your old store still gets glass in their soles. You're the older one, I'm the niece, I shouldn't lecture, but my God! It's thirty years, forty, who knows, give it a rest. It isn't as if I don't know just exactly how you do it, what it's like. What a scene, disgusting! You'll open the box and take it out and cry, and you'll kiss it like a crazy person. Making holes in it with kisses. You're like those people in the Middle Ages who worshiped a piece of the True Cross, a splinter from some old outhouse as far as anybody knew, or else they fell down in front of a single hair supposed to be some saint's. You'll kiss, you'll pee tears down your face, and so what? Rosa, by now, believe me, it's time, you have to have a life.

Out loud Rosa said: 'Thieves took it.'
And she said: 'And you, Stella, *you* have a life?'

If I were a millionaire I'd tell you the same thing: get a job. Or
else, come back and move in here. I'm away the whole day, it
will be like living alone if that's what you want. It's too hot to
look around down there, people get like vegetables. With everything you did for me I don't mind keeping up this way maybe
another year or so, you'll think I'm stingy for saying it like that,
but after all I'm not on the biggest salary in the world.

Rosa said, 'Stella! Would you be alive if I didn't take you out from
there? Dead. You'd be dead! So don't talk to me how much an old
woman costs! I didn't give you from my store? The big gold mirror,
you look in it at your bitter face—I don't care how pretty, even so it's
bitter—and you forget who gave you presents!'

And as far as Florida is concerned, well, it doesn't solve anything.
I don't mind telling you now that they would have locked you
up if I didn't agree to get you out of the city then and there. One
more public outburst puts you in the bughouse. No more public
scandals! For God's sake, don't be a crazy person! Live your life!

Rosa said again, 'Thieves took it,' and went, scrupulously, meticulously, as if possessed, to count the laundry in the cart.

A pair of underpants was missing. Once more Rosa counted everything: four blouses, three cotton skirts, three brassieres, one half-slip
and one regular, two towels, eight pairs of underpants . . . nine went
into the washing machine, the exact number. Degrading. Lost
bloomers—dropped God knows where. In the elevator, in the lobby,
in the street even. Rosa tugged, and the dress with the blue stripes slid
like a coarse colored worm out of twisted bedsheets. The hole in the
armpit was bigger now. Stripes, never again anything on her body with
stripes! She swore it, but this, fancy and with a low collar, was Stella's
birthday present, Stella bought it. As if innocent, as if ignorant, as if *not*

there. Stella, an ordinary American, indistinguishable! No one could guess what hell she had crawled out of until she opened her mouth and up coiled the smoke of accent.

Again Rosa counted. A fact, one pair of pants lost. An old woman who couldn't even hang on to her own underwear.

She decided to sew up the hole in the stripes. Instead she put water on to boil for tea and made the bed with the clean sheets from the cart. The box with the shawl would be the last thing. Stella's letter she pushed under the bed next to the telephone. She tidied all around. Everything had to be nice when the box was opened. She spread jelly on three crackers and deposited a Lipton's teabag on the Welch's lid. It was grape jelly, with a picture of Bugs Bunny elevating an officious finger. In spite of Persky's Danish, empty insides. Always Stella said: Rosa eats little by little, like a tapeworm in the world's belly.

Then it came to her that Persky had her underpants in his pocket.

Oh, degrading. The shame. Pain in the loins. Burning. Bending in the cafeteria to pick up her pants, all the while tinkering with his teeth. Why didn't he give them back? He was embarrassed. He had thought a handkerchief. How can a man hand a woman, a stranger, a piece of her own underwear? He could have shoved it right back into the cart, how would that look? A sensitive man, he wanted to spare her. When he came home with her underpants, what then? What could a man, half a widower, do with a pair of female bloomers? Nylon-plus-cotton, the long-thighed kind. Maybe he had filched them on purpose, a sex maniac, a wife among the insane, his parts starved. According to Stella, Rosa also belonged among the insane, Stella had the power to put her there. Very good, they would become neighbors, confidantes, she and Persky's wife, best friends. The wife would confess all of Persky's sexual habits. She would explain how it is that a man of this age comes to steal a lady's personal underwear. Whatever stains in the crotch are nobody's business. And not only that: a woman with children, Persky's wife would speak of her son and her married lucky daughters. And Rosa too, never mind how Stella was sour over it, she would tell about Magda, a beautiful young woman of thirty, thirty-one: a doctor married to a doctor; large

house in Mamaroneck, New York; two medical offices, one on the
first floor, one in the finished basement. Stella was alive, why not
Magda? Who was Stella, coarse Stella, to insist that Magda was not
alive? Stella the Angel of Death. Magda alive, the pure eyes, the
bright hair. Stella, never a mother, who was Stella to mock the kisses
Rosa put in Magda's shawl? She meant to crush it into her mouth.
Rosa, a mother the same as anyone, no different from Persky's wife in
the crazy house.

This disease! The university letter, like all of them—five, six post-
marks on the envelope. Rosa imagined its pilgrimage: first to the
News, the *Post*, maybe even the *Times*, then to Rosa's old store, then
to the store's landlord's lawyers, then to Stella's apartment, then to
Miami, Florida. A Sherlock Holmes of a letter. It had struggled to find
its victim, and for what? More eating alive.

DEPARTMENT OF CLINICAL SOCIAL PATHOLOGY

UNIVERSITY OF KANSAS—IOWA

April 17, 1977

Dear Ms Lublin:

Though I am not myself a physician, I have lately begun to
amass survivor data as rather a considerable specialty. To be concrete: I am presently working on a study, funded by the Minew
Foundation of the Kansas-Iowa Institute for Humanitarian
Context, designed to research the theory developed by Dr
Arthur R. Hidgeson and known generally as Repressed
Animation. Without at this stage going into detail, it may be of
some preliminary use to you to know that investigations so far
reveal an astonishing generalized minimalization during any
extended period of stress resulting from incarceration, exposure,
and malnutrition. We have turned up a wide range of neurolog-
ical residues (including, in some cases, acute cerebral damage,
derangement, disorientation, premature senility, etc.), as well as
hormonal changes, parasites, anemia, thready pulse, hyperventi-
lation, etc.; in children especially, temperatures as high as 108°,
ascitic fluid, retardation, bleeding sores on the skin and in the

mouth, etc. What is remarkable is that these are all *current conditions* in survivors and their families.

Disease, disease! Humanitarian Context, what did it mean? An excitement over other people's suffering. They let their mouths water up. Stories about children running blood in America from sores, what muck. Consider also the special word they used: *survivor.* Something new. As long as they didn't have to say *human being.* It used to be *refugee*, but by now there was no such creature, no more refugees, only survivors. A name like a number—counted apart from the ordinary swarm. Blue digits on the arm, what difference? They don't call you a woman anyhow. *Survivor.* Even when your bones get melted into the grains of the earth, still they'll forget *human being.* Survivor and survivor and survivor; always and always. Who made up these words, parasites on the throat of suffering!

For some months teams of medical paraphrasers have been conducting interviews with survivors, to contrast current medical paraphrase with conditions found more than three decades ago, at the opening of the camps. This, I confess, is neither my field nor my interest. My own concern, both as a scholar of social pathology and as a human being . . .

Ha! For himself it was good enough, for himself he didn't forget this word *human being*!

. . . is not with medical nor even with psychological aspects of survivor data.

Data. Drop in a hole!

What particularly engages me for purposes of my own participation in the study (which, by the way, is intended to be definitive, to close the books, so to speak, on this lamentable subject) is what I can only term the 'metaphysical' side of Repressed Animation (R.A.). It begins to be evident that prisoners gradually came to Buddhist positions. They gave up craving and began to function in terms of non-functioning, i.e., non-attachment. The Four Noble Truths in Buddhist thought, if I may remind you, yield a penetrating summary of the fruit of craving: pain. 'Pain' in this view is defined as ugliness, age, sorrow, sickness, despair, and, finally, birth. Non-attachment is attained through the Eightfold Path, the highest stage of which is the cessation of all human craving, the loftiest rapture, one might say, of consummated indifference.

It is my hope that these speculations are not displeasing to you. Indeed, I further hope that they may even attract you, and that you would not object to joining our study by means of an in-depth interview to be conducted by me at, if it is not inconvenient, your home. I should like to observe survivor syndroming within the natural setting.

Home. Where, where?

As you may not realize, the national convention of the American Association of Clinical Social Pathology has this year, for reasons of fairness to our East Coast members, been moved from Las Vegas to Miami Beach. The convention will take place at a hotel in your vicinity about the middle of next May, and I would be deeply grateful if you could receive me during that period. I have noted via a New York City newspaper (we are not so provincial out here as some may think!) your recent removal to Florida; consequently you are ideally circumstanced to make a contribution to our R.A. study. I look forward to your consent at your earliest opportunity.

> Very sincerely yours,
> James W. Tree, Ph.D.

Drop in a hole! Disease! It comes from Stella, everything! Stella saw what this letter was, she could see from the envelope—Dr. Stella! Kansas-Iowa Clinical Social Pathology, a fancy hotel, this is the cure for the taking of a life! Angel of Death!

With these university letters Rosa had a routine: she carried the scissors over to the toilet bowl and snipped little bits of paper and flushed. In the bowl going down, the paper squares whirled like wedding rice.

But this one: drop in a hole with your Four Truths and your Eight Paths together! Non-attachment! She threw the letter into the sink; also its crowded envelope ('Please forward,' Stella's handwriting instructed, pretending to be American, leaving out the little stroke that goes across the 7); she lit a match and enjoyed the thick fire. Burn, Dr Tree, burn up with your Repressed Animation! The world is full of Trees! The world is full of fire! Everything, everything is on fire! Florida is burning!

Big flakes of cinder lay in the sink: black foliage, Stella's black will. Rosa turned on the faucet and the cinders spiraled down and away. Then she went to the round oak table and wrote the first letter of the day to her daughter, her healthy daughter, her daughter who suffered neither from thready pulse nor from anemia, her daughter who was a professor of Greek philosophy at Columbia University in New York City, a stone's throw—the philosopher's stone that prolongs life and transmutes iron to gold—from Stella in Queens!

Magda, my Soul's Blessing [Rosa wrote]:

Forgive me, my yellow lioness. Too long a time since the last writing. Strangers scratch at my life; they pursue, they break down the bloodstream's sentries. Always there is Stella. And so half a day passes without my taking up my pen to speak to you. A pleasure, the deepest pleasure, home bliss, to speak in our own language. Only to you. I am always having to write to Stella now, like a dog paying respects to its mistress. It's my obligation. She sends me money. She, whom I plucked out of the claws of all those Societies that came to us with bread and chocolate after the liberation! Despite everything, they were selling sectarian ideas; collecting troops for their armies. If not for me they would have shipped Stella with a boatload of orphans to Palestine, to become God knows what, to live God knows how. A field worker jabbering Hebrew. It would serve her right.

Americanized airs. My father was never a Zionist. He used to
call himself a 'Pole by right.' The Jews, he said, didn't put a
thousand years of brains and blood into Polish soil in order to
have to prove themselves to anyone. He was the wrong sort of
idealist, maybe, but he had the instincts of a natural nobleman. I
could laugh at that now—the whole business—but I don't,
because I feel too vividly what he was, how substantial, how not
given over to any light-mindedness whatever. He had Zionist
friends in his youth. Some left Poland early and lived. One is a
bookseller in Tel Aviv. He specializes in foreign texts and periodicals. My poor little father. It's only history—an ad hoc
instance of it, you might say—that made the Zionist answer.
My father's ideas were more logical. He was a Polish patriot on
a temporary basis, he said, until the time when nation should lie
down beside nation like the lily and the lotus. He was at bottom
a prophetic creature. My mother, you know, published poetry.
To you all these accounts must have the ring of pure legend.

Even Stella, who *can* remember, refuses. She calls me a para-
ble-maker. She was always jealous of you. She has a strain of
dementia, and resists you and all other reality. Every vestige of
former existence is an insult to her. Because she fears the past she
distrusts the future—it, too, will turn into the past. As a result she
has nothing. She sits and watches the present roll itself up into
the past more quickly than she can bear. That's why she never
found the one thing she wanted more than anything, an
American husband. I'm immune to these pains and panics.
Motherhood—I've always known this—is a profound distraction
from philosophy, and all philosophy is rooted in suffering over
the passage of time. I mean the *fact* of motherhood, the physio-
logical fact. To have the power to create another human being,
to be the instrument of such a mystery. To pass on a whole
genetic system. I don't believe in God, but I believe, like the
Catholics, in mystery. My mother wanted so much to convert;
my father laughed at her. But she was attracted. She let the maid
keep a statue of the Virgin and Child in the corner of the
kitchen. Sometimes she used to go in and look at it. I can even

remember the words of a poem she wrote about the heat coming up from the stove, from the Sunday pancakes—

> Mother of God, how you shiver
> in these heat-ribbons!
> Our cakes rise to you
> and in the trance of His birthing
> you hide.

Something like that. Better than that, more remarkable. Her Polish was very dense. You had to open it out like a fan to get at all the meanings. She was exceptionally modest, but she was not afraid to call herself a symbolist.

I know you won't blame me for going astray with such tales. After all, you're always prodding me for these old memories. If not for you, I would have buried them all, to satisfy Stella. Stella Columbus! She thinks there's such a thing as the New World. Finally—at last, at last—she surrenders this precious vestige of your sacred babyhood. Here it is in a box right next to me as I write. She didn't take the trouble to send it by registered mail! Even though I told her and told her. I've thrown out the wrapping paper, and the lid is plastered down with lots of Scotch tape. I'm not hurrying to open it. At first my hunger was unrestrained and I couldn't wait, but nothing is nice now. I'm saving you; I want to be serene. In a state of agitation one doesn't split open a diamond. Stella says I make a relic of you. She has no heart. It would shock you if I told you even one of the horrible games I'm made to play with her. To soothe her dementia, to keep her quiet, I pretend you died. Yes! It's true! There's nothing, however crazy, I wouldn't say to her to tie up her tongue. She slanders. Everywhere there are slanders, and sometimes—my bright lips, my darling!— the slanders touch even you. My purity, my snowqueen!

I'm ashamed to give an example. Pornography. What Stella, that pornographer, has made of your father. She thieves all the truth, she robs it, she steals it, the robbery goes unpunished. She lies, and it's the lying that's rewarded. The New World!

That's why I smashed up my store! Because here they make up lying theories. University people do the same: they take human beings for specimens. In Poland there used to be justice; here they have social theories. Their system inherits almost nothing from the Romans, that's why. Is it a wonder that the lawyers are no better than scavengers who feed on the droppings of thieves and liars? Thank God you followed your grandfather's bent and studied philosophy and not law.

Take my word for it, Magda, your father and I had the most ordinary lives—by 'ordinary' I mean respectable, gentle, cultivated. Reliable people of refined reputation. His name was Andrzej. Our families had status. Your father was the son of my mother's closest friend. She was a converted Jew married to a Gentile: you can be a Jew if you like, or a Gentile, it's up to you. You have a legacy of choice, and they say choice is the only true freedom. We were engaged to be married. We would have been married. Stella's accusations are all Stella's own excretion. Your father was not a German. I was forced by a German, it's true, and more than once, but I was too sick to conceive. Stella has a naturally pornographic mind, she can't resist dreaming up a dirty sire for you, an S.S. man! Stella was with me the whole time, she knows just what I know. They never put me in their brothel either. Never believe this, my lioness, my snowqueen! No lies come out of me to you. You are pure. A mother is the source of consciousness, of conscience, the ground of being, as philosophers say. I have no falsehoods for you. Otherwise I don't deny some few tricks: the necessary handful. To those who don't deserve the truth, don't give it. I tell Stella what it pleases her to hear. My child, perished. Perished. She always wanted it. She was always jealous of you. She has no heart. Even now she believes in my loss of you: and you a stone's throw from her door in New York! Let her think whatever she thinks; her mind is awry, poor thing; in me the strength of your being consumes my joy. Yellow blossom! Cup of the sun!

What a curiosity it was to hold a pen—nothing but a small pointed stick, after all, oozing its hieroglyphic puddles: a pen that speaks, miraculously, Polish. A lock removed from the tongue. Otherwise the tongue is chained to the teeth and the palate. An immersion into the living language: all at once this cleanliness, this capacity, this power to make a history, to tell, to explain. To retrieve, to reprieve!

To lie.

The box with Magda's shawl was still on the table. Rosa left it there. She put on her good shoes, a nice dress (polyester, 'wrinkle-free' on the inside label); she arranged her hair, brushed her teeth, poured mouthwash on the brush, sucked it up through the nylon bristles, gargled rapidly. As an afterthought she changed her bra and slip; it meant getting out of her dress and into it again. Her mouth she reddened very slightly—a smudge of lipstick rubbed on with a finger.

Perfected, she mounted the bed on her knees and fell into folds. A puppet, dreaming. Darkened cities, tombstones, colorless garlands, a black fire in a gray field, brutes forcing the innocent, women with their mouths stretched and their arms wild, her mother's voice calling. After hours of these pitiless tableaux, it was late afternoon; by then she was certain that whoever put her underpants in his pocket was a criminal capable of every base act. Humiliation. Degradation. Stella's pornography!

To retrieve, to reprieve. Nothing in the elevator; in the lobby, nothing. She kept her head down. Nothing white glimmered up.

In the street, a neon dusk was already blinking. Gritty mixture of heat and toiling dust. Cars shot by like large bees. It was too early for headlights: in the lower sky two strange competing lamps—a scarlet sun, round and brilliant as a blooded egg yolk; a silk-white moon, gray-veined with mountain ranges. These hung simultaneously at either end of the long road. The whole day's burning struck upward like a moving weight from the sidewalk. Rosa's nostrils and lungs were cautious: burning molasses air. Her underpants were not in the road.

In Miami at night no one stays indoors. The streets are clogged with wanderers and watchers; everyone in search, bedouins with no fixed paths. The foolish Florida rains spray down—so light, so brief and fickle, no one pays attention. Neon alphabets, designs, pictures, flashing undiminished right through the sudden small rain. A quick lick of lightning above one of the balconied hotels. Rosa walked. Much Yiddish. Caravans of slow old couples, linked at the elbows, winding down to the cool of the beaches. The sand never at rest, always churning, always inhabited; copulation under blankets at night, beneath neon-radiant low horizons.

She had never been near the beach; why should her underpants be lost in the sand?

On the sidewalk in front of the Kollins Kosher Kameo, nothing. Shining hungry smell of boiled potatoes in sour cream. The pants were not necessarily in Persky's pocket. Dented garbage barrels, empty near the curb. Pants already smoldering in an ash heap, among blackened tomato cans, kitchen scrapings, conflagrations of old magazines. Or: a simple omission, an accident, never transferred from the washing machine to the dryer. Or, if transferred, never removed. Overlooked. Persky unblemished. The laundromat was locked up for the night, with a metal accordion gate stretched across the door and windows. What marauders would seek out caldrons, giant washtubs? Property misleads, brings false perspectives. The power to smash her own. A kind of suicide. She had murdered her store with her own hands. She cared more for a missing pair of underpants, lost laundry, than for business. She was ashamed; she felt exposed. What was her store? A cave of junk.

On the corner across the street from the laundromat, a narrow newspaper store, no larger than a stall. Persky might have bought his paper there. Suppose later in the day he had come down for an afternoon paper, her pants in his pocket, and dropped them?

Mob of New York accents. It was a little place, not air-conditioned.

'Lady? You're looking for something?'

A newspaper? Rosa had enough of the world.

'Look, it's like sardines in here, buy something or go out.'

'My store used to be six times the size of this place,' Rosa said.

'So go to your store.'

'I don't have a store.' She reconsidered. If someone wanted to hide—to hide, not destroy—a pair of underpants, where would he put

them? Under the sand. Rolled up and buried. She thought what a
weight of sand would feel like in the crotch of her pants, wet heavy
sand, still hot from the day. In her room it was hot, hot all night. No
air. In Florida there was no air, only this syrup seeping into the
esophagus. Rosa walked; she saw everything, but as if out of invention, out of imagination; she was unconnected to anything. She came
to a gate; a mottled beach spread behind it. It belonged to one of the
big hotels. The latch opened. At the edge of the waves you could
look back and see black crenellated forms stretching all along the
shore. In the dark, in silhouette, the towered hotel roofs held up
their merciless teeth. Impossible that any architect pleasurably
dreamed these teeth. The sand was only now beginning to cool.
Across the water the sky breathed a starless black; behind her, where
the hotels bit down on the city, a dusty glow of brownish red lowered.
Mud clouds. The sand was littered with bodies. Photograph of
Pompeii: prone in the volcanic ash. Her pants were under the sand; or
else packed hard with sand, like a piece of torso, a broken statue, the
human groin detached, the whole soul gone, only the loins left for
kicking by strangers. She took off her good shoes to save them and
nearly stepped on the sweated faces of two lovers plugged into a kiss.
A pair of water animals in suction. The same everywhere, along the
rim of every continent, this gurgling, foaming, trickling. A true
smasher, a woman whose underpants have been stolen, a woman
who has murdered her business with her own hands, would know
how to step cleanly into the sea. A horizontal tunnel. You can fall
into its pull just by entering it upright. How simple the night sea;
only the sand is unpredictable, with its hundred burrowings, its
thousand buryings.

When she came back to the gate, the latch would not budge. A
cunning design, it trapped the trespasser.

She gazed up, and thought of climbing; but there was barbed wire
on top.

So many double mounds in the sand. It was a question of choosing
a likely sentinel: someone who would let her out. She went back
down onto the beach again and tapped a body with the tip of her dangling shoe. The body jerked as if shot: it scrambled up.

'Mister? You know how to get out?'

'Room key does it,' said the second body, still flat in the sand. It was
a man. They were both men, slim and coated with sand; naked. The
one lying flat—she could see what part of him was swollen.

'I'm not from this hotel,' Rosa said.

'Then you're not allowed here. This is a private beach.'

'Can't you let me out?'

'Lady, please. Just buzz off,' the man in the sand said.

'I can't get out,' Rosa pleaded.

The man who was standing laughed.

Rosa persisted, 'If you have a key—'

'Believe me, lady, not for you'—muffled from below.

She understood. Sexual mockery. 'Sodom!' she hissed, and stumbled away. Behind her their laughter. They hated women. Or else they
saw she was a Jew; they hated Jews; but no, she had noticed the cir-
cumcision, like a jonquil, in the dim sand. Her wrists were trembling.
To be locked behind barbed wire! No one knew who she was; what
had happened to her; where she came from. Their gates, the terrible
ruse of their keys, wire brambles, men lying with men . . . She was
afraid to approach any of the other mounds. No one to help.
Persecutors. In the morning they would arrest her.

She put on her shoes again, and walked along the cement path that
followed the fence. It led her to light; voices of black men. A window.
Vast deep odors: kitchen exhaust, fans stirring soup smells out into the
weeds. A door wedged open by a milk-can lid. Acres of counters,
stoves, steamers, refrigerators, percolators, bins, basins. The kitchen of
a castle. She fled past the black cooks in their meat-blooded aprons,
through a short corridor: a dead end facing an elevator. She pushed
the button and waited. The kitchen people had seen her; would they
pursue? She heard their yells, but it was nothing to do with her—they
were calling Thursday, Thursday. On Thursday no more new potatoes.
A kind of emergency maybe. The elevator took her to the main floor,
to the lobby; she emerged, free.

This lobby was the hall of a palace. In the middle a real fountain. Water
springing out of the mouths of emerald-green dolphins. Skirted

cherubs, gilded. A winged mermaid spilling gold flowers out of a gold pitcher. Lofty plants—a forest—palms sprayed dark blue and silver and gold, leafing out of masses of green marble vessels at the lip of the fountain. The water flowed into a marble channel, a little indoor brook. A royal carpet for miles around, woven with crowned birds. Well-dressed men and women sat in lion-clawed gold thrones, smoking. A golden babble. How happy Stella would be, to stroll in a place like this! Rosa kept close to the walls.

She saw a man in a green uniform.

'The manager,' she croaked. 'I have to tell him something.'

'Office is over there.' He shrugged toward a mahogany desk behind a glass wall. The manager, wearing a red wig, was making a serious mark on a crested letterhead. Persky, too, had a red wig. Florida was glutted with fake fire, burning false hair! Everyone a piece of imposter. 'Ma'am?' the manager said.

'Mister, you got barbed wire by your beach.'

'Are you a guest here?'

'I'm someplace else.'

'Then it's none of your business, is it?'

'You got barbed wire.'

'It keeps out the riffraff.'

'In America it's no place for barbed wire on top of fences.'

The manager left off making his serious marks. 'Will you leave?' he said. 'Will you please just leave?'

'Only Nazis catch innocent people behind barbed wire,' Rosa said.

The red wig dipped. 'My name is Finkelstein.'

'Then you should know better!'

'Listen, walk out of here if you know what's good for you.'

'Where were you when we was there?'

'Get out. So far I'm asking nicely. Please get out.'

'Dancing in the pool by the lobby, that's where. Eat your barbed wire, Mr Finkelstein, chew it and choke on it!'

'Go home,' Finkelstein said.

'You got Sodom and Gomorrah in your back yard! You got gays and you got barbed wire!'

'You were trespassing on our beach,' the manager said. 'You want me to call the police? Better leave before. Some important guests have come in, we can't tolerate the noise, and I can't spare the time for this.'

'They write me letters all the time, your important guests. Conventions,' Rosa scoffed. 'Clinical Social Pathology, right? You got a Dr Tree staying?'

'Please go,' Finkelstein said.

'Come on, you got a Dr Tree? No? I'll tell you, if not today you'll get him later on, he's on the way. He's coming to investigate specimens. I'm the important one! It's me he's interviewing, Finkelstein, not you! I'm the study!'

The red wig dipped again.

'Aha!' Rosa cried. 'I see you got Tree! You got a whole bunch of Trees!'

'We protect the privacy of our guests.'

'With barbed wire you protect. It's Tree, yes? I can see I'm right! It's Tree! You got Tree staying here, right? Admit you got Tree! Finkelstein, you S.S., admit it!'

The manager stood up. 'Out,' he said. 'Get out now. Immediately.'

'Don't worry, it's all right. It's my business to keep away. Tree I don't need. With Trees I had enough, you don't have to concern yourself—'

'*Leave*,' said the red wig.

'A shame,' Rosa said, 'a Finkelstein like you.' Irradiated, triumphant, cleansed, Rosa marched through the emerald glitter, toward the illuminated marquee in front. HOTEL MARIE LOUISE, in green neon. A doorman like a British admiral, gold braid cascading from his shoulders. They had trapped her, nearly caught her; but she knew how to escape. Speak up, yell. The same way she saved Stella, when they were pressing to take her on the boat to Palestine. She had no fear of Jews; sometimes she had—it came from her mother, her father—a certain contempt. The Warsaw swarm, shut off from the grandeur of the true world. Neighborhoods of a particular kind. Persky and Finkelstein. 'Their' synagogues—balconies for the women. Primitive. Her own home, her own upbringing—how she had fallen. A loathsome tale of folk-sorcery: nobility turned into a small dun rodent. Cracking her teeth on the poison of English. Here they were shallow, they knew nothing. Light-minded. Stella looking, on principle, to be lightminded. Blue stripes, barbed wire, men embracing men . . . whatever was dangerous and repugnant they made prevalent, frivolous.

Lost. Lost. Nowhere. All of Miami Beach, empty; the sand, empty. The whole wild hot neon night city: an empty search. In someone's pocket.

Persky was waiting for her. He sat in the torn brown-plastic wing chair near the reception desk, one leg over the side, reading a newspaper.

He saw her come in and jumped up. He wore only a shirt and pants; no tie, no jacket. Informal.

'Lublin, Rosa!'

Rosa said, 'How come you're here?'

'Where you been the whole night? I'm sitting hours.'

'I didn't tell you where I stay,' Rosa accused.

'I looked in the telephone book.'

'My phone's disconnected, I don't know nobody. My niece, she writes, she saves on long distance.'

'All right. You want the truth? This morning I followed you, that's all. A simple walk from my place. I sneaked in the streets behind you. I found out where you stay, here I am.'

'Very nice,' Rosa said.

'You don't like it?'

She wanted to tell him he was under suspicion; he owed her a look in his jacket pocket. A self-confessed sneak who follows women. If not his jacket, his pants. But it wasn't possible to say a thing like this. Her pants in his pants. Instead she said, 'What do you want?'

He flashed his teeth. 'A date.'

'You're a married man.'

'A married man what ain't got a wife.'

'You got one.'

'In a manner of speaking. She's crazy.'

Rosa said, 'I'm crazy too.'

'Who says so?'

'My niece.'

'What does a stranger know?'

'A niece isn't a stranger.'

'My own son is a stranger. A niece definitely. Come on, I got my car nearby. Air-conditioned, we'll take a spin.'

'You're not a kid, I'm not a kid,' Rosa said.

'You can't prove it by me,' Persky said.

'I'm a serious person,' Rosa said. 'It isn't my kind of life, to run around noplace.'

'Who said noplace? I got a place in mind.' He considered. 'My Senior Citizens. Very nice pinochle.'

'Not interested,' Rosa said. 'I don't need new people.'

'Then a movie. You don't like new ones, we'll find dead ones. Clark Gable, Jean Harlow.'

'Not interested.'

'A ride to the beach. A walk on the shore, how about it?'

'I already did it,' Rosa said.

'When?'

'Tonight. Just now.'

'Alone?'

Rosa said, 'I was looking for something I lost.'

'Poor Lublin, what did you lose?'

'My life.'

She was all at once not ashamed to say this outright. Because of the missing underwear, she had no dignity before him. She considered Persky's life: how trivial it must always have been: buttons, himself no more significant than a button. It was plain he took her to be another button like himself, battered now and out of fashion, rolled into Florida. All of Miami Beach, a box for useless buttons!

'This means you're tired. Tell you what,' Persky said, 'invite me upstairs. A cup of tea. We'll make a conversation. You'll see, I got other ideas up my sleeve—tomorrow we'll go someplace and you'll like it.'

Her room was miraculously ready: tidy, clarified. It was sorted out: you could see where the bed ended and the table commenced. Sometimes it was all one jumble, a highway of confusion. Destiny had clarified her room just in time for a visitor. She started the tea. Persky put his newspaper down on the table, and on top of it an oily paper bag. 'Crullers!' he announced. 'I bought them to eat in the car, but this is very nice, cozy. You got a cozy place, Lublin.'

'Cramped,' Rosa said.

'I work from a different theory. For everything there's a bad way of describing, also a good way. You pick the good way, you get along better.'

'I don't like to give myself lies,' Rosa said.

'Life is short, we all got to lie. Tell me, you got paper napkins? Never mind, who needs them. Three cups! That's a lucky thing; usually when a person lives alone they don't keep so many. Look, vanilla icing, choco-late icing. Two plain also. You prefer with icing or plain? Such fine tea bags, they got style. Now you see, Lublin? Everything's nice!'

He had set the table. To Rosa this made the corner of the room look new, as if she had never seen it before.

'Don't let the tea cool off. Remember what I told you this morn-ing, the hotter the better,' Persky said; he clanged his spoon happily. 'Here, let's make more elbowroom—'

His hand, greasy from the crullers, was on Magda's box.

'Don't touch!'

'What's the matter? It's something alive in there? A bomb? A rabbit? It's squashable? No, I got it—a lady's hat!'

Rosa hugged the box; she was feeling foolish, trivial. Everything was frivolous here, even the deepest property of being. It seemed to her someone had cut out her life-organs and given them to her to hold. She walked the little distance to the bed—three steps—and set the box down against the pillow. When she turned around, Persky's teeth were persisting in their independent bliss.

'The fact is,' he said, 'I didn't expect nothing from you tonight. You got to work things through, I can see that. You remind me of my son. Even to get a cup of tea from you is worth something, I could do worse. Tomorrow we'll have a real appointment. I'm not inquiring, I'm not requesting. I'll be the boss, what do you say?'

Rosa sat. 'I'm thinking, I should get out and go back to New York to my niece—'

'Not tomorrow. Day after tomorrow you'll change your life, and tomorrow you'll come with me. We got six meetings to pick from.'

Rosa said doubtfully, 'Meetings?'

'Speakers. Lectures for fancy people like yourself. Something higher than pinochle.'

'I don't play,' Rosa acknowledged.

Persky looked around. 'I don't see no books neither. You want me to drive you to the library?'

A thread of gratitude pulled in her throat. He almost understood what she was: no ordinary button. 'I read only Polish,' she told him. 'I don't like to read in English. For literature you need a mother tongue.'

'*Li*terature, my my. Polish ain't a dime a dozen. It don't grow on trees neither. Lublin, you should adjust. Get used to it!'

She was wary: 'I'm used to everything.'

'Not to being a regular person.'

'My niece Stella,' Rosa slowly gave out, 'says that in America cats have nine lives, but we—we're less than cats, so we got three. The life before, the life during, the life after.' She saw that Persky did not follow. She said, 'The life after is now. The life before is our *real* life, at home, where we was born.'

'And during?'

'This was Hitler.'

'Poor Lublin,' Persky said.

'You wasn't there. From the movies you know it.' She recognized that she had shamed him; she had long ago discovered this power to shame. 'After, after, that's all Stella cares. For me there's one time only; there's no after.'

Persky speculated. 'You want everything the way it was before.'

'No, no, no,' Rosa said. 'It can't be. I don't believe in Stella's cats. Before is a dream. After is a joke. Only during stays. And to call it a life is a lie.'

'But it's over,' Persky said. 'You went through it, now you owe yourself something.'

'This is how Stella talks. Stella—' Rosa halted; then she came on the word. 'Stella is self-indulgent. She wants to wipe out memory.'

'Sometimes a little forgetting is necessary,' Persky said, 'if you want to get something out of life.'

'Get something! Get *what*?'

'You ain't in a camp. It's finished. Long ago it's finished. Look around, you'll see human beings.'

'What I see,' Rosa said, 'is bloodsuckers.'

Persky hesitated. 'Over there, they took your family?'

Rosa held up all the fingers of her two hands. Then she said: 'I'm left. Stella's left.' She wondered if she dared to tell him more. The box on the bed. 'Out of so many, three.'

Persky asked, 'Three?'

'Evidence,' Rosa said briskly. 'I can show you.'

She raised the box. She felt like a climber on the margin of a precipice. 'Wipe your hands.'

Persky obeyed. He rubbed the last of the cruller crumbs on his shirt front.

'Unpack and look in. Go ahead, lift up what's inside.'

She did not falter. What her own hands longed to do she was yielding to a stranger, a man with pockets; she knew why. To prove herself pure: a madonna. Supposing he had vile old man's thoughts: let him see her with the eye of truth. A mother.

But Persky said, 'How do you count three—'

'Look for yourself.'

He took the cover off and reached into the box and drew out a sheet of paper and began to skim it.

'That has to be from Stella. Throw it out, never mind. More scolding, how I'm a freak—'

'Lublin, you're a regular member of the intelligentsia! This is quite some reading matter. It ain't in Polish neither.' His teeth danced. 'On such a sad subject, allow me a little joke. Who came to America was one, your niece Stella; Lublin, Rosa, this makes two; and Lublin's brain—three!'

Rosa stared. 'I'm a mother, Mr. Persky,' she said, 'the same as your wife, no different.' She received the paper between burning palms. 'Have some respect,' she commanded the bewildered glitter of his plastic grin. And read:

Dear Ms Lublin:
    I am taking the liberty of sending you, as a token of my

good faith, this valuable study by Hidgeson (whom, you may recall, I mentioned in passing in my initial explanatory letter), which more or less lays the ethological groundwork for our current structures. I feel certain that—in preparation for our talks—you will want to take a look at it. A great deal of our work has been built on these phylogenetic insights. You may find some of the language a bit too technical; nevertheless I believe that simply having this volume in your possession will go far toward reassuring you concerning the professionalism of our endeavors, and of your potential contribution toward them.

Of special interest, perhaps, is Chapter Six, entitled 'Defensive Group Formation: The Way of the Baboons.'

Gratefully in advance,
James W. Tree, Ph.D.

Persky said, 'Believe me, I could smell with only one glance it wasn't from Stella.'

She saw that he was holding the thing he had taken out of the box. 'Give me that,' she ordered.

He recited: 'By A. R. Hidgeson. And listen to the title, something fancy—*Repressed Animation: A Theory of the Biological Ground of Survival.* I told you fancy! This isn't what you wanted?'

'Give it to me.'

'You didn't want? Stella sent you what you didn't want?'

'Stella sent!' She tore the book from him—it was heavier than she had guessed—and hurled it at the ceiling. It slammed down into Persky's half-filled teacup. Shards and droplets flew. 'The way I smashed up my store, that's how I'll smash Tree!'

Persky was watching the tea drip to the floor.

'Tree?'

'Dr Tree! Tree the bloodsucker!'

'I can see I'm involved in a mistake,' Persky said. 'I'll tell you what, you eat up the crullers. You'll feel better, and I'll come tomorrow when the mistake is finished.'

'I'm not your button, Persky! I'm nobody's button, not even if they got barbed wire everywhere!'

'Speaking of buttons, I'll go and push the elevator button. Tomorrow I'll come back.'

'Barbed wire! You took my laundry, you think I don't know that? Look in your dirty pockets, you thief Persky!'

In the morning, washing her face—it was swollen, nightmares like weeds, the bulb of her nose pale—Rosa found, curled inside a towel, the missing underwear.

She went downstairs to the desk; she talked over having her phone reconnected. Naturally they would charge more, and Stella would squawk. All the same, she wanted it.

At the desk they handed her a package; this time she examined the wrapping. It had come by registered mail and it was from Stella. It was not possible to be hoodwinked again, but Rosa was shocked, depleted, almost as if yesterday's conflagration hadn't been Tree but really the box with Magda's shawl.

She lifted the lid of the box and looked down at the shawl; she was indifferent. Persky, too, would have been indifferent. The colorless cloth lay like an old bandage; a discarded sling. For some reason it did not instantly restore Magda, as usually happened, a vivid thwack of restoration like an electric jolt. She was willing to wait for the sensation to surge up whenever it would. The shawl had a faint saliva smell, but it was more nearly imagined than smelled.

Under the bed the telephone vibrated: first a sort of buzz, then a real ring. Rosa pulled it out.

The Cuban's voice said: 'Missis Lublin, you connected now.'

Rosa wondered why it was taking so long for Magda to come alive. Sometimes Magda came alive with a brilliant swoop, almost too quickly, so that Rosa's ribs were knocked on their insides by copper hammers, clanging and gonging.

The instrument, still in her grip, drilled again. Rosa started: it was as if she had squeezed a rubber toy. How quickly a dead thing can come to life! Very tentatively, whispering into a frond, Rosa said, 'Hello?' It was a lady selling frying pans.

'No,' Rosa said, and dialed Stella. She could hear that Stella had been asleep. Her throat was softened by a veil. 'Stella,' Rosa said, 'I'm calling from my own room.'

'Who is this?'

'Stella, you don't recognize me?'

'Rosa! Did anything happen?'

'Should I come back?'

'My God,' Stella said, 'is it an emergency? We could discuss this by mail.'

'You wrote me I should come back.'

'I'm not a millionaire,' Stella said. 'What's the point of this call?'

'Tree's here.'

'Tree? What's that?'

'*Doctor* Tree. You sent me his letter, he's after me. By accident I found out where he stays.'

'No one's after you,' Stella said grimly.

Rosa said, 'Maybe I should come back and open up again.'

'You're talking nonsense. You *can't*. The store's finished. If you come back it has to be a new attitude absolutely, recuperated. The end of morbidness.'

'A very fancy hotel,' Rosa said. 'They spend like kings.'

'It's none of your business.'

'A Tree is none of my business? He gets rich on our blood! Prestige! People respect him! A professor with specimens! He wrote me baboons!'

'You're supposed to be recuperating,' Stella said; she was wide awake. 'Walk around. Keep out of trouble. Put on your bathing suit. Mingle. How's the weather?'

'In that case you come here,' Rosa said.

'Oh my God, I can't afford it. You talk like I'm a millionaire. What would I do down there?'

'I don't like it alone. A man stole my underwear.'

'Your *what?*' Stella squealed.

'My panties. There's plenty perverts in the streets. Yesterday in the sand I saw two naked men.'

'Rosa,' Stella said, 'if you want to come back, come back. I wrote you that, that's all I said. But you could get interested in something down there for a change. If not a job, a club. If it doesn't cost too much, I wouldn't mind paying for a club. You could join some kind of group, you could walk, you could swim—'

'I already walked.'

'Make friends.' Stella's voice tightened. 'Rosa, this is long *distance*.'

On that very phrase, 'long *distance*,' Magda sprang to life. Rosa took the shawl and put it over the knob of the receiver: it was like a little doll's head then. She kissed it, right over Stella's admonitions. 'Good-bye,' she told Stella, and didn't care what it had cost. The whole room was full of Magda: she was like a butterfly, in this corner and in that corner, all at once. Rosa waited to see what age Magda was going to be: how nice, a girl of sixteen; girls in their bloom move so swiftly that their blouses and skirts balloon; they are always butterflies at sixteen. There was Magda, all in flower. She was wearing one of Rosa's dresses from high school. Rosa was glad: it was the sky-colored dress, a middling blue with black buttons seemingly made of round chips of coal, like the unlit shards of stars. Persky could never have been acquainted with buttons like that, they were so black and so sparkling; original, with irregular facets like bits of true coal from a vein in the earth or some other planet. Magda's hair was still as yellow as buttercups, and so slippery and fine that her two barrettes, in the shape of cornets, kept sliding down toward the sides of her chin—that chin which was the marvel of her face; with a different kind of chin it would have been a much less explicit face. The jaw was ever so slightly too long, a deepened oval, so that her mouth, especially the lower lip, was not crowded but rather made a definite mark in the middle of spaciousness. Consequently the mouth seemed as significant as a body arrested in orbit, and Magda's sky-filled eyes, nearly rectangular at the corners, were like two obeisant satellites. Magda could be seen with great clarity. She had begun to resemble Rosa's father, who had also a long oval face anchored by a positive mouth. Rosa was enraptured by Magda's healthy forearms. She would have given everything to set her before an easel, to see whether she could paint in watercolors; or to have her seize a violin, or a chess queen; she knew little about Magda's mind at this age, or whether she had any talents; even what her intelligence tended toward. And also she was always a little suspicious of Magda, because of the other strain, whatever it was, that ran in her. Rosa herself was not truly suspicious, but Stella was, and that induced perplexity in Rosa. The other strain was ghostly, even dangerous. It was as if the peril hummed out from the filaments of Magda's hair, those narrow bright wires.

My Gold, my Wealth, my Treasure, my Hidden
Sesame, my Paradise, my Yellow Flower, my Magda!
Queen of Bloom and Blossom!

When I had my store I used to 'meet the public,' and I wanted to tell everybody—not only our story, but other stories as well. Nobody knew anything. This amazed me, that nobody remembered what happened only a little while ago. They didn't remember because they didn't know. I'm referring to certain definite facts. The tramcar in the Ghetto, for instance. You know they took the worst section, a terrible slum, and they built a wall around it. It was a regular city neighborhood, with rotting old tenements. They pushed in half a million people, more than double the number there used to be in that place. Three families, including all their children and old folks, into one apartment. Can you imagine a family like us—my father who had been the director-general of the Bank of Warsaw, my sheltered mother, almost Japanese in her shyness and refinement, my two young brothers, my older brother, and me—all of us, who had lived in a tall house with four floors and a glorious attic (you could touch the top of the house by sticking your arm far out its window; it was like pulling the whole green ribbon of summer indoors)—imagine confining *us* with teeming Mockowiczes and Rabinowiczes and Perskys and Finkelsteins, with all their bad-smelling grandfathers and their hordes of feeble children! The children were half dead, always sitting on boxes in tatters with such sick eyes, pus on the lids and the pupils too wildly lit up. All these families used up their energies with walking up and down, and bowing, and shaking and quaking over old rags of prayer books, and their children sat on the boxes and yelled prayers too.

We thought they didn't know how to organize themselves in adversity, and besides that, we were furious: because the same sort of adversity was happening to *us*—my father was a person of real importance, and my tall mother had so much delicacy and dignity that people would bow automatically, even before they knew who she was. So we were furious in every direction, but most immediately we were furious because we had to be billeted with such a class, with these old Jew peasants worn out from their rituals and superstitions, phylacteries on their foreheads sticking up so stupidly, like unicorn horns, every morning. And in the most repulsive slum, deep in slops and vermin and a toilet not fit for the lowest criminal. We were not of a background to show our fury, of course, but my father told my brothers and me that my mother would not be able to live through it, and he was right.

In my store I didn't tell this to everyone; who would have the patience to hear it all out? So I used to pick out one little thing here, one little thing there, for each customer. And if I saw they were in a hurry—most of them were, after I began—I would tell just about the tramcar. When I told about the tramcar, no one ever understood it ran on tracks! Everybody always thought of buses. Well, they couldn't tear up the tracks, they couldn't get rid of the overhead electric wire, could they? The point is they couldn't reroute the whole tram system; so, you know, they didn't. The tramcar came right through the middle of the Ghetto. What they did was build a sort of overhanging pedestrian bridge for the Jews, so they couldn't get near the tramcar to escape on it into the other part of Warsaw. The other side of the wall.

The most astounding thing was that the most ordinary streetcar, bumping along on the most ordinary trolley tracks, and carrying the most ordinary citizens going from one section of Warsaw to another, ran straight into the place of our misery. Every day, and several times a day, we had these witnesses. Every day they saw us—women with shopping sacks; and once I noticed a head of lettuce sticking up out of the top of a sack—

green lettuce! I thought my salivary glands would split with aching for that leafy greenness. And girls wearing hats. They were all the sort of plain people of the working class with slovenly speech who ride tramcars, but they were considered better than we, because no one regarded us as Poles anymore. And we, my father, my mother—we had so many pretty jugs on the piano and shining little tables, replicas of Greek vases, and one an actual archaeological find that my father had dug up on a school vacation in his teens, on a trip to Crete—it was all pieced together, and the missing parts, which broke up the design of a warrior with a javelin, filled in with reddish clay. And on the walls, up and down the corridors and along the stairs, we had wonderful ink drawings, the black so black and miraculous, how it measured out a hand and then the shadow of the hand. And with all this—especially our Polish, the way my parents enunciated Polish in soft calm voices with the most precise artic-ulation, so that every syllable struck its target—the people in the tramcar were regarded as Poles—well, they *were*, I don't take it away from them, though they took it away from us—and we were not! They, who couldn't read one line of Tuwim, never mind Virgil, and my father, who knew nearly the whole first half of the *Aeneid by* heart. And in this place now I am like the woman who held the lettuce in the tramcar. I said all this in my store, talking to the deaf. How I became like the woman with the lettuce.

Rosa wanted to explain to Magda still more about the jugs and the drawings on the walls, and the old things in the store, things that nobody cared about, broken chairs with carved birds, long strings of glass beads, gloves and wormy muffs abandoned in drawers. But she was tired from writing so much, even though this time she was not using her regular pen, she was writing inside a blazing flying current, a terrible beak of light bleeding out a kind of cuneiform on the under-side of her brain. The drudgery of reminiscence brought fatigue, she felt glazed, lethargic. And Magda! Already she was turning away. Away. The blue of her dress was now only a speck in Rosa's eye. Magda did not even stay to claim her letter: there it flickered, unfinished like an ember, and all because of the ringing from the floor near the bed. Voices, sounds, echoes, noise—Magda collapsed at any stir, fearful as a phantom. She behaved at these moments as if she was ashamed, and hid herself. Magda, my beloved, don't be ashamed! Butterfly, I am not ashamed of your presence: only come to me, come to me again, if no longer now, then later, always come. These were Rosa's private words; but she was stoic, tamed; she did not say them aloud to Magda. Pure Magda, head as bright as a lantern.

The shawled telephone, little grimy silent god, so long comatose—now, like Magda, animated at will, ardent with its cry. Rosa let it clamor once or twice and then heard the Cuban girl announce—oh, 'announce'!—Mr Persky: should he come up or would she come down? A parody of a real hotel!—of, in fact, the MARIE LOUISE, with its fountains, its golden thrones, its thorned wire, its burning Tree!

'He's used to crazy women, so let him come up,' Rosa told the Cuban. She took the shawl off the phone.

Magda was not there. Shy, she ran from Persky. Magda was away.

1983

The Age of
Grief

JANE SMILEY

Dana was the only woman in our freshman dental class, one of two that year in the whole dental school. The next year things changed, and a fifth of them were women, so maybe Professor Perl, who taught freshman biochemistry, didn't persist in his habit of turning to the only woman in the class and saying, 'Miss McManus, did you understand that?' assuming that if Dana got it, so had everyone else (male). In fact, Dana majored in biochemistry, and so her predictable nod of understanding was a betrayal to us all, and our class got the reputation among the faculty of being especially poor in biochemistry, a statistical anomaly, guys flunking out who would have passed any other year. Of course, Perl never blamed himself.

Dentists' offices are very neat, and dentists are always washing their hands, and so their hands are cool and white and right under the nose, to be smelled. People would be offended if dentists weren't as clean as possible, but they hold it against us. On television they always make us out to be prissy and compulsive. If a murder has been committed and a dentist is in the show, he will certainly have done it, and he will probably have lived with his mother well into his thirties, to boot. Actors who play dentists blink a lot.

Dentists on television never have people coming in like the man who came to me today. His teeth were hurting him over the weekend, and so he went out to his toolbox and found a pliers and began to pull them all out, with only some whiskey to kill the pain. Pulling teeth takes a lot of strength and a certain finesse, one of which the man had and the other of which he lacked. What drove him into my office today, after fifteen years away from the dentist, was twenty-four broken teeth, some in fragments below the gum line, some merely smashed around the crown. Teeth are important. Eskimo cultures used to abandon their old folks in the snow when their teeth went, no matter how good their health was otherwise. People in our culture have a lot of privileges. One of them is having no teeth.

Dana was terrifically enthusiastic about dental school, or maybe the word is 'defiant.' When she came into the lecture hall every day she would pause and look around the room, at all the guys, daring them to dismiss her, daring them, in fact, to have any thoughts about her at all. To me, dental school seemed more like a very large meal that I had to eat all by myself. The dishes were arrayed before me, and so I took my spoon and went at it as deliberately as possible, chewing up biochemistry and physiology, then fixed prosthodontics and operative dentistry, then periodontics and anesthesia and pain control.

I was happy during lab, when we were let loose on the patients. They would file in and sit down in the rows of chairs; then they would lie back, and we would stretch these wire-and-rubber frameworks over their mouths. They were called rubber dams. You lodged the wires in the patient's mouth and then pulled the affected tooth through a tight hole in the rubber sheet. Our professors said that they made the tooth easier to see and get at. Really, I think, they were meant to keep the students from dropping something, a tooth or even an instrument, down that open throat. They also kept the patients quiet. That little barrier let them know that they didn't have to talk. Patients feel as if they ought to make conversation. Anyway, that huge hall would hush, and you would simply concentrate on that white tooth against that dark rubber, and the time would fly. That was the last time that I felt I could really meditate over my work. For a dentist, the social nature of the situation is the hardest thing.

I did well in dental school, but it seemed to me that I deserved more drama in my life, especially after I quit the building crew I had worked on every summer since I was sixteen. I quit the crew because I was making $4 an hour and one day I nearly crushed my left hand trying to lift a bunch of loose two-by-fours. It hurt, but before I even felt the pain (your neurons, if you're tall, take a while) I remembered the exact cost of my first year of dental school, which was $8,792.38. A lot of hours at $4 an hour.

I took on Dana. I felt about her the way she felt about dental school. I dared her to dismiss me, and I was determined to scare the pants off her. I took the front basket off my bike, and then I would make her sit on the handlebars at midnight while we coasted down the longest, steepest street in town. We did it over and over, eight nights in a row once. I figured the more likely outcome, death, was cheaper in the end than just wrecking my hands. Besides, it was like falling in love with Dana. I couldn't stop doing it and I was afraid she could.

After that, we'd go back to her place and make love until the adrenaline in our systems had broken down. Sometimes that was a long time. But we were up at six, fresh and sexy, Dana pumped up for the daily challenge of crushing the dental school between her two fists like a beer can, and me for the daily challenge of Dana. Now we have three daughters. We strap them in the car and jerk the belts to test them. One of us walks the older ones to school every day, although the distance is two blocks. The oldest, Lizzie, would be floored by the knowledge that Dana and I haven't always crept fearfully from potential accident to potential accident the way we do now.

If Dana were reminded these days that she hadn't graduated first in our class but third, she would pretend indifference, but she was furious then. What did it matter that Phil Levine, who was first, hadn't been out of his apartment after dark in three years and his wife seemed to have taken a vow of silence, which she broke only when she told him she was going to live with another guy? Or that Marty Crockett, number two, was a certified genius and headed for NASA as the first dentist in space? The result of her fury was an enormous loan, for office, house, equipment, everything the best, the most tasteful, the most up-to-date, for our joint office and our new joint practice. We had been intending to join two separate and established practices, etc., etc., the conservative path to prosperity. Another result of her fury was that the loan officer and his secretary were our first patients, then his wife, her five children, one of her cousins. The secretary has proved, in fact, an inexhaustible fount of new patients, since she is related to everyone in three counties and she calls them all regularly on the bank's WATS line. I root-canaled three of her teeth last year alone.

Anyway, we dropped without pause from the drama of Dana's four-point grade average into the drama of a $2,500 mortgage payment in a town where we knew no one and that already had four dental clinics. Dana put our picture in the paper, 'Dr David Hurst and Dr Dana Hurst, opening their new clinic on Front Street.' I was handsome, she was pretty, people weren't accustomed to going to good-looking dentists, she said. They would like it. Our office was next to the fanciest restaurant in town, far from Orthodontia Row, as Dana called it. It wasn't easy, and some of those huge mortgage checks were real victories of accounting procedure. As soon as it got easy, just a little easy, Dana got pregnant with Lizzie.

Dana likes being pregnant, even though, or because, each of our fetuses has negotiated a successful but harrowing path through early bleeding, threatened miscarriage, threatened breech presentation, and long labor. She likes knowing, perhaps, that when Dr Dana Hurst comes through the obstetrician's door with the news that she is pregnant, the man had better get out his best machines and give his assistants a little extra training, because it isn't going to be easy, and wasn't meant to be.

Then there was the drama of motherhood—babies in the office, nursing between appointments, baby-sitter interviews that went on for hours while Dana probed into the deepest corners of the candidate's psyche, breasts that gushed in front of the dourest, least maternal patients. Assistants with twins. Those were the only kind she would hire for a while, just, I thought, to raise even higher the possibility that we wouldn't make it through the morning, through the week, through our marriage. I used to meditate over my patients in the dental school, but it wasn't enough. I wanted to be a dentist and have drama, too.

Now the children are all in school, or at least off the breast, we are prosperous and established on a semi part-time schedule, and all Dana has to do is dentistry. Little machines. Itsy-bitsy pieces of cotton. Fragments of gold you can't pick up with your fingers. I think she thought it would get bigger, like Cinerama, and instead it gets smaller and smaller.

If she were writing this, she would say that I was an exotically reckless graduate student, not dental at all, and that she pegged me for that the first day of classes, when I came in late, with my bike helmet under my arm, and sat down right in front of the teacher, stuck my feet into the aisle, and burped in the silence of his pause, loud enough for three rows to hear. But it was the only seat, I was too rattled to suppress my digestive grind, and I always stuck my feet into the aisle because my legs didn't fit under the desk. It was she who wanted me, she would say, to give her life a little variety and color. When I tell her that all I've ever longed for is the opportunity to meditate over my work, she doesn't believe me.

Dana would say that she loves routine. That is how she got through a biochemistry major and through dental school, after all, with an ironclad routine that included hours of studying, but also nourishing meals, lots of sex, and irresponsible activities with me. Her vision of routine is a lot broader than most people's is. You might say that she has a genius for knowing what has to be included. She has a joke lately, though. At night, standing in the bathroom brushing her teeth, she will say, 'There it goes!' or she may get up on Saturday morning and exclaim, 'Zap! another one vanished!' What she is referring to is the passage of the days and weeks. A year is nothing any more. Last fall it happened that we got Lizzie the wrong snow boots, fat rather than thin, and not acceptable to Lizzie's very decided tastes. Without even a pause, Dana countered Lizzie's complaints with the promise that she could have some new ones next year, in no time at all, she seemed to be saying.

It used not to be like this. Time used to stretch and bunch up. Minutes would inflate like balloons, and the two months of our begin-ning acquaintance seem in retrospect as long as all the time from then until now. A day was like a cloth sack. You could always fit something else in, it would just bulge a little more. Routine is the culprit, isn't it? Something is the culprit. The other thing about routine is that it frees you for a more independent mental life, one that is partly detached from the business at hand. Even when I was pulling out all of that guy's teeth today, I wasn't paying much attention. His drama was interesting as an anecdote, but it was his. To me it was just twenty-four teeth in a row, in a row of hundreds of teeth stretching back years. I have a friend named Henry who is an oral surgeon at the University Hospital. He is still excited when he finds someone's wisdom tooth up under the eyeball, where they sometimes migrate. He can talk about his patients for hours. They come from all over the state, with facial disfigurations of all types, no two alike, Henry says. But does his enthusiasm have its source in him or in them? In ten years, is he going to move to New York City because he's tired of car wrecks and wondering about gunshot wounds? Should Dana have gone into oral surgery? I don't know any women who do that.

I sound as if we never forget that we are dentists, as if when someone smiles we automatically class their teeth as 'gray range' or 'yellow range.' Of course we are also parents. These are my three daughters, Lizzie, Stephanie, and Leah. They are seven, five, and two. The most important thing in the world to Lizzie and Stephanie is the social world of the grammar school playground. The most important thing to Leah is me. Apart from the fact that Lizzie and Stephanie are my daughters, I am very fond of them.

Lizzie is naturally graceful and cool, with a high, domed forehead and a good deal of disdain for things that don't suit her taste, for instance, turtleneck shirts and pajamas with feet in them. She prefers blouses and nightgowns. Propriety is important to her and wars with her extremely ready sense of humor. She knows I exploit her sense of humor to get my way, and I would like to get out of the habit of tricking her into doing things she doesn't want to do, but it is hard. The tricks always work.

Stephanie is our boy. She is tall, and strong, and not interested in rearranging the family's feelings. She would rather be out. Sometimes she seems not to recognize us in public. She feels about kindergarten the way people used to feel about going away to college: at last she is out of the house, out of her parents' control, on her own in the great world. I think she has an irrational faith that she won't always be two years younger than Lizzie.

There is a lot of chitchat in the media about how things have changed since the fifties and sixties, but I think that is because nothing has really changed at all, except the details. Lizzie and Stephanie live in a neighborbood of older houses, as I did, and walk home from the same sort of brick schoolhouse. When they get home, they watch Superman cartoons and eat Hershey bars, as I did. They swing on their swing set and play with Barbie and talk about 'murdering' the boys.

They have a lot of confidence, and even power, when it comes to the boys. To hear them tell it, the boys walk the playground in fear. Dana says, 'Don't talk about the boys so much. When you grow up, you're going to resent them for it.' It is tempting, from their school tales, to think of the boys as hapless dopes—always in the lowest reading group, never earning behavior stars for the week, picking their noses, exposing the elastic of their underpants. It is tempting to avoid mentioning that I was a boy once myself.

It's not as if they ever ask. The unknown age they wish to know all about is their own—what were their peculiarities as babies, and toddlers, in the misty pasts of five years ago, three years ago, last year, even. When Dana pulls out a jacket for Leah that was originally Lizzie's, Lizzie greets it with amazed delight—how can it possibly still exist, when the three-year-old who wore it has vanished without a trace?

For Leah, the misty past is still the present, and no amount of future dredging will bring to the surface her daily events of right now—her friend Tessa, at preschool, whose claim on Leah is that she wears a tiny ponytail smack on the top of her head, for example. Were we to move this year, that might furnish her with a memory of this house—a ghostly sense of lines and the fall of light that would present itself to her in some future half-waking state. I wish that Leah's state of mind weren't so unavailable to us all, including herself, because she is driving us crazy.

Dana was glad to get Leah for her third, because Leah was big and cuddly and slept through on the tenth day. There is no subsequent achievement that parent wants of child with more ardor than the accomplishment of eight hours at a stretch, during the night. Leah slept ten, and then, at three months, fourteen rock-solid nightly hours, and woke up smiling. She didn't even crawl until ten months, and could be counted on to stay happily in one place when infants who had been neonates with her were already biting electrical cords and falling down the stairs. At one, when she said her first word, it was 'song,' a request that Dana sing to her. Since the others were already by this time covering their ears and saying, 'Oh, God!' whenever Dana launched into a tune, Dana thought that her last chance for that musical mother's fantasy was a dream come true. Everyone, especially me, liked the way Leah gave spontaneous hugs and said, 'I love you,' at the drop of a hat. She seemed to have an instinctive understanding of your deepest parental wishes, and a need to fulfill them. Patients who had seen her at the office would stop us and say, 'That Leah is such a wonderful baby. You don't know how lucky you are.' My brother would get on the phone from Cincinnati and shout in her baby ear, 'Leah! Cheer up!'

Dana was overjoyed but suspicious. She would say, 'No one grows up to be this nice. How are we going to wreck it?' But she would say it in a smug tone, as if experience alone assured that we wouldn't. Dana felt especially close to Leah, physically close and blindly trusting. They nursed, they sang, they read books, they got lost in the aisles of the grocery store companionably choosing this and that. 'The others are like you,' she often said, 'but she is like me, lazy.' That's what she said, but she meant 'everything anyone could want.' Leah was everything she could want and she, as far as she knew, was everything that Leah could want.

Not long ago, Dana got up first and went into Leah's room to get her out of her crib, and Leah said distinctly, 'I want Daddy.' Dana came back to the bedroom, chuckling, and I got Leah up. The next morning it happened again, but the days went on as before, with Dana sitting in the mornings and me taking the early appointments, then Dana dropping Leah at preschool, where she said, 'Bye-bye, Mom, I love you.'

At three I leave the office and go home to meet the schoolgirls. At five we pick up Leah, at six Dana comes home to dinner. Twelve hours of dentistry at about $100 an hour. We work alternate Saturday mornings, another $500 a week. Simple multiplication will reveal our gross income for part-time work. This is what we went to dental school for, isn't it? Since they got the dental plan over at the university, people ask me if business is better. I say, 'You can't beat them off with a stick,' meaning new patients. The idea of Dana and myself on the front stoop of our office building beating hordes of new patients off with sticks makes me laugh every time.

Anyway, other things were going on. They always are. A patient called me at nine thirty in the evening and said that her entire lower

face was swollen and throbbing, an abscess resulting from a long over-
due root canal. You remove the dead tissue and stir up the bacteria that
have colonized the region and they spread. That's what an abscess is.
I met her at the office and gave her six shots of novocaine, which basically numbed her from the neck up. Meanwhile, at home, Leah
awakened and began crying out. Dana went in to comfort her, and
Leah began crying, 'I want my daddy! I want my daddy!' as if Dana
were a stranger. Dana was a little taken aback, but picked Leah up, to
hug and soothe her, and this made Leah so hysterical that Dana had to
put her back in bed and tiptoe out, as if in shame.

By the time I had taken Mrs Ver Steeg home and put the car in the
garage, all was quiet. I was tired. I drank three beers and went to bed,
and was thus unconscious for the second bout of the night, and the
third. In each instance, Leah woke up crying for me, Dana went to
comfort her and was sent packing. The longer she stayed and the
more things she tried, the wilder Leah got. The first bout lasted from
midnight to twelve thirty and the second from two forty-five until
three forty. Leah began calling for me to get her out of bed at six. I
woke up at last, wondering what Dana was doing, motionless beside
me, and Dana said, 'I won't go to her. You have to go to her.' That was
the beginning.

She lay on the living room carpet, rolled in her blanket, watching
Woody Woodpecker cartoons from the forties. I drank coffee. She was
happy. Between cartoons, she would get up and walk over to me and
begin to talk. Some of the words were understandable, the names
Lizzie and Stephanie, the words 'oatmeal' and 'lollipop.' But more
intelligible was the tone. She was trying to please and entertain me.
She looked into my face for smiles. She gestured with her hands,
shrugged, glanced away from me and back.

When Stephanie and Lizzie came down at seven, attracted by the
opening theme from 'Challenge of the Superfriends,' she retreated to
the couch. When Dana got up and staggered down the stairs in her
robe, looking only for a place to deposit her exhaustion, Leah shouted,
'No! Go away! Don't sit here! My couch!' She would take her oatmeal
only from me. Only I was allowed to dress her. If Dana or Lizzie or
Stephanie happened to glance at her, she would scowl at them and

begin to cry. Dana, forgetting herself, happened to kiss her on the forehead, and she exclaimed, 'Yuck! Ouch!' and wiped the kiss off. When I went to the bathroom and closed the door, she climbed the stairs behind me, saying, 'I go get my daddy back.' We were embarrassed. By eight forty-five, when I was ready to leave for the office, we had run out of little jokes.

It was not simply that she didn't want Dana near her, for she would allow that most of the time, it was also that she had exacting requirements for me and was indignant if I deviated from them in the slightest. If she expected to climb the stairs and find me in my bedroom and I made the mistake of meeting her in the hallway, she would burst into tears and shout, 'Go back in room! Go back in room!' I would have to go back into the bedroom and pretend to be ignoring her, and wait for her to come find me and announce herself.

I don't think this ever happened to my father, who had a plumbing supply business and wore a white dress shirt to work every day. He referred to my brother and sisters and me as 'the kids,' in a slightly disparaging, amused tone of voice that assumed alliance with the great world of adult men, the only audience he ever really addressed himself to. I don't know anyone who calls his children 'the kids.' It would be like calling his spouse 'the wife,' not done these days. We call them 'our children,' 'our daughters,' very respectful. Would Leah thrive more certainly on a little neglect? Should we intentionally overlook her romantic obsession, as our parents might have done naturally?

At any rate, at dinner that night, there seemed no alternative to my serving her food, cutting her meat, sitting as close to her as possible. When I got up and went into the living room without taking her down from her high chair (Dana and Stephanie were still eating, Lizzie wanted me to adjust the television set), she allowed the others to leave the table without asking either of them to get her down. Dana said, 'I can get you down, honey. Let me untie your strap here.' Leah said, 'No! No! Daddy do it.'

I stayed in the living room.

Dana said, 'I'll untie you and you can get yourself down. You're big enough for that.'

'No! No!' said Leah. 'Tie strap! Tie strap!' Dana tied it again. I stayed in the living room. Leah sat in front of her little bowl for ten minutes. Dana sent first Stephanie, then Lizzie as emissaries, first to ask if they could get her down, then if she, Dana, could get her down. Leah was adamant, with the two-year-old advantage that no one knew for sure if she knew what she was talking about, or what any of them were offering. This advantage enables her to be much more stubborn than the average speaker, whose eyes, at least, must register understanding.

After a minute or so, she began calling 'Daddy! Daddy!' in a tone of voice that suggested I was far away but willing. Dana and I looked at each other. She looked hurt and resentful, then she shrugged. I got up and took Leah down from her chair. She did not greet me with the elation I expected, but after we went into the living room, she puttered around me, chattering mostly nonsense and looking to me for approval every so often. I said, 'Let's go along with her for a while. It shouldn't be too hard.'

Dana lifted one eyebrow and went back to her book.

It was nearly impossible. At first I thought the worst thing was the grief at parting: 'Oh, Daddy! Daddy! Daddy!' hardly intelligible through the howls of betrayal. I was only going to the lumberyard or the Quiktrip, ten minutes, fifteen at the outside. Taking a child turns the errand into a forced march. 'She'll be good with you,' Dana would say, and she would, and the household would be relieved of screaming, but at the price of constant engagement with equipment. A snap, two threadings, and two buckles into the car seat. The reverse for getting out of the car seat. Opening an extra door the stroller. Unfolding the stroller, locking it into stroller-rictus, wheeling it around the car, a threading and a buckle into the stroller. Up curbs, through doors, down narrow aisles, all to find a package of wood screws or a six-pack of beer. Or I could carry her, thirty-four pounds. Doing an errand by myself came to seem a lot like flying—glorious, quick, and impossible.

But grief wasn't restricted to my leaving the house. Leaving the room was enough to arouse panic, and the worst thing about it was that at first I was so unaware, and there was the labor of being trained to alert her that I was going outside or upstairs. Then there came the negotiations. One of the first things she learned to do was to tell me not to do what I had originally intended to do. After all, she had her own activities. 'She loves you,' said Dana. 'It won't last.'

There were three more elements, too. I notice that there is a certain pleasure for a meditative person like myself in laying down one thread and picking up another, as if everything isn't happening at once. One of these elements was that Dana's choir group was practicing four days a week so that they might join the chorus of the opera *Nabucco*, which was being given in our town by a very good, very urban, touring company for one night. Dana's choir director was a friend of the musical director of the company from *their* days in graduate school. The text of the chorus had to do with the Hebrews sitting themselves down by the waters of Babylon and weeping. Dana sang it every day, but in Italian. It doesn't sound as depressing in Italian as it does in English.

The second element was our summer house, which we had purchased the fall before, in a fit of response to autumnal color. It is in the mountains not far from where we live. Since buying it, we have also bought a well, a lot of plaster, a coat of exterior housepaint, a heavy-duty lawn mower, a set of house jacks, and a wild flower book. We have identified forty-two different species of wild flowers in the area around the house alone.

The third element was that Dana fell in love with one of her fellow singers, or maybe it was the musical director. She doesn't know that I know that this was an element.

Not too long ago, the single performance of the opera *Nabucco* came and went. Leah stayed home, screaming, with the baby-sitter. Lizzie and Stephanie went along. I paid attention to the music most of the time, and the part that Dana sang about sitting down beside the waters of Babylon was very pretty, to say the least. I closed my eyes, and there were certain notes that should not have ended, that should be eternal sounds in the universe. Lizzie sat in the front seat and fell asleep on the way home. Stephanie leaned against Dana in the backseat, and also fell asleep.

In the midst of all this breathing, still dressed in her Old Testament costume and with her hair pinned up, Dana said, 'I'll never be happy again.' I looked at her face in the rearview mirror. She was looking out the window, and she meant it. I don't know if she even realized that she had spoken aloud. I drove into the light of the headlights, and I didn't make a sound. It seemed to me that I didn't have a sound to make.

When we got home, Leah was still awake. She was thrilled to see me, and while Dana put the others to bed and changed her clothing, I sat next to Leah's crib and held her hand while she talked to me. She talked about the moon, and her books, and her Jemima Puddleduck doll, and something else unintelligible. She perused my face for signs of pleasure. Sometimes she made gestures of ironical acceptance, shrugs of her little baby shoulders. Sometimes she sighed, as if she didn't quite understand how things work but was willing to talk about it. Are these imitations of our gestures? Or does the language itself carry this burden of mystery, so that any speaker must express it?

My eyes began to close, but Leah wasn't finished for the night, and when I slid down the wall to a reclining position, she insisted that I sit up again. It was nearly one by this time. Saturday night. I had root-canaled two, and drilled and filled two, and cleaned two more a very long time before. One of them had insisted upon talking about her sister, who had cancer of the jaw. I had been arduously sympathetic, because, of course, you must. The room was dark and filled with toys. The baby was talking. The moon shone in the window. That was the last real peace I had.

Teeth outlast everything. Death is nothing to a tooth. Hundreds of years in acidic soil just keeps a tooth clean. A fire that burns away hair and flesh and even bone leaves teeth dazzling like daisies in the ashes. Life is what destroys teeth. Undiluted apple juice in a baby bottle, sourballs, the pH balance of drinking water, tetracycline, sand in your bread if you were in the Roman army, biting seal-gut thread if you are an Eskimo woman, playing the trumpet, pulling your own teeth with a pliers. In their hearts, most dentists are certain that their patients can't be trusted with their teeth, but you can't grieve for every tooth, every mouth. You can't even grieve for the worst of them; you can only send the patient home with as many of the teeth he came in with as possible.

After a while, Leah's eyes began to take on that stare that is preliminary to sleep, and her remarks became more desultory. She continued
to hold my hand. I thought about the Hebrews sitting down beside the
waters of Babylon, and I began to weep, too, although as quietly as
possible. I didn't see how I was going to support the total love of one
woman, Leah, while simultaneously relinquishing that of another,
Dana. I wasn't curious. I said my prayer, which was, 'Lord, don't let
her tell me about it,' and shortly after that I must have fallen asleep,
because the next thing I knew it was morning and I had a crick in my
neck from sleeping by the window all night.

I crawled over to the half-open door and slitheted through, so as
not to awaken Leah. I expected to be alone, but I found Dana in her
robe at the table. She was eating cold pizza. Her hair was standing up
on one side, and she hadn't managed to get all the makeup off from the
night before, so there were smudges around her eyes and her lips were
orange. I said, 'What time is it? You look terrible.' She gave me a
stricken look and said, 'I can't believe it's over. It was so beautiful. I
could sing it every night forever.'

'Well, you'll sing other things.' I must have sounded irritable, when
I meant to sound encouraging.

'I don't want to sing other things.' She sounded petulant, when she
must have meant to sound tragic. I have found that there is something
in the marriage bond that deflates every communication, skews it
toward the ironic middle, where man and wife are at their best, good-
humored and matter-of-fact. But maybe there are others who can
accommodate a greater range of exhilaration and despair. Tears came
into her eyes and then began running down her cheeks. I sighed,
probably sounding long-suffering, and sat down beside her and put my
arms around her. Sitting down, it was awkward. I cast around for
something to say. What I hit on was this: 'Mrs Hilton needs to go to
a gum specialist. I scaled her yesterday for an hour, and she is exposing bone around the second and third molars.'

'Have I worked on her?'

'Curly red hair, about thirty?'

'Eight-year-old X-rays of impacted wisdom teeth?'

'Won't have them out till they hurt.'

'I had her. I didn't think her gums were that bad. She could go to Jerry.'

'No dental insurance. Practically no money, I gather.'

Dana sighed. 'Lots of kids, I bet.'

'Five. Sometimes she brings the eighteen-month-old and the three-year-old.'

'Yeah.' Now the tears really began to roll down her cheeks, and she closed her eyes tight to stop them. I had only meant to bring up a mouth, not a life. I held her tightly and repeated my prayer, and it was answered, because although she heaved a number of times, and held her breath as if about to say something, she never did.

Not long after, Lizzie and Stephanie appeared on the scene, the markers came out, the demands for paper, cereal, bananas, and milk went up, and the television went on. Lizzie and Stephanie go head to head on the drawings. Lately, Lizzie's have a lot of writing on them. Wherever the sky would ordinarily be are Lizzie's remarks, in blue, about what the figures are doing. Stephanie can't write yet, but she pays attention. Her skies are full of yellow stars. Dana went into the kitchen and sang her song about the weeping of the Hebrews while dishing up red bowls of Cheerios and bananas. Easter was coming up, and it occurred to me that the choir might go on to something less passionate, but I couldn't imagine what it would be. They would certainly go on to fewer rehearsals every week—maybe only one.

Leah was still asleep. I remembered that I was still in my opera clothes, as formal as we get where I live, which was khaki pants, light blue shirt, sweater vest. Dana came through the dining room, and when I went up to the shower, she was already there, stepping out of her underpants with a sigh. Her breasts are wrinkled and flat from six years of nursing, but the rest of her is muscular and supple. I said, 'May I join you?' Her eyes lifted to my face. It seems to me that they are very beautiful: pale, perfect blue, without a fleck of brown or green. Constant blue. Simultaneously deep-set and protuberant, with heavy, wrinkled lids. Her mother has the same eyes, only even older and therefore more beautiful. I don't know what I expected her to say. She always says yes. Now she said, 'Sure.' She smiled. She got out another towel. I turned on the water, got in first, and moved to the back of the tub. I reached out my hand and helped her in. We got wet, and soaped each other. She was businesslike about it, but friendly. I tried to be the same way. We talked about nitrous oxide, as I remember. We washed our hair, and she washed her face two or three times, asking each time whether the black was off her eyes.

I could not stop looking at her eyes. I wondered if the object of her affections had noticed them yet, in the sense of knowing what he was seeing rather than simply feeling the effect they had on him. She turned her back to me and bent her head under the shower, and I wondered the same thing about her back and shoulders, about the way her neck drops into her shoulders without seeming to spread, like a tulip stem.

Does he appreciate the twist of her wrist when she is picking up little things, the graceful expertise of her fingers working over that mouth, whatever mouth it is? I wondered whether the object of her affections, in fact, was the meditative sort, who separates elements, puts one thing down before picking up another, had it in him ever to have been a dentist, a mere dentist, that laughingstock of the professional community. Every time she saw me looking at her, she smiled, and every time I seemed to be doing something else, she sighed. I said, 'Perk up, Dana. There's always more music.'

'It's a waltz. That's what's so tragic about it. You could dance to it, but you can't.' She got out, saying, 'There's Leah.' I rinsed off hurriedly and wiped myself down while going to Leah's room. She doesn't like to be kept waiting. She was lying on her back with her feet up on the end of the crib, calling, 'Daddy! Dave! Daddy!' When she saw me, she smiled and rolled over, noting with pleasure, I suppose, the wet hair, the dripping chest, the towel, the hurry, all the signs that I had been subdued once again.

I lifted her, stripped her of wet clothes, and wiped her off with my towel. She went to the chest of drawers. I opened the bottom one for her. She chose red shorts, green slacks, and two shirts. I chose a pair of underpants and a pair of socks. She put everything on cooperatively, then admired the effect for a moment or two. I was talking the whole time: 'Good morning, sweetheart! How did you sleep? What a pretty girl! Ready for breakfast? How about some Cheerios with bananas?'

The usual paternal patter. I carried her downstairs, the towel wrapped around my waist, her hands upon my shoulders and her gaze upon my face. We will never know what she sees there until she finds it again, I suppose, in the face of some kid twenty years from now.

Dana was getting ready to go out. She glanced at me, and said with due formality, 'I'm going to the store for milk and the newspaper. Who wants to come along?' But they were all in their nightclothes, except Leah, and so she got away without a single one of them. She looked at me and also said the right thing. 'Back in a flash. Anything you want special?' I shrugged. She left. I went into the kitchen and sliced a banana with one hand, laying it on the counter and chopping at it with the paring knife, because Leah wouldn't let me put her down. Then I unscrewed the cap of the milk with one hand, poured the Cheerios with one hand, kissed Leah, and carried her to her high chair, where she consented to be put for the duration of her meal. Dana had not asked me where I spent the night, although she must have noticed that I wasn't in bed with her.

She was not back in a flash, which has to be interpreted as twenty-five minutes or a half an hour—seven minutes each way to the store, and then a generous ten for milk and newspaper. It took her an hour, and she came back much more serene than she had been since dinner the night before. She carried in her bag, said, 'I got doughnuts for good girls. It's a lovely day out!' and sped into the kitchen. Oh, she was happy, happy, happy, but not exhilarated, not anything blamable or even obvious. She was simply perfectly calm, full of energy, ready for the day. No sighs. No exertion of will. I wondered if he lived nearby, but then I made myself stop wondering about him even before I might start. Leah was standing beside me, and I reached down and swung her into my arms, buried my fatal curiosity in her fleshy, baby smell.

It was a lovely day, and we decided upon a spur-of-the-minute trip to the house, to admire the plaster and the running water and to picnic on the front deck. Lizzie and Stephanie thought it was interesting that you could have a picnic at a house where there was a refrigerator and a stove, and viewed the whole plan as another example of Dana's peculiar but always instructive way of looking at things.

Dana let Lizzie pack the food and Stephanie pack the toys, of which
there have to be enough not only for everyone to have something to
play with every moment of the trip but also to look at, consider, and
disregard. It was fine with me. Dana seemed to me to be sort of like a
hot-air balloon. The more weight we could hang on her, in terms of
children, houses, belongings, foodstuffs, office equipment, and debts,
the harder it would be for her to gain altitude.

The children sat behind us and Dana sat beside me, with her feet on
the lunch basket. My strategy was to talk about patients all the way,
both to remind her of what we shared and to distract her from her sadness, which sprouted as soon as we passed the city limits and grew with
every mile we drove. The older children played together nicely. Lizzie,
in fact, read Stephanie *Green Eggs and Ham*, and Leah was generally
cordial, allowing Dana both to talk to her and to give her pieces of
apple. When the apple was gone, Dana tentatively reached out her
hand, as she had done often in the past, and Leah took it and held it.
I drove and talked.

I have found that it is tempting to talk about every minute of the
past six weeks as if the passing of every minute were an event, which
was what it seemed like. I remember that car ride perfectly—the
bright, early spring sunlight flooding all the windows; my own voice
rising and falling in a loquacious attempt at wit, concern, entertainment, wooing; my repeated glances at her profile; the undercurrent in
all my thoughts of how is she now? And now? And now? As if she
were in some terminal condition.

But it was only a car ride, two hours into the country, 'a dentist'
with 'the wife' and 'the kids.' It could have been 1950. I remember
thinking that then, and wishing that it were—some confused thought
about the fidelity of our mothers' generation, or barring the truth of
that, that at least whatever it was that was present would be thirty-five
years in the past, if it had taken place in 1950. Well, as I say, every
minute had its own separate identity.

Some nights later, we were lying in bed after making love and I was
nearly asleep. Her voice rose out of the blackness of coming somno-
lence like a thread of smoke. She said, 'I wish we were closer.'
Although I was now wide awake, I maintained my breathing pattern

and surreptitiously turned my chest away from her, as if in sleep, so that she couldn't hear my heart rattling in its cage. Now she would tell me, I thought, and then we would have to act. I let out a little snore, counted to twenty, and let out another one. After a minute or so, when my heart had steadied. I turned, also as if in sleep, and threw my arm over her, and hugged her tightly, as if in sleep. My nose was pressed into the back of her neck. She said, 'Dave? David? Are you asleep already?' Then she sighed, and we lay there for a long time until the muscles at the back of her neck finally relaxed and she began to snore for real.

I don't know when she saw him, but I know that she did, because sometimes her sadness was cured. A long time ago, before she joined the choir, when Leah was still nursing five or six times a day, she read a book by some Middle European writer about a man who had both a wife and a mistress. I remember the way she tossed the book down and said, 'You know, I always think of men who have wives and mistresses as having everything, but of women who have husbands and lovers as simply being oversubscribed.' Then she laughed and went on: 'I mean, where would you fit it in? Would you phone him from the grocery store with two old ladies behind you waiting to call the car service and two kids screaming in the basket?' So where did she fit it in? She was always at home when she was supposed to be. She was always in bed with me all night. She never canceled an appointment with a patient. Sometimes she was late coming home from choir practice, once a week, but she had been late in the past, and she was never more than half an hour late. But sometimes she was desperate with sadness and sometimes she was fine, and these states of mind didn't have a thing to do with me, or our household, or the office. And in addition to that, she denied that they even existed, that she was ever in turmoil or that she was ever at peace. I don't mean to say that we spoke of them. I wouldn't have allowed that under any circumstances. But she would catch me looking at her, and she would stare at me with that same stare I remembered from dental school, defiant, daring me to have any opinions about her at all.

I should say that it didn't take long for Lizzie to realize that something was up. Lizzie's situation as the oldest and her observant character make her the point man most of the time, and a lot of our battles have been fought in her digestive tract over the years. The pediatrician, whom I like a lot, does not always go for the psychosomatic explanation. In the case of Lizzie's stomach, he suggests that some children simply suffer more intense peristaltic contractions than others. Any food triggers digestion, which may or may not be painful. And it is certainly true that Lizzie has stomach aches all times of the year, all seasons of the spirit, and also tends to throw up a lot, as does Dana's sister, Frances. It has been routine on every car trip for thirty-seven years for whoever is driving Frances to pull over so that Frances can give her all on the side of the road. It is a family joke, and Frances doesn't get a lot of sympathy for it. Ditto Lizzie. Nature or nurture? My observation is that parents believe religiously in nature, while the hidden family forces that are acting to deform the plastic child are glaringly apparent to any college psych major. At any rate, Lizzie woke up every morning of the week after our trip into the country with a raging belly ache and an equal determination not to go to school, but to stay home and keep her eye on the domestic situation.

Each morning I carried her to school in tears, deposited her in the arms of Mrs Leonard, brushed off her clutching hands, and turned on my heel to the screams of 'Daddy! I need you! I need to be with you!' School, though she always settled down to her work at once, didn't make her forget my betrayal, and explanations, about how sometimes when mommies and daddies argue it makes the children feel bad, did not convince her that she wasn't actually sick. We took her temperature morning and night, promising that if it went up so much as a degree she could stay home.

I took her to the pediatrician, who put his arm around her and said that sometimes when mommies and daddies argue it makes the child feel bad. He also felt her stomach and checked her ears and throat, but she wasn't convinced. I tried to explain to him, because he is rather a friend, and certainly a fellow in the small professional community of our town, that we weren't exactly arguing, but his gaze—warm, sympathetic, resigned—flickered across my face in disbelief. Here was the child, her stomach, her panicked look, the evidence of forces at work. He said, 'The stomach problem she's always had is going to be the focus of all her uneasiness. Some kids get headaches. Some get accident-prone. Every feeling is in the body as well as in the mind.' His voice kept dropping lower and lower, as if he didn't know how to speak to me, a medically trained white male, and it's true, I was rather resentful. More resentful of him than of Dana or the Other. Maybe he was the Other. I wanted to punch him out.

Instead, I took Lizzie to the grocery store and let her pick out dinner. Canned corn, mashed potatoes, pork chops, orange sherbet. Not what I would have chosen, personally. Then I took her home and let her eat a Hershey bar and watch 'The Pink Panther' until it was time for Stephanie to come home.

When Stephanie came home, I noticed for the first time that she had her own uneasiness. She wouldn't look at me or come in the house. She dropped her school bag without showing me any papers and went outside to play on the swings. A few minutes later she saw that one of her kindergarten friends down the street had gotten home as well, and she came and asked to go there, although this is not a friend she particularly likes, and she stayed for the rest of the afternoon, and then called to ask if she could eat dinner there. I suspect that what she would really have liked to do was move in there.

Lizzie began to cry because Stephanie didn't want to play with her, and then we had an argument about whether Stephanie loves her or not, and then I sent her to her room, and then I went up and explained to her that people have to want to play with you on their own, you can't make them, and they can't make you, either. Then I recalled examples of Lizzie not wanting to play with Stephanie, which she denied, and then I gave up, and then I went over to the preschool, leaving Lizzie by herself briefly, and picked up Leah, who, I was told, had put on her shoes and socks all by herself. She was very proud. I was, too.

Since the onset of Leah's infatuation, we had gotten into the habit of dividing the evening's tasks child by child. Dana would serve Lizzie and Stephanie and I would serve Leah. That is how it presented itself to me, although, of course, Lizzie and Stephanie had table setting and clearing to do, and were subject to discipline and the apparent dominance of the parental committee. In view of my determination not to have anything irrevocable communicated to me, this was a pretty good system, and one that I clung to. On this particular day, Dana was feeling rather blue. There was some despairing eye contact across the living room and across the kitchen. I took Leah and went out for beer, lingering over the magazine rack and talking at length with a patient I encountered about real estate taxes. I stayed away for an hour. I missed Dana terribly and wanted only to go home.

The next day at the office I missed her, too. She was right in the next room. I should say that in addition to being dentists, parents, home owners, musicians, and potential or actual adulterers, Dana and I are also employers of four people—two dental assistants and two receptionists—and office society is nearly as complex as domestic society, with the added temptation to think, unjustifiably in my experience, that it can be tinkered with and improved by a change of personnel. The receptionists are Katharyn and Dave, eight to one and one to six, six bucks an hour, and the assistants are Laura (mine) and Delilah (Dana's), eight to two and noon to six, fifteen bucks an hour. Our receptionists are always students at the university, and turn over about every two and a half years. Laura has been my assistant for five years, and Delilah came last year, replacing Genevieve. Both, as I said before, have sets of twins: Laura's fraternal, twelve years old, and Delilah's identical, four years old. Laura and Delilah also have pension plans, so, of course, we are also a financial institution, with policy decisions and long-term planning goals and investment strategies. Dave is a flirt. For convenience, he is known as 'Dave,' while I am known as 'Dr Dave,' even, at the office, to Dana. Dana is known as 'Dana.' Katharyn has been engaged for three years to an Arabian engineer she met during her freshman year. Laura is divorced, edgy, bossy with the patients. Delilah is rounded, soft, an officer in the local Mothers of Twins club, which Laura has never joined. Dave flirts more with Laura than he does with Delilah, which raises the friction potential in the office about twenty-five percent. On the other hand, he is a terrific receptionist—painstaking, well organized, canny about a patient's fear of dentists. He has a sixth sense about whom to call the day before the appointment, and how to say, 'We'll be expecting you, then,' so that the patient doesn't dare 'forget.' He also does the books, so we have been able to let the bookkeeper go. He is graduating next December, a dark day.

I am so used to Laura by now that I don't know what to say about her. She has a raucous, smoke-coarsened, ironic voice, which she uses to good effect in lecturing the patients about dental hygiene. 'What is this, you don't floss? You want your gums to turn to cotton candy? Believe me, if you sat in this chair and watched what comes through the door every day, you wouldn't be so optimistic. Take this. I'm going to show you.' We have never talked about anything but business. Of Delilah I don't know much. She and Dana talk a lot, it seems to me, and for a long time this whispery murmur from the next office has been a kind of comforting white noise at the end of my workday. During the week, after the opera, it falls silent. Dana doesn't have much to say, or rather, what she has to say cannot be said, so she says nothing. I look blankly out the window between patients. I am sure that behind the wall Dana is doing the same thing.

What did I think I was doing on that first day of dental school? Why did I choose to pour the formless me into this particular mold? I hadn't known any dentists except the ones who worked on my own teeth. They didn't strike me as romantic figures. I was, and still am, rather struck by the mystery of teeth, of their evolution and function, of the precisely refined support system in the gums and jaws that enables a person, every person just about, simply to chew. Senseless, mindless objects, teeth, two little rows of stones in the landscape of the flesh, but as sensitive, in their way, as fingertips or lips.

I also felt the mystery of building houses back then—the way lengths of wood, hammered together with lengths of steel, created a space that people either wanted or didn't want to be inside of. I thought of architecture, but architecture was making pictures, not making buildings. Most of my fellow biology majors went to medical school or botany school or zoology school. When I considered doctoring, I used to imagine a giant body laid open on the operating table like a cadaver, but alive, and myself on a little diving board above it, about to somersault in. Not attractive. And I didn't want to spend the rest of my life fighting with some university administration about the age of my lab equipment.

This *is* what I saw myself doing: sitting here, my back hunched, the office cool and clean, the patient half asleep. I am tinkering. Making something little. But perhaps making little things belittles the self. I've noticed at conventions that dentists argue about details a lot. I wish my wife loved me. I wish her constant blue eyes would focus on me with desire instead of regret. I wonder if I haven't always been a little out of the center of her gaze, a necessary part of the life she wants to lead, but a part, only a part.

That was a Friday. The last day of a long, trying week. I suspect that Dana and I measured our time differently that week. For her, maybe, the time fell into blocks of unequal length, pivoting about the minutes she spent wherever, wherever it was that she managed to see him. My week, of course, was more orderly, and it was primarily defined by those trips with Lizzie to school each morning and lying in bed with Dana each night, wide awake and pretending to be asleep so that she wouldn't speak to me. She was, I should add, restless all week. Once, she got up at three and did something downstairs until five ten, then she came back to bed and went back to sleep. My mother used to look at us severely if we complained of not sleeping and say, 'So what have you got a guilty conscience about?'

On Friday the children fell into bed at eight o'clock, practically asleep already. Dana sat knitting in front of the TV. There was an HBO showing of *Tootsie*. I went in and out, longing to sit down, unable to. Every time I went into the living room, I peered at Dana. She seemed remarkably serene, almost happy. I decided to risk it and sat down beside her on the couch. She glanced at me and smiled, pulled her yarn out of the skein with a quick, familiar snap of her wrist, and laughed at the place in the movie where Teri Garr stands up screaming. I settled into the cushions and put my arm around her shoulders. It was tempting, very tempting, not to know what I knew, but I knew that if I relaxed, she would tell me, and then I would really know it. She said, 'Hard week, huh?' She sighed. I squeezed her shoulder.

'Leah doesn't make it easy, does she?'

'What if she's like this forever?'

'Remember when we used to say that about Stephanie? When she was waking up and screaming three or four times every night?'

'Do you think that was the worst?'

'It was pretty bad when Lizzie swallowed that penny.'

'But that night when I had to stay in the hospital with her, I didn't dare think it was bad at all. All those babies in the otolaryngology ward were so much worse.' She bit her lip, looked at the movie, turned her work, looked at me. 'You know,' she said, 'you scare me a little. You always have. Isn't that funny?'

I thought, Compared to whom? But I said, 'I don't believe you.'

'It's true. You don't smile much, not the way most people do. You have this way of letting your gaze fall upon people when they attract your attention, but not smiling, nor reassuring them in any way that you aren't judging them. And you're awfully tall.'

'Awfully?'

'Well, it's not awful. I mean. That's just an intensifier. But you're a lot taller than I am. I don't think about that much, but you must be eleven inches taller than I am.'

'But you've been married to me for ten years. How can you say that I scare you?'

'Remember how you used to sit me on the handlebars of your bike and coast down Cloud Street? How can I say that you don't scare me, after that?'

'Well, back then I was trying to scare you.'

'Why?'

'Because you scared me. You scared everybody. You were so fucking smart.'

She laughed. She turned her work. She said, 'Dave, do you like me?'

I wanted to groan. I said, 'I love you.'

'But do you like me? If you weren't sleeping with me, would you want to talk to me and have lunch with me and stuff like that?'

'Sure.'

She sighed. 'But do you think that we're friends?'

'Sure.'

She looked at me, and sighed again.

'Why are you sighing?' This was risky and could have led to anything, but the temptation to comfort your wife, if you love her, is a compelling one in my experience.

She thought for a moment, then looked at me and said, 'I don't know. Life. Let's go to bed.' She put down her knitting, turned off the light and the television, and led me by the hand up the stairs. She took off my shirt and my pants. Reached up to my awfully tall shoulders and ran her fingers across them. I undid the tie of her robe and cupped her breasts in my hands. She ran her hands down my chest, exploring, trying me out, looking at me again, over her shoulder in a way. I'm not going to say that I could even begin to resist.

I am thirty-five years old, and it seems to me that I have arrived at the age of grief. Others arrive there sooner. Almost no one arrives much later. I don't think it is years themselves, or the disintegration of the body. Most of our bodies are better taken care of and better-looking than ever. What it is, is what we know, now that in spite of ourselves we have stopped to think about it. It is not only that we know that love ends, children are stolen, parents die feeling that their lives have been meaningless. It is not only that, by this time, a lot of acquaintances and friends have died and all the others are getting ready to sooner or later. It is more that the barriers between the circumstances of oneself and of the rest of the world have broken down, after all—after all that schooling, all that care. Lord, if it be thy will, let this cup pass from me. But when you are thirty-three, or thirty-five, the cup must come around, cannot pass from you, and it is the same cup of pain that every mortal drinks from. Dana cried over Mrs Hilton. My eyes filled during the nightly news. Obviously we were grieving for ourselves, but we were also thinking that if *they* were feeling what *we* were feeling, how could they stand it? We were grieving for them, too. I understand that later you come to an age of hope, or at least resignation. I suspect it takes a long time to get there.

On Saturday, Dana asked me to take the children up to the house in the country and maybe spend the night. The beds, she said, were made. There was plenty of firewood. We would, she said, have a good time. She would join us for dinner, after the Saturday-morning office hours. It was very neatly done. I said, 'Maybe that's a good idea. But you could take them and let me do the morning work.' Her face fell into her shoes. I said, 'No, I would like to go into the country, I think.'

It was another sunny day, but cold. Each child was bundled against the weather, her coat vigorously zipped, her hat pulled down over her ears with a snap, her mittens put on and tucked into her sleeves. To each one, Dana said, 'Now you be nice to Daddy, and don't make him mad, okay? I'll finish my work and come for dinner, so I will see you very soon. Tonight we'll have a fire in the wood stove and make popcorn and have a good time, okay?' And each child nodded, and was hugged, and then strapped in. Leah sat in front, eyeing me with pleasure. We drove off.

I couldn't resist looking at Lizzie and Stephanie again and again in the rearview mirror. They were astonishingly graceful and attractive, the way they leaned toward each other and away, the way their heads bent down and then popped up, the way their gazes caught, the way they ignored each other completely and stared out the windows. The pearly glow of their skin, the curve of their cheeks and foreheads, the expressiveness of their shoulders. I felt as if I had never seen them before.

After about an hour, Lizzie began feeling anxious. She asked for milk, said she was hot, subsided. Stephanie sat forward and said, 'Is the pond still frozen, do you think? Can we slide on the pond?'

'I don't know. We'll see.'

'Daddy, my stomach feels funny.' This was Lizzie.

'You shouldn't have drunk so much milk.'

'I didn't. I took three swallows.' Then she panicked. 'I'm going to throw up! Stop! I'm going to throw up!'

'Oh, God,' said Stephanie.

'Oh, God,' said Leah, mimicking her perfectly. I pulled over. Lizzie was not going to throw up, but I got out of the car, opened her door, took her to the side of the road, bent over her, holding her forehead in one hand and her hair in the other. All the formalities. Her face turned red and she panted, but though we stood there for ten minutes, she neither gagged nor puked. I felt her body stiffen, and we straightened up. There were tears in her eyes, and she said petulantly, 'I was going to.'

'I know. It's okay.'

But it wasn't okay with Stephanie. As soon as I pulled onto the highway again, she said, 'I don't see why we always have to stop. She never does anything.'

'I was going to.'

'You were not.'

'How do you know? I was.'

'Were not.'

'Stephanie—' This was me. I looked in the rearview mirror. Stephanie's tongue went out. Leah said, admiringly, 'Stephanie—' The argument subsided, to be resumed later. They always are.

Now Lizzie said, 'Why are we going to the house? I don't want to go. We went there last week.'

'Me, neither,' said Stephanie. 'I was going to play My Little Ponies with Megan.' She must have just remembered this, because it came out with a wail.

'It'll be fun,' I said, but I wasn't as convincing as Dana, who must have cast a spell to get us to leave, because I didn't want to go to the country, either. I glanced at my watch. It was ten o'clock. We could have turned around and been home before lunch, but we didn't. There was no place for us there. At the next K-mart, I turned into the parking lot with a flourish and took them straight to the toy department.

After the dinner that Dana missed and the bedtime she failed to arrive for, I turned out all the lights and sat on the porch in the dark, afraid. I was afraid that she was dead. I wished she had a little note on her that said, 'My family is at the following telephone number.' But, then, a note could be burned up in the wreck, as could her purse, the registration to the car, all identifying numbers on the car itself. Everything but her teeth. I imagined myself telling the children that she had gone off with another man, then some blue-garbed policeman appearing at the office this week or next with Dana's jaw. I would recognize the three delicate gold inlays I had put there, the fixed prosthesis Marty Crockett did in graduate school, when her tooth broke on a sourball. I would take her charred mandible in my hand and weigh it slightly. Would I be sadder than I was now?

Headlights flared across the porch and she drove up with a resolute crunch of gravel. The car door opened. She seemed to leap out and fly up the steps, throw open the door to the dark house, and vanish. She didn't see me, and I didn't say a word. I saw her, though. I saw the look on her face as if my eyeballs were spotlights. She was a soul desperate to divulge information. I got up quietly and walked down the steps, avoiding the gravel, and tiptoed across the front meadow to the road.

So how does the certainty that your wife loves another man feel? Every feeling is in the body as well as in the mind, that's what he said. But the nerves, for the most part, end at the surface, where they flutter in the breezes of worldly stimulation. Inside, they are more like freeways—limited access, running only from major center to major center. I have to admit that I don't remember much Gross Anatomy, so I don't know why it feels the way it feels, as if all your flesh were squeezing together, squeezing the air out of your lungs, squeezing the alveoli so they can never inflate again. More than that, it is as if soon there might be no spaces left inside at all, no conduits for fluids, even. Only the weight of solid flesh, the conscious act of picking up this heavy foot, and then this heavy foot, reaching this cumbersome hand so slowly that the will to grasp is lost before the object is touched. But when the light went on and the door opened and Dana peered into the darkness, I jumped behind a tree as sprightly as a cricket. Every feeling is in the mind as well as in the body. She went back into the house. The light on the stairs went on, then in the upstairs hall, then in the bathroom. A glow from the hall shone in each of the two children's rooms, as she opened their doors to check on them, then the window of our room lit up. It seemed to me that if I could stay outside forever she would never tell me that she was going to leave me, but that if I joined them inside the light and the warmth, the light and warmth themselves would explode and disappear.

I went around the side of the house, placed myself in the shadow of another tree, and watched the window to our bedroom. The shade was drawn, and I willed Dana to come and put it up, to open the window and show me her face without seeing me. She has a thin face, with high, prominent cheekbones and full lips. She has a way of smiling in merriment and dropping her eyelids before opening her eyes and laughing. In dental school I found this instant of secret, savored pleasure utterly beguiling. The knowledge that she was about to laugh would provoke my own laughter every time. I wonder if the patients swim up out of the haze of nitrous oxide and think that she is pretty, or that she is getting older, or that she looks severe. I don't know. I haven't had a cavity myself in fifteen years. Laura cleans my teeth twice a year and that's it for me. The shade went up, the window opened, and Dana leaned out and took some deep breaths. She put her left hand to her forehead and said, in a low, penetrating tone, 'Jesus.' She sighed deep, shuddering sighs, and wrapped her robe tightly around her shoulders. 'Jesus,' she said. 'Oh, Jesus. Jesus Christ. Oh, my God.' I had never heard her express herself with so little irony in my whole life. A cry came from the back of the house, and she pushed herself away from the window, closing it. Moments later, the glow from the hall light shone in Leah's room.

Now I went back to where I had been standing before. The windows in the children's rooms faced north and west, and hadn't received their treatments yet, so everything Dana did was apparent in an indistinct way. She went to the crib and bent over it. She stood up and bent over it again. She held out her arms, but Leah did not come into them. I could hear the muffled staccato of her screams. Dana stood up and put her hands on her hips, perplexed and, probably, annoyed. There was a long moment of this screaming; then Dana came to one of the windows and opened it. She leaned out and said, 'David Hurst, goddamn you, I know you're out there!' She didn't see me. She turned away, but left the window open, so I could hear Leah shouting, 'No! No! Daddy! Daddy!' Now the glow of the hall light appeared in the windows of Lizzie and Stephanie's room, and then Lizzie appeared next to Dana. Dana bent down and hugged her, reassuringly, but the screaming didn't stop. At last, Dana picked Leah up, only with a struggle, though, and set her down on the floor. I didn't move. I was shivering with the cold, and it took all my will not to move. It was like those nights when Stephanie used to wake up and cry. Each of us would go in and tuck her in and reassure her, then go out resolutely and shut the door. After that we would lie together in bed listening to the cries, sometimes for hours. Every fiber in your body wants to pick that child up, but every cell in your brain knows that if you pick her up tonight, she will wake up again tomorrow night and want to be picked up. Once, she cried from midnight until about seven in the morning. The pediatrician, I might add, said that this was impossible. You could say that it is impossible for a man to pull all of his own teeth with only the help of a few swallows of whiskey. Nothing is impossible. I know a man who dropped his baby in her GM Loveseat down a flight of stairs. Having carried that burden uncountable times myself, having wrapped my arms and my fingers tightly around that heavy, bulky object, I might have said that it was impossible for a father to drop his child, but it happened. Nothing is impossible. And so I didn't move.

Stephanie got up and turned on the light in her room. Dana turned on the light in Leah's room. Soon there were lights all over the house. After that, the light of the television, wanly receiving its single channel. I saw them from time to time in the downstairs windows, Dana passing back and forth, pausing once to clench her fists and shout. What she was shouting was, 'So shut up, just shut up for a moment, all right?' A sign that she has had it. They always shut up. Then she opens her fists and spreads her fingers and closes her eyes for a moment and takes a deep breath and says, 'Okay. Okay.' She went out of view. The light went on in the kitchen, and she reappeared, carrying glasses of milk. She went away again. She reappeared carrying blankets and sleeping bags. Then they all must have lain down or sat down on the floor, because all I saw after that was the wall of the living room, with half a Hundertwasser print and the blue of the television flickering across it. I looked at my watch. It was a quarter to two.

At two thirty, lights began going out again, first in the kitchen, then the dining room. The television went off. Dana passed the window, carrying a wrapped-up child, Leah, because that was the room she went into. She went to the window and closed it. Then she carried up Lizzie and Stephanie, one at a time. Don't stumble on those blankets going up the stairs, I thought. The living room light went out. The hall light. The bathroom light. The light in our room. It was three by now. The house was dark. I imagined sleep rising off them like smoke, filtering through the roof and ascending to the starry sky. I stayed outside. The sun came up about six. I went inside and made myself a big breakfast. I sat over it, reading the paper from the day before, until nearly eight thirty, when Dana came down. She was furious with me and didn't speak. I estimated that her pride might carry us through another three or even four days without anything being communicated.

I got up and walked out, leaving all the dirty dishes. Was I furious with her? Was that why I had taken this revenge? In the interests of self-knowledge, I entertained this possibility. Ultimately, however, I didn't care what my motives were. The main thing was that I had invested a new and much larger sum in my refusal to listen to any communications from my wife, and I saw that I would have to protect my investment rather cannily from now on.

For someone who has been married so long, I remember what it was like to be single quite well. It was like riding a little moped down a country road, hitting every bump, laboring up every hill. Marriage is like a semi, or at least a big pickup truck jacked up on fat tires. It barrels over everything in its path, zooming with all the purpose of great weight and importance into the future. When I was single, it seemed to me that I made up my future every time I registered for classes. After I paid my fees, I looked down at that little $4,000 card in my hand and felt the glow of relief. It was not that I was closer to being a dentist. That was something I couldn't imagine. It was that four more months of the future were visible, if only just. At the end of every term, the future dropped away, leaving me gasping.

Dana, however, always had plans. She would talk about them in bed after we had made love. She talked so concretely about each one, whether it was giving up dentistry and going to Mazatlán, or whether it was having Belgian waffles for breakfast if only we could get up two hours hence, at five thirty, in time to make it to the pancake house before our early classes, that it seemed to me that all I had to do was live and breathe. The future was a scene I only had to walk into. What a relief. And that is what it has been like for thirteen years now. I had almost forgotten that old vertigo. I think I must have thought I had grown out of it.

The day after I stayed up all night, which I spent working around the country house, clearing up dead tree limbs and other trash, pruning back this and that, the future dropped away entirely, and I could not even have said whether I would be at my stool, picking up my tools, the next morning. The very biological inertia that propelled me around the property, and from meal to meal, was amazing to me. I was terrified. I was like a man who keeps totting up the days that the sun has risen and making odds on whether it will rise again, who can imagine only too well the deepening cold of a sunless day. I gather that I was rather forbidding, to boot, because everyone stayed away from me except Leah, who clambered after me, dragging sticks and picking up leaves, and keeping up a stream of talk in her most man-pleasing tones.

Dana supported her spirits, and theirs, with a heroic and visible effort. They drove to one of the bigger supermarkets, about twenty miles away, and brought everything back from the deli that anyone could possibly have wanted—bagels, cream cheese mixed with lox, cream cheese mixed with walnuts and raisins, French doughnuts, croissants with chocolate in them, swordfish steaks for later, to be grilled with basil, heads of Buttercrunch lettuce, raspberry vinegar and olive oil, bottles of seltzer for Lizzie's stomach, *The New York Times*, the Chicago *Tribune*, for the funny papers. She must have thought she could lose herself in service, because she was up and down all day, getting one child this and another child that, dressing them so that they could go out for five minutes, complain of the cold, and be undressed again. She read them about six books and fiddled constantly with the TV reception. She sat on the couch and lured them into piling on top of her, as if the warmth of human flesh could help her. She was always smiling at them, and there was the panting of effort about everything she did. I wondered what he had done to her, to give her this desperation. Even so, I stayed out of the way. Any word would be like a spark in a dynamite factory. I kept Leah out of her hair. That is what I did for her, that is the service I lost myself in.

At dinner, when we sat across from each other at the old wooden table, she did not lift her eyes to my face. The portions she served me were generous, and they rather shamed me, as they reminded me of my size and my lifelong greed for food. I complained about the fish. It was a little undercooked. Well, it *was* a little undercooked, but I didn't have to say it. That was the one time she looked at me, and it was a look of concentrated annoyance, to which I responded with an aggressive stare. About eight we drove back to town. I remember that drive perfectly, too. Leah was sleeping in her car seat beside me, Lizzie was in the back, and Dana had Stephanie in her car. At stoplights, my glances in the rearview mirror gave me a view of her unyielding head. At one point, when I looked at her too long and missed the turning of the light, she beeped her horn. Lizzie said that her stomach hurt. I said, 'You can stand it until we get home,' and Lizzie fell silent at once, hearing the hardness in my voice. It was one of those drives that you remember from your own childhood and swear you will never have, so frightening, that feeling of everything wrong but nothing visibly different, of no future. But of course, there is a future, plenty of future for the results of this drive to reveal themselves, like a long virus that visits the child as a simple case of chicken pox and returns over and over to the adult as a painful case of shingles.

I should say that what I do remember about Dana, from the beginning, is a long stream of talk. I don't, as a rule, like to talk. That is why I preferred those rubber dams. That is why I like Laura. Dana is right, people who don't talk and rarely smile seem threatening. I am like my mother in this, not my father, whose hardware store was a place where a lot of men talked. They wandered among the bins of traps and U joints and washers and caulk, and they talked with warmth and enthusiasm, but also with cool expertise, about the projects they were working on. My father walked with them, drawing them out about the details, then giving advice about products . When my father was sick or out of town, my mother worked behind the counter and receipts plummeted. 'I don't know'—that's what she answered to every question. And she didn't. She didn't know what there was or where it might be or how you might do something. It was not that she didn't want to know, but you would think it was from the way she said it: 'Sorry, I don't know.' Snap. Her eyelids dropped and her lips came together. I suspect that 'I don't know' is the main sentiment of most people who don't talk. Maybe 'I don't know, please tell me.' That was my main sentiment for most of my boyhood. And Dana did. She told me everything she was thinking, and bit by bit I learned to add something here and there. I didn't know, for example, until the other night that I don't smile as much as most people. She told me. Now I know.

What is there to say about her voice? It is hollow. There is a vibration in it, as of two notes, one slightly higher than the other, sounding at the same time. This makes her singing voice very melodious, but the choir director doesn't often let her sing solo. He gives someone with purer tones the solo part, and has Dana harmonize. These small groups of two or three are often complimented after the choir concerts. It is in this hollow in her voice that I imagine the flow of that thirteen-year stream of talk. She is a talker. I suppose she is talking now to him, since I won't let her talk to me.

Monday night, after a long, silent day in the office to the accompaniment of extra care by the office staff that made me very uncomfortable, we went to bed in silence. She woke up cursing. 'Oh,' she said, 'oh shit. Ouch.' I could feel her reaching for her feet. When we were first married, she used to get cramps in her insteps from pointing her toes in her sleep. Some say this is a vitamin deficiency. I don't know. Anyway, I slithered under the covers and grabbed her feet. What you do is bend the toes and ankles back, and then massage the instep until the knot goes away. Massage by itself doesn't work at all; you have to hold on to the toes so that they don't point by mistake, for about five minutes. I did. She let me. While I was holding on to her feet I felt such a welling up of desire and pain and grief that I began to heave with dry sobs. 'Dave,' she said. 'Dave.' Her hollow voice was regretful and full of sorrow. In the hot dark under the covers, I ran my thumbs over her insteps and pushed back her toes with my fingers. Your wife's feet are not something, as a rule, that you are tactilely familiar with, and I hadn't had much to do with her feet for eight or nine years, so maybe I was subject to some sort of sensual memory, but it seemed to me that I was twenty-five years old and ragingly greedy for this darling person whom I had had the luck to fool into marrying me. Except that I wasn't, and I knew I wasn't, and that ten minutes encompassed ten years, and I was about to be lost. When the cramps were out of her feet, I knelt up and threw off the covers, and said, 'Oh, God! Dana, I'm sorry I'm me!' That's what I said. It just came out. She grabbed me by the shoulders and pulled me down on top of her and hugged me tightly, and said in a much evener voice, 'I'm not sorry you're you.'

. And so, how could she tell me then? She couldn't, and didn't. I think she was sorry I was me, sorry that I wasn't him in bed with her. But when husbands express grief and fear, wives automatically comfort them, and they are automatically comforted. Years ago, such an exchange of sorrow would have sent us into a frenzy of lovemaking. It did not this time. She held me and kissed my forehead, and I was comforted but not reassured. We went back to sleep and got up at seven to greet the daily round that is family life. Zap, she used to say, there goes another one.

I was worried about her and she was worried about me, and that was an impasse that served my purposes for most of that week. God knows what the bastard was doing to her, but she was very reserved, careful, good, and sad. She went to the grocery store a lot. Maybe she was calling him from there, standing in the phone booth with two children in the basket and a line of old ladies behind her waiting to call the car service.

Each of my children favors one sense over the other. Lizzie has been all eyes since birth. We have pictures of her at nine days old, her eyes focused and glittering, snapping up every visual stimulation. She is terrific at finding things and has been since she could talk. It took us a while to believe her, but now we believe her every time. She doesn't stare, either. She glances. She stands back and takes in wholes. It seems to me that her eyes are the source of her persnickety taste and her fears. She simply cannot bear certain color combinations, for example. They offend her physically. Likewise, what she sees is far away from her, out of her control, and so makes her afraid. She rushes in, gets closer, so that she can look more carefully. But it is hard for her to reach out and touch or rearrange. Fear intervenes. She only looks, she feels no power.

Stephanie is the wild beast who is soothed by music. She has always heard things first, looked for them second. She often looks away from what she is paying attention to, making her seem evasive, but really she is listening. She is the only child I've ever known who doesn't interrupt. I don't even know if she listens to words as much as to tones, to the rhythms of sentences and the pitch of voices. Will she be a musician? She likes music. But she likes the sound of traffic, too, and the sound of cats in the backyard, and the cries of birds and the rustle of leaves. She simply likes the way the world sounds, and she listens to it. She comes closer than Lizzie does, but she doesn't seem to respond to what goes in at all, except with a single, final look, to make sure, maybe, that what is heard has a source. Then she backs away. Is she the one I should worry about?

Leah sat up at five months and reached for the toys that were in front of her. It took her another five months to crawl. Yes, she was big and fat, but more than that, she was satisfied. Her hands were huge, and she could hold two blocks in each of them when she was six months old. Hand to mouth. You couldn't keep anything out of her mouth. Now it seems as though she doesn't recognize anything without touching it. She runs her hands over my face. She holds on tight. She snuggles. Standing in front of a table of toys, she is as satisfied as a human can be, and she has stretches of concentration that Lizzie and Stephanie don't begin to match, although they are five and three years older than she is. If you distract her, she looks drugged for a moment. Drugged by touch.

And so I have three separate regrets. What does Lizzie see? What does Stephanie hear? What unsatisfied, yearning tension does Leah feel in my flesh when she snuggles against me and puts her hands on my shoulders? There is no hiding from them, is there? And there is no talking to them. They don't understand what they understand. I am afraid. I should call the pediatrician, but I don't. I think, as people do, that everything will be all right. But even so, I can't stop being afraid. They are so beautiful, my daughters, so fragile and attentive to family life.

I wish they were boys and completely oblivious, as I was. I could not have said, before I met Dana, whether my parents' marriage was happy or not. I didn't know. She told me. She said, 'Your parents are so dissimilar, aren't they? I mean, your father is sociable and trusting and all business, and your mother just doesn't know what to make of things, does she? They are a truly weird combination.' We were twenty-two. She had spent her first half hour with them, and this was what she came out with, and that is what I have known about them ever since.

The next day a new patient came in, a heavyset, pugnacious man about my age. I poked around in his mouth and said, 'Besides your present cavities, you have some very poorly filled teeth here.' He sat up and looked at me and said, 'You know, I've never been to a dentist who thought much of what was done to your teeth before him. And I'll say this, you'd better be cheap, because five years from now, some guy's going to tell me he's got to redo all your work, too.' He sat back and looked out the window for a second, but he must have thought that the ice was broken, because he started right in again. 'Doctors never say boo about what they see. I mean, some guy could cut off your healthy leg and leave the bad one, and you wouldn't get another doctor to admit the guy had made a mistake.'

'Hmm,' I said.

'I don't know,' he said. 'Things are more fucked every day.'

'Open, please,' I said.

'I mean, I don't know why I'm sitting here having my teeth fixed. It's going to cost me a lot of money that I could spend having the other stuff fixed. By the way, don't touch the front teeth. I play the trumpet, and if you touch the front teeth, then I'll have to change my embouchure.'

I said, 'Open, please.'

'Well, I'm not sure I want to open. I mean, if you don't do anything, then I can spend my money on therapy or something that might really improve my life.'

'We do ask patients to pay for appointments they don't keep. If you're uneasy about the discomfort, we have a lot of ways to make sure—'

'Hell, I don't care if it pinches, like you guys all say. I don't care if it hurts like shit. I just want to feel I'm not wasting my time.'

'Proper dental care is never a—'

'My wife made this appointment for me. Now I've lost my job, and she's kicked me out. But she sent me this little card, telling me to go here, and I came. I mean, I can't—'

'Mr Slater, please open your mouth so that we can get on with it.'

'I can't believe she kicked me out, but I really can't believe she cares whether or not I go to the dentist.'

'I don't know, Mr Slater. But you are wasting my time and yours, too.'

'Didn't you say you'd get paid, anyway?'

'That's our policy, yes.'

'How long does it take you to fill a couple of teeth?'

'About half an hour.'

'Then just let me talk. I'll pay you.'

'I don't like to talk, Mr Slater,' I said. 'I'd rather fill teeth.'

'But I'll pay you the money I should be paying a psychiatrist.'

I put down my mirror and my probe. Dana passed the door and glanced in, curious. Her eyes left an afterimage of blue. Slater said, 'That your wife?'

'What do you want to talk about, Mr Slater?'

He sat back and deflated with a big sigh. He looked out the window. I did, too. Finally, he said, 'Hey, I don't know. Go ahead and fill a couple of teeth. You're probably better at that, anyway.'

'That's what I'm trained to do, Mr Slater.'

He made no reply, and I filled two molars, right lower. He didn't speak again, but every time I changed my position or asked him to do something, he fetched up a bone-quivering sigh. His front teeth, I should say, were a mess. A brittle net, crooked, destined for loss. He left without speaking to me again, and paid with his MasterCard.

After he left I wanted him back. I wanted the navy-blue collarless jacket that he wouldn't take off. I wanted the Sansabelt slacks that stretched tight over his derriere. I wanted the loafers. I wanted him to tell me about his wife. He didn't smile much. He had a rough way of speaking. He was tall and not a pleasant man. It seemed to me that I could have drilled his teeth without novocaine, man to man, and it would have relieved us both.

He was with me all the rest of the afternoon. I imagined him leaving the office when I did. I imagined how he would walk, how he would get in his car, how he would drive down the street—thrusting and pugnacious, jamming the pedals, hand close to the horn all the time. Grief, I saw, had loosened him up, as if at the joints, and up and

down his vertebrae. He had become a man who would do or say anything, would toss back his head or fling out his arms in a gesture
impossible before. He wouldn't leave me alone. I felt bitterly sorry for
him all afternoon. It seemed to me that his fate would be an ill one,
and mine, too. All of our fates.

By the time Dana came home, I couldn't stop doing things as Slater
might have done them. I was talkative and aggressive. I put my hands
on her shoulders and turned her around so that she would look at me.
I wandered around the kitchen, opening cupboards and slamming
them shut. I talked about all of my patients except Slater at boring
length. My voice got loud. Dana shrank and shrank. At first she
laughed; then, with a few sidelong glances in my direction, she began
to scuttle. I wondered if Slater's wife was just then doing exactly the
same thing. But she wasn't. She had kicked him out, and I could certainly see why. Finally I stopped. I just stopped where I was standing,
with my mouth gaping open, and Dana and I traded a long glance. I
said, 'What time is dinner?'

'About half an hour. Dave—'

'I'm going out. I'll be back, okay?' Slater wouldn't have asked in
that way for permission. Neither would Dave Hurst, a month ago. I
slammed out the back door and got into the car.

After I left Dana, Slater left me, and Dana joined me. I had hardly
seen her back at the house, the whole time I was hovering around her,
but now I could practically smell her, feel the vigor of her presence. As
a rule, I don't know what she looks like. I don't think I have known,
since the beginning, before everything about her looks became familiar to me, and saturated with feeling. As I drove along in the car, a
picture of what she looks like came to me for the first time in years.
And I thought, She is pretty, but she is getting a little prim-looking,
with her gold button earrings and the gold chains around her neck.
She wears neat blouses in the office, even now, in the midst of passion.
And as this picture came to me, it also came to me that this passion was
unbearable to her, and that the only way she knew to make it bearable
was to pour herself into it as well as everything else, the way she has
always done. I stepped on the gas, and soon I was streaming down the
interstate at 92 miles per hour. 'Lord,' I said, 'let me fly. Give me that

miracle to ease this pain.' I pushed the car up to 100. I hadn't had a car into three figures in seventeen years, since Kevin Mills let me gas his father's Oldsmobile 98 up to 115 the summer after we graduated from high school. I went fast, but I didn't fly. Instead, I thought of my children and turned back at the next exit. I realized that the object of Dana's affections had refused her.

At the dinner table, Slater invaded me again. I was cutting Leah's meat and she was complaining that the pieces were too large, so I cut them and cut them until they were nearly mush. Then she said, 'I don't like it.' I sat back and looked at her, then around the table at the others, and it seemed to me that I was Slater, visiting for dinner. The woman was blond, sort of pretty and nice enough, I thought, but her children were horrible, the oldest sullen and suspicious—clank, clank-clank went her knife and fork on the plate—the next one an oblivious blonde, masticating her food with annoying languor, and the third irritable and squawking. At last, inevitably, Leah smacked her bowl and it landed upside down on the floor. As Slater, I waited for their mother to do something about it. As my wife, Dana looked at me expectantly. Leah looked at me expectantly. I pretended to be their father. I jumped up and grabbed Leah out of her chair, and said in gruffish tones, 'That's enough. I'm putting you into your bed.' And I carried her upstairs. The windows were dirty and the sills needed vacuuming, and there were toys all over the floor of the child's room. The responsibility for all this seemed put upon me, and I stomped down the stairs, shouting, 'Be quiet! Stop yelling! You can come down in five minutes.'

'Dave,' said Dana.

I answered to this name.

'I don't think you should shout at her like that.'

'Somebody has to. Maybe nobody has enough. You don't. What the fuck is going on around here?'

Dana looked up fearfully. 'Nothing. Nothing is going on, just everything the same. Why don't you sit down and—'

Now I really was Slater. 'Everything's more fucked every day.'

Lizzie and Stephanie had put down their forks and were staring out at me from under their foreheads, as if they couldn't take the full blast of me in their faces, but couldn't resist a look.

Dana said, 'Why are you like this? Why are you so angry all the time? It's unbearable.'

'I'm not angry all the time! I'm not really angry now.'

'Listen to yourself! Can't you hear what you're saying?'

'But it's true, things are more fucked every day! Every day! Every day is worse!'

'No, it isn't! It isn't. Don't say that. I won't listen to that! You've always said that! I hate it.'

'I have not always said that. I just realized it today.'

'You have.' She burst into tears. I was bitterly hurt and angry. Her greatest lifelong sin seemed to me to be that she didn't agree with me about the way the world is. I thought, I could accept anything else, let her love him, let her fuck him, let her talk to him forever, but give me this little agreement that I've never had before. I said, or rather shouted, 'Admit that I'm right. Admit that every day is worse!'

'I won't!'

I could kill you, I thought.

'What did you say?'

'I didn't say anything.'

'You said you could kill me.' I looked into each horrified face and saw that I had said it, or Slater had said it. I groaned. 'I didn't mean to say it.'

'But you thought it.'

'I can't control my thoughts.'

'You thought you could kill me.'

'I don't know what I thought. I thought a lot of things. I think all the time.' I sat down and looked first at Lizzie and then at Stephanie, and I said, 'A person can think anything that they want, because there is no way to make yourself not think things. But you don't want to do everything you think. I'm sorry. I think I'll go out for a little while.' And then Slater and I slammed out of the house and got in the car again, although my father always used to say, in every crisis, 'At least don't get in the car.' And he never did.

Slater kept wanting to stop at a bar. Or at a gas station to pick up a couple of six-packs. Dave didn't think this was an especially good idea, but he did think he deserved something. What Dave really thought was that a responsible professional man, owner of two homes, employer of four persons, parent of three daughters, and lifelong meditative personality ought to be able to control himself. He also thought that his wife, a responsible professional woman, and ditto ditto ditto, if not ditto, ought to have been able to control herself, too. We stopped, Slater and I, at a rest area about thirty miles up the interstate, and there, without the benefit of a six-pack, we stood back from the road in the gloom of a chilly night and we screamed and screamed and screamed. After screaming, while noticing that we had screamed our throat into raw throbbing, we noticed the stars. They lay across the dark blue sky like sugar and diamonds sprinkled together. And Lord, how they shamed the flesh.

In the exhausted backwash of all this verbalizing, I realized that my plan not to be communicated with was at greater risk than ever, because I had made myself so unpleasant that it was likely she would flee to him, or at least flee from me at whatever cost. In fact, my success now rested with his resolution not to have her. Only with that. I wondered what it was about her, her circumstances or her person, that gave him pause. Or maybe it was her intrinsic passion. Maybe he had thought he saw in her cool blondness some sort of astringent distance, and now he saw that between Dana and a desired object there was no distance allowed at all. Maybe he was dazzled by the neat blouses and the deft workmanship into not seeing the defiant, greedy stare. Maybe he saw only the established dentist, not the determined dental student, the stainless-steel blonde in the doorway of the classroom, radiating tensile strength like heat. Appearances aren't deceiving, I think, but you have to know where to look.

I should say that it was hard for me not to see her as a dramatic figure. I always had seen her that way. Maybe, in fact, he only viewed her as something of a bore, a little thing, a mere woman passing through his life. I don't know. I never even saw him. I got home about twelve and sneaked into bed. Dana was already asleep. There is something I have noticed about desire, that it opens the eyes and strikes them blind at the same time. These days, when I lie awake at night and think about those early spring weeks, the objects of the world as they were then appear to me with utter clarity. Edges sharp,

colors bright, movements etched into the silvery mirror of light and
air. When I used to think of the word 'confusion,' I would think of a
kind of gray mist, but that is not what confusion is. Confusion is perfect sight and perfect mystery at the same time. Confusion is seeing
without knowing, as if the optic nerves were still attached but the
hemispheres of the brain were parted. Desire is confusion vibrating in
the tissues.

Confusion and desire also include the inability to keep quiet. One
of the things I remember with embarrassing clarity is all the talking I
did, all the statements I made about every possible thing. They were all
assertions, bombast, a waste of breath. Could I have shut up? The
world was beautiful during those weeks—chill, sunny, gold-green,
severe undecorated shapes of mountains, tree limbs, stones, clouds,
floating together and together in a stream of configurations as the eye
rolled past them. If I had it again, I would look at it better.

About this time we had what Dana would call 'an early warning.'
News of the impending disaster came first to Laura, through her
cousin in California, then to Dave from his mother two states away.
Vomiting, high temperatures in both children and adults, lethargy,
sore throat, possible ear complications. Dana told Dave to rearrange
our schedules for about a week, so that the illness could pass through
the body of the family with as little disruption as possible. It isn't
unusual—the note from the school nurse reporting a case of chicken
pox, the patient confiding, just before he opens his jaws, that he is feeling a little woozy, and then he leans back and out it comes, the miasma
of contagion. Once each winter, if we are lucky, twice if we are not,
the great family reunion that is the flu, or strep throat. The family
patients have their characteristic styles of illness, and Lizzie is truly the
worst, since she can't stand discomfort but fights the medicine. Dana
is hardly any better and seems to get a certain amount of relief from
simply cursing, which doesn't give the rest of us any relief at all. And
me? Dana says that I am the one who haunts the house with a martyred air. I ask for a glass of orange juice, she says, and then, before she
has a chance to get it, I turn up beside the refrigerator, wounded to the
quick by her failure of care, and pour it myself. Yes, yes, yes. I wasn't
eager, given our circumstances, to take on this flu.

The patients, now transformed into vectors, came without cease. I leaned over them. I picked up one instrument at a time and set each down. I wanted to be careful and not angry. I wanted, in fact, not to be myself, but I didn't want to be Slater, either. None of the patients really replaced him in the chair, though, and when Dana passed the door, or spoke in the outer office, his ears pricked with that sleazy curiosity of his. 'That your wife?' he kept saying. My private revenge against him was that I knew that his front teeth were going to disintegrate, and that his embouchure wouldn't be his for long, no matter what. Slater was an insensitive fellow, though, and didn't care what I knew. He also wanted to sit sullenly in the office and eat steak subs with cheese and drink coffee every day for lunch. Dana wasn't the only staff member pretty fed up with him. Laura didn't like his manner at all, and Delilah just stayed away. Only Dave didn't seem to notice.

Anyway, during those lunch hours, Slater and Dr Dave were locked in argument. It was not that they couldn't agree what to do. Neither of them knew what to do. Their concerns were more abstract. Dr Dave wanted to find reasons for his feelings. It would have relieved him to know, for instance, that steak, cheese, and coffee were biochemical poisons that were deepening his anxiety. Slater had never seen anything, heard anything, or felt anything. Slater had no receptors, only transmitters. He wanted to shout and drive and drink and blow his trumpet. He was marvelously contemptuous of every thread Dr Dave wanted to look at. What good had it done him, all these years, Slater declared, to pick up one tool at a time? Income, Dr Dave said, look at my income, look at what people think of me. People, said Slater, think nothing of you. You are just a dentist, another white coat, another small thing. Every day you sit at your stool fashioning things in people's mouths, and then they close their mouths and stand up, and more than anything they want to forget you, and your work never sees the light of day.

But you, Dr Dave said, you know nothing, you stumble through your life without a first notion, pressing yourself and your breath and your music into the world. What good has it done you, Slater, to consume without thought and express without consideration? No good, said Slater. No good. But I know that it does me no good, and you don't even know that.

And then I sit with my head against the wall, waiting for the next patient, and I can hardly move or breathe, and when the tears begin rolling down my cheeks, I just turn my head toward the window, I don't even wonder why they have come or how I might dismiss them. I hear Dana's step pause beside the door, the step of her $120 Italian high heels, for she is very particular about elegant shoes. I can imagine the flash of her curious blue eyes, but she says nothing, and when Delilah speaks from the other office, she turns and goes out, and both Slater and Dr Dave feel gaspingly sorry for themselves. There is nothing meditative about it.

This went on until about Thursday. On Thursday, everyone in the family woke up at a quarter to nine from a sleep that could have been drug- or enchantment-induced. There was no possible consideration of anything except clothing, breakfast, and the fact that the girls were already late for school. Even Lizzie was so somnolent that she gave no thought to the embarrassment of walking into the classroom late. She lifted her arms to receive her sleeves and opened her mouth to receive her Cheerios, and Stephanie wandered around the bathroom as if she didn't know what she was doing there, and Leah let Dana dress her without a word of protest. Dana kept making toast. I kept eating it. It was buttery and delicious. She wouldn't let us hurry. She called the office and said I was busy and would be an hour and a half late, then she called the school and said that the girls would be there in time for recess. She was sleepy, too, and wandered from bathroom to bedroom half-dressed, looking for articles of clothing that were right under her nose. At ten thirty we took Leah early to day care and went to the office together, where Dana worked on the patients I had stood up. I don't think I thought of Slater or the Other or the crisis of my marriage until well into the second patient, and then the patient's malocclusion seemed more immediate, and, even, more interesting. Delilah had brought daffodils from her garden and set them on Dave's desk, and so the day had a refrain, 'Aren't those lovely flowers!'

When I used to work construction, my boss would tell me about the seventeen-inch rule. The seventeen-inch rule has to do with the construction of staircases. If you add together the width of the tread and the height of the riser, they should come out to seventeen inches. If they do, the step will meet the foot. If they don't, the foot will stumble. Sometimes, if he had a remodeling job in an old house, I would check out the seventeen-inch rule, and it was always true. The effort of steps that were too steep or too shallow was always perceived by the knees and the tendons, if not by the brain. And so I would say that we had a seventeen-inch day. Patients came on time and opened calmly. Teeth nearly drilled themselves, or jumped out into my hand. Dana and Delilah chattered and murmured in the next office. Laura and Dave teased each other. At lunch, Dana and I found ourselves on the back step of the office, facing the alley, eating peanut-butter sandwiches with raspberry jam and drinking milk. Our shoulders touched. She said, 'You know, I think Leah told her first joke today.'

'What was that?'

'Well, she was making claws with her hands, and roaring, the way she does, and I said, 'What's the name of your monster?' and she looked at me and said, "Diarrhea." And then she grinned.'

We laughed and our shoulders bumped.

'Do you want the last bite of this?' She held out a piece of her sandwich.

I nodded and opened my mouth. She put it in. I chewed it. We got up and went inside. An hour and a half later I was finished for the day and half expected to be met by Slater on the steps of the office, but the coast was clear. I took out my list of errands and purchases and walked toward downtown. Everything was on sale, including a very nice blue-and-green plaid Viyella shirt, 16-35, $16 marked down from $50. I put it on in the store, something I never do. As a rule I let new clothes sit in the closet for weeks before wearing them. I kept walking, looking at yards and houses and daffodils and crocuses, and felt that spurious permanency that comes with the sense of true peace. For dinner I bought boned chicken breasts and frozen pesto sauce. Dana came home and made fresh noodles.

Leah sat between Stephanie and Lizzie on the couch and they played this game: Lizzie would take Leah's face between her two palms and say, 'Say yes, Leah,' and then she would nod Leah's face up and down. Then Stephanie would take Leah's face from the other side and say, 'Say no, Leah,' and turn her head gently from side to side. None of the three could stop laughing, the two older girls from the sight of it, and from the feeling of their own power, and Leah, perhaps, from the pleasure of their attention, or perhaps from the rattling perspective shifts she experienced as they manipulated her head. I said, 'Careful of her neck.' But they were, without my saying anything. I pretended not to be watching them, but really I was transfixed by the passing of that baby head from hand to hand, by the way Lizzie's and Stephanie's fingers spread and flexed, by how strong their hands were with all their childish pudginess, and by how unconscious they were and yet how sensitive. I went into the kitchen. When I came back a few minutes later, the big girls were at their pictures and Leah was coloring her fingernails with a blue marker. I opened my mouth to remind her not to write on her skin, but before the first word was out, she had drawn a line from her ankle to her diaper. She looked up at me. I said, 'That's naughty. Don't write on yourself.' She knew I would say it, and I did. She refrained from writing on herself then as a formality until I left the room.

These are the trivia of family life, what the children do and say, how the fragrance of dinner wafts through the house, a view of the yard through the glass of the front door, the border collie across the street barking at the UPS man, a neighbor who has been hardly noticed these last weeks bringing the packets of seed you ordered together, looking at you quizzically and with concern, then turning away, making a joke upon herself. One by one they come upon the senses, charge along the neurons, leap the synapses, electrify the brain, and there is a moment, a moment of a specific duration which I don't remember, before the synapses jam, when the ear hears, the nose smells, the eyes see, the fingers sense the cool smooth foil of the seed packets.

We ate dinner.

We watched 'Family Ties,' then 'Cheers.' We put the children to bed and watched 'Hill Street Blues.'

Dana was sitting beside me on the couch. She yawned and turned toward me. I saw my face in the pupils of her eyes, then I saw that she was smiling. She said, 'I can't believe I'm so tired. Are you going to sit up?'

I was, and I did, alone in the silent living room, with the lights off and a beer warming in my hand. It seemed to me that the unexpected peace of the day had left me dizzy with pleasure, such pleasure that its prospective loss made my stomach queasy. Feelings are in the body as well as in the mind, is what he said. I lay back on the carpet, on the floor of the organ that was my house, and felt my family floating above me, suspended only by two-by-fours as narrow as capillaries and membranes of flooring. My pulse beat in my ears and the walls of the house seemed to throb with it. I closed my eyes and took some deep breaths. From China, from California, state by state, patient by patient, the flu had arrived.

I wonder if it is possible to prepare yourself for anything. Of course I lay there, saying, This is the flu, it isn't supposed to last more than two or three days, I should find the Tylenol. In the moment I didn't feel bad, really, a little queasy, a degree feverish. The disease wasn't a mystery to me. I know what a virus looks like, how it works. I could imagine the invasion and the resistance. In fact, imagining the invasion and the resistance took my attention off the queasiness and the fever-ishness. But when I opened my eyes and my gaze fell upon the bookcases looming above me in the half-light, I shuddered reflexively, because the books seemed to swell outward from the wall and threaten to drop on me, and my thoughts about the next few days had exactly that quality as well. I did not see how we would endure, how I would endure.

There are many moments in every marriage that are so alike that they seem to be the same moment, appearing and vanishing, giving the illusion of time passing, and of no time passing, giving the illusion that a marriage is a thing everlasting. One of these recurring moments, for Dana and me, has always had to do with getting ready—finding a clear position to take up before the avalanche of events, like semester exams, births, vacations. Perhaps we practiced for this every night that we coasted down Cloud Street on my bike. That hill was not only long, it curved sharply to the right and had three steep dips. I suppose, looking back, that the precipice, such as

it was, lasted seven or eight blocks before flattening out. Dana's apartment was about a block and a half from the top of the hill, and the
first night I took her out I was so exhilarated that I put my feet on the
handlebars of my bike and coasted all the way to the stoplight, eleven
blocks from Dana's house.

The next time we went out, I suggested that we coast down it
together. I remember the way that her eyelids snapped open at the idea
and her stare locked into mine, but it took her only a second to say yes,
and then we had to do it. I said, 'Sit on the handlebars, then,' and she
did. She put her hands in front of mine, balanced with the small of her
back, and looked straight ahead, straight at the first dip, and I thought,
We are going to die now. I settled the bones of my ass on the seat and
tightened my fingers on the grips. I pushed off and pedaled. I did not
want to drift into it, whatever it was, I wanted to pump into it. It was
agony. The bike was surprisingly front-heavy. I could hardly manage
the dips, and skidded dangerously to the left when the right-hand
curve came up. Our weight carried us a block past the stoplight,
which, fortunately, was green.

After we had stopped, we didn't even speak about it, but resumed
our conversation about dental matters while walking the thirteen
blocks back up the hill. This time we didn't stop at Dana's house, but
climbed to the top, where I stood holding the bike while she hoisted
herself on. Looking back, it is that moment I remember, that recurring
moment, always the same, of her hands and her thighs and her back,
their stillness, the lifting of my foot onto the right pedal. Taking a clear
position. I wonder why she trusted me so. I do not discount the possibility of simple stupidity.

Now, the flu. Three steep dips and a sharp curve to the right.
People without children don't begin to know the test that these ill-
nesses present. But there was no clear position to be taken, and no one
to take it with. I lay on the floor until about three, when I went
upstairs and puked into the toilet. Then I lay in the hallway outside the
bathroom, shivering with fever and waiting to puke again. At six,
Dana found me, gazed down with a knowing look, and went to find
the seltzer, the Tylenol, the thermometer, the cool wash-cloth, my
pajamas, a pillow so that I could remain in the hallway, where I found

a kind of solitary and rigorous comfort. The children thought it was very peculiar and amusing to step over me. I was too dizzy to care.

They abandoned me. The children went to school and day care without a backward look; Dana went early to the office to take care of my patients, with only a shout from the front door that she was leaving now, would I be all right? I got my own juice, my own blanket, drew my own bath, because it seemed as if that would ease the aches and pains. I did everything for myself, because they were all off, doing as they pleased, healthy and happy. I could see out the window that it was a beautiful day, and I imagined them all dazed by the sparkle of the light, on the street, on the playground, all thoughts of me blasted out of them. Lizzie would be working in her reading workbook, Stephanie drawing pictures of the family, Leah making turtles out of egg cartons and poster paints, Dana mixing up amalgam on her tray, all of them intent only on their work, no matter how much I might think of them. Just then the phone rang, and it was Dave. He said, 'Dana wanted me to call and ask if you needed anything.' I said, 'No. I just took some Tylenol.' After that I got into the bathtub and floated there for an hour, resenting the fact that I had left my juice next to the telephone in the bedroom. Drying myself, I was dizzy again and nearly fell down. I entertained myself with thoughts of hitting my head on the bathtub and suffering a subdural hematoma; then I staggered into the bedroom and fell across the bed, already mostly asleep. Three hours later, I resurrected. I was clear-eyed, cool, happy. The forces of resistance had won an early victory.

Lizzie threw up for the first time while she was watching 'The Flintstones' and eating her Hershey bar. She made it to the front hallway, but not to the bathroom. Stephanie was not sympathetic. Leah, carrying her Play Family garage from the living room to the kitchen, could not be prevented from stepping in it. Lizzie had already fled upstairs, Stephanie was hiding her nose in the sofa cushions, and Leah's wet bare footprint followed her into the dining room. I went for paper towels and a bucket, and I heard Lizzie, panicky, shouting from upstairs, 'Daddy! Daddy!' She stumbled from somewhere above my head to somewhere else, and began to retch again. Just then, mop in one hand and bucket in the other, I felt all the grief of the last weeks drain away, to be replaced, not by panic, but by order. I caught Leah, wiped her foot off, and spread some paper towels over the mess in the hall. Then I went to Lizzie, who was draped over the toilet, and carried her into her bedroom, where I laid her on her bed, undid her clothes, and surrounded her with towels. Her face was red and soaked with tears, and I thought, I can't help you. I wiped her face with a cool washcloth, and then Stephanie shouted from downstairs, 'She's going to get in it! She's getting near it! Daddy! Daddy!'

Lizzie said, 'Don't go away.'

That was the beginning.

What is it possible to give? Last fall I was driving to the office in a downpour, and I saw a very fat woman cross the street in front of the bus depot and stick out her thumb. No raincoat, no umbrella. I stopped and let her in. The office was about three blocks down, but I thought I would drive her wherever she needed to go in town. She said she was going to Kinney, a town about ten miles east, and it occurred to me simply to drive her there. She was wearing cloth shoes and carrying all her belongings in a terry-cloth bag. I don't think I answered, but she spoke anyway. She said, 'My husband works out there. I just got in from California, after two months, and the whole time he was sending me these postcards, saying, Come back, come back, and so I bought my ticket.' She fell silent. Then she looked at me and said, 'Well, I called him up to say I'd got my ticket, and he said right there, "Well, I want a divorce, anyway." So here I am. He works out there.'

I said, 'Maybe you can change his mind.'

'I hope so. She works out there where he works, too. I want to get to them before they get into work. If I can't change his mind, I'm going to beat him up right there in the parking lot.' She looked at me defiantly.

I said, 'Why don't I drop you at the Amoco station at the corner of Front Street? You can stand under the awning, and there ought to be a lot of people turning toward Kinney there.'

'Yeah.'

After I got to the office, I thought maybe I could have bought her an umbrella, but I didn't go out and get her one, did I? It perplexes me, what it is possible to give a stranger, what it is possible to give a loved one, the difference between desire and need, how it is possible to divine what is helpful. I might say that I would give Dana anything to ensure her presence in our house, our office, our family, but in saying this I have only traded the joy of giving for the despair of payment. I went downstairs and cleaned up the mess, then I went back upstairs and wiped Lizzie's face again with a newly wrung-out washcloth. If you stimulate the nerve endings in a pleasurable way, the neurons are less capable of carrying pain messages to the brain, and the brain is fooled. Dana was an hour late from work.

I should say that Lizzie heaved twelve times in four hours, so much that we were forcing ginger ale down her throat so that something, anything, could come back up. And she was fighting every drop, and screaming in panic, and throwing herself back and forth among the towels on her bed. We didn't have dinner, of course, but we did laundry, all the nightgowns, all the sheets, all the towels. About eleven, Dana said, 'You're better,' as if she had just noticed.

'Thirteen hours, normal to normal in thirteen hours.'

'That's something, anyway.'

'Not a basis for confidence, though.'

She pursed her lips. 'I wish you weren't always so pessimistic.'

'As long as this lasts, why don't we avoid talking about how we always are?'

'Okay, but no sarcasm, either.'

'A deal.' We shook hands. Lizzie threw up four more times before morning, then six times on Saturday. When I called the pediatrician for a little reassurance and told him she had thrown up twenty-two times, he said, 'That's impossible.'

Dana says that they are formed at birth, and that they spend their whole childhoods simply revealing themselves. With a sort of arrogance that you might say is typical of her, she says that she knew all this in advance, as soon as she laid her mother's hands on them, that Lizzie did not care to snuggle, that Stephanie's neonatal thoughts were elsewhere, that Leah wanted to melt into the warmth of Dana's flesh. Some people cannot, will not be comforted. Lizzie is this way. She tosses off the covers and complains of the cold. Her joints ache, and she won't take the medicine. A swallow of seltzer gives her mouth such cool pleasure that she won't take another. She writhed about among the towels, needing and fighting sleep, and I sat near her, sometimes smoothing her forehead with the wrung-out washcloth and contemplating her doom in much the same way that you contemplate their future glory when they do well in school or learn to read at three and a half. Then she fell asleep about ten and slept all night, not doomed, but saved one more time.

Dana lay next to me in a snore, and I thought of the soul, nacreous protoplasm, ringed in the iron of the self, weak little translucent hands on the bars, pushing, yanking, desperate for release. The moonlight stood flat in the window glass, as if caught there, and I turned and pressed myself against the warmth of my disappearing wife. Leah awakened at four. She would consent to be held only by me, and there was no sitting down allowed, only walking. A torture, in the middle of the night, that could have been devised by the KGB.

That was Sunday, the resurrection of Lizzie and the marathon of Leah, kitchen, dining room, living room, an endless circle. Sometimes Dana handed me food and drink, as in the old Kingston Trio song about the fellow who got stuck on the MTA. Dana kept putting on records, to keep me occupied, and sometimes she took Leah from me, but the screams were unrelenting. Sometimes I put her down in her bed, when she seemed to be asleep, but she always woke up and called out for me. Sometimes I staggered under the weight. Sometimes I got so dizzy from the circling that I nearly fell down. I had a chant: Normal to normal in thirteen hours. Maybe it was a prayer.

For dinner Lizzie and Stephanie wanted pizza. I circled. Leah's head rested back on her neck against my shoulder. Her mouth was open and her eyes were closed. One arm was tossed around my neck and her fingers hung in the collar of my shirt. From time to time I sat down in the rocking chair (this was always accompanied by a groan of protest from Leah) and rocked until the protests grew unbearable. The pizza came and Lizzie didn't want any. Stephanie ate only a single piece, because Lizzie pointed out to her that mushrooms had been put on by mistake. Dana screamed at them, threw away all the rest of the pizza, said we would never order another one, and sent them to their rooms; then she flopped on the couch, ashamed and unhappy, and followed me with her gaze while I circled the downstairs.

She said, 'You're such a hero. I can't believe it.'

'What else is there to do?'

'Yes, but you don't even seem to want to strangle every one of them. I do. Put us all out of our misery.'

I headed for the kitchen and returned. 'Are you miserable?'

Her eyes lifted to mine. She said, 'I expect to be.' I stopped walking and looked at her, then started again. She looked away and shrugged. 'The flu always hits me like a ton of bricks.'

'I didn't have it too badly. Maybe this one is worse for children than adults.'

'But you never really get sick. I always think there's a kind of purity about you. Untouched. You remind me of some kind of flower.'

'A flower?'

'I don't mean that you aren't masculine. You know that. I don't know.' She looked out the window, speculating. 'You know when you lean down and look right into a tulip? You know the way the petals look thick with color, but thin with light, permanent and delicate at the same time?'

'I suppose.'

'That makes me think of you. Always has.'

'Do you think of me?'

She looked back at me. She smiled slightly and said, 'I have been lately, for some reason.'

'Dana—'

'I better go and release them from bondage, or they'll be furious for the rest of the night.' And then the whirlwind swept us up again.

However the flu took Leah, with nausea she couldn't puke out or give voice to, with aches and pains, with lethargy, it took her for three days, and I walked her for most of those three days. At first I was tired and bored: she was heavy, and the urge to put her off was more pressing than hunger, more like a raging thirst. I would panic at the thought of the hours, even the minutes, before me, of walking and carrying until my whole left side, the side she leaned upon, was numb, and my legs were leaden. After a while, though, say late Sunday night, it was as if Leah and our joining had sunk more deeply into me, so that I only did it, didn't think about it, didn't rebel against it. They say that this happens with the KGB, too.

Dana had gone to bed, leaving one lamp in the living room dimly lit. I remember looking at my watch, at the way the time looked there, eleven fifteen, and the previous four weeks of nights, myself lying awake in fear or hope or whirring thought, suddenly seemed like a deck of shuffling cards to me, and yet each moment had been a lengthy agony. That was why the face of my watch was so familiar to me—I had looked at it repeatedly in disbelief at the tormented slowness of time. Then I remember looking down at Leah, whose face, as familiar as the face of my watch, glowed with fever and sleep. Her mouth was partly open and she breathed at me. I felt the tiny rush of it on my lips, where the nerves cluster, on my cheeks, like the first breeze after you have shaved your beard, even on my forehead. There was a fragrance to it, too, sour and pungent, the odor of sick child, but so familiar, so entwined with the lasting pleasure of holding the child's flesh to your own, that I drank it in. I lifted her higher and kissed her hot cheek, hot silk against the searching ganglia. I shifted her over to the right and she settled in. It seemed to me that I had never loved anything—object, or feeling, or person— the way I loved her right now. Love is in the body as well as the mind, a rush of blood to the surface, maybe, an infinitesimal yearning stretch of the nerve endings. I looked at her without seeing her, blinded by the loveliness of her nose, the grace of her forehead, the curl of her upper lip and the roundness of the lower. I will never see her, hard as I try to look past love. My eyes will always cast a light over her, and I will always think that this love, mine for her, is a dear thing. But it is as common as sand, as common as flesh.

After all, it was harder to cherish hers for me. Hard to appreciate the way she climbed the stairs looking for me, held my leg when I was trying to walk across the kitchen, yearned for my presence in the middle of the night, hard even to appreciate her glances into my face, her man-pleasing chatter, the stroke of her baby fingers on my forehead. And these hours of walking were unbearable, although I was bearing them. I stopped and looked down at her, thinking, Open your eyes. After a long while, she opened her eyes with a sigh, and I said, 'Leah, it's time for bed.'

She said, 'Not go to bed.'

'Yes, I'm tired. I'll walk you in the morning.'

'Picky up.'

'I'm going to take you to your bed now. You can have a bottle of juice. Tonight, even the dentist says you can have a bottle of juice.'

'Picky up.'

I carried her into the kitchen, filled a bottle with diluted juice, and began up the stairs.

'No bed.'

'Time for bed. I'll lie down beside you on the floor.'

'No bed.'

I put her in. She was wide awake. I lay on the rug, and she rolled over and looked down at me through the bars. Her eyes were big in the dark. She reached her hand through the bars, and I gave her mine, though it was awkward. She looked at me and held my hand, and I fell asleep. Maybe she never fell asleep. We were up and walking by six. When Dana got up, I said, 'I talked her into letting me get some sleep. I talked her into it.' Dana handed me a piece of toast. I grew, once again, overconfident. The goodness of warm toast, the sweetness of cold orange juice, the attentions of my wife, the new maturity of my two-year-old. 'Two years old!' I said. 'I *talked* her into it.' I thought I knew what I was doing.

We walked all of that day, until about six, when she got down out of my arms to interfere with Lizzie and Stephanie at their Parcheesi game. After dinner her fever went up and we walked until eleven. On Tuesday, we walked from six fifteen in the morning until ten thirty, when she got down for good at the sight of the Barbie bubbling spa boxed up in the front hall closet. I set it up. I found every Barbie and every water toy in the house, all the hair ornaments and four spoons. I gave her Tylenol and a bottle of juice, and then I went into the living room and collapsed on the couch. After a few minutes I could hear her start talking to herself and humming. I ached from the soles of my feet to my chin.

At noon I still hadn't moved, and Leah came in the living room to chat. She said, 'Are you sleeping now?'

I said, 'You're soaking wet.'

She said, 'Are you sleeping on the couch?'

I said, 'Let's go upstairs and change out of your pajamas. Is your diaper wet?' And just then Dana walked in, her face as white as her jacket, which she hadn't bothered to take off. She closed the door behind her and, without speaking, turned and climbed the stairs. I said, 'What's the main symptom?' and she said, 'Aches and pains. My joints feel as if they're fracturing and knitting every second.' Her voice trailed off and I sat up on the couch. Leah said, 'Are you waking up now?'

Stephanie and Lizzie came in at three ten, when I was thinking about dinner. I hadn't thought about dinner in four days, and I was ruminating over steak and baked potatoes and green beans in cheese sauce, my father's favorite meal. They threw down their backpacks and called for milk. While I was in the kitchen, someone turned on the TV. By the time I had returned, Stephanie was face down on the couch. I was nearly jovial. I thought I knew what I was doing. I said, 'Is it your turn, Steph? Have you got it?'

She rolled over. She said, 'I feel bad now.'

'Do you want to go upstairs? Mommy's up there. She's got it, too, but I have a feeling it will go away fast for you and Mommy.' She held out her arms and I picked her up. There was Tylenol in every room in the house, and I grabbed some. She said, 'Ooooh.' It was a long-drawn-out and deeply resigned moan, the sound, it later turned out, of the fever rising in her veins like steam in a radiator. By the time I had carried her to her room, my shirt where she lay against me was soaked with her sweat. She said, 'The yellow one.'

I thought she was asking for a certain nightgown. I said, 'Sweetie, you don't have a yellow one. How about the pink one?'

'Throw away the yellow one. My house.'

I sat her on the bed and counted out five children's Tylenol. She collapsed, and I sat her up, opened her mouth with that practiced dental firmness, and put in the tablets, one by one. Her hair was soaked with sweat. She said, 'Melon. Melon, melon, melon.' I laid her out, and put my hand across her forehead. She was incandescent. I took my hand away and placed it in my lap. From downstairs came the sound of the Superfriends. From down the hall came Dana's voice, low and annoyed, saying, 'Shit. Oh shit.' She is not long-suffering in illness, and generally keeps up a steady stream of expletives as long as she feels bad. I sat quietly, because in myself I felt panic, a little void, needle-thin but opening. The thermometer was on the table next to Lizzie's bed. I stared at it for a long time, then at Stephanie, then at my hand reaching for it, then at my hand putting it in her mouth. The Superfriends broke for a commercial, Lizzie called, 'Daddy!' Dana said, 'Damn I hate this,' and the thermometer, held up to the light, read 104.2.

There is the permanent threat of death. In the fifties, people used to grow trees through the roofs of their houses sometimes, and I often think of death as an invisible tree planted in our living room. When the doors are closed and locked, the insurance paid, the windows shaded, injury and the world excluded so that we, thinking that we know what we are doing, can sit complacently at the dining room table, that invisible tree rustles, flourishes, adds a ring of girth. Any flight of stairs is treacherous, the gas furnace is a bomb waiting to go off, Renuzit may stray, unaided by the human hand, from top shelf to bottom. A child carrying a scissors might as well be holding a knife to her breast; bicycles beside the door yearn to rush into traffic. A tongue of flame can lick out of the wall socket, up a cord carelessly left plugged in, and find the folds of a curtain. From time to time, unable to sleep, I have lain in bed counting household hazards: radon in the basement, petroleum products in the carpeting, gas fumes in the stove. I don't often think of illness, but a child in the next block had meningitis last year. When Eileen, that is the mother, went to the hospital, they looked her in the face and said, 'Twenty-five percent chance of death, twenty-five percent chance of severe brain damage, twenty-five percent chance of minimal brain damage, twenty-five percent chance of full recovery,' and they were so matter-of-fact, Eileen says, that she just nodded and said, 'Oh. Thanks,' as if she were taking a rain check on a sale at K-mart.

I wonder once in a while how my father would have reacted if one of us had died. It seems to me that he would have noticed something missing, that my absence, or my brother's, would have prickled at him

through the day, and he would have upheld the forms of grief, but I
don't know that he ever really looked at us, or perceived enough about
us so that the removal of one of us would have been a ripping of flesh.
Soon enough he would have gotten behind the stove or the clothes
dryer or the dehumidifier with his electrical meter and forgotten about
it entirely, as he did about us alive. Dana said that I often underestimate
him, but in this case, I think he was a wise man, to have addressed himself to the world at large like that, to have stood in front of us, only half
perceiving us, reassured by the shuffle of our feet and our sighings and
breathings that all of us, whoever we were, were back there.

When you are in the habit of staring at your children, as almost
everyone my age that I know is, of talking about them, analyzing
them, touching them, bathing them, putting them to bed, when you
have witnessed their births and followed, with anxious eyes, the rush
of the doctor and nurses out of the delivery room to some unknown
machine room where some unknown procedure will relieve some
unknown condition, when you have inspected their stools and
lamented their diaper rash and, mostly, held their flesh against yours,
there is no turning away. Their images are imprinted too variously and
plentifully on your brain, and they are with you always. When I agreed
with Dana that I wanted to be 'an involved father,' I foresaw the commitment of time. I didn't foresee the commitment of risk, the
commitment of the heart. I didn't foresee how a number on a thermometer would present me with, paralyze me with, every evil
possibility. Stephanie lay there, stupefied with fever. Lizzie came into
the room. She said, 'Didn't you hear me? I want some more milk.' She
sounded annoyed.

'You can pour it yourself.'

'I can't. It's too heavy.'

'Don't talk to me in that tone of voice. Can't you say please?'

'Please!'

'Say it as if you mean it.'

She drew it out. 'Pleeeeease.'

'I'll be down in a minute.'

'It's always in a minute. That's what you and Mommy always say—
in a minute. Then you forget.'

'You aren't the only person in the house, Elizabeth.'

'You always say that, too.' She backed away, not sure how far she could take this discussion. She glanced at Stephanie on the bed. I said, 'Stephanie has a very high fever.'

'Is it dangerous?'

I turned the word over in my mind, because it is a big word in the family vocabulary, a dangerous word, in fact, that always signals to Lizzie that she ought to panic. I was still rather annoyed about her recent demanding tone. I contemplated sobering her up, but I needed her as my ally, didn't I? I said, 'It's not good, but it's not dangerous.' She nodded. I said, 'Do me a favor, and go ask Mommy how she feels.' She turned in the doorway and called, 'Mommy! How do you feel?' Dana groaned. I surveyed Lizzie and wondered, Is this defiance on her part, ill-taught manners, stupidity? I said, 'Go ask her. Be polite. I need you to help me.' Now she surveyed me. I was not kidding. She went into the master bedroom, and I stuck the thermometer back in Stephanie's mouth, thinking that the Tylenol would have had time to take effect. 104.1. Lizzie returned. 'She feels as if she's been run over.'

'What's Leah doing?'

'Watching TV.'

'Can you do everything I say for the next two days?'

'Do you mean like cleaning my room?'

'I mean like getting me stuff and watching Leah, and getting stuff for Mommy.'

She shrugged.

'I think you can. It's important.'

'Okay.' She and I looked at each other. Her eyes are blue, too, but darker blue than Dana's, more doubtful. Simultaneously I thought that this would be a good lesson in responsibility for her and that no lessons, however good, would preserve her from her own nature. I said, 'Go into the bathroom and get a washcloth and wring it out in cold water. I'm going to talk to Mommy for a minute, and then we are going to try and cool Stephie off, okay?'

Dana lay on her side with her eyes closed. The lids were purple all the way to her eyebrows, as if she had eyeshadow on, but the skin of her face was opaquely pale. The blood was elsewhere, heart, brain. She was not sleeping, but I don't think she was aware of me. Her lips formed words, Fuck this, I can't take this, dammit. I leaned down and said, 'Can I get you anything?'

Her eyes opened. She uttered, 'Did you have these aches and pains?'

'Not really.'

'I've never felt anything like it. It must be what rheumatoid arthritis is like.'

'Anything else?'

'A little woozy. How's Stephanie?'

'Temperature.'

'How much?'

'Lots.'

She looked at me for a long moment. 'How much?'

'104.'

'Did you call Danny?'

'He'll just say bring her in at 105. I gave her some Tylenol and I'm going to give her a lukewarm bath.'

'Oh.' Her voice was very low. She closed her eyes. After a moment, tears began to run through the lashes, over the bridge of her nose, onto the pillowcase.

'She'll be all right.'

She nodded, without opening her eyes.

'What's wrong?'

'I'm sad for us.'

'We've had the flu before.'

'I'm sad for us, anyway.' She snorted and wiped her face on the quilt.

'We'll be all right, too.' She opened her eyes and looked at me, sober, speculative, in retreat. Not if she can help it, I thought. I said, 'I love you.'

'I know.' But though she continued to look at me, she didn't reciprocate.

Finally I said, 'Well. I'm going to work on Stephie.' She nodded.

Lizzie was doing a good job. Stephanie lay on her back, with her eyes closed and her chin slightly raised. Lizzie was smoothing the washcloth over her forehead and down her cheeks. She had a look of concentration on her face, the same look she gets when she is writing something. I stood quietly in the doorway watching them and listening to Leah mount the stairs. Soon she came into view, her hand reaching up to grasp the banister, her eyes on her feet, careful. She looked up and smiled. I would like to have all these moments again.

Just then, Stephanie threw out her arm, smacking Lizzie in the face. Lizzie jumped back in surprise, already crying, and I was upon them with reassurances. 'She didn't mean it, honey. Stephie? Stephie? Are you there, sweetie? Do you want to take a little bath?' She was tossing herself around the bed. She said, 'Megan, don't. Don't!' I picked her up to carry her into the bathroom and she nearly jerked out of my arms. She was soaked with sweat and slippery. After the bath, she was still above 104. It was like a floor she could not break through.

I kept a record:

> 6 p.m.: 104.1
> 6:40 p.m.: 104.2
> 8 p.m. (more Tylenol): 104
> 9 p.m.: 104.2
> 10:35: 104.2
> Midnight: 104.4
> 12:30: 104.4
> 3 a.m.: 104.6 (another bath)
> 4 a.m.: 104.4
> 6 a.m.: 104. 2

I longed for some magic number, either 103.8 or 105, for either reassurance or the right to take her to the hospital. She writhed and spoke and sweated and grew smaller in my eyes, as if the flesh were melting off her. I kept reminding myself that the fever is not the illness but the body fighting off the illness. It is hard to watch, hands twitch for something to do. And I was beat, after those nights with Leah, but even if I dozed, I would wake after an hour, and my first feeling was raging curiosity: what would it read this time?

8 a.m.: 104.2

Lizzie walked to school alone and I took Leah to her day care. I ran home, my fingers itching for the thermometer. I was ready to believe any magic, but none had taken effect. I gave her more Tylenol, another bath, took a shower, stepped on the scale. I had lost twelve pounds since Dana's opera. The High Stress Family Diet.

9:30 a.m.: 104.4. Dan, the pediatrician, told me to keep taking her temperature.

11 a.m.: 104.4
1 p.m.: 104.4
3 p.m.: 104.4
6 p.m.: 104.4

After I read it, I shook the thermometer, just to see if the mercury was able to register any other number. I called the pediatrician again. He said that it would go down very soon. I said, 'It's not impossible that it could just stay at this level, is it?'

He said, 'Anything is possible.' I was glad to hear him admit it.

8 p.m.: 104.6
10 p.m.: 104.6

I should say that I talked to her the whole day. 'Stephanie,' I said, 'this stinks, doesn't it? We've been at this for days, it seems to me. Pure torture, an endless task. Sisyphean, you might say. I remember the myth of Sisyphus quite well, actually. We read it in seventh grade. You will probably read it in seventh grade, too. I also remember the myth of Tantalus. He kept trying to bite an apple that would move out of the way when he leaned his head toward it. Sisyphus had to roll a stone up the mountain, and then watch it roll back down again. I think I remember it because that's what seventh grade seemed like to me. Anyway, sooner or later you will know all this stuff. And more. The thing is, after you know it, it will float in and out of your consciousness in a random way, so that if you ever just want to sit and talk to your own daughter like this, not having a conversation but just talking to keep her ears greased, as it were, then all of this stuff will come in handy. But I am here to tell you, Stephie dear, that every word, whatever its meaning, gets us closer to tomorrow or the next day, when you will sit up and look around, and I will breathe a long sigh of relief.' The paternal patter. During the night, it eased toward 105, and I took it every forty-five minutes. At two, Dana got up to spell me, but when I got up at two thirty, I found her passed out in the hallway and carried her back to bed.

She is light. She is only 5′ 4″, though she seems taller to the patients because she always wears those three-inch Italian heels in the office. People marvel at this, but in fact she doesn't stand on her feet all day, she sits on a stool. The shoes flatter her ankles, her hips, her waist, everything up to the back of her head, because everything is connected, of course. She is thin. She weighs 107 or 108. Once I had a good grasp on her, I could have carried her anywhere. She was wearing a white flannel nightgown scattered with tiny red hearts. She was warm and damp, her hair was askew, she would have said that she didn't look her best. A silk shirt, those heels, a linen or cotton or wool skirt, a good haircut, lipstick—that is looking her best, she would have said; a fine-grained surface, a sort of enameling. Women who are more relaxed find her a little cold, or archaic, or formal, but it seems to me that she has poured herself into a sort of dental mold, too. Dentists make a lot of money. Dental conventions are full of dandies. Two dentists in conference in the lobby of the Dallas Hyatt are more likely to be talking about tailors than about inlays. Her body is not yielding. It has a lot of tensile strength that is inherited, I think. Her brother Joe can bench-press 250 pounds, though he doesn't lift weights as a hobby. In any pickup softball game, her sister Frances has amazing power at the plate. To lift Dana in one's arms is to feel not weight but elastic resistance.

To take Dana into one's arms, and to be taken into hers, is to feel, not yielding, but strength. When she holds your hand, she grips it hard. When you hug her, she hugs back. When you kiss her, her lips, which are firm, press against yours. Picking her up reminded me of those things, reminded me that retreat isn't always her mode, is rarely her mode, has never been her mode, is, in fact, a function of point of view, of where you are in the field of her activities. I pushed the covers back with my foot and laid her down. She groaned. I pulled her nightgown over her feet, pulled the sheet up to her chin, then the blanket.

Stephanie had been asleep since about eleven. I opened the curtains of her room partway, and shook down the thermometer by the streetlight outside. I opened her drawer and took out a fresh nightgown. The house was quiet, and I was fully awake somehow, though I hadn't had a full night's sleep in six days, or slept the sleep of the innocent in weeks. The darkness, when I closed the curtains, seemed a presence in the house, sensible, like heat. I let it envelop me where I sat on Stephanie's bed. I might have said that it pressed against my skin, got under my clothes, filtered into my hair, coal dust, blackness itself, sadness. I reached out my hand and put it on Stephanie's small hip under the covers. It submerged her, too, pressed her down against the dark pillow so that I could barely see her face. Even her blond hair, coiled against her neck, moist with sweat, gave off no light. Now the darkness felt as though it were getting into me—by osmosis through the skin, mingled with my inhalations, streaming into my eyes and up the optic nerves to seep among the coils of the brain, replacing meditation. It pooled in my ears. My pulmonary arteries carried blood into my lungs, where it was enriched with darkness, not oxygen, and then it spread through the circulatory system, to toes and fingertips and scalp. The marrow of my bones turned black, began spawning black blood cells. And so thought was driven out at last. Meditation, the weighing of one thing against another, the dim light of reflection, the labor of separating thread from thread, all gone.

I ran my hand gently up Stephanie's back and jostled her shoulder. 'Time, sweetie,' I said. 'I need to take your temperature.' I jostled her again. No response. Now I put the thermometer on the night table and lifted her in my arms. Her head flopped back against my shoulder, and I put the thermometer into her partly open mouth, then held her jaws closed. I was glad she seemed to be getting sounder sleep—she had been restless for two nights now. I counted slowly to 250, then took out the thermometer and laid it gently on the night table. Then I unbuttoned her nightgown and slid her out of it. Her skin was so damp that it was hard to get the sleeves of the clean one up her arms. I stretched her out on the mattress, smoothed the blanket over her. Then I carried the thermometer into the bathroom and turned on the light. 105.2. My hand was still on the switch. I pushed it down and submerged myself in darkness again.

I did not have a thought, but I had a vision, or an image, a fleeting memory of the stars as they looked the night I drove out on the interstate, as many stars as worlds as eras as species as humans as children, an image of the smallness of this one gigantic child with her enormous fever. When each of them was born, Dana used to say, 'There's one born every minute,' but she was grinning, ecstatic with the importance of it. 'Isn't it marvelous what you can do with a little RNA?' she would say, just to diminish them a little. But they couldn't be diminished. So, however many worlds and species and children there were and had been, I was scared to death. I crept to the phone and called the clinic, where, thank God, they were wide-awake. I said, 'Is it possible to die of the flu?' They put a nurse on right away. Was she very sick?

'What does that mean? She has a temperature of 105.2.'

'But how is she acting?'

'She's not acting any way. She's asleep.'

'Is she dehydrated?'

'She urinated at around ten thirty. We've maintained lots of fluids.'

'Is she hallucinating?'

'She's asleep.'

'Is she lethargic?'

'She's *asleep*, goddammit!'

'Is it possible to wake her?' Her voice was patient and slow. Now I had another image, the image of Stephanie's head flopping back on my shoulder and the utter unconsciousness of her state. I said, 'I'll try.' She said, 'I'll hold.'

And then I went in and I sat her up and I shook her and shook her, and I said, 'Stephanie! Stephanie! Wake up! Wake up! Stephanie? Listen to me. I want you to wake up!' She groaned, writhed, protested. She was hard to wake up. I reported this to the nurse and she left the phone for the obligatory hold. After a while she came back and told me to bring her in. Her tone was light enough, as if it were three in the afternoon rather than three in the morning. I began to cry. I began to cry that my wife was unconscious with the flu, too, and that I didn't dare leave the other children in her care, and pretty soon the doctor came on, and it wasn't Dan but Nick, someone whom we know slightly, in a professional way, and he said, 'Dave? Is that you, Dave?' and I of course was embarrassed, and then the light went on and there was Dana, blinking but upright in the doorway, and she said,

'What is going on?' and I handed her the phone, and Nick told her what I had told the nurse, and I went into Stephanie's bedroom and began to wrap her in blankets so that I could take her to the hospital, and I knew that the next morning, when Stephanie's fever would have broken, I would be extremely divorced from and a little ashamed of my reactions, and it was true that I was. They sent us home from the hospital about noon. Dana was making toast at the kitchen table, Leah was running around in her pajama top without a diaper, and Lizzie had escaped to school.

I sat Stephanie at the table, and she held out her wrist bracelet. They had spelled her name wrong, *Stefanie Herst.*

'That's the German way,' said Dana. 'It's pronounced "Stefania." Shall we call you that now?'

Stephanie laughed and said, 'Can I have that one?' pointing at the toast Dana was buttering, and Dana handed it to her, and she folded it in two and shoved it into her mouth, and Dana buttered her another one. They were weak but in high spirits, the natural effect of convalescence. I went into the living room and lay down on the couch. I looked at my watch. It read 12:25. After a moment I looked again. It read 5:12. It was not wrong. Across the room on the TV, Maria and Gordon and some child were doing 'long, longer, and longest.' Leah was watching them, Lizzie was erasing and redoing her papers from school, and Stephanie was coloring. Dana appeared in the doorway, wiping her hands on a towel, then smiled and said, 'You're awake.'

'I'm resurrected. Are you sure I was breathing all this time?'

'We had a nice day.'

'How do you feel?'

'Back to normal.'

'How normal?'

'I'm making fried chicken.'

'Mashed potatoes?'

'Cream gravy, green beans with browned almonds, romaine lettuce.'

'The Joe McManus blue-plate special.'

'I set a place for him at the table, just like Elijah.'

The ironic middle. We were married again, and grinning. We've always made a lot of good jokes together. I heaved myself off the

couch and went to the shower. Not so long ago, Lizzie came home
and said, 'You know when you let the bathwater out and there's a lot
of little gray stuff in it?'

I said, 'Yeah.'

She said, 'That's your skin.'

I stood in the shower for about twenty minutes.

And then it was Friday, everyone in school, day care, work, all
support services functioning, the routine as smooth as stainless steel. I
was thirty-five, which is young these days, resilient, vital, glad to be in
the office, glad to see Laura and Dave, glad to drill and fill and hold X-
rays up to the light. In our week away, the spring had advanced, and
the trees outside my examination room window were budded out.

As soon as the embryo can hear, what it hears is the music of the
mother's body—the *lub-dup* of her heart, the riffle of blood surging in
her arteries, the slosh of amniotic fluids. What sound, so close up, does
the stomach make, the esophagus? Do the disks of the spine creak? Do
the lungs sound like a bellows or a conch shell? Toward the end of
pregnancy, when the pelvis loosens, is there a groan of protest from the
bony plates? Maybe it is such sounds that I am recalling when I sit on
my chair with the door to my office half closed and feel that rush of
pleasure hearing the conversation in the hall, or in Dana's office.
Delilah's voice swells: 'And then they—' It fades. Dave: 'But if you—'
Dana: 'Tomorrow we had better—' The simplest words, words without content, the body of the office surging and creaking. Dana's heels,
click click, the hydraulic hum of her dental chair rising. In my office,
I am that embryo for a second, eyes bulging, mouth open, little hand
raised, little fingers spread. I have been so reduced by the danger of the
last few weeks that the light shines through me. Does the embryo feel
embryonic doubt and then, like me, feel himself nestling into those
sounds, that giant heart, carrying him beat by confident beat into the
future—waltz, fox-trot, march, jig, largo, adagio, allegro? I don't sing,
as Dana does, but I listen. Jennifer Lyons, age fourteen, pushes open
the door, peeps in. 'Hi,' I say, 'have a seat.' And I am myself again, and
the workday continues.

And continued. And continued. She made lasagna for dinner.
Saturday she got a baby-sitter and we went to the movies. Afterward

we stopped at the restaurant next to the office and had a drink. She put her arm through mine. I watched her face. Now I could speak, but what would I say? If there was not this subject between us, I could have talked about the news, our friends, the office, our daughters, but now I could say nothing. We sat close, she put her hand on my knee. I drank the odor of her body into the core of my brain, where it imprinted.

On Sunday there was laundry and old food in the refrigerator. We mopped the floors, and Dana was seized with the compulsion to straighten drawers. I raked mulch off the flower beds and got out the lawn mower and climbed the ladder to clear leaves out of the eaves troughs. Lizzie and Stephanie spent the weekend obsessively exploring the neighborhood, like dogs reestablishing their territory. Leah took this opportunity to play, by herself, with every one of their toys that she had been forbidden over the winter. I liked her touch. She didn't want to damage, she only wanted to appraise. I thought of my temptation to speak on Saturday night with horror. Each of these normal weekend hours seemed like a disaster averted.

Monday at noon Dana and Delilah were late, did not appear. Dave was surprised at my surprise. Man to man. He didn't look at me. He said, looking at the floor, 'Didn't you know that she canceled everything?' Man to man. I didn't look at him. I said, 'Maybe she told me and I wasn't listening. It was a busy morning.' Man to man. We glanced at each other briefly, embarrassed.

She was not at home at three, when I got there to wait for the big girls.

She was not at home at five fifteen, when I got back from the day-care center with Leah, or at five thirty, when I put in the baking potatoes and turned on the oven.

She was not at home at seven, when we sat down to eat our meat and potatoes. Lizzie said, 'Where's Mommy?'

I said, 'I don't know,' and they all looked at me, even Leah. I repeated, 'I don't know,' and they looked at their dinners, and one by one they made up their minds to eat, anyway, and I did, too, without thinking, without prying into the mystery, without taking any position at all.

She was not at home when Leah went to bed at eight, or when Lizzie and Stephanie went to bed at nine.

She was not at home when I went to bed at eleven, or when I woke up at one and realized that she was gone. At first I considered practicalities—how we would divide up the house and the business and the odd number of children. These were dauntingly perplexing, so I considered Dana herself, the object, the force, the person that is the force within the object. In the confusion of dental school, of fighting with my father, of knowing that my draft lottery number was just on the verge of being not high enough, of taking out a lot of student loans and living on $25 a week, I remember feeling a desire for Dana when she first appeared, when she paused in the doorway that second day of class and cast her eyes about the room, that was hard and pure, that contained me and could not be contained, and I remember making that bargain that people always make—anything for this thing.

No doubt it was the same bargain that Dana was making right then, at one in the morning, somewhere else in town.

She was not at home at three, when I finally got up and went downstairs for a glass of milk, or at four, when I went back to bed and fell asleep, or at seven, when Leah started calling out, or at seven thirty, when Lizzie discovered that all the clothes she had to wear were unacceptable, or at eight forty-five, when I checked the house one last time before checking the office. Dave caught my eye involuntarily as I opened the door, and shrugged. At eleven the phone rang, and then Dave came into my examination room between patients and said, 'She canceled again.' I nodded and straightened the instruments on my tray. At two my last patient failed to show, and I went home to clean up for the girls.

She was sitting at the dining room table. I sat down across from her, and when she looked at me, I said, 'Until last night I still thought I might be misreading the signals.'

She shook her head.

'Well, are you leaving or staying?'

'Staying.'

'Are you sure?'

She nodded.

I said, 'Let's not talk about it for a while, okay?'

She nodded. And we looked at each other. It was two thirty.

The big girls would be home in forty minutes.

Shall I say that I welcomed my wife back with great sadness, more sadness than I had felt at any other time? It seems to me that marriage is a small container, after all, barely large enough to hold some children. Two inner lives, two lifelong meditations of whatever complexity, burst out of it and out of it, cracking it, deforming it. Or maybe it is not a thing at all, nothing, something not present. I don't know, but I can't help thinking about it.

1987

I Lock My
Door Upon
Myself

JOYCE CAROL OATES

PART I

1

. . . there on the river, the Chautauqua, in a sepia sun, the rowboat bucking the choppy waves with a look almost of gaiety, defiance. And in the boat the couple: the man, rowing, a black man, the woman a white woman whose face is too distant to be seen. The man is rowing the boat downstream in a slightly jagged course yet with energy, purpose, the oars like blades rising and dropping and rising and again dropping, sinking into the water only to emerge again dripping and impatient; the woman is facing him, close, their knees touching, or so it appears from shore . . . the woman sits straight, ramrod straight, in a posture of extreme attentiveness to the man's and the boat's every move. With one hand she clutches the lurching side of the boat to steady herself, the other hand is shut into a fist, white-knuckled, immobile, in her lap.

. . . past Milburn, past Flemingville, past Shaheen, and then they begin to be seen, to be remarked upon . . . but only when they are a mile above Tintern Falls do people begin to shout in warning and now even the cries of birds at the river's edge lift sharp and piercing with warning. Then about a half-mile above Tintern the rowboat is taken by the swift-flowing current as by a giant hand and now it would require the black man's most strenuous and desperate exertions to steer it from its course yet he lifts the oars and rests them calmly in place as the woman sits continuing to watch him closely, possibly

smiling, are the two of them smiling?—talking together?—hearing
nothing of the shouts from shore and nothing of the increasing roar of
the falls ahead, the sixty-foot drop on the other side of the bridge and
the churning white water beyond . . .

2

That was 1912. Upstate New York in the Chautauqua River Valley,
where dusk and then night come quickly because the steep surrounding cliffs and the foothills beyond cast such long still shadows across the
land, it's as if the darkness, then the night, lift, then thicken, already
there, even in the light, and waiting to take hold.

3

She was my mother's mother but not my grandmother in any terms I
can comprehend and if her mad blood courses through me now I have
no knowledge of it and am innocent of it.

   'Calla': given that name by her own mother as soon as she was
born, in January 1890; as if her mother had known in the agony of
childbirth she could not live, thus wanted to give her infant daughter,
her first- and last-born, a legacy suggestive of the grave.

   So that even as a child my mother's mother was forced to consider
her name specially ordained, fated: a white beyond white: the sweet
waxy glaze of calla lilies, massed funeral flowers.

4

Not 'Calla' but 'Edith Margaret' was my mother's mother's baptismal
name; the name that appeared on official records and would one day

appear, in chiseled script, on her grave marker—in the Freilicht family plot of the First Lutheran Church of Shaheen, Eden County, New York.

'Calla' was the name she insisted upon, as a child. Speaking of herself in the third person, as if stating a fact—'Calla wants to go outside, now,' 'Calla doesn't want to go to bed, she isn't sleepy'—though no one knew who'd told her about that name, given to her by her mother on her mother's deathbed.

From the first, Calla was a difficult child.

5

She had to be disciplined, sometimes hourly, she was that kind of child, too much energy, restlessness, had to be slapped, spanked, paddled. By her father, by her grandmother, by others. There were blows with open hands and blows with closed fists and also pummelings, hair pulling, even shouts of fury and frustration, screams. In those years there was no 'abuse' of children, only 'discipline.'

There was never cruelty in the transaction, only justice.

So she learned to hold herself taut, rigid, her jaws locked against pleading or weeping, her eyes half shut so that milky crescents showed, inside which, stubborn too, vision itself seemed to withdraw; and squatting in front of her, gripping her shoulders, adults were infuriated by the child's refusal to acknowledge them.

My self is all to me. I don't have any need of you.

Once having been drinking hard mash cider for most of a day Calla's father passed a burning match close beneath his daughter's eyes but saw only the reflection of the flame in those eyes, closed to him.

He thought, '—She isn't mine.'

For there was, too, the mere physical fact of her, the anomaly: on neither side of the family was there evidence of such flamey-red hair, thick as a horse's mane; such fine, nervous, aquiline features. Though each summer her skin burnt and eventually tanned her natural color was pale, bloodless, lightly freckled, with a look of translucence; her deeply set eyes were dark brown, so dark as to appear black in certain lights, without any distinction between iris and pupil.

The family said of her, '—If this one isn't ours, whose is she?'

6

In that remote farmhouse north of Milburn—by degrees ramshackle, derelict, and the life of the daily household disorganized—Calla grew up long-limbed, willful, unpredictable; cunning as a half-domesticated creature; so precocious in her manner she might have been, at age eight or nine, mistaken for a child of twelve. Her father was often absent (Albert Honeystone: a farmer forced by crop failures and the manipulation of grain markets wholly beyond his control or even his comprehension to sell off his forty acres of rich dark fertile Chautauqua Valley soil in multi-acre parcels until only three acres remained and then he was a foreman at a sawmill upriver and then a day laborer for the county, and a drinker of hard mash cider and homemade whiskey throughout), and the Honeystone grandparents were slowed by ailments, dazed and embittered country people with their only conviction a sense of the world veering off at angles inhospitable to their interests *No matter how hard you work, God damn bone-aching hard you work* so in that household Calla flourished like the hardiest and most practical of weeds, burdock, sunflower, taking root in any soil and once rooted impossible to extirpate, such households nourish us in ways we can't know and certainly no outsider could guess. Often she stayed out from school to tramp about the fields and woods and along the creek, gone sometimes for entire days when she'd show up at a neighbor's farm like a stray cat or dog *Oh is it Edith Honeystone?* and she'd say *I'm Calla* in that low assured matter-of-fact voice, not so much certain of herself and of her welcome as indifferent; simply not caring; as ready to turn and wander back into the woods as to come into a house and be fed like any normal child.

She grew up devouring, not meals, but food: if at home rarely sitting down at the table and as often outdoors as in.

Eating in the barn with the animals *Oh she's an animal herself—that one.*

She was quickly bored, thus feverish, mutinous, in the single-room country schoolhouse fashioned of crudely hewn logs children from the district were obliged to attend from first through eighth grade, or until the age of sixteen: these wildly disparate grades taught by a female instructor of ravaged middle age who nonetheless had the strength not only to hold such precociously strong children as Calla Honeystone in place as they struggled but to discipline them with swift smarting blows from a willow branch; all but a few times able to prevent them from wresting the branch out of her fingers and striking her with it.

As Calla did, once, with such alacrity and aplomb the other students, even the six-foot-tall farm boys at the rear of the classroom, were astonished: wresting the whipping branch out of Mrs Vogel's fingers and striking her with it full in the face so that her round wire-rimmed glasses went flying *So you can see how she had to be disciplined, just an animal a wild animal just white trash from above Milburn.*

7

The father went off. Joined up with the Army, or drifted west. Or got sick and died in some city where no one knew him or cared so he was buried in a pauper's grave and no one back in Milburn knew, and about this time, in Calla's thirteenth year, she became religious suddenly, though she had long resisted being forced to attend services at the little Methodist church nine miles away in the village of Shaheen where the minister, Reverend Bogey, sometimes wept recalling the sufferings of Christ and the wickedness of the Devil masquerading as mortal men in our midst *Oh he is everywhere—he is legion,* and one week Calla Honeystone sat smirking and chewing her lip and the next there she was crying too, an angry kind of crying, and the tears hot looking and the pale freckled face hot too. Everyone was astonished at the girl's ferocity, how passionately she sang the hymns in her wavering contralto voice, how she began to excel in Sunday school memorizing Bible verses recited with the conviction of kindling sticks burning and crackling and she began to speak of God and of Jesus Christ as if they were in the room with her, bodiless and invisible yet somehow present, active presences. There was a quarrelsome edge to it. People spoke of Calla's face as 'radiant,' 'unearthly.' She learned to play the pump organ, just the rudiments required for playing chords, accompanying the congregation as they sang and she sang too, *for if there is God and if there is Jesus Christ aren't they always with us?—inside us and outside us?—maybe all of us are dead and this is the resurrection?*

8

So maybe, years later, when my mother's mother began her retreat—'retreat' is a way of looking at it, 'exile' might be another—remaining within a single house for a period of fifty-five years *Yes it is unimaginable: that is why I must imagine it* there was this precedent of a kind; this consolation that is beyond mere religious belief, or the wish to believe; a conviction, whether mystical, or simply mad, that God is all in all and inside us and outside us in equal measure, thus why would it matter where one was, in any literal geographical sense?—why, even, who one was?

Who one *is*. Since of course, in God, you don't die.

9

But God did not summon Albert Honeystone back nor did He prevent what little remained of the farm from being taken over entirely by the Yewville Bank & Trust and in pitiless slipping-down degrees He oversaw the tumor-death of first the grandfather and then the grandmother and there was Calla Honeystone tall and skinny yet thriving, her fierce eyes and her amazing hair the color of orange poppies and her prolonged silence—for days, maybe for a week, so they worried she might be mentally defective and then what would they do?—when she went to live with relatives of her dead mother's in the village of Shaheen: this girl so mature in their eyes she might as easily have passed for twenty years of age as for fourteen; who might have been of unusual intelligence and sensitivity as plausibly as she might have been touched in the head.

'Touched in the head': Calla knew what people whispered behind her back, even her mother's people, and she was both outraged in her pride and strangely pleased for, somehow, yes she liked that thought, that idea, 'touched' by the finger of God Himself: compelled to live out a special destiny none of the fools and idiots and commonplace sinners around her could guess.

10

At that time—this was 1905, 1906—it was common practice for banks foreclosing mortgages on certain farm properties to board up the house and out-buildings until the auction was held, sometimes even to raze the house so that the evicted family in their desperation would not creep back by stealth to take up a vagabond residence in their former home; sleeping as criminals on floorboards they themselves had laid, furtively gathering weed-stunted produce they themselves had planted, pumping water from their own wells now forbidden to them under pain of arrest for trespassing.

If they'd done that to me or even tried I would have killed them. Killed whoever. Whoever it was.

Luckily the old farmhouse north of Milburn had not been razed, only boarded up, and that so crudely Calla had no difficulty prying loose boards in order to crawl inside so when after the first time the girl disappeared from her great-aunt's house in Shaheen, no word or warning and seemingly amiable enough the hour before, working beside her aunt in the kitchen, perhaps in her rapt efficient somehow vacant-eyed way, the family knew where she had gone and how to

locate her: a trek of about eight miles as the crow flies from the house
in Shaheen to the house in the country, across fields both plowed and
planted and unplowed and dense with wild rose treacherous as barbed
wire, across creeks and gullies and glacier-gouged landscapes familiar to
Calla Honeystone even by night *Oh I could have walked there in my
sleep—I did walk there, more than once, in my sleep* as, though lacking any
proprietary sense of home, home-owning, property, she was drawn by
an almost physical yearning to a certain point of consciousness; a position fixed not only in space but in time from which, when her eyelids
first fluttered open in the morning, she knew where she was. She slept
on the filthy remains of a mattress in one of the upstairs bedrooms, she
devoured fruit from the overgrown orchard, even raw field corn and
potatoes and counted it no hardship, still less a disgrace, as her mother's
people did.

So they came to bring her back home. Once, and another time, and
yet another time, red-haired gaunt-faced Calla Honeystone silent and
sullen in the back of a rattling horse-drawn wagon, gnawing at her
knuckles until they bled, her skin livid with sunburn like shame and
the odor lifting from her unwashed body a powerful stink as much
earth as animal yet, light-headed with hunger, she associated this state
of being with a state of purity of craving of infinite exalted desire,
hardly listening as her relatives spoke to her in tones of worry, dismay,
disgust, asking what was she doing to herself, was she crazy, did she
want to be put into a county home?—*was* she a wild animal? (for no
term of disapprobation was more extreme: to be called a wild animal
was to be accused of lapsing from humanity itself, a humanity so
recently and tenuously won) and brought back to Shaheen she was
made to bathe, to eat, to dress like the others. She said, 'Let me go—
nobody would know if I lived out there, nobody would know or
care,' and they replied, 'Yes but everyone would know, it would bring
shame on us all,' and she cried, her face heated as if slapped, 'What do
I care about shame: I don't care about shame!'

They perceived there was only one solution: to find a husband for
Calla as quickly as possible.

11

And this task which might have seemed in theory a daunting one turned out to be unexpectedly easy: for Calla Honeystone at seventeen was a striking girl and in the company of strangers could be stirred, for duplicity's sake if for no other, to behave with a childlike yet sensuous charm; like a feral cat knowing instinctively in which direction advantage lay. Thus thinking as she considered the taciturn and seemingly shy, even abashed man proposed to her as a husband *I can keep my distance from that one!*

Despite her cleverness, Calla Honeystone knew little of marriage.

She knew by way of perception how and even why creatures were bound to reproduce themselves but her knowledge did not extend itself to a theory, let alone a principle, that might be applied to *her.*

George Freilicht was thirty-nine years old; a bachelor; not short, nor certainly stunted, but with a look of being undersized, as if his legs were cut off at the knee. His head was large and imposing, set, it seemed, crookedly on his narrow shoulders; his eyes were small and darkly shiny and brooding; inside his bristling yet drooping moustache his lips appeared miniature and bloodless, set over slightly protuberant rabbit teeth in a mimicry of a smile. An ugly little man—but ugly with character, distinction. On nearly every part of his solid body, as a wife would discover, there grew coarse wirelike hairs, graying, springy to the touch, of which the hairs on his head were but the exaggeration, the excess. Freilicht had inherited from his vigorous father a farm of over one hundred acres near Shaheen partly bordering the Chautauqua River; he was not his father, but was willing to work—to work himself and others—to assure a modicum of success, or at least to forestall failure; the creases in his face were marks of worry and weather, and his hands were a farmer's hands—the fingers broad and stubby, scarred, stained, battered, the nails thick as horn. What Calla Honeystone confidently mistook for shyness was a habitual parsimony regarding words, as if words, breath itself, were to be consciously economized. Even in a farming community of German immigrants and their descendants in which qualities of frugality were hardly uncommon George Freilicht was known as tightfisted and meanly scrupulous; it was said of him by his own relatives that the man possessed the pertinacity of a wood-chuck, that most rapacious, cunning, and unkillable of wild creatures.

George Freilicht wanted to marry; or wanted eagerly to be married; or, if he neither wanted to marry nor to be married, he could no longer forestall the entreaties, the pleadings, the naggings, the impor-tunings of his beloved mother and his numerous female relations, that he be married at last, and have children—sons. Before it was too late! Before something happened, and God Himself lost patience, and it was too late!

So Freilicht had been cajoled, even shamed, decidedly pushed into this meeting with—with precisely whom, he did not know, for he left such things to his mother and aunts and cousins, the sifting through of the available women (which were not many: not many, in any case, for George Freilicht of all men) in the Shaheen area; and though this girl with the astonishing red hair and yet more astonishing face was not a Lutheran she *was* a Methodist—a devout Christian, the Freilichts had been assured.

And now the girl, Miss Calla Honeystone, her hair neatly brushed and plaited, her eyes clear, and fingernails perfectly clean, smiled—smiled at *him*.

Did she, the doomed girl, imagine in him, that gnomish little man, an opportunity of a rare kind?—did she see in him an adult less intim-idating than the other adults of her world, as he was, so certainly, less physically imposing?—did she see here a way out of her relatives' house in Shaheen that was not only legitimate but would be blessed, by God and by man?—or was her surge of confidence but a young girl's exulting in her own sexual power?—that mirage of sexual power?

In any case, Calla smiled. With the artlessness of a seductive child. Twined a strand of her wavy flamey hair around a forefinger, and smiled.

And though George Freilicht was too startled to smile in response something did soften about his prim pursed mouth; his coarse-pored skin livened in a blush; the angry little pulse at his temple relaxed. A smile from this young girl where another sort of response had been anticipated was a candle lit impulsively in his heart: it would not burn for long but for the moment, astonishingly, there it was.

12

Only a few photographs survive of the woman who would be my mother's mother.

Family accounts have it, Calla ripped the rest to shreds.

One, badly discolored and dog-eared, shows the bride in a high-necked wedding dress, posed stiffly against a velvet backdrop; the date is November 11, 1907. The wedding dress with its conventionally full skirt is made of something shiny and sleek, like satin; the bodice is tight and lacy and the sleeves are long and tight too, cuffed at the wrists in lace. There is a bridal veil that floats like gossamer on the bride's fussily braided and coiled hair. Inside the glaringly white dress the bride, a mere girl, sits self-consciously, one might guess miserably; her body is lean, not very womanly, with high narrow shoulders, long thin arms, bones prominent at the wrists. The face is strong, oval-shaped, arguably beautiful, but shadowed with a sort of adolescent irony; the eyes too level and direct in their gaze at the camera. There is nothing maidenly or coy here, nothing prettily pleading *Do you like me? Do you like my dress, my face, my hair? You won't judge me harshly—will you?* The feet, long narrow boyish feet, are set flat in their white satin pumps and the knees beneath the satin skirt are a bit spread, as a man might sit; as if the bride is impatient to have her photograph taken, to leap to her feet and escape.

Another less formal photograph shows Calla standing at the rear of the Freilicht house, the backdrop now a grape arbor, overexposed in sunshine.

Here Calla is standing with her arms tightly crossed under her high, small, hard-looking breasts; Calla smiling with half her mouth, sullenly, or sadly, or perhaps indifferently, her gaze abstract and unfocussed. In this photograph Calla is obviously pregnant: still a young girl, grown tall for her bones, angular, awkward, but with a small round belly only partly disguised by the loose skirt of her plain dark dress. Though the photograph is blurry, as if seen through a medium dense and uncertain as time itself, her features are clear—her eyebrows heavy and brooding and darkly defined as if someone has shaded them in with pencil on the matte surface of the photograph. Calla's splendid hair is unbraided

and lustrous, falling past her shoulders; she is standing solidly on her
heels, legs slightly parted and knees bent, to balance the weight of her
belly. No date on the back of the photograph except the terse '1908.'

*And so around me life took on the contour and texture of a dream, though
I was not the dreamer.*

13

Was Calla disappointed in her marriage?—not at all.

Too much pride for that.

Nor was she resentful, or embittered. Nor disgusted.

No emotion at all. No emotion regarding the marriage except to
think *This is how aloneness is: this.*

No emotion regarding the husband; the ugly little doggy-eyed
man covered in bristling grayish black hairs like wires, him with his
clammy feet and toenails gnarled and discolored where they weren't
in fact missing entirely, yes and his tobacco-stained teeth, and the
wormy lips, the belly creases inside the woolly fur and the smell of his
long winter underwear, the touch of it in the laundry, the soapy
churning water never hot enough to get out the stains, the odor of his
body, yes and his breath too as stale at midday as in the morning after
a night of his heavy sweating panting sleep and the rattling breath and
the grinding of his teeth groaning in his sleep twitching and flailing
and his bare bony clammy feet and his flat nasal voice *Edith? Edith?*
and the frown of perplexity between his eyes sharp as if she'd made it
herself with a pen knife but no she felt no emotion for him, too
much pride for that.

'Why should it matter?—when nothing matters.'

These were words she said aloud. Speaking, if to anyone, to God.

Not in complaint either but as mere statement of fact *for of course
God already knows, He is only waiting for us to catch up with His knowledge.*

The aloneness of the soul consoled Calla. And certain immutable
facts: the crows gathering at dusk in the trees down behind the

Freilicht house were the crows gathering at dusk in the trees behind the house of Calla's childhood: the same crows, the same surprising strength and agility in their black bodies, the same harsh inquisitive cries. And the rich smells of rot, of soil, of last year's leaves exposed in spring; the trickling of water in the April thaw; the dripping of icicles, the rivulets making their way down the windows, the ditches, the streams, the creeks making their way veinlike through the hilly countryside to the river, to the lake, the Great Lakes of which Calla had only heard and never seen. And the seeping of her secret blood in her loins. And its cessation: the swelling of her belly which no power of her fevered will could stop. *If this is a dream it is not my dream, for how should I know the language in which to dream it?*

14

The Freilichts did not know what to make of her, their George's young wife. They had thought they would like her, now they were not so sure. The mother, Anya Freilicht, was not so sure. For Calla could never remember to call her husband's mother 'Mother': when she addressed the dwarfish little barrel-shaped woman, she called her 'Mrs Freilicht' as if thrusting away her own rightful name onto another. And Calla, standing tall, a full head taller than the old woman, rarely looked her in the face, at all.

Anya Freilicht had a flushed corroded face inside which a young girl's baffled and furious face was contained, and her eyes that were shrewd damply blinking little pig's eyes shone with the hurt of a young girl as well. 'She thinks she is too good for me, that Edith of yours. Too good for us all,' Mrs Freilicht complained. 'Where does she have the *right*—!'

Freilicht murmured words that sounded like, 'She doesn't think that, Mother,' but he was vague and ashamed, and hid his voice in his moustache, or in his teeth, behind his hand. He was new at all this— new at marriage, had not wanted it, not at all—as new as his bride and as disoriented by the preposterous combination of formality and intimacy that marriage provides, demands. Thus he refused to discuss his wife with any of the family, even his mother. Grinding his teeth he muttered, 'Leave it be, Mother, for God's sake,' turning aside so that the astonished woman could not quite hear, '—you know nothing of her, or me.'

To Calla, who was 'Edith,' he spoke in the same voice, his fingers now fumbling in his moustache and his eyes averted, '—She asks only that you call her "Mother." And that you respect her. If you could try—.'

Calla exclaimed in her bright glib voice, her eyes too averted, 'Oh I do. Yes I *do*. Whenever I think of it I *do*.'

So Freilicht fled the house. Fled to the barns even after dark, after supper. For a farmer with so many head of livestock there is always something to do, there is always more than can be humanly done. He fled to the fields. He hitched up the team in an April hailstorm and plowed fields, and plowed fields. He tramped about the marsh in thigh-high rubber boots, in the muck. He worked beside his hired men, not to spy on them as they naturally thought but, working beside them, to be one of them. He should not have married, but God so ordained. He should not, but—. And now—. He was a bachelor bred in the bone for celibacy and childlessness and he knew now the slow-dawning unspeakable horror that he had surrendered the supreme control of his near-forty years of life to something that could no more be controlled than it could be clearly defined. George Freilicht *had* now a wife; George Freilicht *was* now a husband. The fierce baffled passion he felt for the young red-haired woman who was obliged by marital law to share his bed was nothing of which he could speak to any human being, and that God Himself was a witness to this passion was a source of profound humiliation. He feared he would come in time to hate God too.

So thinking, one day, Freilicht injured his foot in an accident—yes, another toenail had to be picked out with a tweezers, in fragments, out of the bloody stub of a little toe and the pain was a tongue of flame sent by God to cleanse the sinner's soul for however brief a while. *Praise to You in Your infinite wisdom.*

15

In the early weeks of Calla's marriage the man who was her husband dared not touch her.

Though lying panting and stricken beside her touching himself in stealth when he believed her asleep—touching himself with a bachelor's sure swift pragmatic anguished precision as his young wife lay turned from him at the edge of the bed her hands shut into fists and her lower lip caught in her sharp teeth but her breathing rhythmic and placid thinking *How I loathe you, how I wish you were dead dead dead* dropping off to sleep against the grain of her obdurate will.

Then one day in the heat of midsummer Calla found herself with no premeditation, no preparation certainly, simply walking away; having completed a stint of housework under her mother-in-law's supervision, sweaty, her hair in damp ringlets, yet uncomplaining, for Calla Honeystone was never one to complain nor even to betray her innermost feelings *She isn't natural* the Freilicht women murmured among themselves—*she will never make a mother unless she changes*, and now that afternoon in the airless heat-haze there she was stealing away as if her feet had their own volition, their own instinct.

She returned to the old house north of Milburn of course.

Puzzled to see how dilapidated it was, and the out-buildings in even worse condition, everything shabby, weed-choked, roofs covered in a lurid green moss like mange, the floorboards sagging, broken; and everywhere—had years passed?—many years?—the skeletons of birds and rodents underfoot, a little pile of them in a corner of the kitchen beneath the sink, and Calla's eyes filled with tears of hurt and outrage *If You abandon me why then I will abandon You: You and Your Only Begotten Son both* and she lay exhausted on the floor in the room upstairs that had once been hers, too tired and her head pounding too violently for her to mind the dirt, the dust, the cobwebs, the tiny perfect skeletons, the needle-sharp shafts of sunshine that penetrated the walls and ceiling and would have blinded her had she stared at them for long. She lay down, she hugged her knees and gave herself up not to sleep but to death *Why then I will abandon You, I will never be his wife again* and this exalted state of being she associated with purity, with cleanliness, with virginity, she lay with her eyes shut tight frightened of hearing murmurous voices and the rattling of the horse-drawn wagon that meant they were coming for her coming to take her back home not to let her die here but to take her back home, and resolved as she was to stay awake that she might hear them and escape them, she fell into a dazzling sleep and dreamed that, yes, they were here, not only her Shaheen relatives but the man who was her husband, calling *Edith? Oh—Edith?* as one might call a sick person who was also dangerous, and even as she dreamed they were here to return her against her will to that other place, they came for her, and did.

16

Then there were the nights in sweating nightmare succession when husband and wife struggled wordless, seemingly nameless, in that bed, on that horsehair mattress near as hard as any floorboards. This grunting creature who fumbled at Calla's breasts, his clumsy stubby fingers on her belly, the anguish and heat of his breath that smelled, these nights, of alcohol, in shame and desperation he tried to force his knee—his knee that was so hairy! so laughingly hairy! like a gorilla's Calla had seen pictured in a magazine!—between her legs, yes but Calla was too quick for him, too strong, using her elbows and knees and fingernails and even her head for butting so that she was able to force him from her, triumphant. And wordless, each of them wordless. And covered in sweat, and panting.

So for some minutes the man lay still, his heart knocking so hard in his chest that Calla could feel the bed rock beneath them; the floor of the room rock; the very foundation of the old farmhouse; and in her mind's eye she could see the brass lightning rod on the highest peak of the highest roof gleaming with reflected moonlight and this, too, tremulous, quivering with the outrage of George Freilicht's heartbeat.

Then after some minutes the man would turn to her again, though hating her, and hating himself, silent, lips drawn back from his teeth in an arrested grimace, misery, loathing, duty, his disproportionate body damp and frizzed with hair, his muscles straining, and the terse hard rod between his legs tremulous, too, with outrage; so again they struggled wordless and grunting; and again with a surge of strength Calla managed to thrust the man from her; and this time he might give up abruptly for the night, as if released from his travail by an impersonal force or authority, his strength draining rapidly from him, and the rod between his legs immediately gone limp less in shame than in simple animal exhaustion so that he crawled from that place of combat and slept on the carpet so that at dawn Calla woke suddenly amidst the disheveled unspeakably fouled sheets to hear a man's labored wet-rasping breath that seemed to be coming at her from all sides of the twilit room as if he had already died and passed into the very air, like God Himself in Whom in fact Calla was ceasing to believe.

17

And then I weakened, and I died.
And my children were born.

Through the long summer Calla rejoiced in her tender bruised breasts and belly; the discolored flesh of her upper arms and muscular thighs; her backbone that ached from that grim nightly grappling: surveying herself with satisfaction, in secret, knowing that he, the despised husband, was mirrored to her, equally bruised and battered, yet truly humbled as Calla was not. *For she had her pride: always, Calla had her pride.* During the lengthy days, in their clothes, upright, adult, moving sanely among others, husband and wife maintained an air of decorum, courtesy, their eyes tactfully averted from each other and their voices unemphatic. If others watched them calculatingly—not only the ever-vigilant Mrs Freilicht but the several Freilicht relatives who lived in the farmhouse with them, and others who came on Sundays to visit—they gave no indication of seeing. It was as if, by day, neither felt the need to acknowledge a connection with or responsibility for their fevered nocturnal selves. It was as if they had agreed that marital shame need not follow them across the threshold of the bedroom door.

Yet: if Calla were forced to pass close by Freilicht in some cramped space, on the steep narrow staircase for instance, she perceived how the poor man recoiled slightly from her, as if a charge of static electricity leapt between them; if she made an abrupt movement, even if only to set down a plate heaped with steaming food in front of him, she perceived how he shuddered and flinched, or managed to restrain himself from flinching. *Poor man! poor fool!* She knew, for all her studied obliviousness, that crude jokes were being made behind Freilicht's back, about his marriage; about the likelihood, or the unlikelihood, of his ever fathering any children. She knew how people glanced at her, and at him, thinking their lewd thoughts. How some frowned. How some dared smile. And after an accident during wheat harvesting when both Freilicht and another man were injured, though fortunate, as it was said, not to have suffered far worse in the blades of a threshing machine, Calla one midday regarded her husband down the length of the dining room table seeing his stiff graying hair, his creased forehead and cheeks like a much-wrinkled rag, his morose abashed gaze fixed upon her and those small bloodless lips, she saw the pity of him, the pathos, yet a certain kindliness too, a patience beyond all human endurance, and it occurred to her that though she did not love him in the slightest he was perhaps a good man: a man who deserved better than life gave him. So, unthinking, moved by her own impulsive magnanimity, Calla smiled. Feeling no love, no affection, and entirely ignorant of what such a smile might mean to him, from her, Calla smiled—revealing those strong white teeth that were chipped from childhood mishaps but very white, very strong, dazzling to Freilicht who stared at her as if unwilling to believe his eyes.

So I weakened, and I died. And my children pushed forward to be born.

18

Three babies in little more than three years.

A boy, another boy, a girl: and it began to be whispered that Edith Freilicht was not a natural mother, surely there was something wrong with her, how readily she allowed the care of her babies to fall into others' hands, how painful she found nursing them at the breast, and how clumsy, how strained, how vague her manner with them as if they presented to her, in all their mindless heated baby-flesh, the most incomprehensible of riddles. In wonderment she thought *I am drowning, that is what this is* but she felt no terror only a calm and almost logical tranquility as if the waters had risen over her head already and she had only to acknowledge them, and die. Always she had believed that the soul is alone before God: now she did not believe, much, in God. Or, if she believed in God, she had ceased to think of Him. She took solace in the impersonal life that flowed through her like an underground stream; subterranean, secret; the life that generated babies, and ate away voraciously at all organic life, and animated the wind in the trees, and made her heart beat, and beat and beat, without her consent or understanding. She had faith in that life that was unnamable and she thought with a sudden half-angry conviction *I am not drowning, really. I will swim free.*

Soon after Calla became pregnant with the third baby physical relations ceased forever between her and her husband: one night when, tentatively, he touched her, she moved his hand away; and when, another night, he touched her again, again she moved his hand away. And after the baby's birth Calla was ill for some time with an infection, and after her illness subsided there was no proper or inevitable time for Freilicht to touch her again, no moment when, smiling or otherwise, she invited him to do so, thus she had no need to tell him *No, no more* nor had her husband any need to slip from their bed hurt and humiliated and wounded in his masculine vanity.

He's as relieved as I, now he can be a bachelor again.

So Calla began to wander away from the house, as if absentmindedly; at first for an hour or two, then for longer and longer periods of time. Even in chill rainy weather she might disappear for most of a day without having troubled to tell anyone where she was going . . . sometimes in a place she'd never seen before, a birch woods, a hollow by a stream, an old long-abandoned cemetery in no-man's-land, in the ruins of an old settler's cabin, she was overcome by the need to lie down and sleep so that she had no choice but to lie down like an animal overtaken by sleep having time only to assure that she was hidden from view *And how different, in such places, than the sleep of routine and dull domesticity, in a bed, in a room, in a house, within walls shared by others* in that profound sleep that carried her so far she woke restored to herself yet at the same time amnesiac, unable to recall for some minutes where she was, or who she was, or why, or how.

Naturally, the first few times, the Freilichts searched for Calla. But if they saw her it was never in one of her secret places, and never curled up defenseless and asleep: only on her way home, walking along the lane or through a corn-stubbled field, her clothes soiled and untidy, burrs and leaves in her matted hair, face slightly puffy with the balm of unfettered sleep. And the woman would have the audacity to lift a hand in greeting as if she were surprised, delighted at seeing them so unexpectedly: 'Oh—what are you doing *here?*'

19

How strange she was. How . . . strange.

A beautiful young woman so innocent of vanity (or was it self-respect) she scarcely cared how she dressed, even on Sundays; even when company came; like a female derelict sometimes forgetting to wash her hair from one week to the next so that its wavy-red luster turned opaque and there lifted from her a faint warm rank animal smell. Mrs Freilicht, who chided Calla about so many things, chided her about this. And this, and *this.* Why for instance did Calla wear clothes already soiled?—stockings already frayed?—her worst gloves, her shabbiest hat? Why bring in for a bouquet on the dining room table a disorderly handful of those wildflowers—chicory, asters—that would begin to droop and fall within a few hours? *And why was she so loath to look in a mirror?*

Once, asked about the mirror, Calla laughed and said, '—But there's nobody *there.*'

She talked in riddles, sometimes. Mrs Freilicht objected.

What a daughter-in-law: with a habit of murmuring to herself words you couldn't hear; humming, whistling, singing under her breath—'The Old Rugged Cross' and 'Jesus Loves Me This I Know' were her favorite hymns, sung repeatedly in an uninflected deep contralto voice too pure, really, to be her own. And with a habit, too, more disconcerting yet, of lapsing into long spells of silence during which she seemed to hear very little that was said to her, though she pretended otherwise. And there was the time when, working one day in the kitchen, Mrs Freilicht supervising the preparation of a mammoth Sunday dinner to which relatives from upriver were invited, her daughter-in-law dared interrupt her conversation with a cautionary tug of her wrist, saying, 'Shhhh!' and Mrs Freilicht asked, startled, 'Ja?—what is it?' There was the girl standing frozen in the middle of the floor, her head flung back and her jaws rigid, her eyes fixed on something that might have been floating in a corner of the kitchen; and after a long worrisome pause she whispered, '—I was only trying for us two to not be wakened, Mrs Freilicht. If we've been dreaming.'

Calla made an effort, they could see how, against the grain of her nature, she made the effort, repeatedly, with her faint wondering smile and perplexed eyes, to be a mother to her children—a good and attentive and loving 'mother' to these three small children. How could it be said that she was 'cold,' 'unfeeling,' 'unnatural'—a 'bad' mother? Yet the truth was, when Calla was not in the room with her children she tended to forget them.

From the first, much of the care of the babies had fallen to others—the indefatigable mother-in-law primarily, but one or another female relation besides; for always in such farm families there were women not only willing but grateful to take care of babies, lacking their own or having seen their own grow up too swiftly, and these women tended to Calla's babies when she was unwell, or distracted, or absent. And what perverse pleasure in the arrangement: that Mrs Freilicht had the satisfaction of tending to her grandchildren as well as the satisfaction of complaining bitterly of the children's mother.

'She is not right. She does not even look at them *right*.'

But Freilicht, who might have said that after all he had not wanted to marry, and had not chosen his wife, refused to discuss these matters. What God had ordained, God had ordained: he would not die child-less after all; he had not one but two sons. Only to Calla, once, did this taciturn and abashed man bring up the subject of their children, when, after an Easter Sunday spent at a cousin's upriver farm Calla's seeming indifference to her children had provoked comment, and Calla responded, unthinking, immediate, with the air of a child who cannot be relied upon not to speak the obvious, 'Oh—but I didn't really want them, I thought *you* did.'

For a moment Freilicht stared at her, this woman, the mother of his children, *his* children, *his* wife, and could not speak.

His skin was weather coarsened, his small pale lips were quivering, speechless. And that angry little worm-like pulse in his temple begin-ning visibly to beat.

And his hands: those blunt scarred fingers closed themselves into fists, quivering too. This Calla saw, and recognized the sign, but did not step back from him.

Quietly she said, '—You could divorce me. It's done. Send me away. You don't need me, the children don't need me. Let me go away. Don't let anyone bring me back.'

Freilicht composed himself. He managed even to laugh.

'Don't be ridiculous, Edith,' he said, '—you're my wife: you aren't going anywhere.'

Never once in the several years of their marriage had George Freilicht called her Calla, she'd never revealed to him her true name.

20

When I first laid eyes on him it was in innocence for how could I know it was him!

She had been walking, and walking quickly, with no mind for where she was taken. How many miles, and in which direction. It was a warm autumn shimmering with bees. High overhead dense compacted grayish white clouds blew about the sky, the sky was hot with sun, so bright it had no color.

The creek drew her, a nameless creek somewhere east of Shaheen, wide, low, murmurous, with a dank smell, the smell of lichen dried and baked on flat white boulders, the smell of dead fish, a creek that would deepen and begin to move more swiftly, with more purpose and urgency, as it approached the Chautauqua River, snaking through hills lush with vegetation, junglelike, immense willow trees hanging over the water as if crouching and Calla was smelling something rich and fecund and sweetly intoxicating that drew her too: made her smile, and drew her: the apple rot, the fermentation of a compost dump behind an old ruin of a cider mill, the weatherworn boards and steep broken roof and the crude crumbling stone foundation familiar to her or to her mind's eye: *I have been here before.* But the place was no puzzle to her, nor was when she'd seen it previously. Calla's mind was too restless for such speculation.

A low humming-buzzing as of people talking talking talking just out of earshot. She shaded her eyes and saw that it was bees, wasps, flies—amazing clouds of them, glittering imbricated clouds of them above the small mountain of apple compost behind the mill sloping not only to the bank of the creek but into the creek as in an old catastrophe. Above her the cider mill rose hulking and utterly still, though about it the world was buzzing, shimmering, alive.

Calla saw that a man was fishing off the creek bank: a stranger, seemingly: squatting on his heels at the edge of the slow-moving creek, his back to her. She was standing by one of the empty mill windows, looking into a corner of the mill and through another empty window ribbed with broken glass and cobwebs, and attentively she stood on her toes watching this solitary fisherman, oddly dressed for fishing in the backcountry in a new-looking straw hat and a tight-fitting black coat or jacket with a preacherly look to it, surely too warm for this September day, and wasn't there something unusual about the man? something about his dark dark skin, his profile? that held Calla fascinated, and cautious, wary of being seen yet reluctant to move away. She was not by nature a woman given to small nervous fears but she had known since childhood to avoid men, even men whose faces and names she might recognize, in such settings. No man had ever laid a hand on her in her wanderings but a few, a very few, had tried, and Calla did not want to invite misunderstanding here *He's a black man—a Negro* standing as she was so avidly watching, staring, feeling that stab of advantage we feel when we see someone who not only does not see us but has no sense of us entirely. Calla was holding herself on the window ledge, strong enough to balance herself there on her elbows and forearms, not minding how the stone ledge littered with bits of glass and debris hurt her bare flesh, perhaps the odor of sweet apple rot had gone to her head, sweetly befuddling.

In her soft sinuous contralto Calla called, 'Hello!'—too far from the creek for the fisherman to hear her, and again, '—Hello! Someone else is here too!' and now the fisherman lifted his head, turned to look around perplexed, but seeing nothing and no one returned to his fishing line, to the creek that from Calla's angle of vision on higher ground was a broad flat ribbon of light laid down between banks choked with vegetation as in a time so ancient not a one of those living things had a name.

So minutes passed. How many, Calla would not have known.

Calla took delight in observing the stranger, the black man, from her strategic position; bracing herself on the windowsill, her muscles small but hard, strong, bearing her up. In giving birth she had three times bled, and bled, and bled, until that final time she had believed they meant to allow her to bleed to death once the baby was wrenched from her, their baby, and not hers, yet she'd held stubbornly on to the thin stream of life as if with her very fingers, yes she'd held on tight, tight and stubborn, she'd lived and now months later she'd recovered completely from the anguish and ignominy, the unspeakable insult of it, now she was restored to herself again, her body lank yet hard with muscle, ungiving. When hours later or in the morning she returned to the Freilichts it would be bearing her mother-in-law a face masklike with grime, hair wild and tangled, exposed skin stippled with insect bites and scratches and the woman would stare at her with those outraged baffled eyes but not ask her, for she would not stoop, as she claimed, to ask this question another time, where Calla had been: *I do what I do, what I do is what I wanted to have done.*

It seemed Calla's speech was teased out of her by the humming of the insects, the placid glitter of their tiny light-bearing bodies above the sliding heaps of rot, and there was the old mill, too, in its dream-like dilapidation as if its sliding had been arrested, halted, in the very moment of motion, and the creek with no name she could recall, yes and the tall black fisherman in the straw hat and snug-fitting jacket now standing alert and quizzical as if preparing to smile, readying himself to be teased and coaxed again by Calla Honeystone leaning there on the window ledge just out of the fiercest shaft of sun, saying, '—Hello! You! Don't you know someone else is here too!'

But the fisherman could not see her. Tall and attentive and shading his eyes, face plaited in wonder, he could not see her, though he seemed to be looking directly at her. And if he heard her voice he did not hear her words. And if he heard her voice he did not believe it any human voice, thus did not investigate any further, though he did remain standing there on the bank his fishing line forgotten behind him until at last Calla lowered herself to the ground, slipped away almost repentant and released him.

21

It was 1911, in the Chautauqua River Valley.

Aloud Calla said, as if tasting the word, 'Ne-gro.' And black and rich and strange it tasted, like licorice.

For Calla was after all a country girl, rawboned and inexperienced and young for her age, who despite her curiosity and boldness knew little of the world. Never once had she seen a black man or a black woman close up, rarely in fact had she seen blacks save in photographs or drawings and from time to time on the street in the small river city of Derby where the Freilichts shopped on Saturdays occasionally and where Calla managed to slip away from the others to explore afoot the unfamiliar fascinating streets, making her way with less assurance than she did in the country but drawn by the evidence of her eye, these commercial buildings rising five and six and even seven stories above Main Street, these elegant brick houses on High Street, and there were livery stables, and hotels, and a railroad depot, and a granary, and churches and brickyards and open markets but the main thing was people: numberless people: strangers who knew neither her nor her name and if they glanced at her at all (which naturally they did: this tall forthright red-haired young woman who carried herself even in her heavy unstylish skirts like a man) had not the slightest idea where she was from, to whom in all practical terms she belonged.

And among these strangers there were sometimes blacks: Negroes: descendants of slaves, Calla knew; most of them only recently emigrated up from the South.

In Derby, those Saturdays, Calla slipped away from the Freilichts and walked for hours. Beyond the railroad depot and the railroad yards, along the riverfront, the barges, the tugs, the horse-drawn vehicles, and the slaughterhouses where the air pulsed with heat, blood, excrement, death, and it was animal terror she smelled, her nostrils wide with it, her own blood quickened. Where no white woman would walk but she was unfrightened and unembarrassed staring, staring hard, and in the hollow of Negro row houses and shanties, close by the rear of one of the slaughterhouses, across a makeshift bridge spanning a drainage ditch where the brackish water was threaded with rust she was stared at in return, sometimes defiantly, sometimes with blank amazement and wonder, and she would have smiled and lifted a hand in greeting except she knew she had not the right: in their eyes she was a white woman, one of the enemy.

She felt a thrill of horror, amid the blacks. That their immediate ancestors had been *owned*. Not these blacks as individuals for most of them were young, many were children, but their blackness, their essence—that had been *owned*. And now in this city amid the heterogeneous white population of the city they were so relatively few in number—like small dark carp in an immense school of fiercely golden carp, depending upon God knows what precarious law or whim of nature to survive. *Like me they are outcasts in this country. No not like me: they are true outcasts.*

22

Calla's little girl Emmaline was so sick with measles, ice packs could bring her fever down only a degree or two and it hovered meanly at 101 degrees Fahrenheit while the child lay eerily still and uncomplaining, her eyes closed, yet not entirely closed, and Calla paced about the room striking the palms of her hands together as Mrs Freilicht and one of Calla's sisters-in-law fussed and scolded and worried together, and suddenly—this was a windy sunswept morning, April 1912, Freilicht was not at home—Calla's attention was drawn to an unexpected sight out the window: there alongside the house was a man, a stranger: dressed with seeming formality in a preacherly black suit and a black bowler hat and what was he doing there? what was he holding in his hands?—walking slow as a sleepwalker as if measuring something on the ground with his eyes, Calla could see a double-pronged instrument of some kind he was holding at about chest level, and staring down at him, moving along the window as he moved below then going to another window to watch, Calla began to breathe more quickly, staring, seeing the man's skin stained dark as wood with a purplish red sheen in the bright sunshine, thinking *It's him, of course it's him.*

Without a word of explanation to the women who stared at her speechless, nor even a fleeting backward glance at the feverish child in the bed, Calla ran downstairs, heels pounding hard on the stairs and then outdoors into the bright windy day, not taking time even to snatch up a coat or a jacket off the row of pegs by the kitchen door, no time for such prudence: there she was, George Freilicht's very wife and the mother of his three small children daring to run up breathless to a stranger, a Negro, trespassing on her husband's property: demanding who he was? what was he doing? and the black man stared at her for a beat or two before replying, as if whatever he might reasonably have expected, trespassing on a white farmer's property so blatantly, or so hopefully, it surely was not *this*—the black man stared at her and tipped his hat at her saying politely, 'My name is Tyrell Thompson, ma'am, from a ways east of here, by trade I am a water dowser and I been happening to hear there's some farms around here that—' and

Calla saw it *was* a dowsing rod the man held in his hands, a two-branched willow limb of about eighteen inches in length held chest-high like an oversized turkey wishbone, and she laughed, and the color came up in her face, and she said, 'So that's it!'

In this way, Calla met Tyrell Thompson.

Or so it was afterward recounted.

Quickly, as if to forestall embarrassment, Tyrell Thompson explained to Calla that he had not exactly been invited to dowse for water but since he was passing through the valley and he'd been hearing that the water table was low, maybe even he'd happened to hear that the gentleman who owned this property was planning to drill for a new well, yes he was certain he'd heard that mentioned in Shaheen, he'd thought he would make a visit to offer his services gratis—'Like my daddy before me and his daddy before him I never charge any fee for the finding of water, ma'am, it's a sacred calling and must not be profaned, but should I find water, good fresh clear spring-water, and should the gentleman for whom I find it be pleased, I am not averse to accepting—' he paused, knitting his smooth high forehead as he searched for the proper word, '—a gift.' Tyrell Thompson's voice was velvety soft, his diction formal. Calla smiled so hard her face ached and said as if she hadn't heard a word, 'Yes I'm—Calla, I'm Mr Freilicht's wife,' quickly adding, laughing again, as a ragged-looking blush rose into her cheeks, 'I mean—I live here.'

Tyrell Thompson hesitated for the smallest fraction of an instant: then shook Calla's hand.

It was a formal, rather hurried gesture. No sooner had he shaken the woman's hand and felt the strength of her long slender fingers than he let it go.

Calla said, 'Oh I think we've met before—us two.'

Tyrell Thompson said, 'Have—?'

Calla said, 'Oh—you wouldn't remember, that's all.'

Tyrell Thompson regarded Calla in mild indignation that she might be taunting him, or something more cruel. He said, with a little mock bow, gravely, '—Yes, ma'am, but I naturally would remember, you know that, ma'am.'

Calla's blush deepened. As if they'd been quarreling she said, 'My name is Calla—didn't you hear?'

Now Tyrell Thompson stared at Calla frankly perplexed.

Not knowing what to make of her and fearful of her, Tyrell Thompson the itinerant water dowser who was well over six feet in height and two hundred pounds in weight, by his own estimate thirty years in age, and built strong and husky and unmarked by life as a young bull except for trifling scar tissue above his eyes and here and there on his body and a rope burn inflamed like a rash on his neck and that old injury in his right knee that plagued him in damp weather and a fila-gree mark lengthwise on his broad back only a practiced eye would identify as a scar made by barbed wire—not knowing what to make of her Tyrell Thompson bared his teeth in a smile that surprised him, one of those smiles like blows that fall upon us unaware, and said, '—Calla.'

Tall as she was, Calla had to look up to look Tyrell Thompson full in the face, an angle and a posture to which she was unaccustomed. For a moment she felt vertigo as if the sky were tilting.

So that windy April morning as Emmaline lay in her fever doze on the second floor of the old farmhouse, her small body motionless beneath the covers, her eyes showing mucous crescents beneath her reddened lids, Calla and the Negro water dowser Tyrell Thompson were to be observed, and indeed were observed scrupulously and incredulously, making their way with slow deliberate steps about the house, the one in his tight-fitting black suit and black bowler hat holding the dows-ing rod delicately in front of him and the other avidly watching and talking, talking animatedly—but what did George Freilicht's wife who was so silent within her household, so maddeningly vacant-eyed and strained in her smiles find to talk about with *him?*—that big burly dan-gerous-looking colored man?—why did those two smile at each other, at first shyly and fleetingly, then with more boldness, and why was their joined laughter so staccato and breathless, with a sound of shat-tering glass—which the women inside the house heard clearly in their imagining if not in their ears?

True: the water table on Freilicht's property had been gradually sinking for years, the previous summer he'd had to pay to have

drinking water hauled from town but it had not been declared that
George Freilicht intended to drill a new well, frugal as the man was,
and cautious about spending money until there was no recourse but to
spend it, thus how had the Negro water dowser known to come out
here, unbidden?—and why had he come at a time when the owner of
the farm was not home? All the years of her remembered life, a life
now spanning beyond seven decades, Mrs Freilicht had been unswerv-
ing and certain *You can't trust colored ever—except maybe if you know them
by first and last names both and who their families are and who they work for
and where they live and even then you can't trust them behind your back, you'd
be a God-forsaken fool if you did* and now there was her George's wife
cavorting and prancing out there for anyone to see in the company
of—

'How can she! Like a common slut! Our Edith!'

Now a bit of time had passed, Calla and the water dowser Tyrell
Thompson were more at ease with each other: Calla chattering away
telling Tyrell Thompson things she hadn't ever told anyone and
wouldn't ever have thought of telling, such as when she'd been a little
girl a water dowser had come by her father's farm to locate water for
a well and yes he'd found it and afterward she'd played trying to work
a dowsing rod for herself but without success, the willow branch just
stayed fixed in one position unless on purpose she made it move
which was cheating so she wondered was water dowsing a gift you had
to be born with or was it a skill to be acquired by practice and good
intentions and Tyrell Thompson told her it was both, so far as he
knew—'A human being is born with a gift for water like for singing
or dancing or preaching or fighting but then it's God's will you refine
it. That means discipline, and hard work, and a right way of thinking
so that what is sacred is not cast down in the mud.'

Tyrell Thompson explained that any sacred calling was profaned in
the marketplace of a country like the United States or even if displayed
for vanity's sake, yet there comes a time in a man's life when he may
have to humble himself and risk profanation since the majority of
God's progeny can't be lilies of the field, toiling not, yet being nour-
ished and protected by the lifelong labor of others who spend their
lives cutting away at the weeds choking the lilies' roots, so long as the

laborer is properly humbled in his pride and is worthy of his hire God should not judge harshly, some say it is even His will, as in dowsing for water for instance where fresh clear spring-water is discovered in earth, in mud, in muck, in the very place of filth, to be drawn up for the benefit and glory of mankind. He explained that being able to detect water as he did—not smelling it exactly but somehow knowing it's there, 'As it's said, "like calls out to like"'—in truth he would not require an actual dowsing rod but that was how it had always been done, how he'd learned from his daddy and his daddy had learned from *his*, going back to the first water dowser who lived, it was like say you're a blind man drawn to sound no one else could hear, but he, Tyrell Thompson, believed in using the willow branch as a visible sign others could see and identify, and touch.

As Tyrell Thompson spoke—and his speaking was like singing with no music, yet paced to the subtle rhythms of music—he continued to walk with the dowsing rod held at chest level, so delicately, Calla was fascinated. She saw that his fingers were nearly twice the size of hers. A dark dark brown on the outsides, with a purplish red sheen beneath like fine wood many-layered in shellac, and on the insides a tender-looking pale pink, flushed and pink as her own, so a stab of feeling ran through her, and she said, '*Can* I touch it, then?—try it myself?' indicating the dowsing rod with a forefinger; and Tyrell Thompson frowned and said, '—When it's time.'

If the man was having difficulty locating water on Freilicht's property he kept his difficulty to himself, never gave any indication of doubt. One of the clear facts about Tyrell Thompson.

Another was: he had faith.

It was not, yet it surely seemed, a deliberate taunting of those several pairs of eyes inside the Freilicht house, that Calla and the black man never remained in sight more than a few minutes but continued to circle the house in widening concentric rings; vanishing for bits of time altogether; so that eyewitnesses to the spectacle were forced to renegotiate their positions, window to window, room to room. Mrs Freilicht and one or another of George's sisters or aunts or cousins were speechless with wonderment and revulsion that that woman who held herself so proud in their company who shrank from being touched even by her own children was now walking so close by this stranger it seemed she brushed the sleeve of her dress against the sleeve of his coat, even once or twice blundered into him when he paused to regrip and refocus the dowsing rod *How dare she: like common white trash: like a slut: and that nigger black as sin like he'd climbed up out of the ground exactly the kind to slice your throat without asking any questions, yes and then he'd wipe the knife on your clothes when he was finished* until by teasing degrees they moved, now a seeming couple, farther and farther from the house, farther from those pairs of aghast eyes, down beyond the kitchen garden that was a tangle of dead vines and plants and lop-sided bean poles from the previous year, and the grape arbor, and the present well which was an ordinary stone-and-concrete well (that if you leaned into cupping your hands to your mouth and calling out you would hear an echo immediate yet seeming to come from the bowels of the earth, a hollow sonorous sound having nothing to do with you in daylight standing with your feet flat and solid on the surface of the earth), until at last they came to a wide shallow grassy space bordering a pasture where in that harsh morning sunshine white-faced cattle browsed placid and motionless as painted cattle: and here Tyrell Thompson snorted 'Huhhhh!' as unmistakably the willow branch squirmed, and jerked, and the prong pointed down.

'Here. Here's water. Right where we are standing.'

Though truly Calla did not disbelieve, she'd seen it herself, she insisted upon taking the branch from Tyrell Thompson, and held it erect herself in wishbone position, and again it squirmed and jerked in her fingers and the prong pointed down—'Oh it's alive like a snake!' she cried.

Tyrell Thompson said, modestly, 'It *is* alive. Like we are alive. And the water too—"like calls out to like."'

Tyrell Thompson located a sizable rock to lay on the grass marking the spot beneath which water was to be found.

Calla observed him gravely. By this time her hair was wind whipped and her lips blue with cold, the tips of her fingers like ice yet she never felt it, not a bit of discomfort, so rapt an attention did she give Tyrell Thompson. Expressing a wifely doubt she did not truly feel, she said, as Tyrell Thompson prepared to leave, '—But if he goes to all the trouble and expense of—of drilling—and if—if there's no water—'

Tyrell Thompson tipped the rim of his smart bowler hat with a flicker of impatience, and said, 'Mrs Freilicht, ma'am, my word is as good as my life.'

So Calla stood silenced and corrected.

By morning of the following day, who knows how such things spread, word was everywhere in the valley that George Freilicht's wife, one of those impoverished Honeystones from up around Milburn, had hired a Negro, a stranger, against her husband's wishes, not simply to dowse for water on Freilicht's property but to drill for a new well. And more.

23

Though Calla was guiltless at the start, relations between her and Freilicht were altered forever: and in that grassy hollow by the pasture Tyrell Thompson's rock remained untouched for weeks, months. Freilicht saw it frequently but chose not to speak of it. To haul it away would be to acknowledge it, thus he did not haul it away, nor ask that one or another of his farmhands do so. Or maybe in fact he did not see it?

The Freilicht property, acquired in the mid-1800s along the south shore of the Chautauqua River, its considerable acreage, and the several barns, and the red-brick house, and the livestock, and the farming equipment, and numberless possessions under the roof of the house, were George Freilicht's: thus he had the privilege of seeing what he wished to see, and no more.

And of hearing what he wished to hear, and no more.

Each time Calla dared bring up the subject of a new well Freilicht said coldly that so long as there was water in the present well they could hang on a little longer. Calla persisted, 'At least we must pay him. We owe him—' but she could not think what sum of money might be appropriate: twenty-five dollars, seventy-five dollars, one

hundred dollars? Or only five dollars?—for Calla rarely handled money
and rarely gave it a thought. 'But it can only be a gift, it can't be direct,'
she said. 'A water dowser of Tyrell Thompson's quality can't accept
money for his services outright.'

Freilicht said, 'Oh can't he!'

Freilicht said, his voice rising, '*You* might owe him, *I* don't: if that
nigger sets foot on my property again I'll shoot him down like a dog.'

Rainfall during the summer was light and intermittent and by late
August and early September there were lengthy rainless stretches and
a heat wave of two weeks' duration when the cloudless bleached-blue
sky gave off blinding heat from all directions and the daytime temperature climbed beyond 100 degrees Fahrenheit and by night rarely
dropped below 80 degrees Fahrenheit and the creeks and water holes
began to shrink and the river turned mud color revealing gouged-
looking banks disfigured with the exposed roots of trees like astonished
veins or nerves . . . and the husks of dead insects gathered underfoot,
even inside the Freilicht house; and leaves curled, and browned, and
fell from the trees; and the well required ever more pumping to yield
its increasingly tepid, rust-specked water.

By mid-September the water table had dropped so low that
Freilicht was again obliged to haul in water; yet still stubbornly the
man resisted, awaiting rain, ever certain that God would not humili-
ate him and fail to send rain . . . though when rain did come in
scattered explosive showers it was not sufficient to replenish his well.
By this time Calla no longer spoke of water and the water dowser and
what might or might not be owed the man, Calla was rarely present to
speak to Freilicht at all, but others in the family begged him, Mrs
Freilicht herself begged him, so finally in late September Freilicht
gave in and arranged for a Yewville company to drill a new well on his
property by which time Tyrell Thompson's marker had mysteriously
disappeared so when at last a new well was dug after five or six fruit-
less exploratory drillings there was no way of knowing or
demonstrating that Tyrell Thompson had been the one to first discover
the ideal site there in the grassy hollow by the pasture where thirty-six
feet below the surface of the earth beyond loamy pebbly soil and

serrated sheets of shale an underground stream flowed miraculously bright, sparkling, plenteous, with a taste pure as ice crystals on the tongue, and so cold it felt like fire.

And by that time, too, rumors had begun to spread through the valley about Calla and Tyrell Thompson, surely untrue, that the two were seen together hurrying in stealth, on country roads in the Shaheen area, in Tintern Falls, in the city of Derby, a tall beautiful red-haired white woman *he never should have married, that poor fool* and her black lover who was in some versions a water dowser clad in black near seven feet tall with a glass eye and a bad limp, in other versions a preacher with a scarred face and rope burns showing on his neck where he'd been hanged and left for dead *or maybe he's got nine lives, did actually come back from the dead vowing revenge* and in others a 'rogue' of a Negro escaped from a chain gang in Georgia *come North to seduce white men's wives and take his pleasure and his revenge in one.*

PART II

24

And when her life was split irrevocably in two though not in half she would recall that night, those nights when it did seem at least at the first that the dream that contained her was a dream of her own deepest purest most passionate wish and not a dream beyond her control or comprehension, those nights that were a single night *At first there was no moon, then like an eye opening there was a moon almost blinding* and the man who was her husband slept his heavy sullen wetly rasping perspiring sleep seemingly unknowing and unsuspecting and Calla slipped out from beneath the suffocating covers, not needing to breathe, not needing to see in the familiar dark, but how her heart beat! her pulse wild to leap in her wrist! for she had heard him call for her *Calla oh Calla! Calla!* and she could not deny him.

She had not in fact denied him, other times. And by crude blunt brash daylight.

I do what I do: what I have done is what I have wanted to do taking up her clothes where she'd carelessly laid them, moving silently, barefoot and eager on her toes, and it's as if she is sleepwalking, with such uncharacteristic grace and caution her feet scarcely touch the floor, she dresses in an alcove of the upstairs hall swiftly bunching her hair up in a knot at the nape of her neck hearing him cry *Calla! oh Calla!* his voice light and mournful-sounding as the loons on the river that keep her awake these late-summer nights, her heart beating rapid as pain with desire with what she had not known was desire, and now she stands at the window seeing how, like hoarfrost, reflected light lies on the roof below her, and on the high-peaked roofs of the outbuildings, and on the conical metal roof of the silo, her eyes dilated now, almost entirely pupil, and it's impossible to determine in the moonlight in this world so drained of normal color where grass leaves off and earth begins; where earth leaves off and sky begins; where in the wind-rippled shadow of the hay barn Tyrell Thompson in his black clothes stands beckoning to her.

Calla oh Calla!

That name she'd taught him. Taught him to say. And each time he'd faltered shying from it out of habit murmuring *ma'am* or worse yet to her ears *Mrs Freilicht*, she'd snatched up his hand in hers and squeezed the fingers hard digging in her nails so he laughed and winced *My name is Calla: Calla is my only name*, her face bright and fierce with what she hadn't known was desire, the terrible pulse of it, the hunger.

Now she is making her way down the narrow stairs at the rear of the house, those stairs pitched at a treacherous angle, steeper by night they seem than by day, and the youngest child Emmaline wakes in her sleep on the floor above open-eyed suddenly and terrified hearing the wind in the eaves, the wind blowing the clouds across the sky, there's the sound of a door being opened downstairs at the rear of the house, the sound of something slammed in the wind but heedless Calla is running across the wide moonlit space to the shadow of the barn where her lover Tyrell Thompson is waiting for her, thinking *It's true there is no shame in me: only hunger* and wordless he catches her in his arms strong enough to lift her in the crook of one arm and they embrace, they kiss, there's a kind of anger in their kissing, wanting to hurt *I love love love you* Calla wrapping her arms around the man, yes and her muscular legs too, fitting herself to him so he draws back his head laughing in mock alarm *Calla you going to be the death of me.*

They have to flee, they can't remain here, there's a dog barking and that man in the house if he wakes from his heavy sullen sleep has a shotgun, both barrels loaded, and laughing they make their way along the lane, their feet barely skimming the earth, arms around each other's waist they are running past the dessicated cornstalks shivering in the wind and past the marshy land where mosquitoes stir warmed by the scent of their blood and on the far side of the marsh there are birds singing faint and sweetly tentative as if it's morning—morning already—but the moon is still shining overhead *I was drawn after that man like water sucked by wind, shaping my shape to his* and it was true, in his arms in one of their snug hiding places in a no-man's-land by the river Calla screamed and screamed and screamed, wept, sobbed herself to sleep shaped to his shape curled like a baby waiting to be born like the lost memory of one of Calla's own babies snug and hot tight up inside her waiting to be born.

25

Most nights, there was a moon.

Or those nights recalled as if the doomed ferocity of certain emotions *I love only you God damn you I want only you, I'm no more a coward than you are* had been imparted to the night itself, the very sky that drew them out with a promise of giving shelter.

26

. . . lying there on the hearth by the fireplace downstairs in the musty parlor in a state between sleep and wakefulness warming herself with

a little fire she'd built in haste but the birch wood seemed to be damp,
gave off a warmth meager and grudging and the smoke made her
cough behind her knuckles and her eyes water as if with hurt or grief
Calla oh Calla! and now she was sprawled there shivering slattern her
long snarled hair fanned out on her shoulders to dry, wavy red hair
stippled with twigs, burrs, cobwebs, her hair needed washing, her
face and her hands needed washing, there she was lying on the floor
where no normal or sober or self-respecting woman would lie, her
clothes looking as if slept in, the skirt mud stained . . . yes and her
frayed stockings were wet and muddy, she'd kicked her ruined shoes
off *from tramping about in the muck like a madwoman, you'd think her husband or his people would put a stop to it for very shame* neither asleep nor
entirely awake half-sensing she was in danger but her eyelids were
heavy, hair luxuriant fanned on her shoulders so the very sight of it, of
her, that puffy slumberous look to her face would madden him, it was
very early in the morning, just dawn, and sunless, a chill wan grudging light barely penetrating the lace curtains hanging from the parlor
windows year after year prim and functionless save to accumulate by
slow degrees that thin near-invisible film of dust that must then be
laundered out of them, so carefully, by hand, gentle soap and no agitation and hung to dry out of the sun to prevent yellowing and
shrinking and Calla might have been thinking how the rawboned
young girl who had wandered the back roads and woods and fields and
creeks was dead, now she was a mature woman, breasts, belly, thighs,
loins, yes and even her face showing it, the eyes pinched at their corners, the mouth fleshy, puffy, much kissed, knowing, and Calla wiped
roughly at her eyes with the back of her hand and happened then to
see Freilicht standing there in the parlor doorway with the shotgun in
his arms, certainly it was the shotgun but in that instant Calla had no
clear thought *It's a gun, I'm going to die* seeing Freilicht's face as he
advanced upon her grimacing, the eyes shining with conviction, glass-
ily drunk, or beyond drunkenness, the jaws stubbled with gray-glinting
wires, he was a man unfamiliar to her, ravaged and triumphant weaving drunkenly toward her having been drinking much of the previous
day despite the family's pleas for him to stop, and through the long
night, locked upstairs in that bedroom alternately praying on his knees

and drinking whiskey waiting for the woman who was his wife to
come back, so he had by this hour the look of a man drowned and
hauled out of the water in mad triumph revivifying in air saying softly,
'—You whore! *Whore!*' striking Calla in the face with his fist clumsy
and off balance so he nearly fell on top of her, a second blow missed
but her nose was spurting blood as she scrambled on her hands and
knees rising to fight him, he struck her again and she clutched at his
wrist, the shotgun was an impediment to them both as Freilicht
sobbed and cursed her and Calla in grim silence struggled knowing it
was her life *I can't die, not like this, it isn't time* as upstairs in their beds
the children lay wakened and terrified hearing what they could not
know yet understood were the sounds of struggle, that single raised
despairing voice they could not know yet understood was their father's
voice, and Calla snatched up the fire tongs, Calla crouched, panting,
the tongs raised, as in her stocking feet she circled away from Freilicht
and his mad eyes, shouting words she didn't hear, she was panicked yet
calm with no time to recollect *You don't want to be hurt,—no you don't
want to be hurt the way white people hurt black people* and she was backing
away with the tongs upraised, as if that were a defense against the shotgun, as wavering and clumsy Freilicht leveled it at her, fully at her face,
saying something incoherent-sounding like '—that's what you will,
will you—you will, will you—yes?—eh?—whore—' as by design or
accident he shifted the barrel so that when he pulled the triggers, and
he pulled both triggers, the deafening blast was aimed at the window
beside her and Calla this time was spared.

27

*And then it was like we didn't belong to ourselves any more, like something
had been started that couldn't be stopped.*

*Yes we kept a careful distance between us for I don't know how long but it
didn't change things because everyone knew and that couldn't be erased and it
got so I would hear him calling my name at night when he wasn't anywhere
near, sometimes when I'd given up on him too and vowed I would forget but*

*when I saw him again he told me the same thing with him, the same exact
thing he said—'It's like it can't be stopped except by one way.'*

I never asked what that way would be.

28

Those months through the width of the Chautauqua Valley three
hundred miles from east to west and up into the mountains and down-
state as far as the Pennsylvania border people told of Calla and Tyrell
Thompson without knowing their names: a wild red-haired white
woman who had abandoned her children to run off with a black man,
in some versions of the tale as it fructified like vegetation in steamy
heat the white woman's husband and his kin were tracking them
down meaning to kill them, in some versions of the tale the black man
was an ex-convict from the South pretending to be a Christian minister carrying a Bible in one hand and a dowsing rod in the other—a
dowsing rod that never failed to find water no matter how rocky or
clayey the soil—and, strapped to one of his calves hidden up inside a
trouser leg, an eight-inch deadly-sharp knife with which he'd slit the
throats of many a white man between Georgia and here.

In fact, he'd slit the throat of the woman's husband.

In fact, the husband had tracked him down and killed him with a
double-barreled shotgun.

In fact, the white woman had come home abandoned by her black
lover and there she'd given birth to his baby, a coal-black creature,
black and sinister as the Devil, and she'd gone crazy seeing it and the
family had taken it away at once to do which of several things with it,
no one knew for sure: give it to a Negro orphanage in Buffalo, or
deliver it to the black man himself living in some slum tenement or
dirt-floor shanty with his own wife and barefoot children or maybe
did they out of shame and meanness drown the creature in the river?—
yes but there endured a version of this tale that for all its being wholly
illogical and even comic was nonetheless stubbornly told and retold for
decades until it was finally unattached to any specific individuals or

even to any specific locale except the Chautauqua backcountry in the old days when even normally law-abiding Christians were capable of such extravagances of behavior: *the outraged family had drowned the baby in their well . . . the very well the black man had helped them dig.*

There were stories and rumors less cruelly fantastical, thus more vexing in their own way since they might be believed even by people who knew the Freilichts: such as, George's wife came from a white trash family up around Milburn with a history of alcoholism and mental instability, her own mother had run off after she was born leaving her to be brought up by her father and now it was being said that Calla had had a mental collapse and the family was trying to keep it a secret, wouldn't call in a doctor for her and wouldn't allow anyone to see her including her own relatives in Shaheen, unless it was Calla herself who wouldn't see them, wouldn't see anyone including her own children *And that's the insult of it, how always it comes back to a woman being a 'good' mother in the world's eyes or a 'bad' mother, how everything in a woman's life is funneled through her body between her legs.* Yet it was said, too, that Calla was still seeing Tyrell Thompson, going sometimes on foot to beg a ride with someone to Derby poor thing like she'd been bitten by a rabid creature so the craziness was in her blood for him, a rumor circulated that the family was going to commit her to the state hospital at Erie especially now she was drinking and they couldn't control her and Tyrell Thompson was a known drinker too, belligerent and dangerous, and still she was slipping away to see him, the two of them turning up in Derby, in Yewville, in Tintern Falls, in the lowest of lowlife taverns which were the only places people like that could be seen together *Because it's unnatural and disgusting, the races mixed like that just to look at it you feel sick.* And one of George Freilicht's cousins not otherwise known for his irresponsibility or excitability swore he'd seen Calla and Tyrell Thompson together on the Fourth of July, the two of them laughing together strolling by the river in Derby their arms around each other's waist behaving as if they'd been drinking and didn't give a damn for who saw them out in public displaying themselves like that *Like they were inviting trouble and were surely going to get it.*

In fact, as the Freilichts knew, Calla had been home with her family on that day, she'd been home with her family for weeks, impassive, silent, moving like a ghost among them. As if she had no physical being *like we didn't even belong to ourselves any longer, just parts scattered like animal carcasses the dogs have torn at* since Freilicht had aimed the shotgun at her and in a way she'd died but George Freilicht's cousin not otherwise known for his irresponsibility or excitability insisted he had seen her, yes he'd seen her, cavorting there in public with her black lover Tyrell Thompson.

29

Among the lurid tales of those months when the lovers were apart there was one that was true, and Calla perceived as true, because so terrible.

In the heat of a summer night in Derby, Tyrell Thompson was hunted down by a gang of drunken white men, beaten and kicked and stripped of his clothes, and his ankles bound with cord and they'd pushed him off a bridge into the Chautauqua River yelling, 'See can you save yourself, water dowser,' and 'See how you like white women where you're going, nigger,' and they stood at the railing watching as Tyrell Thompson began to drown, sinking, then surfacing, keeping himself afloat by the sheer desperate struggle of his arms, and he held his head erect like a seal refusing to drown, to die, to be bested, and as the current carried him downstream he managed to untie his ankles until at last before the eyes of astonished witnesses the man began swimming, saved himself from a drowning death *As if it was true, what he'd always boasted—water was his friend and in his power* just swimming away downstream and off into the night, and where he came staggering and panting to shore a mile or so down below the railroad yard and the slaughterhouses along the debris- and waste-befouled shore of the Negro section of town, no one of those white men on the bridge could see.

And hearing this story told her surreptitiously by a young woman cousin from Shaheen, Calla burst into bitter tears, the first tears of her adulthood, not simply because Tyrell Thompson had been so cruelly treated and so courageous but because, hearing of his cruel treatment and of his courage, Calla knew she had no choice but to see him again.

And what he wanted to do with her, what he would expect of her as his woman, she would have no choice, she would have no will, except to acquiesce.

30

They met by the river, they made love, fierce, wordless, wanting to hurt, Calla clutched Tyrell Thompson tight to her and in her smelling his sweet-sour whiskey breath and knowing long before she had reason to know that, yes now she was pregnant: now, at last, seed taken into her she wanted, now she was capable of such easy tears. *Why you cryin, honey, you just make the both of us feel bad.* And he'd gripped her throat in his huge hands not to choke her nor even to frighten her and not seemingly to silence her but—perhaps—to suggest the idea of silence to her so Calla would carry the imprint of his fingers on her skin, the weight of those fingers defining her very bones, for the remainder of her life. *Ain't nobody forcing you to love me, honey, don't you know that, smart white woman like you?*

That night when Calla became pregnant with Tyrell Thompson's child the western sky above the river was banked in clouds like gigantic boulders, or human brains, stacked thick, high, ponderous, massive, terrible to see. A mist lifted thinly from the water and invisible loons were calling to one another in harsh melancholy shreds of sound and all the way back to the house, to her home, stumbling, wiping hard at her eyes with her knuckles, Calla could see herself on her knees in the wet grass and there was Tyrell Thompson rising and swaying above her adjusting his clothing, she heard his lightly mocking murmurous words, the whiskey rhythm beneath them, she saw his fumbling fingers and felt again their hard sure hinting touch *But I love you, I would die for you, you only you you you* but it was a touch that released her finally and not without tenderness. How tall, how big his body, he was bareheaded and his tight kinky oily hair fitted his head snug as a cap defining its size, suggesting its weight, she saw the whites of his large intelligent eyes moving in their sockets smooth as grease. She wished he'd strangled her: that would be an ending. She could not bear it that since loving Tyrell Thompson she'd become one of those women she had always scorned, quick to tears, bones like water, raw and demeaning hunger shining in her face *Love me, love me don't ever stop I will die if you stop* and maybe in fact Tyrell Thompson did have a wife, a black woman with whom he lived in Derby when the mood struck him, maybe he had a number of women, and more children than he could recall, in the river towns he visited on foot making his restless way from east to west and from west to east dowsing for water or plying whatever trade might nourish him from one season to the next, as he'd hinted—cardplaying, gambling, blacksmithing, livery stable hand, common laborer *like my daddy before me and his daddy before him God's progeny can't all be lilies of the field white and pure and blessed Oh no ma'am we can't.*

31

In continual quarrel with him Calla murmured aloud, '—I didn't choose the color of my skin, how can I be *blamed*.' And, 'No more than you I can't be blamed.' Yet unspoken between them was the understanding that she would come to him, when he wanted her.

Now she was pregnant the heedlessness of a true pregnancy was upon her. Not the sick dull vague resigned and merely physical pregnancies of her early marriage but a fevered condition by day and by night as if she held a giant seashell pressed against her ear, its roaring always with her, thus she was incautious in remarks she sometimes made aloud that might be overheard by others, knowledge of her secret self carried away from her and out of her power, to be used against her. It was not even that her condition was a secret so much as the fact that to Calla it had nothing to do with anyone apart from Tyrell Thompson and herself, how then could she speak of it, or wish to speak of it, to others.

She thought obsessively of the man who was her lover, her lover now mysteriously inside her, carried safe inside her, protected by the warmth of her very flesh, yet she rarely allowed herself to think of Tyrell Thompson as a man among men, a black man among white men in a world as steeped in racial injustice as in the unacknowledged breathable element of air, a world she might ignore as it touched upon herself—her, Calla, 'George Freilicht's wife'—yet could hardly ignore as it touched upon Tyrell Thompson. For in that world all the man might be outwardly was defined for him and granted him by his enemies, as the finest bred racehorse no matter its beauty, its strength, its courage, its speed, is defined and limited by the space of the intolerable penned corral or pasture into which his owners have forced him.

'—why didn't you strangle me then, that would have been an ending.'

But she didn't mean it of course.

For never had Calla Honeystone been happier.

Outwardly during this fevered interim of about eight weeks in the fall of 1912 Calla behaved tractably, cooperatively, with no sign of resistance or sullenness or even of recalling, in Freilicht's embarrassed presence, the fact that he had threatened her life. Husband and wife were courteous to each other, like convalescents. Elderly but ever-vigilant and ever-suspicious Mrs Freilicht wondered if Calla was repentant of her sins and hopeful of making amends—a woman of surpassing vanity, she would allow herself to be courted by her husband's wife.

Calla was suffused with the bloom of pregnancy: she was well: did not listen to much of what the Freilichts told her or discussed in her presence but still she heard, unfailingly she heard, and threw herself with energy and even zest into those mindless mechanical household chores that allowed her a fierce and undivided concentration upon her interior life. The most seemingly communal tasks Calla made into solitary occupations; there was something almost voluptuous in her absorption in the dumbly tactile, the close-at-hand. Only the intrusion of others—of her children, her Freilicht children as she thought them—threw her into disequilibrium. Looking up from the limp bloodless pimpled carcass of, say, a butchered chicken she was cleaning on the back porch, her mind miles away, Calla would see her little girl Emmaline, who'd just spoken to her, or asked a question of her she had no idea how to answer since she hadn't heard and had no wish to hear. A smile, a quick kiss, a pretty frowning admonition—'Momma is busy, dear, why don't you run along and play with—' her mind already releasing the child to that sublunary vagueness, that dim uncharted periphery of household inhabitants or guests or visitors or pets Calla had rarely, since coming there to live, made the slightest effort to know.

32

Emmaline a half-century later: 'Did I hate her?—no, she was my mother. I only lived in terror that she would finally go away.'

33

And then so abruptly, when her lover summoned her, she did go away.

Though saying beforehand to Freilicht, '—Let me go: I won't take anything,' but Freilicht stiffened in rage, hurt, resignation, saying, 'You'll take everything,' so softly Calla could barely make out his words. His eyes shone a sickish yellow, his weatherworn face was creased as if it had been crumpled, cruelly, by hand; Calla thought, staring at him, *Does he love me after all? But why?*

She was in a hurry. She was too distracted for pity.

Impatiently she cried, '—I'm pregnant with another man's child.'

And turned her back on him, and walked away. And if Freilicht wished at that moment that he had in fact killed her with his shotgun, yes and turned the gun then on himself, Calla could not know, had no time to consider, Calla was already gone.

34

They met behind the ruins of the old cider mill, they made love there, a final time, had no intention of falling upon each other as they did with such desperation, such need—but that was what happened. And afterward sitting so close together in the shade of the collapsed building amid the drunken hum of bees and wasps and flies above the sweet-reeking landslide of apple compost it was as if they drank from the same bottle, the same unmarked whiskey bottle, with the same mouth.

Calla had not known what her lover meant, at first. Something about a rowboat he'd found upstream. Or had he maybe stolen it?— 'Ain't nobody going to miss the old scrubby thing till it's too late.'

Calla had not known if she was being tested as to her courage. As to whether, set beside a Negro woman, the women of the kind Tyrell Thompson knew, she would be found lacking, no true match for a man of Tyrell Thompson's quality, she was reckless in any case, excited with love and lovemaking and her lover so close beside her after weeks of deprivation when she'd half feared she would never see him again so she said, love-warmed and whiskey-warmed nudging her head against his hard enough to give them each a little bolt of pain, '—You think I won't do it?' liking perhaps the impromptu nature of it, the defiance, the flaunting and self-display and madness of it, the two of them rowing downstream to Tintern Falls on a day when anyone might see them who chose to see them, setting their course deliberately for the falls at Tintern that had not the power—so he boasted, or gave the air of boasting—to withstand Tyrell Thompson's God-given mastery over water.

Or maybe he just wanted to kill them both. And this, so extravagant a way of making an ending.

Calla said, 'You think I won't do it, damn you?—is that what you think?'

Tyrell Thompson said, laughing, 'Sure you will, honey.'

Calla said, 'I will. I'll do it.'

Tyrell Thompson said, 'Sure you will, honey. Just like that.'

Calla said, her voice rising, 'God damn you I *will*.'

She'd told him, earlier, lying in his arms in the shade of a collapsed wall of the mill, about the baby-to-be. And she'd felt him—was it stiffen? shiver? stifle a spasm of laughing?—and take it all in silence, not a word.

Calla cried, 'Oh you bastard you'll see!' scrambling to her feet leaning heavily against Tyrell Thompson who grabbed at her hips laughing and they wrestled together fondly and a little roughly and then they were making love again, harder and with less ceremony than before, and Calla screamed and clutched at her lover so close against her she could not see his face, her eyes shut tight against his face as the huge man pumped his life's blood into her, groaning and burrowing helpless as a resentful child, 'Uh-uh-*uh*,' he moaned forcing her by painful little inches backward in the dirt until at last it was over and Calla lay dazed, tears running from the corners of her pinched eyes and her entire body aching as if she'd been flung from a great height to lie here spread-eagled and powerless on her back trusting to a giant of a black man not to smash her bones to bits or smother her with his weight and though now he was saying how he loved her *Oh honey oh honey* she felt her consciousness close to extinction seeing overhead the sky lightly fleeced with clouds, layer upon layer of pale clouds, so empty, so without consolation or even the illusion of such, Calla felt her mouth shaping an involuntary smile.

When had I stopped believing in, what is it—God?—and Jesus Christ His only begotten son? After loving Tyrell Thompson, or before?

She made her way through the prickly underbrush to where he'd dragged the rowboat up onto the red-clayey bank of the creek, the creek was only two or three feet deep at this point so he'd simply waded in it: and there the rowboat was: larger than Calla had expected, maybe twelve feet in length, unpainted, moderately weathered and splintery to the touch and there was a puddle of brackish water in it but the oars were in good condition and the seats had been strengthened recently, fresh boards nailed across, certainly this was a boat that belonged to someone, a fisherman's boat, some farmer or his son who lived close by, so Tyrell Thompson had stolen it, certainly. Calla drew her hand tentatively across the hull, Calla swallowed hard. The beat

beat beat of the pulse in her loins seemed to her so powerful and so terrible she could not endure it. She squinted at where Tyrell Thompson in his somber black attire was crouched incongruously in the stream, trouser legs rolled up, stooping to wash his face in his cupped hands, she called out harshly, gaily, '—I told you: I'm ready.'

And so they set out.

And so, once their course was set, they would not turn back.

The creek, a nameless creek, would empty into the Chautauqua River five or six miles to the north and once on the Chautauqua at a point about parallel with Milburn they would make their way swiftly and unerringly past Flemingville, past Shaheen, toward Tintern Falls and wherever it was they were going. The single bottle of whiskey which would have to do for them for hours in the pitiless September sun was still three-quarters full, which was a good thing.

If this is a dream it is not my dream for how should I know the language in which to dream it.

35

So, there, on the river, in the slanted sunshine, the stolen weatherworn rowboat bucking the waves with a look almost of gaiety, defiance. Yes certainly defiance: the big broad-shouldered black man at the oars rowing not quite rhythmically but with strength, purpose, deliberation, the oars lifting dripping from the water and sinking again at once; with a look both antic and violent, and facing him her knees nudging his knees, the white woman with the long tattered wind-whipped red hair, a blaze of it in the sun as she sat so unnaturally straight in a posture of amazement or delight or terror or simple child-like entrancement staring at the wide river so much wider, and rougher, than you know from shore, and watching the tangled banks that seemed to be passing in drunken spasms, and now they were beyond the mill at Flemingville the very sawmill at which Mr Honeystone had worked when his farm failed him and shortly thereafter came the houses at Shaheen so oddly, illicitly glimpsed from their rears, lightning rods, glass winking in windows, clothes and white-glaring linens hanging from clotheslines, and there was the high-arched Shaheen bridge with its nightmare spidery look, floorboards that rattled when wagons were drawn across it, rivets glinting coldly in the sun and everything perceived as unfamiliar from Calla's new lowered angle of vision on the river and what was Tyrell Thompson saying to her?—telling her another time as if he'd forgotten he'd told her before about his young mother years before he was born, fourteen years old she'd been taken by night by slavery abolitionists across the Potomac at Martinsburg, Virginia, taken from house to house with a small group of terrified young slaves and finally into the large farmhouse of a Quaker family in Pennsylvania and from there to New York State and onto a railroad running up through the northern part of the state to the Canadian border thus out of the reach of slave catchers, and the white railroad workers were ready to help—for a fee, and so Tyrell Thompson came north sixteen years before he was born, and who his momma's people were back down in Virginia he was never to know, never even to inquire, and Calla returned his hard grimace of a smile, their knees companionably nudging, sweat in rivulets running down their faces like tears as, now, they were beginning at last to attract serious attention on shore, men in shirtsleeves by the dock behind a granary staring at them shading their eyes to see who they were, this defiant mismatched couple *A nigger and a white woman!—look!* and Tyrell Thompson did not slacken in his vigorous rowing, his tight-fitting black coat straining across his muscular shoulders as he rowed taking pleasure in the ache of his body in the mindlessness of such effort, and Calla saw this, Calla drank from the whiskey bottle and passed it back to Tyrell Thompson with his fine-scarred purplish-red black skin, a skin that looked many-layered and not thin like Calla's, she smiled refusing to beg her lover to change his mind and very likely in her mesmerized state she did not want him to change his mind, she was in dread of him turning coward in her place *I do what I do, what I have done is what I have wanted to do* she saw he was perspiring big oily globules of sweat, his coat and shirt soaked in sweat, and what a fine rancid odor lifted from him, the cuffs of his trousers wet as well, like the soiled hem of Calla's skirt, they smiled and winked at each other, Calla bumped his knees hard with her own and leaned forward precipitously to seize his face between her hands and kiss the lips greedily and the snubbed oily nose, she made a gesture of licking his sweat-begrimed forehead but the boat was lurching and Tyrell Thompson urged her gently back onto the seat *I wanted to scream and scream, scream my legs wrapped around him to squeeze the very life from him* and Calla relented seeing how her skin was visibly burning from the sun, she stared seeing the luminous pale-freckled skin turning pink in the humid sunshine and she thought with regret of how her face would peel, shredded and scarified like the beginning of death when her enemies laid her out gloating to contemplate her one final time praying God to have mercy on her sluttish unredeemed soul.

Not far east of Tintern Falls there came hurtled at the couple in the bucking rowboat isolated shouts, crude warnings but they were aloof to the commands of strangers; the woman meant to maintain till the very end her stiff alert posture; the black man hunched, rowing, and then straight, his shoulders straightening in pride meaning to resist the natural tug of his bones toward the earth, then again hunched with the effort of maneuvering the boat always a little faster than it could go, and now in the suddenly frothy rapids above the falls the little boat began seriously to dip, to plunge, to shudder, to cavort, so that Tyrell Thompson's smile looked startled for a perceptible instant and Calla felt that stabbing vertigo in the pit of the belly that signals acute danger but she gripped both sides of the boat and steadied herself as with drunken swiftness they flew beneath the bridge at Tintern Falls where faces gaped down at them, white faces, men, a boy or two, arms and fists were waved, the air rang with shouts of warning and upset and incredulity, but the couple in the boat paid no heed, it was queenly and kingly, their defiance of all who witnessed their flight and were bound to speak of the spectacle for years, decades, lifetimes, still they paid no heed to strangers, looking at each other their eyes drowning in each other as the roar of the falls ahead began by odd fast jumps to increase in volume more rapidly than one might expect and the sky had dissolved in white spray and froth and the world was finite enough now to fit inside a twelve-foot battered rowboat stolen out of a marshy

inlet and Calla thought *I'm ready* and Tyrell Thompson by now had
carefully lifted the oars to place them in the oarlocks so he might be
observed should witnesses care to observe him sitting erect and alert
and unafraid his arms folded across his broad chest and his big hands
tight beneath his armpits, not a glimmer of apprehension in that stoic
masklike face, not a glimmer of apprehension in the woman's face so
if you were a witness to this spectacle at Tintern Falls in September
1912 you knew and could hardly not know how these two were a
couple bonded in love, and more than love.

PART III

It is the remainder of her life of which I find it so difficult to speak:
except to see her shut her door, lock her door upon herself, one of
those large drafty rooms at the top of the old farmhouse, but not a
room she was obliged to share with her husband or with anyone and
which only at rare intervals during the subsequent years were visitors,
even her children, allowed to enter.

My mother has said *People lived differently then, they did things for life,
made gestures that lasted for life* and it was fifty-five years Calla chose to
remain in seclusion in that farmhouse that was never home to her,
caring to leave the house and the property no more than a half-dozen
times and each of these times exclusively for the purpose of attending
a funeral, the final occasion being March 1928 when her husband died
and was buried in the hilly cemetery behind the First Lutheran
Church of Shaheen beneath a granite marker already engraved to
include *Beloved Wife Edith* 1890—.

She would die finally in 1967 at the age of seventy-seven by which
time she had outlived her husband by forty-three years and her lover
by fifty-five years and I think how quaint, how diminished they must
have seemed to her by then, like images seen through the wrong end
of a telescope but perhaps I am mistaken for how can I speak of that

woman let alone speak for her who scarcely knew her: she who was my mother's mother yet as distant to me as any stranger.

Because I was mad, or because I was never mad?

I cannot bear to think of her yet I think of her continuously.

I cannot solve the puzzle, the riddle, the mystery she embodies: Calla Honeystone, a young woman at the time of her initial retreat, from all that I've been able to learn only semi-invalided and intermittently unwell (both her legs were broken in the plunge over the falls, one kneecap seriously shattered, and there were many lacerations, and, to come, migraine headaches and spells of blindness and 'fits') yet she chose to withdraw inside the Freilicht household and inside the farmhouse itself—roof, walls, windows—to define herself as, not Edith Freilicht, for she was never apparently that woman, but a presence of no distinctive name or being or volition or wish, performing household chores with an unfailing concentration and indifference, coming downstairs from time to time—when not 'unwell'—to sit at the table with the others, even to make a polite pretense of showing interest in grandchildren as they were presented to her, though without troubling to remember names, for what after all are names, to what purpose the distinction of individuals, what futility, vanity *It isn't that one day resembles the preceding day, or the following day, in your room at the top of the house dreaming at your high window watching the river through the trees glittering like a snake's scales but one day is in fact that day, all days are identical.*

Once when I was a small child three or four years old my mother had driven back to that place she called home, her mouth downward turning around the word *home*, the very sound of it, like *family* too, like *mother*, the old farmhouse of dim red weatherworn but still sturdy brick at the end of a snow-bordered lane of pines so straight and so tall they seemed to reach into the sky beyond my range of vision craning my neck in the car, and it was the week following Christmas and I'd climbed the stairs to see what it was I'd been warned against disturbing and there was my mother's mother's door ajar at the end of the hall, perhaps two inches ajar, as if in invitation, the woman shy, shy inside the chill averted gaze and the face both ravaged and beautiful, the bones sharp in the cheeks and socketing the eyes and the hair metallic gray carelessly braided and left to hang between the gaunt shoulder blades like a noose and I crept to the door and looked inside smelling a faint odor of camphor and there in the twilit textured light my grandmother's pale face, her figure, dark-clad, shading into the shadows of the room or into the very wallpaper, but there seemed for an instant to pass between us a small stab of recognition *Because we are linked by blood and blood is memory without language* and she spoke to me questioningly, her voice harsh as if it had been unused for some time, very likely she was asking if I would like to come into her room but I shrank away my fingers jammed in my mouth and ran downstairs and beyond that the memory dissolves in a mist of childish shame and adult regret *Because we are linked by blood, thus irrevocably.*

Never did she speak to the Freilichts of Tyrell Thompson, nor did they speak to her of him. Of the baby—the baby-to-be—the bloody miscarriage amid the catastrophe of the plunge over the falls, the smashed rowboat, the flailing drowning broken bodies, of course no one spoke and *no one was ever to speak.*

In families there are frequently matters of which no one speaks, nor even alludes. There are no words for these matters. As the binding skeleton beneath the flesh is never acknowledged by us and, when at last it defines itself, is after all an obscenity.

How have I come by this knowledge: by way of fragments, whispers, half-heard reproaches. In point of fact as I was growing up I heard of my mother's mother the 'crazy' woman as much from girlfriends and from their mothers as I did from my own mother, for to her, Emmaline, the mystery of Calla Honeystone was a deep and abiding embarrassment. Years before Calla died in 1967 Emmaline would say *Let the dead past bury the dead* it was a fervent prayer for her, an appeal to God and His sense of fair play.

She shut her door, she locked her door upon herself early in the winter of 1913 as soon as she'd sufficiently recovered from the trauma done to her body, able to walk with difficulty yet with stubborn persistence using a cane and her thin shoulders hunched, head bowed to protect her watery squinty eyes from the sun glaring fierce as a razor on the dullest of surfaces, and ever after that as the seasons reeled past, the years, the decades, Canada geese flying north above the highest peak of the highest roof of the house, Canada geese flying south issuing their hoarse melancholy cries, and the invisible loons on the river, and the warning calls of red-winged blackbirds in the marshes, moons too flying by, twin moons reflected calmly in her wide calm staring eyes as she thought *No hunger is ever satisfied if it is a true hunger.*

She believed that river water remained in her lungs, the dark brackish taste of it, the faint scent of vomit.

She'd vomited convulsively when they dragged her to shore. Her broken useless legs, her hair trailing like seaweed in the churning white water, eyeballs rolled up in her head like a great doll's so she hadn't been a witness to what was whispered later through the valley, that the men had allowed Tyrell Thompson to drown there amid the boulders and the screaming white rapids *No but he slipped through our fingers, big black bastard got away his head split like a pumpkin spilling brains* but they'd relented, finally dragging him from the water a half-mile downstream, his broken battered body like the carcass of an animal floating in the river for days, the stink and heaviness of death lifting from it and where the water dowser was buried, and who mourned him, which black woman, or women, how many children scattered in the river towns east to west and west to east along the Chautauqua no whites were to know, certainly not the white woman who had nearly died with him at Tintern, plunging over the falls with him in a rowboat that had shattered about them like kindling tossed up shrieking amid the granite rocks and boulders and the cascading white water rabid with froth like old men's beards as she'd think of it afterward mute and broken her bones in traction in a city hospital where for some time she was not expected to recover until one whitely glaring morning her eyelids fluttered open and Calla woke to full horrific consciousness and began screaming *Just screaming and screaming what you wouldn't ever expect from the lips of a woman like that: 'Jesus! Jesus! Jesus!'*

Fifty-five years.

A life split in two but not in half, the weight of it in the past and all that remained a protracted repetition of minutes, of peace. As standing at a high window as night comes on you observe how by slow

ineluctable degrees the outer world diminishes and your own reflection defines itself without color, or texture, or depth, or soul. *Did you
know it was Death that summoned you, a dowsing rod in his hand? Or was
it Love? And were you faithful to him however bitterly however purposelessly
all the days of your long life? Or did you forget him, and this inevitably, helplessly, as, as life passes through the seasons, the decades, the calm mad minutes
of the ticking of household clocks, we are bound to forget, all, everything, our
very selves?*

Still she stands there, at the high window with its view of the river
a quarter-mile away, as night comes on.

Once my mother divorced the man who was, who is, my father, and
left him behind in Shaheen, and moved away to a city at the western
border of the state, the visits back home were infrequent and were primarily visits with my mother's brother Edward and his family, my
thick-set kindly taciturn uncle Edward who had inherited the farm
when his father died of a massive coronary in 1928 and who did quite
well with it relative to his farming neighbors once he shrewdly sold off
half the acreage and kept the most fertile and tillable land for himself in
addition to long lovely sloping stretches of deciduous woods and pas-
tureland along the Chautauqua River: Edward Freilicht grew wheat,
soybeans, and corn, razed the old rotting orchards and laid in acres of
Cortland apples and Bing cherries, rebuilt the old barns, refenced the
pastures, renovated part of the old farmhouse and painted its tall
narrow shutters an unexpected white, and became at about the time of
his mother's death in 1967 an officer of the New York State Farm
Bureau to whom state legislators were obliged to listen with a modicum of respect. My mother and Edward were not much alike (my
mother often said she'd resembled, she'd been adoring of, their older
brother, Enoch, who had been killed in the Philippines in World War
II) nor did they give any outward appearance of being sentimental
people but they were linked of course by family obligations, family history, family memory and expiations, they were avid to speak together
*And how is Mother? Unchanged? Always unchanged?—it's the others of us
who change isn't it?* in privacy together while sometimes through an
entire visit of two or three days my mother's mother would remain out

of sight, there might be creaking floorboards overhead and we'd imagine a sound, a hesitant contemplative sound, of footsteps on the stairs descending and then abruptly retreating back up to whatever it was there in her room under the eaves furnished so sparely yet so seemingly completely, where when I was a girl of fourteen and fifteen I dreamt of her as a figure static as the wallpaper of that room of which I'd had a glimpse (I believed I'd had a glimpse: had memorized: a lacy floral pattern of no discernible color overlaid upon a pale background of no discernible color, the pattern in vertical rows) since wallpaper consists of aesthetic configurations that appear to move even as they repeat themselves endlessly, a calm steady confining repetition from wall to wall to wall to wall thus the prison of that room, the sanctuary of that room, for a woman, for that woman, perhaps for me since I am a woman, perhaps it is the woman's womb, she is imprisoned there in her womb or is it a sanctuary?—so I would offend my mother and my uncle asking why my grandmother kept so much to herself, rarely stepped out of the house except to go into the barns sometimes or the chicken coop, she hadn't left the property itself in years and why, why if she wasn't actually ill, wasn't mad, or senile, why didn't she at least visit neighbors, relatives, go to church with the family?—and they would assure me that my grandmother had been offered many opportunities to leave the house, to visit anywhere she wished, there was a tacit understanding that her son would drive her anywhere but no one wanted to anger her by making these suggestions that had been made countless times over the years and the fact was that the woman lived the life she chose, she was happy in that life and it was no one's business after all but her own, my uncle's face darkening with blood as he spoke, my mother's fair fine skin pink as if smarting yet still I persisted, for I thought it such a horror, such a grief, yes and an embarrassment too, I said, 'She's made a prison of this house, it's like she's a nun, it must be to punish herself,' and my mother said quietly, angrily, 'You don't know—what do you know! People do what they want to do.'

But I could not, could not believe that terrible truth, don't expect me to believe such a terrible truth, it's pitiless, it leaves no room for mercy, it isn't the world as I would have imagined it.

*

In the Chautauqua area it was generally believed that Calla had gone mad: not raving mad but quietly, even placidly mad, as women some-times did, women of her generation, or the generations preceding, worn out with childbirth or female maladies whose very Latin names evoked distaste, of course there were madmen too, living alone on isolated farms in the foothills or at the outskirts of one or another slowly developing town, recluses, hermits, the men living alone in ramshackle farmhouses or log cabins or tarpaper shanties or in some desperate instances in old packing cases in the township dump, while the women tended to withdraw within actual households often with the implicit support or encouragement of husbands, parents, children, ministers, parish priests willing to come to the house to deliver com-munion and to pray with the afflicted party, who might in truth not be considered afflicted but perversely independent, blessed, requiring nothing of the profane world's vanity but subsisting within the walls of a single house a single household performing the routine and wholly satisfying mindless tasks of housewifery, as Calla did once she was recovered from the worst of her trauma, her old zeal returning, her former rapt concentration, those strong deft fingers, rather mus-cular arms, a predilection for such solitary tasks as ironing clothes, scrubbing floors, polishing furniture and silverware and washing win-dows and sewing, at first by hand and then at the wonderful little gleaming black Singer sewing machine with the foot pedal and the flying needle with its eye so curiously at its point: just to watch that needle was bliss! *Like the flash of heat lightning that tells you all that is, is now.*

Yet it was not true that Calla kept solely to herself, within even a year of the scandalous incident at Tintern Falls. Often she was to be found working companionably with her female in-laws, especially at the preparation of meals (and especially at harvest when Freilicht would have hired on as many as twelve extra hands), and it so strangely developed that the elderly Mrs Freilicht who had endured years of per-petual disapproval and outrage regarding her headstrong daughter-in-law became not only forgiving of the young woman but protective of her now she was broken and humbled and even her beauty marred by rivulets of tears, or were they scars, or stains, if it was not a genuine

Christian repentance that glimmered in those eyes it had the look of one *Praise be to God from Whom all blessings flow, praise Father, Son, and Holy Ghost that a sinner is returned to the fold!* thus among the reversals of Calla's life came this odd belated flowering, though almost entirely unvoiced, of a deep maternal interest on the part of the elder woman whose strength of will and indefatigable energy allowed her dominance in her son's household well into her eighty-sixth year and whose brief illness and collapse and death Calla was to mourn with the shock of fresh grief as if she had thought, still so young, hardly thirty years old, that one death, one violent bitter loss, was all that God would have required of her forever.

When Calla accompanied the family to church, and to Mrs Freilicht's gravesite, dressed entirely in black, a black veil covering her face from forehead to chin, leaning on George Freilicht's arm, moving stiffly, her gaze downcast and unreadable, it was the first time church members and neighbors had seen her for years: since the incident at Tintern Falls and Calla's return to the Freilichts and what was generally if vaguely understood to be her 'strangeness': and it would be years, in fact six years, before they had the satisfaction of seeing her again, this time at Freilicht's funeral and burial, at which occasion she, just widowed, seeming scarcely to have changed since Mrs Freilicht's death, would be dressed again entirely in black, a shapeless oversized black linen coat borrowed from a sister-in-law, a black straw hat and a coarse black veil covering her face from forehead to chin, Calla this time leaning on her elder son Enoch's arm and yielding to curious eyes no outward sign of grief or of the stoic suppression of grief so they, those others whose faces, let alone names, she had never troubled to learn, murmured together in communal outrage and gratification *Look at her! so young! she'll outlive them all! she'll inherit! all that land! she'll take up with another nigger and bring him home and this time she'll have nigger babies right here in Shaheen with nobody to stop her!* which turned out to be utterly utterly mistaken.

After her death (quietly in her sleep of heart failure, one May night in 1967, no warning beforehand: she appeared a young seventy-seven) the family discovered her girlhood Bible left open on her bureau, the

tissue-thin pages dog-eared and worn with a look of having been read
repeatedly so it was a consolation to the Freilichts to think that she had
had faith, still, in God, in the Christian religion, and particularly in the
teachings of Martin Luther, in the forgiveness of sins and the redemption of sinners through Jesus Christ our Savior, for all the Freilichts and
their kin and farming neighbors were unquestioning Christians in
those days *I asked him do you believe in God?—just tell me and he shrugged
his shoulders wide as the length of another man's arm and laughed and said,
Why certainly, honey, you know I believe in God: had better, so I said,
You're lying, you're too smart to believe in any god white men have got up in
their own image, so he made this snorting laughing noise of his like a horse
almost, I knew I had him now, I had him now, so he granted I was right, he
said, Now look: a white man's god ain't much certainly but he's a whole lot
better than nothing, to keep them white men from the full nastiness they'd naturally like to be* which was their way of redressing certain imbalances in
life, for instance sinners who suffered insufficiently in this world would
suffer sufficiently, and forever, in that other world, and the uncomplaining faithful, meek and mild and abrogating their militancy to
formal governments, armies, legislated laws, would inherit what
remained, and even if in so many—so many!—instances the balm of
Eternity might not erase the heartbreak of Time these good Lutherans
would at least know that their Savior knew, they would at least know
that their Savior knew.

For long spells of the life that remained stretching out seemingly without end Calla was physically disoriented; inhabiting her body as if it
were another's; in such stasis pain came at unpredictable intervals sharp
and stabbing as a bird's beak and she would lie motionless as a dead
woman on her bed in that room sequestered beneath the eaves, a
damp cloth over her eyes to assuage the curious pain that rose and
broke, rose and broke, rose and broke like cascades of glittering white
water in which she yearned to drown except her strong lungs refused
to fill, choking and vomiting she rid herself of it repeatedly yet lay
unmoving on the horsehair mattress beneath the wool-and-silk quilt of
three hundred sixty-five squares her mother-in-law had sewed for her
in her first illness when it was clear that Calla Honeystone was broken

and could not ever mend properly, thus she lay floating as beyond her locked door the clocks of the household ticked their smug time and her children grew older not by degrees it seemed but in sudden pleats and jumps, their faces hard with bone as her own, their eyes wary, intelligent, evasive, Enoch and Edward and Emmaline were their names but these were not sacred names Calla whispered to herself in moods of distress as a mother might, nor did she whisper the name of her late husband George Freilicht except to regret at the time of his death that she had not been able to love him as any man of his strength and industry and Christian charity deserved, and there was too the elderly woman whom she had never called Mother, now dead, and beyond the locked door of her room the century rushed headlong as over a series of cataracts into its future of wars, financial collapse, boom times, and new presidents of the United States, and new wars, and the area around Shaheen acquiring roads paved in asphalt, the River Road itself at the end of the Freilicht's quarter-mile lane not only paved but widened considerably, and there were motorcars and no longer horse-drawn wagons, there were tractors and no longer horse-drawn plows, there were combines, and threshers, and telephones, and radios, and television, newspaper headlines and photographs flaring up as if, thrown onto the fire, they existed forever in that moment before consumption when every detail is irradiated as if from within and given the deluded significance of immortality, so Calla lived however disoriented and bemused and cynical at times and at other times simply grateful thinking *I was never unhappy, I regret nothing* for otherwise she would never have known him: her lover: whose name she did not say either as if doubting it had been the man's true name but she could see him distinctly outside the window, a stranger, down there holding his dowsing rod in both hands like a prayer at mid-chest, that trespasser, black suit fitting him tight in the shoulders and a frayed white shirt some woman had ironed and starched for him but not for a while, and that black bowler hat snug on his head and that light in his eyes like the ivory of old piano keys when she'd told him *My name is Calla.*

Yet for years they were seen together and tales of such sightings repeated, seen always at a distance so that their exact identities were in doubt yet everyone in the Chautauqua Valley knew who the red-haired white woman and the giant of a black man were glimpsed at dusk walking together by the river their arms defiantly around each other's waist their smiling faces lowered together conspiring and then again in the ruins of the old mill above Shaheen where other illicit lovers sometimes met, or was it in Derby at the lower end of town in one or another riverside tavern or café where a black man with a white woman would not arouse immediate outrage or at least the violence that such outrage as cultivated by white men usually entailed, and yes of course on the Chautauqua itself they were frequently sighted in the doomed little rowboat, Tyrell Thompson rowing with that air of precision and desperation and the white woman gripping the sides of the boat in belated alarm for years, for decades until finally the descendants of the descendants of those individuals who had actually seen Calla and Tyrell Thompson on that day or who had at least heard firsthand breathless accounts from those who had were all dead, or had grown too infirm to remember, or had moved away from that remote region in upstate New York to which they might return if they chose to return only as temporary visitors: strangers.

That final time. The summer before her death and my mother and I were visiting the farm and so little seemed to have changed, I was sitting restless on the top step of the veranda a few feet away from her in the dusk, she was sitting in one of the high-backed wicker rockers but she wasn't rocking just sitting there still with one of the barn cats drowsy in her lap so I could hear the cat's low throaty purring and we didn't speak and my heart began to beat rapidly urging me to speak since I wasn't a child any longer, I was a young woman needing to ask of my mother's mother certain crucial questions before it was too late *for as each dies, a part of that old world dies with her* but I was wary of offending her, provoking her into rising and walking away stiff with arthritic dignity as I'd witnessed upon occasions when others however well-intentioned tried to draw Calla into casual conversation, I sat silent thinking *Was it for love you threw your life away?—did you throw your life away?* but I said nothing as darkness began to lift from the grass and the fireflies began winking in the shadows and suddenly there were dozens of them, hundreds, tiny lights beating and pulsing and the urge to confront my mother's mother subsided and after some minutes she remarked as if we'd been talking this way, the two of us, companionably, easily, all along, '. . . when I was a little girl, I went to school up in Milburn . . . a one-room school . . . in winter it got dark early so the teacher, Mrs Vogel, lit our lanterns for us one by one so we could see our way home . . . and we'd be walking, a string of us, along the road . . . and the children would turn up onto lanes, or other roads, going over hills . . . the fireflies always remind me of that, the lanterns we'd carried . . . the lanterns going off across the hills and into the dark and I'd go on by myself, finally I was the last one on our road and by the time I got home it was night, and cold,' and I sat there listening entranced for never had I heard my mother's mother speak in so prolonged and so purposeful a way, never to me, sitting there in the high-backed wicker rocker one of the Freilichts had built by hand a scruffy barn cat drowsing on her lap, though in the dim light I couldn't see her face just the outline of her glimmering hair, I said, 'Grandmother, oh when was that?' and she replied after a pause as if she were bemused at my tone or maybe she was actually calculating, counting the years and it was that that bemused her, '—A long time ago.'

1990

Hey, Have You Got a Cig, the Time, the News, My Face?

BARRY HANNAH

His dreams were not good. E. Dan Ross had constant nightmares, but lately they had run at him deep and loud, almost begging him. He was afraid his son would kill his second wife. Ross often wanted to kill his own wife, Newt's mother, but he was always talking himself out of it, talking himself back into love for her. This had been going on for thirty-two years. E. Dan Ross did not consider his marriage at all exceptional. But he was afraid his son had inherited a more desperate fire.

Newt had been fired from the state cow college where he taught composition and poetry. Newt was a poet. But a friend of Ross's had called from the campus and told him he thought Newt, alas, had a drinking problem. He was not released for only the scandal of sleeping with a student named Ivy Pilgrim. There was his temper and the other thing, drink. Newt was thirty. He took many things very seriously, but in a stupid, inappropriate way, Ross thought. There were many examples of this through the years. Now, for example, he had married this Ivy Pilgrim. This was his second wife.

The marriage should not have taken place. Newt was unable to swim rightly in his life and times. The girl was not pregnant, neither was she rich. If she had made up that name, by the way, Ross might kill her himself. He could imagine a hypersensitive dirt-town twit leeching onto his boy. Newt's poetry had won several awards, including two national ones, and his two books had been seriously reviewed in New York papers, and by one in England.

Ross did not have to do all the imagining. Newt had sent him a photograph a month ago. It was taken in front of their quarters in the college town, where they remained, Newt having been reduced in scandal, the girl having been promoted, Ross figured. Ross was a writer himself. He was proud of Newt. Now he was driving to see him from Point Clear, Alabama, a gorgeous village on the eastern shore of Mobile Bay. Ross and his wife lived in a goodly spread along the beach. He worked in a room on the pier with the brown water practically lapping around his legs. It was a fecund and soul-washed place, he felt. He drove a black Buick Riviera, his fifth, with a new two-seater fiberglass boat trailing behind. It was deliberately two-seater. There would be no room for the girl when they went out to try the bass and bream.

He saw ahead to them: The girl would be negligent, a soft puff of skin above her blue jeans, woolly 'earth sandals' on her feet, and a fading light in her eyes, under which lay slight bags from beer and marijuana and Valium when she could get it. Newt's eyes would be red and there would be a scowl on him. He will be humming a low and nervous song. He will be filthy and misclothed, like an Englishman. His hands will be soft and dirty around the fingernails. He'll look like a deserter on the lam. This is the mode affected by retarded bohemians around campus. Cats would slink underfoot in their home. Cats go with really sorry people. If anybody smokes, Newt and Ivy will make a point of never emptying the ashtray, probably a coffee can, crammed and stinking with cigarettes. Somebody will have sores on the leg or a very bad bruise somewhere. They will have a guitar which nobody can play worth spit. A third of a bottle of whiskey is somewhere, probably under the sink. They'll be collecting cash from the penny bowl in order to make a trip to the liquor store. This is the big decision of the day. Old cat food would lie in a bowl, crusted. Shoes and socks would be left out. Wherever they go to school or teach it is greatly lousy, unspeakably and harmfully wrong. This was his son and his wife, holding down the block among their awful neighbors in a smirking conspiracy of sorriness; a tract of rental houses with muddy, unfixed motorcycles and bicycles around. Somebody's kid would sit obscene-mouthed on a porch.

E. Dan Ross, a successful biographer, glib to the point of hackery (he prided himself on this), came near a real monologue in his head: Your son is thirty and you see the honors he has won in poetry become like cheap trinkets won at a fair and now you know it has not been a good bargain. A bit of even immortal expression should not make this necessary. It should have brought him a better woman and a better home. Your son has been fired in scandal from a bad school. Newt must prevail, have a 'story.' These poets are oh, yes, insistent on their troubled biography. The fact is that more clichés are attached to the life of a 'real' writer than to that of a hack. Every one of them had practically memorized the bios of their idols and thought something was wrong if they paid the light bill on time. When I talk to my son, Ross thought, it is comfortable for both of us to pretend that I am a hack and he the flaming original; it gives us defined places for discussion, though I have poetry in my veins and he knows it, as I know damned well he is no real alcoholic. The truth is, Newt would drink himself into a problem just for the required 'life.' Nobody in our family ever had problems with the bottle. It is that head of his. He did not know how to do life, he did not know how to cut the crap and work hard. He did not know that doomed love would wreck his work if he played around with it too much. There is cruelty in the heart of those who love like this. There is a mean selfishness that goes along with being so deplorable. You will say what of the life of the spirit, what has material dress to do with the innerness, the deep habits of the soul, blabba rabba. Beware of occasions that call for a change of clothing, take no heed for the morrow, Thoreau and Jesus, sure, but Newt has no mighty spiritual side that Ross has seen. Newt's talent, and it is a talent I admit, is milking the sadness out of damned near everything. Isolating it, wording it into precise howls and grasping protests.

Newt swam in melancholy, he was all finned out for tragedy, right out of the nineteenth century, à la Ruskin, wasn't it? Look deep enough into the heart of things and you will see something you're not inclined to laugh at. Yeah, gimme tragedy or give me nothing. My heart is bitter and it's mine, that's why I eat it. He would squeeze the sadness out of this Buick Riviera convertible like it was a bright black sponge. Ross agreed that his son should win the awards—he was good, good, good—but he could make you look back and be sorry for having had a fine time somewhere. You would stand convicted in the court of the real for having had a blast at Club Med, or for seeing the hopefulness at a christening. Ross had been offered university jobs paying four times what his son made, condo included. But Newt's readers—what, seventy world-wide?—rejoiced in the banal horror of that. They were, doubtless, whiskered Philip Larkinophiles in shiny rayon pants, their necrotic women consorts sighing through yellow teeth. The job Newt had thrown away, his allegiance to the girl for whom he had thrown it all away, had paralyzed him. There *must* be love; it has to have been all worthwhile. Ross took an inner wager on Newt's having a pigtail. He now sang with a punkish band. Odds were that he had not only a pigtail but some cheap pointless jewelry too around his wrist, like a shoelace.

Ross intended to talk his son out of this Ivy Pilgrim. A second brief marriage would go right into the *vita* of a modern poet just like an ingredient on a beer can. No problem there. Lately his son had written 'No poems' in every letter, almost proudly, it seemed to Ross. But this was more likely a cry beneath a great mistake. In the back seat of the car were a CD player and a superior piece of leather Samsonite oversize luggage, filled with CDs. It was not a wedding gift. It was to remind Newt, who might be stunned and captured in this dreadful cow-college burg, that there were other waters. Sometimes the young simply forgot that. The suitcase was straight-out for him to leave with. Ross was near wealthy and read Robert Lowell too, goddammit. And 'The Love Song of J. Alfred Prufrock' was his favorite poem. Had poetry done any better in this century? No. There were inklings here and there, Ross thought, that his boy was better than Elliot, if you take away the self-prescribed phoenix around his neck, this thing with women. Newt had a son from his first wife, a college beauty who had supported his melancholy. Already Newt was at odds with his seven-year-old son, who was happy and liked sports and war toys. He cursed his ex-wife and raised her into an evil planetary queen, since she sold real estate and had remarried a muscled man who had three aerobic salons. But Ross recalled the time when this woman was the source of Newt's poems, when it was she and Newt against the world, a raving dungeon teasing the eternally thirsty and famished.

This little Ivy Pilgrim had to be a loser and Newt would kill her one day. He had threatened his last wife several times and had shot a hunting arrow into his estranged house. Ross projected seeing Newt in the newspaper, jailed and disconsolate, Ivy Pilgrim's corpse featured in his bio, Newt not remembering much, doomed forever. Then bent on suicide. Or a life of atonement, perhaps evangelism. Or teaching prison poetry workshops, a regular venue for worthless poets nowadays.

Everett Dan Ross (given, not a pen name; how he despised writers who changed their names for whatever reason!) could see Ivy Pilgrim in the desolate house. Hangdog and clouded, nothing to say for herself. It made him furious. He predicted her inertia, a feckless, heavy tagalong. The bad skin would tell you she was a vegetarian. At best she would be working a desk out of a welfare office someday. Or 'involved' in an estate settlement (meticulous leeching of the scorned dead). One always appreciated those who gave attention to one's son, but she would have a sickening deed to him, conscious that they were a bright scandal at this dump of a college ('Oh yes, they don't know what to do with us!') in the Romantic vein. When the truth was, nobody cared much. They might as well have been a couple of eloped hamsters. She was a squatter, a morbid lump, understanding nothing, burying him with her sex. She'd favor the states of 'laid back' and 'mellow,' as if threatened crucially by their opposites.

Ross, through life, had experienced unsafe moments. He knew where Newt's melancholy came from. It was not being sued by that true hack whose biography Ross had done. It wasn't Ross's fault the man was too lazy to read the book before it came out, anyway, though Ross had rather surprised himself by his own honesty, bursting out here at age fifty-two—why? Nor was it the matter of the air rifle that always rode close to him. Nor was it a panic of age and certain realizations, for instance that he was not a good lover even when he loved his wife, Nabby. He knew what was correct, that wives liked long tenderness and caressing. But he was apt to drive himself over her, and afterwards he could not help despising her as he piled into sleep for escape. She deserved better. Maybe his homicidal thoughts about her were a part of the whole long-running thing. The flashes of his murderous thoughts when she paused too long getting ready to go out, when she was rude to slow or mistaken service personnel, when she threw out something perfectly fine in the trash, just because she was tired of it or was having some fit of tidiness; even more, when she wanted to talk about them, their 'relationship,' their love. She wondered why they were married and worse, she spoke this aloud, bombing the ease of the day, exploding his work, pitching him into a rage of choice over weapons (Ross chose the wire, the garrote, yes!). Didn't she know that millions thought this and could shut up about it? Why study it if you weren't going to *do* anything? She did not have the courage to walk out the door. *He* did, though, along with the near ability to exterminate her. She also called his work 'our work' and saw herself as the woman behind the man, etc., merely out of cherished dumb truism. But none of these things, and maybe not even melancholy, could be classified as the true unsafe moments.

Especially since his forties, some old scene he'd visited, made his compromises with, even dwelled with, appeared ineffably sad. Something beyond futility or hopelessness. It was an enormous more-than-melancholy that something had ever existed at all, that it kept taking the trouble to have day and eyesight on it. He felt that one of them—he or it—must act to destroy. He would look at an aged quarter—piece of change—and think this. Or he would look at an oft-seen woman the same way. One of them, he reasoned, should perish. He didn't know whether this was only mortality, the sheer weariness of repetition working him down, calling to him, or whether it was insanity. The quarter would do nothing but keep making its rounds as it had since it was minted, it would not change, would always be just the quarter. The woman, after the billions of women before her, still prevailed on the eyesight, still clutched her space, still sought relief from her pain, still stuffed her hunger. He himself woke up each morning as if required. The quarter flatly demands use. The woman shakes out her neurons and puts her feet on the floor. His clients insisted their stories be told. He was never out of work. Yet he would stare at them in the unsafe moments and want the two of them to hurl together and wrestle and explode. His very work. Maybe that was why he'd queered that last bio. The unsafe moments were winning.

Ross's Buick Riviera, black with spoked wheel covers, was much like the transport of a cinematic contract killer; or of a pimp; or of a black slumlord. There was something mean, heartless and smug in the car. In it he could feel what he was, his life. Writing up someone else's life was rather like killing them; rather like selling them; rather like renting something exorbitant to them. It was a car of secrets, a car of nearly garish bad taste (white leather upholstery), a car of penetrating swank; a car owned by somebody who might have struck somebody else once or twice in a bar or at a country club. It was such a car in which a man who would dye his gray hair might sit, though Ross didn't do this.

He kept himself going with quinine and Kool cigarettes. All his life he had been sleepy. There was nothing natural about barely anything he did or had ever done. At home with his wife he was restless. In his writing room on the pier he was angry and impatient as often as he was lulled by the brown tide. Sleeping, he dreamed nightmares constantly. He would awaken, relieved greatly, but within minutes he was despising the fact that his eyes were open and the day was proceeding. It was necessary to give himself several knocks for consciousness. His natural mood was refractory. He'd not had many other women, mainly for this reason and for the reason that an affair made him feel morbidly common, even when the woman displayed attraction much past that of his wife, who was in her late forties and going to crepey skin, bless her.

It could be that his profession was more dangerous than he'd thought. Now he could arrange his notes and tapes and, well, *dispense* with somebody's entire lifetime in a matter of two months' real work. His mind outlined them, they were his, and he wrote them out with hardly any trouble at all. The dangerous fact, one of them, was that the books were more interesting than they were. There was always a great lie in supposing any life was significant at all, really. And one anointed that lie with a further arrangement into prevarication—that the life had a form and a point. E. Dan Ross feared that knowing so many biographies, *originating* them, had doomed his capacity to love. All he had left was comprehension. He might have become that sad monster of the eighties.

Certainly he had feelings, he was no cold fish. But many prolific authors he'd met were, undeniably. They were not great humanists, neither were they caretakers of the soul. Some were simply addicted to writing, victims of inner logorrhea. A logorrheic was a painful thing to watch: they simply could not stop observing, never seeing much, really. They had no lives at all. In a special way they were rude and dumb, and misused life awfully. This was pointed out by a friend who played golf with him and a famous, almost indecently prolific, author. The author was no good at golf, confident but awkward, and bent down in a retarded way at the ball. His friend had told Ross when the author was away from them: 'He's not even here, the bastard. Really, he has no imagination and no intelligence much. This golf game, or something about this afternoon, I'll give you five to one it appears straightaway in one of his stories or books.' His friend was right. They both saw it published: a certain old man who played in kilts, detailed by the author. That old man in kilts was the only thing he'd gotten from the game. Then the case of the tiny emaciated female writer, with always a queer smell on her—mopwater, runaway mildew?— who did everything out of the house quickly, nipping at 'reality' like a bird on a window ledge. She'd see an auto race or a boxing match and flee instantly back to her quarters to write it up. She was in a condition of essential echolalia was all, goofy and inept in public. Thinking these things, E. Dan Ross felt uncharitable, but feared he'd lost his love for humanity, and might be bound on becoming a zombie or twit. Something about wrapping up a life like a dead fish in newspaper; something about lives as mere lengthened death certificates, hung on cold toes at the morgue; like tossing in the first shovelful of soil on a casket, knocking on the last period. 'Full stop,' said the British. Exactly.

Ross also frightened himself in the matter of his maturity. Perhaps he didn't believe in maturity. When did it ever happen? When would he, a nondrinker, ever get fully sober? Were others greatly soberer and more 'grown' than he? He kept an air rifle in his car, very secretly, hardly ever using it. But here and then he could not help himself. He would find himself in a delicious advantage, usually in city traffic, at night, and shoot some innocent person in the leg or buttocks; once, a policeman in the head. Everett Dan Ross was fifty-two years old and he knew sixty would make no difference. He would still love this and have to do it. The idea of striking someone innocent, with impunity, unprovoked, was the delicious thing—the compelling drug. He adored looking straight ahead through the windshield while in his periphery a person howled, baffled and outraged, feet away from him on the sidewalk or in an intersection, coming smugly out of a bank just seconds earlier, looking all tidy and made as people do after arranging money. His air rifle—a Daisy of the old school with a wooden stock and a leather thong off its breech ring—would already be put away, snapped into a secret compartment he had made in the car door which even his wife knew nothing about. Everett Dan Ross knew that he was likely headed for jail or criminal embarrassment, but he could not help it. Every new town beckoned him and he was lifted even higher than by the quinine in preparation. It was ecstasy. He was helpless. The further curious thing was that there was no hate in this, either, and no specific spite. The anonymity of the act threw him into a pleasure field, bigger than that of sexual completion, as if his brain itself were pinched to climax. There would follow, inevitably, shame and horror. Why was he not—he questioned himself—setting up the vain clients of his biographies, his fake autobiographies, some of whom he truly detested? Instead of these innocents? They could be saints, it did not matter. He *had* to witness, and exactly in that aloof peripheral way, the indignity of nameless pedestrians. He favored no creed, no generation, no style, no race. But he would not shoot an animal, never. That act seemed intolerably cruel to him.

Assuredly his books raised the image of those he wrote about. Ross had developed the talent long ago of composing significance into any life. He had done gangsters, missionaries, musicians, politicians, philanthropists, athletes, even other old writers. He could put an aura on a beggar. Then with the air rifle, he would shoot complete innocents to see them dwindle. He would swear off for months but then he would come back to it.

It had happened often that Ross was more interesting than his subjects. He was certainly not as vain. Writing his own autobiography would not have occurred to him. But there was a vain and vulgar motive in everybody he depicted: *look at me*, basically. The ones who insisted on prefaces disclaiming this howling fact made him especially contemptuous. It was not hilarious anymore, this 'many friends have beseeched me to put down in writing,' etc. Blab, blook, blep. It was astounding to Ross to find not one of his biographees conscious of this dusty ritual in their own case. *Their* lives were exempt from the usual flagrant exhibitions of the others. His last chore on a porcine Ohio hack writer—the suer, as Ross called him—a sentimental old fraud who'd authored one decent book a century ago when he was alive, then rode like a barnacle the esteem of the famous who suffered him the rest of his life, dropping names like frantic anchors in a storm of hackism and banality. Ross had to pretend blithe unconsciousness to the fact that the man 'was ready for his story to be told,' and had sent friends to Ross to 'entice you to sit down with shy, modest X.' Ross also had to watch the man get drunk about seventy times and blubber about his 'deep personal losses,' his 'time-stolen buddies.' The depth of his friendship with them increased in proportion to their wealth and fame. Ross kept a bland face while the obvious brayed like a jackass in the room. The amazing fact was that the man had lived his entire life out of the vocabulary and sensibility of his one decent book. There seemed to be no other words for existence since 1968, no epithets for reality outside the ones he'd bandaged on it twenty years ago. He'd written his own bible. Most of all he adored himself as a boy, and wept often now about his weeping then. Ross gutted through, and one night, as it always did, the hook fell out to him gleaming—the point of the biography: history as a changeless drunken hulk, endlessly redundant; God himself as a grinding hack. The sainthood of no surprises. The Dead Sea. This truth he sedulously ignored, of course—or thought he had—and whipped out a tome of mild hagiography. This was his fifteenth book and sold better than the others, perhaps because it celebrated the failure of promise and made the universal good old boys and girls very comfortable. The hack was a Beam-soaked country song.

The fact that Ross himself was a sort of scheduled hack did not alarm him. There weren't many hacks of his kind, and that pleased him. He dared the world to give him a life he could not make significant on paper and earn some money with. So didn't this indicate the dull surprise that nobody was significant? Or was it the great Christian

view—every man a king? Ross had no idea, and no intention of following up on the truth. Years ago he had found that truth and the
whole matter of the examined life were overrated, highly. There were
preposterous differences in values among the lives he had thrown himself into. Even in sensual pleasure, there was wide variance. He himself
thought there was no food served anywhere worth more than ten dollars. No woman on earth was worth more than fifty, if you meant bed
per night. Others thought differently, obviously. The young diva who
put pebbles in her butt and clutched them with her sphincter (she
insisted he include this)—well, it was simply something. It made bor-
derline depraved people feel better when they read it. Also, when
would the discussion about love ever quit? He could be deeply in love
with most of the women in every fashion magazine he'd ever flipped
through. The women would have to talk themselves *out* of his love,
stumble or pick their noses. Usually he did not love Nabby, his wife,
but given an hour and a fresh situation he could talk himself into adoring her.

What he loved was his son.

What was love but lack of judgment?

So if God judged, he was not love, eh?

This sort of stuff was the curse of the thinking class. You went away
to college and came back with such as that to nag your sleep till you
dropped.

Best to shut up and live.

Best to shoot anonymous innocent citizens with an air rifle and shut
up about it. The delicious thing was that the stricken howled and bore
the indignity as best they could, never to have an answer. He saw them
questing through the decades for the source of that moment. He saw
them dying with the mystery of it. Through the years the stricken had
looked up at the top of buildings, sideways to the alleys, and directly
at passersby. Once he had looked directly at a policeman, beebeed,
rubbing his head and saying something. Twice people had looked
deeply at Ross and his car—another year, another Riviera—but Ross
was feigning, of course, sincere drivership. What a rush, joy nearly
pouring from his eyes!

In Newt's neighborhood his car was blocked briefly by some

children playing touch football on the broken pavement. They came around and admired his car and the two-seater boat towed behind as he pulled in between dusty motorcycles in front of a dark green cottage, his son's. Already he wanted away from it, on some calm pond with the singing electric motor easing the two of them into cool lily-padded coves, a curtain of cattails behind their manly conversation. They had not fished together in ages. Newt used to adore this beyond all things. Ross had prepared his cynicism, but he had prepared his love even more. The roving happy intelligence on the face of little Newt, age eleven, shot with beauty from a dying Southern sun as he lifted the great orange and blue shellcracker out of the green with his bowed cane pole—there was your boy, a poet already. He'd said he had a new friend, this fish, and not a stupid meal. He'd stroked it, then released it. You didn't see that much in the bloody Southern young, respect for a mere damned fish. He'd known barbers to mount one that size, chew and spit over it for decades.

They seemed to have matched Ross's care in his presents with (planned?) carelessness about his arrival. This sort of thing had happened many times to Ross in the homes of celebrities, even in the midst of his projects with them. Somebody would let him in without even false hospitality: 'Ah, here is the pest with his notes again,' they might as well have said, surprised he was at the front door instead of the back, where the fellow with their goddamn mountain water delivered.

The girl indicated somebody sitting there in overalls who was not Newt, a big oaf named Bim, he thought she said. Yes, there always had to be some worthless slug dear to them all for God knew what reasons hanging about murdering time. Bim wore shower shoes. He did not get up or extend a hand. Ross badly wanted his cynicism not to rise again, and made small talk. The man had a stud in his nose. He dressed like this because the school *was* a cow college, Ross guessed. It was hip to enforce this, not deny it, as with Ivy League wear, etc.

'So where do you hail from, Bim?'

'Earth,' said the man.

Drive that motherfucking stud through the rest of your nose, coolster, thought Ross. Ross looked straight at Bim with such bleak amazed hatred that the man rose and left the house as if driven by pain.

Ross stood six feet high and still had his muscles, though he sometimes forgot. There wasn't much nonsense in him, and those who liked him loved this. The others didn't. He might seem capable of patient chilly murder.

'I don't know what you did, but thanks,' said Ivy Pilgrim. 'He's in Newt's band and thinks he has a title to that chair. Can't bear him.'

'Bimmer has a fine sensitivity. Hello, Dad.' Newt had entered from the back. There were only four rooms. 'Where'd Bimmer go?'

Newt did not have a ponytail. He had cut off almost all his hair and was red in the face around his beard. He wore gold-rim glasses set back into his black whiskers, and his dark eyes glinted as always. His head looked white and abused, as just shoved into jail. The boy had looked a great deal like D.H. Lawrence since puberty. Here was the young Lawrence convicted and scraped by Philistines. But he didn't seem drunk. That was good.

'I don't believe Bimmer liked me,' said Ross.

'He moves with the wind,' sighed his son.

'Mainly he sits in the chair,' said Ivy Pilgrim.

Ross looked her over. She was better than the photograph, an elfin beauty from this profile. And she wasn't afraid of Newt.

'You have the most beautiful hair I've seen on a man about forever. That salt and pepper gets me every time,' she said to Ross.

'Thank you, Ivy.' Watch it, old man, Ross thought. Other profile suggests a kitten, woo you silly.

'What instrument does Bimmer play?' he asked.

'Civil Defense siren, bongos, sticks,' said Newt seriously.

'So you're in earnest about this band?'

'I've never been more serious about anything in my life.' Since Newt was twenty, Ross was wary of asking him any questions at all. He'd get the wild black glare of bothered pain.

Who could tell what this meant? Though with his bald head it seemed goony and desperate.

Ross was parched from the road. He sat in Bimmer's chair, big and tweedy. The place was not so bad and was fairly clean. There were absolutely no books around. He wondered if there were a drink around. He'd planned to share some iced beer with Newt, by way of coaching him toward moderation, recovering what a man could be—healthy in a beer advertisement. He was throwing himself into the breech, having lost the taste for the stuff years ago.

'I'm either going to sing or go into the marines,' said Newt. Was he able to sit still? He was verging in and out of his chair. *Acasthia*, inability to sit, Ross recalled from somewhere. It was a startling thing when one's own went ahead and accumulated neuroses quite without your help. Ross looked at the girl, who'd come in with a welcome ginger ale, Dr Brown's.

'Newt remembered you liked this,' she said.

This was an act that endeared both of them to him. At last, a touch of kindness from the boy, though announced by his wife.

'Well, I need a splash with mine,' said Newt. He went to the kitchen and out came the Rebel Yell, a handsome jug of bourbon nearly full. However, this was histrionic, Ross was sure. Newt did not look like he needed the drink. He had affected the attitude that a man of his crisis could not acknowledge ginger ale alone. Ross, having thought more than usual on the way up to Auburn and presiding too much as father to this moment, sincerely wanted to relax and say to hell with it. He wasn't letting anybody live. The marines, singing? So what? Give some ease. He himself had been a marine, sort of.

Where was it written in stone, this generational dispute? Are fathers always supposed to wander around bemused and dense about their young? Wasn't it true old Ross himself had nailed the young diva, weeping runt, with her heavy musical titties bobbling, right in the back door? While Nabby, loyal at home—source of Newt right in front of him—was shaking her mirror so a younger face would spill out on it? Not very swell, really, and his guilt did not assuage this banal treachery. Old, old Ross, up the heinie of America's busty prodigy. Awful, might as well be some tottering thing with a white belt and toupee, pot, swinging around Hilton Head. What a fiend for one of Newt's poems, but really beneath the high contempt of them.

'So how's the poetry-making, anyway, sport?'

Newt was tragic and blasé at once, if possible, gulping down the bourbon and ginger.

'Nothing. It's the light. Light's not right.'

'But you're not a painter, Newton. What light?'

'He means in his *brain*,' explained Ivy.

'My love for Ivy has killed the light.'

Newt had to give himself his own review, this seriously? Good gad. Save some for the epitaph.

'I like it that way,' Newt added hurriedly, but just as direly.

Ivy seemed upset and guilty, yearning toward Ross for help. 'I didn't want to be any sort of killer.'

He liked this girl. She had almost not to say another thing in her favor. *She* had the pigtail, pleasant down the nice scoop of her back.

'Well, can't we open the shroud a little here, Newton? Look outside and see if you can see a little hope. Maybe some future memories, son.'

Newt shuffled to the door and looked at the car and boat a whole minute, too long. Ivy got Ross another Dr Brown's. The last thing Ross might say in a hospital room someday in the future, nurse turning out of the room: 'Nice legs.' Good for little Ivy. Would it never stop? Ross had long suspected, maybe stupidly but as good as any genius, through life and his biographies, that women with good legs were happy and sane. Leg man as philosopher. Well, Nabby's seemed to persuade mostly joy out of the day, didn't they? Even given the sullen, jagged life he sometimes showed her. Get out of my skin and look, he thought: Was I ever as, oh, *difficult* as Newt myself? Probably, right after he'd fired himself from the war, though he hid it in Chase's house in San Pedro.

'So what do you see, Newt?'

'No wonder Bimmer left,' said Newt.

'Now, can you explain that?'

'Bimmer's father is a man of . . . merchandise.'

Hold off, *hang fire*, with Henry James. Ross cut himself off. With a new enormous filtered Kool lit—stay with these, and you've got at most twenty-five years, likely; we don't have a clumsy century of discord to work it out, Newt, for heaven's sake—he thought, Don't give me that *merchandise* crapola, young man. I bred you in Nabby. You know very well my beach house and all of it could burn up and not impress me a great deal, never did. Let's take off the gloves, then. *I* came here.

'Is that why your man Bimmer dresses like a laid-off ploughboy? Missing the fields and horse shit over to the back forty?'

Newt smiled. Maybe this was the real turf, here we were. The smile was nice, at last, but why did he have to destroy his head? His son's hair was black and beautiful like his used to be.

'So let me declare myself and your mother finally. The quick wedding, there wasn't any time for presents much.'

Ivy went with him to the Riviera. She saw the CD player inside and gave a gasp of pleasure. It was the piece of luggage full of CDs she wound up with.

'This wonderful suitcase. I'll bet you want us to get out of this dump p.d.q?'

Ross felt very mean for his previous plans for the bag.

'Where are *you* from, Ivy?'

'Grand Bay, close to Bayou La Battre. Right across the bay from you. The poor side, I guess. But I loved it. And I'm not broke.'

'Fine. Very 'fine.' Unnecessary, but necessary, on the other hand. She'd won him.

'So there we are. Boat, motor, the player. And *voilà*! (Ross opened the bag, nearly a trunk). Some late wedding music.'

'Must be fifty discs there!' cheered Ivy.

'Thought you and I might break in the boat and pursue the finny tribe this afternoon,' said Ross, brightly.

Christmas in May, he was feeling, was really an excellent idea. Look down, son.

Newt barely glanced into the suitcase.

'Fishing? That's pretty off the point, Dad.'

'Oh, Newton!' Ivy jumped right on him.

'What's . . .' Don't, Ross. He was going to ask what *was* the point, you bald little bastard?

'I've promised the kids I'd play some touch with them. Just about to go out there. Then there's the band tonight. You can come with Ivy if you want.'

'Newt takes the band very seriously,' said Ivy. This seemed to be a helpful truth for both the men. Ross forgot Newt's rudeness. Or did he *know*? What part of loony Berryman or Lowell had he researched?

Newt glanced at Ivy dangerously. This brought Ross's nightmares right up, howling. This was the feared thing. His son seemed to want to beat on this strange idiot who'd just opened her mouth.

Ross couldn't bear it. He went out with a fresh Kool and the remains of the ginger ale and stood in the yard near his sleek Buick, gazing through some cypresses to a man-provoked swamp behind the hideous cinder blocks of an enormous grocery, some kind of weeds native only to the rear of mall buildings, ripping up through overflowed mortar on the ground.

Here he was back in 'life,' shit, man with twenty-five years to go, wearing a many-pocketed safari shirt next to a pimp's car. What did an old American man *wear* rightly, anyway? Fifty-two *was* old. Cut the hopeful magazine protests. You spent half your time just trying not to look like a fool. What intense *shopping*. Hell, shouldn't he have on a blazer, get real in a gray Volvo? Disconnection and funk, out here with his killer Kool, pouting like a wallflower; son inside wrecking the afternoon with bald intensity. Back to his nightmares, the latest most especially: Ross, as an adult, was attending classes in elementary school, somehow repeating, but bardlike, vastly appreciated at the school by one and all for some reason, king of the hill, strolling with the children, glib, but why? The school was paying him a salary while he was doing what? But at the school gate he was in a convertible with two girls, and two men—one of them Newt—jumped in the car and rammed long metal tongs through the skulls of the girls. Their screams were horrible, the blood and bone were all over Ross. Then policemen appeared and drove metal tongs through the skulls of Newt and the other man. The screams of Newt were unbearable, loud! He'd awakened, panting. Ross almost wept, looking at the back of that grocery now. But it was a dry rehearsal, with only a frown and closed eyes.

Ivy touched him on the arm. 'Sometimes you've just got to ignore him. I'll go fishing with you. Please, I'd love to. And I love everything you brought. Thank your wife, Nabby, for me.'

Marriage was a good cause, thought Ross. On a given day chances were one of you might be human. Was D.H. Lawrence a rude bastard, even into his thirties?

He saw the kids gather and Newt go out as the giant weird quarterback. The day was marked for gloom but he was going to have something good out of it. He did not want to watch his son play football. But thanks, Lord, for providing him with the dread image: Newt had once embarrassed him playing football with young kids.

He was home from graduate school—Greensboro—at Christmas. He was invited over to an old classmate's house in Daphne. Ross came later to have a toddy with the boy's father. It was another big modest beach house with a screened porch all the way across the back. They took their hot rums out to the old wooden lounges and watched Newt and his friend quarterback a touch game with his friend's nephews and nieces, ages five to twelve. Ross was pleased his boy cared about sports at all. It was a stirring late December day, cool and perfect for neighborhood touch, under the Spanish moss and between the hedges. But then Ross saw his contemporary staring harder out there and when Ross noticed, things were not nice. Newt was hogging the play and playing too rough, much too rough. He smashed the girl granddaughter of this man into the hedge. She didn't cry, but she hung out of the game, rubbing her arms. Then Newt fired a pass into the stomach of a boy child that blew him down into the oyster shell driveway. The kid was cut up but returned. Newt's friend implored him and the children were talking about him, but he remained odd, yes, and driven. Ross was looking at something he deeply despised seeing. He did not want to think about the other examples. They called the game. The children came up on the porch hurt and amazed, but gamely saying nothing around Ross. They were tough, good children, no whiners. In the car home, he said to Newt, 'Son, you were a mite fierce out there. Just kids, *kids*.' Newt waited a while and came back, too gravely: 'You want me to smile all day like a waitress?'

This *fierceness*, off the point, that was it.

So they drove around and Ivy, who did not change from her short skirt and flowered blouse to go fishing, directed him through town to pick up Newt's bounced checks—this tavern, that grocery, the phone company. Ross didn't mind. He'd expected financial distress and had brought some money. With some irony of kinship he'd brought up a fairly big check from Louisiana State University Press to sign over to Newt. This concern had published Newt's books. Ross had just picked up a nice bit of change from a piece of his they were anthologizing. Christ, though, the kid might make something out of it. But not a kid. He was thirty. Newt's sister Ann was twenty-eight, married in Orlando, straight and clean as a javelin, thanks. Ivy Pilgrim (her real name) wanted to know all about Ann and Nabby. Then they did go fishing.

Auburn had some lovely shaded holes for fishing in the country. Erase the school, and it was a sweet dream of nature. Ross, a Tuscaloosa man, could never quite eliminate his prejudice that Auburn U should have really never occurred, especially now that it had fired his boy. There had been some cancerous accident among the livestock and chicken droppings years ago, and, well, football arose and paid the buildings to stay there and spread. These farmboys, still confused, had five different animal mascots, trying to get the whole barnyard zoo in. Ivy was amused by these old jokes, bless her, though he really didn't mean them. She was in architecture, hanging tough. How could Newt have attracted *her*? he thought, instantly remorseful.

She thought Newt would return to his poems soon. Improbably, she *understood* his books and wanted him to move on to—pray for rain!—some *gladness*, bless him. The poetry had won her over, but as a way of life it sucked wind.

'Newt is proud of you and he wants to be glad,' she said.

'Honestly?'

'Honestly.'

Once he had been to an inspirational seminar with one of his clients. The speaker was a man who had been through unbearable, unlucky, unavoidable horror. He told the crowd he intended never ever to have another bad day. He just wouldn't. He was going to force every day to be a good day. Ross was heeding the man now. He was glad he'd remembered. He concentrated on Ivy, who was a good fisherman. She had sporting grace. They caught several blue-gills and one large bass. There was never any question but that she'd clean them and put them in the freezer, since Ross was buying her supper.

'I suppose, though, Newt is casting around for other work?'

'It's the band, the band, the band. He writes for it, he sings. He says everything he's ever wanted to say is in the band.'

Ross had noted the late gloomy competency in American music, ever a listener in his Riviera. Electricity had opened the doors to every uncharming hobbyist in every wretched burg, even in Ohio. You could not find a dusthole without its guitar man, big eyes on the Big Time beyond the flyspecked window, drooling, intent on being wild, wild, wild. America, unable to leave its guitar alone, teenager with his dick: 'Look here, I've got one too.' He saw Newt, late-coming thirty, in the tuning hordes, and it depressed him mightily. As witness the millions of drips in 'computers' now. Yeah, toothless grizzled layabout in the Mildewville Café: 'Yep, my boy used to cornhole bus exhausts, he's now in computers.' Look down at a modern hotel lobby, three quarters of them were in 'computers,' asking the desk clerk if the sun was shining. His daughter's husband, a gruesome Mormon yuppie, was 'in computers.' Then Ross's ears harked to the Riviera speakers—something new, acoustic, a pro-tolesbian with a message. Give people a chance, Ross corrected himself: you were a G-22, Intelligence, with the marines in the worst war ever, by *choice*, dim bulb in forehead. Whole squad smoked by mortars because of you, put them on the wrong beach. A gloomy competency would have been refreshing, ask their mothers. I could have stayed home and just been shitty, like the singer Donovan, hurting only music.

Back at home, she showered while Ross set up the CD player with its amazing resonant speaker boxes. What a sound they had here with Miles Davis. She heard it while the water ran. Ross was excited too. In his fresh shirt, blazer, trousers and wingtips, he emerged from his own shower, opened the mirror door of the medicine chest to check Newton's drugs, and caught Ivy Pilgrim sitting naked on her bed, arms around her breasts, sadly abject and staring at the floor. Ross looked on, lengthening the accident. This is my daughter, my daughter, he thought, proud of her. The brave little thing.

There was a great misery she was not sharing with him. Doomed or blessed—he couldn't know—he froze at the mirror until she looked over at him in the reflection and saw him in his own grief. Ross felt through the centuries for all chipper wives having to meet their in-laws. Holy damn, the strain. She was such a little lady, revealed. He smiled at her and she seemed to catch his gratitude instantly. Oops, slam the mirror. Nice there was nothing ugly here. I won't have a bad day, I won't. This was the best of it, and later he thanked the highway rushing in front of him for it.

The place was a converted warehouse rank with college vomit, beer in Astroturf, a disinfectant thrown contemptuously over it. The spirit of everywhere: spend your money, thanks, fuck you. Chicken-yard hippies, already stunned by beer, living for somebody right out of suburban nullity like them, 'twisted' on his guitar stroking: 'He don't *give* a damn.' Couple of them so skinny they looked bent over by the weight of their cocks. Ivy had quit beaming. Since the mirror there had been a honest despair between them.

Newt and his truly miserable band came on, tuning forever as the talentless grim do. Ross was sorry he was so experienced, old. He could look at the face and bald pate of the drummer, comprehending instantly his dope years and public sorriness, pushed on till damned near forty, no better on drums than any medical doctor on a given Sunday afternoon with the guys. Then came Bimmer, a snob in overalls, fooling with his microphone like some goon on an airport P.A. system. Then a short bassman so ugly he *had* to go public. The sax man could play, but he was like some required afterthought in a dismal riot of geeks. Then there was a skinny man near seven feet tall who just danced, male go-go. What an appalling idea. Then Newt, not contented with the damage he'd done on backup guitar, began singing. He was drunk and fierce, of course. The point seemed to be anger that music was ever invented. It was one of the ugliest episodes Ross had ever witnessed. He smiled weakly at poor Ivy, who was not even tapping her foot. She looked injured.

At the stage, Ross saw the chicken-yard hippies and a couple of their gruesome painted hags, hateful deaf little twats who might have once made the long trip to Birmingham. They loved Newt and egged him on. This was true revolt. Ross wondered why the band had bothered to tune.

He had had dreadful insights too, too often nowadays, waking up in a faraway hotel with his work sitting there, waiting for him to limn another life. The whole race was numb and bad, walking on thin skin over a cesspool. Democracy and Christianity were all wrong: nobody much was worth a shit. And almost everybody was going to the doctor.

'Professional help' for Newt flashed across his mind, but he kicked it away, seeing another long line, hordes, at the mental health clinic, bright-eyed group addicts who couldn't find better work waiting inside. Ross had known a few. One, a pudgy solipsist from Memphis, had no other point to his life except the fact he had quit cigarettes. A worthless loquacious busybody, he'd never had a day of honest labor in his life. What did he do? He 'house-sat' for people. But the fellow could talk about 'life' all day.

Then things really got mean.

Newt, between sets, red-eyed, hoarse, angrily drunk, drew up a chair ten feet away from Ivy and his father, muttering something and bearing on them like some poleaxed diagnostician. Ross at last made out that Newt was disgusted by his blazer, his shoes, his 'rehearsal to be above this place.'

'This place is the whole world, sad Ross-daddy. You won't even open your eyes. There's nowhere else to go but here! No gas, no wheels, no—' He almost vomited. Then he walked his chair over to them, still in it, heaving like a cripple. He was right in their faces, sweat all over him.

'Good-looking pair, you two. Did you get an old touch of her, Pops?' He reached around and placed his hand over Ivy's right breast. 'But I tell you. Might as well not try. You can't make Ivy *come*, no sir. She ain't gon come for you. Might as well be humping a rock, Rosser!'

Crazy, mean, unfinished, he laid his head on the table between them. The sweat coming out of his prickly head made Ross almost gag. Then he rose up. His eyes were black, mad. He couldn't evict the words, seemed to be almost choking.

Ross handed over the endorsed check and stood to leave.

'What are you going to do for work, son?'

'S'all that bitch outside says. Job, job, job.'

'Well, bounced checks, bounced checks, bounced checks is not your sweetest path either.' He hated Newt. An image of Newt, literally booted out the window by an Auburn official, rose up and pleased him.

'Shut up, you old fuck,' said Newt. 'Get home to Mama. And remember, remember . . .'

'What? Be decent, goddammit.'

'Let the big dog eat. Always fill up with supreme.'

Ross looked with pity at Ivy. Given the tragedy, he could not even offer to drive her home.

Outside the turn at the Old Spanish Fort, Ross knew he would lie to Nabby. All was well in Auburn. Save Nabby, God, he asked. She was a fine golfer, in trim, but all those days in the sun had suddenly assaulted her. Almost overnight, she was wrinkled and the skin of her underchin had folds. The mirror scared her and made her very sad. Ross, for all his deskwork and Kools, and without significant exercise, was a man near commercially handsome, though not vain. There was something wrong with the picture of a pretty fifty-two-year-old fellow in a Riviera, anyway. In the mirror, he often saw the jerk who'd got eleven young men mortared over there—a surviving untouched dandy. A quality in all of Ross apologized and begged people to look else-where.

Newt, by the way, had married somebody much like his mother. Small, bosomy, with slender legs agreeable in the calf. Probably he wouldn't kill Ivy. Ross would make a good day of this one, be damned. It was only midnight. Nabby was up.

He caressed her, desperate and pitiful, wishing long sorrowful love into her. She cried out, delighted. As if, Ross thought, he were putting a whole new son in Nabby and she was making him now, with deep pleasure.

Newt had left some books in the house a while back. Ross wanted to see what made his son. He picked up the thing by Kundera with the unburdening thesis that life is an experiment only run once. We got no second run, unlike experience of every other regard. Everything mistaken and foul is forever there and that is you, the mouse cannot start the maze again; once, even missing the bull's-eye by miles, is all you got. It is unique and hugely unfair. No wonder the look you see on most people—wary, deflected, puzzled—'What the hell is happening?' Guy at a restaurant, gets out of his car and creeps in as on the surface of the moon. Ross liked this and stopped reading. There would be no Newt ever again, and whatever he'd left out, fathering the boy, it was just botched forever, having had the single run. Forgiven, too, like a lab assistant first day on the job. And then Ann, not a waver, twice as content as Ross was, almost alarmingly happy. She was the one run too. He could call Ann this instant and experience such mutual love it almost made him choke. There was the greedy Mormon, her husband, but so what? You didn't pick her bed-mate out of a catalogue.

The old hack suing E. Dan Ross backed off, unable to face the prospect of any further revelations on himself the trial might bring. He called up Ross himself, moaning. He was a wreck, but a man of honor too, a First Amendment champion after all. Ross, who'd never even hired a lawyer, felt sorry for what the erupting truth had brought to both of them. He feared for his future credit with clients. But the hack was invited on television, in view of his new explosion of hackery, a photo album valentine to every celebrity he'd let a fart off near. He became a wealthy man, able to buy a chauffeur who took him far and wide, smelling up the privacy of others.

For months they did not hear from Newt, only two cards from Ivy thanking them for boat, motor, luggage and Newt. This sounded good. Around Christmas they got a letter from Newt. He was in the state asylum in Tuscaloosa, drying out and 'regaining health and reason.' The marriage was all over. He was smashed with contrition. There'd been too many things he'd done to Ivy, unforgivable, though she'd wanted to hang in right till the last. What last nastiness he had done was, after her badgering, he'd written her a poem of such dev-astating spite there was no recovery. It was a 'sinful, horrible thing.' Now he still loved her. She'd been a jewel. He was a pig, but at least looking up and out now. He pleaded with them not to visit him. Later, out, when he was better. He still had health insurance from the school and needed nothing.

. . . And Dad, the boat and motor was wonderful. Bimmer stole it, though. He proved to be no real friend at all. I ran after him down the highway outside the city limits with a tire tool in my hand. They say I was raving, my true friends, and they brought me up here. True. I was raving. No more 'they said.' Please forgive me. I'm already much better.

Love, Newton

Nabby and he held hands for an hour. Nabby began praying aloud for Newt and then blamed the 'foreigners at Auburn and all that dreadful radioactivity from the Science Department.' Ross was incredulous. Nabby was going nuts in sympathy. Have a good day, Ross, have a good day. He walked out to the pier, into his writing room, and trembled. For no reason he cursed the Bay of Mobile, even the happy crabs out there. What could a man take?

Then, next week, another blow lowered him. Chase's wife called and told him Chase was dead. He'd taken a pistol over to Long Beach, threatened his ex-wife, and was killed in a shoot-out with the police. God have mercy. Chase was a policeman himself.

Ross recalled the street, the long steep hill down to Paseo del Mar from Chase's house, with thick adobe walls around it. Ross had needed the walls. He was badly messed up and stayed that way a month, having fired himself from the war, G-22, all that, after he misdirected the Seals to a hot beach and got them mortared. Chase met him in a bar and they stayed soaked for five weeks. Chase was a one-liner maniac. All of life had a filthy pun or stinger. Ross thought it was all for him and appreciated it. But when he got better and wouldn't drink anymore, Chase kept it up. Ross needn't have been there at all, really, he found out. Chase became angry when Ross quit laughing. Not only were the jokes not funny anymore, Ross knew he was witnessing a dire malady. Chase kept hitting the beer and telling Ross repeatedly about his ex-wife, whom he loved still even though married to Bernice, a quiet thin Englishwoman, almost not there at all but very strong for Chase, it seemed to Everett D. Ross, before he was E. Dan Ross. Ross heard of vague trouble with the woman in Long Beach and the law. But Chase was selfless and mainly responsible for

Ross's recovery, giving him all he needed and more. Chase had also
adopted a poor street kid, a friend of his daughter's. He was like that.
He would opt for stress and then holler in fits about it. When Ross
told him he was leaving, taking his rearranged name with him back to
Mobile where his wife waited, hoping for his well-being, Chase went
into a rage and attacked him for ingratitude, malingering, and—what
was it?—'betrayal.' Not of the Seals. Of Chase. It was never clear and
Chase apologized, back into the rapid-fire one-liners. Chase was very
strange, but Ross had not thought he was deranged. The shoot-out
sounded like, certainly, suicide, near the mother of his children. Too,
too much. A man Ross's age, calling happily to the ships at sea around
L.A. Harbor over his ham set. Raving puns and punchers.

The very next day he heard that a classmate of his, the class joker,
had shot himself dead in a bathtub in San Francisco. Wanted to make
no mess. Something about money and his father's turning his back on
him. Ross could not work. He stayed in his pier room rolling up paper
from his new biography—of an old sort of holy cowboy in San
Antonio. Talked to animals, birds, such as that. Four wives, twelve
children. The balls of paper lay in a string like popcorn on the meager
tide, going around the ocean to California where the dead friends
were. Ross thought of the men not only as dead but as dead fathers.
Children: smaller them, offspring of grown pranksters, gag addicts.
Ross thought of his air rifle. His classmate, last Ross had seen of him,
right before he went over to Vietnam, was in the National Guard. He
did something hazy for athletic teams around Chicago, where Ross last
saw him. It didn't take much time. His real life work was theft and
happy cynicism about others. Bridge could level anybody with mor-
dant wit. He'd kept Ross and others howling through their passionate
high school years. Once, on a lake beach in late April, a class party
where some of the girls were in their bathing suits sunning themselves,
first time out this spring, Bridge had passed a couple of lookers and
stopped, appreciative, right in front of them: 'Very, very nice. Up to
morgue white, those tans.' The boys howled, the girls frowned, mor-
tified. Given everything by his psychiatrist parents, Bridge still stole,
regularly. Ross heard he'd been kicked out of the university for stealing a football player's watch from a locker. Bridge was an equipment

man. He deeply relished equipment, and ran at the edge of athletic teams, the aristocracy in Southern schools. In Chicago, he'd taken Ross up to his attic. Here was a pretty scary thing: Bridge had stolen from his unit a Browning .30-caliber machine gun and live ammo and enough gear to dress a store dummy, stolen somewhere else; he had set the dummy behind the machine gun among a number of sandbags (the labor!) so that the machine gun aimed right at the arriving visitor. Ross jumped back when the light was turned on. Bridge, Bridge. Used to wear three pairs of socks to make his legs look bigger. Used Man Tan so he was brown in mid-winter. Children, money and booze. Maybe great unrepayable debt at the end.

Ross knew he was of the age to begin losing friends to death. But more profound was the fact that he was not the first to go. Fools, some thirty of them from his big high school in Mobile, had gone over to Asia and none of them was seriously scratched or demented on return. It was a merry and lusty school, mental health or illness practically unheard of. What was his month of breakdown? Nothing. What was he doing, balling up the hard work and watching it float off? Nothing.

His son in a nut ward, Nabby collapsing, he took down a straight large glass of tequila and peered strongly across the bay to where Ivy Pilgrim had grown up. Did she have to be all disappeared from Newt, forever? A smart young woman, very sexy, plenty tough, endowed, couldn't cure him. He missed her. Ross, frankly, was glad Newton didn't want him at the asylum. But he sat down and wrote him a long letter, encouraging his strengths. The tequila gave him some peace. He took another half glass. His friend, Andy the pelican, walked into the room and Ross began talking to him, wanting to know his adventures before he opened a can of tuna for him.

He confessed his grief and confusion to the pelican. The absurd creature, flying bag, talked back to him: Tell me. It's rough all over, pard. Lost my whole family in Hurrican Fred.' One thing about the sea, thought Ross, sneering toward it, it doesn't care. Almost beautiful in that act. Maybe we should all try it.

Next thing they heard, Newt was visiting his sister in Orlando. She and her husband lent their condo at New Smyrna Beach to him. He was sunning and 'refining his health' at pool and oceanside. He was working on poems and didn't know how he felt about them. Walker, Ann's husband, came by frequently and chatted. He liked Walker a lot. He wasn't going to impose on them forever. The world was 'over there' and he knew it. Ross and Nabby's music was helping, thanks. Especially Bach. Had they ever listened to the Tabernacle Choir? Glorious. Newt said that he wanted 'excruciatingly to walk in the Way.' Grats extreme too for the money. He was just beginning his life and would be reimbursing everybody soon. 'Truly, though, people, I like being poor and I am going to get used to it.'

Ross had written himself neutral. He rewrote what he had thrown to sea, it didn't matter, there it was all back and the life of the saintly cowboy wrote itself. He wrote twenty pages one night, nonstop, and recollected that he could not remember what he had said. When he read the pages, however, they were perfect. The words had gone along by themselves. Ross seemed not to have mattered at all. His mind, his heart, his belly were not engaged. Entailed was a long episode of murder, rape, and the burning alive of a prized horse. A short herd of people were killed, the cowboy wounded in the throat. It was some of Ross's best writing, but he had not particularly cared. Even hacks sometimes cared, he knew. This business was too alike to the computer goons he despised. Ross was bleak. He'd just gotten too damned good at his stuff. He was expendable. Nothing but the habitual circuitry was required.

Otherwise, it was a good year. Nabby did not say any more insane things. But she badly wanted a face-lift. Felt sure she was falling apart and would not show herself near sunlight. Back in her room the ointments overblew the air. She kept herself in goo and almost quit golf. They had had separate rooms since Newt went to the asylum. She felt ugly. Ross felt for her deeply. This emotion was a constant tender sorrow and that was what he had instead of the eruptions of love and homicidal urges. It was much better, this not too sad little flow. Their love life was much better, in truth. A sort of easy tidal cheer came over Ross, fifty-three. He was appreciating his years and the pleasant gravitation toward death. It had a sweet daze to it. He could look at his tomb and smile, white flag up in calm surrender.

Why not a face-lift, and why not love? Things were falling together even though he was a disattached man. He rushed to finish the book before the old cowboy died. Blink, there it was. The old man's children read it to him and he liked it very much. They told Ross his eyes, like a robin's eggs, brightened. He blessed the author. He had never thought his life made any sense. He had never meant to be famous or read about. He wished he could read. By far he was the most pleasant subject Ross had ever worked with.

Nabby, fresher at the neck though a little pinched at the eyes after her face-lift, wanted the children to visit over Thanksgiving and have a family portrait made. They'd not heard much from either of them lately. Newt was teaching night classes at a community college in Orlando. He had his own place.

But when Nabby called he could hear his daughter was not right. Something had happened. The upshot was Newt had converted to Mormonism, very zealously, and had simply walked out of town and his job and his apartment, without a word to anyone. Nobody knew where he was. He had destroyed all his poetry two months before. He left everything he owned.

Ross could see his wife, blank in her new face, holding the phone as if it were a wounded animal. She cradled it and stroked it. Ross had never seen an act like that. Ann's voice continued but her mother listened at the end, when Ross took the phone, as if death were speaking to her directly. Ann's husband, Walker, came on and detailed the same version.

'What do Mormons, new Mormons, do?' asked Ross.

'There's no place, like a Mecca, if that's what you mean,' said Walker.

'I mean how should they act?'

'It's inside, Ross. They affirm. They attend. They practice. They study. A great deal of study.'

'What *did*, damn it, Mormonism—or *you*—do to Newton?'

'He wasn't raving. It's not charismatic.'

'Would he be in some fucking airport selling flowers?'

Walker hung up. His reverent tongue was well known. All told, he was a Boy Scout with a hard-on for wealth; the boy so good he was out of order. He wouldn't even drink a Coke. Caffeine, you know.

When Ross lit a Kool, Walker looked at him with great pity. Ross hated him now, smug and square-jawed, wearing a crew cut. He saw him dripping with a mass of tentacles attached to him, dragging poor Newton into the creed, 'elders' spiriting him away. The cult around Howard Hughes, letting him dwindle into a freak while they waited on his money. Clean-cut international voodoo. Blacks and Indians were the tribes of Satan, weren't they? Ross always rooted against BYU when they played football on television. Sure. Hard-working, clean-limbed boys next door. Just one tiny thing or three: we swallow swords, eat snakes, and ride around on bicycles bothering people for two years. Nabby lay on her bed with her new face turned into the pillow. Ross petted her, but his anger drove him out to the pier again, where for a long time he searched the far shore for the image of his lost daughter-in-law, Ivy, naked and in grief, hugging her breasts.

So. The colleges wouldn't have him anymore. There goes that option. He had a great future behind him, did Newt.

'Destroyed his poems.' Right out of early Technicolor. Have mercy on us. What kind of new Newton did we have now? Fig Newton, Fucked Newton. He tried hard again not to detest his boy. He tried to picture him helpless. Mormons probably specialized in weak depressed poets. Promise him multiple wives, a new bicycle. But more accurately Ross detested Newton for the sane cheer of his letters. What a con man, cashing Ross's ardent checks. Venal politician. Ross could hit him in the face.

From Ann he had heard that Ivy was at home with her father, who was sick and might die. They'd cut a leg off him just lately. Ross wanted to take the form of Andy the pelican and fly over there to her.

This did not feel like his home right now. He did not like Nabby collapsing again, especially with her expensive new face. He reviewed his grudges against her. Five years ago, at the death of his father—an ancient man beloved by everyone except Nabby, who thought he was an awful chauvinist who loved to be adored too much: true—she had not shed a tear until later in the car when she told Ross some woman had alluded slyly to her sun wrinkles. She began cursing and crying for herself, his father barely in the ground. Ross almost drove the Riviera off the road. He said not a word all the way home from Florida.

Nabby, jealous of the dead man who'd upstaged her own dear plight; the funeral a mere formality while huge issues like sun wrinkles were being battled.

Feeling stranded, he'd driven over to Bayou La Battre four days later. He didn't call ahead. The Pilgrims lived just off Route 90 in a little town called Grand Bay. A healthy piece of change from the old cowboy's book had just arrived. He was anxious to spend money on something worthwhile. How impoverished were the Pilgrims? The mother had been a surprise. He'd not told Nabby about it, for the first time in his life with her.

Their home was neat. On the front were new cypress boards, unpainted. The house was large and the yard was almost grassless, car ruts to one side, where he parked behind a jeep with an Auburn sticker on the rear window. Over here you got a sense of poor Catholics, almost a third world, some of them Cajun and Slavic and Creole. He'd always loved this country. Most of your good food came from these people; your music, your bonhomie, your sparkling black-eyed nymphs. Upland, the Protestants had no culture. If anything, they were a restraint on all culture, especially as it touched on joy. He thought of Newton, now even odder than they were, beyond them, in a culture of how much crap can you swallow, unblinking, and remain upright. Close by was the great shipyard at Pascagoula, where Ivy's father had worked. You threw a crab net in the water and thought of submarines the length of football fields close under you, moving out with fearsome nukes abroad. Almost a staggering anomaly, these things launched out of the mumbling-dumb state of Mississippi.

Ivy and one of her brothers, also a painter at Ingalls, met him at the door. They were very gracious, though mournful. It didn't look like their father was going to make it. An hour from now they would go back to the hospital in Mobile. Surprising himself, Ross asked if he might go with them, drive them. They thought this was curious, but would welcome a ride in his Riviera, which the brother thought was the 'sporting end.' He had a coastal brogue. Ivy had got rid of hers. Maybe it would not go with a career in architecture. Ivy looked radiant in sorrow. When he mentioned Newt, the brother left for the back of the house, where it smelled like Zataran's spices and coffee.

'I've heard a few things, none of them very happy. I'm afraid I don't love him anymore, if you wanted to know that,' she said.

The finality hurt Ross, but he'd expected it. He did not love the boy much either.

'He was in the shipyards "witnessing." My brothers saw him. Some security guys took him out of the yard. He had a bicycle. He told my brother he was going to places around large bodies of water.'

'Did he have "literature"?'

'The Book of Mormon? No, he didn't. You'd know that Newt would be his own kind of Mormon or anything. He'd stretch it.'

Ross recalled his hideous singing.

'Did you ever think of Newt's age?' she asked him.

Ross went into a terrible cigarette cough and near-retching, reddening his face. Father of Newt, he felt very ugly in front of her; a perpetrator.

'His age. Thirty-one. Jesus Christ was crucified at age thirty-three. A Mormon is a missionary, all the males, for two years.' Ivy revealed this much in the manner of a weary scientist. The evidence was in: cancel the future.

'You figured that out, Ivy. Do you . . . How . . . Would you like him dead?'

'Oh *no*, Dan!' She was shy of using his first name, but this brought her closer to him. 'A friend of mine from Jackson, big party girl, said she saw him at the Barnett Reservoir north of the city. He was "witnessing" outside a rock and roll club and some drunk broke his ribs. The ambulance came but he wouldn't get in.'

'He rode a bike to Jackson, Mississippi?'

'I suppose so. Don't they have to?'

At the hospital he was useless, pointless, and ashamed of his good clothes, a pompous bandage on his distress. He smoked too much. He looked for a Book of Mormon in the waiting room. One of the nurses told him no flatly and looked at him with humor when he asked if there were one around. An alien to their faith, he was being persecuted anyway. The world was broken and mean.

The only good thing about the trip was the sincere goodbye hug from Ivy in her yard. She was on him quickly with arms tight around his neck, not chipper anymore, and she cried for her father, him and Newt, too, all at once. The strength of it told him he would probably never see her again. So long, daughter. I will not have a bad day, will not. He crashed into early night.

In Mobile, on Broadway beneath one of the grandfather live oaks 'bearded with Spanish moss'—as a hack would write—Ross beheld a preacher, a raver, with a boom box hollering gospel music beside him on the sidewalk. He was witnessing through the din, screaming. Heavy metal would be met on its own terms. Three of the curious peered on. It was a long red light. Ross unsnapped the chamber, lower left, where his air rifle was hidden. He badly needed to shoot. But for that reason, he did not. He saw it was in there oiled, heavy with ammo, *semper fidelis*, a part of his dreams.

The next option was to buy a tramp and hump her silly. Make a lifelong friend of her. Nice to have a dive to dip into, young Tootsie lighting up in her whore gaud. Calamity Jane. Long time, no see, my beacon. Miserable bar folks withering around their high-minded big-time copulation. Relieve himself of wads, send her to South Alabama U, suckology. Nabby bouncing dimes off her face back home, considering a mirror on the ceiling and her own water tower of ointment.

He cruised home, shaking his head. He was having another bad day, and the clock was up on legs, running.

The next day he set out for Jackson, got as far as Hattiesburg, saw a bicycle shop, hundreds of bikes out front, sparkling spokes and fenders under the especially hired muttering-dumb Mississippi sun, and grew nauseated by chaos. Too many. He'd never find Newt, going on one mission from one large body to the next. He feared his own wrath if he found him. Two more years of life for him, if you listened to Ivy, who might know him better than Ross. Newt's conversion still struck him as elaborately pretended, another riot of fierceness. In Salt Lake City, he would have turned Methodist. What was he 'witnessing'—what was his hairy face saying? He wouldn't sustain. He was a damned lyric poet, good hell, having a crucifixion a day, maybe even broken ribs, but chicken when the nails and the hill hove into view.

They did not know where he was for nearly a year. Minor grief awoke

Ross every morning. Nabby almost shut down conversation. Some days he woke up among his usual things, felt he had nothing but money and stuff, was crammed, pukey with possessions—its, those, thingness, haveness. One night in April he tore up a transistor radio. Nothing but swill came out of it, and he always expected to hear something horrible about Newton. He dropped his head and wanted to burn his home. The men he'd got mortared called to him in nightmares, as they had not ever before. The tequila, nothing, would help. The murdered men begged him to write their 'stories, our stories.' Their heads came out on long sprouts from a single enormous hacked and blasted trunk. He got to where he feared the bed and slept on the couch under a large picture of him and Nabby and the kids, ages ago. Everybody was grinning properly, but Ross looked for precocious lunacy in the eyes of young Newt, or some religious cast, some grim trance. He fell asleep searching for it.

What was religion, why was he loath to approach it on its own terms? You adopted it, is what you did, and you met with others you supposed felt as you did, and you took a god together, somebody you could complain to and have commiserate. Not an unnatural thing one bit, though inimical to the other half of your nature, which denied as regularly as your pulse out of the evidence of everyday life. For instance the fact that God was away, ancient and vague at his best. Also there was the question of the bully. Ross had never been a bully. Better that he had been, perhaps. He had never struck a man in a bar or country club. Ross's mother was a religious woman, aided in her widowhood by church friends and priest, who actually seemed to care. He had never bullied her. Rather the reverse. She'd used the scriptures to push him around, guiltify him. There was no appeal to a woman with two millennia of religion behind her. Ross suddenly thought of the children Newt played football with, or *at*, hurting them, oppressing them. A thin guy, *he* was the bully, as with his little wives. A lifelong bully? Bullying the happiness out of life. Bullying his parents—a year and a half without a word.

When Ross was in his twenties, he went to Nabby's family reunion up in Indiana. Most of her relatives were fine, scratchy hill people, amused by the twentieth century, amused by their new gadgets like weed-eaters, dishwashers and color televisions. They were rough, princely South Americans. Ross thought of Crockett and Bowie, Travis, the men at the Alamo. But then the pastor of the clan came on board, late. It was Nabby's uncle, against tobacco, coffee, makeup, short dresses, 'jungle music' and swearing. Stillness fell over the clan. The heart went out of the party. That son of a bitch was striding around, quoting the prophets, and men put away their smokes, women gathered inward, somebody poured out the coffee, and he was having a great time, having paralyzed everybody before he fell on his chicken. So here was Newt? Indiana preacher's genes busting out, raiding the gladness of others.

They received a letter, finally, from Newton, who was not too far from them, eight hours away in Mississippi. He was superintendent of a boys 'training school' and taught English. The school had a storm-wire fence around it, barbed wire on top, armed guards, and dogs for both dope and pursuit at the ready. Tough cases went there. Sometimes they escaped out to the country and beyond to create hell. Parents had given up, courts had thrown in the towel and placed them here, the last resort. Occasionally there were killings, knifings, breakages; and constant sodomy. A good many of the boys were simply in 'training' to be lifelong convicts, of course. Much of their conversation was earnest comparison of penal situations in exotic places, their benefits and liabilities. Many boys were planning their careers from one joint to another as they aged, actually setting up retirement plans in the better prisons they considered beds of roses. A good half of them never wanted outside again. The clientele was interracial, international and a bane to the country, which was always crying out for more protection and harsher penitence. Newt wrote that he had to whip boys and knock them down sometimes, but that 'a calm voice turneth away anger,' and he was diligently practicing his calmness. He was married yet again. His wife was pregnant. She was plain and tall, a Mennonite and recovering heroin addict, healthy and doing very well. This love was honest and not dreamy. Newt apologized for much and sent over twelve poems.

They were extraordinary, going places glad and hellish he'd never approached before.

Ross cried tears of gratitude. His hands shook as he reread the poems: such true hard-won love, such precise vision, such sane accuracy—a sanity so calm it was beyond what most men call sanity. He raised his face and looked over Dauphin Island to the west, taken. Nabby trembled the entire day, delirious and already planning Christmas three months ahead. Newt was bringing his wife over to meet them and visit a week, if they would have him. He invited Ross to visit him at the school as soon as he could get over. His voice on the phone when Ross called seemed a miracle of quiet strength. He made long patient sentences such as Ross had never heard from him before. Ross would leave that night.

His brand new navy blue Riviera sat in the shell drive. It was a sweet corsair, meant for a great mission: nothing better than the health and love of the prodigal son. Bring out the horns and tambourines. Poor Ann. There was no competition. All she was now was nice, poor Ann. He wanted to pick up his wealth in one gesture and dump it on Newton.

Outside Raymond, Mississippi, he pushed the hot nose of his chariot into a warm midmorning full of nits, mosquitoes, gnats and flying beetles. His windshield was a mess. Ross was going silly. He felt for the bugs and their colonies. Almost Schweitzer was he, hair snowier, fond, fond of all that crept and flogged.

They were very stern at the gate, sincere cannons on their hips, thorough check of the interior, slow suspicious drawls rolled out of the lard they ate to get here. While they repeated the cautions three or four times—about stopping the car (don't) and watching his wallet ('hard eye if I's yoo') and staying some lengths away from everybody, they acted as if Newt were a great creature on the hill ('Mister Ross he fonk nare boot cup, nard').

Ross had not been searched thoroughly since the war, when at the hospital they feared briefly for his suicide, and in a strange way he felt flattered by these crackers taking the time around his own domain. Only when he was driving up to Newt's house did he go cold, as splashed with alcohol. They'd missed the air rifle, which he had forgotten was there. Then he fell back, silly. It was an *air* rifle only. There would have been no trouble, only shy explanation about its presence and the snap compartment, where there should have been, if he were mature he supposed, a sawed-off pump for danger on the road. The times they were a-changing, all the merciless ghouls prowling for you out there, no problem. A shotgun would be easier to explain than a Daisy. Over here was the *home* of the peacemakers racked across the rear windshield, handy to the driver. Could always be a fawn or doe out of season to shoot, Roy Bob. Over here they considered anybody not in the training school fair gubernatorial timber.

So this was Newt's new job, new home, new Newt. He'd not said how long he'd been here. A job like this, wouldn't it take a while to qualify? But this was the Magnolia State. He'd probably beaten out somebody who'd killed only two people, his mother and father; little spot on his résumé.

Some boys were walking around freely, gawking at his car. This must be how a woman felt, men 'undressing her with their eyes,' as that Ohio tub of guts might 'inscribe.' Those kids would probably tear this car down in fifteen minutes. My God, they had skill-shops here to give them their degrees in it. Ross noticed that almost every boy, whether gaunt or swaybacked, chubby or delicate, had on expensive hightop sneakers. Crack and hightops were probably the school mascots. But he saw more security men than boys outside. He'd glanced at the Rules for Visitors booklet: no sunglasses, no overcoats, no mingling with the student body. Do not give cigarettes or lighters if requested. Your auto was not supposed to have a smoked glass windshield or windows, but they had let him through because he was the father of 'Mister Ross.'

At Newt's WPA-constructed house, like the house of a ranger in a state park—boards and fieldstone—Ross hugged his son at the door, getting a timid but then longer hug back. His wife was still getting ready. They had just finished a late-morning breakfast. There had been trouble last night. Three boys cut the wire and escaped, APBs were issued, the dogs went out, and they were brought back before they even reached Raymond, where they were going to set fire to something.

Ross was thinking about the appearance of Newt's pregnant wife. Why had he thought it necessary to describe her as 'plain' in his letter, even if she was? It was something too deliberate, if you worried the matter. Revenge? Against Ivy, his first wife, his mother? Ross's handsome world scorned? He hoped not.

She, Dianne, was very tall, taller than Newt by three inches and close to Ross's height. She sat at the dining room table, very long and big-stomached, about seven months along. Her father had run this place before Newton. He was retiring and Newton, well, was right there, ready, willing, able—and with (she placed her hand over Newton's at the salt and pepper shakers) the touch of the poet.

Ross did not want to ask his boy the wrong questions and run him away. He was gingerly courteous—to the point of shallowness, he realized, and hated this. It made him feel weak and bullied and this couldn't go on long. But Newt was forthright.

'Not just the broken ribs over at the reservoir, Dad. I was saying my thing at Tishomingo, on the boat dock, and her' (he smiled over at Dianne, who looked fine although a bit gawky—old romantic history a-kindling) 'boyfriend, this tattooed, ponytailed "ice" addict, stabbed me with a knife right in the heart.'

'You're not telling me—'

'Right *in* the heart. But Dianne knew, she was once a nurse and still will be when she gets her license back. She wouldn't let me or anybody pull it out. The knife itself was like a stopper on the blood.'

'That's true,' said Dianne. 'He went all the way to the hospital with it still in him and you could see it pumping up and down with Newton's heart. They helicoptered him to Memphis.'

'She followed me in a car, without her boyfriend.' Newt giggled. 'She was strung out, violently sick herself, but drove all the way over, couple hundred miles.'

'The love got me through, don't you see, Mr Ross? I was already in love with him, like a flash. It pulled me through the heroin, the withdrawal. I sat out there in that waiting room, sick as a dog. But there is a God, there is one.'

'Or love. Or both, sure,' said Ross. 'He stuck you for being a Mormon, Newt?'

Newt still smiled at his father. He looked much older, used, but his grown-out hair was long, like a saint's or our Lord's, thought Ross.

Now the spectacles gentled him and he seemed wise and traveled, much like his new poems.

'Pa, don't you know me? I was Mormon, I was Jew, I was Christ, I was Socrates, I was John the Baptist, I was Hart Crane, Keats, Rimbaud. I was everything tragic. I'm still outcast, but I'm almost sane.'

His son giggled and it was not nervous or the giggle of a madman. It was just an American giggle, a man's giggle—'What the hell is going on?'—full blooded and wary.

'You love these boys? I suppose they're helping you back to . . . helping you as . . .'

'Hell no, I don't love them. I hate these bastards. It might not be all their fault, but they're detestable vermin and utter shits, for the main part. I love, well, five. The rest . . . What you find most often is they've been spoiled, not deprived. Like me. Nobody lasts long here. They try to love but it gets them in a few months. Dianne's father lasted, but he's the meanest, toughest son of a bitch I've ever met.'

Dianne assented, laughing again, about this paternal monster, just a solid fact. The laugh surely lit up that plain face nicely.

'Come eat with me in the big hall and I'll show you something,' said Newt.

'Is this a bad question? What are you going to do? Stay here *because* you hate it?'

'No. I'll do my best. But I'm in fair shape for a job up at Fayetteville. They've seen my new work and I guess they like post-insane poets at Arkansas. Actually, a lot of folks like you a lot when you straighten out a little. The world's a lot better than I thought it was.'

Ross considered.

'Newt, do you believe in Christ?'

'Absolutely. Everything but the cross. That never had anything to do with my "antisocial" activity. I'll still holler for Jesus.'

'I love you, boy.'

'I know it. Last month I finally knew it. Didn't take me forever, is all I can say.'

'Thanks for that.'

'There's some repaying to do.'

'Already done. The new poems.'

Dianne wept a little for joy. This was greatly corny, but it was magnificent.

In the big hall, eating at the head table among the boys, Ross got a drop-jaws look at real 'antisocial' manners. Guards were swarming everywhere, but the boys, some of them large and dangerous, nearly tore the place apart. They threw peas, meat, rolls, just to get primed. Two huge blacks jumped on each other jabbing away with plastic knives. A half grapefruit sailed right by the heads of Ross and Newt. It had been pegged with such velocity that it knocked down the great clock on the wall behind them. Whoever had done it, they never knew. He was eating mildly among them, slick, cool, anonymous, wildly innocent, successful. Right from that you could get the general tenor. Unbelievable. Newt and he were exiting when a stout boy about Newt's height broke line and tackled him, then jumped up and kicked him with his huge black military-looking hightops. Newt scrambled up, but was well hurt before the guards cornered the boy, who'd never stopped cursing violently, screaming, the whole time. With their truncheons the guards beat the shit out of the kid and kept it up when he was handcuffed and down, maybe unconscious. None of the other boys seemed to think it was unusual. They neither cheered nor booed.

Newt wanted him to sleep over so they could go fishing early the next day. He knew a place that was white perch and bass heaven. Dianne insisted, so he did.

They did fairly well on the fish, again in a pond so dark green and gorgeous you could forget the training school and human horror everywhere.

'I guess, like I heard anyway, you went to bodies of water because, well, because what?' Ross asked.

'Because in the South, I figured, the men who change the world mostly go fishing?' He laughed at his father with the flyrod in his hands, so sincere. 'They want *out* of this goddamned place.'

Next morning he left them cheerfully, driving out, but then, as he neared the gate, he circled back—out on his own hook, cautious in the car with smoked windows. He had seen what he wanted, set it up, had found his nest. There was a place in the parking lot for officials and staff that the Riviera nestled into, uniform in the ranks of autos and pickups, as you might see in a big grocery lot. Behind his smoked window he was unseen. Sixty feet away was the entrance to a shop or snack bar. Anyway, a lot of the boys were gathered there, allowed to smoke.

Ross unsnapped the compartment and withdrew the Daisy. My, it had been months, years. Thin, tall, lumpy, sneering, bent, happy, morose, black, white, Indian. It didn't matter. He rolled the window down just a tad, backing up so the barrel wasn't outside the window.

He began popping the boys singly, aiming for the back of their necks and, if lucky, an ear. That was about the best pain he could inflict. A boy leapt up, howling, holding his wound. He got another right on the tit. Did he roar, drop his cigarette, stomp and threaten the others? Yes. He popped another in the back of the head, a hipster with tattooed arms mimicking sodomy. Many of them were questioning, protesting, searching the trees in the sky and other inmates.

Ross rolled up the window and watched them through the one-way glass.

That's it, lads. Start asking some big questions like me, you little nits. You haven't even started yet.

1993

Caroline's Wedding

EDWIDGE DANTICAT

It was a cool September day when I walked out of a Brooklyn court-room holding my naturalization certificate. As I stood on the courthouse steps, I wanted to run back to my mother's house waving the paper like the head of an enemy rightfully conquered in battle.

I stopped at the McDonald's in Fulton Mall to call ahead and share the news.

There was a soap opera playing in the background when she picked up the phone.

'I am a citizen, Ma,' I said.

I heard her clapping with both her hands, the way she had applauded our good deeds when Caroline and I were little girls.

'The paper they gave me, it looks nice,' I said. 'It's wide like a diploma and has a gold seal with an official-looking signature at the bottom. Maybe I will frame it.'

'The passport, weren't you going to bring it to the post office to get a passport right away?' she asked in Creole.

'But I want you to see it, Ma.'

'Go ahead and get the passport. I can see it when you get it back,' she said. 'A passport is truly what's American. May it serve you well.'

At the post office on Flatbush Avenue, I had to temporarily trade in my naturalization certificate for a passport application. Without the certificate, I suddenly felt like unclaimed property. When my mother was three months pregnant with my younger sister, Caroline, she was arrested in a sweatshop raid and spent three days in an immigration jail. In my family, we have always been very anxious about our papers.

★

I raced down the block from where the number eight bus dropped me off, around the corner from our house. The fall was slowly settling into the trees on our block, some of them had already turned slightly brown.

I could barely contain my excitement as I walked up the steps to the house, sprinting across the living room to the kitchen.

Ma was leaning over the stove, the pots clanking as she hummed a song to herself.

'My passport should come in a month or so,' I said, unfolding a photocopy of the application for her to see.

She looked at it as though it contained boundless possibilities.

'We can celebrate with some strong bone soup,' she said. 'I am making some right now.'

In the pot on the stove were scraps of cow bones stewing in hot bubbling broth.

Ma believed that her bone soup could cure all kinds of ills. She even hoped that it would perform the miracle of detaching Caroline from Eric, her Bahamian fiancé. Since Caroline had announced that she was engaged, we'd had bone soup with our supper every single night.

'Have you had some soup?' I asked, teasing Caroline when she came out of the bedroom.

'This soup is really getting on my nerves,' Caroline whispered in my ear as she walked by the stove to get some water from the kitchen faucet.

Caroline had been born without her left forearm. The round end of her stub felt like a stuffed dumpling as I squeezed it hello. After my mother was arrested in the sweatshop immigration raid, a prison doctor had given her a shot of a drug to keep her calm overnight. That shot, my mother believed, caused Caroline's condition. Caroline was lucky to have come out missing only one forearm. She might not have been born at all.

'Soup is ready,' Ma announced.

'If she keeps making this soup,' Caroline whispered, 'I will dip my head into the pot and scald myself blind. That will show her that there's no magic in it.'

It was very hard for Ma to watch Caroline prepare to leave us, knowing that there was nothing she could do but feed her.

'Ma, if we keep on with this soup,' Caroline said, 'we'll all grow horns like the ones that used to be on these cows.'

Caroline brushed aside a strand of her hair, chemically straightened and streaked bright copper from a peroxide experiment.

'You think you are so American,' Ma said to Caroline. 'You don't know what's good for you. You have no taste buds. A double tragedy.'

'There's another American citizen in the family now.' I took advantage of the moment to tell Caroline.

'Congratulations,' she said. 'I don't love you any less.'

Caroline had been born in America, something that she very much took for granted.

Later that night, Ma called me into her bedroom after she thought Caroline had gone to sleep. The room was still decorated just the way it had been when Papa was still alive. There was a large bed, almost four feet tall, facing an old reddish brown dresser where we could see our reflections in a mirror as we talked.

Ma's bedroom closet was spilling over with old suitcases, some of which she had brought with her when she left Haiti almost twenty-five years before. They were so crowded into the small space that the closet door would never stay fully closed.

'She drank all her soup,' Ma said as she undressed for bed. 'She talks bad about the soup but she drinks it.'

'Caroline is not a child, Ma.'

'She doesn't have to drink it.'

'She wants to make you happy in any small way she can.'

'If she wanted to make me happy, you know what she would do.'

'She has the right to choose who she wants to marry. That's none of our business.'

'I am afraid she will never find a nice man to marry her,' Ma said. 'I am afraid you won't either.'

'Caroline is already marrying a nice man,' I said.

'She will never find someone Haitian,' she said.

'It's not the end of creation that she's not marrying someone Haitian.'

'No one in our family has ever married outside,' she said. 'There has to be a cause for everything.'

'What's the cause of you having said what you just said? You know about Eric. You can't try to pretend that he's not there.'

'She is my last child. There is still a piece of her inside me.'

'Why don't you give her a spanking?' I joked.

'My mother used to spank me when I was older than you,' she said. 'Do you know how your father came to have me as his wife? *His* father wrote a letter to my father and came to my house on a Sunday afternoon and brought the letter in a pink and green handkerchief. Pink because it is the color of romance and green for hope that it might work. Your grandfather on your papa's side had the handkerchief sewn especially in these two colors to wrap my proposal letter in. He brought this letter to my house and handed it to my father. My father didn't even read the letter himself. He called in a neighbor and asked the neighbor to read it out loud.

'The letter said in very fancy words how much your father wanted to be my husband. *My son desires greatly your daughter's hand*, something like that. The whole time the letter was being read, your father and I sat silently while our parents had this type of show. Then my father sent your father away, saying that he and my mother wanted to think about the proposal.'

'Did they consult you about it?' I asked, pretending not to know the outcome.

'Of course they did. I had to act like I didn't really like your father or that at least I liked him just a tiny little bit. My parents asked me if I wanted to marry him and I said I wouldn't mind, but they could tell from my face that it was a different story, that I was already desperately in love.'

'But you and Papa had talked about this, right? Before his father came to your father.'

'Your father and I had talked about it. We were what you girls call dating. He would come to my house and I would go to his house when his mother was there. We would go to the cinema together, but the proposal, it was all very formal, and sometimes, in some circumstances, formality is important.'

'What would you have done if your father had said no?' I asked.

'Don't say that you will never dine with the devil if you have a daughter,' she said. 'You never know what she will bring. My mother and father, they knew that too.'

'What would you have done if your father had said no?' I repeated.

'I probably would have married anyway,' she said. 'There is little others can do to keep us from our hearts' desires.'

Caroline too was going to get married whether Ma wanted her to or not. That night, maybe for the first time, I saw a hint of this realization in Ma's face. As she raised her comforter and slipped under the sheets, she looked as if she were all alone in the world, as lonely as a woman with two grown daughters could be.

'We're not like birds,' she said, her head sinking into the pillow. 'We don't just kick our children out of our nests.'

Caroline was still awake when I returned to our room. 'Is she ever going to get tired of telling that story?' she asked.

'You're talking about a woman who has had soup with cow bones in it for all sixty years of her life. She doesn't get tired of things. What are you going to do about it?'

'She'll come around. She has to,' Caroline said.

We sat facing each other in the dark, playing a free-association game that Ma had taught us when we were girls.

'Who are you?' Caroline asked me.

'I am the *lost* child of the night.'

'Where do you come from?'

'I come from the inside of the *lost* stone.'

'Where are your eyes?'

'I have eyes *lost* behind my head, where they can best protect me.'

'Who is your mother?'

'She who is the *lost* mother of all.'

'Who is your father?'

'He who is the *lost* father of all.'

Sometimes we would play half the night, coming up with endless possibilities for questions and answers, only repeating the key word in every sentence. Ma too had learned this game when she was a girl.

Her mother belonged to a secret women's society in Ville Rose, where the women had to question each other before entering one another's houses. Many nights while her mother was hosting the late-night meetings, Ma would fall asleep listening to the women's voices.

'I just remembered. There is a Mass Sunday at Saint Agnès for a dead refugee woman.' Ma was standing in the doorway in her night-gown. 'Maybe you two will come with me.'

'Nobody sleeps in this house,' Caroline said.

I would go, but not her.

They all tend to be similar, farewell ceremonies to the dead. The church was nearly empty, with a few middle-aged women scattered in the pews.

I crossed myself as I faced the wooden life-size statue of a dying Christ, looking down on us from high above the altar. The chapel was dim except for a few high chandeliers and the permanent glow of the rich hues of the stained glass windows. Ma kneeled in one of the side pews. She clutched her rosary and recited her Hail Marys with her eyes tightly shut.

For a long time, services at Saint Agnès have been tailored to fit the needs of the Haitian community. A line of altar boys proceeded down the aisle, each carrying a long lit candle. Ma watched them as though she were a spectator at a parade. Behind us, a group of women was carrying on a conversation, criticizing a neighbor's wife who, upon leaving Haiti, had turned from a sweet Haitian wife into a self-willed tyrant.

'In New York, women give their eight hours to the white man,' one of the worshipers said in the poor woman's defense. 'No one has time to be cradling no other man.'

There was a slow drumbeat playing like a death march from the altar. A priest in a black robe entered behind the last altar boy. He walked up to the altar and began to read from a small book.

Ma lowered her head so far down that I could see the dip in the back of her neck, where she had a port-wine mark shaped like Manhattan Island.

'We have come here this far, from the shackles of the old Africans,' read the priest in Creole. 'At the mercy of the winds, at the mercy of the sea, to the quarters of the New World, we came. Transients. Nomads. I bid you welcome.'

We all answered back, 'Welcome.'

The altar boys stood in an arc around the priest as he recited a list of a hundred twenty-nine names, Haitian refugees who had drowned at sea that week. The list was endless and with each name my heart beat faster, for it seemed as though many of those listed might have been people that I had known at some point in my life.

Some of the names sent a wave of sighs and whispers through the crowd. Occasionally, there was a loud scream.

One woman near the front began to convulse after a man's name was called. It took four people to drag her out of the pew before she hurt herself.

'We make a special call today for a young woman whose name we don't know,' the priest said after he had recited all the others. 'A young woman who was pregnant when she took a boat from Haiti and then later gave birth to her child on that boat. A few hours after the child was born, its precious life went out, like a candle in a storm, and the mother with her infant in her arms dived into the sea.'

There are people in Ville Rose, the village where my mother is from in Haiti, who believe that there are special spots in the sea where lost Africans who jumped off the slave ships still rest, that those who have died at sea have been chosen to make that journey in order to be reunited with their long-lost relations.

During the Mass, Ma tightened a leather belt around her belly, the way some old Haitian women tightened rags around their middles when grieving.

'Think to yourself of the people you have loved and lost,' the priest said.

Piercing screams sounded throughout the congregation. Ma got up suddenly and began heading for the aisle. The screams pounded in my head as we left the church.

We walked home through the quiet early morning streets along Avenue D, saying nothing to one another.

★

Caroline was still in bed when we got back.

She wrapped a long black nightgown around her legs as she sat up on a pile of dirty sheets.

There was a stack of cards on a chair by her bed. She picked it up and went through the cards, sorting most of them with one hand and holding the rest in her mouth. She began a game of solitaire using her hand and her lips, flipping the cards back and forth with great agility.

'How was Mass?' she asked.

Often after Mass ended, I would feel as though I had taken a very long walk with the dead.

'Did Ma cry?' she asked.

'We left before she could.'

'It's not like she knows these people,' Caroline said. Some of the cards slipped from between her lips.

'Ma says all Haitians know each other.'

Caroline stacked the cards and dropped them in one of the three large open boxes that were kept lined up behind her bed. She was packing up her things slowly so as to not traumatize Ma.

She and Eric were not going to have a big formal wedding. They were going to have a civil ceremony and then they would take some pictures in the wedding grove at the Brooklyn Botanic Garden. Their honeymoon would be a brief trip to the Bahamas, after which Caroline would move into Eric's apartment.

Ma wanted Eric to officially come and ask her permission to marry her daughter. She wanted him to bring his family to our house and have his father ask her blessing. She wanted Eric to kiss up to her, escort her around, buy her gifts, and shower her with compliments. Ma wanted a full-blown church wedding. She wanted Eric to be Haitian.

'You will never guess what I dreamt last night,' Caroline said, dropping her used sheets into one of the moving boxes she was packing. 'I dreamt about Papa.'

It had been almost ten years since Papa had died of untreated prostrate cancer. After he died, Ma made us wear mourning clothes, nothing but black dresses, for eighteen months. Caroline and I were both in high school at the time, and we quickly found ways to make wearing black a fashion statement. Underneath our black clothes we were supposed to wear red panties. In Ma's family, the widows often wore blood-red panties so that their dead husbands would not come back and lie down next to them at night. Daughters who looked a lot like the widowed mother might wear red panties too so that if they were ever mistaken for her, they would be safe.

Ma believed that Caroline and I would be well protected by the red panties. Papa, and all the other dead men who might desire us, would stay away because the sanguine color of blood was something that daunted and terrified the non-living.

For a few months after Papa died, Caroline and I dreamt of him every other night. It was as though he were taking turns visiting us in our sleep. We would each have the same dream: Papa walking in a deserted field while the two of us were running after him. We were never able to catch up with him because there were miles of saw grass and knee-deep mud between us.

We kept this dream to ourselves because we already knew what Ma would say if we told it to her. She would guess that we had not been wearing our red panties and would warn us that the day we caught up with Papa in our dream would be the day that we both would die.

Later the dreams changed into moments replayed from our lives, times when he had told us stories about his youth in Haiti or evenings when he had awakened us at midnight after working a double shift in his taxicab to take us out for Taste the Tropics ice cream, Sicilian pizzas, or Kentucky Fried Chicken.

Slowly, Papa's death became associated with our black clothes. We began carrying our loss like a medal on our chests, answering every time someone asked why such young attractive girls wore such a somber color, 'Our mother makes us do it because our father is dead.'

Eighteen months after his death, we were allowed to start wearing other colors, but nothing too bright. We could wear white or gray or navy blue but no orange, or red on the outside. The red for the world to see meant that our mourning period had ended, that we were beyond our grief. The red covering our very private parts was to tell our father that he was dead and we no longer wanted anything to do with him.

'How did you dream of Papa?' I asked Caroline now.

'He was at a party,' she said, 'with all these beautiful people around him, having a good time. I saw him in this really lavish room. I'm standing in the doorway and he's inside and I'm watching him, and it's like watching someone through a glass window. He doesn't even know I'm there. I call him, but he doesn't answer. I just stand there and watch what he's doing because I realize that he can't see me.'

She reached into one of her boxes and pulled out a framed black-and-white picture of Papa, a professional studio photograph taken in the nineteen fifties in Haiti, when Papa was twenty-two. In the photograph, he is wearing a dark suit and tie and has a solemn expression on his face. Caroline looked longingly at the picture, the way war brides look at photographs of their dead husbands. I raised my nightshirt and showed her my black cotton panties, the same type that we had both been wearing since the day our father died. Caroline stuck her pinkie through a tiny hole in the front of my panties. She put Papa's picture back into her box, raised her dress, and showed me her own black panties.

We had *never* worn the red panties that Ma had bought for us over the years to keep our dead father's spirit away. We had always worn our black panties instead, to tell him that he would be welcome to visit us. Even though we no longer wore black outer clothes, we continued to wear black underpants as a sign of lingering grief. Another reason Caroline may have continued to wear hers was her hope that Papa would come to her and say that he approved of her: of her life, of her choices, of her husband.

'With patience, you can see the navel of an ant,' I said, recalling one of Papa's favorite Haitian proverbs.

'Rain beats on a dog's skin, but it does not wash out its spots,' Caroline responded.

'When the tree is dead, ghosts eat the leaves.'

'The dead are always in the wrong.'

Beneath the surface of Papa's old proverbs was always some warning.

Our Cuban neighbor, Mrs Ruiz, was hosting her large extended family in the yard next door after a Sunday christening. They were blasting some rumba music. We could barely hear each other over the crisp staccato pounding of the conga drums and the shrill brass sections blaring from their stereo.

I closed my eyes and tried to imagine their entire clan milling around the yard, a whole exiled family gathering together so far from home. Most of my parents' relatives still lived in Haiti.

Caroline and I walked over to the window to watch the Ruiz clan dance to the rumba.

'Mrs Ruiz has lost some weight since we saw her last,' Caroline said.

'A couple of months ago, Mrs Ruiz's only son had tried to hijack a plane in Havana to go to Miami. He was shot and killed by the airplane's pilot.'

'How do you know such things?' Caroline asked me.

'Ma told me.'

When we were younger, Caroline and I would spend all our Sunday mornings in bed wishing that it would be the blessed day that the rest of Caroline's arm would come bursting out of Ma's stomach and float back to her. It would all happen like the brass sections in the Ruizes' best rumbas, a meteoric cartoon explosion, with no blood or pain. After the momentary shock, Caroline would have a whole arm and we would all join Mrs Ruiz's parties to celebrate. Sometimes Sunday mornings would be so heavy with disappointment that we thought *we* might explode.

Caroline liked to have her stub stroked. This was something that she had never grown out of. Yet it was the only part of her that people were afraid of. They were afraid of offending her, afraid of staring at it, even while they were stealing a glance or two. A large vein throbbed just below the surface, under a thick layer of skin. I ran my pinkie over the vein and felt it, pulsating against my skin.

'If I slice myself there, I could bleed to death,' Caroline said. 'Remember what Papa used to say, "Behind a white cloud, a bird looks like an angel."'

Ma was in the kitchen cooking our Sunday breakfast when we came in. She was making a thick omelet with dried herring, served with boiled plantains. Something to keep you going as if it were your only meal for the day.

'Mass was nice today,' Ma said, watching Caroline balance her orange juice between her chin and her stub. 'If you had gone, you would have enjoyed it a lot.'

'Yes. I hear it was a ball,' Caroline said.

'You two have been speaking for a long time already,' Ma said. 'What were you discussing?'

'This and that,' I said.

'I've been jealous,' Ma said.

That night I dreamt that I was at a costume ball in an eighteenth-century French château, with huge crystal chandeliers above my head. Around me people were wearing masks made from papier-mâché and velvet. Suddenly, one of the men took off his mask. Beneath the mask was my father.

Papa was talking to a group of other people who were also wearing masks. He was laughing as though someone had just told him a really good joke. He turned towards me for a brief second and smiled. I was so happy to see him that I began to cry.

I tried to run to him, but I couldn't. My feet were moving but I was standing in the same place, like a mouse on a treadmill. Papa looked up at me again, and this time he winked. I raised my hand and waved. He waved back. It was a cruel flirtation.

I quickly realized that I would never get near him, so I stood still and just watched him. He looked much healthier than I remembered, his toasted almond face round and fleshy. I felt as though there was something he wanted to tell me.

Suddenly, he dropped his mask on the ground, and like smoke on a windy day, he disappeared. My feet were now able to move. I walked over to where he had been standing and picked up the mask. The expression on the mask was like a frozen scream. I pressed the mask against my chest, feeling the luxurious touch of velvet against my cheek.

When I looked up again, my father was standing at the foot of a spiral staircase with a group of veiled women all around him. He turned his back to me and started climbing the long winding staircase. The veiled women followed him with their beautiful pink gowns crackling like damp wood in a fire.

Then, the women stopped and turned one by one to face me, slowly raising their veils. As they uncovered their faces, I realized that one of them, standing tall and rigid at Papa's side, was Caroline.

Of the two of us, Caroline was the one who looked most like Papa. Caroline looked so much like Papa that Ma liked to say they were *one head on two bodies. Tèt koupé.*

I started screaming at the top of my lungs. Why were they leaving me out? I should have been there with them.

I woke up with my face soaked with tears, clutching my pillow.

That morning, I wrote down a list of things that I remembered having learned from my father. I had to remind myself, at least under my breath, that I did remember still. In the back of my mind, I could almost hear his voice saying these things to me, in the very same way that he had spoken over the years: 'You have memory of walking in a mist at dawn in a banana jungle that no longer exists. You have lived this long in this strange world, so far from home, because you remember.'

The lifelines in my father's palms were named after Caroline and me. He remembered everything. He remembered old men napping on tree branches, forgetting the height of the trees and the vulnerability of their bodies. He remembered old women sitting sidesaddle on ancient donkeys, taking their last steps. He remembered young wives who got ill from sadness when their men went to the Bahamas or the Dominican Republic to cut sugarcane and were never heard from again. These women lived in houses where they slept on sugar sacks on the floor, with mourning ropes around their bellies, houses where the marital bed was never used again and where the middle pillar was sacred.

He remembered never-ending flour fogs in the country market-place, fogs that folks compared to the inside of a crazy woman's head. He remembered calling strangers 'Mother,' 'Sister', 'Brother,' because his village's Creole demanded a family title for everyone he addressed.

My father had memories of eating potato, breadfruit, and avocado peels that he was supposed to be feeding to his mother's pigs. He remembered praying for the rain to stay away even during drought season because his house had a hole in the roof right above his cot. Later he felt guilty that there was no crop, because he thought that it was his prayers that had kept away the rain.

He remembered hearing his illiterate mother reciting poetry and speaking in a tongue that sounded like Latin when she was very ill with typhoid fever. This was the time he tried to stuff red hot peppers into his mother's nose because he was convinced that if the old woman sneezed three times, she would live.

It was my father's job to look for the falling star that would signal his mother's impending death, and when he saw it crash in a flash behind the hills above his house, he screamed and howled like a hurt dog. After his mother died, he stuffed live snakes into bottles to imprison his anger. He swam in waterfalls with healing powers. He piled large rocks around his mother's house to keep the dead spirit in the ground. He played King of the Mountain on garbage heaps. He trapped fire-flies in matchboxes so he would not inhale them in his sleep. He collected beads from the braids in his mother's hair and swallowed them in secret so he would always have a piece of her inside of him. And even when he was in America, he never looked at a night sky again.

'I have a riddle for you. Can you handle it?' he would ask.

'Bring it on. Try me.'

'Ten thousand very large men are standing under one small umbrella. How is it that none of them gets wet?'

'It is not raining.'

'Why is it that when you lose something, it is always in the very last place you look?'

'Because once you find it, you look no more.'

He had a favorite joke: God once called a conference of world leaders. He invited the president of France, the president of the United States, the president of Russia, Italy, Germany, and China, as well as our own president, His Excellency, the President for Life Papa Doc Duvalier. When the president of France reached the gates of Heaven, God got up from his throne to greet him. When the president of the

United States reached the gates of Heaven, God got up to greet him as well. So, too, with the presidents of Russia, Italy, Germany, and China.

When it was our president's turn, His Excellency, the President for Life Papa Doc Duvalier, God did not get up from his throne to greet him. All the angels were stunned and puzzled. They did not understand God's very rude behavior. So they elected a representative to go up to God and question Him.

'God,' said the representative, 'you have been so cordial to all the other presidents. You have gotten up from your throne to greet them at the gates of Heaven as soon as they have entered. Why do you not get up for Papa Doc Duvalier? Is it because he is a black president? You have always told us to overlook the color of men. Why have you chosen to treat the black president, Papa Doc Duvalier, in this fashion?'

God looked at the representative angel as though He was about to admit something that He did not want to.

'Look,' he said. 'I am not getting up for Papa Doc Duvalier because I am afraid that if I get up, he will take my throne and will never give it back.'

These were our bedtime stories. Tales that haunted our parents and made them laugh at the same time. We never understood them until we were fully grown and they became our sole inheritance.

Caroline's wedding was only a month away. She was very matter-of-fact about it, but slowly we all began to prepare. She had bought a short white dress at a Goodwill thrift shop and paid twelve dollars to dry-clean it. Ma, too, had a special dress: a pink lace, ankle-sweeping evening gown that she was going to wear at high noon to a civil ceremony. I decided to wear a green suit, for hope, like the handkerchief that wrapped Ma's marriage proposal letter from Papa's family.

Ma would have liked to have sewn Caroline's wedding dress from ten different patterns in a bridal magazine, taking the sleeves from one dress, the collar from another, and the skirt from another. Though in her heart she did not want to attend, in spite of everything, she was planning to act like this was a real wedding.

'The daughter resents a mother forever who keeps her from her love,' Ma said as we dressed to go to Eric's house for dinner. 'She is my child. You don't cut off your own finger because it smells bad.'

Still, she was not going to cook a wedding-night dinner. She was not even going to buy Caroline a special sleeping gown for her 'first' sexual act with her husband.

'I want to give you a wedding shower,' I said to Caroline in the cab on the way to Eric's house.

There was no sense in trying to keep it a secret from her.

'I don't really like showers,' Caroline said, 'but I'll let you give me one because there are certain things that I need.'

She handed me her address book, filled mostly with the names of people at Jackie Robinson Intermediate School where we both taught English as a Second Language to Haitian students.

Eric and Caroline had met at the school, where he was a janitor. They had been friends for at least a year before he asked her out. Caroline couldn't believe that he wanted to go out with her. They dated for eighteen months before he asked her to marry him.

'A shower is like begging,' Ma said, staring out of the car window at the storefronts along Flatbush Avenue. 'It is even more like begging if your sister gives one for you.'

'The maid of honor is the one to do it,' I said. 'I am the maid of honor, Ma. Remember?'

'Of course I remember,' she said. 'I am the mother, but that gives me claim to nothing.'

'It will be fun,' I tried to assure her. 'We'll have it at the house.'

'Is there something that's like a shower in Haiti?' Caroline asked Ma.

'In Haiti we are poor,' Ma said, 'but we do not beg.'

'It's nice to see you, Mrs Azile,' Eric said when he came to the door.

Eric had eyes like Haitian lizards, bright copper with a tint of jade. He was just a little taller than Caroline, his rich mahogany skin slightly darker than hers.

Under my mother's glare, he gave Caroline a timid peck on the cheek, then wrapped his arms around me and gave me a bear hug.

'How have you been?' Ma asked him with her best, extreme English pronunciation.

'I can't complain,' he said.

Ma moved over to the living room couch and sat down in front of the television screen. There was a nature program playing without sound. Mute images of animals swallowing each other whole flickered across the screen.

'So, you are a citizen of America now?' Eric said to me. 'Now you can just get on a plane anytime you feel like it and go anywhere in the world. Nations go to war over women like you. You're an American.'

His speech was extremely slow on account of a learning disability. He was not quite retarded, but not like everybody else either.

Ma looked around the room at some carnival posters on Eric's living room wall. She pushed her head forward to get a better look at a woman in a glittering bikini with a crown of feathers on her head. Her eyes narrowed as they rested on a small picture of Caroline, propped in a silver frame on top of the television set.

Eric and Caroline disappeared in the kitchen, leaving me alone with Ma.

'I won't eat if it's bad,' she said.

'You know Eric's a great cook,' I said.

'Men cooking?' she said. 'There is always something wrong with what he makes, here or at our house.'

'Well, pretend to enjoy it, will you?'

She walked around the living room, picking up the small wooden sculptures that Eric had in many corners of the room, mostly brown Madonnas with caramel babies wrapped in their arms.

Eric served us chicken in a thick dark sauce. I thrust my fork through layers of gravy. Ma pushed the food around her plate but ate very little.

After dinner, Eric and Caroline did the dishes in the kitchen while Ma and I sat in front of the television.

'Did you have a nice time?' I asked her.

'Nice or not nice, I came,' she said.

'That's right, Ma. It counts a lot that you came, but it would have helped if you had eaten more.'

'I was not very hungry,' she said.

'That means you can't fix anything to eat when you get home,' I said. 'Nothing. You can't fix anything. Not even bone soup.'

'A woman my age in her own home following orders.'

Eric had failed miserably at the game of Wooing Haitian Mother-in-Law. Had he known—or rather had Caroline advised him well—he would have hired a Haitian cook to make Ma some Haitian food that would taste (God forbid!) even better than her own.

'We know people by their stories,' Ma said to Caroline in the cab on the way home that night. 'Gossip goes very far. Grace heard women gossip in the Mass behind us the other day, and you hear what they say about Haitian women who forget themselves when they come here. Value yourself.'

'Yes, Ma,' Caroline said, for once not putting up a fight.

I knew she wanted to stay and spend the night with Eric but she was sparing Ma.

'I can't accuse you of anything,' Ma said. 'You never call someone a thief unless you catch them stealing.'

'I hear you, Ma,' Caroline said, as though her mind were a thousand miles away.

When we got home, she waited for Ma to fall asleep, then called a car service and went back to Eric's. When I got up the next morning, Ma was standing over my bed.

'Did your sister leave for school early again?' she asked.

'Yes, Ma,' I said. 'Caroline is just like you. She sleeps a hair thread away from waking, and she rises with the roosters.'

I mailed out the invitations for Caroline's wedding shower. We kept the list down to a bare minimum, just a few friends and Mrs Ruiz. We invited none of Ma's friends from Saint Agnès because she told me that she would be ashamed to have them ask her the name of her daughter's fiancé and have her tongue trip, being unable to pronounce it.

'What's so hard about Eric Abrahams?' I asked her. 'It's practically a Haitian name.'

'But it isn't a Haitian name,' she said. 'The way I say it is not the way his parents intended for it to be said. I say it Haitian. It is not Haitian.'

'People here pronounce our names wrong all the time.'

'That is why I know the way I say his name is not how it is meant to be said.'

'You better learn his name. Soon it will be your daughter's.'

'That will never be my daughter's name,' she said, 'because it was not the way I intended her name to be said.'

In the corner behind her bed, Caroline's boxes were getting full.

'Do you think Ma knows where I am those nights when I'm not here?' she asked.

'If she caught you going out the door, what could she do? It would be like an ant trying to stop a flood.'

'It's not like I have no intention of getting married,' she said.

'Maybe she understands.'

That night, I dreamed of my father again. I was standing on top of a cliff, and he was leaning out of a helicopter trying to grab my hand. At times, the helicopter flew so low that it nearly knocked me off the cliff. My father began to climb down a plastic ladder hanging from the bottom of the helicopter. He was dangling precariously and I was terrified.

I couldn't see his face, but I was sure he was coming to rescue me from the top of that cliff. He was shouting loudly, calling out my name. He called me Gracina, my full Haitian name, not Grace, which is what I'm called here.

It was the first time in any of my dreams that my father had a voice. The same scratchy voice that he had when he was alive. I stretched my hands over my head to make it easier for him to reach me. Our fingers came closer with each swing of the helicopter. His fingertips nearly touched mine as I woke up.

When I was a little girl, there was a time that Caroline and I were sleeping in the same bed with our parents because we had eaten beans for dinner and then slept on our backs, a combination that gives bad dreams. Even though she was in our parents' bed, Caroline woke up in the middle of the night, terrified. As she sobbed, Papa rocked her in the dark, trying to console her. His face was the first one she saw when Ma turned on the light. Looking straight at Papa with dazed eyes, Caroline asked him, 'Who are you?'

He said, 'It's Papy.'

'Papy who?' she asked.

'Your papy,' he said.

'I don't have a papy,' she said.

Then she jumped into Papa's arms and went right back to sleep.

My mother and father stayed up trying to figure out what made her say those things.

'Maybe she dreamt that you were gone and that she was sleeping with her husband, who was her only comfort,' Ma said to Papa.

'So young, she would dream this?' asked Papa.

'In dreams we travel the years,' Ma had said.

Papa eventually went back to sleep, but Ma stayed up all night thinking.

The next day she went all the way to New Jersey to get Caroline fresh bones for a soup.

'So young she would dream this,' Papa kept saying as he watched Caroline drink the soup. 'So young. Just look at her, our child of the promised land, our New York child, the child who has never known Haiti.'

I, on the other hand, was the first child, the one they called their 'misery baby,' the offspring of my parents' lean years. I was born to them at a time when they were living in a shantytown in Port-au-Prince and had nothing.

When I was a baby, my mother worried that I would die from colic and hunger. My father pulled heavy carts for pennies. My mother sold jugs of water from the public fountain, charcoal, and grilled peanuts to get us something to eat.

When I was born, they felt a sense of helplessness. What if the children kept coming like the millions of flies constantly buzzing around them? What would they do then? Papa would need to pull more carts. Ma would need to sell more water, more charcoal, more peanuts. They had to try to find a way to leave Haiti.

Papa got a visa by taking vows in a false marriage with a widow who was leaving Haiti to come to the United States. He gave her some money and she took our last name. A few years later, my father divorced the woman and sent for my mother and me. While my father was alive, this was something that Caroline and I were never supposed to know.

We decorated the living room for Caroline's shower. Pink streamers and balloons draped down from the ceiling with the words *Happy Shower* emblazoned on them.

Ma made some patties from ground beef and codfish. She called one of her friends from Saint Agnès to bake the shower cake cheap. We didn't tell her friend what the cake was for. Ma wrote Caroline's name and the date on it after it had been delivered. She scrubbed the whole house, just in case one of the strangers wanted to use our bathroom. There wasn't a trace of dirt left on the wallpaper, the tiles, even the bathroom cabinets. If cleanliness is next to godliness, then whenever we had company my mother became a goddess.

Aside from Ma and me, there were only a few other people at the shower: four women from the junior high school where we taught and Mrs Ruiz.

Ma acted like a waitress and served everyone as Caroline took center stage sitting on the loveseat that we designated the 'shower chair'. She was wearing one of her minidresses, a navy blue with a wide butterfly collar. We laid the presents in front of her to open, after she had guessed what was inside.

'Next a baby shower!' shouted Mrs Ruiz in her heavy Spanish accent.

'Let's take one thing at a time,' I said.

'Never too soon to start planning,' Mrs Ruiz said. 'I promise to deliver the little one myself. Caroline, tell me now, what would you like, a girl or a boy?'

'Let's get through one shower first,' Caroline said.

I followed Ma to the kitchen as she picked up yet another empty tray.

'Why don't you sit down for a while and let me serve?' I asked Ma as she put another batch of patties in the oven. She looked like she was going to cry.

When it was time to open the presents, Ma stayed in the kitchen while we all sat in a circle watching Caroline open her gifts.

She got a juicer, a portable step exerciser, and some other household appliances from the schoolteachers. I gave her a traveling bag to take on her honeymoon.

Ma peeked through the doorway as we cooed over the appliances, suggesting romantic uses for them: breakfasts in bed, candlelight dinners, and the like. Ma pulled her head back quickly and went into the kitchen.

She was in the living room to serve the cake when the time came for it. While we ate, she gathered all of the boxes and the torn wrapping paper and took them to the trash bin outside.

She was at the door telling our guests good-bye as they left.

'Believe me, Mrs Azile, I will deliver your first grandchild,' Mrs Ruiz told her as she was leaving.

'I am sorry about your son,' I said to Mrs Ruiz.

'Now why would you want to bring up a thing like that?' Mrs Ruiz asked.

'Carmen, next time you come I will give you some of my bone soup,' Ma said as Mrs Ruiz left.

Ma gave me a harsh look as though I had stepped out of line in offering my belated condolences to Mrs Ruiz.

'There are things that don't always need to be said,' Ma told me.

Caroline packed her gifts before going to bed that night. The boxes were nearly full now.

We heard a knock on the door of our room as we changed for bed. It was Ma in her nightgown holding a gift-wrapped package in her hand. She glanced at Caroline's boxes in the corner, quickly handing Caroline the present.

'It is very sweet of you to get me something,' Caroline said, kissing Ma on the cheek to say thank you.

'It's very nothing,' Ma said, 'very nothing at all.'

Ma turned her face away as Caroline lifted the present out of the box. It was a black and gold silk teddy with a plunging neckline.

'At the store,' Ma said, 'I told them your age and how you would be having this type of a shower. A girl there said that this would make a good gift for such things. I hope it will be of use.'

'I like it very much,' Caroline said, replacing it in the box.

After Caroline went to bed, I went to Ma's room for one of our chats. I slipped under the covers next to her, the way Caroline and I had come to her and Papa when our dreams had frightened us.

'That was nice, the teddy you got for Caroline,' I said. 'But it doesn't seem much like your taste.'

'I can't live in this country twenty-five years and not have some of it rub off on me,' she said. 'When will I have to buy you one of those dishonorable things?'

'When you find me a man.'

'They can't be that hard to find,' she said. 'Look, your sister found one, and some people might think it would be harder for her. He is a retard, but that's okay.'

'He's not a retard, Ma. She found a man with a good heart.'

'Maybe.'

'You like him, Ma. I know deep inside you do.'

'After Caroline was born, your father and me, we were so afraid of this.'

'Of what?'

'Of what is happening.'

'And what is that?'

'Maybe she jumps at it because she thinks he is being noble. Maybe she thinks he is doing her a favor. Maybe she thinks he is the only man who will ever come along to marry her.'

'Maybe he loves her,' I said.

'Love cannot make horses fly,' she said. 'Caroline should not marry a man if that man wants to be noble by marrying Caroline.'

'We don't know that, Ma.'

'The heart is like a stone,' she said. 'We never know what it is in the middle.'

'Only some hearts are like that,' I said.

'That is where we make mistakes,' she said. 'All hearts are stone until we melt, and then they turn back to stone again.'

'Did you feel that way when Papa married that woman?' I asked.

'My heart has a store of painful marks,' she said, 'and that is one of them.'

Ma got up from the bed and walked over to the closet with all her suitcases. She pulled out an old brown leather bag filled with tiny holes where the closet mice had nibbled at it over the years.

She laid the bag on her bed, taking out many of the items that she had first put in it years ago when she left Haiti to come to the United States to be reunited with my father.

She had cassettes and letters written by my father, his words crunched between the lines of aging sheets of ruled loose-leaf paper. In the letters he wrote from America to her while she was still in Haiti, he never talked to her about love. He asked about practical things; he asked about me and told her how much money he was sending her and how much was designated for what.

My mother also had the letters that she wrote back to him, telling him how much she loved him and how she hoped that they would be together soon.

That night Ma and I sat in her room with all those things around us. Things that we could neither throw away nor keep in plain sight.

Caroline seemed distant the night before her wedding. Ma made her a stew with spinach, yams, potatoes, and dumplings. Ma did not eat any of the stew, concentrating instead on a green salad, fishing beneath the lettuce leaves as though there was gold hidden on the plate.

After dinner, we sat around the kitchen radio listening to a music program on the Brooklyn Haitian station.

Ma's lips were moving almost unconsciously as she mouthed the words to an old sorrowful bolero. Ma was putting the final touches on her own gown for the wedding.

'Did you check your dress?' she asked Caroline.

'I know it fits,' Caroline said.

'When was the last time you tried it on?'

'Yesterday.'

'And you didn't let us see it on you? I could make some adjustments.'

'It fits, Ma. Believe me.'

'Go and put it on now,' Ma said.

'Maybe later.'

'Later will be tomorrow,' Ma said.

'I will try it on for you before I go to sleep,' Caroline promised.

Ma gave Caroline some ginger tea, adding two large spoonfuls of brown sugar to the cup.

'You can learn a few things from the sugarcane,' Ma said to Caroline. 'Remember that in your marriage.'

'I didn't think I would ever fall in love with anybody, much less have them marry me,' Caroline said, her fingernails tickling the back of Ma's neck.

'Tell me, how do these outside-of-church weddings work?' Ma asked.

'Ma, I told you my reasons for getting married this way,' Caroline said. 'Eric and I don't want to spend all the money we have on one silly night that everybody else will enjoy except us. We would rather do it this way. We have all our papers ready. Eric has a friend who is a judge. He will perform the ceremony for us in his office.'

'So much like America,' Ma said, shaking her head. 'Everything mechanical. When you were young, every time someone asked you what you wanted to do when you were all grown up, you said you wanted to marry Pélé. What's happened to that dream?'

'Pélé who?' Caroline grimaced.

'On the eve of your wedding day, you denounce him, but you wanted to marry him, the Brazilian soccer player, you always said when you were young that you wanted to marry him.'

I was the one who wanted to marry Pélé. When I was a little girl, my entire notion of love was to marry the soccer star. I would confess it to Papa every time we watched a game together on television.

In our living room, the music was dying down as the radio station announced two A.M. Ma kept her head down as she added a few last stitches to her dress for the wedding.

'When you are pregnant,' Ma said to Caroline, 'give your body whatever it wants. You don't want your child to have port-wine marks from your cravings.'

Caroline went to our room and came back wearing her wedding dress *and* a false arm.

Ma's eyes wandered between the bare knees poking beneath the dress and the device attached to Caroline's forearm.

'I went out today and got myself a wedding present,' Caroline said. It was a robotic arm with two shoulder straps that controlled the motion of the plastic fingers.

'Lately, I've been having this shooting pain in my stub and it feels like my arm is hurting,' Caroline said.

'It does not look very real,' Ma said.

'That's not the point, Ma!' Caroline snapped.

'I don't understand,' Ma said.

'I often feel a shooting pain at the end of my left arm, always as though it was cut from me yesterday. The doctor said I have phantom pain.'

'What? The pain of ghosts?'

'Phantom limb pain,' Caroline explained, 'a kind of pain that people feel after they've had their arms or legs amputated. The doctor thought this would make it go away.'

'But your arm was never cut from you,' Ma said. 'Did you tell him that it was God who made you this way?'

'With all the pressure lately, with the wedding, he says that it's only natural that I should feel amputated.'

'In that case, we all have phantom pain,' Ma said.

When she woke up on her wedding day, Caroline looked drowsy and frazzled, as if she had aged several years since the last time we saw her. She said nothing to us in the kitchen as she swallowed two aspirins with a gulp of water.

'Do you want me to make you some soup?' Ma asked.

Caroline said nothing, letting her body drift down into Ma's arms as though she were an invalid. I helped her into a chair at the kitchen table. Ma went into the hall closet and pulled out some old leaves that she had been saving. She stuffed the leaves into a pot of water until the water overflowed.

Caroline was sitting so still that Ma raised her index finger under her nose to make sure she was breathing.

'What do you feel?' Ma asked.

'I am tired,' Caroline said. 'I want to sleep. Can I go back to bed?'

'The bed won't be yours for much longer,' Ma said. 'As soon as you leave, we will take out your bed. From this day on, you will be sleeping with your husband, away from here.'

'What's the matter?' I asked Caroline.

'I don't know,' she said. 'I just woke up feeling like I don't want to get married. All this pain, all this pain in my arm makes it seem so impossible somehow.'

'You're just nervous,' I said.

'Don't worry,' Ma said. 'I was the same on the morning of my wedding. I fell into a stupor, frightened of all the possibilities. We will give you a bath and then you lay down for a bit and you will rise as promised and get married.'

The house smelled like a forest as the leaves boiled on the stove. Ma filled the bathtub with water and then dumped the boiled leaves inside.

We undressed Caroline and guided her to the tub, helping her raise her legs to get in.

'Just sink your whole body,' Ma said, when Caroline was in the tub.

Caroline pushed her head against the side of the tub and lay there as her legs paddled playfully towards the water's surface.

Ma's eyes were fierce with purpose as she tried to stir Caroline out of her stupor.

'At last a sign,' she joked. 'She is my daughter after all. This is just the way I was on the day of my wedding.'

Caroline groaned as Ma ran the leaves over her skin.

'Woman is angel,' Ma said to Caroline. 'You must confess, this is like pleasure.'

Caroline sank deeper into the tub as she listened to Ma's voice.

'Some angels climb to heaven backwards,' Caroline said. 'I want to stay with us, Ma.'

'You take your vows in sickness and in health,' Ma said. 'You decide to try sickness first? That is not very smart.'

'You said this happened to you too, Ma?' Caroline asked.

'It did,' Ma said. 'My limbs all went dead on my wedding day. I vomited all over my wedding dress on the way to the church.'

'I am glad I bought a cheap dress then,' Caroline said, laughing. 'How did you stop vomiting?'

'My honeymoon.'

'You weren't afraid of that?'

'Heavens no,' Ma said, scrubbing Caroline's back with a handful of leaves. 'For that I couldn't wait.'

Caroline leaned back in the water and closed her eyes.

'I am eager to be a guest in your house,' Ma said to Caroline.

'I will cook all your favorite things,' Caroline said.

'As long as your husband is not the cook, I will eat okay.'

'Do you think I'll make a good wife, Ma?'

'Even though you are an island girl with one kind of season in your blood, you will make a wife for all seasons: spring, summer, autumn, and winter.'

Caroline got up from the tub and walked alone to Ma's bedroom.

The phone rang and Ma picked it up. It was Eric.

'I don't understand it, honey,' Caroline said, already sounding more lucid. 'I just felt really blah! I know. I know, but for now, Ma's taking care of me.'

Ma made her hair into tiny braids, and over them she put on a wig with a shoulder-length bob. Ma and I checked ourselves in the mirror. She in her pink dress and me in my green suit, the two of us looking like a giant patchwork quilt.

'How long do I have now?' Caroline asked.

'An hour,' I said.

'Eric is meeting us there,' Caroline said, 'since it's bad luck for the groom to see the bride before the wedding.'

'If the groom is not supposed to see the bride, how do they get married?' Ma asked.

'They're not supposed to see each other until the ceremony,' Caroline said.

Caroline dressed quickly. Her hair was slicked back in a small bun, and after much persuasion, Ma got her to wear a pair of white stockings to cover her jutting knees.

The robotic arm was not as noticeable as the first time we had seen it. She had bought a pair of long white gloves to wear over the plastic arm and her other arm. Ma put some blush on the apple of Caroline's cheeks and then applied some rice powder to her face. Caroline sat stiffly on the edge of her bed as Ma glued fake eye-lashes to her eye-lids.

I took advantage of our last few minutes together to snap some instant Polaroid memories. Caroline wrapped her arms tightly around Ma as they posed for the pictures.

'Ma, you look so sweet,' Caroline said.

We took a cab to the courthouse. I made Ma and Caroline pose for more pictures on the steps. It was as though we were going to a grad-uation ceremony.

The judge's secretary took us to a conference room while her boss fin-ished an important telephone call. Eric was already there, waiting. As soon as we walked in, Eric rushed over to give Caroline a hug. He began stroking her mechanical arm as though it were a fascinating new toy.

'Lovely,' he said.

'It's just for the day,' Caroline said.

'It suits you fine,' he said.

Caroline looked much better. The rouge and rice powder had given her face a silky brown-sugar finish.

Ma sat stiffly in one of the cushioned chairs with her purse in her lap, her body closed in on itself like a cage.

'Judge Perez will be right with you,' the secretary said.

Judge Perez bounced in cheerfully after her. He had a veil of thin-ning brown hair and a goatee framing his lips.

'I'm sorry the bride and groom had to wait,' he said giving Eric a hug. 'I couldn't get off the phone.'

'Do you two know what you're getting into?' he said, playfully tap-ping Eric's arm.

Eric gave a coy smile. He wanted to move on with the ceremony. Caroline's lips were trembling with a mixture of fear and bashfulness.

'It's really a simple thing,' Judge Perez said. 'It's like a visit to get your vaccination. Believe me when I tell you it's very short and pain-less.'

He walked to a coat rack in the corner, took a black robe from it, and put it on.

'Come forward, you two,' he said, moving to the side of the room. 'The others can stand anywhere you like.'

Ma and I crowded behind the two of them. Eric had no family here. They were either in another state or in the Bahamas.

'No best man?' Ma whispered.

'I'm not traditional,' Eric said.

'That wasn't meant to be heard,' Ma said, almost as an apology.

'It's all right,' Eric said.

'Dearly beloved,' Judge Perez began. 'We are gathered here today to join this man and this woman in holy matrimony.'

Caroline's face, as I had known it, slowly began to fade, piece by piece, before my eyes. Another woman was setting in, a married woman, someone who was no longer my little sister.

'I, Caroline Azile, take this man to be my lawful wedded husband.'

I couldn't help but feel as though she was divorcing us, trading in her old allegiances for a new one.

It was over before we knew it. Eric grabbed Caroline and kissed her as soon as the judge said, 'Her lips are yours.'

'They were mine before, too,' Eric said, kissing Caroline another time.

After the kiss, they stood there, wondering what to do next. Caroline looked down at her finger, admiring her wedding band. Ma took a twenty-dollar bill out of her purse and handed it to the judge. He moved her hand away, but she kept insisting. I reached over and took the money from Ma's hand.

'I want to take the bride and groom out for a nice lunch,' I said.

'Our plane leaves for Nassau at five,' Eric said.

'We'd really like that, right, Ma?' I said. 'Lunch with the bride and groom.'

Ma didn't move. She understood the extent to which we were unimportant now.

'I feel much better,' Caroline said.

'Congratulations, Sister,' I said. 'We're going to take you out to eat.'

'I want to go to the Brooklyn Botanic Garden to take some pictures,' Caroline said.

'All set,' Eric said. 'I have a photographer meeting us there.'

Ma said, 'How come you never told me you were leaving tonight? How come you never tell me nothing.'

'You knew she wasn't going back to sleep at the house with us,' I said to Ma.

'I am not talking to you,' Ma said, taking her anger out on me.

'I am going to stop by the house to pick up my suitcase,' Caroline said.

We had lunch at Le Bistro, a Haitian Restaurant on Flatbush Avenue. It was the middle of the afternoon, so we had the whole place to ourselves. Ma sat next to me, not saying a word. Caroline didn't eat very much either. She drank nothing but sugared water while keeping her eyes on Ma.

'There's someone out there for everyone,' Eric said, standing up with a champagne glass in the middle of the empty restaurant. 'Even some destined bachelors get married. I am a very lucky person.'

Caroline clapped. Ma and I raised our glasses for his toast. He and Caroline laughed together with an ease that Ma and I couldn't feel.

'Say something for your sister,' Ma said in my ear.

I stood up and held my glass in her direction.

'A few years ago, our parents made this journey,' I said. 'This is a stop on the journey where my sister leaves us. We will miss her greatly, but she will never be gone from us.'

It was something that Ma might have said.

The photographer met us at the wedding grove at the Botanic Garden. Eric and Caroline posed stiffly for their photos, surrounded by well-cropped foliage.

'These are the kinds of pictures that they will later lay over the image of a champagne glass or something,' Ma said. 'They do so many tricks with photography now, for posterity.'

We went back to the house to get Caroline's luggage.

'We cannot take you to the airport,' Ma said.

'It's all right, Mother,' Eric said. 'We will take a cab. We will be fine.'

I didn't know how long I held Caroline in my arms on the sidewalk in front of our house. Her synthetic arm felt weighty on my shoulder, her hair stuck to the tears on my face.

'I'll visit you and Ma when I come back,' she said. 'Just don't go running off with any Brazilian soccer players.'

Caroline and I were both sobbing by the time she walked over to say good-bye to Ma. She kissed Ma on the cheek and then quickly hopped in the taxi without looking back. Ma ran her hand over the window, her finger sliding along the car door as it pulled away.

'I like how you stood up and spoke for your sister,' she said.

'The toast?'

'It was good.'

'I feel like I had some help,' I said.

That night, Ma got a delivery of roses so red that they didn't look real.

'Too expensive,' she said when the delivery man handed them to her.

The guy waited for her to sign a piece of paper and then a bit longer for a tip.

Ma took a dollar out of her bra and handed it to him.

She kept sniffing the roses as she walked back to the kitchen.

'Who are they from?' I asked.

'Caroline,' she said. 'Sweet, sweet Caroline.'

Distance had already made my sister Saint Sweet Caroline.

'Are you convinced of Caroline's happiness now?' I asked.

'You ask such difficult questions.'

That night she went to bed with the Polaroid wedding photos and the roses by her bed. Later, I saw her walking past my room cradling the vase. She woke up several times to sniff the roses and change the water.

That night, I also dreamt that I was with my father by a stream of rose-colored blood. We made a fire and grilled a breadfruit for dinner while waiting for the stream to turn white. My father and I were sitting on opposite sides of the fire. Suddenly the moon slipped through a cloud and dived into the bloody stream, filling it with a sheet of stars.

I turned to him and said, 'Look, Papy. There are so many stars.'

And my father in his throaty voice said, 'If you close your eyes really tight, wherever you are, you will see these stars.'

I said, 'Let's go for a swim.'

He said, 'No, we have a long way to travel and the trip will be harder if we get wet.'

Then I said, 'Papa, do you see all the blood? It's very beautiful.'

His face began to glow as though it had become like one of the stars.

Then he asked me, 'If we were painters, which landscapes would we paint?'

I said, 'I don't understand.'

He said, 'We are playing a game, you must answer me.'

I said, 'I don't know the answers.'

'When you become mothers, how will you name your sons?'

'We'll name them all after you,' I said.

'You have forgotten how to play this game,' he said.

'What kind of lullabies do we sing to our children at night? Where do you bury your dead?'

His face was fading into a dreamy glow.

'What kind of legends will your daughters be told? What kinds of charms will you give them to ward off evil?'

I woke up startled, for the first time afraid of the father that I saw in my dreams.

I rubbed the sleep out of my eyes and went down to the kitchen to get a glass of warm milk.

Ma was sitting at the kitchen table, rolling an egg between her palms. I slipped into the chair across from her. She pressed harder on both ends of the egg.

'What are you doing up so late?' she asked.

'I can't sleep,' I said.

'I think people should take shifts. Some of us would carry on at night and some during the day. The night would be like the day exactly. All stores would be open and people would go to the office, but only the night people. You see, then there would be no sleeplessness.'

I warmed some cold milk in a pan on the stove. Ma was still pressing hard, trying to crush the egg from top and bottom. I offered her some warm milk but she refused.

'What did you think of the wedding today?' I asked.

'When your father left me and you behind in Haiti to move to this country and marry that woman to get our papers,' she said, 'I prepared a charm for him. I wrote his name on a piece of paper and put the paper in a calabash. I filled the calabash with honey and next to it lit a candle. At midnight every night, I laid the calabash next to me in the bed where your father used to sleep and shouted at it to love me. I don't know how or what I was looking for, but somehow in the words he was sending me, I knew he had stopped thinking of me the same way.'

'You can't believe that, Ma,' I said.

'I know what I know,' she said. 'I am an adult woman. I am not telling you this story for pity.'

The kitchen radio was playing an old classic on one of the Haitian stations.

Beloved Haiti, there is no place like you.

I had to leave you before I could understand you.

'Would you like to see my proposal letter?' Ma asked.

She slid an old jewelry box across the table towards me. I opened it and pulled out the envelope with the letter in it.

The envelope was so yellowed and frail that at first I was afraid to touch it.

'Go ahead,' she said, 'it will not turn to dust in your hands.'

The letter was cracked along the lines where it had been folded all of these years.

My son, Carl Romélus Azile, would be honored to make your daughter, Hermine Françoise Génie, his wife.

'It was so sweet then,' Ma said, 'so sweet. Promise me that when I die you will destroy all of this.'

'I can't promise you that,' I said. 'I will want to hold on to things when you die. I will want to hold on to you.'

'I do not want my grandchildren to feel sorry for me,' she said. 'The past, it fades a person. And yes. Today, it was a nice wedding.'

My passport came in the mail the next day, addressed to Gracina Azile, my real and permanent name.

I filled out all the necessary sections, my name and address, and listed my mother to be contacted in case I was in an accident. For the first time in my life, I felt truly secure living in America. It was like being in a war zone and finally receiving a weapon of my own, like standing on the firing line and finally getting a bullet-proof vest.

We had all paid dearly for this piece of paper, this final assurance that I belonged in the club. It had cost my parent's marriage, my mother's spirit, my sister's arm.

I felt like an indentured servant who had finally been allowed to join the family.

The next morning, I went to the cemetery in Rosedale, Queens, where my father had been buried. His was one of many gray tombstones in a line of foreign unpronounceable names. I brought my passport for him to see, laying it on the grass among the wild daisies surrounding the grave.

'Caroline had her wedding,' I said. 'We felt like you were there.'

My father had wanted to be buried in Haiti, but at the time of his death there was no way that we could have afforded it.

The day before Papa's funeral, Caroline and I had told Ma that we wanted to be among Papa's pallbearers.

Ma had thought that it was a bad idea. Who had ever heard of young women being pallbearers? Papa's funeral was no time for us to express our selfish childishness, our *American* rebelliousness.

When we were children, whenever we rejected symbols of Haitian culture, Ma used to excuse us with great embarrassment and say, 'You know, they are American.'

Why didn't we like the thick fatty pig skin that she would deep-fry so long that it tasted like rubber? We were Americans and we had *no taste buds*. A double tragedy.

Why didn't we like the thick yellow pumpkin soup that she spent

all New Year's Eve making so that we would have it on New Year's
Day to celebrate Haitian Independence Day? Again, because we were
American and the Fourth of July was *our* independence holiday.

'In Haiti, you own your children and they find it natural,' she
would say. 'They know their duties to the family and they act accord-
ingly. In America, no one owns anything, and certainly not another
person.'

'Caroline called,' Ma said. She was standing over the stove making
some bone soup when I got home from the cemetery. 'I told her that
we would still keep her bed here for her, if she ever wants to use it.
She will come and visit us soon. I knew she would miss us.'

'Can I drop one bone in your soup?' I asked Ma.

'It is your soup too,' she said.

She let me drop one bone into the boiling water. The water
splashed my hand, leaving a red mark.

'Ma, if we were painters which landscapes would we paint?' I asked
her.

'I see. You want to play the game of questions?'

'When I become a mother, how will I name my daughter?'

'If you want to play then I should ask the first question,' she said.

'What kinds of lullabies will I sing at night? What kinds of legends
will my daughter be told? What kinds of charms will I give her to
ward off evil?'

'I have come a few years further than you,' she insisted. 'I have
tasted a lot more salt. I am to ask the first question, if we are to play the
game.'

'Go ahead,' I said giving in.

She thought about it for a long time while stirring the bones in our
soup.

'Why is it that when you lose something, it is always in the last
place that you look for it?' she asked finally.

Because of course, once you remember, you always stop looking.

                                                              1995